Author's Note

The (common) religion of the Isles is based on Sumerian cult and ritual, but the magic itself comes from the Mediterranean and is mostly Egyptian in its original source. The *voces mysticae* which I've referred to as "words of power" in the text represent the language of demiurges; that is, they are intended to have meaning to beings which can then translate human desires to the ultimate powers of the cosmos. I have copied them from real spell manuscripts of the classical period.

I don't personally believe that the *voces mysticae* have power over events, but millions of intelligent, civilized people *did* believe that. I don't pronounce the *voces mysticae* aloud when I'm writing.

Rather than invent literary sources for the background of *Servant of the Dragon*, I've used real ones. The actual quotes are from poems by Horace and Ovid; my translations are serviceable, but Horace in particular deserves better than anyone can give him in English.

In addition there are passing references to Homer, Vergil, Hesiod, Athenaeus, and Plato. The fascinating thing about going to original sources is that it's the best way to learn not only what people distant in time thought but also how they went about thinking.

And you know, when you've seen the differences between us and the ancestors of our Western culture, it may make you—as it certainly has made me—a little more tolerant of the beliefs of different modern cultures. That wouldn't be a bad thing for the world.

—Dave Drake
david-drake.com

Prologue

The deeps trembled, shaking a belfry which had not moved for a thousand years. Eels with glassy flesh and huge, staring eyes twisted, touched by fear of the power focused on the sunken island. Cold light pulsed across their slender bodies.

A bell rang, sending its note over the sunken city. It had been cast from the bronze rams of warships captured by the first Duke of Yole. A tripod fish lifted its long pelvic fins from the bottom and swam off with stiff sweeps of its tail.

Ammonites, the Great Ones of the Deep, swam slowly toward the sound. They had tentacles like cuttlefish and shells coiled like rams' horns. The largest of them were the size of a ship.

The powers supporting the cosmos shifted, sending shudders through a city which nothing had touched for a millennium. The bell rang a furious tocsin over Yole.

The island was rising.

The Great Ones' tentacles waved like forests of serpents in time with words agitating the sea. In daylight their curled shells would shimmer with all the colors of the sun. Here the only light was the distant shimmer of a viperfish flashing in terror as it fled.

The dead lay in the streets, sprawled as they had fallen. Over them were scattered roof tiles and the rubble of walls which collapsed as the city sank. Onrushing water had choked their screams, and their outstretched arms clutched for a salvation which had eluded them.

The bodies had not decayed: these cold depths were as hostile to the minute agents of corruption as they were to humans. Some corpses had been savaged by great-fanged seawolves which had swept into the city on the crest of the engulfing wave; other victims had been pulled into the beaks of the Great Ones and there devoured. For the most part, though, the corpses were whole except where sluggish, long-legged crabs had picked at them.

Tides of light touched the drowned buildings and gave them color. Faint tinges of blue brightened as the island rose. At last even the roof tiles regained their ruddy tinge.

The Great Ones swam slowly upward, accompanying Yole its return. The movements of their tentacles twisted the cosmos.

The belfry of the duke's palace, the highest edifice in Yole, broke surface. Water cascaded from stones darkened by the slime which crawled along the sea's deepest trenches.

Moments later the Great Ones surfaced, their shells a shimmering iridescence in the dawnlight. They swam slowly outward so as not to be trapped by the rising land. The S-shaped pupils of their eyes stared unwinking at the circle of wizards who stood in the air above the rising city.

Three of the wizards wore black robes with high-peaked cowls over their heads. Their faces and bare hands were blackened with a pigment of soot and tallow. Only their teeth showed white as they chanted words of power:

"*Lemos agrule euros . . .*"

Three wizards were in robes of bleached wool, white in shadow and a mixture of rose-pink and magenta where the low sun colored the fabric. They had smeared their skin with white lead so that their eyes were dark pits in the ghastly pallor of their faces.

"*Ptolos xenos gaiea . . .*" the wizards chanted.

The earth rumbled. Torrents thundered from doorways and windows of Yole, spilling in echoing gouts along the broad streets that led to the harbor. Corpses flopped and twisted in the foaming water. Each syllable could be heard over the chaos, though the words came from human throats.

The wizards' leader was black on his left side, white on the right. He chanted the words of power which his fellows echoed, syllable by syllable. From the brazier standing before him, strands of black smoke and white smoke rose, interweaving but remaining discrete.

"Kata pheinra thenai . . ."

Facing the leader was a mummified figure whose head the wizards had unbandaged. The mummy's sere brown skin bore the pattern of tiny scales, and the dried lips were thin and reptilian. Its tongue, shrunken to a forked string, flickered as the figure chanted. Words of power came from its dead throat.

The belfry continued to shudder, but the bell's voice was lost in the greater cataclysm. Seabirds wheeled in the air, summoned from afar as the sea thundered away from the newly risen land.

"Kata, cheiro, iofide . . ." chanted the wizards.

The ghost of a pierced screen hung in the air beyond the wizards, a filigree of stone that wavered in and out of focus. The screen's reality was that of another time and place, but the incantation had drawn it partway with the wizards.

The soil of Yole touched the wizards' feet. The island gave a further convulsive shudder, then ceased to rise. Waves, shaken away by Yole's reappearance, returned to slap its shore in a fury that slowly beat itself quiescent.

In the harbor the Great Ones floated. Their tentacles waved in a ghastly parody of a dance.

Gulls and frigate birds dived and rose again in shrieking delight. Yole's rise had swept creatures of the deep to the surface faster than their bodies could respond to the changes in pressure. Birds carried away the ruptured carcasses in their beaks.

The six lesser wizards collapsed on the dripping cobblestones of a plaza, gasping in exhaustion from the weight of the spell they had executed. Their leader raised his arms high and shouted, *"Theeto worshe acheleou!"*

Momentary silence smothered the world, stilling the

waves and even the screams of the gulls. Sunlight winked on the armor of soldiers and the jewelry of ladies who had arrayed themselves in their finest, not knowing that they were dressing for their own deaths. A child's hand still clutched an ivory rattle; it too gleamed in the sun.

The leading wizard remained standing. His mad peals of laughter rang across the dead city.

The mummy stood also, motionless now and silent. Its sunken eyes were on the wizard, and its reptilian features were twisted into a mask of fury.

Chapter One

Prince Garric of Haft, Heir Presumptive of Valence III, King of the Isles—and already by any real measure the ruler of the kingdom—faced his Council of Advisors. Down the table from him were the chief nobles of the island of Ornifal, some of the most powerful men in all the Isles. They were waiting for him to make known his wishes as Lord Waldron, commander of the Royal Army, argued with Lord Attaper, commander of the Blood Eagles—the royal bodyguards.

Garric's wishes were to be back home in Barca's Hamlet, the village on Haft where he'd been raised for all but the first days of his eighteen years. Life was a lot simpler then, although it had seemed complicated enough at the time.

"You can't go back, lad," whispered the ghost in Garric's mind: Carus, the last king of the united Isles, whom wizardly had drowned a thousand years before. *"Even if duty didn't keep you here in Valles, Barca's Hamlet isn't really your home anymore."*

"May I remind both of you gentlemen that soldiers have to be paid!" said Lord Tadai, now Royal Treasurer in place of a well-meaning incompetent who'd held the position under Valence. Tadai wiped his round face with a handkerchief embroidered with the arms of his house, the bor-Tithains.

Everyone was getting to his feet and shouting. Royhas bor-Bolliman, Garric's chancellor and closest to being Garric's friend of the men present, snarled, "And speaking of money, Tadai, the honor of the kingdom is being tarnished by your failure to pay—"

"Gentlemen," Garric said in a mild voice. He knew no one would listen to him, but his father had raised him to be polite.

Liane bos-Benliman, a dark-haired girl of Garric's age, sat beside Garric and a half-step back, making it clear that she had no right to speak during the deliberations. In this room she was acting as Garric's secretary. She met Garric's eye and smiled, but there was concern in her expression.

Liane was the only living person present who wanted the things Garric wanted and no more: peace and unity for the Kingdom of the Isles, which wizardry had shattered a thousand years before and which wizardry now threatened to crush to dust. In Garric's eyes Liane was the loveliest woman in the Isles, and a more neutral judge might have concurred.

"The money's there, you just won't release it as your duty demands!" Royhas cried, leaning over the table from his side. Tadai, leaning toward the chancellor with his face the color of his scarlet handkerchief, said, "If you're so set on finding jobs for all your relatives, Royhas, then I suggest you find the money for them as well!"

Garric's index finger touched the conference table. It was of burl walnut, polished to a glassy sheen that brought out the richly complex pattern of the grain. In Barca's Hamlet men shaped wood with an adze or a broadaxe. Garric had never seen a saw or a sawn plank until fate took him from him his home. A table like this was fit for the Queen of Heaven and Her consort, not mortals like Garric or-Reise.

"And besides *that*—" Royhas said.

Garric slammed his fist down. The table, large enough to seat twelve and heavy in proportion, jumped on the stone floor.

No one spoke for a moment.

Garric hadn't eaten since . . . well, he'd had an orange and a roll baked from wheat flour at dawn, with nothing since. Maybe that was why he felt queasy.

"Gentlemen," he said, "I'm going to adjourn this meeting because I'm obviously not in condition to keep it under control."

"I'm sorry, Your Highness, but—"

"I didn't mean to—"

"Of course, Garric, I'll—"

"Well, *really*, Pr—"

"*Silence!*" Garric bellowed. The conference room shutters were slatted to let in summer breezes while maintaining privacy from the eyes of folk wandering through the palace grounds. They rattled against their casements. Even Liane jumped, though she immediately grinned as well.

"Gentlemen," Garric continued in the quiet tone he preferred. "We'll resume this meeting tomorrow in the third hour of the afternoon. I know that some of you have written proposals. Leave them with Liane and I'll review them before that time."

Garric's eyes flicked from Royhas to Tadai. Both men had their mouths open to speak. They saw Garric's expression, as grim and certain as a sword edge.

"Quite so," the chancellor murmured as he took from his wallet a scroll of parchment bound with a red ribbon. He handed it to Liane with a courtly flourish.

Lord Tadai had a similar document, though his ribbon was pale yellow, dyed with the pollen washed from beehives. "There's an annex which one of my aides will bring you shortly, Lady Liane," he said in an undertone.

The conference room was one of the many separate buildings in the grounds of the royal palace in Valles. The councillors passed out one by one to meet their aides and bodyguards, the latter carrying ivory batons instead of swords. Only the Blood Eagles and folk the king particularly wanted to honor were permitted to go armed within the palace grounds.

The last councillors remaining were Attaper and Waldron. The two warriors stepped to the doorway together and halted. After a moment Attaper grinned tightly. "I trust you not to stab anyone in the back, Lord Waldron," he said. "Even me." He swept through the door ahead of the older man.

"Puppy!" Waldron muttered as he strode out in turn. He left the door open behind him: opening and closing doors was beneath the concern of a man of Waldron's lineage.

A servant peered into the conference room to see what those still within might wish. Liane shook her head minusculely and closed the door herself.

"It was perfect!" Garric said with a grin. "I almost broke out laughing when you cited Sourous chapter and verse about the worthless parasite he thinks is his friend. Ilna couldn't have done it better!"

Garric thought about the friends he'd grown up with: his sister Sharina, tall, blond, and (like Garric himself) able both to read the classics and to put in a full day's work at their father's rural inn; Cashel or-Kenset, an orphan since his father's early death, almost as tall as Garric and as strong as any two other men—

And Cashel's twin sister Ilna: dark-haired, pretty; a weaver whose skill passed beyond art to wizardry. Ilna's tongue was as sharp as the bone-cased knife she kept for household tasks and to cut the selvage of her fabric. Ilna might well have dressed Sourous down in that fashion, but—

"Ilna would've enjoyed it," Garric said sadly. "*I* enjoyed it while it was happening, but I shouldn't have. Sourous is a fool, but that's not a crime. I liked to see him squirm because I'm tired and frustrated."

Garric slid his chair back to stand. He kept knocking his elbows on the chair arms of solid black wood. He wondered what people would say if he had the chairs in this conference room replaced with benches.

King Carus laughed at the unspoken thought. Garric echoed the laughter aloud; it broke his mood.

"I don't feel that I'm getting anywhere," he said in a more cheerful tone than he would have used a moment before. Having a companion who knew your every thought

and who was always willing to laugh with you—or at you—was a good thing for a ruler. Garric knew both from Carus' memories and from his own experience that kings were generally lied to.

He was luckier than most kings: neither Liane nor the friends he'd grown up with would lie, to Garric or to anybody else. But he was lucky also to have a friend and advisor like Carus.

"You've done more in the past few months than any King of the Isles managed in his whole reign," Liane said with a hint of sharpness. "Anyone since the Old Kingdom, I mean. There's a Royal Army—and more important, there's a royal administration that does more than accept whatever pittance the local landholders claim they owe the state."

"We've got the start of an administration," Garric agreed, "but just a start and that's only here on Ornifal. The rulers of the other islands go their own way. The only reason the Earl of Sandrakkan and the Count of Blaise haven't proclaimed themselves kings of their own islands is that they both think that if they play the game right they can claim the whole Isles."

"And now that they see the king in Valles isn't a weakling who can be pushed aside," said Carus, "they'll be thinking very hard about independence. We'll need to deal with that."

Garric patted the coronation medal of King Carus which he wore on a ribbon under his tunic. The king's presence in Garric's mind frequently laughed but was always alert. Carus was an older version of Garric himself, wearing flamboyantly colored clothing. The right hand of his image was never far from the hilt of his long, straight sword.

"When we have Ornifal organized, you'll be able to extend your administration right across the Isles. After all, it's not just the kingdom that's better for having fair taxation and honest justice, it's all the *people* of the kingdom."

Garric laughed. "All the people except the ones profiting

by the present chaos," he said. "Which means most of the people in power already."

"In the long run—" said Liane. Emotion had raised spots of color on her cheekbones. Liane was so passionate about the plan to reunify the Isles that sometimes she couldn't see the problems for all her sharp intelligence. She couldn't *bear* to see obstacles in the way of what she knew with all her soul was right.

"People don't think about the long run," Garric said quietly. "They think about what they have in their hand today."

Liane started to speak, then swallowed the retort with a grimace. She was tired too.

"Remember, you and I know the dangers," Garric said. He put his fingertips on the backs of Liane's hands. She'd watched a demon disembowel her father. Magical forces were again rising to their thousand-year peak. No one understood better than Liane what would happen to the Isles if those forces were allowed to shatter even the fragile peace which had returned since the fall of the Old Kingdom. "Most people don't, and it's most people that we have to deal with."

Liane turned her right hand and squeezed Garric's. "And some people, even if they did know what we know," she said, "would keep right on robbing their peasants instead of trying to build a community of honesty and justice. Well, you have the Royal Army too."

"*And so you do, lad,*" agreed King Carus. "*A good one, and getting better each day. Just don't be as quick as I was to use your sword instead of talking; and don't forget that however good my army was, there was a wizard who could sink it and me to the bottom of the Inner Sea.*"

Garric laughed. Liane smiled through her puzzlement: no one but Garric himself heard the words of his ancestor. "I'm reminding myself that wizardry is a danger no matter how good our army is," Garric said, to explain what he was thinking about. It took a particular kind of gallows humor to laugh at the thought, though.

Along the room's sidewalls were leather-covered benches where aides would sit during the meetings they were allowed to attend. For most of his life Garric had slept in a garret room with a bed even narrower than the benches. "What I need most now is a nap. Is there anything so pressing that . . . ?"

"I'll tell the guards that you're not to be disturbed by anyone but me," Liane said as she rose, folding her travel desk with the same graceful movement. "And I'll be in the service building next door. There's a couch there too. I'm going to fall asleep on my feet unless I manage to lie down first."

"Things are bound to settle down someday," Garric said as he held the door for Liane. A servant tried to take the little desk from her; she motioned him away peremptorily and stepped toward the adjacent building, throwing Garric a parting smile.

Garric shrugged out of his vermilion robe of state. Underneath he wore a tunic of thin wool rather than silk: wool *felt* right against his skin, because that's what he'd always worn. He settled on the bench, kicking off the silly-looking slippers of gilded leather that he had to wear with the heavy robe.

"Maybe things settle down for some people when they die," said his grinning ancestor. *"Not for all of us, though."*

And as Garric plunged into the darkness of sleep too long delayed, Carus added, *"And besides, what would folk like you and me do if a miracle brought us peace, lad?"*

Cashel or-Kenset was learning to dance in the city fashion. It was a more stately business than what went on at weddings and harvest feasts in the borough.

"Oh, Lord Cashel, you are so masterful!" said his partner, Lady Besra bos-Balian—a woman Cashel had at first thought resembled his sister. Besra was as dark and petite as Ilna, but she lacked Ilna's principles, her loyalty, and her wit.

In particular, Besra didn't have enough wit to know that while Cashel wasn't smart the way his friends Garric and Sharina were, he wasn't nearly stupid enough to be taken in by Besra's act. She liked to call herself a girl, but Cashel guessed she must be at least thirty—and by the lines at the corners of her eyes beneath a layer of powdered chalk, they'd been hard years most of them.

"No, Lady Besra," Cashel said patiently. "I made a mistake. I swung left when I should've swung right."

He turned his head and nodded to the dance mistress, Lady Kusha. She was, well, ancient.

Lady Kusha had been a maid of honor, whatever that was, to the wife of the first King Valence, grandfather of the man now on the throne. She had black eyes and always wore garments of stiff black linen as though she'd just been widowed. Sharina said that in fact, Kusha had never married.

"Sorry, Lady Kusha," he said sincerely. "I'll get it right the next time."

"I'm sure you will, Master Cashel," Kusha said. "You have an instinct for the dance; it just needs to be tutored into the proper forms."

Unlike Besra and too many more of the people in Valles, Kusha never tried to flatter Cashel by addressing him as "lord." Cashel's father was a miller's son who'd drunk himself to death a few years after he'd come back to Barca's Hamlet with infant children and no wife to mother them.

False honor rubbed Cashel the wrong way, though he'd given up trying to train the Besras of this world out of using it. Cashel didn't set much store by nobility—he hadn't yet met a noble who was better at any of the things Cashel thought were important—but it bothered him to be given something that he knew he didn't have a right to.

There were three men in the marble-floored salon besides Cashel. Two were musicians playing a descant recorder and a kit violin, a tiny stringed instrument which

was bowed instead of being plucked like the lutes Cashel was familiar with.

The third man was Lord Evlatun. All of Cashel's teachers seemed to be noble or claim to be, though they didn't have much besides the name and generally the attitude. Evlatun joined with Lady Kusha in measures which needed four dancers.

Evlatun was Besra's partner; whether the partnership was as formal as marriage, Cashel couldn't guess and didn't care. The blond, balding fellow smiled brightly whenever he saw Cashel looking at him, but the times Cashel had caught his unguarded expression, well . . .

If Evlatun had been a snake, he'd have been poisonous. Cashel wouldn't have thought twice before breaking his back with a quarterstaff stroke.

There seemed to be a lot of people like that in Valles. Maybe it was just that the palace drew them, the way you found flies on a manure pile.

"You're the most graceful man I've ever danced with, Lord Cashel," Besra said. She laid her right hand on his biceps, sliding her fingers under the fringed sleeve of his embroidered tunic. It was a costume he had to wear for these sessions. Had to, because Sharina had to go through the same business and he didn't want to embarrass her.

Cashel turned slightly to rotate himself away from the woman. Evlatun watched, grinning like a man dying of lockjaw.

"Um," Cashel said. "We dance in Barca's Hamlet, it just isn't the same steps."

He *was* graceful, that he knew. Besra hadn't been the first person surprised at that, though. Cashel was big, so he moved carefully: big, strong men who aren't careful break things. He'd spent much of his life moving at the pace of sheep or a team of plow oxen, and he'd learned they get where they're going just as sure as more excitable animals do.

Folks tended to think that a big man who counted on his fingers would be awkward besides. Awkward people don't work with axes and heavy weights, not and survive with all their limbs. Ever since he got his growth Cashel had been the fellow folk in the borough called on when they needed a tree felled just right, or a boulder shifted from a space too tight for oxen.

He wasn't slow, either, not when there was need to move fast. Now and again a drover's guard had too much to drink at the Sheep Fair and challenged Cashel to a bout with quarterstaves or of all-in wrestling. The ones who were lucky staggered away from the flagged ring afterward; the others were carried by their friends.

Besra moved close to Cashel; he turned to face the dancing mistress, putting his back to Besra. He could swear he heard Evlatun's teeth grinding. "I'm ready to go on, Lady Kusha," he said.

"We'll start from the rigadoon," Kusha said. She tapped her fan toward the musicians; the folding tortoiseshell leaves made a muted clack. "Positions, please!"

The salon was the large central room of a building meant for entertainment. There were two-story wings on either end, providing separate suites for the male and female guests to leave their outerwear and their servants. Like the rest of the sprawling palace on the outskirts of Valles, the building had decayed badly during the last few years, but repairs were well under way. The crumbled stucco copings on the east end had been replaced, and a pair of workmen were repainting the gilt highlights on the coffered ceiling during the intervals between Cashel's dancing lessons.

There was a tap on the door from the men's suite. Kusha turned imperiously and said, "Begone! This room is engaged!"

The door opened anyway for a man wearing the blue-gray robe of a palace servant. The tassel on his matching soft cap was gold as a sign of rank. He was the chamberlain, and Cashel knew well him well.

"Begone, I said!" Kusha shrilled. Her lanky body seemed to expand like that of a toad facing a snake. "I am Lady Kusha bos-Kadriman, here at the express request of

the Lady Sharina. I am not to be interrupted by a mere hireling!"

It seemed to Cashel that being palace chamberlain was a lot more impressive than being dancing mistress, but that wasn't the point. "Here, it's all right," he said. "Master Reise's a neighbor of mine."

The chamberlain bowed low and drew an S curve in the air with his right hand. It had something or other to do with what they considered manners here. "I beg your pardon most sincerely, Lady Kusha," he said, "but a matter has arisen which I needed to communicate to Master Cashel as soon as possible."

"Did you hear the lady?" Evlatun said, his voice an octave higher than usual. He swaggered a step forward and put his hand on his sword hilt.

"Besides," Cashel added as an afterthought, "he's Garric's father. Prince Garric, I mean."

"You're joking," Kusha said. She and all the others were staring at the chamberlain. "Surely you're joking, Master Cashel."

Reise surveyed the three nobles with a sardonic expression. It was hard to connect this self-assured official with Reise the Innkeeper, henpecked, vaguely comic, and sourly angry with his life in a hamlet of sheepfarmers.

Of course, it was hard for Cashel to connect the simple shepherd he knew he was with the fellow who'd battled demons and beaten them . . . which Cashel had done also. Life was a lot more complicated than it had seemed when he was growing up in Barca's Hamlet.

"I was amanuensis to Countess Tera of Haft," Reise said to Kusha. Besra was staring at Cashel again. The pair of musicians were interested spectators of the whole business, pleased to be entertained instead of entertainers. Evlatun was pop-eyed with amazement.

"The countess gave birth the night of the riots which cost her life," Reise continued calmly. "My wife and I saved the infant, Garric, and fostered him along with my wife's daughter Sharina. So yes, I did have the honor of fostering Prince Garric."

"But you're a *servant*," said Lady Besra. Her wondering tone sounded like she was saying, "But you have three heads."

"Prince Garric felt he needed someone trustworthy to run his household when . . . after King Valance adopted him," Reise said. His smile was as faint and cold as a curl of condensate on smooth gray stone. "He asked me to return to Valles, where I had at one time served in the palace; and of course I was duty bound to accept."

Kusha was motionless except for blinking twice. It was like watching the inner lids flick across the eyes of a lizard waiting for prey to come within range of a quick lunge. When she'd put the pieces of what she'd just heard into their places, she said abruptly, "Come, you lot, quickly! Master Cashel has private business to transact!"

Thrusting out her arms like a black-clad mantis, Kusha chivied the dancers and musicians through the ladies' suite ahead of her. The violinist bent to pick up his book of tunes picked out in shaped notes; he'd dropped it, likely in the commotion when Cashel was dealing with Evlatun. Kusha whacked the poor fellow with her fan and sent him off at a run. He'd have a welt for sure across the back of his thighs.

Cashel felt a sudden flash of concern. "Ah, Sharina's all right, isn't she, Reise? Master Reise, I mean."

"She was fine when I conducted a delegation to see her earlier this afternoon," Reise said as coolly as if he were only the chamberlain—not Sharina's father also. "She remarked that she was looking forward to seeing you when she'd heard the group out. They were landholders with concerns relating to taxation, as I understand it."

He changed the subject by clearing his throat. "I'm here, however, to tell you that your uncle Katchin would like to speak with you."

"My uncle?" Cashel said. He was as amazed as Lady Kusha had been when she learned who Reise really was.

Praise for David Drake

'Unlike most modern fantasy, David Drake's *Lord of the Isles* is an epic with the texture of the legends of yore, with rousing action and characters to cheer for'

Terry Goodkind

'*Lord of the Isles* has it all – treacherous queens, faithful and faithless courtiers, peasants and shepherds who are more than they seem, wizardry fair and most foul, quests, love beyond the grave, and all manner of despicable plotting and unabashed heroics . . . A fast-reading and complex fantasy adventure.'

L. E. Modesitt, Jr.

'True brilliance is as rare as a perfect diamond or a supernova. *Lord of the Isles* is truly brilliant. Plot, pace, excitement, characterization, but most of all the finely honed and superb use of language mark this as one of those exceptional books you will want to have bound in leather and pass on to your grandchildren.'

Morgan Llywelyn

'Some authors are powerful storytellers. Others evoke images that we did not believe existed. When the two are combined you have a powerful writer. *Lord of the Isles* is a magnificent example.'

Gordon R. Dickson

'A genre fantasy with more suspense, action, and horror than most . . . Drake's magic is more complex than fantasy magic, and the dangers of uncontrollable power form an important theme here. His settings and magical creatures provide surprise and drama as well as plenty of color. This substantial fantasy, in which moral and physical threats are serious and the actions of the characters have real consequences, will appeal to those tired of watered-down myth.'

Publishers Weekly

Acknowledgments

Dan Breen, my first reader, describes himself as a scribe. This is valid; but while I value the way he catches grammatical errors, I gain even greater benefit from his more general criticisms. Though I often disagree (though I most often disagree), he forces me to consider why I did the particular things that I did.

If there's an author photo on this book, it's probably the one John Coker took in 1986 (I'm grayer but I wear the same trouser size). John is not only a fine photographer, he's one of the nicest people you could ever hope to meet. I really appreciate his permission to use his picture.

Things go wrong in publishing, just as they do in every other form of human endeavor. Stephanie Lane at Tor works hard to fix errors. This is no more common in publishing than it is anywhere else, so I feel very fortunate to work with her.

My mean time between failure with computers is about six months. Losing three of them during the writing of this novel was pretty remarkable, though. My thanks to Mark L. Van Name, Allyn Vogel, Ruben Fernandez, and Rich Creal, whose help made a series of frustrating experiences nonetheless survivable.

The text of this paperback edition is cleaner than that of the hardcover in part because of the efforts of Sharon Pigott and Rick LaBach. Sharon read the proofs of my first book also, so this wasn't a new experience for her. I had a difficult time during the course of writing this book. (See the paragraph immediately above for a lot of the reason.) My friends and especially my wife, Jo, were unfailingly supportive. My sincere thanks to all of them.

To Jamuna devi dasi, AKA Melissa Michael,
who makes the world a better place

SERVANT
of the
DRAGON

David Drake

The right of David Drake to be identified as the author
of this work has been asserted by him in accordance with
the Copyright, Designs and Patents Act 1988.

First published in Great Britain in 2000 by
Millennium
An imprint of Victor Gollancz
Orion House, 5 Upper St Martin's Lane,
London WC2H 9EA

To receive information on the Millennium list, e-mail us at:
smy@orionbooks.co.uk

A CIP catalogue record for this book
is available from the British Library

ISBN 1 85798 950 3

Printed in Great Britain by
Clays Ltd, St Ives plc

"Katchin the Miller wants to see me? What's he even doing in Valles?"

"I suspect he's trying to gain a position in the new government," Reise said. He gave Cashel a dry smile. "That's only an assumption; your uncle and I didn't exchange confidences even when we were neighbors in Barca's Hamlet."

Cashel nodded as he let the information sink in. The miller and the innkeeper were successful businessmen in a community where most everyone else depended on farming or sheep. Katchin was probably wealthier; certainly he spent more on personal show. He'd also become bailiff for the Count of Haft's interests in the borough—not that the count had many dealings in an out-of-the-way place like Barca's Hamlet. Katchin treated Reise as his rival.

Reise hadn't seemed to give much thought to Katchin one way or the other. Seeing Reise here as palace chamberlain, Cashel could understand why: the difference between the top and the bottom of society in Barca's Hamlet was too slight to notice for a man who'd served in the royal palace when he was a youth.

"And strictly speaking, your uncle didn't want to see you either, Master Cashel," Reise continued. "He asked to see Prince Garric, whom he chose to call 'my old friend Garric.' I wasn't about to allow that, of course; but when he asked for you as an alternative, I felt the blood relationship made it my duty to bring the matter to your attention."

Reise seemed calm here. Back home—back in Barca's Hamlet—the innkeeper sizzled with frustration and an anger that rarely came to the surface. In another man it'd have been something the neighbors kept in mind. With Reise, though—well, everybody knew that if Reise started screaming and flailing about with his meat cleaver, he'd manage to trip on a wash kettle and knock himself silly before he hurt anybody.

Funny how little you know about somebody you've known all your life. Funny how little you know about yourself even.

Cashel shrugged. "Sure, I'll talk to my uncle," he said. He guessed it was a duty, like checking the sheep each night for fly sores. "Where do I go?"

Reise nodded. "He's waiting in the male servants' room," he said, turning his eyes toward the door from which he'd entered the salon. "I'll bring him in, or you can see him there—or see him anywhere you please, of course, sir."

Cashel shook his head in amazement. Garric's father calling *him* "sir." "I'll go there," he said, walking toward the door.

Cashel had been a little surprised that his uncle hadn't come bursting into the salon if he was so close by. When he entered the waiting room he saw why. Katchin was there, all right, red-faced and puffing; but with him were two husky palace ushers carrying ebony staffs of office with silver knobs on either end. The rods weren't a patch on a proper quarterstaff like Cashel's, but they were surely enough to keep Katchin in his place.

Here in the palace, Katchin's place was wherever the chamberlain said it was. No wonder the miller looked mad enough to chew rocks.

"Good afternoon, Uncle," Cashel said. "I wasn't expecting to see you here."

And Duzi knew, that wasn't *half* the truth.

Katchin twisted his mouth into a smile. He had a flowing mustache, maybe to make up for the way the hair on his head had thinned to a speckly band above his ears on either side. He ate too much and drank too much; it showed in his face, in his belly, and most of all in the way the flesh of his fingers puffed up around the rings he wore on every finger.

"Well, my boy, you must have known I'd come as soon as I heard you and our Garric needed help!" Katchin said.

"Master Cashel?" said Reise in a voice as dry as a salt-cured ham. "I'll leave the ushers at the outer door. They'll guide your visitor to wherever you tell them at the end of your interview."

He bowed—to Cashel, not to Katchin—and stepped through a back doorway, drawing the ushers with him. One of them winked at Cashel as he left.

Cashel surveyed his uncle. Katchin's clothing was brand new: layered tunics, the outer one striped beige and maroon crossways; a sash of gold brocade from which hung a sword that was even more of a toy than the one Cashel had just bent double; and on his head, a peaked cap with a swan's feather dyed a sort of muddy purple. Katchin looked like a juggler come to the Sheep Fair, though Cashel knew the rig-out must have cost the price of a farm in the borough.

"I'm sorry you did that, uncle," Cashel said. "Garric hasn't said he needs your help, and I surely don't. You'd be happier back home, I guess."

"I can't believe I'd hear ingratitude from the child I raised!" Katchin said. He probably meant it, too. Katchin didn't exactly lie, but he managed to remember events in whatever way served him best. "Prince Garric needs trusted men to help him govern. I came to him as soon as I heard his need."

Cashel shook his head sadly. Katchin was such a *little* man. Cashel had never noticed it before. The bluster had made Katchin seem larger in Barca's Hamlet. Here he was just a buffoon come to the city from some sheepwalk nobody in Valles had ever heard of.

"Uncle," Cashel said, "you ought to go home. If you won't do that, at least get rid of those silly clothes. Put on a clean wool tunic and be yourself, not a joke for the palace servants to laugh at. You saw how the ushers looked at you."

Katchin's face went dark with a rage he couldn't swallow down. "And who are you, beggar boy, to lecture on fashion to Count Lascarg's bailiff?" he shouted.

"I never begged," Cashel said. He didn't get angry over words, and those particular words were too foolish to get angry over anyway. "And as for what I know of fashion, well, I don't guess I could live with Ilna all these years and not know something. Merchants came all the way from Valles to buy the cloth she wove, you know."

Katchin's mustache fluffed with the force of his breathing. He'd break something inside if he wasn't careful. "Look, Cashel, my boy," he said in forced jollity. "Just take me to see our Garric and he'll understand what he's being offered. You're a strong, honest lad, but this is a business beyond your understanding."

Cashel smiled. "I guess you're right, Uncle," he said. "But that's why you shouldn't have come to me. Garric has people to tell him who he's going to see. I don't know enough to go against what they decide."

He gestured to the door. "Go back home, Katchin," he said. It embarrassed Cashel to say things that shouldn't have to be said at all. "You'll like being a big fish in Barca's Hamlet better than you will being bait in Valles."

Katchin's mouth opened and closed, but fury choked his words for several moments. Finally he said, his voice breaking, "And I suppose *you* belong here, Cashel the Shepherd?"

"I belong wherever Sharina is, Uncle," Cashel said. A year ago he'd have been tense as a chain on a heavy drag if he'd had to talk about this sort of thing. "I guess I always did. It's just that now I know it."

He gestured toward the door again with a scooping motion, as though he was shooing a puppy out from where it didn't belong. Choking on bile, Katchin obeyed.

Cashel smiled at the thought he'd just had: he knew he belonged with Sharina; and Sharina knew she belonged with him, too.

Sharina's meeting with the delegation of Western Region landholders had been moving along at approximately the speed of mortar setting on a humid day. Watching mortar set would have been a good deal more interesting.

"It's not that the assessor sent to my parish is a bad lad," the delegate now holding the floor said. Sharina had tried to memorize their names, but she just couldn't: she was tired, sick and tired, and they were all the same. It was like trying to make individuals out of twelve peas. "He doesn't understand us, is all. Why, it's hard for us to understand him with that twang of his, not that I have any quarrel with him being a Northerner born and bred."

A hummingbird whistled by, pausing to drink from the trumpet-shaped scarlet flower of a lotus. Another hummingbird whirred toward the first. The pair disappeared deeper into the gardens, chittering angrily at one another.

The delegation in the tiled gazebo consisted of eleven men and one woman—a representative of each parish of the three western counties of Ornifal. They wore high-laced boots and tunics with ribbon ties down the front so that the lower half could be cinched into breeches when work required it. The delegates were substantial people in every sense—physically, they were built like so many tree stumps topped with gray moss—but the Western Region was a patchwork of smallholdings unlike the great estates of northern Ornifal. All the delegates had guided a plow themselves at some time in their lives, and most of them probably still lent a hand during the furious demands of the harvest.

The parishes of the Western Region were similar to the borough on the east coast of Haft where Sharina grew up, in fact. She could understand their concerns better than they themselves probably imagined.

The trouble was, the twelve of them individually were so like Katchin the Miller that he could have sat at the end of the row and no one would find him out of place. Puffed-up little people full of personal pride, with a vision as parochially narrow as that of the most mincing dandy among the palace courtiers.

A different parochial vision, of course.

"Just the same for us!" said the delegate from one of the coastal parishes: he had a rhomboid representing a turbot worked in silver thread onto the breast of his tunic, and a similar pin on his velvet cap. 'Where do I buy peat for my cook fire?' he asked me. Peat! And when I said we burn wood here, he looked at me as if I were mad! 'You can afford wood to burn, here?' he said, and I could just see the silver eagles tumbling around in his mind!"

"Just the same!" echoed other delegates like the chorus of a play. Three then started to tell their own detailed version of the injustice of having outsiders sent into their parishes to assess the taxes.

Eight of those present had had their say thus far in the afternoon. The speeches could have been interchanged or even intercut sentence by sentence without making any real difference. It all boiled down to "Outsiders don't know how we do things here in the West."

A clerk brought down from an estate in the north whose waterlogged soil didn't support trees might very well be surprised that heat for homes and food came from dead limbs rather than bricks of peat cut from the bogs and dried under shelters. That didn't mean he wouldn't adapt to the new circumstances: tax assessments were made on the local value of produce, not what the produce might have brought if it were transported somewhere else to be sold.

The real problem—and the one that the delegates speaking so earnestly to Sharina, making broad flourishes with their arms to emphasize their points, had no intention of raising—was that because Garric's new assessors were from outside the local power structure, they were working for the government in Valles instead of on behalf of themselves and their cronies. Oh, they could be bribed—they were human, after all, and could be expected to have human failings. But district supervisors kept an eye on the assessors, comparing individual revenues against those of similar parishes under different men.

Besides, it isn't nearly as easy to bribe a stranger as it is a man you've known all your life. Like any other criminal conspiracy, bribery requires that the parties trust one another. How do you trust a fellow with a funny accent and weird ideas about food?

There was a faint chime from the nympheum in the center of the palace grounds, where the giant water clock stood. A bronze bowl had flipped on its axis, spilling into the pool the water that had filled it drop by drop. The servant watching it struck a tuned rod. Other servants waiting at crosswalks throughout the grounds called, "The fifth hour has sounded!," their voices seeming to echo as those farther away took their cue from the ones nearest to the nympheum.

Sharina rose to her feet. The three delegates who were speaking simultaneously fell silent, though with nervous looks at one another. They were afraid—rightly—that Lady Sharina intended to end the audience before they'd had time to say everything *they* wanted. Sharina had learned from months of listening to similar representations that the thing all the delegates wanted most was a chance to hear their own voices. More than a reduction in taxes, more than better roads, more than a restoration of local tolls which they'd been pocketing to the detriment of trade and communication through their bailiwick . . .

"Mistress and masters," Sharina said, nodding to the woman and then to the eleven male representatives in a general sweep of her head. "During the past three hours, I have listened to your concerns. I sympathize with you, and I'll discuss what you've said with the officials in whose charge these matters lie."

The truth was that after three hours with these people, Sharina wouldn't have been able to manage much sympathy for them if they were being boiled in oil. Sharina's maid had dressed her as a private citizen of high rank. Chancellor Royhas had picked the outfit to emphasize that Sharina wasn't a court official and therefore couldn't bind the government by anything she chanced to say.

Sharina understood the purpose. She even managed not to feel too insulted that Royhas was treating her like a silly girl who might want to remit a district's taxes or promise a governorship to some charlatan who claimed to be a royal bastard. Royhas was simply being careful, and it was to the benefit of the kingdom that the Isles have a careful chancellor.

The problem was that the garments worn by a private Ornifal citizen of high rank were even heavier and more confining than court dress of beige silk robes with a stripe on the side to indicate the wearer's rank and position. Sharina's blond hair was teased up in a vast pile supported by ribbons and gold combs. Her tight-laced bodice was cloth-of-gold over a robe of heavy green silk, with appliqué panels showing the birth and exploits of the mythical hero Val.

For comfort, Sharina had decided to hold the meeting in a water garden of the palace. Cypresses shaded the slate-roofed gazebo; streams played from the mouths of stone dolphins to plash into the encircling lotus pond, cooling the air.

Nothing could make this clothing acceptably cool! Sharina had been more comfortable—less uncomfortable—tending the bread oven in the middle of the summer. The garb was as stiff as armor and as stifling as the steam baths that were a Cordin specialty which the elite of Valles had begun to take up.

"While I promise you consideration . . ." Sharina continued. *Royhas would be pleased at my diplomacy.* ". . . I can't tell you that there'll be an immediate change in the principle that the government has instituted. You see—"

The one female delegate—Mistress Alatcha—said, "Princess, the king's your brother! Can't you tell him we deserve to be ruled by our own folk?"

Physically there wasn't much to distinguish Alatcha from her colleagues. When she was standing—she was seated now—her tunic fell to her ankles instead of being knee-height, and there was a narrow band of lace dangling from her hat brim to do duty for the veil of respectable widow. Her sex had emboldened her to interrupt with the protest that the male delegates were swallowing, however.

Sharina smiled to show that she'd accepted the interruption in good part. She nodded—very carefully, because the mass of combs and hair was heavy enough that she worried what would happen if she leaned too far—and said, "I'll certainly discuss the matter with my brother Prince Garric, Lady Alatcha"—thank goodness she'd at least remembered that one name out of the twelve—"though I hasten to remind you that Valence III is King of the Isles. Like yourselves, my brother and I are the king's loyal subjects."

Mild as Sharina's statement was, the male delegates edged away from Alatcha as though she'd suddenly begun frothing at the mouth. Garric and the advisors who'd helped make him the real power in the Kingdom of the Isles were extremely careful to maintain the fiction that Valence was still king. To do otherwise would stir up trouble on Ornifal as well as probably pushing the rulers of other islands to declare their independence.

Alatcha looked frozen with fear. To take the unmeant threat out of her correction, Sharina stepped forward and offered the woman her hand. Alatcha gripped it as though she'd been drowning.

"But since you've raised the point, I'll address it directly," Sharina said. She patted Alatcha with her free hand, then disengaged and stepped back to survey the entire delegation. "Your taxes are being levied by people you don't know, and perhaps you've heard—I'll tell you now if you haven't—that within the year circuit courts under royal judges will begin hearing all cases of manslaughter and civil matters where more than twenty silver eagles are in dispute."

"Oh!" said one of the standing delegates. His colleagues, nodding grim-faced, had obviously heard the rumor already. In embarrassment the fellow sat down. The two others who'd been standing to speak sat also. For the first time this afternoon, the delegates were listening to something other than their own voices.

"The men who are coming to your districts were clerks in the households of northern landholders," Sharina said. "They're being paid by the treasury, though. Their loyalties, like their responsibilities, are to the whole kingdom rather than to one nobleman or another."

She paused, wishing she had a mug of the sharp, dark germander ale that her father had brewed in his inn. A swallow of that would cool her throat and clear the phlegm from it.

"But they don't know *us*," one of the delegates said, giving frustrated urgency to the point the speakers had been repeating with embellishment all afternoon.

"They'll get to know you," Sharina said forcefully. "But they'll serve the king. And if you think you're unhappy at having to deal with folk from the North, you can imagine how those northern nobles feel about assessors who come from the commercial houses here in Valles. Can you imagine how many times I've heard, 'But you can't propose that Lord So-and-Which pay taxes like some plowman in West Bay!' "

The delegation broke up in guffaws of delight. "Is that so?" a delegate cried in wonder.

"Well, Prince Garric *does* expect all the fine lords to pay their taxes," Sharina said. "And he expects the Valles shippers to pay theirs as well, which they will since they're being watched over by some of your own sons and daughters. Isn't that true?"

Over the general murmur of agreement, a man whose mustaches divided his face into two florid parts said, "Aye, my nephew Esmoun's one of them, he is. The king pays him seventeen eagles a month, a *month* that is, and in cold, hard cash!"

During the crisis just past, when the queen strove through wizardry to gain the kingdom, taxes due from the outlying regions had generally gone unpaid. There were two reasons the new government had money to pay its employees. First, the conspirators who'd opposed the queen—when King Valence was too weak to do so himself—were wealthy men in their own right. They'd backed the new government with their purses as well as their lives.

The second reason was that the queen had amassed enormous wealth before her defeat. Some had been looted, more was destroyed in the riot that made Garric the heir to the kingdom; but a great deal of the queen's treasure remained, and Lord Tadai had been quick and efficient in bringing that wealth into the royal treasury.

It was an open question whether Tadai would have been quite so scrupulous to avoid further enriching himself in the process had he not known that Chancellor Royhas was keeping very close track of matters. In the event, Tadai knew that he *was* being watched, so Tadai's worst enemy couldn't complain about the way he carried out his duties as treasurer.

"And Rohan, he's the second son of Robas, the miller in Helvadale, he went off to the king in Valles too," another delegate agreed. "Sharp as a bodkin, that boy, but what was there for him if he'd stayed in the parish? You can't split a gristmill, can you? Nor can you keep two families on what a mill brings in, not in Helvadale, you can't."

There was a pause for general consideration. Mistress Alatcha rose carefully to her feet. "Lady Sharina, you'll tell your brother that the Western Region is loyal, won't you?" she said. "I mean, we're used to the folk here in Valles treating us like we were scrapers to clean the muck from their boots—and we won't have that!"

Several representatives cried "No sir!" or something similarly agreeable. One launched into a story about an absentee landowner who didn't keep up his fences, but a pair of his fellows hushed him immediately.

"But we'll stand for the kingdom if the kingdom stands for us!" Alatcha concluded. The men around her bellowed "Aye!" and "Hear, hear!" in voices that threatened to rattle the roof slates. Servants and minor officials passing nearby craned their necks to see what was going on. Here in Valles, that many people shouting at the same time probably meant a riot rather than cheerful enthusiasm.

Sharina sighed internally with relief. She'd gotten through to this group, at least. She felt a rush of kinship for the delegates, peasants like herself, who were satisfied to be treated fairly.

Most of the people who came to Lady Sharina—because Royhas and Tadai made sure they couldn't get to Prince Garric—didn't care about what was fair or even what was necessary for the Kingdom of the Isles to survive the crisis it was facing. They wanted more for themselves, and their concept of justice balanced on the belief that the world (and certainly the kingdom) should operate to give them everything they wanted.

"Mistress Alatcha," Sharina said. "Masters—I'll be glad to assure my brother that the Western Region is loyal. For your own part, feel free to communicate with your government either in person as today or by written petition. But I ask for your patience as well, and your awareness that the burdens you and your neighbors carry are there for the kingdom's sake."

Sharina thought about the way the royal income was spent. She suspected there might be a way to run the palace that didn't require quite so many servants standing around with self-important expressions . . . but maybe not. Her father had made a success of a rural inn where there was no margin for waste. Now he was running the palace, and she didn't imagine he'd changed his principles with his new position.

The palace had requirements that went beyond simple efficiency. It had to cater to the expectations of the people who came here, folk like this delegation and embassies from other islands as well. Maybe you *needed* a network of servants calling the time for the same reason that Sharina was wearing expensive garments when bare feet and a simple woolen tunic would have answered the demands of decency. How would Mistress Alatcha have reacted to Sharina looking like a peasant?

She grinned. The delegates thought she was smiling at them as they mouthed their goodbyes. Actually, she was thinking about how good it would feel to change into a tunic and take off the high buskins which encased her feet.

Ushers, summoned in some fashion Sharina didn't understand, stood ready to guide the delegates back to the palace entrance. She ought to ask her father how servants, discreetly out of sight, suddenly appeared when they were needed.

The delegates moved off slowly, murmuring among themselves. Mistress Alatcha turned and waved where the walkway swept around a bed of osiers in a flooded planter; all of her fellows had to stop and do the same. Sharina held a frozen smile and waved back until the last of the twelve had disappeared.

Sharina's maid Diora came up to her quietly. Sharina lowered her hand and said quietly, "I've never been so glad in all my life to see a stand of osiers."

"Milady?" said the maid, frightened because she didn't understand what Sharina meant. Servants could never be sure how their employer would react to ignorance. Even in Barca's Hamlet, an occasional merchant or drover would aim a blow at a servant who hadn't performed as the guest thought was proper.

That didn't happen twice. Not when the broad-shouldered Garric or-Reise was the innkeeper's son, and every man in the borough would back Garric if the guest's guards took exception to the way their master was being rammed face-first into the inn's manure pile.

"That's all right, Diora," Sharina said. "I was just talking to myself. Can you help me let down my hair right now? I suppose I'll have to wear the rest of this ridiculous outfit until I get back to my suite."

She'd see Cashel as soon as she'd changed. She wished he were here already, not that there was anything he could really do for her. Sharina giggled, imagining Cashel carrying her to her suite like a woolsack. He was strong enough to lift two of her, even in the heavy garments she was wearing, but it would cause as much scandal as if Lady Sharina decided to strip down to her linen undertunic here in the gazebo. People—here and everywhere—worried more about the way things looked than the real decency or indecency of what was going on.

Diora plucked out combs with quick fingers. Sharina

hadn't liked the thought of having servants, but there wasn't any choice. She could no more have dressed herself in this garb than she alone could have rowed all hundred and seventy oars of a trireme.

Diora was quietly cheerful, good at her job, and—perhaps the most important thing from Sharina's standpoint—completely a child of Valles, so that she could pilot her mistress through the shoals of palace culture. There were many times that without Diora, Sharina would have been as lost as, well, as the maid would be if dropped into the middle of the common woodland adjoining Barca's Hamlet.

"Ah, milady?" Diora said hesitantly as she removed the last few combs, twisting them slightly so that Sharina's massed hair fell loose instead of following the teeth. Bits of gold rang softly and sweetly against other bits. "I wonder if you might have a moment to talk to some . . . other people?"

Sharina felt her stomach knot. *She couldn't take more of this* . . .

But she could. So long as she stayed in Valles, she had to. It was her duty.

"What other people would those be, Diora?" Sharina said in what she hoped was a tone of friendly curiosity. She started down the path toward her suite; the maid quickly stepped ahead of her and took Sharina's hand in the one that didn't carry the bag of combs. Sharina couldn't see her own feet while wearing this stiff, puffed outfit, so she needed a guide to keep from falling on her face.

Newly hired gardeners were repairing the ravages of years of neglect, but there was a lot of work yet to do. The roots of a stately elm had grown across the walk. Workmen had stacked the flagstones on one side and dumped a load of gravel ballast to the other, but they hadn't gotten around to sloping the ballast over the humped roots and relaying the flagstones.

"Up here, milady," Diora said. "Higher—there, now your left, and high again . . . There! You have it, milady."

Once they were past the awkward stretch, Diora released Sharina's hand. The maid continued to walk ahead as they passed between beds of zinnias flaring in vivid pastels, so that her mistress couldn't see her face. She said, "You see, milady, these are people from my old neighborhood. In the Bridge District, where I lived before I got my place here in the palace."

"Ah," said Sharina noncommittally. She didn't know where the Bridge District was—well south on the River Beltis, she supposed, because that was where the only bridge was. Valles had three districts on the west side of the river, she knew, but Sharina understood that only ferries and small boats connected them to the municipality's other fifteen districts.

"You see, milady, they can't get anybody to listen to them!" Diora said. "My mam's near out of her mind with it! I said that you were a *real* lady, not just a painted statue, and that I thought you'd maybe, you know, if you had a moment free . . . ?"

The girl was speaking faster than she normally did and clipping her syllables. That was the way people talked in the streets of Valles, not here in the cultured sanctity of the palace.

Sharina smiled faintly. She was trying to avoid the Haft lilt that came into *her* voice when she spoke without thinking. The lilt made her sound different from everyone around her, though of course nobody would mention it to her face.

Her face sobered. The delegates from the Western Region would have gone away happy if Sharina had claimed that tomorrow the rivers would run with wine and pies would grow on trees. The important thing was that Lady Sharina had listened to *them*, had talked to *them*, and they could carry that memory back to their parishes with as much joy as if it had been a casket of golden crowns fresh from the royal mint. She knew that what she was doing was important, but it *felt* as empty as trying to sweep back the tide with a broom.

And now her maid was bringing a deputation to her. Well, Reise hadn't raised his children to shirk their duties.

Diora risked a glance over her shoulder; Sharina's silence had worried her. They'd almost reached the building that was Sharina's own, a suite of neat little rooms about a central atrium with a skylight over a little pool. The janitor had removed the glazed cover for this hot weather; rain sent the pool's lacy-finned carp scurrying about the lily pads.

Sharina thought of asking if she could change clothes first, but that would be an insult—a way of saying that Diora's kin and friends weren't as important as the delegates who'd just left. Sharina's job was to make people feel *good* about their government.

Anyway, she'd been miserable all afternoon. Being miserable for another hour or however long wasn't going to kill her.

"Of course I'll see your neighbors, Diora," Sharina said. "Will your mother be among them?"

"Oh, no, milady!" Diora said in amazement. "My mam wouldn't think of pushing in to a business like this. I said to send the leading men of the neighborhood, six of them, and that's who's waiting on you now ... if that's all right?"

"Of course it's all right," Sharina repeated. Diora didn't seem to see anything incongruous about only men being fit to meet with the Important Personage ... who happened to be a woman. She thought of what Ilna would say, and as a result Sharina was giggling as she entered the hall to greet the delegation from the Bridge District.

The delegates waited in the atrium with their backs to a mural. Sharina's doorkeeper watched over them with a carefully neutral expression, ready to bellow at them as intruders if Lady Sharina showed displeasure at seeing them. The men themselves couldn't have been more frightened if they were waiting to be thrown to real gryphons and chimeras like those painted against a black ground behind them.

"Good afternoon, masters," Sharina said with a smile. "I'm glad to meet friends of Mistress Diora. She's been a wonderful help to me since I came here."

There was a general sigh. Sharina thought the big fellow with welts burned into his forearms by flying sparks—a farrier, beyond doubt—might faint from relief.

"Master Alswind," Diora said. The oldest man nodded stiffly. He wore a purple tunic which might have fit him twenty years before, when the noble to whom he was in service gave it to him as a castoff. That had been a good forty pounds ago, and if Alswind made a full bow he or the garment would burst.

"Master Rihholf, Master Aldern, Master Dudo"—the farrier—"Master Demaras, and Underpriest Arpert."

Sharina made the slight bow that was all the movement her stiff bodice allowed. Alswind wasn't the only one here trapped by clothing. "I'm pleased to meet you gentlemen," she said. "Will you be seated?"

There were benches with zebrawood seats and legs of pierced bronze on either side of the entrance door. Sharina gestured to them.

The delegates looked startled. "Oh, we could never sit in front of you, mistress!" said Rihholf, a plump man wearing a shoulder cape which must have been very uncomfortable in this weather—and which didn't quite cover the awkwardly darned moth hole in the breast of his tunic.

"She's not a mistress, you pigeon-brain!" Dudo snarled at him. "She's a *lady*!"

Sharina pointed at the benches. "Sit!" she said. She'd handled unruly diners in the inn's common room. If somebody didn't take charge promptly, midnight would come and nobody would have explained why these men had come to her.

Sharina stepped aside so the delegates could get to the benches without stumbling over her. There was a brief hesitation while they decided which man would sit where. Diora solved that by pointing to positions, three to a bench, and announcing each sitter's name in a crackling whisper.

The residents of the Bridge District might defer to the *concept* of maleness, but there didn't seem to be any nonsense about women waiting for the decisions of men who obviously didn't have a lick of sense.

"Master Arpert?" Sharina said. "Speak. Tell me why you're here to see me."

Arpert opened his mouth, closed it, and looked aside to his fellow delegates. "*Speak*, the lady says!" Dudo muttered. "Or so help me—"

"Right," said Arpert, suddenly focused. "We came to see you, lady, because we can't get anybody else to listen to us and Gunna's girl Ora here—"

"*Dio*ra," Alswind whispered. He'd managed to sit without splitting himself, but his back was as straight as if he'd been impaled.

"Diora, that's right," Arpert continued, "she said that you listened to people that nobody else would, and that you could maybe help. It's about the bridge, you see. It shouldn't be there, but it is again. At night. And there's the sounds, and it's getting worse."

"Folks're scared to death," said another man; maybe Demaras, but Sharina couldn't have sworn to his name if her life depended on it. She was tired, and there'd been *so* many names in the last three months. "I don't mean just the babies and the old women neither."

"The City Watch, they say it's no affair of theirs and they just stay away," said Arpert. "Which is what they mostly do anyway. Who cares if somebody's robbed in the Bridge District? That's how *they* feel about it."

The men nodded gloomily to one another. Sharina bit her tongue to keep from shouting in frustration. If these dimwits had gone into a Watch station mumbling nonsense the way they were doing here, she didn't blame the Watch officers for brushing them off!

But that wasn't fair. Arpert and his fellows weren't the poorest of the poor—they probably didn't think of themselves as poor at all; for that matter, they probably had as much ready cash as folk whom Barca's Hamlet considered prosperous farmers. Still, they were frightened and knew they were badly out of place here in the palace. Sharina was seeing them at their most flustered.

Which meant she'd have to help them if she wanted to complete the interview before dawn broke. "You say the bridge shouldn't be there," Sharina said. "Why not? You live in the Bridge District."

"Oh, not for hundreds and hundreds of years, mistress," Rihholf said, repeating his error of a moment before. Dudo, wrapped in greater worries, didn't correct him this time. "There was a bridge from the Old Kingdom, but it fell back nobody knows how far. There's still the abutment on our side, but on the left bank even that got swept away in the floods when Isnard the Bold was city proctor and tried to make himself king."

Three generations ago, Sharina translated mentally. For the most part the library Reise brought to Barca's Hamlet was of Old Kingdom classics, written a thousand years and more in the past. There'd been a few volumes of contemporary Ornifal history, though, since Reise was an Ornifal native and had been a palace steward before he fled to Haft for reasons he'd never made clear to his children.

"But the bridge is back now at night," maybe-Demaras said earnestly. "Or something is, all blue light that doesn't look like anything on this earth!"

"One moment, please," Sharina said. "Brogius"—her doorkeeper—"would you send an usher to Mistress Tenoctris and tell her there's a matter on which I would appreciate her counsel immediately? In fact, will you go yourself? I want Tenoctris to hear what these citizens have to say."

"Yes, milady," Brogius said. He paused only to put down his ceremonial axe—the double bitts were pierced brass and shaped like eagle heads, the symbol of Ornifal—and trotted off on his errand.

People spoke just outside the doorway. The door re-opened and sandals whispered on the mosaic floor of the anteroom. Sharina turned with an angry expression. If someone had decided to walk in on her unannounced because her doorkeeper was temporarily absent, that person was going to learn that Sharina didn't need servants to get rid of unwanted intruders.

Brogius stepped back into the atrium, followed by a birdlike woman in green silk robes. "Milady?" he said. "She was coming—"

"To see you, Sharina," Tenoctris said, stepping past the doorkeeper with her usual bright smile. "I was hoping you and Cashel—and perhaps your brother as well—might join me while I look for the source of a disruption."

Tenoctris was tiny and seventy years old in terms of normal aging—but cast into this era from a thousand years in the past. The sparkle of her personality lit up any gathering of which she was a part. She looked at the men on the benches to either side of her and added, "But I didn't mean to intrude. Let me wait—"

"No, no," Sharina said, taking the old woman by the hand. "Masters?" she said to the expectant men. "This is my friend Tenoctris the Wizard. She's the person I was bringing here to listen to what you have to say."

She cleared her throat, drawing warmth from the older woman's hand. Sharina had gone cold when she heard Dudo's description.

Because that bridge of shimmering blue light could only be the result of wizardry; and Sharina had seen enough wizardry to know the terrible dangers it could pose for the Kingdom of the Isles.

Ilna os-Kenset stood in her garden, weaving a memorial for those whom wizardly had killed at her side. Her fingers moved the shed and the shuttle of the double loom, quickly and absolutely without error.

Another weaver would have had to concentrate her whole being to work on a design as complex as this arras. Ilna let her fingers choose the wrap threads while she thought about the path which had brought her where she was.

A thread could go as many different places as there were cords in the weft, but there was only one correct choice for each pattern. Ilna supposed that was true of lives as well. She didn't complain about that; but occasionally she wondered what life would have been like if her pattern had been a little different.

Her fingers flew. The tapestry grew with the steady ease of a tide rising.

Ilna was dark-haired and petite. From a distance she looked pretty. Close up, especially if you looked into her eyes, she was beautiful; but Ilna's beauty was that of a sword edge.

Ilna's eyes were as clear as pools mirroring Truth. If you didn't want to hear the truth as Ilna saw it, you'd best go elsewhere—quickly.

She'd been a skilled weaver before she surrendered to evil and gained inhuman abilities. Ilna had escaped from evil in the end; but she couldn't escape knowledge of the things she'd done, and she still had the skills she'd learned in Hell.

Each strand had a story that Ilna absorbed much the way that her nostrils drew in the perfume of the flowers about her in the garden. *Lambs gamboled on a slope overlooking a pond whose margin had been trampled to mud. A shepherd bowed a three-stringed rebec and sang to his flock . . .*

Garric had played the pipes. Ilna, standing at her loom in the dooryard of the mill, had often heard the clear sweet notes soothing sheep in the meadow.

That was in another life, gone now for both of them. And even if the tides of time and space hadn't thrown the wizard Tenoctris onto the shore of Barca's Hamlet, the future wouldn't have gone the way Ilna had dreamed it would. Garric, strong and handsome and educated by his father to a level few youths in the great cities could reach, would never have married an illiterate peasant like Ilna os-Kenset.

Someone knocked imperiously on the door of Ilna's bungalow. A guard opened the barred eyeslit and spoke to the visitor.

Her house in the palace grounds was three rooms off a tiny atrium—plus the gorgeous garden where Ilna worked while the weather allowed. It was more space than she and Cashel needed here; but Ilna by herself had kept their half of the millhouse in Barca's Hamlet clean, and that was larger yet.

From what Ilna had seen, the maids available in Valles were mostly slatterns; and if they weren't, well, she didn't want them in her home anyway. She and Cashel had no servants here.

Ilna did have guards, though. At Garric's personal orders a pair of Blood Eagles stood watch at all times, changing shift at every fourth hour.

Ilna had protested. Garric had listened politely, then told her that while his friends lived in the palace, they were in danger because they *were* his friends. Ilna—and Liane, Sharina, and Tenoctris—would have guards, however they felt about the matter. He had guards himself.

Garric hadn't assigned guards to Cashel. A smile wasn't the most frequent expression on Ilna's face, but she smiled now at the thought of a couple of Blood Eagles trying to protect her brother better than he could protect himself.

The argument at the door continued; loudly on the part of the men outside demanding entrance, quietly but with increasing harshness from the two guards within. Ilna could have let the Blood Eagles handle it, but the intruders' business was properly with her, and she'd never been one to leave her tasks for others to do.

Ilna closed the shed of her loom and stepped through an aisle of twisted columns into the atrium. "I'll handle this," she said to the guards.

The Blood Eagles wore helmets and breastplates of iron scales cushioned by quilted leather vests. The armor was hot, uncomfortable, and probably unnecessary; but the guards were there in the first place in case the improbable happened. One of them was grizzled and in his fifties, but his younger companion seemed to be in charge.

Instead of stepping aside, the younger man closed the eyeslit with a bang and said to Ilna, "The president and two councillors of the Temple of the Protecting Shepherd are here to see you, mistress. How would you like us to .deal with them?"

If I said that I'd like them disemboweled here in the garden, would you do that? Ilna wondered. She found soldiers disquieting not because they were capable of doing terrible things, but because they might do terrible things if somebody else told them to.

The Blood Eagles provided both a royal bodyguard and a pool from which junior officers were drawn for the regular regiments. The older man of this pair would never go anywhere: he wore the black uniform because he was brave, loyal, and a good soldier, but he had no more brains than a large dog.

The younger man was of another type: a veteran, because he'd had to prove himself to be enrolled as a Blood Eagle, but alert and clearly ambitious. With Garric's expansion of the Royal Army under way, this fellow would be promoted in the near future.

Different as they were, they shared a willingness to kill people they'd never met, simply because they were ordered to do so. Perhaps there was a need for such men just as there was a need for sharp knives, but Ilna would have preferred not having them around.

"I'll take care of them myself," she said calmly. She slid the bar aside and pulled the door open.

And if I really thought they should be disemboweled, I could manage that myself also.

Ilna was accurate to a hair in judging strangers' wealth and social standing by their clothes. The three men on her arched porch were wealthy businessmen, but not of the highest class. They dressed in Valles fashion with layered tunics and sashes of colored silk, but only the pale, cadaverous man at the head of the trio was born on Ornifal.

"I am Velio or-Elvis, president of the Temple of the Protecting Shepherd," he said. He spread his right arm in a rhetorical gesture. The stocky man to his right had to jump back to avoid being struck; he muttered and glared at Velio.

"My companions are Councillor Casses and Councillor Ermand," Velio continued in a slightly chastened tone. "We're here to discuss with you the arras which you're providing to screen the image of the Protecting Shepherd."

Ilna's face didn't change as she decided how to deal with the intrusion. "Come in," she said after a moment, stepping back to pull the door fully open, "but you've wasted your trip. I told your temple clerk that I'd finish the cloth tomorrow. You can save yourself a lot of trouble in the future by assuming that I mean what I say."

The stocky councillor, Casses, wore a long-sleeved tunic to minimize the tattoos on both arms. He'd been a sea captain at one time, though now he must have a shoreside business in order to sit on a temple council.

Ermand was a much more polished sort. He held his right hand out palm down in a courtier's gesture, offering it for Ilna to touch lightly with her fingertips.

Ermand oozed a sort of charm that would have floated on water. No question how *he* came to his present affluence.

Ilna ignored the hand. "Come and sit if you must," she said, turning away from the trio. "I can offer you water or good ale. There's bread and cheese as well, and I suppose we can find something fancier in the palace if your tastes demand it."

Ilna had to live in a society of human beings who didn't listen and who wasted their time in foolish ways. She was trying to train herself to be a part of that society, but it was very hard. Generally she felt like a shuttle in a world of warp and weft: acting on the pattern, but never really a part of it.

Sometimes Ilna wondered how it would feel not to be lonely, but she didn't expect she'd ever learn.

The councillors entered, looking puzzled. Ermand laced and unlaced his fingers in a nervous gesture. The guards closed and barred the door, then stepped discreetly through the bead curtain into a darkened side room. They could watch and listen unobtrusively to what was taking place under the skylight in the atrium.

But the only furniture in the atrium was a pair of wicker stools. There was a stool in each of the bedrooms as well, but—

"Come out into the garden," Ilna decided aloud. "There're benches set into the wall under the colonnade."

They trooped out through the back of the atrium, Ilna leading the three men. She didn't know what they were doing here, but she understood who they were.

When she'd decided what sort of memorial would be appropriate, Ilna had gone to Liane bos-Benliman for advice. Others could have told Ilna how the bureaucracy of a temple in Valles was organized. Asking Liane, Garric's Liane, for advice was Ilna's way of apologizing for the unjustified anger she felt toward the other girl. It wasn't Liane's fault that she had the culture and education a peasant like Ilna lacked. . . .

The councillors seated themselves carefully. Pear trees planted at either end of the masonry bench had been espaliered flat against the wall. Their branches interlocked in a network too spiky to lean against.

Ilna stood with one hand on the frame of her loom, eyeing her guests. Temple councils provided status for people who lacked it by birth and breeding, and who didn't have enough wealth to buy their way into the real upper circles. Councillors were responsible for upkeep of the building itself and the cult statue it housed. In exchange, they wore ornate costumes to major ceremonies and had an annual banquet in the temple precincts.

"Will you have refreshments?" Ilna repeated. At one time she would have been irritated at losing daylight to a foolish interruption. Since she returned from Hell, though, she could weave in the dark if necessary.

She was still irritated, but she was determined not to let it show. Much.

Velio stared at the loom. This panel, the last Ilna was completing, would form the center of the three-part hanging. Only a small portion of the design was visible from where the councillors sat.

"But *you're* weaving the arras, mistress," Velio said.

"Yes, of course," Ilna said. "I arranged it with your clerk last month: a screen for the Shepherd's image, to commemorate the salvation of Valles from the Beast. That's what you're here about, isn't it?"

The councillors goggled at her, and she wondered if her own face didn't wear a similarly stupid expression. What did they think they were getting if not a—

"We thought you were hiring people to weave the arras, mistress," Councillor Casses said. "We didn't know you were going to weave part of it yourself."

Ilna smiled coldly now that she understood the confusion. "I'm weaving all of it myself, Master Casses," she said. "I assure you I'm qualified. I told your clerk that I would provide your temple with a hanging like no other you will ever see, and so I shall. I'll have the panels joined when you return at the time we've arranged tomorrow. The completed work will speak for itself."

Casses frowned and sucked in his lips. It struck Ilna that the former sailor was probably the smartest of the three. He was watching her as he might in other times have eyed a cloud on the horizon, wondering if it was going to grow into a life-threatening storm.

Velio cleared his throat and said, "Well, it's not who makes the hanging that brings us here, mistress. You see, it's traditional that the sponsor of an offering to the temple provide a trust to maintain the gift in perpetuity. We haven't heard from your bankers as yet."

"A large cloth like this requires expensive care, you understand, Mistress Ilna," Ermand put in unctuously. He was beaming at her with the false smile that he must have practiced on scores of wealthy women over the years. "Of course you want the best f—"

Ermand broke off in midsyllable; his expression changed. He must actually have looked into Ilna's eyes for the first time.

"I don't have a banker, Master Velio," Ilna said pleasantly. "Not here in Valles, at any rate. There are sums—people—I could call on in Erdin, but that's not the point."

Ilna really was trying to avoid the anger that was the only thing in the world she feared, but her voice still hardened as she went on, "My offer was to provide your temple with a hanging that would remind all who saw it of the city's salvation and of the sacrifice of those who made that salvation possible. If you misunderstood my clear words, I regret it. Now, masters, I wish you good day, because I have work yet to accomplish on my part of the bargain."

She gave a quick flip with two fingers of her right hand as if she were hooking the councillors to their feet. They stood up obediently, but Velio continued to frown.

"Mistress," he said, "you live in the palace. I understand that you may not have money of your own, but—"

Casses gripped the president's elbow in a vain attempt to stop the fool before he blurted, "—won't your protector—"

The analytical part of Ilna's mind had foreseen the question just as Casses had done. She reached into her left sleeve and brought out the clutch of cords which she kept there at all times. Her fingers twisted them into a pattern with the same cold certainty as water flows through rapids.

"—provide the endowment if you ask him in the right—"

Ilna stepped forward and drew the cords tight in front of Velio's face. He started to scream, but even that sound choked in his throat.

Bubbles formed between the president's lips. His eyelids couldn't blink. Neither of his companions spoke or moved.

Ilna collapsed the design with a shudder and drew back.

She was shivering in summer sunlight. She heard Velio gag as he started to recover.

To the loom—she didn't dare face Velio for a few moments yet—Ilna said, "I have a terrible temper, Master Velio. I'm already doing penance for the evil which my anger drew me into in the past."

She cleared her throat and turned. Casses was holding Velio to keep the president from slumping onto the ground.

"I've just shown you the sort of place to which my anger would consign anyone who called me a whore," Ilna said. "I no longer let my anger rule me, so there was no danger of that happening."

She cleared her throat again, swallowing the lie she'd just spoken. "And anyway, you didn't really mean the insult, did you?"

Velio shook his head. He couldn't speak, and he finally had to cover his eyes with his hands before he could blink away the dryness.

Casses gave Ermand a nudge, starting him off toward the atrium with a spastic jolt. He guided Velio in the same direction.

"We'll leave you to your work, mistress," Casses said in a voice as polite and careful as that of a shopkeeper to a wealthy client. "The endowment won't be a problem, I assure you. We'll have no difficulty finding a patron to sponsor work that *you* do."

"I'll expect you tomorrow," Ilna said. Her throat was dry. She felt dizzy with reaction to what she hadn't permitted herself—quite—to do.

She didn't belong in this world! She had to stop acting as if she had a right to correct people who behaved badly. She had power, but using her power on ordinary people was like using a hammer to fix everything that breaks. Sometimes a hammer's the right tool, but more often it makes the problem worse.

The guards had returned to the atrium when Ilna led her guests out the back. They opened the door for the councillors without expression. If the Blood Eagles had an opinion of what they'd seen happen, they kept it professionally to themselves.

"Why didn't somebody warn us she was a wizard?" Councillor Ermand wailed to his fellows as they stepped off the porch. Though she was still standing by her loom, Ilna had a view through the axis of her house. She watched the backs of the shaken men as they went down the path bowered by peach trees.

A servant with the ebony staff of an usher trotted around the trio on his way toward Ilna's dwelling. The Blood Eagles saw him also; the younger man turned to catch Ilna's eye.

"Yes, of course I'll see him," she said, answering the guard's unspoken question. She walked into the atrium. The few people who might send a palace usher for her all had a claim on her time.

The usher reached the porch. He hadn't brought a message to Ilna before, so he'd expected to find a doorkeeper. He hesitated, not sure how to proceed when faced with two Blood Eagles and an intense young woman dressed too simply to be a palace servant.

Focusing his eyes past Ilna's shoulder to the empty interior of the house, the usher announced, "Lady Tenoctris requests that Mistress Ilna os-Kenset join her and their friends in Prince Garric's apartments immediately, if it is convenient for her to do so."

Ilna nodded. The words "if it's convenient" meant that Tenoctris didn't see whatever was happening as an immediate crisis. On the other hand, the old wizard wouldn't have bothered gathering Ilna "and their friends" for a merely social occasion.

Ilna smiled faintly. Tenoctris was if anything less given to socializing than Ilna herself.

"Yes, of course," Ilna said. "While you're here, you can help these men and me bring the loom inside in case it rains. It's double width, so it's awkward."

The usher opened his mouth, perhaps to protest. The older Blood Eagle put an arm around the usher's shoulder and squeezed him with a hand callused from wielding a sword. "Sure, it's your job, boy," he said with a nasal accent from the north of Ornifal. "Just like it's our job. You put that pretty stick down and come help us so you can get right back to sitting on your fanny for most of the day."

Ilna stepped briskly back to the loom to tie off the shuttle before they moved it. Behind her the old soldier added in a husky whisper, "You'll like it a lot better than you do hopping like a toad for the rest of your life; and that's not the worst might happen if you got snorky about helping the lady. Understand?"

Ilna shivered, but she pretended she hadn't heard the comment.

Chapter Two

Garric's body continued sleeping on the couch in the conference room. His mind got up from it and strolled out of the building. He didn't have any control over his movements, though that didn't concern him at the moment. He supposed he was dreaming.

Garric's legs swung in their usual long stride, but he was moving faster than a walking man and not traveling through space alone. He recognized all the places he passed, but many were in Barca's Hamlet, not Valles, and some were from out of the waking world.

The people Garric met were shadows, but sometimes they spoke to him and he replied. He couldn't hear the exchanges, even the words that came from his own lips.

He was alone for the first time since his father had given him a coronation medal of King Carus. When Garric hung that ancient gold disk against his chest, he and Carus had begun to share an existence closer than twins, closer than spouses. But now—

Garric felt for the medallion. It lay back with his sleeping self. He straightened his shoulders and let the dream carry him where it would.

He reached a bridge and started across. Behind him was Valles; beyond . . . he couldn't be sure. Sometimes Garric saw shining walls; other glimpses were of ruins which might once have been the same buildings. The structure underfoot felt more solid than stone, though to Garric's eyes he was walking on a tracery of blue light, a fairy glow without substance.

Garric reached the far end of the bridge. It was daylight here, though it had been early dusk in Valles when he left his couch. Before him was a city which at the time of its glory must have been magnificent; it was breathtaking even now. He strode toward it.

Modern Valles might be larger; Carcosa in the days of King Carus and the Old Kingdom was far greater yet. In the richness of its fittings, though, nothing Garric knew from his own day or the past could compare with what this place must once have been.

He was walking up an esplanade paved with slabs of red granite, each as wide as Garric was tall and twice as long. The labor of cutting and smoothing such hard stone made him blink.

The blocks were cocked and broken, by time and the roots of trees crawling from the median plantings. The surface should have been as hard to walk on as a seascape frozen in the middle of a lashing storm. In this dream existence, the footing didn't hinder Garric.

Pedestrian porticos flanked the roadway. Some of the arches had collapsed. The core was fitted stones rather than the concrete and rubble of similar constructions in ancient Carcosa.

The buildings to either side were stone also, but originally metal had covered them. Some had worn tin, decayed now to powdery tendrils trailing from the cracks between close-fitting blocks. Others had been clad in sheets of copper and bronze whose blue-green revenants still stained the walls.

Garric frowned. He'd heard of this place, but as a myth of the final days before the fall of the Old Kingdom. A fragment from a discourse of the philosopher Andron, captured in a quirky anonymous compendium entitled *The Dress of All Peoples in All Times*. He couldn't remember the exact words or the claimed location, but he recalled the description of residents wearing striped clothing which reflected variously according to the color of the mirroring walls they passed beside.

A dream of a myth? *These* ruins had a solid reality.

He walked toward the vast building at the end of the esplanade. The three stages of its façade were supported by pillars of equal height, but those of the middle level were more slender than the massive columns beneath them, while delicate pairs of banded travertine chosen for appearance rather than strength formed the uppermost range. The wooden casements and shutters of the upper-story windows had rotted to dust.

The ground-floor entrance was recessed deeply within a pointed arch, but the door itself was small and so strongly made that it yet survived. Flanking the porch were fountains. Rains had left a stagnant scum in the orichalch basins, but the bronze statues from which water had once played were twists of verdigris which gave no hint of their former shapes.

The city was silent save for the wind soughing through the walls.

A broad helical staircase twisted from the ground to the building's roof. The pillared tower was styled to match the main structure, but the two were only connected at the top.

Garric climbed the stairs. Their pitch was shallow, too shallow for his long legs, and should have been uncomfortable. In his present dream state he only noticed what he had no muscles to feel.

He wondered if King Carus missed Garric's presence as

much as Garric did his. Did Carus even realize that Garric was gone?

As Garric mounted the stairs, his view of the city through the columns broadened. The streets were laid out in concentric circles centered on this building, though the docks of what had been a thriving seaport ate an arc out of one edge. The ships were gone, but the quays and stone bollards remained. The port didn't have sloping ramps up which oar-driven warships could be drawn to prevent their light hulls from decaying while not in use.

At the very edge of his vision Garric thought he saw a wall of shimmering light like that which formed the bridge. It was too faint for him to be sure. Though daylight suffused the sky, there was no sun.

Garric stepped onto the roof. It was covered with granite like the boulevard and esplanade, but these slabs were as nearly level as the common table in Reise's inn. The foundations must sink down to the bowels of the earth.

The roof was a vast plaza decorated by a score of stone planters like buttons tucking the horsehair of an upholstered seat. Grass and weeds grew in them now, and from one sprouted a twisted apple tree—the progeny many times removed of the tree placed there when the building was new. Roots had burst out the sides of other planters in the distant past, spilling the soil for rains to wash into a film of mud; only the lone apple had been able to reseed itself.

The roof was an audience ground. At the end opposite the staircase was a chamber with a screen of pierced alabaster for its outward-curving front wall. Garric walked toward it, his feet taking him where he would have gone of his own volition.

The translucent alabaster was no more than a finger's thickness. Light both reflected from and refracted through the milky stone, giving the air a soap-bubble sheen. The piercings were not simple holes or even a repetitive pattern. As Garric stepped close he saw a tracery of images, each as subtle and unique as the starlings of a flock wheeling in autumn.

The cut-out shapes had meaning—of that Garric was sure. His conscious mind couldn't grasp what the meaning was, however. Would Tenoctris understand?

The screen permitted citizens to see and hear their ruler close at hand, while still preventing them from touching him—or her, Garric supposed. It was carved from a seamless sheet of alabaster and had no door. A twig with a few dried leaves was caught in one of the small holes.

In ancient Carcosa the King of the Isles addressed the people assembled in the Field of Heroes from a high balcony on the back of the palace. Since the Dukes of Ornifal had become Kings of the Isles, they'd practiced a cooler sort of kingship. The populace had seen Valence III in formal processions and at ceremonies before the great temples, but he'd never addressed them directly. Anything the king had to say to his people came through the mouths of underlings.

That was going to change. It had *already* changed, beginning the day a combination of pragmatism and fear forced Valence to adopt Garric as his son and successor. Garric thought the idea of a podium or high balcony was a better choice than this screen, but the notion was an interesting one.

The screened audience chamber had solid walls on the other three sides. The windows in the sidewalls had screens of electrum filigree, and the door in the back wall had a grate over the viewport.

The room was empty save for dust and a bier of travertine marble. Discolored patches on the floor showed where bronze hardware had decayed. What—

Garric stepped through the alabaster as he had the door of the conference room when he started this journey. He felt momentary surprise, but he was too busy taking in his changed surroundings to marvel at inconsequentials.

Now that Garric was inside, he saw a plump old man in a tasseled tunic on the bier. Over him a serpentine shape waxed and waned, never fully visible but casting a glow like a golden blanket.

The old man's eyes opened. He rose with a cheery smile, pulling with him a tail of the quilted velvet covering the stone. "Good day, sir!" he said, extending his arm to clasp Garric's. "And who would you be?"

The old man paused. His smile slipped into an expression half-wary, half-peevish. "Or have we met? Do I know you? Tell me!"

It was late evening. The sky, visible through the electrum grating, was a sullen red. Crowds were looking up from the streets. Ships packed the quays, moored several deep in some cases, but no vessels were under way in the harbor.

"Sir, I don't think we've met," Garric said. He stepped forward, offering his arm though the old man had jerked his own back as doubt struck him. "I'm Garric or-Reise of Haft."

He swallowed. "But I think I'm dreaming."

The old man's smile returned like the sun flashing after a summer shower. They clasped, hand to elbow so that their forearms joined. The old man's grip was firm; his flesh resilient and vaguely warm.

"Dreaming?" he said to Garric. "Nonsense! You're here, aren't you? How can you be dreaming?"

The room was the same as when Garric viewed it through the alabaster, except that now signs of occupancy littered it. A cushioned pad covered the bier, and wooden bookcases lined all three walls: shelves for codices and pigeonholes for scrolls.

The cases were empty. Here and there a locked screen hung askew, wrenched off as the library was ransacked with brutal haste.

Garric stepped back. The old man looked around him with dawning puzzlement. "Sir, may I ask your name?" Garric said politely.

"What?" said the old man, again with a querulous tone. "I'm Ansalem, of course!"

He'd been looking at the glowing shape rippling in and out of existence above the bier. It seemed to be a serpent with a short, fat body, but sometimes the head appeared to be on one end, sometimes on the other.

Ansalem paused and fingered a wall niche large enough to have held a life-sized statue. It, like the bookcases, was empty. "I think I am, at least," he said. "But I don't understand. If I'm Ansalem the Wise . . ."

He turned to Garric, his face wrinkling in an expression of concern foreign to it. "If I am, then where are my books? And where are the baubles I've gathered over the years?"

Ansalem's expression flowed suddenly into something as cold and inhuman as the ice of a pond at mid winter. "Have you taken them?" he demanded. "You must return them at once! They're objects of power. They aren't safe for anyone else to have, you see. I know better than to use them, but anyone else might—" He snapped his pudgy fingers in a sound as sharp as nearby lightning. "—blast this world to dust! I'm not joking, young man. You must return them at once!"

"Sir," Garric said. "I haven't taken your property or anyone else's. I just arrived, and I don't even know where I am."

His mouth was dry. Ansalem was as unpredictable as the sky in summer, changing from sun to storm before a shepherd has time to call his flock.

And for all his general good nature, Ansalem was more dangerous than any storm. Garric didn't recognize the name, but he knew that the old man was a wizard. If he'd brought Garric here, he was a wizard of incalculable power.

"Where you are?" Ansalem said, his sunny disposition reasserting itself. "Why, you're in Klestis, in my palace. Don't you know?"

He gestured broadly. That made him notice the empty cases again; his face slipped back into a worried frown. "Where can—"

Ansalem stopped. He fixed Garric with an analytical gaze and took the youth's chin between finger and thumb. He twisted Garric's head from one profile to the other.

Garric accepted the attention, though he felt a surge of anger at being treated like a sheep being sold. Ansalem was an old man and obviously confused.

Ansalem wasn't a bit more confused than Garric, though, if it came to that.

"Are you sure I don't know you?" Ansalem asked, not harshly but with a note of sharp interest. "Surely we've met! Now where, I wonder?"

He turned to the bookcase on his right, obviously reaching for a volume that was no longer there. He froze, his face taking on the terrible icy hardness Garric had seen before.

"Where are my acolytes?" Ansalem demanded. "Have you seen them, Master Garric? Purlio will know what's going on here."

"Sir, I don't know anything," Garric said. "I've never heard of you, and the only Klestis I know of is a fishing village on the south coast of Cordin."

"Fishing village indeed!" Ansalem said in a tone of amazement. He beckoned Garric to the window looking onto the harbor. "Does this look like a fishing village, sir?"

"No sir," Garric said, "but—"

"But what's wrong down there?" Ansalem said, looking himself at the scene and finding it different from whatever he'd meant to show Garric. "Everyone's standing in the streets and staring up . . ."

He spun on Garric with another flash of mercurial temper. "What have you done with my acolytes?" Ansalem said. "Purlio, come here at once!"

"I—" Garric said.

Ansalem stepped to the bier from which Garric had awakened him. He ran his hand through the air, seeming to caress the flickering serpent. "The amphisbaena is here," he said, "but not the other objects. Some of them are too dangerous to use, even for me! Don't you understand?"

Ansalem patted the tall niche, then touched other alcoves and ran his fingers over the top of a marble plinth standing empty beside the door in the back of the chamber. He moved with the quick, jerky motions of a toad hopping, desperate in its terror.

"You must bring them back!" Ansalem said. "They won't do you any good, I assure you. There's nothing there but destruction for whoever uses them!"

The chamber grew foggy as another world began to interpenetrate it. "Bring me . . ." Ansalem cried in a voice as high as a distant gull's.

The words faded. Garric felt his soul rushing back the way it had come. He was a shimmer in existence like the current of a rushing stream.

"Garric?" a voice said. Not Ansalem, but—

Garric opened his eyes. He lay on a bench in the conference room. Liane stood beside him, holding a lamp; the light through the open door was the last red of sunset. His friends were watching him with guarded concern: Cashel and Sharina, Tenoctris and Ilna, and Liane, thank the Lady; Liane, her worry clear in her dark, limpid eyes.

"I was dreaming," Garric said as he sat up cautiously. "And I'm *very* glad to see you all."

"You didn't wake up," Sharina said. "We thought— well, Tenoctris says there's something dangerous going on."

"Something very powerful which I don't understand, at any rate," the old wizard explained. She cocked Garric a wry smile. "Which I suppose means it's dangerous, true enough."

She sobered. "I need to learn what the—source of power—is. It's already causing disruption on this portion of the cosmos. There's a nexus nearby; somewhere in Valles."

"I'm going with Tenoctris to, well, fetch and carry," Cashel said with a grin. To protect the old woman, Cashel meant; he was carrying the hickory quarterstaff he'd shaped with his own big, capable hands. "Sharina and Ilna are coming too. We know you're busy, but we thought we'd ask if you wanted to come along. Like old times, you know."

"You're scheduled to dine with Chancellor Royhas tonight," Liane said, meeting Garric's eyes but speaking with a careful lack of emphasis. "I was going to suggest that a more relaxed evening might be a good idea anyway."

"I've seen you lots of times after you've plowed all day in the hot sun," Cashel said. "That sweated you down to a nub, but you never looked as bad as you do now."

Ilna nodded. She'd stayed arm's length behind the others, unwilling that anyone might think she was pushing herself forward even though she and Garric had been friends for all their mutual lives.

"You're stretched too far," she said crisply. "Anyone can see that. I can't imagine how a meal with your chancellor can be a strain, but you obviously think it is. Only a fool would break himself by going to dinner instead of getting the sleep he needs."

"I don't need to go with Tenoctris," Sharina said apologetically. "Garric, why don't you get proper rest in a bed tonight. I'll meet with Lord Royhas if it's just a formal meal."

Garric looked at his friends. "It's not just a formal meal," he said. "It's part of the biggest problem I've got as, as whatever I am now."

"*As King of the Isles, lad,*" whispered Carus through the ages. The king was back in Garric's mind; as straight as an ancient pine, and as great a support to the youth he guided. "*That's what you are.*"

"The greatest problem I've got as King of the Isles, I mean," Garric said, correcting himself with a rueful smile. This was no place for self-deprecation. "And sure, I need sleep, but this nap's been enough to hold me. What I really need is to talk to my friends about the kingdom."

"Garric, I don't know anything about kingdoms," Cashel said. "Maybe Sharina . . . ?"

Garric stepped forward and embraced Cashel. It was like hugging a warm boulder. Garric was taller than his friend— by a bit—but Cashel had a solid strength that went beyond that of any other human being Garric had met.

"I need to talk to people I trust," Garric said. "You five are the only people on earth I can trust to want exactly what I want—peace for all the people of the Isles."

He stepped back and glanced toward the wizard. "Tenoctris?" he said. "Can the thing you're looking for wait for us to eat and talk first?"

"Yes," Tenoctris said. Frowning as she tried to explain to people who couldn't see the varied forces that worked the cosmos the way she saw them, she continued, "It isn't a hostile intrusion, not a thing of Malkar or a wizard allied to Malkar."

To Malkar: to evil, the force of absolute black evil that was the abnegation of all light and good.

"It's just very powerful," Tenoctris added, spreading her hands.

Garric nodded. "Half the buildings in the palace compound haven't been repaired yet," he said. "Let's find a quiet spot in one of them and I'll cook supper like I would if we were watching the flock overnight in the North Pasture. All right?"

"Cook?" Liane said. She clapped her left fingers to her lips in embarrassment the instant the question slipped out.

"Cook," Ilna repeated with emphasis. "If the stewards can't supply Prince Garric with flour, cheese, and onions promptly, I suspect the chamberlain will have replaced them all before morning."

"And a flitch of bacon," Garric said, laughing with the relief of not being Prince Garric of Haft for this one evening. "We'll eat like rich folk tonight, with meat for dinner!"

He shrugged to loosen his muscles. He needed to exercise more than he'd been doing recently.

"After we talk and eat," Garric said, "we'll find the nexus Tenoctris is looking for. And if it's a problem, then we'll deal with it."

"As we've done before," boomed King Carus. He stood

with his thumbs hooked in his sword belt, grinning at the youth whose mind he shared. *"And as we'll keep on doing until the Isles have the peace I wasn't able to give them alone!"*

Chapter Three

The big kitchen had served the servants' dormitories when all the palace staff were housed within the compound. That had been under Valence II, a generation previous; the site had been abandoned since then. Within the past week a team of gardeners had cleared the honeysuckle off the long building and rolled it into a bale higher than a man was tall.

The gardeners would burn the vines as soon as they'd dried. Ilna guessed that the flames would glare from the bases of clouds. Honeysuckle blazed as hot and fierce as anger . . . Ilna's anger, at any rate. She smiled.

A pair of cook's helpers had deposited a hamper of food and a jar of beer—on Ornifal they carried liquids in tarred earthenware instead of wooden casks—on the brick floor of the kitchen. They waited doubtfully for orders. Liane glanced toward Garric, but he and Sharina were too busy looking over the range to notice the servants.

"Go on, then," Ilna said to the helpers. "We'll take care of anything further ourselves."

Garric glanced up and nodded, but the servants were already scampering back to wherever they normally sat on their hands. No point in them hanging around *here* looking silly. Ilna wouldn't trust either one to sort carrots from parsnips.

"Garric, I can do the cooking," Sharina said as she

straightened from the range. She glanced at Ilna and smiled. "Or Ilna can."

The heavy iron bars of the grill were still solid though rust and ancient grease caked them. Ilna suspected that even when the kitchen was in daily use the cooks' standards of cleanliness had been lower than any she—or Reise's children—would have permitted if they were in charge.

"And do a better job, I know," Garric said. "But I'll do well enough, and I feel like it."

Sharina grinned at her brother. "Then I'll chop firewood," she said agreeably. "There's no lack of fallen limbs here, is there?"

Firewood was a valued resource, but this great compound was royal property. While Valence lost his grip on power, dead wood had been allowed to rot on the ground instead of being put to productive use.

Sharina wore a thin tunic with a black, knee-length linen cape for modesty. It was a common outfit in Valles among women of middling station who wanted to be comfortable while they were doing the day's shopping.

The metal kitchenware had gone when the kitchen went out of service, but there was sufficient pottery remaining to feed a packed common room, let alone the six of them. Sharina unpinned the clasp of enameled gold and hung the cape on a peg meant for a skillet. Belted to her waist where the cape had hidden it was a very unladylike weapon: a Pewle knife in a sheath of black sealskin.

The knife's heavy blade was straight and as long as Sharina's forearm, with a deep belly that put the weight of a blow at the tip. A Pewle knife would chop wood as well as an axe and let a life out as quickly as a sword. Its former owner, the hermit Nonnus, had used the knife for both purposes until the night he died protecting Sharina.

Sharina had carried the knife ever since. More as a memorial than a weapon, Ilna supposed, but she'd never asked and Sharina had never volunteered her feelings on the matter. It was good to have it around to chop kindling since there wasn't a hatchet by the side door as there was in most prosperous houses in the borough.

Ilna laughed. Everybody looked at her, even Cashel, who was checking an overturned bowl to see if he'd have to clean it before he used it to carry water.

"It's hard to live in a normal way in a palace," Ilna explained. "The normal things aren't here unless you ask for them specially."

Garric smiled, but he looked tired at a level deeper than muscle or even bone. Ilna would have hugged him if . . . well, if she hadn't been Ilna os-Kenset. And nobody was to blame for *that* but her.

"I don't even know what normal is anymore," Garric said. "But I know I'm glad I have friends who make do with what's available. If there were more people in Valles and the kingdom who—"

He stopped himself. "Well, maybe there will be when people see that there's a real chance for unity and peace," he concluded. "And if not, well, we'll make do, won't we?"

Liane looked at Garric, worried by the tone of his voice. She put her hand on his and squeezed it.

"I saw loofas growing in the kitchen garden," Ilna said as she turned away. "I'll fetch some to clean the grill."

She walked quickly around the building, blinking at tears. The garden had been abandoned when the kitchen was, but some crops survived. The row of asparagus had grown into a thicket and the gourds had continually re-seeded themselves. Ilna squatted and reached for the paring knife she carried in her sash.

"I'll help," said Liane.

Ilna looked over her shoulder. Liane knelt beside her. She'd drawn a double-edged dagger from its hidden sheath. The blade was only a finger long, but the steel was better than anything seen in Barca's Hamlet. It was the sort of weapon a wealthy lady kept by her while traveling, insurance if her retinue of guards and servants wasn't enough to prevent the unexpected.

Despite the jeweled hilt and gold filigree on the blade, it would open gourds just as well as the knife Ilna used for the tasks of kitchen and household.

Liane's tunics, inner and outer both, were simply cut but made of silk. Her sandals were vermilion leather with decoration in gold thread; one of them had sunk ankle-deep in soft earth on the way to this nook in the palace grounds. Ilna didn't bother with footwear within the compound, though she wore clogs when she went out on the hard cobblestone streets beyond.

But just as the fancy dagger was able to do this job, so was its fancy owner.

"Yes, all right," Ilna said, twisting the vine and then slicing through the woody fibers which still held the gourd. "I'll need about a dozen of them, I'd judge, as filthy as those grills looked."

Liane snipped off a loofa in a close approximation of what she'd seen Ilna do. "And I'll help with the cleaning, though you'll probably have to show me how to do that too," she said as she reached for another vine.

Ilna swallowed. "I wonder . . ." she said, keeping her eyes on her task. "You were reading a poem the other day. Something about bees weaving?"

" 'I've a jar of wine in its ninth year, Phyla, and in my garden the bees weave crowns . . .' " Liane said, "Yes, isn't that lovely? It's Celondre."

"I wonder if you could go over that for me till I can remember it all through," Ilna said, dropping a third gourd into the lap of her outer tunic. She cleared her throat again. "There was something about knowing your station, too."

"Well, Celondre thought of himself as an aristocrat," Liane said apologetically. "But I'd love to do that. Right now, if you'd like."

Ilna smiled wryly. "Yes, I'd like that," she said.

" 'Only pursue the things you're worthy of,' " Liane said, running over the verse for herself. " 'Shun what is above you.' "

Someone, something, with skill greater than Ilna's own

was weaving a pattern of which she was a thread. Ilna couldn't see the end yet; perhaps she never would.

But she was sure there was one.

Cashel stirred the porridge with a spoon he'd shaped with his iron knife after Sharina had cut down a willow sapling for him. He hadn't asked to borrow the Pewle knife because he knew Sharina was more than strong enough to shear through the soft wood herself—and besides, Cashel felt a little uncomfortable about that knife. Nonnus the Hermit had treated Sharina as if she'd been his own child. He'd protected her when Cashel was far away, and had *died* protecting her. Cashel was as grateful as could be about the hermit's sacrifice, but sometimes he felt that he had to measure himself against a saint; and Cashel couldn't convince himself that he came off well in the comparison.

"The thing that keeps throwing me . . ." said Garric. He paused to turn a strip of bacon with his dagger. The silvered steel glittered in the light of the lantern Liane had hung from a swivel hook in a disused hearth. The long, tapered blade was pretty fancy, but it did a cooking fork's job well enough.

"It isn't the crises themselves," Garric went on as the bacon spluttered, a salty smell in the woodsmoke that made Cashel think of home. "Though the Shepherd knows it's been one thing after another. And now whatever it is you've found, Tenoctris."

He grinned to show that he wasn't blaming the old wizard for bringing him a warning. Garric looked five years younger here than he had when Cashel and the others awakened him this afternoon.

"The latest is we've gotten word that both the Earl of Sandrakkan and the Count of Blaise are planning to call themselves king. Of their own islands, not Kings of the Isles, but it'll cause about as much trouble as the other would. Valence III beat the Earl of Sandrakkan at the Stone

Wall twenty years ago, but the kingdom's never recovered from the strain."

"Can you trust the rumors?" Sharina said, speaking to her brother but glancing at Liane, who had charge of the confidential reports.

Liane looked at Garric; he nodded. "Yes," she said. "In this case we can. The only thing that's holding them back is that they're both afraid of being first. They remember the Stone Wall too."

"Even without spies," Garric added, "it's what you'd expect them to do. The title didn't matter so much when they could ignore whoever was sitting on the throne in Valles. Now that it looks like the Isles'll have *real* unity, they're likely to act."

"When the forces that turn the cosmos peak," Tenoctris said musingly, "they put all society in a kettle on a hot fire. Once a millennium everything comes to a boil. It isn't just that wizards now have more power than they dreamed of a few years ago."

She grinned and added, "Some of us don't have very much power even now, of course."

Cashel believed Tenoctris when she said that she wasn't a powerful wizard, but he knew—as she certainly knew—that a lot of times strength wasn't as important as knowing how to use the strength you had. Tenoctris saw and understood the sources of power, while other wizards used them blindly. There was much the old woman couldn't do, but Cashel had never seen her do a single thing she didn't mean to.

He grinned broadly. Cashel knew better than most how important it was to be careful. You broke things otherwise, and sometimes you broke yourself.

Garric nodded. "I *might* have an army that could defeat one or the other of them," he said. "But I don't have a way to get the army *to* Sandrakkan or Blaise. And anyway, winning would be just about as bad as losing for what it'd do to the kingdom. Knocking heads isn't the way out."

"We need time," Liane said with a worried expression.

"A few months might be enough. If the rulers of the other islands see that Ornifal's better off under a real king, that may keep them quiet better than the threat of the army alone."

Fleetingly Cashel wondered who she meant by "we." Probably "the Isles," and anyway, it wasn't his business to worry about.

Ilna sniffed from where she sat in a corner, plaiting rushes into pads. "So long as you still have the army. Some heads *should* be knocked."

Garric nodded, more to show that he was listening than because he'd heard anything he thought was a solution. "We—the government of the Isles, *my* government—could find a way to deal with Blaise and Sandrakkan."

He sighed and began turning the rest of the meat as he continued, "The trouble is that my council's fighting itself and I don't know what to do to change things. Nothing's getting done—or it isn't getting done right— because people who are supposed to be on the same side are squabbling between themselves. We needn't worry about evil if the folks on our side do evil's work."

Cashel thought for a moment. "You mean Attaper and Waldron are at each other's throats about running the army?" he said. He didn't know anything about politics, but he knew how rival males acted. None better than a countryman to understand *that*.

Garric laughed with relief at being able to talk freely. "No, not quite," he explained, "because Attaper and Waldron are both of them too dangerous. Neither one will give the other an inch, but they don't play silly games. They both know that the other has killed more men than they can remember. They don't goad each other, because the other man *will* go for his sword if pushed, and they've both been down that road too often to go again for little reasons."

Sharina sat on a chopping block that she'd covered with reed pads that Ilna had woven with a few twitches of her fingers. "So it's Lord Tadai and the chancellor who're fighting?" she said.

"And how!" Garric agreed. He swept the bacon to a brick support to drain while he cooked the remaining rashers. "Any project Royhas proposes has to wait forever for funding. Any revenue proposals that come from the treasury go unstaffed or get staffed with people you wouldn't trust to pluck a chicken. Things aren't getting done, and they need to get done!"

"But you're the king," Cashel said, speaking aloud not so much to get an answer as because sometimes he understood things better if he heard himself say them. "You can tell them what to do."

"As I could tell a flock of sheep which way to take to pasture," Garric said. "And have about as much chance of them obeying me. The sheep'll go their own way because they know what's best. It takes more than a little shouting to change their minds."

Cashel smiled. Garric caught his unspoken thought and said, "Right, the path the sheep takes probably *is* the best one. The trouble is, here I've got two different leaders. Maybe they've both got good ideas, but I can't—the Isles can't!—go both ways at the same time."

"Sometimes you get two ewes like that," Cashel said, continuing to puzzle over the problem aloud. He withdrew the spoon and licked it; the porridge was warm through to the center. "If they're both worth something, you sell one out of the district. If one of them's nothing special for milking, well, you've got to cull the flock before winter anyway, right?"

He lifted the pot from the fire. They didn't have hard bread for trenchers, but Sharina had sliced birchbark to eat from while there was still daylight. Liane wouldn't be used to everybody dipping a hand into the pot.

"You said ewes, Cashel," Liane said. "Don't rams fight too?"

Besides being Garric's friend, Liane was a real lady, but she was always nice to Cashel. He had the feeling that a lot of people in the palace laughed at him behind his back. He was used to that. Folks in the borough had been the same way. "Big as an ox and just as stupid," he'd heard often enough before he got his full growth, and he knew they still said it, though not where he could hear.

They might even be right, but Cashel didn't like it; and he didn't like the people who treated him that way. Liane was different, so instead of snorting in amazement he glanced at Garric—who shrugged.

"You don't need but one ram for a herd, mistress," Cashel said. "There's no point in wasting fodder on something that's just going to make problems for you."

"Oh," said Liane, blinking. She was a smart girl, no question, but Cashel had noticed that city folk generally didn't understand how hard rural life was and how hard rural people had to be as a consequence.

"In fact, Tadai and Royhas *are* both valuable," Garric said. "And perhaps more to the point, they're both too powerful to be kicked out in the cold without causing real trouble for the kingdom. They conspired against Valence when they thought it had to be done, even though he'd been their friend in earlier years. Neither man is *my* friend."

Cashel tried to get his mind around the situation. Liane noticed his frown and said in a friendly voice—not talking down, just talking, "A lot of people on Ornifal don't like having a government that does what's right instead of what it's been bribed to do. With a man like Tadai or Royhas either one to lead them, that sort of people would be a danger."

Cashel nodded. "And you don't want to kill them," he said; not asking and *certainly* not suggesting, but just getting the facts straight in his mind.

"I'm not willing to do that," Garric said simply. "I think it'd be bad policy anyway, but the truth is that I just won't do it. Kill a man because it's awkward having him around."

He forced a laugh to change the subject. "I think we've

got a meal ready," he said, sliding the last of the bacon off the grill. "Let's eat!"

Sharina squatted to eat, the point of her shoulder braced against Cashel beside her. The fire had sunk to winking coals. The wood had aged on the damp ground, rotting to punk that burned sullenly rather than with a clean, hot flame; it had been good enough for the porridge and bacon, but it burned away too quickly to keep the hearth warm on a winter night.

"Lerdoc, Count of Blaise, has begun wearing a diadem in public," Garric said as he daubed up porridge on the willow spoon Sharina had trimmed while her brother was cooking. "He hasn't formally changed his title to king; he's probably wondering what I'm going to do. I'm wondering too."

He grinned. Garric sounded tired but he wasn't as bitterly *worn* as he'd seemed every time Sharina saw him during the past two weeks.

"Lerdoc may be hoping that his diadem will convince the Earl of Sandrakkan to take an overt step," Liane said. Cashel had upturned a large pot as a seat for her; Liane had never learned to squat, and she probably wasn't used to sitting cross-legged on the ground for any length of time either.

"And he may be right about that," Garric agreed. "Earl Wildulf has called a muster of the Sandrakkan militia for the twentieth of next month. Our agents think he's checking to see how many of his nobles show up with their troops before he decides whether to proclaim himself King Wildulf the First. That's what his granduncle did . . . the year before he died at the Stone Wall."

Sharina liked the porridge, though the flavor had surprised her. This was the first time since she'd arrived in Valles that she'd had a meal like what most of the people here ate. It was subtly different from what she was used to. The meal, leeks, and chives were the same as she'd used in Barca's Hamlet more times than she could remember, but the cheese Cashel had stirred in came from goat's milk instead of ewe's.

"Carus faced the same sort of problems when he was crowned King of the Isles," Garric went on with a wry smile. "Usurpers, rebels, secessions—on Haft and all over the Isles. Carus met his problems with a sword in his hand and an army none of them could equal . . . until the day a wizard sank him and his army to the bottom of the sea."

Tenoctris watched Garric with sharp attention. Earlier in the evening she'd gone to a corner of the long building to work a spell. Sharina had seen red wizardlight flickering between the old woman's cupped palms, but she hadn't asked the purpose or the result.

"I don't have an army that good," Garric said. "Besides, I don't particularly want to wind up drowned."

He smiled again, though Liane beside him winced at the words. Since Garric began wearing the medal of King Carus, he'd gained a sense of black humor. He'd once told Sharina that you needed laughter on a battlefield worse than you did anywhere else, so you'd better be able to laugh at what you found there.

"I've thought of taking the army to Sandrakkan, then Blaise," Garric went on musingly. "Not attacking Wildulf and Lerdoc, just arriving on their doorsteps with enough strength to make them think again about declaring their islands independent."

"That may work while your troops are *on* Sandrakkan," Liane said. From her tone, she and Garric had held this discussion in the past. "But when they leave for Blaise, what happens then? And what happens here in Ornifal?"

"I'm going to have to do something soon," Garric said with a flash of irritation. "If not that, what?"

"Send ambassadors," Sharina said. Everyone looked at her in surprise. "Instead of taking your army."

Sharina had mulled the plan ever since Garric described his problem. Her solution fit. The empty round of Sharina's days had driven her to distraction, but it was that frustration which gave her the key to Garric's greater difficulties.

"We have envoys in Erdin and Piscine already, Sharina," Garric said. "And Wildulf and Lerdoc have envoys in Valles as well."

"Ready to fund anyone on Ornifal with courage enough to rebel," Liane added with an edge in her voice. "We're watching them carefully."

"No," Sharina said. "You've sent professional diplomats, petty nobles who've spent their lives learning to say safe things in a smooth manner."

Garric nodded. He was cleaning grease from his dagger with a wad of cattail pith, and he had the sharpening stone from his belt pouch ready to touch up the weapon's point.

"What you should do is send someone to Earl Wildulf that he'll listen to because he knows the person is one of the most important people in your court," Sharina explained. "Send Tadai or Royhas."

"Oh!" gasped Cashel in delight. "Oh, Sharina!"

"By the Shepherd, Sharina," Garric said softly, "that *might* work. Not an open threat, but somebody they'd have to listen to."

He looked toward Liane. "I'll send Tadai," he said, asking the girl for confirmation rather than permission. "I can spare him better—though I *wish* he and Royhas could work together."

"He'll take your orders to go?" Ilna asked with the detached curiosity that was so much a part of her personality.

"In this?" Garric said. "Yes. Tadai knows that something has to change quickly for the kingdom to survive. He can't back down to Royhas—"

"Won't," Liane said.

Garric shrugged. "Can't, won't, it's the same thing. Tadai will take an honorable way out of the tangle he and Royhas have gotten themselves into if one's offered. I'll make him ambassador to Erdin with full powers to negotiate Sandrakkan's status within the kingdom—that's a royal position, and he'll take it."

Garric stood and stepped to the threshold to look out

into the night. He sheathed his long dagger without needing to check where the point was in relation to the mouth of the scabbard. "Also, Tadai will go because he knows that I'll have to remove him from the council if he doesn't. One way or the other, he'll go."

Garric's voice was as detached as Ilna's, and it had an underlying hardness that surprised Sharina. She remembered her brother in Barca's Hamlet, whistling a cheery tune at any time his lips weren't smiling. They weren't in Barca's Hamlet anymore. . . .

"And send me to Blaise, Garric," Sharina said, feeling a shiver as the words came out. She didn't regret them, though. "Send the Lady Sharina, your sister."

Cashel alone didn't react to what Sharina had said. His arm was steady as an oak trunk, supporting her shoulder as Cashel had always supported her.

Sharina turned and hugged him. "Cashel, I'm sorry," she said. "I should have talked to you about this before I said anything, but I just worked it out now."

Cashel smiled faintly. Either he was blushing or the fire-light had painted a flush on his cheek. "That's all right, Sharina," he said. "I don't mind Valles, but it's not a place I'll mind leaving, either. I'm here because you're here."

Garric cleared his throat. "Ah, Sharina?" he said. "Is there some reason you want to go to Blaise? Because Pitre bor-Perial might make an even more satisfactory ambassador than Tadai. Except that I don't need to get rid of Pitre, of course."

"I'm going out of my mind, doing what I am here," she replied bluntly. She stood; Cashel rose beside her so that they looked like a willow growing at the side of a boulder. "Every day I see people who want something they can't have. If there were a prayer of them getting what they're petitioning for, they'd be seen by somebody with real authority."

"It's an import—" Garric began.

"Yes it is," Sharina said, cutting across her brother's objection. "It's an important job, but it's a job that King

Valence himself can do better. Isn't that true?"

Garric pursed his lips. Liane, still seated, said, "Not better, no, but he can do it. Valence—rightly—trusts Lord Royhas, and he'll allow the chancellor to guide what he says."

Liane's eyes narrowed slightly as she looked at Sharina. "You know, a task that brought the king into contact with his citizens might well be good for his state of mind. As well as for the kingdom."

"As you just said, Garric," Sharina said, "going to the count at Piscine with full power to negotiate is a real job. I don't want to leave you—"

She looked around the gathering. "Any of you," she went on; Cashel smiled with placid assurance. "But if we're to save the Isles from chaos, there are more important jobs for me to be doing than listening to a deputation from the Bridge District about the noises they hear in the night."

"All right," Garric said with kingly decisiveness again. He'd listened, been convinced, and was acting promptly on his decision instead of tramping back and forth over the same ground. "We'll meet with Royhas tomorrow to decide exactly what to offer Blaise. But you'll have full powers to make whatever arrangement seems best when you've viewed the situation."

He smiled oddly. "But it's funny that you should mention the Bridge District. I was dreaming about a bridge when you all waked me. A bridge, and a man named Ansalem . . ."

"Ansalem?" Tenoctris said, her face lifting slightly. She'd listened to the earlier discussion, but it seemed to Garric that she'd suddenly become intensely alert. "Ansalem the Wise, do you mean?"

Garric nodded, feeling his mouth go dry. "That's what he said his name was," he agreed. "He said the city where I dreamed I was seeing him was Klestis. And I think—"

He coughed to clear his throat.

"—that he's a wizard."

Tenoctris nodded and opened her mouth to speak. Before she could, a rush of memory flooded Garric: not *his* memories, but those of King Carus opening like a window within Garric's mind.

Ships and boats formed a double line in the harbor Garric had viewed from Ansalem's chamber. Bunting hung from their masts and stays, and on their decks people cheered and waved pennons as the trireme bearing Carus, King of the Isles, passed between the lines.

"I went to Klestis on an embassy, lad," Carus said. *"That was in the fall before the summer when I drowned. I thought if I came alone and talked to Ansalem myself, I could convince him to help me. 'Help the kingdom' is what I said, and maybe that's what it was; but back then I was a little too quick to think whatever I wanted was what the kingdom needed."*

The boulevards which Garric had dreamed in ruins were lined with joyous citizens in striped garments. Sunlight on the buildings' metal façades threw a dazzling splendor over the city, brighter even than the sea surrounding a ship becalmed at midday.

Carus marched with the twenty Marines from his ship. The remainder of the trireme's complement, the two dozen sailors who handled the rigging when the vessel was under sail and the hundred and seventy oarsmen, remained at the harborside.

The Marines were in embroidered tunics rather than armor, but even as a guard of honor they wore their swords. They were the only armed men visible; perhaps the only armed men in all Klestis.

"Ansalem had made Klestis great by his wizardry," Carus said. *"His people worked for their livings, but they lived a hundred times better than they could have anyplace but in his city. Buildings rose overnight, and the streets were clean every morning."*

Instead of climbing the circular stair tower, Carus and his guards approached the entrance to the palace itself. Young girls in pastel frocks blocked the door alcove, giggling and tossing flower petals at the score of armed men. The door behind them remained closed.

"A great wizard, Ansalem," Carus said grimly, *"and a great ruler, although he didn't have any formal title beyond Citizen of Klestis. And he absolutely refused to have anything to do with violence."*

An older man in a tunic of wool bleached white— sober garb for Klestis—stepped out of the bevy of girls, bowed respectfully to Carus, and spoke in the king's ear as the Marines glowered.

Carus nodded curtly and unbuckled the long double tongues of his sword belt. The grizzled captain of his guards protested with increasing vehemence. Carus looked at him with a face of iron and snapped one word. The captain and the other Marines stiffened.

Carus offered his belt and sword to the palace official—who jerked back as though the king had thrust a viper at him. Carus handed the weapon instead to his captain.

The door opened and the girls backed to either side, still giggling. The old official bowed Carus into the palace.

"I could have built a fleet of two hundred warships with the value of the orichalch sheathing one single building in Klestis," Carus said musingly. *"And for the tin that covered another one I could have paid the crews for a year.*

I hated the very thought of wizards, but I'd have pretended I didn't know the city's wealth came from wizardry if I could've gotten my hands on it."

The entrance hall of the palace was windowless, but ribbons of pale light twisted in the air about the high arches. The coffered ceiling was decorated with scenes from rural festivals, peasants who danced and cheered friends competing in races, wrestling, and throwing the stone.

The memory—Garric's memory now—made his eyes sting with tears for the world he'd left forever. But life in Barca's Hamlet hadn't all been feasts and balmy days; and without Garric and his friends to protect them, there'd be little enough joy for any of the folk of the Isles before long.

Seven wizards wearing robes embroidered with signs in the Old Script awaited Carus in the vaulted hall. No servants or ordinary officials were present. The wizards' leader was epicene and completely bald, though Garric guessed he was a young man . . . if indeed he was a man rather than a sexless neuter.

The leader nodded to the king instead of bowing. He turned and led Carus to a staircase hidden behind a pillar carved from a block of chalcedony in three interwoven strands like a fig tree braided for decoration. The other wizards, four men and two women, followed silently like pages bearing a lady's flowing train.

"No one's ever called me a coward," Carus said simply. *"But I'd rather have carried as many spiders in my hands than gone anywhere in the company of those seven."*

The staircase kinked back on itself a dozen times on its way to the roof of the building. The treads and railing were of myrrhine. Bands of light shimmered through the stone, illuminating crystals of blue and

purple as well as white calcite inclusions bigger than
a man's fist. The soft stone gleamed, its polish unaffected by the feet of those who had passed this way.

At the top of the stairs was the shallow anteroom
of the audience chamber where Garric had met Ansalem in his dream. A cadaverous doorkeeper sat there
on a stool, holding a two-year-old boy on his lap. He
rose as Carus and the wizards entered, shifting the
smiling boy to the floor beside him. Hanging from a
chain around the doorkeeper's neck was a hollow disk
with the flares of the sun's corona on its outer edge.

The man was easily seven feet tall. He was thin,
but his limbs had the knobbed muscularity of a goat's.
Though the doorkeeper didn't carry a weapon, Garric
wouldn't have wanted to wrestle him; even Cashel
might have frowned at the thought.

The doorkeeper eyed Carus with a depth of understanding that nobody else in this enclave of peace had
demonstrated since the king arrived. The leader of the
seven snapped a curt order. The doorkeeper ignored
him. He stepped back against the panel and called a
question through the grilled viewport. The answer
must have been affirmative, because he slipped the
bolt and pulled the panel open.

The little boy stood upright by clinging to the wall
with both hands. He beamed at the king.

Carus entered the audience chamber alone. In the
doorway he stopped and bowed to the keeper.

"His name was Castigan," Carus said. *"I asked later.
When I met Castigan I knew that Ansalem wasn't a complete fool, however peaceful he might be for choice."*

The audience chamber was as Garric remembered it
from his dream, though the bookcases were filled and
even overfilled. Many of the pigeonholes held two
rolls, or even three if they were slim ones. Additional

codices were stuffed atop the ranks of those shelved normally.

Ansalem too was the same cheerful soul Garric had met. He stepped forward and clasped Carus' arm. The cushioned travertine bier was the only seat within the chamber. Ansalem led his guest to it and sat beside him hospitably, continuing to hold Carus' hand.

"Have you ever tried to talk to somebody sitting alongside you instead of facing?" Carus said. *"It feels all wrong. It sounds silly, but I'd have been less uncomfortable if he'd held a dagger to my throat the whole time. Not that I was going to convince that wizard to help me, no matter how we held the discussion."*

A membrane of thin, hard fabric had been drawn over the exterior of the alabaster screen, protecting the chamber from weather and the sun's harshest rays. The pierced symbols stood out white against the creamy texture of the stone.

In the tall niche facing the bier stood the mummy of a creature with scaly skin and a long reptilian jaw. Age-browned bandages bound the mummy's arms across its chest, and beads of amber replaced its sunken eyes. They watched Carus and his host with a cold yellow luster, not malevolent but clearly inhuman.

"Ansalem was as friendly as anyone could ask," Carus recalled. *"It was like talking to a three-year-old, though. He'd listen to me, but he completely ignored all my arguments about why he had to help me hold the Isles together. I was furious. He agreed that I was King of the Isles, but he didn't care about that any more than he did about the name of a bird from Shengy. Both things interested him, but they didn't really matter."*

Carus jerked his hand away from the plump wizard and got up abruptly. He stalked to the door, his fists knotted. King Carus had been an intimate guest in Garric's mind for the months since Garric began wearing the coronation medal.

He'd seen the king laughing in the midst of slaughter and facing dangers to soul as well as body. Never had he imagined Carus in the kind of frustrated rage that Garric saw him now.

On the pedestal which Garric had seen empty in his dream was a fossilized ammonite. Its coiled shell had been replaced by crystals of marcasite, which gleamed a sulfurous bronze color in the sunlight filtering through the screen. The creature had not been a large example of its kind: the coil was no more than a foot in diameter, while Garric had seen examples which were the size of a house.

There was a psychic depth to this fossil, however; it was a pit into the fiery heart of evil. Carus had walked by the thing unnoticed when he entered the chamber. As he stamped out in fury he almost collided with the pedestal. He recoiled, then hammered the shell with the bottom of his fist.

The ammonite didn't move. Carus pushed at the door; it was barred from the outside. Only when the doorkeeper had looked through again did he open it to release the king.

"Don't hit things because you're angry, lad," Carus said in a tone of mild reminiscence. *"My arm was numb for a week after that piece of foolishness. Because of what the thing was, of course; stone wouldn't have hurt me like that."*

The vivid recollections faded, returning Garric to the present instant before his friends were aware that he'd left them. In the back of his mind, he heard King Carus mutter, *"Wizardry!"*

"Ansalem was a wizard of my time," Tenoctris was saying. "I'd never met anyone like him, then or since."

"You did meet him, though?" Garric said. He was dizzy with the onrush of memory he'd just absorbed. Carus, attentive at the back of his mind, was a pillar supporting Garric while time and space fused into present reality.

"I'd heard of him as a great scholar and wizard," Tenoctris said with a nod. "He ruled Klestis, on the south coast of Cordin. He let others use his library if they liked, so I visited Klestis."

She smiled and toyed with a lock of her short gray hair. "I visited when I managed to raise the passage money from where I was living on Blaise, that is. I wasn't a powerful enough wizard to command great sums, nor a good enough showman to earn my living by tricks."

"But you understand things, Tenoctris," Liane said.

"Yes," the old wizard agreed, "and wisdom by itself is a good way to starve. Which is all right—I didn't need very much, you see, a modest amount of food and books to continue my studies. It just took me longer to visit Ansalem than it otherwise would have."

She smiled again, looking decades younger than she had a moment before. "And since I left again almost immediately, I had even less need of money than I'd expected."

"What did Ansalem do to you?" Cashel asked. He hunched slightly forward, a motion that wouldn't have meant anything to people who didn't know him as well as the friends now present did.

Sharina had been sheltering against Cashel's strength; now she put her hand on his shoulder to settle him. Insults rolled from Cashel like water from a rock, but nobody mistreated Cashel's friends twice in *his* presence.

"I don't think Ansalem could hurt anyone or anything," Tenoctris said. She spoke calmly, as though she were unaware of the storm her previous comment had set to rumbling in Cashel's heart. "He had a truly childlike innocence. It must have been the source of his power. He was a little vain—but only a little, considering his power.

And occasionally petulant as well, but never enough to do real harm."

Tenoctris lowered her eyes, smiling at the memory but shaking her head in wonder as well. "I called Ansalem 'childlike,' " she went on. "But he was a true scholar as well. My equal, I think."

Her lips pursed. "Perhaps my equal," she qualified, grinning at herself for the implied boast.

Garric and the others grinned back. Pride was the most human of emotions. Tenoctris was always quick to note that she wasn't a powerful wizard; but though her knowledge and skill were those of a jeweler rather than a blacksmith, she'd accomplished a great deal worth being proud of.

"Ansalem had gathered books from all over the Isles," Tenoctris continued. "Works on all subjects, not just wizardry. And I think he must have searched time as well as space, because there were things in his collection that couldn't have survived even hours without a wizard's art to preserve them, let alone the ages since they were written. There was a poem written in the scales from butterfly wings mounted on a spiderweb. . . ."

"An incantation?" Sharina asked.

"Just a poem," Tenoctris said, shaking her head again in wonder at a world that included the things she had seen. "An epitaph, I suppose. 'The pious child I nurtured grew to save me from the foe's fury. When peaceful death claimed me, he raised my mound on this green hill.' "

"But why did a wizard have that?" Cashel asked. He laced his fingers together and frowned in concentration.

Tenoctris flipped her palms up and smiled, a little wanly. "I don't know," she said. "And I don't know why someone would have written it in gossamer and butterfly wings instead of carving it on stone. . . . But I've never forgotten the verse, Cashel, even though I don't know who or what it was about."

Her face sobered. Lamplight emphasized the age-etched lines on her cheeks. "There were incantations in Ansalem's library that even the most powerful wizard should not, I think, have dared to attempt; but that wasn't what concerned me. Ansalem also collected objects which act as nexuses for enormous powers."

Tenoctris rose to her feet as a nervous reaction to the events she remembered. "Ansalem's palace was a storm of energies that warped the very cosmos. No one but Ansalem himself could remain near such things safely. I certainly couldn't."

Garric thought of the objects he'd seen displayed in the audience chamber: the reptilian mummy; an athame of some metal that cast a bluish glow on the niche in which it rested; a fist-sized globe that blazed like flame made solid; and of course the marcasite Great One.

"Why didn't it bother Ansalem?" Cashel asked. "Because he was so powerful?"

Tenoctris shook her head. "Because he was so innocent," she said. "I don't think it's possible to be powerful enough to resist such forces, but there was nothing in Ansalem for them to grip and twist as they would a normal human. A normal wizard, at any rate."

"Even you, Tenoctris?" Liane asked.

"Even me," the old woman said. "There was no wisdom but flight."

She pressed her palms together and closed her eyes as she remembered. "One of the objects Ansalem had collected was the shell of one of the Great Ones, changed to marcasite in the aeons before man. It was as close to pure evil as anything that can exist in the waking world."

Garric nodded agreement. Not even Tenoctris knew how completely he understood what she meant.

"I'd have liked to use Ansalem's library," Tenoctris said. "Even the little taste of it I had was a delight I still treasure. But if I hadn't left at once, I'd have been torn apart by the storm of evil swirling about the palace."

"There were other wizards with Ansalem, though, weren't there?" Garric said. He kept his palms flat on his thighs. When the memories he recalled were those of Carus, some of Carus' fierce hatred for wizards and wizardry bled through as well.

Wizardry was merely a tool. In Tenoctris' hands it was a key of great subtlety that unlocked hidden truths. It wasn't the tool's fault that most wizards used their art like a sledge in the hands of a blind madman.

"Yes there were," Tenoctris said evenly. "Seven of them at the time I visited Klestis; Ansalem called them his acolytes. I'm sure they weren't twisted by anything they learned from him, but . . ."

She shook her head with a grimace. "If I'd been in doubt about the risks of staying in the palace," she said, "seeing what it had done to those seven would have convinced me. They were powerful wizards in their own right, though, particularly the one named Purlio of Mnar."

No one spoke for a moment. Ilna got up and stepped to the doorway; she checked the time by the height of the moon. In passing close to Garric, she held out her hand as if to guard herself from contact; that, or as a caress without touching.

"We're done eating," she said. "Tenoctris, you gathered us to look at events in the Bridge District. If we're going to go . . . ?"

Tenoctris gave Ilna a half bow. "Yes," she said. "We should do that. Nothing I've heard tonight suggests that the reports are *less* important than I feared they might be."

Chapter Four

The driver called "Whoa up!" to his pair of horses, bringing the coach to a rumbling halt. There was a last jolt as a front tire slipped with a clang into the crack between cobblestones.

Garric flung the door open and hopped down, ignoring the mounting step. He didn't know that he'd ever been happier to have his feet on the ground again.

The coach had crashed and swayed all the way here. Garric's ears were still numb from the roar of iron tires on the stone streets, though now that they were stopped he became aware of the murmur of the crowd gathered on the plaza. Hundreds of people stood in small groups, watching the river.

The vehicle didn't have royal markings, but no carriage was nondescript in a working-class district like this one. Folk at the back of the crowd turned to eye the new arrivals.

Cashel climbed down from the box beside the driver. His quarterstaff wouldn't fit inside a coach crowded with five other people, and he didn't choose to leave it behind. He smiled at Garric and said, "I'd as soon have walked, but I guess this is faster; and the driver knew where he was going. Were you able to make plans?"

"We weren't able to think!" Sharina said, getting down after Garric. The postilion was handing Liane and Tenoctris out the other side; Ilna waited for Sharina, then stepped down with an expression of disdain for the experience just over. "What a terrible lot of noise!"

"Well, Tenoctris couldn't have walked the distance," Garric said, "and Liane wanted to check her book of sailing directions. I thought that if we came in a coach instead of them in chairs and the rest of us walking, we could talk."

He shook his head ruefully. "I'll know better the next time."

During the Old Kingdom, the inn at Barca's Hamlet had been a stop on the coaching highway up the east side of the island. The road had been paved—Garric could see the broad way in Carus' memory—but the storms of a thousand winters had crumbled all but a few protected stretches into the sea.

Wealthy merchants sometimes rode horses to the Sheep Fair, and occasionally an overweight drover arrived in a palanquin borne by six or eight bearers across the hilly track from Carcosa on the west coast. "Carriage" had only been a word to Garric until the past few months, and even after he left home he'd never expected to ride in one.

"King Carus visited Klestis once," Garric said, speaking particularly to Tenoctris. He didn't discuss how he came by the information, though the others had probably guessed by now. Garric was just embarrassed to be speaking with, *living* with, a man dead for a thousand years. "There wasn't any bridge there at the time."

The driver and postilion could hear him; so could the people at the back of the crowd, though many had returned to their own conversations. Other people listened and watched Garric. That couldn't be helped and anyway, it was a part of life.

Nobody in a palace—or a rural village—had any realistic expectation of privacy. Whether you had servants or you lived in a hut of wattle and daub, your business was going to be the business of everybody else if it was interesting enough to notice.

"If we're going to see a bridge," Ilna said, not harshly, but in a tone of cool dispassion, "then we need to get closer to the water."

"Right," said Garric, wondering if they'd have to force their way to the levee. "Let's move up."

They could push forward, of course, with him and Cashel in the lead. Garric hadn't brought a detachment of guards because he didn't want to cause a stir. It hadn't occurred to him that although his government didn't have an inkling about whatever was happening in the Bridge District, word was certainly out among the citizens of Valles.

And beyond, apparently. Some of the spectators were obvious countrymen in dark wool tunics and hats with wide leather brims. There were also folk—most of them sailors, but not all—in the garb of at least six other islands, including a Dalopan with bone ornaments.

Some knots of spectators were families, others waited as

a handful of friends. For the most part men stood with men and women with women. Children played with a degree of nonchalance, but their mothers kept a worried eye on them. There were no servants in these homes to watch children if the parents chose to go out of a night.

Cashel eyed the crowd. "There's room," he said. He started forward.

Because those watching were in discrete groups, it wasn't as much of a problem to move through them as Garric had expected. People talked to their friends, their backs to similar clots of people. They were uncomfortable about the event they waited for, but that hadn't formed the crowd into a mob. This was something they wanted to see in the company of those closest to them.

"Like the way trees in the woods don't quite touch their branches," Cashel said over his shoulder in mild amusement.

He shuffled forward sideways, though even so his bulk cleared a wide path for his friends. Occasionally his arm or chest bumped people apart, but the contact wasn't heavy enough to raise anger. Some folk looked around, but Cashel's size quieted even the mild protest that might have been made.

"Klestis stopped paying tribute to the Duke of Cordin when Ansalem became ruler," Garric said to Tenoctris, who followed Cashel closely. Garric was right behind her. Protected as she was by the two big youths, there was no danger that the old woman would be crushed. "The gifts Ansalem sent to the duke at Ragos were worth many times what the tribute would have been, but he made it clear that he didn't *owe* anything to Cordin or to the Isles."

"That was my experience as well," Tenoctris agreed. "Ansalem was a thoroughly pleasant man, delighted to entertain a fellow scholar, but he was completely self-willed. I'd been told that Ansalem was unworldly, but he didn't really ignore the world. He chose to detach himself from it in every possible fashion."

She eyed Garric. The only light on the plaza was that

of the partial moon, but that was sufficient to show the concern in her expression. "Almost anything might be possible for a wizard as powerful as Ansalem," she said. "But even he could make a mistake."

Cashel reached the levee and turned. The crowd directly overlooking the River Beltis was less dense than it had been twenty feet back from the masonry dike. Furthermore, none of the people Garric noticed in this front row were from the Bridge District. Many were foreigners, and there were several groups of nobles accompanied by shoals of guards and servants.

Garric stepped aside, forming a pocket into which Liane, Ilna, and Sharina could fit along with Tenoctris. He and Cashel had worked together so often on jobs where timing had to be perfect to avoid danger—tree felling and similar tasks involving heavy weights—that the process of making room for the women was a matter of reflex.

"Excuse, sir," Garric murmured to a sailor with a cloudy emerald set in the lobe of his ear, pressing back the fellow with his chest instead of using the point of his shoulder. Garric's shoulder would have been arrogance and challenge; a bump from his ribs was accidental contact caused by too little room.

Cashel made space on the other side by looming over a footman in a lace-hemmed tunic, never quite touching him but forcing him back by sheer bulk. The footman scooted around to the other side of the group he was part of, throwing a black look over his shoulder at Cashel.

Liane squeezed close to Garric. He grinned down at her—like Ilna, she only came up to his shoulder. Sharina was within a hand's breadth of Cashel's height, and Cashel wasn't much shorter than Garric himself. Liane smiled a reply, but concern underlay her cheerful expression.

All of them knew that there was danger in wizardry; but Liane had watched her father blight his life, then lose it, through mistakes in what he called his art. Garric had never seen Liane flee from danger, whether natural or otherwise;

but dealing with wizardry took a particular effort of will for her.

"The sailing directions I just searched are Serian," she said. She was speaking to all of them, but particularly to Garric and Tenoctris, standing on either side of her. "They follow a different tradition than those of rest of the Isles."

Garric nodded. Liane's father had been a great traveler for the whole of his life. He'd used Serian bankers and often Serian ships as well, so his daughter had connections that would be unavailable even to Garric in his persona of Prince of the Isles.

The sailing directions were a notebook of thin bamboo sheets Liane had brought to read on the way from the palace. The oil lamps on either side of the coach lighted the interior through isinglass panels, but it must've taken enormous concentration to read during the jolting, thunderous ride.

"Serian sailing directions are really just a compilation of landing places on a stretch of coastline," she said, lifting the booklet from her left sleeve to identify her subject. "They give the political circumstances to the degree that a merchant needs to worry about them, and a list of imports and exports for each landing."

Garric nodded to show he was listening to Liane, though his eyes were on the river. The Beltis ran more swiftly here than it did a few miles south, where it broadened into a delta that reached the Inner Sea through three mouths. Nothing moved on the surface but moonlight and flotsam.

"This set is centuries old," Liane continued. "Too old for use, but a shipper who'd had dealings with my father still kept it in his library. It says that Klestis is a little fishing port of no particular importance—"

"Right," said Garric. That's what Ornifal sea captains had told agents of the royal courier service when Garric asked about the place.

"But it also says that Klestis used to be the greatest harbor on the southern coasts," Liane said. "And that the old city sank into the sea as part of the same cataclysm that engulfed Yole."

Tenoctris pursed her lips. Her expression reminded Garric of a robin deciding where—or whether—to probe for a worm.

"That's possible, I suppose," she said. "And of course I was snatched away from Yole during the cataclysm, so I have no personal knowledge of what else might have happened at the same time. But I don't think Ansalem would have made the kind of mistake that would destroy Klestis that way."

She paused, considering how to explain what she felt. With a quizzical grin she went on, "Ansalem truly *was* Ansalem the Wise, but his wisdom went beyond mere scholarship like mine. He had an understanding of the cosmos that was more than simply human. In that he reminds me very much of Cashel and Ilna."

Tenoctris looked toward the pair, acknowledging them so that she wouldn't seem to have spoken behind their backs. Cashel hadn't heard her; Ilna grimaced, her eyes on the river.

There was a cold shimmer above the water. "It's happening!" a young woman cried in a voice quivering with wine and excitement.

"Yes," said Ilna as a tracery of blue light formed, stretching from the levee into infinite distance. "It is."

Tenoctris seated herself on the bare stone pavement. She moved with a jerky suddenness, like a tree that rot has finally overcome. She was too old and brittle to be graceful when she tried to move fast. Ilna reached to help her, but Liane was standing between the two of them and was quicker yet.

There was nothing wrong. Even as she sat, Tenoctris was fumbling out a bundle of the bamboo slivers with which she often worked her incantations. Other wizards used specially made tools, often an athame forged with the help of spells and inscribed to increase the power of incantations. Tenoctris made do with simple wands—bamboo, twigs; a stalk of grass—and discarded them after one use so that she didn't stain a spell with the residues of a previous one.

Ilna approved of her care. If Tenoctris had been a weaver, her designs would be small, tight, and absolutely perfect in execution.

Tenoctris drew a figure on the grime of the pavement—the cobblestones were so irregular that Ilna couldn't be sure whether it was intended for a square or a circle—and wrote around the outer edge. There wouldn't be any unintended results from the spell she was preparing to work.

Ilna returned her attention to the tracery of blue light which wavered above the river. Sometimes it touched the knees which once had supported the first arch of the ancient bridge. Individual flickers had no more direction than the glow of a single lightning bug, but if Ilna let her eyes absorb the pattern she could visualize a smooth curve mounting toward not the other shore of the Beltis but rather the distant horizon.

She wasn't sure she'd have thought of it as a bridge except that everybody else called it one. It felt to Ilna more like a fishing line cast from somewhere else to here. It wasn't a threat, precisely, but it was here for a purpose—and that purpose wasn't to benefit Ilna or those close to her.

"And who are *you*, my pretty?" a man said. His tone made the hairs on Ilna's nape bristle even though the words weren't directed at her. She turned her head while her right hand twitched the hank of cords out of her left sleeve.

The youth who'd spoken was no older than Sharina, whose neck he was fondling. His blond hair would have been shoulder length if it was hanging down, but tonight he'd had it slicked with scented oils and worked up into a chaplet of roses. He wore a diaphanous silk tunic next to his skin. Instead of an ordinary outer tunic, he wore a cutwork garment of gilded leather over it.

The fashion was new to Ilna but obviously expensive. The fellow had come over from a group—a gang—consisting of three similar youths, four women with the patina of highly paid professionals, and a dozen servants. The youths all wore swords, but any serious violence would come from their quartet of bodyguards.

Ilna expected Sharina to slap the perfumed *worm*; instead she shook her head and moved back behind Cashel as though he were a boulder on a plain. "Return to your own party, sir," she said.

The youth stepped after her. Tenoctris was mumbling an incantation with her eyes closed, unaware of what was going on around her. Liane spread her arms between the older woman and the youth, trying to protect Tenoctris from being trampled. Garric threw the right flap of his cape over his shoulder, displaying the hilt of his long sword. His hand didn't touch it.

Cashel picked up the youth by the neck and lifted him back to where he'd been standing. It was quite a gentle gesture, rather like a mother cat carrying a kitten. Ilna had seen her brother crack pecans between his fingers.

"Go away," Cashel said. He sounded amused rather than angry. A little fellow like this was just a yapping puppy to Cashel. "I don't want to hurt you."

"Emrich!" the youth shrieked to his bodyguard. "Dispose of this rabble!"

People—including the whores and ordinary servants of the noble party—had spread away from the altercation. Sharina and the rest of Garric's party were dressed simply for choice and didn't have servants along, so the youth had taken them for poor folk from this district. That meant he could do as he pleased with them. The notion was so foreign to what Ilna was used to in Barca's Hamlet that it shocked her.

A smarter man—or a more sober man, at any rate—might have noticed that while Garric wore a plain tunic, his sword was worth a year's income for a farm in the borough. The four bodyguards *had* noticed that, but they'd started to draw their own blades anyway. They might try to talk things out, but they'd do so from what they thought was strength—four men to two.

Ilna didn't doubt that Garric and her brother could handle the matter, but she could handle it better herself. She'd knotted four cords together. The pattern formed when she tossed them spinning in the air.

She'd have preferred better light, but the bleached wool caught enough of the moon to draw the guards' eyes. As one they cried out and fell to the pavement, clutching at their faces and torsos as though they'd been caught in a net.

"Don't let the spider get me!" Emrich screamed. "Don't let it get me!"

The youth turned and goggled at the writhing guards, their weapons forgotten. His three fellows watched with more interest than concern; one swigged from a silver-mounted drinking horn. They'd come for a spectacle, after all, and this was proving even better than the supernatural display they'd been expecting.

The youth touched his own sword, probably for lack of any other thought in his head. Cashel closed his own left hand over the youth's, squeezing it for an instant and then lifting it from the hilt. Garric stepped forward and took the sword belt in both hands. He twisted, snapping the silver buckle like a dry cornstalk instead of bothering to unbuckle it.

"What are—" the youth said. Cashel gave him a little push backward. The youth's feet pedaled for a step or two; then he fell over with a thump. Garric tossed the sword—belt, scabbard and all—into the Beltis.

Garric and Cashel started laughing. Cashel passed his quarterstaff from his right hand to his left so he could clasp arms with his friend. They worked together like the two stones of a mill. . . .

"Do you know what that sword was worth?" shrilled a servant, shocked beyond concern for his own safety by his amazement at what had just happened.

"It was very nearly worth this little ponce's life," Garric said, toeing the youth. The fellow began hunching backward across the cobblestones, staring up with eyes as wide as a frog's.

Smiling lazily, Garric turned to Ilna. "Are they going to be all right?" he asked, flicking the fingertips of his left hand in the direction of the guards. His *left* hand, Ilna realized, because his right was clenching and unclenching as though it wanted to grip his sword.

She looked at the guards. They'd grown still. For a frozen moment Ilna thought that her fingers had added one knot more to the pattern, the knot her brain hadn't meant to tie. . . .

The men were still breathing. They'd simply exhausted themselves in struggling with the web that only they could see. Ilna's knees buckled with relief.

"Garric, catch her!" shouted a voice, Liane's voice, and Ilna wasn't falling any more. Garric's arms, strong as hoops of hickory, encircled her and she felt his heart hammering with the fierce anger that had ruled him as it had Ilna herself.

"They'll be all right when the knots are loosed," Cashel heard his sister moan from against Garric's broad chest. "But oh! I was ready to kill them. I almost killed them!"

Cashel squatted beside the guards and looked them over. Their eyes stared back at him. None of them moved; their arms were close at their sides, as though they were wrapped in wet sheets. Emrich, something of a dandy in silver-studded harness and a silk neck scarf, mouthed the word, "Please . . ."

"You didn't kill them, though," Garric said, patting Ilna's back with his right hand. "And because of you, Cashel and I didn't have to kill them either."

Garric's eyes had been a thousand miles away right after the trouble, but they were coming back to normal now.

Cashel himself hadn't been that worked up about the business. It had all been so silly.

He picked up the cords Ilna had knotted. The pattern didn't mean anything to him—it seemed as random as the way wind might have whipped the four bits if they'd been dangling alongside one another. He started to hand them to his sister. He saw she was still sobbing with reaction, though, so he picked the knots apart himself.

Cashel knew how much it took out of you to do what Ilna had done. It wasn't wizardry the way Tenoctris did it, with words and written symbols, but it did some of the same things.

And more. Cashel had faced real wizards, and when they'd each taken their punch it had been Cashel or-Kenset who was still standing. He didn't understand what it was he did—it was different from Ilna's tricks with fabric, that was certain—but there were powers they both tapped when they needed to.

Cashel chuckled at a further thought: it was harder work than rolling a boulder uphill all the day, that was for sure. Well, he didn't mind work, nor did Ilna.

Though the knots were tight, they came apart easily under the touch of Cashel's big fingers. Ilna saw patterns, Cashel saw the way things balanced against one another. It was close to being the same thing, he guessed.

He stood. The guards shuddered as Cashel smoothed the cords straight in the palm of one hand with the index finger of the other, the hand that held his quarterstaff. He wondered if it really would've come to killing except for what Ilna had done. It could have at that: the guards had swords and there wouldn't have been time for delicacy.

Cashel shook his head in wonder. So silly!

Ilna was standing on her own, now; Liane offered her a hand, but Ilna shook it away.

Garric walked over to the nobleman who'd started the trouble. The fellow started to get up, then changed his mind and lay back on the cobblestones. He put his hands over his private parts, of all things!

"Who are you?" Garric asked, in friendly enough fashion but sounding like he expected an answer. Being king or the next thing to it surely did suit him!

"I'm Lord Mos bor-Moriman," the fellow said in a squeaky voice. "My friends and I—"

He glanced backward, desperately looking for support. The other nobles and their entourage watched the fallen man like gulls waiting to peck a stranded fish to death.

Cashel kept an eye on the guards, though, just in case one of them decided to try Garric from behind. That'd be a pretty dumb thing to do—Garric saw everything around him when he got keyed up, and Ilna was watching with a grim expression and another selection of cords—but enough dumb things had happened already that Cashel didn't take the risk.

"Well, Lord Mos," Garric said, "do you know who I am?"

One of the guards sprawled at Cashel's feet muttered, "May the Sister drag me down! He *can't* be."

"By the Lady!" Emrich said. "He is! Prince Garric, we didn't know!"

Emrich hunched his arms under him and glanced toward Cashel; Cashel nodded, giving him permission to get to his feet. Emrich at least was smarter than a sheep, though Cashel wouldn't say as much for his noble master.

Having risen, Emrich knelt again before Garric. "Your Majesty," he said, speaking to the dirty pavement, "our lives are yours, but we didn't know."

The other guards were rising cautiously. Cashel noticed with amusement that two of them were more worried about the cords in Ilna's hand than they were about his own iron-shod quarterstaff. They might be right about that, too.

"You're Prince Garric of *Haft*?" Mos said. Then he said, "You're Prince Garric! Well, I don't see how you expect people to—"

"Hush," Garric said. "Or I'll toss you in after your sword, as I'm rather inclined to do already."

Garric wore heavy-soled boots now, as always when he

went onto the hard streets of Valles. He pointed the toe of one at Mos' lips, just short of touching him. Mos hushed.

"Lord Mos," Garric went on, "your choice is to endow a hostel for the orphans of this district. A representative of the chancellor's office will call on you tomorrow to discuss the details."

"A choice?" squeaked Mos. He looked like a beetle on his back, which was close enough to the truth. "What do you mean a choice? You're just giving orders!"

Garric grinned. "It's a real choice, milord," he said, "but you *won't* like the other option."

Just so they got the point—not that Garric's tone hadn't been clear enough—Cashel rapped the lower ferrule of his staff on the pavement with a sparkling *crack*!

Garric winked at him, then turned to the group of nobles with a face as threatening as a thundercloud and said, "You will leave now, taking your toad of a friend here with you." His boot prodded Mos in the side; not hard, but hard enough to be noticed. "I recommend that you not come back."

He looked at the four guards. "Not you," he added. "I have something more to say to you."

The nobles exchanged glances. One of them snapped an order to a pair of servants. They in turn eyed Garric, then leaped forward and helped Lord Mos to his feet. The entourage moved back through the crowd, silently at first but with a gabble of mutual complaints as they got out of sight.

"Prince Garric?" Emrich said. His face was set with fear of what Garric was going to say next. The four guards stood stiffly, as though they were being inspected by their commander.

"In the morning," Garric said easily, "you're to report to Lord Waldron's office in the Arsenal. You'll probably see one of the adjutant's clerks rather than the commander himself, but that won't matter. Tell him that you're reporting for assignment to one of the new regiments."

Sharina moved close to Cashel, though she didn't cling to his arm as he'd half-hoped she would. That could get in the way if he needed to use his staff, but he was sure by now that he wouldn't. Sharina had pulled the edge of her cape forward again, covering the big knife which she'd resheathed.

"You'll be paid on a scale determined by your skill and experience," Garric continued, "but I don't suppose the wages will be as high as what you were making until tonight."

"You'll be working for a man, though," Ilna put in, her words clacking out like boards striking together. "You may find that a pleasant change."

"You trust us to appear, Your Majesty?" another of the—former—bodyguards said; an older man than Emrich. His mustache and sideburns were very full. His cap still lay on the pavement where he'd been squirming, revealing that he was completely bald.

"You'll appear or you'll have left Ornifal before tomorrow sunset," Garric said. "I trust you to know that you can't hide on this island from me and my friends here."

Ilna grinned like a skull. She dangled her hank of cords before the men for a moment, then replaced them in her sleeve.

"May the Shepherd shield me with His crook," whispered a guard. His face had gone sallow. "May the Lady cover me with the cloak of Her mercy."

"Come on," muttered Emrich to his fellows. The older guard picked up his cap. Instead of putting it on at once, he faced Garric and slapped it against his chest with his arm at a stiff angle.

To Cashel's surprise, Garric responded by thumping his clenched right fist on his opposite shoulder. It was a military greeting of some sort, Cashel supposed; a salute, or maybe two different kinds of salute. Garric had become a wonder since his father gave him that medal to wear!

The guards moved off, close together and silent. The trouble had cleared twenty feet of open space around Cashel and his friends. Cashel grinned. That mightn't have been enough. The Shepherd alone knew how far a sword might have spun if Cashel's quarterstaff had whacked it out of somebody's hand.

Garric surveyed the watching crowd and called, "Is this sort of business frequent? Rich fools coming here to swagger about and use their guards to punish anyone who objects?"

Nobody spoke for a moment. A girl stepped forward. Cashel had seen her before, though dressed fancier than she was now: Sharina's maid Diora. She dragged an older, rounder woman out of the crowd with her.

"Come on, Mam!" Diora said. "Tell him! Tell Prince Garric the truth!"

The older woman opened and closed her mouth several times, but she couldn't force the words out. Diora turned from her mother with a look of disgust and anger. Shrilly she said, "Not every night, but them and their sort come here to do as they please, and nobody does anything about it!"

"They like poking a chained dog!" a male voice shouted from anonymously farther back. "They know if a few of us get together with cobblestones for an answer, the army'll march in to put down the riot!"

Garric nodded. "All right," he said. His voice echoed from the tenement façades. "I'll have a discussion with the city prefect tomorrow. There'll be a detachment of the watch stationed here of nights to insure courteous behavior by *all* citizens of the Isles."

Garric laughed aloud and looked about him, his fists on his hips. At this moment he was older than the lad Cashel had grown up with, and he looked very, very strong.

"And if that doesn't work," he shouted, "there'll be a new city prefect, and he'll *live* in District Twelve until he's found a way to solve the problem. This is a kingdom of all citizens, not just of fools with money and a title!"

People started cheering. Garric looked startled and embarrassed, as though he'd suddenly remembered who he was.

Cashel grinned in delight at his friend. He was Prince

Garric, that's who he really was. Nobody could listen to that speech and doubt it!

Garric raised his arms to acknowledge the cheers, then put his back to the crowd. "And one way or another," he added quietly as he viewed the apparition hanging above the river, "we're going to deal with this thing too. But I hope somebody else can tell me how!"

Sharina thought for a moment that Diora was going to come over to her, but at the last moment the maid lost her nerve and burrowed deeper into the crowd, out of sight.

Telling her mistress privately about the bridge had been one thing. This time, though, Diora had addressed Prince Garric himself in front of all the world. No wonder she was terrified.

Smiling slightly, Sharina turned her attention back to the bridge wavering above the Beltis. Tomorrow she'd calm Diora and assure her that she'd been right to speak—as she certainly had. There was nothing to be done tonight that wouldn't just scare the girl worse. Sharina rested her fingertips lightly on Cashel's forearm.

The structure seemed to have been outlined in pastels. During the coldest winter in living memory, the Northern Lights had hung above Barca's Hamlet. The bridge looked only a little more solid than those. It wasn't frightening, exactly, but it *was* uncanny.

"I see people moving there," Cashel said. His eyes narrowed. "At least I think I do."

Garric glanced at Tenoctris. She still sat on the stones, murmuring as her bamboo sliver tapped time. Liane had hovered protectively over the old wizard while the rest of them were concerned with Lord Mos and the others. "Does she . . . ?" Garric asked.

Liane turned a palm up in the equivalent of a shrug. With a wince of embarrassment she then resheathed the little dagger she'd concealed in her other hand. "She hasn't said anything, Garric," Liane said. "Except for the spell."

"That bridge isn't anything like the one that used to cross the Beltis here," Garric said. He spoke loud enough for all of them to hear him, but it seemed to Sharina that her brother was really organizing his thoughts. "The one King Carus knew. It doesn't even look like a bridge, though it was one when I crossed it in my dream."

"This is where you visited Ansalem?" Liane asked.

"It's *how* I went," Garric said with a smile. "I'm not sure it's really a 'where,' either here or in my dream."

A shriek that couldn't have been human—it was too loud, too loud even for a horse—keened through the night. Cashel spun around, but the sound didn't come from nearby.

Sharina took her hand from the hilt of the Pewle knife. It probably didn't come from this world at all, any more than the structure glimmering in the air did.

Tenoctris gave a muted sigh and set her stylus down. She wavered and might have fallen over herself if Ilna hadn't knelt and put an arm around her in time.

Ilna looked up with an expression of cool achievement. Sharina met her friend's eyes and grinned. Liane had been protecting the old wizard from being trampled, but Ilna had been watching Tenoctris herself.

"Help me up, please," Tenoctris said. Ilna rose, straightening at the knees and supporting the older woman with the arm around her shoulders. Garric held out a hand; Ilna acknowledged the offer with a nod, but she didn't need the help and had no intention of accepting it.

Sharina tried to imagine a world in which everybody was like Ilna. It would be a polite place and everything would be done right.

It would also be a very frightening world; a lot like walking over a crust of stone and knowing that a volcano bubbled just underneath. Not that Ilna would ever let loose the rage and power within her....

Sharina reached over and squeezed Ilna's arm. Just a friendly touch, a friend's touch. Ilna gave her a wry smile as though she understood what Sharina had been thinking, and agreed.

Tenoctris straightened and took a deep breath. "Do you know what it is then?" Garric asked. He couldn't hide his impatience, but he managed to sound apologetic about it.

"I won't know that for a very long time," Tenoctris said. She attempted a smile, but she was too exhausted to carry it off. Some things could only be learned or accomplished by wizardry, but its use required brutal effort and great danger even if the wizard didn't make a mistake.

When wizards *did* err, the only question was how many others they dragged with them to Hell. It was error as much as intent that had smashed the Old Kingdom to bloody shards, and another wizard's blunder now would end all hope of civilization for the Isles.

Because the crowd had grown still at the shriek, Sharina could hear other voices.

They were too high-pitched to be human, and she couldn't tell whether they were laughing or gibbering in terror. Like the bridge itself, the sounds faded in and out of awareness.

The frogs that normally formed a shrilling chorus in the shallows at the river's margin were silent also. A fish slapped the water far out in the current, leaping away from some perceived danger.

"What I was trying to do tonight . . ." Tenoctris said. She gathered strength with each word. Now she patted Ilna's hand in thanks and release, then stood upright on her own. ". . . is determine whether the force we're witnessing is cyclical or is increasing in magnitude. If I thought it were going to go away by itself, I'd be inclined to let it do so."

She gave them a weary smile. "Unfortunately, it'll grow until it's removed, and removing it will be as difficult as moving Valles to the north coast of Ornifal. Or perhaps simply shifting the whole city to Haft."

Cashel stretched his arms upward, holding his staff crossways over his head where it wouldn't threaten any of the people around him. He grinned. "So," he said. "Do we start moving Valles a building at a time, or does it have to be the whole place at once?"

Tenoctris laughed transformingly. She was still obviously tired, but no longer did her face wear a patina of desperate concern. Cashel had reminded the old wizard that she was among friends, and that these friends—*her* friends—had halted onrushing chaos before.

"Well, what I think we'll do is to get help," Tenoctris explained. "More precisely, we'll find the wizard who's responsible for this appearing and convince him to remove it."

"Ansalem?" Garric asked.

Tenoctris shrugged. "It might be Ansalem," she said, "if he were alive. Ansalem was like no one, no *thing,* I've ever met. It's not a bridge exactly; that's just how our human minds perceive it. It's a point where planes of the cosmos merge. It isn't really evil, but the amount of damage it can do simply by—"

There were screams; and this time they were human. A man flung himself into the river, bellowing in hoarse terror. A thing of rosy light loped through the crowd, looking as desperately frightened as the people trying to get away from it.

It was man-sized or almost and built—almost—like a man. It had two arms and two legs, but they were shaggy and the legs bent the wrong way. They ended in goat hooves which clacked on the pavement when the creature looked most solid.

The faun faded to a pale blur which ran through a sedan chair and the bejeweled young woman seated in it. She screamed, but she'd been screaming already. Sharina couldn't see that she was any the worse for her experience.

Two strides beyond the sedan chair, the faun's outline sharpened into the solidity of a red jasper statue. He—the faun was unclothed and there was no doubt about his sex— was running down the esplanade in the general direction of Sharina and her friends.

He leaped. A husky man in a butcher's leather apron

dodged in the same direction. They collided. It was the man who went down, though the faun gave a despairing bleat as he caromed off.

He was headed straight toward Sharina. His pointed face was a mask of panic. She drew her Pewle knife, but Cashel stepped in front of her with his quarterstaff beginning to rotate. The faun bounded upward like a deer—

And vanished in midair, leaving only a smudge of dissipating scarlet flickers where he'd been.

"Oh . . ." said Sharina, feeling the muscles over her ribs relax. She felt as she had the day a hornet—swift, mindless, and viciously dangerous—had flown at her face.

The butcher lay on the stones, moaning and trying to stanch the blood with his hands. The faun's sharp hooves had sliced through the apron and deep into his left thigh, cutting like paired knives. A woman and a boy were helping the butcher—the one tearing a bandage from the hem of her tunic, the other cradling the older man's head and mumbling reassurance while tears ran down his face.

Most of the other spectators had fled from the riverside. The noblewoman stood in her sedan chair, sobbing uncontrollably. Her three guards ringed her, their swords drawn, but the bearers who should be carrying her away in the vehicle had instead fled unencumbered. After a moment's discussion, the group made off on foot. Two of the guards helped their mistress over the cobblestones.

Cashel didn't relax, though he lowered his quarterstaff. "What was that?" he asked quietly.

"Someone who shouldn't be here," Tenoctris said. "Not a danger in himself—not much of one, at any rate—but a symptom of what the problem is. So long as the connection is here, things fall through holes in the cosmos. Some of them could be very dangerous indeed."

Sharina saw something in the sky above the bridge. At first she thought it was a remnant of the sparks into which the faun had dissolved. It shimmered like haze at sunrise; then it had winged shape, a bird stroking slowly in the direction of Sharina and her friends.

The red light faded. The bird wavered out of focus, then reappeared.

"I think we can return to the palace now," Tenoctris said. "I've learned all I can here tonight."

She smiled wanly. "In part because I'm too tired to do any more."

Sharina glanced back. Their carriage waited forlornly at the edge of the esplanade, now generally deserted. The butcher limped away, supported by the woman and a man of his own age who'd returned to help him.

Liane was speaking to Garric. Sharina looked to see if the bird had vanished the way the faun did. It was still in the sky—and huge.

"All right—" said Garric.

"What's that?" Sharina asked, pointing upward. Immediately she felt uncomfortable about the gesture, as though she'd called attention to herself when she shouldn't have.

Cashel looked up and frowned. He stepped between Sharina and the bird. Was it too large to call a bird? When Sharina first saw the creature, she'd thought of it as a gull. It was growing. Now it had a span of forty feet.

Garric had begun to sheath his long sword. He hesitated, then slammed the blade home in its scabbard after all. A naked sword was an awkward thing to hold. Garric had shown he could clear the weapon in a heartbeat if the situation required that.

The bird's wings flapped again. The slow stroke didn't bring it closer, but the thing grew enormously in size. Its pinions were scaly and a hundred feet across. The creature had a toothed beak and three clawed fingers at the elbow joint of each wing. It cocked its long head sideways, fixing Sharina with the glare of one fiery eye.

"Get down!" Garric shouted, sweeping his sword out again. "Cashel, you and me!"

Liane took Tenoctris in her arms and lay down, covering the old woman with her body. Sharina drew the Pewle knife, but she realized that Garric was right: he and Cashel needed a clear field to use their strength and weapons. She flattened on the stones, her face turned to the side so she could watch the sky. Her own knife, the sharp little blade Liane carried, and Ilna's noose were all effective enough in the right circumstances; but not against a monster like the one now filling the night sky.

Sharina doubted that Garric's sword could do much either. Cashel, though . . .

Cashel set his staff rotating with the deliberation of a careful craftsman. He held the hickory at either side of the balance, then crossed his wrists as the staff turned; and again, and again, and—

The spinning circle was a common technique with a quarterstaff. The stout hickory protected the staff-wielder, and he could strike out of the circuit with either end if the enemy pressed him.

In Cashel's hands, however, the staff was more than a physical object. Sparkles of blue fire, then sizzling trails of light dripped from both ferrules as the quarterstaff spun before him. His legs were set and braced, facing the threat and determined to beat it or die.

The bird banked slightly. A flash of ruby fire showed its massive reptilian form in the jeweled detail of dew on a morning spiderweb. Its beak opened to call.

It was on them. Garric's sword swung forward, Cashel's staff was a disk of solid sapphire light, and the bird—

The bird vanished as though it never was.

Sharina got to her feet. Liane covered Tenoctris, supporting her own weight on her palms. She raised her head to make sure the danger had passed, then began helping the older woman up.

Ilna stood gracefully and coiled her silken noose around her waist. She caught Sharina's eye and gave her friend a wry smile. "I didn't know what good it was going to do either," she said, "but I felt better with it in my hands."

Sharina grinned and sheathed the Pewle knife in reply.

The driver of the carriage was fighting with the reins, and the postilion clung to the off-horse's harness. The beasts were neighing in terror even now that the danger was over. Only the servants' skill—and courage—had kept the team from bolting down one of the narrow streets entering the esplanade. The carriage would inevitably have smashed on the corner of a building.

Garric was still wild-eyed. He'd spun on the balls of his feet as though he expected to find the bird behind him. It was simply gone, spit from present existence the way the faun had been. He shuddered.

"I don't think I'm going to be able to get used to that sort of thing," he said mildly. "Though I suppose it's better than trying to fight something bigger than a trireme."

Cashel gave a great sigh. He set one end of his quarter-staff on the ground and leaned against it. He looked as weary as if he'd just tried to lift the world on his shoulders.

Sharina stepped close and clasped his right arm between both of hers. Cashel's skin was hot, and she could feel the hairs on his arm raised and prickly.

"I didn't see where it went," he said. "I don't remember exactly. . . ."

"It just disappeared," Garric said. He sheathed his sword and seemed doubtful as to whether he should offer Cashel a hand in support. "Tenoctris, do you know what it was?"

"Something else that got in through the crack the bridge is causing," Tenoctris said. "There'll be other visitors coming; and more frequently, I'm afraid, until we remove the burden from the cosmos."

"I thought it was coming for us," Liane said in a calm voice.

Ilna gave a minuscule nod. "Us, or one of us," she said. "I thought that too."

"Well, we'll get back—" Garric said.

People screamed hoarsely. Sharina looked up. The bird sailed toward them over the tenements. It had circled in whichever plane of the cosmos to which it had faded; now it was returning from behind them. A flash of scarlet wizardlight shivered over the vast, dark-hued form. Its braying call shook foam-tipped wavelets from the river.

Sharina turned, trying to put herself between the monster

and Tenoctris. Cashel swayed, lifting his staff again; Garric
was drawing his sword. If anything happened to the old
wizard, the rest of them wouldn't know what to do, let
alone be able to do it.

The sky went black. Air sliding past the monster's scaly
wings whispered like a forest in springtime.

"Sharina!" Cashel cried.

Horny talons the size of human arms clenched about
Sharina from behind. She tried to draw her knife, but the
pressure clamped her arms to her sides. *Like a vole
snatched by an owl,* she thought; but the claws held her
instead of piercing her through the way an owl's would
have done its victim.

She looked down. The ground lurched away. The Beltis
was below, the bridge a shimmering mirage on its surface.

The bird's leathery wings stroked, and the whole universe vanished in a thunderclap.

Chapter Five

S harina squirmed as gray mist swirled in the stroke of
the creature's wings. The bird's talons were harder than
horn; harder even than iron, perhaps. They held her as
securely as millstones did a wheat kernel in the moment
before they crushed it.

The haze congealed into a reality again, though not anything of the world from which Sharina had been snatched.
The sea tossed close below them. The sun was low on the
horizon, though Sharina couldn't be sure whether it was
rising or setting.

The bird's pinions were reflected in the black water. She
could see herself as a pale blur clutched close to the dark
body.

Something rose slowly from the sea ahead. It had the streamlined shape of the seawolves which Sharina knew from their rare forays onto the shores of Barca's Hamlet: marine lizards with flattened tails and jaws which could crush a sheep's hips—or a man's.

A big seawolf might be twelve feet long. This creature was the size of a ship, or even bigger. Its fangs winked in the red sun.

The bird's wings stroked in their slow rhythm. The sea and the monster on it broke into scatters of rainbow light which faded to gray. Sharina was alone with the vast creature which had caught her. Its scaled, leathery skin never lost definition, though all else blurred away.

She wriggled again, but the talons meshed like the wards of a lock. They weren't so tight that they hurt her, but she couldn't even get a hand free to sweep her hair back.

The wings stroked slowly down. Sharina thought of her friends. The sting of her whipping hair was bringing tears to her eyes. . . .

Ilna sat straight-backed and prim in a corner of the pavilion while the others reacted in their several ways. *She* was still and calm; all except for her fingers, which wove and picked loose the yarn of designs which could have blasted minds if she'd chosen to display them.

"Well, we've got to rescue Sharina," Cashel said. At a casual glance he seemed calm, but his was the tense stillness of an ox when a great horsefly buzzes back and forth about it, choosing a place to land. At any moment Cashel might burst out in a fury that would tear down everything in his path.

"I don't think Sharina is in immediate danger," Tenoctris said. She didn't know Cashel as well as Garric or Ilna herself did, but she was still trying not to offend the big man. "I can't tell who sent the creature, or what his purpose in taking Sharina could be—"

Tired as she was, the old wizard had worked a spell at

the riverside before she allowed them to take her back to the palace. She'd said that the bridge of wizardlight gave her incantation greater effect, though it also required even more than her usual care.

At the end of the whispered spell, Tenoctris had collapsed. Ilna and Liane had cradled her between them on the carriage seat during the trip back, trying to lessen the wheels' hammering vibration for the older woman.

"—but he has a purpose beyond simply doing her harm," Tenoctris concluded.

Cashel snorted. "It's not Sharina's purpose," he said. "And by the Shepherd! it's not mine. I'm going to bring her back, and I don't care what it takes to do it!"

Oil lamps with silver reflectors hung from each pillar of the colonnade supporting the pavilion's slate roof. Moths blundered into the reflectors and made the flames flicker with the beat of their wings. Ilna marveled to see so much light during nighttime.

"It might be best to close the hole first," Garric said. He'd been pacing but he knew how nervous that made him look. Now he sat on the stone bench running along the center of the pavilion, squeezing his fists together knuckle to knuckle. He still looked as tense as a drawn bow. "Get rid of the bridge I mean. When Tenoctris recovers, we can plan what we're going to do."

Cashel looked at his friend. "I told you what I'm going to do," he said in a quiet voice blurred slightly by its growling undertone. "I'm going to find Sharina and bring her back. If I was half the man she deserves, I'd have moved fast enough to stop that bird."

He turned and slammed his fist into a pillar. It was stuccoed wood, not stone as Ilna had thought. The column shuddered violently, shedding its plaster in flakes and dust. The projecting lamp flailed wildly, showering drops of oil. There was a smudge of blood on the shaft.

Ilna stood and stepped quickly to her brother. The others remained wisely motionless. Cashel gripped the column in both hands as if the shaft was a throat he wanted to throttle.

Ilna put her hands on his cheeks, turning his head toward her by touch alone. No amount of force could have diverted Cashel's anger.

"It was my fault," he said in a choked whisper.

"If the worst thing on your conscience," Ilna said in a harsh voice, "is that when you'd worn yourself out guarding your friends something managed to slip in behind you—then you're a saint, not a man! Are you a saint, Cashel or-Kenset?"

He stiffened in embarrassment. "No ma'am," he said. "No, Ilna, you know I'm not."

Ilna kept her face stern as a knife's edge, her natural expression, but a cold smile played at the back of her mind. If a saint was someone so blessed by the Great Gods that he could walk through fire and over the sea, the way the hymns to the Lady said the righteous could—no, Cashel wasn't a saint. But being righteous—as best Ilna could tell from the way the priests from Carcosa behaved when they led the images of the Lady and the Shepherd through the borough at the annual Tithe Procession—was a matter of offering the Gods more money than either of Kenset's orphan children could even imagine until they left Barca's Hamlet.

You couldn't ask for a kinder, gentler fellow than Cashel, unless you went well out of your way to make him an enemy. He and Ilna were twins. It seemed to her that they'd each gotten more than their share of emotions that other people had in moderate proportions. Different emotions, of course.

She put her hands down and stepped back. "Then stop beating on the house," she said more mildly. "That doesn't do it any good, or you either. Liane, will you look at my brother's hand, please? Or should we call a healer?"

"It's all right," Cashel muttered, his embarrassment even deeper. Ilna took his wrist in both hands and tugged it toward Liane; Cashel didn't fight her, though he was obviously unhappy to be fussed over.

Liane turned his hand palm-down. Her fingers positioned

Cashel's bloodied knuckles under one of the lamps so that she could view them.

"I know she could be dead," Cashel said. He stared out through the portico. Nothing moved in the darkness except the yellow-green flicker of fireflies. "I know that Sharina could be dead."

Sharina hung in a gray haze that had no temperature. The bird's wings stroked and reality coalesced again about her. The air was cool with a hint of recent rain. They were overflying plains. The landscape spread as broadly as the sea had earlier, and it seemed to have as little in the way of distinctive elements.

The tall grasses were yellow, and auburn seedheads weighed many of the stems into arcs. The vast shadow of Sharina's captor sent waves of lesser birds fluttering from the autumn bounty with calls of peevish concern.

Grazing animals, some of them shaped like horses but only a little bigger than sheep, looked up at the giant bird. A score of mixed herds began fleeing in as many different directions. The animals called out in a chorus of blats and neighs, unpleasant individually and hideous in combination.

The great bird flew on. The landscape dissolved into colorless mist.

The wings were silent. The talons clutched Sharina so close to the leathery belly that she couldn't see the bird's head. Could the creature think? Could it even hear?

"Where are you taking me?" she shouted. Her words were flat and echoless. "Who are you?"

The sound of her voice was worse than the silence it replaced. In this gray limbo Sharina was alone in a way that no one in waking reality could be alone.

She and the bird swept into a vision of light and springtime. Spires of sunstruck crystal rose from a landscape of pools and gardens. Pavilions gleamed in the air, each dangling from a gossamer tendril so fine that only the quivering light showed how it was attached to a nearby tower.

There were people here, the first she'd seen since the bird snatched her away. They strolled through the gardens, wearing flowing robes and laughing as breezes blew spray from the fountains over them. Some reclined in the pavilions, drinking from goblets. A dozen youths danced and wound ribbons about a pole rising from a serpentine lake. Their feet were supported only by air.

"Help me!" Sharina cried. She could hear the laughter of the folk below, so she knew they must be able to hear her. "Help me get free!"

Some of the people looked up. A girl Sharina's age was standing in a crystal eyrie hundreds of feet above the ground. She waved a scarlet ribbon and smiled.

The youths continued to dance. The bird's wings beat again, lifting it and Sharina out of this reality.

"Help me!" Sharina repeated, though she alone could hear the words.

"Cashel," Garric said, "I may need your help here. The kingdom may need your help."

Cashel looked at his friend, feeling embarrassed again and frustrated. Things seemed obvious to him. He didn't know how to explain them to Garric if Garric didn't see them already.

"I have to find Sharina," he said. "I'll come back as soon as I can, but I need to find her first."

"The kingdom—" Garric said. He was frowning like he had a heavy job to do and wasn't sure how to go about it. People did that a lot when they were talking to Cashel.

"I don't know about the kingdom," Cashel said. He shrugged. "I know about sheep, that's all. And I know what *my* duty is. Garric, you're the king and you have to worry about everything. I'm Sharina's friend, and I guess she needs my help worse than you do."

Cashel had left his quarterstaff outside the pavilion because he'd known he shouldn't have it in his hand when he was angry like he'd been. He'd calmed down now that he'd figured things out, and the familiar smoothness of the hickory would have felt good.

But he didn't need it. He didn't *need* anything but to get Sharina back.

Garric suddenly laughed and clapped Cashel on both shoulders. They were back to being friends who'd grown up together; friends who knew each other better than maybe either of them knew himself.

"If I were as sure you were wrong as I am of the sunrise," Garric said cheerfully, "then I still couldn't change your mind. And I'm not that sure."

"Sometimes I wonder about the sunrise," Liane said, sitting on the central bench with her hands folded in her lap. She gave Cashel an affectionate smile. Liane was about as nice a person as you could ask to meet.

Garric sat down again, a little closer to Liane than he'd been before he got up this last time. He gave a weary sigh, and when the laughter left his face he looked frustrated enough to chew on rocks.

Garric was really smart. Nobody here in Valles had anything on him for brains . . . but that wasn't always the advantage people thought it was.

Garric and the rest could see all sorts of ways and twists and questions. A lot of times they weren't sure which way to go because they knew how many different paths there were.

Cashel just went straight on ahead. Like this business of getting Sharina back from whatever the thing was that took her. What did the kingdom matter compared to that?

Cashel didn't even know what a kingdom was. Even Barca's Hamlet, small as it was compared to Valles, wasn't *a* thing: it was a lot of families, a lot of people, all going their own way. Garric must see something more than that, and Cashel didn't doubt that whatever his friend saw was really there—

For Garric. But it wasn't anything that was going to turn Cashel away from a friend who needed his help.

"I know you think it's important that we all fight evil," Cashel said apologetically. "But you know, I'm going to take a lot of convincing before I believe that bird and whoever sent it are good."

Even Ilna grinned. Her face sobered when her gaze shifted to Liane and Garric together on the stone bench, though. Aloud she said, "Cashel's right, of course. The pattern is so vast that if you try to understand it completely you won't be able to do anything. And some things are worth doing."

She smiled without humor. "In human terms at least," she added. "For my own part, I'm going to complete a tapestry and then leave for Erdin. I have unfinished business there."

Garric grimaced, but he didn't protest. He knew as well as Cashel did that you'd have as much chance of teaching a tree to dance as you would of changing Ilna's mind once she'd decided what she ought to do.

"Lord Tadai is going to Erdin shortly as well," Garric said, "though he doesn't know that yet. He keeps late hours, so I suppose I'll see him tonight."

He gave Cashel a wry smile. "It's always best to do an unpleasant job first," he said, "so you don't have it hanging over you. Though Duzi knows, there's enough unpleasant jobs in being king that I don't think I'm going to run out of them any time soon."

Ilna stood and looked around the group, giving anyone time to ask for her help if they thought they needed it. Ilna didn't volunteer, but Cashel had never seen his sister turn down a request anybody made her. Mind, her tongue might flay the hide off the person asking, telling him why he was such an idiot to need the help—but he'd get the help regardless. It was a matter of what was important to you.

Nobody spoke now, though Garric and Liane rose to their feet. Ilna nodded to Cashel, to Garric, to Tenoctris—and then gave Liane a quick hug. Cashel blinked. That was the biggest surprise of the night, though it was a lot more pleasant than to see that huge bird coming out of nowhere to snatch Sharina. Ilna's set expression was the one Cashel had seen her wear while she cleaned the mill's dovecote, but she was really trying to be friendly.

Ilna started out of the pavilion. Cashel touched her shoulder as she went by and said, "Hey? Take care of yourself, all right?"

"And you too, Cashel," she said. She smiled, but there was a tear glittering at the corner of her eye as she walked swiftly toward the dwelling she and Cashel shared.

Garric and Liane were ready to leave also. Cashel gave his friend a quick signal and said to Tenoctris, "Mistress? Can I see you to your house? Ah—I could carry you if you liked."

"And not for the first time," Tenoctris said as she rose. "But I'm well enough tonight to walk home with your company."

Cashel gave the old wizard his right arm; the quarterstaff leaned against one of the entrance pillars and he took it in his left. A pair of servants waited with lanterns, ready to light the couple to where they were going. There was a first-quarter moon, plenty to see by.

"No, we don't need you," Cashel said gruffly. He hadn't meant to sound so unfriendly, but he didn't want ears around when he asked for help.

"I can't come with you to find Sharina, Cashel," Tenoctris said, answering a question that he wouldn't have dreamed of asking. "I wish I could, but the need here is too great."

"Oh, I knew that!" Cashel said. "I was hoping maybe you could get me pointed in the right direction, though. But if you can't, I'll understand."

They walked through an arbor overgrown by honeysuckle. The vines were a terrible pest; they'd choke even a tree if there was sunlight enough for them to grow the way they liked. But Cashel loved the smell of honeysuckle in early summer, so he was glad the gardeners hadn't gotten around to clearing this away.

"I guess you think I'm doing the wrong thing," he added quietly. He hated to disappoint his friends.

Tenoctris chuckled. "I don't think you're capable of doing the wrong thing, Cashel," she said. "The choices you make are always going to be the right ones for you."

Cashel cleared his throat. A fountain plashed behind a boxwood hedge. He liked the waterworks here in the palace grounds. It reminded him of the way Pattern Creek rippled through the pasture south of Barca's Hamlet.

"Well," he said aloud. "There's a lot of things I don't understand."

"There are things you don't consciously understand," Tenoctris said. "I haven't seen you deal with anything important that you didn't understand at a basic level, though. I wish I could say as much about myself."

After a pause she added, "Cashel, if you feel that you need to leave us now, you're almost certainly right. I don't know why, but whatever you decide will be what we—what Good, if you will—need."

"You think the Shepherd's guiding me?" Cashel said bluntly.

"No," said Tenoctris. "But if I believed in the Great Gods, I *might* think that."

A handcart loaded with gravel lay across the walkway where workmen had left it when they quit work at sundown. Cashel lifted the old woman in the crook of his arm and carried her around the obstruction. There was no need for her to ask or him to offer his help: they'd worked together in the past. Cashel was used to being Tenoctris' legs and strong right arm.

Tenoctris had deliberately chosen a bungalow at a distance from the busy quarters of the palace. The workmen repairing decades of neglect hadn't gotten this far, and the overgrown surroundings meant she had greater privacy. Wizardry made normal people uncomfortable, even if they worked in a palace and thought they were sophisticated.

Cashel put Tenoctris down on the other side of the obstruction. They resumed walking side by side. "I think the

best help I can give you . . ." she said. "Is to send you to
someone who's probably better suited to what you need
than I would be even if the bridge didn't require my presence here. His name is Landure."

"All right," Cashel said. "How do I find him?"

They were nearing the three-room bungalow Tenoctris
had chosen for herself. Half the roof tiles had needed to
be replaced, but it didn't matter to Tenoctris that water
damage had cracked most of the plaster off the inside
walls.

There should have been a lamp burning on the porch,
but Rimara, Tenoctris' maid, had no virtue beyond staying
calm at the thought of serving a wizard. Since Rimara was
generally asleep, Cashel wasn't sure she even knew Tenoctris *was* a wizard.

"I'll have to send you to him," Tenoctris said. "He's not
on this plane, but neither is Sharina herself, I'm sure. Landure is . . ."

As Tenoctris paused, searching for the right word,
Cashel stepped ahead of her and opened the door. The
porch overhang put the step in shadow. As weary as Tenoctris was, she could easily stumble.

"I've never met Landure," Tenoctris continued. "I know
him only by reputation. He's a haughty and imperious man
by all accounts, but he's also a fierce opponent of chaos
and evil. And he's a very powerful wizard."

Cashel lifted her through the doorway. "Tsk!" she said.
"I can still walk."

"Hoy!" Cashel said as he set the old woman on the
bench he knew was just inside the door. "Rimara! Fetch a
light!"

"Do you have to shout like that?" a sleepy voice protested from the side room. Iron clicked querulously against
a flint.

"I think Landure will be willing to help you," Tenoctris
said. For all her protest at being carried up the two entrance
steps, she sounded as faint as the tinge of moonlight leak-

ing around the window shutters. "And I'm afraid I don't have a better answer just now."

Wavering yellow light bloomed in the side room. Rimara came out wearing a dirty smock. She carried a tallow-soaked rushlight in one hand and rubbed her eyes with the other.

"That's all right," said Cashel, running his right palm along the quarterstaff. He was checking for cracks in the polished hickory, a familiar gesture and one that always calmed him. "I don't need a lot of help. Just someone to show me where Sharina is. I guess I can take care of the rest."

Just show me where Sharina is, he repeated silently. The maid saw his face and, mistaking the reason for the grimness, began to gabble empty apologies.

The great bird stroked out of gray limbo. Sharina's nose wrinkled at the stench of sulfur. She sneezed, bruising her ribs against the inexorable grip of the talons. They sailed over a darkness lit by volcanoes on the horizon and lines of bright lava seeping across the plain below where armies battled.

Swordsmen wearing horned helmets and carrying iron shields fought giants with writhing snakelike legs and four arms, each bearing a club. Club-strokes rang on shields like a raucous knell.

Occasionally a monster went down, shrieking and squalling. Men stood about the victim, hacking with the fury of automatons. Sometimes their swords fouled one another, throwing red sparks into the night.

Men fell too, their brains dashed out or their torsos crushed when a club battered through their defenses. They made no sound either in triumph or agony.

The lava continued to spread, forcing the combatants inward from the cracks that fractured the plain. When molten rock lapped over the fallen, hair burned sullenly and the flesh popped and sizzled. In a few days all the plain from horizon to horizon would be a sea of bright lava, but those fighting seemed to have no thought for the future.

Sharina closed her eyes. She felt the wings of the great bird rise and stroke downward with the majesty of a celestial event. This time the transition from reality to a place beyond reality was a blessing. She closed her eyes until dry air bathed her skin.

The terrain over which the bird flew was arid and stony. There was no sign of the sea in any direction, but Sharina saw the glitter of ice cliffs across the whole northern horizon.

Winds and freshets had carved the landscape into knobs. On the flanks of the buttes, bands of yellow, magenta, and even purple soil set off the brown and dun Sharina found more familiar.

Though dry, this world was no desert. The north slope of each hillock was terraced with the retaining walls raised high enough to protect the narrow fields from wind. Any rain that fell would seep down three levels or four, watering a separate crop at each terrace. That and the dew squeezed from the air each morning was enough to support barley and several types of bean.

There were no houses or other buildings. A nude woman carrying a woven satchel turned when the bird's great shadow fell across her. She gave a piercing call, somewhere between a whistle and a trumpet blast, and hurled herself headfirst into the hole beside her.

Warning cries echoed from every hilltop across the barrens. The human forms—they *were* human, beyond question—blended so well with the landscape that Sharina hadn't seen them as figures, only as motion as they vanished into the ground.

The bird's wings lifted, unconcerned with the panic it had sown on the world beneath. It cared as little for its route through the cosmos as a sandal does for the stones over which it treads. A gray that was neither light nor lightless replaced the badlands and their scurrying human dwellers.

How far could the bird carry her? Would she starve in limbo interspersed with scenes from worlds not her own?

Sharina started to laugh. She knew as much about her own future as anyone else did about theirs: nothing at all. She'd go on, doing her best and knowing that her friends were doing the same. If the Gods were with them, that would be enough; and if not, well, nobody would say that they hadn't tried.

The room which Lord Tadai had taken for his office in the palace had been intended as the bedroom of a richly appointed suite. From it a pillared loggia looked out over a pond which, now that gardeners had thinned the mimosa and removed the choking weeds, was quite lovely by daylight.

The pond still made its presence known in darkness by the croaks and piping of frogs in and around it. Garric smiled faintly. To him that was at least as good as a glimpse of pink flowers lifting in the sun above the lotus pads. There hadn't been lotuses back home, but there had been frogs.

Being king, well, prince, meant Garric had to do a lot of things that he didn't like; but it also meant he didn't have to live in multistory buildings standing side by side the way most people in Valles did. It wasn't exactly compensation: Garric wouldn't have been here at all if he hadn't been told the Isles needed him—

"And I'll tell you again if you don't choose to believe what you've seen yourself!" interjected Carus in a tart whisper.

"I believe it," Garric said, smiling faintly. And he did. What he *didn't* really believe was that Garric or-Reise was the person whose life he seemed to have been living since he left Barca's Hamlet.

"What's that, Your Majesty?" said Tadai, who'd risen from a desk lighted by multibranched oil lamps when his pair of guards ushered Garric into the office.

"I was thinking that having trees and frogs around me keeps me sane," Garric said, letting his smile widen slightly and feeling the king within him do the same. "More or less sane, I suppose."

"I'm a city man myself," Lord Tadai said. He was as slick and soft to look at as if molded of butter. Even now, well past midnight on a day he'd been working since dawn, Tadai was perfectly attired in a blue silk robe and gilt sandals whose straps were picked out in enamel that matched the cloth. "I've thought of ordering wagons to drive around the building while I'm working here, but I suppose that won't be necessary."

He looked at the two aides present: one young and of noble birth, the other much older and probably not. "Aradoc and Murein, you can go home now. Tell the guards to turn away any further visitors."

Smiling with a bitterness Garric had never seen on his face before, Tadai added, "Any visitors for me, that is."

The younger aide stared at Garric transfixed. Garric was pretty sure he'd seen the fellow before, waiting against the wall behind Tadai during meetings of the council, though he couldn't have put a name to the face with better than an even chance of being correct.

The older man jerked the youth's elbow, keeping his own eyes averted. They scurried together out the door by which Garric had entered. The guards closed the panel—from the outside.

"I was expecting you, of course," Tadai said, standing as straight as a rabbit lured by a lamp. He looked a little silly; and in this as in many things about Lord Tadai, looks were deceiving. "You or a detachment of Blood Eagles."

Tadai's chairs were of ivory cut in sweeping curves and fretted into traceries that looked as delicate as spiderweb. Spiderwebs trapped remarkably large prey on occasion, and Garric knew his about-to-be-former treasurer didn't let his love of artistry completely stifle his pragmatic core.

Garric lifted a chair from against the wall, set it in the center of the room facing Tadai, and sat down . . . carefully. He pointed to the silver urn resting in a ceramic bowl filled with damp moss or, just possibly, moss over a bed of ice preserved at great expense from last winter. "I'd take a glass of wine, if it were offered," he said, crossing his ankle over his knee.

Tadai gave an embarrassed cough. "It's sherbet, actually," he said as he turned and dipped one, then two, of the tiny matching silver goblets into the urn. "If I drank wine while I was working, I'd have much shorter days. The parts I'd remember, at any rate."

Garric took the goblet and sipped while Tadai turned around the chair at his desk and reseated himself. The sherbet was tart and cool, an unfamiliar flavor but one Garric could come to like. He didn't think he'd ever get used to tasting metal while he was drinking, though, no matter how skillfully the artist had etched a scene from the life of the wine god Fis on the silver.

"And you didn't really imagine I was fool enough to send troops instead of coming myself," Garric said as he lowered the goblet. "Besides, you'd have had more than two guards here if you thought that might happen."

Tadai sneered. "Would more guards have made any difference?" he said.

"If you'd misread the situation that badly," Garric said, letting an edge of anger show in his voice for the first time, "you'd have been stupid enough to think your men could fight the Blood Eagles, yes! Now, let's act like two of the men on whom the safety of the Isles depends, shall we?"

Tadai stiffened. He gave Garric a tiny nod. "I apologize, Your Majesty," he said quietly. "I've been under a good deal of strain recently."

"I prefer 'Garric,'" Garric said, mildly again. He met Lord Tadai's eyes over the edge of the cup he was lifting. "When I stop feeling that way, it'll be time for me to muck out stables for a while to remind myself of who I am."

Tadai laughed. "No one else in this room is in doubt as to who you are, Garric," he said. "Though I have no doubt that you're quite capable of cleaning stables as well. You have the advantage of me on both ends of the range of endeavor."

"I want you to go to Earl Wildulf," Garric said, "and bring Sandrakkan back into the kingdom on the terms you think best. We can break him, but I would prefer any other reasonable choice. I will be bound by your decision."

Garric set the cup down beside his chair. It was a tiny little thing, emptied in two sips. He gestured. "I'll give you documents saying that to show the earl, with seals and ribbons all over them. But I'm giving you my word, now."

"Ah," said Tadai, without inflection. His own goblet remained poised in his hand, midway to his lips.

"I planned for my sister to go to Blaise on a similar mission," Garric continued. "A bird took her away tonight, a bird or a monster. I'd welcome your recommendation of a replacement to send as envoy to Count Lerdoc."

He was using what happened to Sharina—*whatever* had happened to Sharina, capture or death or just possibly worse—as a tool to get Tadai's sympathy. The part of Garric that had been raised in Barca's Hamlet hated the words his tongue was speaking; but the king within him, and the king Garric had to be if the Isles were to survive, knew that kings did many worse things out of duty.

"The lady Sharina?" Tadai said. A series of emotions crossed his face, disbelief followed by anger at being duped—and then as quickly, real affection and concern. "A monster has taken Lady Sharina?"

Everybody liked Sharina. She was polite, beautiful, and smart. And perhaps most important, Sharina never had to give orders that other people didn't want to hear.

"Yes, and that's something I'll have to deal with later," Garric said; not angrily, but with a crispness that had a lot to do with the number of things he was going to have to deal with, and Duzi help him if he knew how. "But it's not why I'm here, Lord Tadai."

"Yes, I see," Tadai said musingly. "Waldron has a younger brother, a half-brother, actually: Warroc bor-Warriman. He's at least as intelligent as Waldron, and he's far more clever in political terms. Rather too clever, in fact. He'd make an excellent envoy."

Garric frowned. "You wouldn't be concerned that he might think making common cause with Count Lerdoc would be a better bargain for him?" he said.

"If anything," Tadai said, "Warroc is more of a chauvinist than his brother is. Hard though you may find that to believe. He wouldn't do anything that would hurt his standing with the only people he really regards as people—the great landholders of Northern Ornifal. Becoming Count of Blaise himself wouldn't repay him for that."

Tadai rose and dipped a fresh goblet in the urn. "On the other hand, my friend Garric, *you* should watch your back if Warroc returns a hero for the arrangement he's managed with Blaise."

He held the goblet to Garric, adding, "Though clever as Warroc is, I rather doubt he'll make a better job of it than I will in Erdin. I know things about the Earl of Sandrakkan's finances that he probably doesn't know himself. And he really needs to, for reasons that I'll make quite clear to him in our private discussions."

And to think he'd been secretly afraid Tadai would turn down the offer! Garric gave a bellow of laughter of a sort that probably wasn't often heard in chambers as delicately appointed as these. Well, maybe it should be!

"Lord Tadai," he said, "you'll know better than I do what the requirements for your mission will be. Give me a list and I'll see to it that it's filled."

Garric took the sherbet from Tadai's steady hand and tossed it down. He was acting more unconsciously than not, but the astringence and tiny portion shocked him into awareness of what he'd just done.

"I'll bid you good night, then," he said. "I have—"

He and King Carus laughed together. "Right, we all have a great deal to do. The kingdom is fortunate to have a minister as resourceful and intelligent as you, Tadai."

"And fortunate to have a prince of your quality, Garric," Tadai said, taking the empty goblets and setting them on the table for a servant to clear when the room was empty. "Quali*ties*, rather; remarkable ones in a man of any age, I should have said, let alone someone of your youth."

As Garric turned with a smile toward the door, Tadai added to his back, "And you've certainly managed to make my life more interesting than if you'd never appeared in Valles!"

The bird's wings stroked. A frozen plain shivered into reality with the speed of a tropic dawn. The sun far to the south was bright but tiny, and the wind cut Sharina marrow-deep.

The bird glided parallel to the face of a glacier stretching from horizon to horizon. Dirt and boulders lay on the white surface of the broad ice-river, but through cracks in its face Sharina could see crystal as pure and blue as the finest sapphire.

The ice was receding, if slowly. A coarse scree covered the plain south of the ice face, the debris of past millennia released when the glacier carrying it dissolved. Tunnels at the base of the ice oozed meltwater. It meandered in braided streams through the rocks and gravel and finally vanished in the emptiness.

Occasionally the sun glinted on metal—a gilded helmet, the silver boar's-head boss of a round shield; an ivory sword hilt wound with electrum wire. Verdigris had concealed the blade in the stone's blue-gray shadow until Sharina's eyes caught the rich mountings and traced the weapon's full lines.

There was clothing, too; brocades and fabrics embroidered with gold and silver. Metal cups sewn to the fabrics held jewels. Light winking from them woke counterfeits of life in the bleak expanse. Wind-driven grit had shredded furs and woven goods.

Occasionally Sharina caught a glimpse of wood: a broken spearshaft, an axe helve sticking vertically from the gravel where the head moldered. Nowhere did she see a body or even a scrap of bone.

The bird continued its swift progress, the huge left wing tilted minusculely higher to catch the updraft from the escarpment of ice. Sunlight shining through the lifted van showed unexpected mottling in scales on the skin stretched between elongated fingerbones.

This was the longest the bird had remained in a single reality since it snatched Sharina from among her friends. Did it nest here in this lifeless—

There was life after all. A shape hunched out of a tunnel and stood, staring at the bird with faceted eyes. Despite the foreshortening from Sharina's vantage point, she could see that it was big: eight feet tall, perhaps ten. The creature had an exoskeleton like an insect and six limbs, but it was standing upright on the back pair.

The other four limbs held human bodies, long-dead soldiers it had dug from the ice. They wore rich accoutrements, and the hands of one were frozen to a cross-staff holding a silver boar's head on a red field.

When the creature saw the great bird, it dropped the corpses and spread its four upper limbs. The hands had crab pincers, toothed to mesh like a crocodile's jaws. Its mandibles swung sideways and gave a rasping cry.

Similar creatures shambled from nearby tunnels. They projected a mindless malevolence, a desire to feed at any cost.

The bird's wings stroked again and the scene dissolved. In the empty grayness Sharina continued to think of the frozen world she had just escaped.

It had been like watching worms writhe in hog manure. . . .

Chapter Six

Ilna looked back through the atrium when she heard the front door open. The guard who'd entered—the pair on duty this morning were new to her—called, "The chamberlain's here, mistress. Want to see him?"

The Blood Eagles lacked the air of solemn formality that Sharina's doorkeeper projected—Ilna tried to imagine that self-important fellow shouting across the hall instead of approaching his mistress and murmuring the name of the caller—but they didn't seem to resent doing servants' work for lack of anyone else being around. Ilna wondered if the Blood Eagles had been warned that she hadn't wanted them either, and that she was likely to tell them so if they objected to doing what their presence made necessary.

As indeed Ilna would have done, in a fashion those listening would remember.

"Reise's here?" Ilna said, smiling at the thought of dealing with people who thought there was any honest work that they were too good for. She walked toward the door. "Yes, I'd be glad to see him."

Her mouth pursed in wry disgust. She often wished that the thoughts that gave her pleasure had more to do with joy and kindness; but correcting fools *did* make the world a better place. Presumably there were other folk who dispensed joy and kindness.

Garric's father entered. He'd been a tallish, awkward fellow in Barca's Hamlet; respected for his learning and the success he'd made of a run-down inn, but loved by no one. Here, though dressed in the gray of a palace servant, Reise was a different and much more impressive man.

He bowed and made a complicated hand flourish, not

because Ilna demanded it but because his position did. Ilna knew that she could no more have stopped Reise from giving her the marks of respect due any palace resident than he could have made *her* accept a chambermaid to tidy her baskets of yarn. Ilna didn't like court ceremony; but she very much liked the determination with which Reise followed his principles wherever they led.

As he always had, she knew. And as he'd raised his son and daughter to do.

"I'm intruding because of a personal matter, mistress," he said as he straightened.

"Garric?" Ilna said, her muscles suddenly cold and very hard.

"I misspoke," Reise said. His wince of embarrassment meant that he understood more than Ilna wished he did. But after all, the whole world seemed to—except for Garric himself. "Your uncle Katchin visited the palace yesterday. He met your brother, but I thought you should be told directly as well."

Ilna sniffed. "You're not intruding," she said. "Come out in the garden, won't you? I'll show you the work I've just finished."

As she stepped into the columned walk she added, "And you were right that I hadn't heard Katchin was here. Cashel tends to forget things that aren't important, and neither of us considers our uncle very important."

Ilna hadn't stitched the three pieces together because she didn't have a room high enough to hang the arras complete. Instead she'd arranged the portions for temporary display on the west—shaded—side of the colonnade. The theme of the action was consecutive through the three bands anyway, so it was much easier to view the details here than it would be when the tapestry hung as a whole before the statue of the Protecting Shepherd.

Reise strolled along the arras. Initially he had his fingers tented, but after a few steps he crossed his wrists behind him as if to prevent himself from touching the fabric. When he reached the end of the third—the bottom—section, he turned and walked back to Ilna. He didn't speak, and his face had no expression.

"You're the first person to see it complete," Ilna said carefully. She wasn't one to demand praise, but she'd certainly expected some reaction. "Do you have any comment?"

"Why do you ask that, mistress?" Reise said in a trembling voice. "I feel exactly what you wanted me to feel. You know that! Anyone who sees this will feel all those things that you made them feel."

"I . . ." Ilna said in embarrassment. People didn't expect emotion from Reise the Innkeeper. Well, they didn't expect it from Ilna, the orphan who lived next door to the inn either. "With something this complex, I didn't know . . ."

"This . . ." Reise said. He looked over his shoulder at the hanging, then twisted his head away with an effort of will. "The image of my, my s-s . . . of Prince Garric fighting the Beast made me . . ."

Reise rubbed tears from his eyes and added, "Mistress, I didn't believe in the Great Gods. Oh, I'd make the usual offerings—I had to in a place like Barca's Hamlet, after all. But now I thank the Lady; and I thank you."

"I don't believe in the Great Gods now," Ilna said harshly. "And anyway, the place I learned to weave the way I do now had nothing to do with the Lady or anything you could call good."

She laughed; the sound was brittle, but she couldn't help that. It was all she could do to avoid letting the sound trail off into hysteria as she remembered the gray place and a tree with limbs like snakes writhing.

"Mistress?" Reise said. Then, sharply, *"Ilna."*

Ilna blinked. Her body swayed like a slowing top. The chamberlain offered his arm; Ilna gripped it. *Funny to be getting support from clumsy, henpecked Reise!* She laughed, with amusement this time, and that steadied her properly.

"I've been working hard," she said in apology. That was true, and she supposed it was part of the reason as well.

Ilna had wanted to finish the arras quickly so that she could leave Valles. She didn't grudge Garric and Liane the happiness they found in one another—she didn't! Each was a wonderful person who deserved someone as wonderful as themselves.

But though she wasn't sorry for their happiness, it tore her heart out to watch them. Besides, Ilna had debts to pay in Erdin, where she'd ruined lives with the skills she'd learned in Hell.

"The arras shows the world the son you raised, Reise," Ilna said, looking with a critical eye at the neighbor she'd known from her first youth. "You can be proud of him, and he of you."

"*Prince* Garric," Reise emphasized. "Whom I fostered."

"Don't tell *me* that!" Ilna snapped. "Do you think I can't read lineage as surely as I can tell you the kind of mulberry trees that fed the worms who spun your robe? No doubt Garric is the offspring of Countess Tera and heir to the blood of the ancient Kings of the Isles; but no doubt he's Garric, son of Reise, as well."

Reise made a sound that was halfway between a bark and a gasp. "May I sit down?" he said, gesturing to one of the benches placed between alternate pairs of columns.

"Of course," Ilna said, though she was a little surprised. "I have beer, bread, and cheese, if you'd like."

She grinned tightly. "Though the beer isn't as good as your own."

Reise smiled vaguely, a polite response to words he hadn't really listened to. His eyes were on a patch of wall that had been frescoed in a brick pattern; the sheathing was badly cracked, and a portion had flaked away from the rubble core.

"Tera was a lovely woman," Reise said. He looked toward Ilna. "There was nobody I could say that to, you know. I couldn't talk even to you if we'd both stayed in Barca's Hamlet."

You don't have to talk to me now, since it's of no interest to me, Ilna thought; but she stopped the thought short of her tongue by an effort of will. Back in the borough Reise had treated her and Cashel exactly as he treated anyone else: with brusque, carping honesty. He hadn't been a friend to the orphans—or to anyone else in the world— but he hadn't tried to take advantage of them either. Reise wasn't easy to like, but his virtues were real and his flaws were ones that Ilna found easy to understand.

"And Count Niard?" Ilna said; out of kindness, she supposed. She'd created a chance for Reise to speak as he felt he needed to because he'd treated her decently when others did not.

"He was Sharina's father," Reise said quietly. Now he was looking at the tapestry again, viewing the figure of the tall, blond woman who danced through beastmen and fiends of living flame. "Not a bad fellow, Niard, though we used to joke that every time he had a second thought in the same day, one of his ears fell off . . . and he still had both ears. He ordered me to marry Lora as cover for his affair with her; and I did, because it was protection for Tera as well."

He shook his head at ancient memories. "Lora does the best she can," he said.

"And a poor enough job it is!" Ilna said. Lora with her palace airs and shrewish temper had been harder to take even than Uncle Katchin.

Reise turned his head toward her. "Yes, a poor job," he said. "But she fostered another woman's child without complaint."

He smiled faintly. "That was perhaps the only thing in this world or the next that she *didn't* complain about, I'll grant. And of course she didn't realize that Sharina was her own daughter and that Garric was the fosterling; only the midwife and I knew that."

"She treated Sharina like royalty," Ilna said bitterly, "and Garric as badly as she did . . ."

She stopped *that* thought short of her tongue also, but only just. She met Reise's eyes with a grimace.

He laughed and rose heavily from the bench. "As badly

as she did me?" he said. "Yes, more or less. But it's a sign of Sharina's strength that Lora's treatment didn't ruin her ... and I'm afraid that strength isn't something the children got from me."

Reise nodded toward the arras. "Mistress Ilna, I appreciate being shown your work. I am honored to know you."

Ilna sniffed, leading the chamberlain back into the house. He was ready to leave, and she had to join the others shortly to see Cashel off on his search for Sharina. "Katchin was after a job, I suppose?" she asked as they crossed the atrium.

"Yes, I assume so," Reise agreed. "A position with a great deal of show and public honor, at any rate. He'll not find it here, not with my son in charge."

Reise made his formal bow and flourish, then paused with his hand on the latch lever. "Katchin should go back home," he said. "I did."

He gestured broadly, indicating the palace where he'd worked as a youth and the city beyond, where he was born. "And I'm *much* happier here."

Ilna chuckled as she followed her guest onto the front porch. It was easy to say that Reise had enormous power in the royal palace whereas all Katchin had to look forward to was being the leading man in a rural borough of an island nobody cared about nowadays. But the chamberlain's duties combined real power with outward subservience, which Katchin wouldn't have been able to manage. And Reise had made a remarkable success in Barca's Hamlet, for all that no one imagined that he belonged there.

Reise started down the path, then turned. The Blood Eagles to either side of Ilna shifted minuscule, though it wouldn't quite be correct to say that they tensed. "I hope you learn where home is, Ilna," he said.

"My home is my work, Reise," she called back. She knew the words were true as soon as she spoke them.

She just wished that the truth made her feel happier than it did.

*   *   *

"I never saw the Altar of Harmony myself, lad," King Carus said as the group made its way up Straight Street—which wasn't, unless you viewed it in half-block sections. *"I'd heard it was supposed to be really fancy—it was ancient even in my day, of course. But when I visited Valles, I had more pressing business than sightseeing."*

Through Garric's mind flashed a montage of Carus' memories: a banquet in the Hall of the Combined Guilds—it still existed in the center of Valles, though it'd been converted to a shopping arcade in the past millennium; a meeting of the Ornifal nobility in a temple, the chairs set up in arcs beneath an enormous chryselephantine statue of the Lady; a dozen of Valles' top bankers in a sumptuously appointed conference room, their faces giving away nothing.

"Though I might just as well have stayed on Haft for all the good I did trying to convince people here that they couldn't stay neutral when I was trying to hold the Kingdom together and twenty-odd usurpers wanted to tear it apart," Carus added. *"Ornifal was so sure it could buy peace by paying off every pirate or usurper—the Kingdom go hang!"*

"Hey, watch where you're going there!" shouted a waterseller who carried his two jugs on a short staff over his left shoulder. He'd paused to dip a drink for a housewife from the smallest of the three graduated cups chained to a collar that he could shift from the neck of one jug to the other. The staff stuck out into the crowded street, and one of the leading Blood Eagles had bumped it.

"Shut up and get out of the way of your betters!" the soldier replied. He and the man in the next rank grabbed the waterseller by both arms and walked him backward into pavement racks selling old clothing and old—definitely old—vegetables. The waterseller and the two old women minding the racks squalled in unison.

"Enough of that!" Garric shouted. "Sir, we didn't mean

to jostle you, but this is a street. And Captain Besimon, remind your men that we take up a good deal of room ourselves, so a little charity toward the encroachments of others is called for."

Liane grinned at Garric and squeezed his hand.

They were a lot more of a procession than Garric would have liked, but he didn't see much way around it. There were ten Blood Eagles in front and ten more behind. They'd need the troops for a cordon at the altar where Tenoctris had decided to speak the incantation that would send Cashel off in his pursuit of Sharina.

The wizard herself rode in a litter. Cashel walked beside it, chatting with her and looking every inch of what he was: a countryman wandering in the big city. His quarterstaff was awkward on the cramped pavements, but nobody was going to complain to Cashel even if they happened to get bumped.

Ilna was right behind her brother. She was close enough to join the conversation, but Garric hadn't noticed her do so.

"I think we're nearby," Liane murmured to Garric. "Mistress Gudea didn't take us to see the altar on our history walks, because of the location."

She giggled. " 'Not a suitable venue for young ladies' was how she put it, though I've seen—"

Liane nodded demurely in the direction of the balconies on either side of a lane joining Straight Street. Barebreasted women with cinnabar-accented eyes called laughingly to the soldiers who passed stone-faced.

"—quite a number of young ladies since we've been in the district. We looked down from the Citadel, though, so I know we're close."

"Here we are, sir," called Besimon, the commander of the guard detachment. A niche, half natural but improved by the hand of man, bit into the rocky bluff to the left. The first settlers of Valles had built their walled encampment on top of the steep hill for protection.

The Citadel had remained the center of the city during

the Flag Wars. After Ornifal was unified, wealth and government had abandoned the Citadel and the poorly drained district at its foot for more comfortable climes. The Temple of the Lady of Valles still stood on the Citadel; and at the hill's base the first Duke of Ornifal had built the Altar of Harmony to symbolize the unity the island had achieved centuries before Lorcan of Haft became Lorcan, the King of the Isles.

"It must have been lovely when it was whole," Garric said. He'd seen a lot of impressive monuments through Carus' eyes and no few on his own, in the Isles and on more distant worlds that he'd traversed while he struggled to halt Chaos; but the Altar of Harmony was unique and in some ways uniquely beautiful. "Even now . . ."

The altar stood within a large, roofless enclosure entered by a ramp. The enclosure's marble walls were carved with vignettes of men and Gods within frames of acanthus vines. Age had blackened the stone except for streaks of bubbling white decay.

The enclosure's west wall had collapsed in the distant past. A roof of rushes and a curtain wall of rubble on either end of the ornate altar had converted the remaining space into a dwelling of sorts. No, a tavern—

"Clear this place," Besimon ordered curtly. "Mistress Tenoctris needs it empty for her work."

The Blood Eagles were in half-armor—cuirasses and helmets—and carried their spears as well as a sword and dagger on each man's equipment belt. Six of them immediately thrust their spears butt-first into the curtain wall and levered it apart.

"Hey, what do you think you're doing?" said the bouncer as he and four startled-looking patrons came running out into the open. He held a spiked club, but he dropped the weapon immediately when he saw the detachment of troops.

The roof started to sag. The villainous-looking owner strode out brandishing a hook-bladed knife. He was missing three fingers from his left hand, and the way he combed his hair forward meant that he'd been branded T for Thief on the forehead. That last was a Blaise custom, Carus noted in the same detached fashion that the king judged where his first swordstroke would go if the business turned ugly.

"Who're you to turn me out?" the owner snarled. He didn't drop the knife. A Blood Eagle gripped his arm and bent it back; bones would have broken shortly, but another soldier rapped the fellow's knuckles hard with a spearbutt, numbing the hand to release the weapon.

"I'm a citizen," Garric said, surprised at how angry he felt at what he'd found here. "You've taken what should be an honor to the whole city, to the whole *kingdom*, and said it's yours because you've got a knife and a thug to enforce your claim!"

A Blood Eagle judged his placement, then stamped his hobnailed heel on the knife. It broke at the cross guard against the cobblestones; the hilt spurted sideways, shedding its bone scales.

Ten of the Blood Eagles were facing outward, but the gathering crowd cheered ironically at the entertainment. The taverner didn't seem popular.

"Poor people are no more likely to want criminals for neighbors than anybody else is," Liane said from Garric's side. She counted two silver coins from her purse into her palm, then with a judicious frown added one of the double-weight bronze coins called a Crowned Sheaf for the design on the obverse. "Judging from the clientele, this was the worst sort of dive."

"What?" said the taverner. He sounded genuinely amazed. "Hey, I paid good bronze to One-Eyed Tahsin when I took over this stand!"

The guard released him, though Garric knew it wouldn't take much for the taverner to meet another spearbutt, this time in the pit of the stomach. That wasn't called for, but part of Garric wouldn't have minded seeing it happen.

At Besimon's command, four of the soldiers used their spears as levers to lift the roof and throw it off the back of the enclosure. Inside was a wooden bar and two jugs of

wine. Those went over the back wall with as little ceremony as the roof had.

A soldier braced himself to lift one of the carved stone
blocks being used as stools. "Leave them," Tenoctris ordered. "They were part of the enclosure wall."

On one stone, a priest led a garlanded bullock with
knob-tipped horns. It was probably part of the sacrificial
procession at the time the altar was dedicated.

"The Altar of Harmony will shortly be rebuilt into the
monument it was meant to be," Garric said. "It's not yours
to appropriate, nor mine either. It belongs to all the people
of Ornifal. And there's never been a time in the past thousand years that people needed harmony more than we do
now!"

He stepped forward so that it didn't look as though he
were hiding behind a rank of black-armored guards.
Though he faced the taverner, he pitched his voice so that
he could be heard throughout what was by now a considerable crowd.

"Hey!" cried someone in delight. "That's Prince *Garric*!
The prince is here!"

"Prince Garric?" repeated the taverner. "What're they
talking about?" He mumbled the question to the soldier
who'd disarmed him. The locals—his bouncer among
them—had backed well away as though from fear of con-
tagion.

How am I ever going to pay for rebuilding this? Garric
thought despairingly. He didn't know why he'd spoken,
though now that he'd said the words they would stand.
Pterlion bor-Pallial, the new treasurer, would scream.
*There's so many better places to spend what little money
the kingdom has!*

"*And again, lad,*" King Carus whispered through the
ages, "*sometimes the symbol is the thing. There's worse
uses for money than convincing the people in tenements
that they're part of the kingdom and that the king cares
about them.*"

"But it's just old stones," the taverner said, protesting

more at the idea than for his loss. "I keep an honest house—"

Ilna sniffed. The taverner looked at her. He wouldn't be likely to understand the net of cords in her hand, ready to be drawn tight before him, but the sneering disbelief of her expression was as obvious as the cobblestones.

"Well, anyway," the man muttered, "I paid—"

"And I'm going to pay you for your loss," Garric said sharply. "But the payment comes with a warning: Don't be here when the workmen arrive in the next day or two."

Could he get the job under way that quickly? Probably. The odd thing about being king was that while for the most part Garric didn't seem to be able to do anything, the specific things that he *could* do happened almost before he finished thinking about them. If only harmonizing Ornifal's regional tax structures were as easy as getting an ancient building renovated!

Liane stepped forward holding the three coins, the Double Sheaf and the two Ladies, fanned between her left thumb and forefinger. The taverner gaped to see the wink of silver. He would have snatched the money, but he noticed the way a soldier shifted to butt-stroke him into a state of greater respect.

The taverner bowed and held his cupped hands out before him with his face lowered. Liane dropped the coins into them and stepped back, dusting her palms together unconsciously. The taverner really *was* a disgusting brute, and even the almost-contact of paying him was unpleasant.

"If you are here when the workmen arrive, still misappropriating public lands," Garric continued in a pleasant voice, "then you'll join the chain gang repairing the city wall. For the rest of your life."

He flicked his fingers. The former taverner popped the coins in his mouth and scampered off. Scampered into the crowd, at least; there seemed to be a number of voices claiming he owed them debts. The fellow made it into an alley but not, from the sound of it, very much farther.

Captain Besimon grinned faintly. He felt no more inclination than Garric did to interfere with the local administration of justice. Not in this case.

The soldiers had cleared the enclosure with a brisk thoroughness that impressed Garric. Under Attaper if not before, the Blood Eagles had been more than a ceremonial force—and more even than a true bodyguard, capable of preserving the king's life on the field at the cost of their own. They were trained in all the construction and engineering duties that an army in the field required. This business, emptying a small building of the debris that choked it, was nothing to them.

"Troops who can't fortify their camp before they go to sleep after a march," King Carus noted approvingly, *"are going to wake up before dawn one day with the enemy in bed with them."*

Besimon looked at Garric for orders. Garric raised a hand to show he was aware of the situation and said, "Tenoctris? What would you like us to do next?"

The old woman had bent to examine the remains of the central altar. Cashel stood beside her, quietly solid with his staff and a wallet on a heavy shoulder strap. Cashel didn't have the cowhorn with a wooden mouthpiece that he carried to give the alarm when he watched the sheep of the borough; otherwise he looked exactly as he would have any morning back home.

He *was* that same person, Garric realized; it was just that there had been more to Cashel than anybody in Barca's Hamlet had seen. He guessed he was the same Garric or-Reise as well. It was hard to remember that sometimes, when everything around him was so different.

Liane smiled at him. Well, "different" didn't always mean "bad."

"I think if the men will keep the crowd at a distance . . ." Tenoctris said as Liane helped her rise. "There's nothing for anyone to do except for me. And Cashel, of course."

"Besimon," Garric said, nodding, "Mistress Tenoctris will be working where the altar was. Please have your men cordon the open side of the enclosure to give her room."

Besimon gave Garric a bleak grin. "That shouldn't be hard," he said. "Not when people—"

He lifted his chin toward the spectators. Hawkers carrying doughnuts on short sticks, baskets of fruit, and a tray of amulets of the Lady and the Shepherd—"Genuine silver, or the Sister drag my soul to Hell!"—were working the spectators. The event was quickly turning into a street fair.

"—figure out that it's wizardry going on here."

The Blood Eagles fell in across the west and northern arc of the enclosure. Their faces were toward the crowd and they held their spears crosswise at waist height to form a continuous bar. There wasn't any serious jostling. Garric was pleased to note that the troops were doing their job in a good-humored fashion.

He joined Tenoctris and the others in the center of the enclosure. The altar top and the four slabs of its sides had collapsed over the years. The taverner or some similar entrepreneur of time past had stacked the marble on the altar pedestal to form a support pillar.

Across the uppermost slab walked men, women, and children, wearing peaked hats and chained together with garlands of roses. Some played slender horns with outturned bells, others shook tambourines. The children's mouths were open in song.

Someday we'll have harmony again, Garric thought. The king in his mind grinned wryly; Garric grinned in response. *Well, we'll have as much harmony as they* really *had when they were building the altar.*

Tenoctris took a bamboo sliver from the packet Cashel handed her. He always carried the wizard's paraphernalia when they were together. Garric noticed when Cashel opened the flap of his wallet that there was nothing else inside but a round of hard bread and a wedge of cheese wrapped in a dock leaf.

Somebody else setting out as Cashel was doing might try to figure all the dangers he'd face and prepare against them. Cashel wasn't reckless; anybody who'd seen him with sheep remarked on the way he guessed any fool thing the beasts might do, because he'd seen them do it before.

But there was a lot of life you couldn't plan for, you just had to deal with it as it came up. Cashel had a slow grin, a quarterstaff, and strength that nobody else in the borough could match. Cashel was very good at dealing with the unexpected.

"This place is a focus of power," Tenoctris explained. "That makes it easier for me to send Cashel to where I hope he'll find more accomplished help. This place—"

She glanced at the blackened marble walls, then up the bluff to the ancient Citadel. Grasses and vines swathed the coarse limestone; here and there the roots of a gnarled tree had found lodging.

Apologetically Tenoctris returned her attention to her friends. "I was daydreaming," she said. "About the past, about the future. I suppose I'm trying to delay executing the spell. Difficult jobs don't get easier for being put off, as you all have taught me."

She patted Cashel's arm. He smiled, but his eyes were focused on the horizon and the immediate future.

"I was going to say," Tenoctris resumed, "that this place has a connection to Landure. That's why we're here."

Tenoctris looked judiciously at the wand she held. "Cashel," she said, "would you cut me a fresh twig instead? Something you've made yourself will make my task easier."

She gave her quick grin. "And I need all the help I can get."

Cashel snipped off a sprig of lamb's tongue growing at the corner of the wall and trimmed it with the simple iron knife he wore through his sash. It was the all-purpose tool of every peasant, used to cut his bread, clear grass from a clogged plow coulter, or trim leather for a harness strap.

He handed the wand to Tenoctris. The woody stem was thin but stiff enough for her purposes. She knelt again to scribe a circle and words in the Old Script in the hollow of the altar. The supple withy didn't leave marks on the stone that Garric could see, but they were presumably enough for Tenoctris herself. *Sometimes the symbol is the thing. . . .*

Garric stepped over to Cashel and hugged him. "I wish I was going with you," Garric said as they separated. The huskiness in his voice surprised him.

Cashel smiled. "Well, I'd like the company, but you've got things to do here," he said. He didn't sound worried, but then he never did.

If you didn't know Cashel well you could believe he wasn't aware of danger. Garric knew better than that. Cashel understood exactly what he was letting himself into; he just didn't let it affect what he was doing.

Ilna murmured goodbyes to her brother. She stood as stiffly upright as Cashel's staff and looked as hard. Which she was, of course. Quite a woman, Ilna.

Garric looked at Cashel and thought of the number of times he'd sent other people into danger. The king in his mind stirred, reminding Garric of how often King Carus had done the same in his longer life. It was so much easier to go yourself than to send a friend. And it was so much easier to be a peasant than it was to be a king.

Though . . . a peasant makes life-and-death decisions also. In a prosperous community, which Barca's Hamlet was by its own lights, folks would help a neighbor who suffered a disaster; but there were limits. Even in Barca's Hamlet there were stories about the way babies born during an especially hard winter sometimes disappeared.

"There," Tenoctris said as she straightened. "Cashel, if you'll stand in the center of the circle—" The words of power were barely a shadow on the stone, but the altar itself framed the spot accurately. "—when you're ready, I'll begin."

"I'm ready," Cashel said without emphasis. Liane hugged him in turn. She backed away and the tension went out of his expression. He stepped carefully over the markings and stood with his staff close to his body so that it didn't reach over the scribed boundary.

"Cashel, one final warning," Tenoctris said. "Landure is

a powerful wizard, but by reputation he's also a very hard, haughty man. He may refuse to help you."

Cashel shrugged. "If Master Landure doesn't want to help, then there'll be someone else who does," he said. "Or I'll find my own way to Sharina. But I *will* find her."

The wizard gave a quick, birdlike nod. "Garric," she said, "I'll have to speak this spell myself. But if you could kneel with me and hold my arm so that I don't fall over, it might be a help. Perhaps I'm being unduly pessimistic."

She smiled. Garric understood the attempt to treat the matter lightly, but it wasn't very successful. He put his big hand on Tenoctris' shoulder, noticing as he always did when he touched her that the wizard had no more meat on her bones than a quail does.

Tenoctris seated herself cross-legged. She closed her eyes briefly to recruit her strength, then bobbled the wand in time with the syllables as she said, *"Chai aphono apaphono . . ."*

There was a murmur through the crowd as they understood what was going on. Garric's back was to the spectators, but he'd seen the way wizardry made ordinary people draw away. Sane people didn't like wizardry. There were infinite mistakes for a wizard to make, and any one of them could cost the lives or souls of those nearby.

"Echaipen panaitos epaipen . . ." Tenoctris said, her voice as measured as drips from a water clock. A faint blue haze spread about Cashel's stolid figure.

"Semon seknet thallassosemon . . ." Tenoctris said. Liane was at Garric's other side, standing with her fingertips on the point of his shoulder. The touch strengthened him the way touching the stirrup leather makes it possible for a foot soldier to run alongside a cavalryman.

Cashel looked as steady as before, but a sphere of blue fire wrapped him. His body hung in the air at right angles to the way it had stood a moment before. He gave no sign of realizing there had been a change.

"Agra bazagra oreobazagra!" Tenoctris said, her voice cracking. The wand split in her hand, its tough fibers frayed

apart by friction not of this world. She started to topple. Garric reached around her and scooped her up in his arms.

Cashel's body rotated sunwise in a ball of light that cast no shadow on the stone. His body shrank as though he were falling away; his expression was unconcerned, his staff straight in his hands.

Tenoctris sighed in exhaustion. The light turned in on itself and vanished. Garric's mind held an afterimage of his friend spinning and growing ever smaller, like a doll dropped into deep, clear waters.

The great bird broke out of limbo and banked in a sunwise curve. Below Sharina, a harbor nestled into a wooden shoreline. It was late afternoon.

Initially Sharina saw no sign of human activity, but as the bird continued to wheel she spotted several boats drawn up on one of several stretches of sandy beach within the bay. A hilltop overlooking the sea had been cleared in a ragged yellow scar. A palisade protected the clearing; in it stood a dozen oval huts with thatched roofs on low field-stone walls. One was slightly larger than the others and set within a fence of its own.

People wearing garments of leather and coarse grass looked up at the bird, then ran inside. Sharina heard cries of warning. Mothers snatched up children too small to flee.

The bird continued to wheel, losing altitude noticeably. The treetops were only about fifty feet below. They were hardwoods, clothed in the lush foliage of high summer.

The rudimentary settlement was on the western jaw of the land. The bird's curving flight followed the belly of the embayment. A wild tangle of vegetation spilled down to the tideline except for the patches of sand too close to support the roots of anything more substantial than sea oats.

Abruptly the bird overflew more structures, an enormous complex of quarried stone on the peninsula opposite the human settlement. These buildings were in sweeping curves rather than square lines. The individual stones of the construction were smaller than Sharina would have expected and of irregular shapes, but they fitted together with the precision of a mosaic floor.

Trees choked the ancient city, their roots squeezing and prying into cracks that must have been too tight for a knife to enter when the stones were laid. Many of the buildings had collapsed into overgrown rubble; Sharina wouldn't have been aware of them had she not been swept just above the foliage.

Even so the masonry resisted. The trees growing from the stone were stunted, short and wizened compared with their kin on the surrounding hills, from which they were seeded. A wave of starlings swept from one treetop to another, moving like a single amorphous creature. There was no sign of human life.

The great bird reversed direction with a grace as ponderously amazing as that of a whale broaching in the open sea. The left wingtip rose, the right wing dipped to point directly at the ground. Sharina, immobile in the creature's talons, swung in a sickening arc.

A strong breeze blew down the throat of the harbor and onto the land. The bird's wings opened to it like the sails of a vessel immeasurably larger than humans could build even in dreams. It hung for a moment like a seagull hovering for thrown scraps, then settled over the trees at the harbor's edge. The powerful legs, drawn up to hold Sharina against the scaly breast, extended.

The bird lurched in the air; the talons opened to deposit Sharina on the beach. The operation was as gentle as that of a mother cat transferring one of her kittens.

Sharina's limbs were numb from tight constraint. She rolled away. Her legs wouldn't hold her when she first got them under her, but she raised the Pewle knife to hack at the beak if it stabbed down to finish her.

The bird's body, nearly vertical as its feet touched, arched again into the wind and the open sea beyond the harbor. The wings stroked with the slow grinding strength of a glacier.

The bird, a shadow on the sky, slid forward in the air. It flew just above the harbor's surface, trapping the evening breeze between the water and its wings. White-capped compression waves shivered across the mild surf.

Before the first slow beat of the wings was complete, the bird vanished like a sand castle when the tide rises. Sharina was alone on the sea-lapped edge of a forest.

In the near distance, a horn was winding.

Ilna frowned as she viewed the woven figure of Sharina. She'd pictured her friend writhing free of a sculptured beastman, using the finest silk thread for her blond hair. The result still didn't do Sharina justice.

Ilna wondered where Sharina was now; and wished, as she sometimes wished, to believe enough in the Gods that she could offer a prayer for her friend without hypocrisy. Ilna knew of no other help she could offer.

"There's the people come to see you about the weaving, mistress," a Blood Eagle called across the garden from the arch to the atrium. "Shall we send them through?"

"Yes, do that," Ilna said. She winced to hear herself and added, "Please."

She needn't have bothered; the guard was already shouting the answer to his partner at the front door. One benefit of dealing with soldiers was that they didn't resent getting brusk orders. It was a benefit if you were thoughtlessly discourteous as a matter of course, that is.

Sharina would be all right. She was clever as well as capable, and she had a knack for finding friends who could do things that she could not. Friends like Cashel, for example.

Ilna smiled. The delegation from the Temple of the Protecting Shepherd took the expression as directed at them. Master Velio relaxed noticeably, which made Ilna smile more broadly.

She honestly didn't mean to frighten people. Most of the time.

The Blood Eagle leading the delegation stepped aside to let by Velio and a stranger, with Casses and Ermand following on the graveled path and behind *them* Lord Tadai and a girl of nine or so whose features bore a family resemblance. His daughter, perhaps? Ilna recognized the— former—royal treasurer from public events where he'd accompanied Garric. Ilna could have attended council meetings, she supposed, but she couldn't imagine why she would have wanted to.

"Mistress Ilna os-Kenset . . ." Velio said. He didn't let his eyes meet Ilna's, but his voice didn't break. "May I introduce Lord Jalo bor-Jarial of the Board of Religious Affairs—"

Jalo was the stranger, a sour-looking, narrow-faced man of about thirty. His layered tunics were new and of decent quality—the embroidery was more expensive than it was good, but it wasn't *bad*. His shoulder cape, however, had been turned and relined to hide the wear on the other side. The cost of dressing up to his title was breaking Lord Jalo, and the snap when he broke would probably please most of the people who had to deal with the nasty little fellow.

He didn't bow to acknowledge Ilna; she was a commoner, after all. Ilna didn't know Jalo well enough yet to wish him ill. She expected that by the end of this meeting she would, however.

"And Lord Tadai bor-Tithain, Councillor of the Prince, Ambassador Plenipotentiary—"

Tadai stepped forward, waving a hand before Velio to silence him. Tadai's fingernails were trimmed to perfect almond shapes.

"Mistress Ilna knows as much of me as she needs to, Velio," he said. "And I know Mistress Ilna by reputation, so I don't want to play the fool by trying to impress her with empty titles."

Tadai bowed deeply, though he didn't make hand flourishes as Reise—or a toady—would have done. Ilna's eyes narrowed. Tadai had carefully judged the boundary between what Ilna would take as respect and the excess she'd find insulting. He'd guessed quite accurately . . . which meant that he—his underlings—had studied her the way she would go over a hank of yarn, with a cold dispassion.

She supposed she should find it flattering. In her heart of hearts, though, the last thing Ilna wanted was to be known. She lived by the truth, but she was quite certain she had nothing to gain by other people knowing the truth about her.

"Mistress," Tadai resumed. His manners had the ease of a man who'd always been at least the equal of everyone around him and who therefore knew he had nothing to prove. "Allow me to present my niece and aide, Lady Merota bos-Roriman."

The child made a curtsy with some kind of complicated footwork in the middle of it. Ilna avoided a grimace, but only just. She bowed in response, because Merota was being courteous and didn't deserve a sneer for being able to make a gesture that Ilna thought was silly.

Sharina could curtsy. Lora had insisted that her daughter learn all the court nonsense that Lora had learned herself.

"Merota will accompany me when I leave for Erdin," Tadai explained, "which will be as soon as the ships are ready. That's why I'm anxious to arrange for the delivery of your arras immediately."

He smiled. The anxiety beneath the expression was unmistakable. "I'm not a good traveler," he said. "I hope the gift will be enough to gain us the protection of the Shepherd. If not, it will perhaps keep memory of me alive for a time."

Ilna stepped back so that the delegation could view the arras. She gestured them forward. "I take responsibility for the weaving," she said. "Anything else is out of my hands."

Tadai strolled to the first of the three pieces. Merota walked with him, but she turned to gaze at Ilna as she passed. The girl's eyes were large, brown and intelligent. She had a clear complexion and, like her uncle, a tendency

toward softness that irritated Ilna though there was no reason that it should.

The three members of the temple council followed Tadai
to the tapestry with nervous impatience. They lacked the
nobleman's air of unconcern, but they were unwilling to
push ahead of their social superior.

Lord Jalo, on the other hand, sneered at Ilna as he sauntered past. "I think it would be a mistake for you to get
involved with this clothwork, Lord Tadai," he said. "For a
man of your stature, there are much better ways to commemorate your generosity. For example—"

"We've already arranged for the hanging, Jalo," said
Councillor Ermand. Ilna smiled faintly, the only emotion
that she permitted to reach her face. Jalo was a slug, and
squashing him would foul the sole of her foot. . . .

"*You* have," Jalo said. "And you did it without clearing
your action with the Board of Religious Affairs. You—"

"There's no requirement to bribe a gang of noblemen's
byblows!" Casses snarled. If he'd had a belaying pin in his
hand, Jalo would have risked a dent in the center of his
thinning blond hair.

The Blood Eagle escorting the group grinned at Ilna. So
long as she wasn't threatened, the others present could
slaughter themselves so far as the guard was concerned.
Soldiers tend to take a narrow view of orders, a necessary
safety device given that their duty may require them to
follow those orders through to horrific conclusions.

Tadai walked along the tapestry. His expression, a vague
smile, remained unchanged. At his side his niece drew
more and more into herself. At the break between the middle section of the arras and the last, she looked at Ilna. Ilna
raised an eyebrow to encourage a question, but Merota
instead returned her attention to the hanging.

"The new temple of The Lady of the Seas has been
getting most of the profitable departure gifts recently, Lord
Tadai," Jalo said. He didn't respond verbally to Casses'
insult, but the splotches of color on his cheekbones showed
that either the reference to bribes or—more likely—the

claim that Jalo was illegitimate had gotten home. "There's always the concern that a bequest to an underfunded temple will be used to pay for wine at the council dinner instead of the purpose for which it was intended."

"Look, you!" Casses said. He lifted a hand.

Velio had been staring at the arras, though he hadn't moved from the first panel. He turned and touched Casses' arm. "We aren't involved in this," he said to his colleague.

He looked at Ilna and bowed, his face drawn. "Our concern is merely to keep the bargain we made with Mistress Ilna," Velio added, facing her though he was supposedly addressing Casses.

Ilna dipped her head in curt agreement.

Jalo wore an increasingly frustrated expression. Lord Tadai wasn't paying any attention to him, and he didn't understand what was going on between Ilna and the temple council.

Jalo hadn't, Ilna noticed with some amusement, looked even once at the arras. His concern was entirely because arrangements for the hanging had been made without the involvement of his organization, the board which synchronized the activities of Valles' religious orders so that they didn't compete too openly.

"I don't understand," said Ermand. He'd followed along behind Tadai and Merota, peering intently at the rippling action woven into the fabric. "It's a great piece of art—I wouldn't mind buying it myself. But the *Shepherd* isn't anywhere in the design."

Tadai turned. His fingers were tented before him. That was more than a gesture. Despite the nobleman's deliberate calm, white pressure bands marked the flesh beneath his perfect nails.

"No one can look at that arras and not be moved by the power of the Great Gods," he said to Ermand. His voice had grown slightly rougher.

Tadai looked Ilna in the face. "*No* one," he repeated.

"It doesn't matter what's on the cloth," Velio said. "Everyone will want to have his actions blessed at the temple where this hangs. Do you understand? Ermand, Casses? *Our* temple will be famous!"

"Why, you *perfume* merchant!" Jalo exploded. The real cause of his anger was probably the way Tadai refused to take notice of him, but the temple councillors were a safer target. "When the Board of Religious Affairs lifts its approval from your little pile, then you'll see exactly what your backdoor deals with this weaver are really worth!"

"Lord Jalo," Tadai said. He didn't raise his voice, but it cut like an axeblade. "The Board of Religious Affairs has a public duty, but it's not overseen by any government ministry, is that correct?"

"Why, yes," Jalo said. "We're an entirely private organization, funded by the contributions of our membership."

Jalo's smile had brightened because the wealthy nobleman was addressing him. He wasn't a particularly quickwitted man, and he hadn't yet grasped the direction the conversation was about to go.

Ilna *did* understand. She too smiled.

"Given that you're obviously corrupt and a fool as well," Lord Tadai continued in a pleasant, faintly ironic tone, "that needs to be changed. If I were staying in Valles, I'd bring your board under the treasury; since I'm not, I'll suggest to Chancellor Royhas that the chancellery take charge immediately. I'm sure my friend Royhas will humor me in this."

"What?" said Jalo. "What did . . . ?"

He stared at the faces around him. Casses looked on the verge of cheering; Ermand was as puzzled as Jalo; and Velio had no expression at all.

"What are you saying?" Jalo suddenly shouted at Tadai. "You can't do that!"

"Mistress?" Tadai said to Ilna. His niece had flinched back at Jalo's outburst. "I realize your guards won't take orders from me, but I'd appreciate it if they escorted this person—"

He indicated Jalo by wrinkling his nose.

"—out of our presence. I'm not sure who invited him to begin with. I certainly did not."

"He invited himself," Velio said. "He said we shouldn't have done anything without the board's approval, and that he'd make sure we knew our place the next time."

"Sister take me, I'll move him along!" said Casses. The stocky ex-seaman caught Jalo by a wrist and shoulder, twisting the nobleman's arm expertly behind his back. He started toward the house, ignoring Jalo's jabbers of pain.

The Blood Eagle raised an eyebrow. Ilna shrugged. The Blood Eagle grinned and bellowed to his partner, "Let Lord Jalo out, Ramis. He's overstayed his welcome."

Tadai ignored the byplay once he was sure that it was under control. "You aren't in the tapestry either, Mistress Ilna," he said softly. "But rumor says that you were the most important of all in defeating the Beast."

"If rumor says that, rumor is a fool," Ilna snapped. "And you're a fool if you believe it."

Tadai smiled. "I'm not such a fool that I completely disbelieve the rumor, mistress," he said.

"It's from her eyes," the child said unexpectedly. She watched Ilna as she spoke. "The tapestry *is* her, Uncle."

"Yes, I suppose it is," Tadai agreed with a nod. He looked into Ilna's eyes. She wondered what he saw there. "Anyway," Tadai continued, "I'll underwrite the cost of the arras' immediate hanging in the Temple of the Protecting Shepherd. And the endowment for care, of course."

He nodded to Ilna. "Will you oversee the process, mistress?" he asked. "I'd like the task done quickly, because we'll be leaving as soon as possible after it's complete. But it has to be done correctly, of course."

"Of course," Ilna agreed. "If these gentlemen are willing—"

The councillors would be willing to turn cartwheels all the way to the temple, she suspected, if she told them to. Casses was returning to the garden with a pleased expression on his face.

"—then I think we can do that immediately."

"I'll send a messenger to the temple at once," Velio said quietly. "The staff will be waiting for our arrival."

"I realize you didn't do this for money," Lord Tadai said. He was speaking with the care of someone who knows he's treading dangerous ground. "But if an honorarium or simply a defrayal of your costs would be permissible, I would—"

"No," Ilna said. She didn't snarl, because she knew the offer was well meant as well as being polite. "This is my monument to those who died while I lived. I can't take your money, any more than I could sell their bones."

She smiled. The expression was terrible. "Not that their bones are in any place they could be found now, I'm afraid."

No one spoke for a moment. Ilna cleared her throat and went on, "However, there's a favor I would appreciate if it's practical. I too would like to get to Erdin quickly."

She sneered mentally at her words. The truth was that she wanted to leave Valles, where seeing Liane and Garric together ate her bowels like a cancer.

"If there's room on your vessel that I could buy passage . . . ?"

"Buy, no," Lord Tadai said. "But to travel as an honored member of my suite, yes of course. The ships leave tomorrow afternoon, however."

"It can't be too soon for me," Ilna said grimly. "It can't be too soon."

Chapter Seven

Pull for the wife who's glad to see the back of you!" sang the scarred sailor calling the cadence. He wasn't one of the ship's officers: Ilna noted that each of them wore a broad leather belt as a mark of authority. She supposed the chanteyman just had experience and a good voice.

"Pull!" roared the lines of men on the ropes.

The two triremes had been rigged from the arsenal and loaded with the extensive baggage of Tadai bor-Tithain and his suite. Now seamen were sliding the first of the vessels down the ramps of the drying shed.

Ilna stood on the pier, waiting with the other passengers to board when the ships were afloat. She held her own baggage—a cloak rolled tightly over an extra tunic, and a modicum of cheese and hard biscuit because she didn't care to be without provisions of her own in event of shipwreck. Besides food, the only things she needed in life were yarn and a loom. She'd be able to buy them in Erdin.

"Pull for the child who'll never see your face again!" sang the cadence caller. The sheds were supported by pillars instead of walls so that air could circulate freely among the warships' slender pine hulls. His voice echoed down the colonnades, becoming at last a whispering descant to itself.

"Pull!" bawled the men on the ropes.

The keel of the trireme smoked and squealed even though workmen had tallowed the grooved skidway before they began drawing the vessel down it. Ilna smiled faintly to watch the mechanism that cranked the ship forward while the chanting sailors lunged in place against the drag. The tracery of ropes and pulleys wasn't as complex as the patterns she wove, but the sheer scale of the hawsers gave it a certain majesty.

And perhaps some thing or some one wove with human lives. Ilna could only hope that whoever that was, God or Fate or Chance, knew what it—

She smiled more broadly.

—what *She* was doing.

"Pull for the girl who's waiting at the other shore!" the chanteyman sang. He was a short fellow, less than a hand's breadth taller than Ilna herself, but he had broad shoulders over a trim waist, and he strutted like a cockerel as he called cadence.

He saw Ilna looking in his direction. Sweeping off the bandanna he wore as a cap, he waved it to her in a flourish. Her face went glacially cold.

"Pull!" called the sailors, hauling on the ropes.

Lord Tadai stood with a group of aides and the two ship's captains. The latter wore helmets and gorgets of polished brass. Neither of them looked any more nautical than Ilna herself was, and she didn't even *like* sea travel.

She thought, *Be fair. You don't like most things,* and grinned at herself.

Tadai's niece Merota wore what her minders had been told was proper grab for a sea voyage: tunic and breeches of tightly woven linen, waxed and secured to her wrists and ankles by ties. The poor child must be sweltering! You had to be rich to be that *stupidly* miserable, though the poor seemed to manage the business well enough.

"Pull for the fish that're waiting for their bite of you!"

Merota was under the charge of a severe-looking companion whose black garments looked equally uncomfortable but weren't obviously intended to be waterproof. The companion suddenly pushed through the cordon of Blood Eagles around the delegation, shouting to a sailor aboard the slowly moving trireme. Apparently he was doing something—or she thought he was—to her baggage.

"Pull!"

Merota glanced sideways at her uncle, saw that he was occupied in his discussion, and ducked through the guards. One of the Blood Eagles started to grab her, then snatched his hand back. They weren't baby-sitters, and Lady Merota bor-Roriman was a noblewoman—albeit a young one.

The pier was made of coarse volcanic stone. Years of foot traffic and wheeled carts had worn it down, but the stone's porous surface gave a good grip even now when wet from an early-morning rain shower. Merota's sandals had gold appliqués and bells on the upturned toes, a concession to fashion even when the rest of her costume was so absurdly "practical." Her feet skipped *skritch*/tinkle, *skritch*/tinkle, as she trotted quickly toward Ilna.

"Good morning, Mistress Ilna," Merota said with a little bow. "I'm glad that you're traveling with us."

"Good morning," Ilna replied. She wasn't going to call this child *Lady* Merota. The sudden realization that perhaps Merota expected the honorific hardened Ilna's expression and froze her tongue, though she hadn't intended to be unfriendly.

The girl looked nervous and miserable. With a bright falseness that should have been beyond her years, she said, "Will you be boarding the same ship as Uncle Tadai and me, mistress? It's the *Terror*."

Ilna looked at Merota in puzzlement. Probing questions got Ilna's attention in an unpleasant fashion, but the girl seemed so desperately earnest. . . . "I really don't know," Ilna said. "That's up to your uncle and I suppose the ships' officers. I rather assumed I'd be traveling on the other ship with the soldiers."

Tadai's embassy required two triremes. The warships were being used to carry passengers because they didn't depend on the vagaries of the winds, which at high summer on the Inner Sea were whimsical at best. The problem with triremes—apart from the pay of the oarsmen—was that a full crew of 170 rowers, plus a score of officers and riggers for the sail, completely filled the belly of the vessel. Tadai—Garric, really—had gotten around that by manning only one of the three oarbanks, but even so the enormous paraphernalia of a high nobleman's suite was more than a single ship could accommodate.

In addition to Tadai's dozen civilian aides, a rank of thirty Blood Eagles—a tenth of the royal bodyguard—accompanied him. The Blood Eagles weren't intended to protect the ambassador from a real attack. The Earl of Sandrakkan had several thousand troops in his standing army, and it took nothing away from the courage and skill of Garric's bodyguards to say that they couldn't win against odds of a hundred to one.

Their presence with Lord Tadai emphasized his status, however: only those closest to Prince Garric would be accompanied by members of his black-armored elite. Even so, Tadai and his friends wouldn't want to be bothered by the presence of uncouth soldiers during the voyage. There wasn't much they could do about the presence of uncouth sailors, of course.

Ilna's smile didn't have anything to do with Merota, but the girl took it as a friendly sign anyway and said with obvious relief, "Oh, mistress, won't you please come with me? I'd so like you to be with me!"

"Why on earth do you say that?" Ilna said. Surprise washed away all her previous grim thoughts about rank and society.

Merota opened her mouth to answer. At that moment the black-clad woman noticed the girl was gone. She let out a wordless shriek, then called, "Lady Merota! Lady— ah, there you are!"

She plunged through the waiting Blood Eagles. "You come away from that person immediately!"

Ilna smiled. The girl squeezed closer to her, but Ilna wasn't really aware of Merota for the moment. "Excuse me, mistress, but did I hear you address me as 'that person'?" Ilna asked in a pleasant voice.

"I—" said the companion. Ilna had stepped forward to meet her. The older woman was probably twice Ilna's size, tall and thick-boned if not precisely fat, but at the instant they looked like a cicada facing a small, furious scorpion.

The companion stopped. "I'm Mistress Kaline, Lady Merota's tutor," she said. "I'm responsible for the child's safety and instruction."

The shriek had drawn Tadai's attention. He looked around, frowned; then, realizing the confrontation for what it was, strode over with a professionally opaque expression. His suite and the guards followed like the wake foaming behind a vessel's cutwater.

"Mistress Ilna," Tadai said as he swept past Kaline, "I hope you're not being inconvenienced?"

"*Her* inconvenienced!" said the older woman.

"Not at all," Ilna said. "Your niece and I were having a pleasant conversation. Is there any problem with that?"

"Of course not," the plump nobleman said in relief. "Mistress Kaline, come away if you please."

He made a curt motion with his right hand, as though he had a gaff in it and were jerking the tutor along with him.

"But . . ." said Mistress Kaline. Tadai glared at her. One of the aides, himself an older man, reached for the tutor. She hopped away from Ilna to avoid the touch of the fellow's hands. "But I don't understand," she wailed.

"Obviously," Ilna murmured with a satisfied expression. Merota giggled and moved up from behind to beside her again.

"*You* understand things," the girl said. "I knew that as soon as I saw your tapestry. I don't understand anything at all."

Merota's cool demeanor broke. "Oh!" she wailed. "I'm so afraid. They tell me I'm going to find a husband in Erdin, and, and . . ."

"Your uncle tells you that?" Ilna said. She felt cold again, and her eyes followed Lord Tadai as he resumed his discussion with the captains.

"Mistress Kaline did," the girl said. "But it's true. My parents died. We had a house in Valles. The queen tried to buy it, but my parents wouldn't sell. Then the house burned and everyone in it, but I was off at school . . . and the queen bought the land to build her own mansion."

"Ah," said Ilna, without emphasis. "I've heard something about that. The queen is dead now."

"But so are my parents," said Merota reasonably. "There wasn't much money left after everything burned. Uncle Tadai's been taking care of me, but Mistress Kaline says it's only common sense that he marry me to a wealthy man who wants a noble wife."

"Ah," Ilna repeated. Her face had no more expression than a block of marble. Her eyes were on Lord Tadai, talking with his fellows. The tutor stood with her back to the others in feigned disregard for all that was taking place around her.

Tadai wasn't a bad man, as these things were judged. So far as Ilna was concerned that proved how low the standards of judgment were, since they permitted a fellow to sell his young niece to a newly rich foreigner to save himself the trouble of looking after the child himself.

The first of the two triremes was fully afloat in the pool below the drying shed. Sailors were casting off the hauling tackle and making her fast bow and stern to the pier. Some of the aides started for the boarding bridge.

"Hold on!" called one of the brass-helmeted captains. "Wait till the *Ravager*'s in the water and the crews're aboard. They'll climb right over you if you don't."

The aides stepped back, murmuring. Had they thought the scores of oarsmen would somehow levitate to their benches without disturbing the passengers thronging the vessel's limited deck space?

"What do you think about my being married, mistress?" Merota said, staring up at Ilna's rigid face.

Ilna looked at her. "I don't think very much of it," she said. "But neither do I think that it's any of my business."

The crewmen were carrying the drag tackle to the other trireme. There was a noticeable sullenness among them. Because the vessels were part crewed, the effort of launching was much greater for the men doing it. There seemed to be more to it than that, though.

The chanteyman caught Ilna's eye and gave her another ironic salute. She ignored him.

A squad of Blood Eagles approached the pier at a swinging pace. More passengers? That seemed pointless, but Ilna didn't pretend to understand things that were meant for show instead of for use.

There were several hundred spectators lining the levee on either side of the drying sheds. Some of them were simply layabouts who had no better place to be of a morning, but most were friends and kinsmen of sailors going off in the ships. The wives and friends of members of Tadai's suite were with the men on the pier, but the guards kept commoners at a distance.

Ilna thought about her friends. Sharina had been snatched off no one knew where. Cashel had gone after her. Which left Garric, of course, but Garric had important things to do.

And Garric had Liane. . . .

"May I call you 'Ilna'?" the girl asked. Her soft voice broke into Ilna's bleak reverie.

"Of course!" she snapped. "What else would you—oh, sorry."

Ilna squatted so that she looked up rather than down as she met the girl's eyes. "There's no need for friends to call each other 'mistress,' " she said. "Please call me 'Ilna,' Merota."

She cleared her throat. "Or would you prefer to be called Lady Merota?" she asked.

The child laughed brightly. Ilna hadn't realized she was capable of it. "Oh, no!" she cried. "Mistress Kaline calls me that all the time and I want to scream!"

Ilna straightened her legs and stood. "And as for helping you," she said, "I come from a place where people expect to help one another. I'll do what I can for you, and you'll do the same for me. That's how it works."

The squad of soldiers had stopped near their fellows around Lord Tadai. The commander was Captain Besimon; Ilna recognized him from previous meetings. One of the Blood Eagles came toward Ilna and the girl, his shield strapped to his back and a broad-bladed javelin in his hand. What on earth was he—

"Oh," Ilna said. She smiled; the big soldier smiled back. "I only saw the uniform," she said.

"That's why I wore it," said Garric as he put his arms around her and hugged her to his armored chest.

* * *

"Even Tadai didn't recognize me," Garric said, shaking his head. "I wouldn't have been able to get out of the palace if I hadn't changed into this. Everybody has something they need to tell Prince Garric."

"Everybody wants a piece of the king," Carus agreed. *"That's one of the reasons I spent so much time fighting . . . until the fish got all the pieces there were of me."*

He bellowed with laughter in Garric's mind. Garric smiled in response. Willingness to laugh at death wasn't the only virtue there was in the world, but it was a good virtue for a king to have; and it was a virtue that Garric would never lack while he had the spirit of his ancestor with him.

"Would you introduce me to your friend, Ilna?" Garric said as he stepped back. He knew he was trembling a little, as though he were riding a mettlesome horse which wanted to take the bit in its teeth.

Carus, who'd been the foremost man-of-war of his day, was always close when Garric wore armor or handled a sword. When Garric donned his panoply there was a constant struggle to keep the ancient king from clothing himself in Garric's flesh while Garric watched as a spectator through his own eyes.

"I'm Merota," the girl said. How old was she, anyway? The play of emotions across her clear face could be anywhere from eight years old to twelve. "And I know who you are: you're Prince Garric, and you're Ilna's friend."

"I wonder about the first one sometimes," Garric said with a wry smile. "But not the other."

The second trireme was sliding down the ways. Warships were flimsy, hard to preserve, and absurdly expensive to build and crew; but they were lovely things in the water, all curves and sleekness.

He looked at Ilna. "I won't waste my breath trying to change your mind," he said. "About this or about anything else. But I'll miss you when you're gone."

Ilna shrugged with more tenderness than she usually showed. "The world goes its way, whatever people wish it did instead," she said. "Maybe there's another world where the rules are different. Though . . ."

She gave Garric a smile that was either sad or as cruel as a gut-hook. With Ilna you could never be sure, and either one was a good bet. "I don't suppose I'd really want to change with anybody, even the Ilna in that other world if there was one. But sometimes I wonder what it might be like."

The second trireme splashed into the pool. The crews began carrying their ropes and pulleys back to the hooks where they hung under cover for the next use. Some of the men were already trooping aboard the first-launched of the vessels.

"The crews were part of the revolt under Admiral Nitker while the queen was in power," Garric said, contemplating the oarsmen with grim concern. "That isn't anything against them on its face—Lord Royhas and the rest of us revolted as well, or near enough. But the morale of the survivors is terrible since Nitker got most of their fellows slaughtered, and I wouldn't say they were the most loyal subjects of the new government either."

His lips grinned; his mind did not. Nor did Ilna, watching him.

"I wish the cross-training of the new phalanx as oarsmen had gone fast enough that I could give you a hundred of them for crews," Garric said, "but for now I think using the remnants of the old fleet is probably the better choice."

Ilna sniffed. "We use the materials we have at hand," she said. "It's usually been enough."

The coldness of her usual expression gave way to a smile. "For both of us, Garric."

To his surprise, she stepped forward and hugged him as he'd hugged her when he arrived. Then she broke away and, shouldering her rolled cloak, held her free hand out to Merota. "Come along, girl," she said. "It's time to board."

Her back as straight as a spearshaft, Ilna strode away from Garric without a look behind. He watched her moving down the narrow central deck between the oarsmen on the outer bank. Baggage filled the hollow of the hull where the rest of the crew would normally man two more ranks of benches.

When Ilna and Lord Tadai's niece reached the far bow where a catapult would have been mounted if the vessel were going to war, they turned. Garric waved his helmet. Merota waved back with her scarf.

And after a long moment, Ilna waved as well.

Sharina had thought she could reach the settlement by walking around the shoreline of the bay, but the tide was in. She had either to struggle through mud in waist-high salt water or to climb up on the low overhang and battle vegetation luxuriating in the unstinted sunlight from the open seaside.

It had taken her over an hour to get a hundred yards beyond the edge of the beach where the bird had dropped her, and part of that way she'd hacked with the Pewle knife. Then she ran into the bamboo.

Sharina paused, panting. She was almost ready to cry from fatigue. The bird's grip had left her bruised, cramped, and cold. The trek thus far had been difficult, and she knew from past experience with bamboo that she had no more chance of forcing her way through a stand of this magnitude than she could have bored through rock.

The horn continued its long, hooting calls. Sharina knew where the settlement was, but the sound echoed from the opposite headland to reach her. If she hadn't seen the huts and palisade from the air, she'd have turned in the wrong direction to reach the settlement.

Though of course she wasn't making much headway in the right direction.

She entered the forest, skirting the bamboo. To her surprise, she found that it was easier to walk among the trees than it had been along the shoreline where the vegetation wove densely among itself.

Sharina didn't recognize any of the trees by species, but they seemed ordinary enough hardwoods. Vines swathed many of them, but there was less undergrowth than she'd have expected in the woods back home. The bamboo was a light green mass thrusting into the blacks and darker greens of the great trees, but so long as she kept outside of that she made good progress.

She smiled again. Not that it was progress in the direction she'd wanted to go.

A trail wound its way along the northern edge of the bamboo thicket. Sharina hesitated only an instant before turning onto it. This wasn't merely a track worn through the forest by the hooves of wild hogs, though it might have started that way. Axes had improved the passage. Saplings lay beside their hacked-off stumps, and in one place they'd cut through the trunk of a fallen tree so that the path could continue without diversion.

Sharina now heard only the lowest notes of the horn. It had no direction at all. With the sun out of sight above the canopy, she wasn't sure where she was going. The path must lead to the settlement, though—unless it led away.

There were animals in the foliage, because sometimes she found piled droppings that were too large for birds— or at least birds of a size to fly within the tight confines of this forest. The chirps and hooting from above her could have been anything—birds or squirrels or lizards, and perhaps some other creatures still. Maybe fish climbed trees in this place.

Sharina touched the hilt of her Pewle knife. She didn't expect to meet anything in the forest as dangerous as she could be herself. Not until she reached the settlement, at least. The folk there might be nervous about a stranger, even a lone woman, but Sharina didn't see any choice but to join them.

Perhaps they could tell her where she was. It wasn't likely that they could tell her how to get back home, though.

Sharina rounded an oak which so dwarfed all those

nearby that its spreading limbs had opened a clearing at ground level. Another path joined the one she was following. Three women chattering in friendly nervousness were coming down it. They stopped wide-eyed.

Sharina turned her hands out to her sides. "Hello?" she said. Her voice was friendly, but it caught in the middle of the short word.

The women screamed and ran, dropping some of their tools and equipment. The path wasn't straight. They vanished up it, their voices fading almost as quickly in the vegetation as sight of them did.

Sharina swallowed. She hadn't expected *that*. Had they seen the knife? Even if they had, she'd been careful to keep her hands away from the hilt. Nobody could have taken her greeting as hostile unless they were already badly frightened.

She looked at one of the fallen tools. It was a digger made from a length of stout sapling with a flint blade lashed by withies into the split end. Another of the women had dropped a basket of bark cloth. It held bamboo shoots, severed by a tool with a serrated edge. One of the women had a chopper thrust through her sash, a section of gnarled root to which shark teeth had been cemented.

Sharina continued up the path. She wanted to run, but that would look as though she were chasing them. Were they afraid of the bird that brought her here? Or was there something more that she didn't know about?

That she didn't know about *yet*.

The horn calls had stopped. Sharina walked on, keeping her hand away from her knife by conscious effort.

The ground gradually rose and became rockier underfoot. The forest changed slightly; there were conifers among the hardwoods, though again no varieties that Sharina could name precisely.

She came out into an area cleared by ringing the bark of the trees. The trunks still stood, but the leafless branches let through enough sunlight to sprout the barley planted among the sprawling roots. Swathes of bark hung from the dead gray boles like the hair of corpses.

The palisaded community was on the high ground beyond. Picking her way among the dead trees, Sharina made her way toward the gateway.

The grain plots hadn't been plowed: the soil was too stony and root-laced for that. The farmers had planted kernals in individual holes prodded into the earth with a pointed stick. The barley didn't look healthy to Sharina, but she might be wrong in estimating that the season here was late summer. All she knew for sure was that the great bird had taken her a very long way from her world and her friends.

Everything had a raw look. The trees hadn't been dead for even a year. The bare soil was orangish and unhealthy, gullied by recent rains.

The trees nearest the settlement had been cut down for use, leaving ragged stumps. For the most part, though, the wood was being wasted in a fashion that Sharina found as shocking as she would a human sacrifice.

Did they practice human sacrifice here?

Somebody must have been watching from between the logs of the palisade, because a warning cry sounded moments after Sharina came out of the uncut forest. She heard a babble of voices but she couldn't make out the words. She wasn't even sure they were speaking a familiar language, though the rhythms seemed normal enough.

A shark's head was impaled as a standard on the peak of the timber gateway. It was the real thing and badly preserved. Sharina was approaching from downwind. Her nose wrinkled, but the heavy effluvium of the dead fish wasn't really worse than the sourness of human waste coming more generally from the settlement.

Three men wearing full armor stepped into the gateway, filling it with their great bull-hide shields. Each wore a bronze helmet with a plume, eagle feathers dyed red for the men on either side and a spray of peacock tail feathers for the man in the center. They were barefoot but bronze greaves covered their shins; those of the man in the center were molded with demon heads. The metal had been recently polished, so sunlight winked from it.

They lowered their bronze spearheads and began advancing on Sharina. The man in the center took longer strides than the other two and drew slightly ahead.

More people came out of the palisade behind the warriors. Some of the men had crude bows, but most carried sticks or tools—stone-headed axes and hoes, dibbles, and even threshing flails. The women had stone knives or held rocks to throw. There were a dozen children in a crowd that totalled about eighty. They were a hundred yards away from Sharina, beyond range of a flung rock and probably even bows of that quality; but they were coming closer.

Sharina stopped and raised her right hand, palm forward. "I'm a stranger who would be your friend," she called in a clear voice. "You needn't be afraid!"

Why *were* they afraid? She was a lone woman.

The group—the mob—coming toward her was dressed mostly in coarse bark cloth, but some of the folk wore furs and there were a number of garments made from more finished textiles. The cloak of the leading warrior was of excellent wool but dyed a muddy russet color.

One of the women Sharina had seen on the path raised her shark-tooth chopper. "Dragonspawn!" she shrieked in a thick accent.

The woman behind her, the one who'd lost the basket of bamboo shoots, threw a rock. It bounced back from a dead trunk and almost hit a warrior, anonymous in a helmet whose flaring cheek panels left only a T-shaped slot for him to see and breathe through.

The three warriors clashed their spear blades against their mottled shields and called a muffled war cry. They raised the spears overarm and began to stump forward, shouting each time their left feet hit the ground.

The rest of the community followed, spreading to either side. Stones flew and a number of arrows wobbled in Sharina's direction. There was a mixed bellow of, "Kill!" and "Die!" and especially, "Dragonspawn!"

Sharina turned and ran, making for the track the settlers had cut. Plunging into the forest proper would be suicide, an invitation to anyone following to find her gripped in brambles or facing another wall of impenetrable bamboo.

She glanced over her shoulder. They were pursuing, all of them, emboldened by their own numbers and the fact that their prey was fleeing. The unencumbered civilians left the warriors behind.

"Dragonspawn!"

They'd connected her with the great reptilian bird, of that there was no question. Was there more to the settlers' fear?

Sharina ran with the long-limbed grace that had been hers since early childhood. No one in the borough could chase her down if she got a bit of a lead, not even her brother. Certainly none of the stocky, dirty folk pursuing her now.

But she didn't know how far they'd follow. And though the settlement had been a poor hope for helping Sharina to get home, it was the only hope she had.

Branches whipped her. At every pumping stroke of her arms, her fingertips brushed the black horn hilt of the Pewle knife. If they did catch her—outrun her, trap her, circle her while she slept, as at some time she'd have to sleep . . . if they did, they'd learn that the business wasn't over yet.

Cashel watched the world spin about him, wondering when the business would be over. He was standing still. He *knew* that, as surely as he knew his own name. Everything around him changed in a series of eyeblinks.

His friends rotated and vanished. A blue haze congealed, then vanished like dew in the sunshine. Cashel stood at the base of the same bluff as before, but the vegetation twisted along the ground and had a maroon tinge. Shallow water that was choked with bluish algae stood where the street had been. A pair of eyes looked up from the water's surface, but the thing's body remained a vast dark mass which the algae mottled.

Everything shifted again. The water swung vertical; the bluff behind Cashel was a flat plain for the instant before a hard, ruby glare encompassed him and everything vanished.

Cashel was under the pale green sea. A fish faced him, hanging in place with quivering motions of its pectoral fins. The pressure of forty feet of water squeezed Cashel and started to lift him.

He twisted, wondering if he'd drown before he reached the surface. The bluff behind him was covered with sponges and soft corals whose fans waved in the current.

A red light enveloped Cashel again. He breathed hot, dry air and his staff was firmly planted on stony soil. His skin and clothes were sopping, and he could taste salt water on his lips.

Three figures goggled at him. They looked like toads standing on their hind legs, their broad lipless mouths gaping white. They wore copper bangles around their wrists, ankles, and the thickening beneath their heads that would have been the neck in a human being. The toads carried no tools or weapons, but one had a whisk of something that might have a beast's tail, grass, or even some fibrous mineral.

The blue glare wrapped Cashel, then opened to release him. He stood in a forest glade, beneath the same rocky hillside as in every other scene. This time he stumbled and thrust out his staff to catch himself.

In the side of the bluff was a thirty-foot gateway framed by pillars of pinkish-gray granite like no stone Cashel had seen in Valles. He looked up. From his steep angle he couldn't be sure about the scene on the triangular pediment above him, but it looked like a montage of men and demons battling or perhaps just torturing one another. The figures were sculpted from the same dense stone; the job must have been almost as difficult as carving crystal on the same scale.

The door in the gateway was bronze and stood ajar. Its surface was chased with writing in the sweeping letters that Cashel knew to call the Old Script. He couldn't read himself and could barely write his name in modern letters, but he'd seen the script often enough in the recent past. It was the form which wizards used to write their spells before they spoke them.

Cashel took a deep breath. The woods around him looked ordinary, though he hadn't been in this particular place before. There were oaks, beeches, and hickories; where the light was good enough, hornbeams formed a lower story. The air had the heavy natural smell of decay, the scent of late summer when growth has stopped and the leaves of dogwoods and sweetgums have already begun to turn.

Cashel spun his staff, using one hand and then both. He was loosening his muscles and making sure everything—his body as well as the hickory—was in balance.

A squirrel chattered above him. Cashel let the staff swish to a halt and called back with his tongue against the roof of his mouth. Startled, the squirrel fell silent.

Cashel pursed his lips and looked around him. It was nice to be out of the city again, though he preferred meadow to woodland. If your sheep got into the woods, they usually got in trouble. Of course, they got in trouble in open meadows too—if there was a sillier animal than a sheep, Cashel hadn't met it—but in open country you could get to them easier before they managed to drown or hang themselves in the crotch of a sapling.

He grinned. He knew about sheep, but he couldn't say he missed being around them all the time since he'd left the borough.

Cashel figured he was where Tenoctris meant him to come, but he didn't see any sign of Landure. The open bronze door was one way he could go, and there were three trails through the forest converging here.

The cave breathed out the way caves do when the open air is cooler than that in their depths. The forest wasn't *that* cool, Cashel would have thought, and he didn't like the sulfur tinge from below.

His nose wrinkled. He guessed he'd try one of the trails.

At least this was a better place to be than any of the ones he'd flashed through in coming here. The toadmen hadn't looked unfriendly, exactly, but the sea would've been a real problem for somebody who didn't swim any better than Cashel did. Though he guessed he'd have managed.

He started up the trail that led through a bed of galax for no reason beyond his needing to pick one path or another. He hadn't taken the second step when a woman with a hand over her bleeding thigh came running toward him past a stand of yellow birches.

She saw Cashel the same time he saw her. "Help please!" she cried desperately. "He means to kill me!"

She was about as pretty as any woman Cashel had ever met. Her hair was black and long, but she wore it in twin braids bound on top of her head like a turban. Her skin was white except for her lips, and the nails of her fingers and bare toes must have been painted with something to give them such a metallic red color.

The wound couldn't have been too bad, though it had soaked the lower right side of the linen tunic that was all the clothes the woman wore. If it'd been deep enough to get the artery, she'd have been dead as quick as if her throat was slit, and she ran too well for any big muscles to be cut.

Cashel dropped his staff crossways in front of him. "Keep back of me," he said, his voice suddenly husky. He didn't know what was going on, but this wasn't something he was going to walk away from. Finding Landure and then Sharina could wait a bit.

The woman gave him a grateful look and obediently swung herself behind Cashel's solid form. He hoped she'd know to keep *well* back, because a seven-foot quarterstaff takes up a lot of room when it's being used for serious work. He couldn't waste time worrying about her now, though; a man with a long bloody sword in his hand came through the birches in pursuit.

"Hello there!" Cashel said, his legs braced and his hands spread about the center point of the staff, ready to spin or strike. "What is it you plan to do here?"

The man stopped. His expression changed from momentary amazement to mottled fury. He was a tall fellow with a full black beard and shoulder-length hair. He wore a headband of red leather with symbols drawn on it in gold, and some sort of red apron over his tunic, also embroidered in gold. On the middle finger of his left hand was a ring with a purple-black stone, nearly opaque but larger than a walnut.

The man looked Cashel over. "Don't meddle in matters that are none of your business, boy," he said. His words seemed to echo from the open gateway behind Cashel.

He pointed his left index finger toward the cowering woman. "Get down there, Colva," he ordered, "or I'll treat you as you deserve!"

"If you take another step with that sword . . ." Cashel said. He had to force the words; his anger was like a mouthful of pebbles, choking him. "Then you'll make it my business."

"May the Lady preserve me from fools!" the man snapped. He closed his left fist and held it toward Cashel as though the big ring was a buckler for protection. "Strike him down!" he said.

A bubble of red light swelled from the sapphire like sap dripping from a wounded pine. It grew to the size of a brood sow, flame-shot and still expanding to fill the distance between Cashel and the stranger who thrust it at him.

Cashel stabbed with his quarterstaff, leading with his right hand. The blow was instinctive. The ferrule met the bubble with a blue flash that jolted him as though he'd slammed his staff into a boulder.

The bubble vanished. The wizard—no doubt about that

now—flew over on his back, even though he'd been a good ten feet from the quarterstaff when Cashel struck.

"Bad idea, master!" cried a piping voice Cashel couldn't identify. "A really bad idea! Get down on your knees and beg, *that's* what you need to do now!"

The wizard paid as little attention to the disembodied voice as Cashel himself did. He got to his feet with the smooth, slow care of a man who's letting caution temper his obvious rage. "Will you, do you think?" he said to Cashel in a hoarse voice. "By the Lady, you will not!"

He stepped forward and cut overhand at Cashel. Cashel brought the staff around again, left ferrule leading this time, and caught the sword in midstroke.

The blade rang on the iron butt-cap. The wizard kept his grip on the humming weapon, but the shock spun him face-down on the ground.

"Not used to fighting people who fight back, are you?" Cashel growled in a voice he wouldn't have recognized as his own if he'd had leisure to think about it. "Go on about your business, fellow. And I *don't* mean your business with this lady!"

The wizard rose again, watching Cashel with an expression of cold anger. His eyes were as black as chips of jet.

He began circling to his right. He'd lost his headband the second time he hit the ground, so his hair hung in loose strands across his face. He brushed it away with his left hand; the swordpoint quivered in narrow circles in line with Cashel's heart.

Cashel turned easily with his opponent; the woman kept behind him. She'd torn off the hem of her tunic and was binding it over the slash in her thigh as she moved.

The wizard was a strong man to be able to keep his sword up the way he did, but he hadn't done a lot of fighting. The blade gleamed with a high polish. It'd rung like steel when Cashel struck it aside, but the sheen of the metal was more like silver or even glass.

The high voice jeered, "He's right, you know, master. You're always pushing people around, telling them to do this, do that. And now it's time for you to—"

"Shut up!" the wizard said in a voice like thunder.

"Oh, sure," chirped the disembodied voice. "You're my master, so I'll shut up. But you're not his, that's for—"

The wizard slid his booted right foot forward on the loam, extending his right arm and sword in a long lunge. Cashel's quarterstaff stabbed, the right hand guiding the hickory and the left ramming the shaft straight out like a battering ram.

The staff was twice the length of the wizard's blade. The ferrule caught him on the bridge of the nose, smashing his skull and flinging his body back into the doorway in the bluff. Cashel felt the shock all the way up his left arm. He stepped back, wheezing from the tension of the fight.

"You killed him," the woman said. She stepped past Cashel with a serpentine grace despite her wound. Her fingertips brushed the bunched muscles of his left arm, as gently as a breeze.

"Keep away!" Cashel said. "He may not be . . ."

But the wizard really was dead. Cashel knew that as surely as he knew the sun rose in the morning.

"I didn't mean to kill him," Cashel muttered. "I don't even know who he was."

The woman knelt beside the body. Cashel thought she was holding the corpse's left hand, but when she turned to face Cashel again he saw that she'd covered the ring with a wad of soft dirt.

"He was a monster of the pit," she said, rising supplely to her feet. "He escaped while my husband Landure was absent for a few days. I tried to force him back into the Underworld, but he was too strong for me. If you hadn't arrived, stranger, he would certainly have killed me—or taken me down with him to a worse fate."

She bent and deliberately wiped the dirt from her hands on the dead man's rich apron. Her eyes, large and honey-colored, were fixed on Cashel.

"The ring is a demon," she explained as she straightened. "It speaks, and it's almost as dangerous as the demon-lord who wore it."

Her tongue licked her lips. "My name is Colva," she added.

Cashel cleared his throat. "I'm Cashel or-Kenset," he said. He was having a hard time collecting his thoughts. "My friend, that is, the wizard Tenoctris sent me here to find your husband. I, ah, I'm looking for my friend Sharina. Lady Sharina."

Colva smiled at him. "The Gods must have sent you to me," she said. "Don't you think so, Cashel?"

The sound of her voice made him feel like he was being licked by a cat's tongue, warm and tickling and sticky as well. It made it hard to think.

"I don't know about the Gods," Cashel said. "I—Can you direct me to Master Landure?"

"Come," said Colva, putting her right hand in his left and leading him up the path by which she'd first appeared. "I'll take you to our mansion, where you can wait for my husband Landure to return. It'll only be a few days."

Cashel glanced over his shoulder. "How about the, the dead man?" he said.

Colva looked up into his eyes. "Let him stay where he lies," she said. "He'll be a warning to others of his sort who might want to come up to plague the waking world."

She tugged Cashel's hand. Beneath the soft, pale skin, Colva had the muscles of a cat. "Come," she repeated.

Hand in hand, she and Cashel went up the path. No birds or squirrels chittered in the leaves; the woodland had gone silent. Colva began to sing, but the tune was in a minor key and Cashel couldn't make out the words.

Chapter Eight

As soon as it was decently dark, Ilna crawled out of the luxurious tent Lord Tadai had forced on her. She didn't want to insult the nobleman, but she'd sooner have slept on a mattress of human bones.

Bones didn't speak to Ilna. Fabrics did, and the flooring of silk rugs knotted by the fingers of tiny children—the knots were closer because the hands tying them were so small—spoke in tones of wailing misery.

Ilna was no romantic. Farm labor was hard, and children in the borough worked almost from the time they were weaned. Even so, she preferred to sleep outside wrapped in the cloak she'd woven rather than on gleaming rugs under a canopy of silk and cloth-of-gold.

The two triremes leaned on braced oars so that when the tide came in they wouldn't fill and sink. Their anchors were set high up the sand with the flukes pegged down to hold against the water's tug. They'd been beached on one of the many nameless islets which dotted the Inner Sea when the tide had just begun to ebb.

A girdle of barren sand stretched down to the water, but there was thick vegetation in the center of the island which only the highest spring tides washed. Ordinary trees couldn't have survived the occasional baths in salt water, but beach plums and a number of other low-lying woody plants bound the soil with their roots.

On the east side of the islet were mangroves, dropping roots into the shallow sea. Their gnarled stems and the driftwood carried from distant islands fed the sailors' fires on the wet sand, while the passengers dined in lamplit tents on the higher ground. Salt colored the sparks blue and green and sometimes a flash of gleaming purple.

Carrying her cloak—the air was warm, but not so warm that she'd want to sleep under the sky with only her tunic—Ilna walked away from the circle of tents. Guards and servants may have noticed her, but none of them commented that she could hear. She'd wondered how Lord Tadai and his companions could manage to pack the ships with so much baggage, but when she saw the tents, betasseled and brocaded, begin to come out of the narrow hulls, she understood.

Ilna had been looking for privacy, but as she started up the slope from a swale where the sand was fluid even with the tide this low, she realized that sailors had gathered on the other side of the ridge. They had a fire, but it was a low one and she was nearly to the line of groundsels on the top of the rise before she saw the sparks.

Ilna paused, wondering which direction to go. She wanted the crewmen for company as she slept even less than she did the members of Tadai's suite.

"There's no end to the riches," said a voice drifting to her on the breeze. "Gold lies in the streets, armlets and broaches and headbands of jeweled foil. If you want more, there's the treasure rooms of noblemen and of merchants richer than any who live today."

Ilna knelt, dropping the cloak behind her as an encumbrance. She worked her way forward among the fleshy leaves of the groundsel to where she could see. Her face was a mask without feeling. Without thinking what she was doing, her hands twitched loose the silken rope she wore over her waist sash. On one end was a running noose which would do everything but talk when Ilna used it.

There were thirty sailors in the depression. It was a cup, not a trough, shielding them from view on all sides. Vonculo, the sailing master of the *Terror*, squatted near the fire. He was the navigator and highest-ranking seaman on the vessel, though titular command was that of the noble captain, Lord Neyral.

Vonculo wasn't in charge here either. Standing beside

him to address the gathering was Mastyn, the bosun. Ilna had taken note of Mastyn already on the voyage: a close-coupled man who shaved his head and eyed the nobles with angry contempt when he thought none of them saw him.

Ilna had no quarrel with Mastyn's opinion, but the man's furtiveness repelled her. Anyone who wanted to know where Ilna os-Kenset stood had only to ask her.

A sailor anonymous in the crowd asked a question in a voice too low for Ilna to hear. The fire cracked out a gout of white sparks as if for emphasis.

Mastyn hooked his thumbs in his broad belt. "Aye!" he said. The bosun's voice had a hoarse rasp from bellowing orders in storms where a missed command meant death and ruin. "What of the captains and the fine nobles that're drinking wine while we huddle here with hard bread and bad water? The only reason they didn't have us executed for mutiny when we followed Admiral Nitker is that they need us for a time. How much longer, though, do you think it'll be when the usurper Garric has his own crews trained?"

"We've got pardons," a sailor called, with more doubt than denial in his voice. "All of us who survived."

"All the handful who survived!" Mastyn snarled. "Pardons as good as the word of nobles who laughed when the beastmen killed our fellows, killed them and *ate* them! That's how good the pardons are!"

"He should've been a politician, shouldn't he, our Mastyn?" murmured a voice at Ilna's side. She looked sideways, her fingers curving to cast the noose, but the chanteyman's fingers closed on her wrist before she could move. Not hard, but there was iron under the touch.

"Gently, lass," the fellow said. He grinned. In the low moonlight, the scar on his right cheek seemed to continue the line of his mouth into the gape of a laughing frog. "They'd not care to be spied on, I think; by either of us, but especially you."

Ilna nodded agreement and deliberately turned back to watch the gathered sailors. The chanteyman released her wrist. The calluses on his thumb and forefinger were tough as boot leather.

"My name's Chalcus," he said. His voice was soft but clear. "And you're Mistress Ilna, the wizard."

"Others have said that," Ilna said. "No such nonsense has come from *my* mouth."

"The rulers of the place know how to reward bold men," Mastyn said. He bent to retrieve the bundle lying at his feet. The outer wrapping was of goatskin bound with the hair side inward, but within was a layer of silk that gleamed scarlet in the firelight. "They have need of sailors, and those who join them early will live like the kings of other isles."

"Oh, aye," murmured Chalcus. "The rivers run with wine, and roast ducks hop onto your platter, begging you to eat them."

Ilna couldn't help but smile. The chanteyman's words were so close to what she'd been thinking that they might have come from her own mouth.

A sailor asked a question; only worry reached the ears of those listening from above.

"We'll take care of the guards," Vonculo said. He rose to his feet with the sudden catch of a man who'd been squatting too long. He swore under his breath, then continued, "There'll be no fighting. No harm to them, even, if you're squeamish about those who never cared about you."

Mastyn unwrapped the last covering from the object he held. It was a box of gold and mother-of-pearl, amazingly delicate in the bosun's hands. He raised the lid, then inserted a key into the side and began to turn it.

Chalcus leaned forward, watching intently. He wore a gold ring in his left ear. Close up Ilna could see that his skin was pocked with more scars than were likely to come to most men. Honest ones, at any rate. The semicircle of pits on Chalcus' shoulder was surely from an animal's bite.

Mastyn removed the key. The slowly uncoiling spring drove the mechanism of the box. Tiny silver notes sang across the sand, waking false memories in Ilna's mind. She found herself thinking of drowned palaces, streets along which fishes swam. Treasure lay on the pavements, all the wealth that Mastyn had spoken of and more. . . .

The music slowed, then stopped with a final plangent tone. The gathered sailors were silent, and Mastyn himself seemed transfixed.

Mastyn shook himself alert. "So, lads," he said, "what do you say? Will it be more gold than you can carry, or will you bow and scrape to fools like Neyral until they choose to hang you?"

A sailor asked a question. Mastyn looked at the sailing master. Vonculo nodded twice and said, "Nothing for now. We're speaking to the rest of the men. When it's time, you'll be told."

Ilna eased back from the ridge. Dried leaves crackled beneath her weight, though no one could hear the rustling at any distance. Chalcus backed also, making as little sound as a weasel.

"So, lass," the sailor whispered. "Where do you stand? For wealth by the armload?"

"The wealth may be there," Ilna said. "What comes with it though, I wonder? Nothing those monkeys prating of riches are going to talk about, of that I'm sure."

She found her cloak and gathered it under her left arm, leaving the right hand free with the noose. Not that she expected to need it.

"Aye," Chalcus said with a knowing grin. "Promises too good to be true are just that, I've found: too good to be true. I've come close losing my neck to such—"

He continued smiling, but his index finger traced a scar running from the lobe of his right ear down his throat and under his V-neck tunic.

"—and I don't choose to repeat the lesson. But most of the crews will jump for it, don't you think?"

"I can't be bothered with what other people do," Ilna snapped. The sailor's grin irritated her. She had the feeling that Chalcus really *did* understand the things he mocked— Ilna os-Kenset among them.

Ilna turned and walked quickly back in the direction she'd come. She didn't want to be caught by the conspirators as they dispersed.

For all her brave words, Ilna was well aware that what others did might very well bother her. And the child Merota, if it came to that.

Garric lay on a couch whose bronze frame was inlaid with ivory and ebony in an interwoven pattern. The black-and-white striped horsehair cushions had probably been chosen to match, but either color alone would have been a better choice. The fabric looked coarse in comparison with the subtlety of the intarsia as Garric gazed down at his sleeping body.

He walked out of the palace, through solid doors, walls, and landscaping. Nothing was a barrier to him.

It must have been midnight. The detachment of Blood Eagles on guard in the hall outside his sleeping chamber was changing. He'd walked through men who continued to watch his sleeping body.

Time compressed, or at any rate didn't run the way it would have done in the waking world. Each step Garric took was in a different hour of the day, though noontide was as likely to precede dawn as it was to follow.

Garric reached the bridge. He'd known that was where he was going, though he had no control over his movements and no concern about what they implied. It made him vaguely angry to be shifted the way a chessplayer places a pawn, but the force controlling Garric had stripped away all volition.

The bridge was no tracery of light to Garric in his present state: rather it was solid gray sandstone, bound with iron cramps which had rusted red stains across the ashlars. Garric's feet slapped the pavement, jarring him even in his dream.

Garric heard other feet echo faintly to his left. He turned his head and saw Carus, forcing a smile. The king wavered in and out of focus. He opened his mouth to call something, but the words were lost.

Garric shut his eyes and gripped the coronation medal hanging against his chest. For a moment he held the thin gold stamping, warm with his own blood's heat; then he was holding the callused right hand of a swordsman.

Garric opened his eyes and grinned. He and King Carus walked together, hand in hand, across the hard stone. Lightning flashed among the clouds, but no thunder reached the pavement below.

They were approaching the ruined city that Garric had visited before in this fashion. "That's Klestis, all right," Carus said. His voice seemed deeper than it had when Garric heard his ancestor in the silence of his own mind. "It's worse for wear, isn't it?"

He chuckled. He opened his hand, releasing Garric's wrist. They continued to walk side by side. Caressing the hilt of his sword, Carus added, "Though Klestis is in better shape than my Carcosa is today, lad. There were hogs rooting in the Field of Monuments when you saw it, weren't there?"

"There's life in Carcosa," Garric said. "All that Klestis has is stones and the landscaping run wild. And Ansalem, I suppose."

His left hand tingled with the strength of Carus' grip. Garric wondered what effort it had taken to draw the king through the barrier into an enchantment meant for Garric alone. Carus' worst enemies can never have doubted the king's strength and determination.

The bridge ended at the esplanade in the center of Klestis. Garric was walking normally again, though he wondered what would happen if he tried to turn and run.

His face hardened, though his expression was technically a smile. He wasn't going to run, from Ansalem or from anybody. Especially not when the eyes of his ancestor were on him.

"There were people who next to worshipped Ansalem," Carus said musingly. "I heard them say that the Yellow

King formed mankind out of dust, and that men would return to dust again when Ansalem died."

He laughed, but there was a touch of unusual bitterness in the king's voice as he added, "It wasn't quite dust, what the kingdom fell into; but it was close enough at that. Maybe I should have listened to all those frightened doomsayers."

"Most folk wouldn't say it was Ansalem's death that brought down the Old Kingdom," Garric said. "Besides, Ansalem seemed lively enough when I last saw him, as do you. And I've learned from you that it's never good to listen to fear."

"Oh, I never told you that," King Carus said cheerfully. "Fear's a useful thing, lad; it keeps you from getting overconfident. But you can't let it rule you, no. Not and still be a man."

They strode toward the palace, going forward boldly to avoid being driven. Pride wasn't worth much when you were completely in another's power, but it was all Garric had. Pride in himself, and in the ancestor who'd overcome the will of a great wizard to join him.

"Klestis grew all its own food," Carus said as he and Garric entered the palace, this time through the small front entrance. "You can see the fields from the roof here; I caught only a glimpse when I was visiting Ansalem. Wheat kernels each the size of my thumbnail and oranges as big as melons. Ansalem's doing, I suppose."

Age had ruined the building's interior. A few scraps of tapestry—mostly the metal strands which had been part of the weave—clung to the hooks beneath the cornice moldings, but for the most part the rotted hangings clogged the floors as dust. The furniture had fallen apart as well. Statues and urns set into wall niches remained, though some had toppled in the ages since they were brought here.

No one had walked in the palace for decades, perhaps centuries. Garric felt the debris cling to his bare feet. He and Carus both were leaving footprints. The king followed the line of Garric's eyes; he nodded.

They climbed the stairs by which servants had led Carus to Ansalem in past times. Had that been in the past? Though surely as many years had passed in this place as they had in the Isles.

The king laughed suddenly. "It doesn't seem dangerous in the least, does it?" he said. "So why do I feel this way?"

Garric shrugged. A right turn of the stairs followed a left turn, so that each man alternately had to lengthen his stride at the landings.

"A hen's got a pretty good life too," he said. "Nothing to do but come to the kitchen door where the wife scatters grain in the morning, and then grub for herself the rest of the day. Then one morning the wife wrings the hen's neck and she's that day's dinner."

Garric exchanged glances with Carus. "Not that we know whoever's bringing me here is planning dinner," he added. "But there isn't a lot I can do about it if he is."

Carus laughed again. "We'll see what we can do," he said.

Garric noticed that the king's fingers twitched his sword up a finger's breadth to make sure it was loose in the scabbard. It was an unintended gesture; neither of them consciously thought that weapons would be of any use against the force controlling them. But it also showed that to Carus, the danger was theirs together and not Garric's alone.

Garric gripped the king's shoulder and squeezed it. Both men smiled, though neither spoke.

There was no one in the anteroom at the top of the stairs. The door that the tall man had guarded was barred from their side. Carus slid back the untarnished electrum bolt without difficulty, pulled the door open, and bowed Garric in ahead of him ironically.

Ansalem was sitting on the stone couch again, apparently oblivious of the double-headed serpent, the amphisbaena, which shimmered in and out of view through him. He looked up eagerly, then frowned when he saw Garric and Carus entering the room.

"Dear, dear," Ansalem said as he rose to greet them.

"I've met you before, haven't I? Both of you. Or are you both the same person? King Carus, isn't it?"

"I'm Carus," the king said with an easy smile. "This is my many-times-grandson Garric."

His quick glance took in the whole room. The mid-morning sun would enter through the alabaster as well as through the holes in a creamy effect that softened what would otherwise have been glare.

"And we've met before, yes," Garric said. "When you brought me here the first time, Master Ansalem."

"Did I really?" Ansalem said, peering around the littered room with a puzzled expression. "Oh, I scarcely think I did that, my boy. I couldn't have, surely. This chamber is closed off from all the rest of the cosmos. You don't really exist, you see: you're just my dream."

Instead of answering, Carus rapped his knuckles on the window grille beside him. The electrum frame bonged musically.

Ansalem nodded, looking even more puzzled than before. "Yes," he said, "that *is* strange, isn't it? But you can't be real."

He reached toward a bookshelf and paused with a moue of frustration when he realized that all his books were gone. "Purlio!" he shouted. "Master Purlio, come here at once!"

His voice echoed. There was no other sound.

"I think my acolytes must have closed me off here," Ansalem said. He sounded more interested than concerned. "Why do you suppose they did that? You haven't seen them, have you, Purlio and the rest? But no, you couldn't have. You don't really exist."

"I met your Purlio when I was here in my own flesh," Carus said bluntly. "I thought he was a nasty piece of work, and the other six with him not much better."

"What?" said Ansalem in mild surprise. "Oh, they're not so bad. Quite clever, all of them, though—"

His cherubic face clouded.

"—they really shouldn't have walled me off here while

I was so tired from removing Klestis from the waking world. I was going to . . ."

Ansalem's eyes suddenly focused on Carus. Garric, watching the old man, suddenly saw that beneath the child-like innocence was a core as powerful and amoral as the lightning.

"You were very angry that I wouldn't join the great crusade you were mounting against all your enemies, weren't you, Carus?" the old man asked.

Carus shrugged grimly. "They were the enemies of civilization, but"—he smiled; with some humor, though not a great deal—"yes, I did tend to confuse myself with civilization back in those days. As for angry, no. Not with you, at least."

Carus turned to the windows and looked out. In the streets below, the terrified citizens stood in the gleaming streets of ancient Klestis.

"I thought you were a shortsighted fool," the king said, returning his attention to Ansalem. "As indeed you were. But with the advantage of hindsight, I realize I was a shortsighted fool as well in trying to solve all my problems with my sword arm."

"I knew I didn't have enough power to save all the Isles," Ansalem said, protesting mildly rather than flying into one of the petulant rages Garric had seen the first time he was brought to this place. "Besides, the kingdom wasn't my business. My duty was only to Klestis and its citizens, so that's who I saved."

"You didn't save them, sir," Garric said. "The city's as dead as the sea bottom now. Despite what you see from the window here."

"Is it really?" Ansalem said. He sat on the bier again, knitting his fingers together in concern. "I wasn't able to complete my plan, you see, because I'm still sleeping here. How much time has gone by? I'm afraid it's very long, isn't it?"

"A thousand years," said Carus. "Garric here is my descendant a thousand years after the time I drowned, Ansalem."

The old wizard sighed. "Yes, I was afraid of that," he said. "It really had to be for you to enter my dreams this way, you see. Only when the forces are at a millennial peak would that be possible."

Ansalem stood, showing for the first time the weariness of old age. He touched places on his bookshelf, here caressing a missing codex, there tapping the roller of the scroll that should have been in a particular pigeonhole. "You see," he went on, "when you died, Carus—"

He turned toward the king with the quickness of a frog snatching prey.

"You did die, didn't you?" Ansalem asked with the sharpness of one who expects to get an honest answer, and promptly.

Carus shrugged. "My body drowned," he said. "I'm not a philosopher or a priest to tell you about the rest. But I'm here, now."

"Here in my dream, yes," Ansalem said, genial again. "Well, I had no need of scrying mirrors or divination spells to know what would happen to the Isles when you'd finally failed. I took Klestis out of time to preserve it from the chaos to come. Next . . ."

He turned and surveyed the empty bookshelves and the niches which had held objects to focus the powers on which the cosmos turned. This time he didn't try to touch the missing treasures. His visage was momentarily hard and old in an inhuman fashion, the way a mountain is old.

"I was very tired, you see," Ansalem continued quietly. "It was a great work. I alone could have achieved it!"

He glared at Garric and Carus as if daring them to gainsay him. The old wizard was a child again with a child's boastfulness—and the power to move a city out of time, as he clearly had done.

Garric folded his hands over the sash of his sleeping tunic of plain wool, the only garment he wore in this dream state. He nodded agreement. It was like facing a caldera

of bubbling rock, wondering if the next instant would bring
a burp of fire to incinerate him and all else around.

Ansalem sighed, shrinking into himself. "I was tired and
I slept," he said softly. "When I awakened I would have
moved Klestis a thousand years into the future when peace
and stability were reestablished. I didn't want my people
to suffer through the ruin to come."

Garric smiled wryly. "I wouldn't call the present—my
present, I mean," he said, "either peaceful or stable, but
I'll grant that it's better than what happened immediately
after the collapse of the Old Kingdom. For the time being,
at least. The trick will be to keep it that way, and your
bridge from Klestis to our world is making that harder,
sir."

"Bridge?" said Ansalem. "I don't remember making a
bridge. But there's so much I don't remember. You say
it's all gone out there?"

He gestured, not to the window overlooking the city but
rather to the alabaster screen from behind which the be-
nevolent despot Ansalem the Wise granted audience to the
folk of Klestis. From inside this chamber Garric could see
fruit trees growing in the planters and the bordering beds
of portulaca that waved in a mild breeze. There were no
people here, however.

"Yes," said Carus. "All gone. There's nothing but a
waste. There aren't even goats to crop the grass in the
streets."

"That's because I never woke up," the old wizard said,
shaking his head in an attempt to understand what he knew
had happened. "Why do you suppose Purlio and the others
would have sealed me in here in my dreams? They must
have known that Klestis couldn't survive without me.
Didn't they?"

"Maybe they didn't care," Carus said. He hooked his
thumbs in his sword belt, facing Ansalem like the grim
statue of a war god. "Certainly they didn't care."

"Sir?" said Garric. "We need to break the enchantment

and return you to where you belong. Can you tell us how to do that?"

"Oh, you can't do that, boy," the old wizard said with a dismissive wave. "Only the amphisbaena could do that, and—"

As Ansalem spoke, Garric felt a force snatch him with the suddenness of a released bowstring. The chamber blurred. Garric was rushing through time and space, watching the cosmos reverse about him.

Faintly through the gray darkness he heard Ansalem saying, "—the amphisbaena is here with me!"

Sharina had a stitch in her side from straining against the bird's unmoving talons. She hadn't noticed it in her relief at being dropped at last on the beach, but she surely did now.

The rib muscles were a lance of gasping pain every time her right leg extended, and another punishing jolt when her toes touched the ground to take her weight.

She dodged a dome of multiflora roses. They were lovely in season—the season was past—but also the worst brambles in the woods. Because Sharina was tired and hurting, she didn't allow enough clearance. A tendril drew three long cuts across her left forearm and snatched threads from the tip of her crimson sash as well.

That'll show them I passed this way, she thought. But the villagers were following anyway, as relentless as yellow jackets and as murderously inclined. Sharina heard them not very far behind her, calling to one another in vicious glee.

The armored warriors would be a long way back. That didn't help, because if a score of peasants with rocks and choppers ringed their victim they were more than a match for even a swordsman like Garric—if they were willing to pay the price.

The Pewle knife hung on a broad belt drawn tight so that it didn't flop while the wearer was in violent motion.

Sharina didn't touch the hilt at the thought—it would have thrown off her stride—but she smiled grimly all the same. There'd be a price to pay before they brought this lone woman down, too.

The track she'd followed away from the settlement had dribbled to nothingness half a mile back. Sharina kept running, picking her route with an eye well accustomed to the woods; but not *these* woods, and night was falling.

"Lady," she mouthed. She was too fatigued for a proper prayer. "Lady, help me Your servant."

A clearing—it wasn't really a clearing; it was a broad swath on which all the growth was stunted—cut through the forest at a diagonal to Sharina's path. She swung left rather than make the acute angle to the right that would have brought her back more in the direction of her pursuers. The villagers might know, must know, about this stretch of relatively easy going. They'd be cutting through the woods already to block their prey if she tried to double back on it.

Sharina didn't try to hide in the taller growth on the other side instead of running in one direction or the other along the track. Her cape wasn't long enough to cover her bleached-wool tunics, and they'd flash like fire in the moonlit forest. Her skin was paler yet, and her hair was a bright blond flag to signal those who wanted her life.

She thought at first that she was following a seam of dense volcanic rock, less permeable to water and seeds struggling to root themselves than the limestone that underlay most of the terrain. The path was too straight, though, and too broad: twenty feet across, and more regular that most of the streets in Valles.

This was a boulevard: an ancient roadway laid with such skill that the only purchase for roots was the thin layer of soil that had drifted over the pavement during centuries of disuse.

Sharina brushed aside a stunted pine and strode through the bed of ivy that carpeted a wide stretch of the path. Her toes easily tore the stems, tossing behind her a trail of the soft, broad leaves.

Birds lifted from overhanging branches in a chorus of whirrs and the clatter of wings against the foliage. She'd disturbed doves or perhaps quail who'd already roosted for the night.

The roadway intersected an overgrown wall at a corbeled arch that must have been thirty feet tall when it was complete. The top had fallen in. The head that had originally glared down on those passing through the entrance now lay in the gateway on a pile of the small squared stones into which it had been set.

The head was that of a serpent, sculpted in a squared idiom that made it more, not less, awesome to unfamiliar eyes like Sharina's. The jaws were large enough to envelop her torso had they been flesh and not stone; a forked tongue curled out of them. Florid carvings, some of them lesser heads, covered all the surfaces of the great bust.

Sharina put her hand on the cold stone as she slipped past, slowing lest she turn an ankle on the jumble of overgrown stones.

She'd reached the great complex she'd seen while she hung in the bird's claws. She couldn't turn aside now. The boulevard was a notch in the canopy, allowing more sunlight to penetrate to ground level than it did elsewhere in the forest. In that bounty the vegetation to either side had grown impenetrable with honeysuckle and thorns.

It didn't matter: Sharina couldn't run much farther with this fire in her side, and perhaps it was time to make a stand anyway.

She stepped out of the direct sight of those pursuing and took stock. A street extended the line of the boulevard. The building to her immediate right was a ruin whose original outline was beyond imagining. A gigantic oak tree grew from piled rocks whose squared corners were the only evidence that the mound wasn't natural.

Beyond that ruin was a structure at least a hundred and fifty feet long. Like the exterior walls and all the other visible buildings, it was made from granite rather than the limestone Sharina had seen along the seashore and in outcrops in the settlers' clearing. Flecks of mica and other glittering inclusions winked in the waning skyglow.

Roses and long-needle pines grew up the building's high façade; in many places their roots had levered off the ornamental moldings. Piles of richly carved ashlars, some of them broken when they fell, lay against the front wall, blocking two of the entrances and almost the third nearest Sharina.

It was as good a covert as any. She patted the knife, then mounted the heaped stones to the opening at the very top of the corbeled arch. She climbed with all four limbs, holding rough-barked trunks for support while her toes found purchase in the carved faces of monkeys, lizards, and less identifiable creatures.

Another serpent head projected above the sharp peak. Sharina squirmed beneath it and into the darkness of the building's interior.

The piled debris was much steeper on this side. In order to keep from falling head first, Sharina grabbed the notch which must ages ago have held a wooden doorframe. Carefully she swung her torso around and found footholds so that she could wait just below the opening with her knife ready. She opened her mouth wide so that her gasps wouldn't give her away.

Though the villagers would learn where she was as soon as one of them tried to crawl through this hole. They had to come at her one at a time unless they decided to pull down a mass of hard stones woven about by brambles and tree roots. That wouldn't be an easy job or a short one, even by daylight.

Neither would getting through the existing hole while Sharina waited with a knife that could whack through a wrist-thick sapling with a single stroke. She smiled with a dark humor. She hadn't asked them to become her enemies.

As Sharina's hammering pulse slowed, she heard her

leading pursuers arrive. Voices, all of them male, were arguing in nervous, winded tones. She couldn't make out the words. They seemed to be some distance away still.

Deciding that being able to see her enemies was worth the risk, Sharina raised her eyes slowly over the lip of piled debris. Dim light and the pale stone of this city would confuse her outline even if one of the villagers was looking straight at the opening.

As she'd thought, her pursuers had halted at the gate pillars. They peered through the opening while trying to keep their distance from the serpent head. There were half a dozen young men and one fellow with a stone-gray beard and ridged muscles on his arms and bare thighs. More villagers arrived as Sharina watched.

The argument continued, obviously going nowhere. Each newcomer spoke; those already present answered in tones of increasing frustration. The light was failing.

The older man squatted with a flint knife and a handful of pithy canes he'd gathered from the margins of the boulevard. He arranged his fireset, then struck a quick blow to the end of a piston igniter. He spilled pressure-heated shavings onto the waiting punk and blew the glow to full life.

The warriors arrived along with their flunkies and at least a score of the settlement's women. Each warrior carried his own spear, but other men bore the helmets; they must've left the ox-hide shields by the palisade. Full battle armor was scarcely necessary for three men fighting a single woman.

The warriors donned their bronze helmets, adjusting the webs of leather straps that cushioned them on their skulls. The grizzled man rose with the pine knot he'd lighted, holding it away from his body as he eyed the opening where Sharina waited. She resisted the impulse to duck down: motion would give her away while the blur of her face would not.

The grizzled man smiled. He hadn't joined the conversation that circled among the rest of the villagers. If they came for her, *that* would be the man to watch out for.

Though she suspected that he was far too canny a hunter to put himself at the point of the head-on assault that would certainly be the plan of his fellows.

One of the warriors strode forward. He shouted and thrust his spear through the archway, but he didn't—he carefully didn't—let his leading foot cross the line of where the gate would have been. Still blustering, the warrior backed away.

Sharina looked behind her. Her eyes had adapted enough to see that the room was empty except for a few stones fallen from the roof and a more general litter of the stucco that had once covered the interior surfaces. A crosswall with a post-and-lintel doorway separated the adjacent portion of the long structure. Presumably that was the room which the middle of the three outside doorways gave onto.

Voices rose again outside. Sharina raised her head cautiously. Villagers were trying to light crude torches from the burning pine knot which the grizzled man had butted in the ground. He seemed the only one present who was really comfortable in the woods. He watched in stony wonderment as his fellows tried to ignite fallen limbs that had decayed into soggy punk and lengths of sapling too green to burn in anything less than a roaring blaze.

The villagers started back the way they'd come. The warrior with the peacock plume shook his spear toward the ruins and bellowed in a thick accent, "Rot in Hell, dragonspawn!"

He turned and gave a curt order to the grizzled man. That fellow nodded and picked up the flaring pine knot. After a final long glance toward Sharina's hiding place, he started toward the settlement with the torch held high. He was lighting the way for the warriors, though they were going to be lucky not to fall on their faces unless they removed their helmets again.

The lights vanished quickly into the forest. Villagers complained as they stumbled into trees or thorns caught at them. Sharina was sure they'd given up, but she waited at the opening while the moon climbed higher by the width of two fingers at arm's length.

She sighed and sheathed the Pewle knife, then climbed down into the building. She was thirsty and she'd probably be very hungry in the morning, but she couldn't go exploring in the dark. At best she'd waste her time, and there was a good chance she'd manage to turn an ankle or worse.

The folk who'd settled the opposite headland feared the reptilian bird who'd carried her, they feared this place with its reptilian carvings, and they feared Sharina herself. In a more charitable mood Sharina might have said that she didn't blame them; but she did.

The interior door was a rectangle of light fainter than a will-o'-the-wisp. Sharina frowned. The glimpses of moonlight that penetrated the foliage barely outlined the opening by which she'd entered. Had the roof of one of the more distant rooms collapsed, leaving it open to the sky?

Sharina walked across gritty stucco toward the connecting door. She stepped carefully onto, then over, a stele that had tilted out of its wall niche and broken on the floor. The slab's back had been carved as well as the front.

She entered the central room. The light—and it was too faint to be called "light" against anything but the absolute darkness framing it—came from the doorway on the other side. Against the room's back wall a statue of butter-smooth jade faced the outside doorway, now blocked by rubble. The carven figure stood twice Sharina's height: more than life-sized, she supposed, but she couldn't be certain of that.

The statue was not of a man but rather of a scaly, man-shaped creature with pointed teeth in a long reptilian jaw. The eyes of rock crystal glittered at Sharina. In this light she couldn't be sure, but she suspected the rest of the figure had been shaped from a single block.

Dragonspawn, she thought. She walked past. The statue wasn't trying to kill her, and the humans out there certainly were.

Bats didn't roost in the building's dry interior the way

Sharina would have expected. She'd have smelled them even if they were already out hunting. The air did have a dry odor that she couldn't place; it wasn't a vegetable smell, but it might have come from the stone itself.

One of the interior doorposts had tilted slantwise across the opening. Sharina ducked under it and entered the third room.

The roof was whole, the outer doorway a solid mass of roots and rubble. The light—blue if it had any color— came from an alcove in the end wall of the building. Shapes moved in it, or seemed to.

Sharina stepped forward. She slid the Pewle knife out without consciously meaning to do so. As she got closer, she could see courses of tight, mortarless masonry behind the light. The alcove wasn't really there.

Sharina looked back in case she was seeing the reflection of illumination behind her. There was nothing but the doorway, so blurred that she couldn't make out the post that she knew lay across it.

She turned again, more puzzled than afraid, and saw— in/on/through the solid wall—a figure seated behind a desk. It was man-sized and man-shaped, but it was reptilian and had eyes of lambent blue fire.

"Hey!" Sharina shouted, raising the knife to split the creature's skull if it leaped at her.

"I'm not your enemy, Sharina os-Reise," the figure said. Its lipless mouth moved, but she heard the words only in her mind. They had a dry coolness that reminded her of the odor she'd noticed as she walked through the building.

The figure gestured with a three-fingered hand. A stone bench was built into the back wall of this room, kitty-corner to the insubstantial desk of glow and shadow.

"Sit down, won't you?" the cold voice said. "I have a proposition for you."

Colva hugged Cashel's left arm as they climbed out of the silent woods. "I'm so lucky that you arrived to save me," she said. "No reward could be too great for a hero like you."

Cashel held his arm as rigid as the quarterstaff in the opposite hand. He couldn't very well fling her away. Besides, he didn't want to. "I'm not a hero," he muttered.

Landure's palace was a tall, austere building built up the side of a crag which rose from a gentler grassy slope. The façade was flat, but the sides and back formed a smooth half-circle as though a gigantic stone tree had been halved down the middle for puncheons. The upper stories stood away from the crag's slight inward slope, making them a tower of sorts, though the domed roof wasn't quite as tall as the rock behind it.

The view across the valley should have been remarkable, but Cashel didn't see any windows unless those narrow vertical slots penetrated the walls completely. Opening or not, they were the only embellishment on the severe structure.

Colva pulled away slightly. They'd both paused when they saw the tower. "He built it as a pin to fasten the structure of this plane," she said in a dispassionate voice. "My husband, Landure, did. What do you think of it, Cashel?"

Cashel cleared his throat. "Well, it's interesting," he said. He didn't see what there was to say. The building was as bluntly utilitarian as a watering trough. Cashel could feel that, though he wasn't sure why. "Ah, are we going inside?"

He could use something to drink, buttermilk for choice. A fight dried his throat even though he hadn't been shouting. He guessed he had shouted, come to think. Afterward he could never remember all what had gone on.

"Yes, of course we will, Cashel," Colva said, squeezing his arm again. "We'll do that now."

The door set flush with the flat front of the palace was a comfortable height for a tall man but not built to impress visitors. At a distance Cashel thought the panel was made of age-darkened wood, but close up he realized that it was sheathed in silver or some other metal that blackened but didn't decay on exposure. The handle, a vertical bar, gleamed where the hands of users had polished it.

"Will you open the door for me, Cashel?" Colva said. She smiled, her head cocked sideways. Her fingertips rested on his left biceps like drifting gossamer.

"What?" said Cashel. "Oh, sure. Sorry."

He shook his head, angry at himself. He wasn't thinking straight. He'd been waiting for Colva to swing back the door because it was her house, when he should have remembered that she was a little wisp of a thing.

The door was just as heavy as it looked. Cashel pulled steadily; you don't jerk at a heavy weight, not unless you want to snap something that might be your own back muscles. There was a gasp of released suction; the panel moved as smoothly as milk pouring from a pail. Cashel wondered how the door was hung to swing without any hint of a catch.

"Thank you, Cashel," Colva said as she stepped high over the threshold. The lintel, jambs, and transom were the same smooth metal as the panel itself, but the door didn't have a latch.

"There's no lock," Cashel said, pausing to examine the panel. The more substantial houses in the borough had pin-and-tumbler locks, and even the doors of poor folks' huts had bars on the inside.

"The creatures of the Underworld couldn't open the door," Colva said, looking around the interior of the palace with an avid gleam in her eyes. "Landure doesn't fear anything else."

"But when you're alone . . . ?" Cashel said. He entered, raising his bare foot the way Colva had so as not to brush the lintel. He guessed maybe she was protecting the tight metal-to-metal seal.

"Oh, you mean the monster chasing me?" she said with a smile. "He found me outside, you see. But you came by to save me, my hero."

She brushed him again. Cashel didn't know how to take

the woman's, well, banter, he supposed. He was used to not understanding other people's jokes. The only thing was, he wasn't sure Colva was joking. Not quite sure.

He cleared his throat. "Could you get me something to drink?" he said. "Water would be fine. I'm really dry."

"Of course," the woman murmured. She surveyed the room with the bright-eyed curiosity of a mouse entering a pantry, then walked with small, quick strides to a metal hamper.

Cashel looked around also, trying not to knock something with his staff. It was hard to tell in this place what was real and what was just a, well, reflection.

The scorings on the side of the building were windows after all. Anyway, light came through them, but it didn't come in slices the way it did when the shutters were ajar on a normal casement. Streaks of pure color flooded the air. Sometimes they overlaid one another to form a third hue, sometimes they stood as discrete as the squared stones of the seawall in Barca's Hamlet.

Cashel reached out, watching red, blue, and then a yellow as pale as clover honey flow across his skin. It seemed to him that he ought to be able to *feel* colors so intense, but they had no more weight than any other light did.

The effect made Cashel uncomfortable, but there wasn't anything wrong with it. He'd felt uncomfortable at formal banquets in Valles, too.

The interior of the palace was a single half-round room. It went all the way up to—

Cashel paused to estimate the height of the ceiling against that of the building's exterior. He couldn't use numbers the way Garric and Sharina did, but he wouldn't have been much good at felling trees if he hadn't been able to guess exactly how high a tree grew and what arc its spreading branches would sweep on their way to the ground.

This was no different. The ceiling was—Cashel splayed the fingers of his left hand, closed them, and spread the index and middle finger again—seven times his own height. From the outside the building was twice more his height to the top of the roof dome. That meant there was one more floor above this one—and maybe a sleeping loft, though he didn't guess a palace would be built that way.

A steep, narrow staircase followed the arc of the curved wall to a framed opening in the ceiling. There wasn't a railing.

"Here, Cashel," Colva said, returning to him with a decanter and a single crystal tumbler. Varying light washed across her face, turning it violet, then orange, and suddenly throwing a negative of the true colors onto her features. Colva's teeth were black, her skin a gray touched with amber, and her hair a dark forest green.

She smiled and filled the tumbler with liquid which had no more hue than the container of rock crystal did. "To your health, my hero," Colva said. She took a tiny sip from the tumbler, then held it out to Cashel.

"Is it water?" he asked; but it didn't matter, his throat was so dry that he croaked like a pig frog. The liquid was cool and washed his mouth with a prickly numbness. He swallowed, feeling warmth and well-being blossom slowly through his body.

"What is it?" he said, lowering the tumbler. Not wine, surely; he'd tasted wine and didn't care for it. This was more like water if the water was, well, *alive.*

"Do you like it, Cashel?" the woman said. "Have some more."

She refilled the tumbler. Cashel wanted to protest, but he *did* like the taste. And he was very thirsty.

Cashel drank again. He tried not to gulp this time, but when he lowered the tumbler he found half its contents gone. Colva smiled at him and poured it full.

The floor had a mosaic border as wide as a man's arm where birds and animals went about their business in a forest like the one outside. The pictures were real and alive even though the artist had been drawing with bits of stone.

Cashel felt a pang of homesickness to see a mockingbird on a branch of a dogwood scolding the squirrel midway up the trunk. His eyes told him that if he bent and touched the floor, he'd feel the tree's rough bark instead of chips of glass and colored marble.

The central image was just as vivid as the woodland border, but it showed swords of light driving monsters toward the bronze portal where Cashel had appeared in this world. The snarling creatures within the ring of fire included some beasts that seemed to have been made from parts of other animals, but others were as human as the man Cashel had killed to save Colva. A few were human-*like*, but too slimly lovely to be really human; and, from what looked out of the windows of their eyes, too evil to live.

Cashel swallowed. He'd emptied the tumbler again. "Who made this floor?" he said. He wondered if his tongue had slurred the words the way it seemed to.

"Landure himself," Colva said. "My husband."

She laid her fingertips on the side of Cashel's neck and guided him toward what he supposed was a couch. He could feel his pulse throbbing against the light pressure of her fingertips. "Come sit," she said.

Landure's furniture was as spare as the architecture of his palace. The couch had curved legs of bronze with a lavender undertone where a wedge of white lighted one end. The seat was of the same material, contoured but cushionless. It looked really uncomfortable and flimsy besides.

"Will it, ah, hold me?" Cashel said. He didn't want to complain, but he didn't want to smash his host's furniture either. He wondered if Landure was a wizened little fellow, a male equivalent of Tenoctris' aged frailty.

"Of course, Cashel," Colva said, drawing him down beside her. The legs of the couch scraped against the stone flooring, but they took his weight easily.

Cashel looked around to avoid focusing on the warm presence at his side. The sparse remainder of the furniture was of the same style as the couch. In the center of the room was a high desk with a spindly-legged stool for the person using it. A codex with silver clasps and a cover of scaly gray leather lay closed on the slanted writing surface.

The waist-high chest from which Colva took the liquor was one of several along the curved wall. They were made of bronze like the other furniture and chased with scenes of forest life. In the mansions of Valles Cashel had seen tapestries and wainscots carved with hunters and their prey, but Landure's designs were of birds and animals involved with their own affairs.

The panels weren't peaceful, exactly: Cashel, like any countryman, knew there was little real peace in nature. Here a weasel leaped for a leveret's throat, there a black-snake squirmed toward a wren's nest while the parent birds dived shrieking on the reptile. Still, it was nature's violence, not man's.

At the middle level of the high room, metal beads rotated slowly around their own axes, around other beads, and as a whole around the glowing gold ball in their center. Cashel couldn't be sure in this odd lighting just how many beads there were, but he thought at least a dozen. He couldn't see any wires to support them.

His vision blurred. He grunted and rubbed his eyes. The crystal tumbler clattered on the floor. He'd forgotten he was holding it. Had it broken?

The spasm of dizziness passed. Cashel rose to his feet, bracing his quarterstaff on the floor. "I think I'm tired," he said in a thick voice. "If you've got a shed I could sleep in . . . ?"

Colva had been leaning against him. She twisted supplely to remain upright when the support of his shoulder pulled away. Standing with the grace of mist rising, Colva said, "No, Cashel, you must have my husband's bed. He'd want that, for the hero who saved me."

"I don't need anything but the bare floor," Cashel muttered, but he was too tired to argue with the woman. She reached back with her left hand and led him to the curving staircase. Her fingertips rested on Cashel's extended wrist.

Cashel's right shoulder would be against the wall while

he mounted the stairs. He switched his staff to his left hand. Colva twisted sideways so that now her right hand held Cashel's right.

They climbed with her in front of him because the stairs weren't wide enough for two to walk abreast. Cashel blinked away dizziness again. He didn't worry about falling. He'd crossed streams on rainswept logs while so fatigued he couldn't have said whether it was day or night. He could go on, putting one foot in front of the other, even when his mind had lapsed to a low hum.

Colva's touch was like a bracelet of live coals. Cashel wondered whether it had been the fight that made him so tired, or if the crystal warmth from the decanter was responsible.

They reached the top of the staircase. Cashel's foot rose for a step that didn't exist and jolted down on the floor of the mansion's upper room. His eyes focused. He hadn't closed them, but he wasn't really seeing his surroundings.

He clashed his staff on the floor, waking echoes. Colva jumped back, startled by the sound or the fat red sparks the iron ferrule had struck against the stone.

The night sky gleamed above him. "Where's the ceiling—" Cashel said, and with the echo realized that he was looking at a dome with glowing dots for stars rather than the real vault of heaven.

The constellations were just as they should be, though; and as Cashel watched in openmouthed wonder, a shooting star traced across the purple-black to vanish again. Or had that simply been a flash of light within his eyes, another sign of how tired he was?

"Here's your bed, Cashel," Colva said in a voice like warm honey. "Landure's bed, but yours tonight."

The room's only furniture was a metal couch similar to the one downstairs. The thin bronze was as springy as a mattress of willow withies, though there were no blankets or other bedclothes.

This one had a U-shaped headrest molded into one end. A man lying on it could look up at the false sky, his feet to the flat side of the building where the southern horizon would be in real life.

"I can't take your bed," Cashel muttered. He could curl up on the stone floor. At home he'd slept in the kitchen of the millhouse, leaving the upstairs bedroom to his sister Ilna.

"Not my bed, Cashel," the woman said. "Landure's bed, and tonight yours because you saved me."

"I can't . . ." Cashel repeated, but Colva was drawing him to the couch and he was too tired to do anything but follow. He sat down, hearing the bronze feet scrape like woodland insects.

Colva put her hand, both her hands, on Cashel's forehead with a gentle pressure. After a moment he let himself lie back. He was still able to wonder why the bed wasn't wide enough for two, but he was asleep before he felt his head touch the metal cushion.

Cashel dreamed. He was a statue lying on a barren plain. The man he killed before the bronze gates was a giant standing before him, railing in a loud voice. Cashel couldn't understand what the giant was saying. Maybe the sounds were only angry thunder.

Around the shouting giant capered an imp of purple light whose face looked like he'd been made from broken glass. Sometimes he swooped close and mocked Cashel with crackling laughter, then flashed away again. When he turned on edge he vanished like he'd been only a reflection.

The moon rose. Its cool light penetrated the giant and the dancing midget, washing away their color. The giant raised his fist in fury, but his flesh grew transparent and then his bones wasted to shadows as well.

The figures were gone. The moon climbed higher above the silent plain.

The air was very cold. The moon was taking on human features, becoming a woman's smiling face. Cashel was sure he knew her, but he couldn't put a name to her now.

He was a fallen statue, and he was freezing.

A winged skull came out of the night, chattering its teeth together. It nipped at Cashel and was gone; flown away, flashed away. Its teeth burned like the touch of frozen iron.

There were more skulls. Their wings whispered and he heard the click of their teeth, but he couldn't see *them* anymore. They bit and vanished, taking each time another morsel of Cashel's life. He tried to slap them, but his arms wouldn't move.

The moon's laughter rolled in silvery peals. There was greed in her lovely woman's eyes; greed and triumph, and when her smile grew broader Cashel saw the points of her teeth.

Cashel's limbs were stone and as cold as the ashes of stars, but he *would* not be mocked by this thing. He lunged upward, feeling his body shatter when he forced it to move. His hands clasped to throttle the laughing, bodiless face.

There was something sinuous in his fingers. It pulled free, but Cashel was awake now.

He'd overturned the bronze couch. He half-knelt, half-sat on the floor of Landure's bedchamber, lighted by the glow of the false sky.

The thing which called itself Colva had twisted away from him. Its features were more delicate than those of a human, and they were the denial of all good. From the thing's bald scalp came tendrils of gray light, still questing toward Cashel like leeches scenting blood.

Cashel stood. His quarterstaff lay across the couch. He took it in his hands, feeling a cleansing touch in the smooth hickory.

Colva laughed and spread her arms out from her sides. Her nude body was as sexless as a frog's. The gray mass from her scalp reached toward Cashel like the many arms of an ammonite extending to seize prey.

Cashel slashed his staff through them. Where the gray limbs touched the iron ferrule, they shriveled like slugs in the sun. Cashel stepped forward.

Colva shrieked in dismay and sudden terror. Cashel

cocked his staff for the straight, iron-shod thrust that would crush this *thing* against the wall behind her.

Colva leaped for the opening to the stairs and dropped out of sight. Cashel, holding his staff out for balance, stumped along behind her. He was weak, perhaps weaker than he'd been since infancy, but he was strong enough to finish this before he died.

Colva screamed as she ran through the blocks of pure light. The gray phosphorescence burned away from her scalp like chaff in a bonfire. She stumbled at the base of the stairs, catching herself with a jerk like that of a broken-backed serpent.

Cashel followed. He bumped the writing desk aside, hearing it clang to the floor like an angry carillon. He was focused on his task, crushing through anything that got in his way.

Colva reached the entrance. The silver panel stood ajar as she'd left it after Cashel opened the door to admit her. She jumped, but the struggle had weakened her as well. Her hand brushed the silver jamb.

Colva screamed. There was a sizzle like bacon frying and a stench like that of a reopened grave. Wailing in pain and fury, she staggered out into the night.

Cashel reached the doorway and slammed backward. He'd been holding his staff crossways before him. He gasped, "Duzi help . . ." but he no longer needed help.

All he needed now was sleep. Cashel felt his body slide to the welcoming floor. He still gripped his quarterstaff, holding it across the threshold.

Chapter Nine

Garric's consciousness rushed upward from sleep like a high-diver clawing for the surface of the pool into which he's plunged. His mind was full of a torrent of recent images, Ansalem's face and Ansalem's parting words. King Carus was a presence within him rather than standing at Garric's side like a champion.

Liane took Garric's hands in hers. His skin was as cold as if he'd been caught by a winter storm far from shelter.

"Tenoctris said we shouldn't wake you," Liane whispered. She looked at the floor as she rubbed warmth into his fingers. "I could only tell you were breathing because you fogged the mirror I held to your lips."

"I wasn't sure we could awaken more than your body," the old wizard said apologetically. "The person who called you out of your flesh was too powerful. Was it Ansalem again?"

"Yes," said Garric. He wondered how long he'd been dreaming. Tenoctris had brought a brazier into the room and burned written spells on its charcoal.

Garric stood, marveling that the tunic he wore was no more real than its shadow had been in his dream. The fine-spun goat's wool had the same soft texture. . . . "I was taken to him, at any rate," he added. "Ansalem didn't say he'd summoned me."

The room's shutters had been thrown back; the sun well up. Liane would have come for Garric by candlelight before dawn to start work, and found him—

Garric smiled grimly. Next to dead, apparently. And summoned Tenoctris at once.

Garric touched the hands of both women and said, "I'm

sorry I frightened you. I don't think Ansalem intends any harm, though he can make mistakes. Which is why he's asleep alone in a city he took out of time a thousand years ago."

"Out of time?" Tenoctris said sharply. "What exactly did Ansalem say?"

Servants hovered against the wall of the bedchamber. Tenoctris made a hand gesture; a pair of pages grabbed the legs of the tripod supporting the brazier and trotted outside with it. Unlike Garric and his friends from Barca's Hamlet, the two women were familiar from birth with ruling a houseful of servants. Garric would have removed the brazier himself without thinking, and no doubt scandalized the servants by doing so.

Garric cleared his throat as he looked into memory for the correct words. "He said he'd taken Klestis out of its plane of the cosmos when King Carus died," he said. "He planned to shift the city and its people to our time to avoid the chaos to come in his day, but he fell asleep from exhaustion before he could. And while Ansalem was asleep, his acolytes walled him off in his room so that he'd never awaken. Does that make any sense?"

Tenoctris nodded. There was a folding stool with ivory legs and a seat of silk brocade near where the brazier had been. She felt for it with her hand, then seated herself before a servant could slide the stool closer.

"It makes sense," Tenoctris said, nodding. "But—imagine that Ansalem had told you that he'd danced on his tiptoes while carrying his palace on his back. What you've just told me is much more remarkable than that. Did he mention what he used for a source of power?"

Garric frowned as he tried to concentrate. "He said he'd used his amphisbaena," he said. "That's a—"

"I know what the amphisbaena is," the old woman said in an unusually curt fashion for her. What Garric had said must have struck her deeply. "Though he must have gotten it after I visited him. And he said his acolytes had trapped him?"

"He thought they must have," Garric said. "He said the only way to reach him was by the amphisbaena, but that it was inside the, the spell with him."

Liane had released Garric's left hand, but she continued to knead his right with both of hers. The blood had returned to his skin and he was no longer shivering.

"Poor Ansalem," Tenoctris said softly. "He was such an innocent man, really. He should have known that none of the wizards who joined him would be safe from the power of the objects he thought were toys."

"If Ansalem had been worldly enough to understand human frailties," Liane asked, "would *he* have been safe, Tenoctris?"

Tenoctris nodded approvingly. "No, he wouldn't," she agreed. "And if I'm going to wish for things to be different from what they are, I can find more important things to change than Ansalem's knowledge of human nature."

"What happened to the acolytes, do you suppose?" Garric said. "When I was there, the palace was completely empty except for Ansalem himself."

Tenoctris shrugged. "They were powerful wizards, especially Purlio," she said. "And they had Ansalem's cabinet of artifacts to increase the power of their spells."

She looked out the window at the sunlit garden. "It's the objects themselves that I'm more worried about," she said. "Some of them really were pretty toys. There was a music box which created visions of the place whose tune its keys were set to play. But there were others. . . ."

The old woman shivered. Garric stepped to the stool and put his hands on her shoulders, offering his strength to her when she needed it.

"There was the shell of a Great One," Tenoctris said, "changed to marcasite. It was a thing of enormous, evil power. If a wizard uses that, I . . ."

Tenoctris spread her hands, palm up. "I don't know what will happen," she said. She smiled wryly. "Except that we won't like it, my friends."

* * *

Lord Tadai's large tent was suspended from an external framework of blackwood poles gilded with flowing vines. Blood Eagles in half-armor guarded the front, back, and both long sides. Lantern light seeped beneath the tent's front and middle portions; Ilna heard the murmur of speech. The tent's rearmost third, where Tadai would sleep when he finally retired, was dark.

A sailor played a double-pipe at one of the fires on the islet's sandy margins. The shrill notes sounded like bird cries and were almost as unpleasant to Ilna's ears, but the musician's fellows laughed and danced in a circle nearby.

Garric had played the shepherd's pipe in Barca's Hamlet, six reeds of graduated length with wax-stopped ends. Ilna thought his tunes were the sweetest music in the world. She wondered if Garric ever found time to play now that he was a prince.

"I need to see Lord Tadai," Ilna said to the guards. Though she didn't know their names, she recognized two of the four Blood Eagles at the tent's entrance; they'd guarded her bungalow in the palace during past months.

"Wait here, please, mistress," said one of them. He rapped his spearshaft against the entrance crosspole for attention and waited for a steward to open the tent from inside.

While Mastyn spreads his poison to another score of sailors, Ilna thought, but she didn't let the anger warm her normal cold expression. She knew the Blood Eagles were going to carry out their task exactly the way they'd been told to, even though they knew Ilna and very possibly feared her. She couldn't quarrel with people doing their jobs correctly, even when it got in her way.

The steward, a handsome fellow no older than Ilna herself, slid the entrance curtain sideways on its ring mountings. "What's the matter with you?" he said peevishly to the guard.

Through the opening Ilna saw that an interior hanging

separated the front of the tent into an antechamber and servants' quarters. While this man answered the summons, his three fellows reclining on couches continued to drink from goblets of glass etched with scenes of nymphs and satyrs. Tadai himself would be in the room beyond.

"Mistress Ilna os-Kenset to see Lord Tadai," the guard said.

The steward looked at Ilna, letting his lip curl. "Lord Tadai is working on his personal accounts," he said. "They've been sadly neglected because of his public duties. He doesn't want to be disturbed."

Ilna's stomach tightened. Another soldier turned and touched the steward's nose with an index finger that looked sturdy enough to drive stakes with. "How about you ask him anyway," the soldier said. "That'll keep him from being disturbed by you squealing like a pig when the butcher clamps its nose."

The steward's eyes opened, but he turned and flounced away. The other servants had put down their cups and were sitting upright on their couches, though none of them seemed inclined to get involved.

The steward spoke to someone on the other side of the curtain. Ilna said, "Thank you," in a low voice without turning her head toward the guards.

The soldier who'd offered the bland threat snorted. "Jumped-up little ponce," he said. "Thought he was too good to do his job, *he* did."

"Lord Tadai will see you now, mistress," the steward said as he trotted back to the entrance. Spots of color brightened his cheekbones. He swept the curtain aside with a clatter of suspension rings, resolutely refusing to notice the soldiers grinning at him. When Ilna entered, the steward closed the curtain—*He probably wishes it was a door he could bang*—and hustled ahead of her to open the inner curtain as well.

Thick rugs overlay one another on the tent's floor. Ilna kept her face stiff, but she wished she was wearing slippers instead of going barefoot. Suffering was the way of the world. She didn't know why it should bother her just because this time it happened to be children doing the suffering. She didn't *like* children!

Lord Tadai reclined on a couch, holding a lap desk. Notebooks made from laced sheets of wood and ivory lay on the cushions beside him. His two aides sat at traveling desks whose legs folded out of the bottom and were braced with silver hardware. There was a carafe of wine in a parcel-gilt stand, but this was clearly no drinking party.

"Mistress?" Tadai said. "I'd rise, but I'm afraid I'd lose such organization as we've managed to achieve tonight." He waved a negligent hand at the litter of documents that would skid to the floor if he moved incautiously.

Ilna shook her head curtly. "I've been listening to the crew," she said without bothering about small talk that would only waste time. "There's a mutiny brewing. I think the leader's a bosun named Mastyn, but the sailing master of our ship, Vonculo, is part of it too."

The younger aide started to speak. Tadai hushed him with a hand and called, "Appun! Come here please."

The curtain slid back so quickly that the steward on the other side must have been leaning close to the cloth to hear what was being said to his betters. "Yes, milord?" he asked obsequiously.

"Bring Lieutenant Roubos at once, please," Tadai said. "And Lord Neyral as well, I suppose."

The steward turned away so quickly that his bow of obedience was bestowed quite generally across the interior of the tent. His three fellows were on their feet also, their wine cups cautiously removed from sight.

"Would you like a seat, mistress?" Tadai offered. "We can have a couch brought in, or a stool if you prefer."

Ilna shook her head with a pinched grimace. The rugs were more distracting to stand on than live coals would have been. Pain was something she could wall off, but not the despairing wails. *Why* hadn't she worn sandals?

Roubos, commander of the Blood Eagle detachment, entered the tent barefoot and still buckling his equipment belt.

He was a middle-aged man with a pronounced limp; a solid sort who'd taken wounds in service that didn't quite require his retirement but which made him a good choice for a ceremonial command like this embassy. "Milord?" he said, saluting by placing his right hand over his heart.

"Mistress Ilna here says the crew is plotting mutiny, Roubos," Tadai said. He nodded toward Ilna. His tone wasn't ironic, but there was no hint of excitement or urgency in it either. "Is that possible, do you think?"

There was a bustle in the antechamber. Lord Neyral, the captain of the *Terror*, entered. His face was flushed. As he pushed past, Ilna smelled as much wine on Neyral's breath as he'd managed to spill on the front of his tunic.

"What's this, Tadai?" he demanded. "Sister take it, man, couldn't it wait for morning?"

"Your men are plotting mutiny," Ilna said, trying to keep the contempt out of her voice. She wasn't particularly successful at doing so. "If you arrest Mastyn and Vonculo immediately, you can nip it in the bud."

"What?" said Neyral in amazement. "Are you out of your mind? I don't know who this Mastyn is, but without Vonculo we might as well stay here on this mudbank. Unless you know how to navigate a ship, *mistress*."

Ilna went cold. Her hand reached into her sleeve, but she didn't bring out her bunch of cords. That wouldn't help; and the kind of satisfaction she'd take in—watching Neyral strip off his clothes and hop like a toad out of the tent, say—would be one more matter for regret when she next wakened before dawn.

"Let me have some of that wine, Tadai," the captain said. "It's the least you can do, dragging me out of my tent for this nonsense."

"Lieutenant Roubos?" Tadai asked calmly. "What's your opinion of the matter?"

"I don't know what a bunch of rowers are going to do," the Blood Eagle said. "They don't have weapons beyond belt knives and I suppose clubs. I can keep my men in full gear, if you like, and transfer the rest of them over to your ship. But even the six of us aboard now could cut through fifty sailors about as quick as we'd butcher sheep."

"You'll have to row yourself if you do," Neyral said, looking up from the wine that he'd started to pour. "Look, I don't see why we're talking about something so silly. The men won't mutiny—they get paid at the end of the voyage!"

Ilna looked at the captain who didn't recognize the name of his own ship's bosun. "Mastyn tells them he'll take them to a place where gold lies in the streets," she said, controlling the angry tremble in her voice. "He has—"

He has a music box that makes people see visions? As Ilna's mind formed the words, she knew better than to speak them. "He's very persuasive," she concluded lamely.

Neyral chuckled and winked at Tadai over the cup he'd just filled.

"Pardon me, mistress," the younger aide said, his voice just on the side of politeness. "You say you heard the men plotting. This was in a dream vision?"

"No, I got up and went outside to sleep," Ilna said. "I don't have visions."

"Perhaps you dreamed you walked outside, mistress?" the aide pressed. Tadai and Roubos exchanged a glance; knowing and very possibly pitying. "No doubt the voyage is a great strain on you. Leaving your friends behind, that is."

"I'm telling you what I heard, not what I imagined!" Ilna snapped. The children wailing underfoot were goading her into a fury. She had to get off these accursed rugs!

"Well, we'll take precautions," Lord Tadai said in a soothing voice. "Roubos, you'll see to it?"

"Yes, milord," the soldier said. "We'll be especially alert. We're here to guard you with our lives."

Ilna opened her mouth, then closed it. She wanted to blast them all screaming to Hell—and she could do that, she really had that power. She wouldn't, though, because that sort of action would take her to Hell along with her

212 / DAVID DRAKE

victims, and she'd already spent all the time there she
wanted to in this lifetime.

Ilna turned and walked out of the tent, blind with anger.
Behind she heard a voice calling, "Mistress Ilna, please sit
with us for a moment," and another voice saying, "Is she
drunk? She'd leave us without a navigator or a crew!"

The sea breeze filled her tunic. The atmosphere inside
the tent had been stifling. The servants wore garlands of
silk flowers with perfumed ointment as they sat drinking,
but Ilna knew that wasn't what she was reacting to.

There was a rustle beside her. "Mistress Ilna?" Merota
whispered.

Ilna put an arm around the girl fiercely and walked away
from the tent and the fools inside it. When they were ten
paces out in the darkness she demanded, "What are you
doing here?"

"I slipped under the side of my tent when you were
talking to my uncle," Merota said. "Mistress Kaline was
asleep. She snores."

Ilna looked at the girl. Merota was wrapped in a black
shawl much too big for her. Ilna touched the garment and
let the wool tell her of an aging, stiff-necked, poor woman
whose secret pride was that she believed her real father
was a noble and not her mother's saddle maker husband.
She was quite wrong about that.

"This is your tutor's shawl," Ilna said.

Merota nodded agreement. "I wore it because it was
black and I could get close to the tent to hear what you
were telling my uncle," she said. "The guard was listening
too."

Ilna laughed bitterly. "Nobody was listening," she said.
"They made that quite clear, though some of them more
politely than others."

They'd reached an outcrop of porous stone standing
above the tideline. Coral, perhaps? Ilna knew little about
rocks and cared less. She sat down, spreading the lower
edge of her cloak to make a seat for the girl beside her.

The shawl's loose weave was no protection from the damp ground.

"The men think you were Prince Garric's mistress," Merota said as she seated herself daintily, crossing her legs at the ankles. "They think he's getting rid of you because he has Lady Liane now and you're just raving because you're so angry. But that's not true."

"No," said Ilna, holding her hands very still because she was afraid of what she might otherwise do with them. "That's not true. But it explains the way they treated me tonight. There's always a reason for why things happen the way they do."

Her hands didn't move, but she couldn't prevent the images forming in her mind. She could lead them all into the sea after her: the plotters, the forsworn sailors, the soldiers smug in their armed strength and the nobles with their entourage smirking at the little peasant girl who thought she could be more than a bit of slap-and-tickle for a prince. . . . They would walk off the beach in line, each one holding the hand of the victim in front of him, and they would drown in terror, unable to struggle against their doom.

And Ilna os-Kenset would drown first of all, never again to be troubled by fools and by lies!

"Are you really going to do that, Ilna?" Merota asked in a small voice.

Another group of sailors was dancing, this time to a beat shaken out on a tambourine and a pair of castanets. Stringed instruments wouldn't last long at sea.

"I spoke aloud?" Ilna said.

"Yes, Ilna," Merota said. The shawl covered all the girl's face but the white band in which her eyes were gleaming pools.

"Well, I'm not going to do that," Ilna said with a sigh. "It wouldn't help anything. Not that I can see what I could do that would help."

"I'm glad," Merota said. She was shivering.

Ilna put an arm around the girl again and hugged her in embarrassment. "This isn't a world for people like me,

Merota," she said as she stared at the mild surf. "Other people don't react to things the way I do. They don't care, or anyway they don't care the same way I do."

She felt tears forming at the corners of her eyes. She couldn't stop them any more than she could stop her heart beating. Merota's arm wove under Ilna's so that she could hug the older woman also as they sat side by side.

"It's their world, you see, Merota," Ilna said, "so it's me that has to be wrong. And I suppose I could be wrong about the sailors' fantasies too. What Mastyn promises can't possibly be true. Anybody can see that once they think it through."

"I hope so, Ilna," the girl said in a soft voice.

Ilna grimaced. "Come," she said. "We'll find softer ground and get some sleep. My cloak will cover two."

Maybe if she slept she could manage to forget Chalcus saying how it was easy to get people to believe in what anybody should have known was too good to be true. And also forget Chalcus' knowing smile.

"Where am I?" Sharina asked. She started back instinctively, though she felt embarrassed at once. The long jaws would look the same whether the creature were smiling or leaping to tear her throat out.

"You're on an island that doesn't have a name as yet, Sharina," the creature said. "In your day—in the age from which you come—it will be called Cordin."

If she turned her head even slightly she could no longer see him; he was a blur of smoke and faint light visible from only one angle. His voice rang in her head as if someone played the words on tiny metal strings instead of speaking them through a normal throat.

Sharina forced herself to breathe slowly, but she couldn't help the way her heart hammered. She wondered if she was really listening to a reptile man or if this was a hallucination from the stress of the past—hours? How long had it been since the great bird snatched her away from her friends?

"You can put your knife away," the creature said. "I mean you no harm. And besides, it's no threat to me. Even in this age, I've been dead for longer than you can imagine."

He made a trilling sound in her head like the call of a leopard frog. Sharina supposed it was laughter; and it did relax her, for no reason she could have explained.

She slid the knife home in its sheath, closing the tongue of sealskin around the hilt and into the socket on the other side. "Who are you?" she asked. "You already know my name."

The creature shrugged. "The colonists call me the Dragon," he said. His long jaw swung and dipped, indicating the direction from which Sharina had entered this chamber. "The people like you, that is. *My* people are long dead."

"Why do they want to kill me?" Sharina said. "What have you done to them to make them so afraid?"

"They have no more reason to fear me than I, who am dead, have to fear them!" the Dragon said. His mouth shut so sharply on the last syllable that Sharina heard the *clop* that the jaws would have made if they were real. "They're barbarians who know no response but fear or violence."

He bent forward slightly—though Sharina noticed that he never took his four-fingered hands from the table nor leaned beyond its ghostly edge. "Nor have you, Sharina. If you wish, you can walk away from here without let or hindrance. But if you do—"

Sharina touched her index finger to the black horn hilt of her knife. She knew it was useless as a weapon, but the smooth coolness of it helped her retain her calm.

"—you should realize that you will never see your home again. Alternatively, you can choose to serve me. If you do so, you and your friends will gain by it."

Sharina put her hands to her side and stood straight. "I won't serve evil," she said in a clear voice.

The Dragon responded with more trilling laughter. "I am not evil, Sharina os-Reise," he said. "Or good either, if it comes to that. If you enter my service, you *will* serve me. But I promise that if you serve me well, you will find me a good master."

She realized that the real oddity of the creature's voice was not how she heard it, but rather that she heard it without echoes. Her words waked their own chorus whenever she spoke.

Sharina chuckled. What was the choice, after all? To go back to the settlement? The only question there seemed to be whether they would simply kill her or instead would kill her with refinements.

The Dragon's jaws opened in a toothy grin. His voice in her mind said, "They aren't a very refined group, I'm afraid. Though perhaps they'd make an exception for you."

He hears what I think!

Sharina interlaced her fingers and stretched them. "But of course you would, wouldn't you?" she said, deliberately speaking aloud.

"If you enter my service, you will have far to travel," the Dragon said, continuing the previous thread of conversation with an ophidian determination. "Though the path will be toward your home, you will find the way hard. I will give you guidance on the way, but I cannot protect you."

He didn't blink the way a human does, but as he spoke membranes flicked sideways across his eyes, the right one and then the left. The effect was disconcerting; but then, everything about Sharina's situation was.

She bent and began to massage the soreness from her calf muscles with both hands. "If I served you, what would you have me do?" she asked without looking up from her task.

Abduction and being chased through the forest had taken a lot out of Sharina. She'd have liked to sit, but there was no chair or bench and sitting on the floor would have put her at the Dragon's feet. Did his toes have claws? His fingers looked normal enough by human standards, though fine scales covered them in place of bare skin.

Instead of answering immediately, the creature stood deliberately and set his right foot on the table before him. His jaws smiled. His high buskins were of gilded leather. If the foot within the boot's pointed toe had claws, they were small ones.

"I will direct you to a place," the Dragon said. "You will find an object there. You must destroy the object, an undertaking even more dangerous than the journey itself."

Sharina stood straight again. Even wearing the thick-soled footgear, the Dragon was shorter than she was. He sat again as he waited for her reply.

"What sort of object?" she asked, though in a way it really didn't matter.

"A mummified body," said the Dragon. "The mummy of my own body, as a matter of fact."

The Dragon's laughter shrilled again in Sharina's mind. His fingers splayed and closed on the shimmering table in what Sharina guessed was a meaningful gesture to the creature's own race.

"I was a great wizard, you see," he explained. Hints of merriment continued as an undertone to his words. "My flesh retains certain authority over the powers I controlled when it clothed me. Those who are using that flesh for their own ends should have remembered that—"

The humor vanished. The reptilian cheekbones didn't have muscle over them and therefore lacked a mammal's range of facial expression, but Sharina suddenly knew what a snake looks like to a rabbit in its last moments of life.

"—by doing so they may call up the spirit which once wore the flesh."

"Who's using your mummy?" Sharina asked. Her mind flashed through the implications of what she was being told, vivid images of danger framed by the greater blackness of the unknown.

"Wizards," the Dragon said. His long thumbs tapped the

table together; soundlessly, because neither they nor the furniture had material existence. "Fools."

He smiled broadly. "No friends to you and yours, Sharina. You have my oath on that."

The Dragon leaned toward her again. "But I will have your oath too, Sharina os-Reise. If you enter my service, you bind yourself by your honor and your soul that you will keep on until you have accomplished the task I have set you."

The black, bulging eyes watched her. The creature was still and silent.

"If you keep faith with me," Sharina said, slowly and distinctly, "then I will keep faith with you. I swear this by the Lady, the Queen of Heaven."

"My art has shown me many things," the Dragon said, "but I have never seen the God my own people worshipped. Nor your Gods either, human."

Sharina let her lip curl. She said nothing.

"Perhaps I look with the wrong eyes," the Dragon said at last. She thought she heard—felt?—an undertone of approval. "I accept your oath, Sharina os-Reise. If you survive, you will be glad of our bargain."

Sharina felt a rush of relief. She'd been taken away from everyone and everything she knew. She hoped that the Dragon would return her to those she loved; but whether he did or not, she had a place again in the cosmos. She'd stopped being a chip adrift on the seas of time and space.

Sharina grinned. She'd never expected to be the servant of a prehuman wizard, but she hadn't expected to be a princess surrounded by servants and sycophants, either. Aloud she said, "I've had jobs I liked less."

"To business, then," the Dragon said. "You will leave this building and walk toward the arch at the end of the avenue—opposite the gate by which you entered. Slide off the seat of the throne that faces the arch. In the hollow base you will find a snakeskin and a gold plaque."

The Dragon's image had a wavering insubstantiality like that of the creatures which appeared in Valles at the site of the bridge; but the giant bird, at least, had proved itself quite real. Sharina massaged her left shoulder where the talon's grip had bruised her.

"Carry the snakeskin with you," the Dragon continued. His lipless mouth moved in synchrony with the words in Sharina's head, but she doubted that those reptilian jaws could have made the sounds she could hear with her ears. "You will want it when you reach your destination. The plaque you will sell for money to keep you while on your journey."

"Sell it in the settlement here?" Sharina said in cautious concern.

The Dragon laughed. "To those folk, trade is what you do when the other party has as many spears as you do," he said. "Besides, they wouldn't understand what you meant by coinage. But their descendants will have progressed to a degree, at least; you will sell the plaque at the next station on your way."

Sharina nodded but said nothing. Her interruptions had slowed the transfer of information, so she bit back the further question she'd started to ask.

The Dragon gave a soft hiss of approval. "When you have the skin and the plaque," his cold, inhuman voice continued, "stand under the arch and wait for the moon to reach zenith. When that occurs, you will be transported to the next stage."

Sharina thought of where the moon had been when she slid to safety in this building. Frowning she said, "That won't be long."

"You are correct," the Dragon said. "Occupy yourself in the place to which the arch has sent you until I contact you with further instructions."

"How long will that take?" Sharina asked.

"However long it takes," said the Dragon. "Go now and deal with my affairs, Sharina."

The alcove of light and illusion faded into a haze of discrete dots, then vanished entirely. Had it been in Sharina's mind, as the voice certainly was? When she turned, her eyes were as well adapted to the dark as if no light had impinged on them for the past half hour. She could see the interior doorway, a rectangle of moonlight which had seeped the length of the building from the hole by which she had entered.

That was the only exit, also. Sharina started back, wondering how long it would take her to find the arch. No more than minutes, she hoped, because the moon was already near zenith.

When she passed the statue in the central room, the odor she'd noticed earlier was gone.

Sharina's subconscious had identified it, by now. She'd smelled something similar the year a storm in early spring had toppled a great oak. The roots had pulled open the den of vipers wintering beneath them.

Chapter Ten

Warm sunlight falling through the mansion's open doorway had brought Cashel back to consciousness. Back to life, pretty close. He'd felt strength returning slowly to his limbs as if he was a bean sprout unfolding in the bright sun.

The woods had a balm of their own, though, because they were bubblingly full of life. Landure's mansion and the sloping meadow on which it stood were coldly pure. That was well enough in itself, but it wasn't an atmosphere that Cashel would've wanted to stay in for very long.

He smiled, maybe a little sadly. You got that feeling around Ilna sometimes, when she was having a bad day. Which was more days than not, when you came right down to it.

Cashel sauntered along at the pace he'd have used if

he'd been following sheep. He ached all over, and he felt weak as a kitten besides. On a better day he'd have moved a mite faster, though he'd rarely seen as much need for haste as pushier folk did.

Thinking about it, Cashel spun his quarterstaff around in a half circle in front of him, then crossed his wrists and finished the rotation. The staff moved as easily as water down a mill's spillway.

He grinned. Not quite as weak as a kitten, then.

Plants called spring apples carpeted the ground, though high summer had shriveled their leaves. Their swelling fruit was already a bright shade of orange.

Cashel didn't have to hurry this morning. Landure wasn't going anywhere.

When Cashel had to deal with wizardry, it always took a lot out of him. The business with Landure—killing Landure—was maybe why he felt like he'd been dragged behind a wagon for most of a day.

But Colva had done something to him too. She'd like to sucked the life out of him, and he wasn't sure a few hours' sleep and bright sunlight had been enough to recruit the strength the woman drained with those tendrils of gray ugliness. Colva had stood there like leeches grew from her scalp, smiling the way a weasel does as it rips the throats out of chickens.

Colva was loose in the world because Cashel had let her loose. There was no point in pretending that it hadn't happened that way.

Air ruffled the treetops. Not much of the breeze reached down here to the forest floor, but when the broad leaves of the big white oak fluttered, sunlight touched Cashel and the viburnum sprouting beside the path. It felt good.

Cashel was sorry as anything that he'd knocked in the head of the fellow that Tenoctris sent him to for help, but looking back on it he didn't see much he could've changed. If Landure had bothered to explain instead of throwing out orders the way a man does to his dog, well, things might've worked out better.

Chances are Landure would claim there hadn't been time enough for him to go into the whys and wherefores. Well, maybe not; but Landure doing things his way had gotten him time aplenty. Given the way it worked out, even the wizard would say he should've been more polite to a stranger.

A crow in a hickory cawed an angry warning. Cashel looked up. The bird swooped away, putting the crown of the tree between itself and the man on the ground. It called again, a sound as harsh as a branch splitting in a storm.

Cashel came around the stand of birches and saw the great bronze doors set into the bluff before him. He stopped and reflexively crossed his quarterstaff before him.

Landure wasn't quite where he'd fallen after all. A group of little animals had dragged the body off the threshold and—*by the Shepherd!*—were digging a trench alongside it for a grave.

The raccoons had already vanished into the spicebushes fringing the base of the hill, though Cashel caught a glimpse of a ringed tail. Two of the possums were ambling in the same direction, though the third blinked several times at Cashel before swaying off toward cover.

The squirrel stood its ground, hissing and chattering with its head low and its slashing tail held high. Before the little rodent lay the white length of root it'd chopped out of the deepening grave.

"Go on!" Cashel said, flicking the tip of his staff in the squirrel's direction. "Shoo!"

The squirrel's hind legs bounced up and down. Cashel didn't remember the last time he'd seen anything so mad at him. Things had tried to kill him now and again, but that was generally because of what was in their head rather than for anything Cashel had really done.

He'd done this, all right. He'd killed Landure.

Keeping his eye on the squirrel, Cashel squatted down and felt for a pebble in the damp clay soil. Squirrels were agile little critters, no mistake, and their teeth were no joke. If Cashel tried to swat this one, chances were good it'd come swarming up the staff at him; and if the staff did connect with a solid blow, well, he wasn't in the mood just now to kill something that maybe had right on its side.

Though what Cashel had been supposed to do when Landure came at him with a sword, *that* he didn't see.

He cocked his arm back with the stone. "Get on off!" he said, a last warning and meaning it. He didn't often miss when he shied stones at targets as close as the squirrel was.

The squirrel either figured as much or just generally ran out of meanness. It spun sideways, then sprang for the branch of a dogwood high off the ground. The critter bobbed and cussed him for some moments more, then disappeared like the other animals and birds that ought to be going about their noisy business among the trees.

Cashel grimaced. *What's done is done,* he thought. They'd mounded up the soil at either end and the near side of the would-be grave. He walked around it, then squatted to view Landure close up.

Nobody looks grand with his forehead dished in, but Landure had a strong jaw and pretty impressive shoulders for a fellow who wore robes as fancy as his. His bleached white tunic would show dirt like a cloud in a clear sky if you did any real work in it, and the apron was thick brocade and stiff with gold embroidery besides.

Cashel wasn't sure what he ought to do. Carry Landure back to his house and bury him on the hillside, he supposed. Or maybe just finish the grave the forest animals had started? He wondered if there was a shovel somewhere. He hadn't seen tools when he was at the house, but there might be an outbuilding on the other side.

There were more questions too, pushed toward the back of Cashel's mind by the need to do what he could for the dead man. He didn't see how he was going to get from here to where Sharina was, now that he'd killed the man Tenoctris had planned would help him. As a matter of fact, it was hard to see how Cashel was ever going to get out of this place, period.

Well, he had to go back to the house to look for a shovel so he might as well take the body with him. If he decided to finish the grave here, he'd just carry Landure back again.

Cashel set his quarterstaff down and started to reach under the body. The wizard had been dead long enough that the stiffness had passed, leaving his muscles as flaccid as wet wool. Cashel would take the staff in his hands again as soon as—

"Now what?" a shrill voice demanded. "You've already loosed a monster on the world and killed the guardian. Do you plan to eat the body to end the business with a flourish?"

Cashel jumped, spinning in the air so he came down facing the other way. His left hand snatched the quarterstaff and brought it up across his body.

He'd thought somebody had crept up behind him. Nobody was there.

"Cute," the voice said. "Do you balance a plate on your nose for the next act?"

Cashel spun again. He peered into the open portal to see if somebody was hidden there. The cave went a long way back into the bluff, but there was nobody standing in it for as far as the sunlight penetrated. Besides, echoes would thicken the voice of anybody speaking from inside the rock. What Cashel heard chirped like a cicada.

He turned to the forest again. "Who said that?" he called. His legs were spread and he dug his toes into the ground to give him a firm base if he needed to swing the staff.

"Well, let's consider the possibilities," the voice piped. It was coming from *beneath* him. "There's Landure, but I guess he'd have a hard time speaking with his upper jaw broken into about twenty pieces. Not to mention his brains leaking out."

Cashel knelt, reaching for Landure's right hand. The wad of mud Colva had smeared over the ring had fallen off when the body was moved.

"Or there's you talking to yourself," the voice continued. "Personally I wouldn't be a bit surprised if you did talk to yourself, but I doubt you make this much sense when you do. And last—"

Cashel turned the ring to look at the jewel in the setting. It was a huge thing, the size of a duck's egg, polished instead of being faceted to sparkle more. Deep in the stone's purple-black depths was a wavering star of light, five streaks like a stick figure's head and limbs.

"—there's me, Krias, the demon of the ring," said the voice. Cashel could feel the ring vibrate like the breast of a stunned bird against his palm. "Which do you suppose the right answer is? Being it's you, I'll give you three chances."

Cashel slid the ring off the dead man's finger and held it so that a shaft of light fell across the setting. It was a sapphire, he guessed, but so dark it wouldn't be worth much to the gamblers who came to Barca's Hamlet during the Sheep Fair. They wanted jewelry that flashed and tricked their victims' eyes away from what the gamblers' fingers were doing.

The dim star in the jewel's heart had changed. Now the stick figure stood arms-akimbo. "Well?" the ring demanded.

"Good morning, Master Krias," Cashel said politely. "I'm a stranger in these parts, and I'm hoping you can help me get my bearings."

Master Koprathu, the chief clerk of the Fleet Office, stood at the left end of the dignitaries who watched with Garric as the warships maneuvered in the river. "Your Highness," he said, "this is a bad course, a *dangerous* course for the kingdom!"

On the other end of the line Lord Waldron snarled, "Sister take this nonsense of soldiers pulling oars, boy! You need real soldiers to keep the kingdom, not rowers with spears—and not a mob of artisans and city layabouts, either!"

"That's probably the first time those two agreed on any-

thing in their lives," King Carus murmured with a smile even broader than his usual. *"Not that they'd have had much call to stand in the same place before you took over."*

"In truth, I thought they were shaping rather well," Garric said mildly. He tried to keep his own amusement out of his voice. "It seems to me that they keep stroke as well as anyone could ask, Koprathu; and stamina will of course come with practice."

The demonstration was taking place in the basin formed when the River Beltis' burden of silt formed a natural impoundment below Valles. From here water drained to the Inner Sea through three mouths. The first squadron of the Royal Fleet, ten triremes, was crewed with pikemen from the new phalanx.

The basin was deep enough for a fully laden warship. Its breadth was enough to allow a squadron to practice evolutions without danger—much danger—to commercial shipping. Finally, the enclosing shores were vastly safer than the open sea for new-minted sailors who'd never before been in a body of water larger than the puddles that formed in the streets below their tenements after a rain.

"Why, most of those fellows never set foot aboard a ship before you hired them on as oarsmen, Your Highness!" Koprathu said, as though he were reading Garric's mind. Of course Koprathu put a different emphasis on the undoubted fact.

At the time of Admiral Nitker's rebellion, Koprathu had been quartermaster and in real charge of the naval arsenal in Valles, though a nobleman had the title of Lord of the Arsenal. Most of the fleet's bureaucracy had perished when the queen's forces overran the naval base on the small island of Eshkol off the mouth of the Beltis. Garric had promoted Koprathu to the responsibility of outfitting the fleet. For the most part, the warships themselves had survived the rebellion, but Garric was having to rebuild the personnel from the waterline up.

"I'm more concerned about what they do now, Master

Koprathu," Garric said. "And it appears to me that they're doing quite well for two months' training."

Lord Zettin, a former Blood Eagle promoted to Admiral of the Fleet over Waldron's protests, must have spotted Garric watching this afternoon. The squadron paused in facing divisions of five ships each. The flagship blew a three-note call, two long trumpet blasts followed by a clash of cymbals.

"May the Lady save me!" Koprathu gasped. "That titled idiot is going to sink himself and all the ships' furniture that I had in store!"

"Master Koprathu, watch your tongue!" Garric said loudly. He wasn't terribly concerned about the clerk's language. He knew that if he didn't react instantly, however, Lord Waldron would very likely reprove the commoner with the back of his hand—if he didn't use his sword. Waldron didn't have any use for Lord Zettin, but he was very punctilious about the deference owed a nobleman.

Garric was re-forming the kingdom's military on the model of King Carus' phalanx of oarsmen: former urban and rural laborers who could row the fleet to the shores of a rebelling island, then disembark carrying light shields and twenty-foot pikes. A phalanx of pikemen could stop heavy cavalry like a stone wall and drive through opposing infantry the way a cobbler's awl pricks holes in shoe leather.

Unless the phalanx was very well trained, it was dangerously unwieldy: slow to turn and unable to react to a flank attack except by collapsing into rout. That wasn't a reason not to use the formation, but it made close training absolutely necessary.

The same was true of what Admiral Zettin was attempting right now. Garric frowned. Zettin *wasn't* an idiot, but Garric was willing to agree that he was acting like one. The admiral had ordered his ships to execute a sweep-through.

The sections began to stroke toward one another. The ships were operating in pairs, each against the vessel facing it in line.

If warships struck one another straight on, ram to ram, they were likely both to sink. In a sweep-through, the helmsman guided his vessel to graze its opponent instead. At the last instant the rowers on the side to the enemy drew in their oars so that their vessel's bow swept through the other's extended oars. The oarshafts broke and the looms flailed within the enemy's hull, wrenching limbs, crushing chests, and completely disabling the stricken vessel.

That was if your own crew got its oars in in time. If not, you'd disabled your own ship as well.

The ten triremes were up to ramming speed, a fast walk. Top speed was used only for maneuvering, since too fast an impact would smash the attacker's hull as well as that of the victim. Doubled by the fact that the lines were approaching, even the ships' moderate speed closed the gap with shocking abruptness.

Cymbals clashed again. For a moment Garric heard only the hiss of water past the lithe hulls. Then—

Wood crackled; then the screams started. Two of the vessels drifted sideways in a tangle. The screaming continued.

Lord Waldron was cursing; Master Koprathu moaned at the damage to his stores, half a dozen oars at least on one of the triremes. The other councillors gasped or gaped depending on whether they were more horrified or entertained by the spectacle.

Garric was glad that Liane was in the palace, arbitrating in the handover of accounts between Lord Tadai's aides and those of Pterlion, the new treasurer. She knew better than most of the men what the carnage would be like within the vessel whose crew had been too slow.

Carus watched through Garric's eyes, grimly approving. *"Not bad, considering,"* he murmured silently. *"They're coming along."*

"There're men *dead* there," Garric said, barely aloud.

The king in Garric's mind shrugged and said, *"Lose a few in training, or lose an army the first time they do it for real. You've got a good commander in young Zettin."*

"I doubt you'll ever make scum like that into sailors," Waldron growled. "And I know on my oath as a bor-Warriman that they'll never be soldiers!"

"I disagree, milord," Attaper said, politely but without deference. His family was as good as Waldron's, though the older man could buy Attaper a hundred times over. They were careful to keep emotion out of their exchanges, but neither was willing to pass a point where it looked like the other was grasping for power or status. "I can't say what they'd be like fighting as individual duelists, but that isn't what they're trained to do. Shoulder to shoulder in a block sixteen ranks deep, they'll stand as firm as the Customs Tower."

"If the Kingdom of the Isles is to be more than Ornifal," Garric said, "the rulers of other islands have to believe we're able to force them to our will if needs must."

"We beat the Earl of Sandrakkan at the Stone Wall and put King Valence on the throne!" Waldron snapped. "Using proper soldiers, landholders and not lower-class dirt who can't even afford to buy their own pikes and shields!"

"Aye!" said Garric. Carus spoke through him, and it took all of Garric's control to prevent his hand from straying to the hilt of his sword. "And the king's soldiers lay becalmed for three days on the sailing ships that carried them, baking in the heat and puking their guts up as they rocked on the swells. How near was it that Valence left his head on a Sandrakkan spear, Waldron, and the Earl of Sandrakkan became King of the Isles as a result? How near?"

"Fagh!" Waldron shouted. His right hand clenched. Blood Eagles standing discreetly in the background suddenly shifted their attention from spectators eyeing the group of dignitaries to the dignitaries themselves. Lord Attaper reached up with his left hand and loosed the clasp of his cloak; he was preparing to wrap the garment around his left arm for a shield.

Waldron turned his back, then kicked angrily at the servant standing nearby with a tray of gauze-covered marzipan for the councillors to nibble as they watched. The fellow yelped and leaped back, but he didn't drop the tray.

"Lord Waldron," Garric said. He was shuddering; furious at his ancestor's temper and furious at himself for not checking it sooner. "I apologize for my tone. I will not be swayed from my plan of using a phalanx of oarsmen as the core of the kingdom's battle line, but I meant no disrespect to you. *Your* troops held at the Stone Wall."

"Sorry, lad," whispered Carus. *"I won't let you down again."*

Waldron nodded, but he didn't trust himself yet to turn. "You weren't born when we fought at the Stone Wall, boy," he said in a voice like stones sliding. "Prince Garric. I commanded our left wing, and I say to you—"

At last he faced Garric, forcing his lips into a jagged smile.

"Never again! I think you'd do better to use yeomen rather than gutter sweepings, but I gave my oath to serve you. The kingdom can't survive another battle like the Stone Wall; and as you say, it barely survived the first one."

Garric took two strides and clasped right arms with Lord Waldron. Royhas and Attaper hopped out of the way, blank-faced.

"I've a notion for using more heavy infantry on the ships to protect the flanks of the phalanx," Garric said. His voice still trembled. "Trireme hulls with one set of oars and a double crew of pikemen to row in shifts, with the third set of benches for your Northern District yeomen. But for now the pikemen are better value for the money, at a silver Lady a day instead of the two a heavy infantryman earns."

Waldron nodded understanding, though a frown he couldn't control furrowed his brow. They stepped apart, both of them glad nothing worse than words had eventuated.

"He's smart enough," Carus said, assaying Waldron through Garric's eyes, *"and he's a better than fair general. But though he can see the advantage of being able to get*

*troops where they're needed without waiting on winds,
he's frightened by how fast things are changing. Just don't
use the word 'frightened' to his face."*

"We've been able to manage thus far on the wealth the
queen had sequestered," Royhas said, surveying traffic on
the river to avoid looking at Garric and Waldron. "That
can't continue forever, though."

Garric had returned property when the owners or their
heirs could be identified, but a great deal of the queen's
treasure came from no certain victim or from families
which had perished utterly in the queen's ruthlessness.
Those monies had paid the expenses of government since
Garric took charge.

"It won't have to, Royhas," said Pterlion in a peevish
tone. The chancellor's comment had trespassed on the treasurer's domain, and Pterlion was as much at pains as any
householder to prevent encroachment by his neighbors.
"The taxes are coming in quite nicely, and I'll see to it
that they continue to do so."

"Which should be easy enough, now that the Royal
Army isn't a joke anymore," Attaper said with a grim
smile.

Garric looked at the commander of the Blood Eagles.
He liked and respected Attaper, but . . .

"Lord Attaper," he said, "my ancestor Carus used to
think that a strong sword arm was the best way to insure
his orders were obeyed. If he stood before you now—"

Garric's smile and that of the king in his mind were
identical.

"—he'd be the first to tell you that he was wrong in that
belief. Our soldiers aren't tax gatherers."

Garric paused, letting his grin grow broader. "Though
there might be a case when marching a few well-
disciplined regiments through a district would convince the
folk there that their taxes were being well spent."

The ships in the basin had re-formed. The triple call
sounded. The triremes started toward one another again, all
ten of them, though the vessel with a dozen dead or injured

crewmen on its narrow deck lagged behind the others in its division.

"Oh, may the Sister drag me down!" Koprathu moaned. "He's going to do it again!"

Lord Waldron unexpectedly laughed. "I don't know that I'd care to serve under your friend Zettin, Attaper," he said. "But I wouldn't mind having a bold man like him at my side if it came to strokes."

Attaper gave a nod and a slight smile to acknowledge his rival's apology. It was as close as Waldron could come to an apology, at any rate. "The kingdom can use bold men, Waldron," he said aloud, "though I hope Zettin doesn't prove overbold."

The warships coasted past one another. The rowers had all shipped their oars in time. The vessels passed noticeably farther apart than they had in the first sweep-through.

"It's better to lose a few men in training," Garric said with a wry smile that only the man he was quoting would understand, "than to lose a fleet the first time they do it for real."

Attaper and Waldron looked at Garric oddly. They were both hard men when the need was; it surprised them, though, to hear a youth like Garric sounding just as pragmatic as they were.

Zettin's trumpets blew a long attention call, followed by a quick tattoo of cymbals. The triremes formed in line ahead and followed their leader upriver to the sheds at a stately pace. Water slipped in silver showers from the oar-blades as they feathered and dipped for another stroke.

"In a few months," Garric said, "before the end of the sailing season, at least, I'll pay a friendly visit to Sandrak-kan and Blaise in the new Royal Fleet. The Lady and the general contrariness of fate permitting, of course."

"Wildulf and Lerdoc can either one put more troops in the field than we'll have trained by then, Your Highness," Attaper warned. Even in private, where the other councillors said "Garric" with Garric's full approval, the Blood Eagles' commander used formal address for his prince.

"So they can," Royhas said, entering the discussion as chancellor of the Kingdom of the Isles that he and Garric alone of this group foresaw. The others members of the council were Ornifal nobles first, last, and only. They visualized the kingdom as an extension of Ornifal power in the rare cases that they thought about the kingdom at all. "In a week, would you say, Lord Waldron?"

The old soldier snorted. "In two weeks they might have half the nobles' household troops gathered. The rest won't dribble in for two months, those who show up at all. As I know well."

He grinned wryly, obviously thinking of the struggle he'd had to raise support from his fellow northern landholders to garrison Erdin against the queen's return. "As for the local militias, anywhere from a month to never, not that they'd be much use except for skirmishers anyway."

"We're building a kingdom for every citizen of the Isles," Garric said. His voice filled and deepened, but without the harsh, hectoring tone of minutes before when he faced Waldron's disparagement of folk not of his own class. "Lerdoc of Blaise and Wildulf of Sandrakkan want to go their own ways, but that makes it harder for them to convince their own nobles to jump to what the count or the earl says."

"Many a local landholder would rather see a strong king off in Valles," King Carus noted. His grin widened into a broad smile. *"Or Carcosa, it may be once again—than they would their own baron a few hours away have all the power* he *wants. And they're right to feel that way!"*

The triremes had passed out of sight into the channel leading to the naval arsenal. Garric sighed, knowing it was time to return to the palace but enjoying the last of these moments of relative freedom.

The noblemen had come in their individual carriages. The vehicles waited on the margin of the highway, each driver grooming his pair of horses while the postilions polished brightwork or the leather seats. Garric had chosen to ride with Pterlion to get a feeling for how the fellow—a distant cousin of Tadai's—was doing in his post, and to make it clear to Royhas that the new treasurer was a full member of Garric's council. Like so many of the suggestions that guided Garric through political snares and deadfalls, this one had come from Liane.

The Blood Eagles' horses cropped coarse grass nearby. Normally cavalry operating dismounted would detail every fifth man as a horseholder. The bodyguards—who considered themselves mounted infantry rather than cavalry anyway—brought grooms for the purpose so that all of them were ready to protect the prince with their swords and their lives.

"I promised Liane I'd be back before midday to go over the petitions," Garric said aloud, "and it's almost that now. Royhas, if you don't mind I'll ride—"

A trim carriage trotted down the road from the city behind a handsome pair of mules. The only thing that made it different from a wealthy shopkeeper's vehicle on the way to a riverside picnic was its escort: four mounted Blood Eagles leading, and four more riding behind.

"As the Lady smiles on me!" Garric said. "That's Liane driving!"

And Tenoctris in the seat beside her, Garric saw. His councillors turned to peer beyond the backs of the guards around them.

Few but professional teamsters and the scions of wealthy households could drive with any skill. Liane had learned on the vast estates her father owned on Sandrakkan before wizardry led to his disgrace. Now that opportunity returned she was indulging her hobby with considerable panache. Tenoctris' lips pursed with concern as Liane drove the carriage over the paved drainage swale bordering the highway, bouncing first one wheel and then the other high in the process.

"My lords and Master Koprathu," Garric resumed, "I believe we're done here. I thought to share your coach on the trip back, Royhas, but it seems that other arrangements have been made."

"I regret losing the chance to discuss district assessors with you, Your Highness," Royhas said—smiling, but with an undertone of real dismay in his voice. "You'll certainly have more attractive company this way, however."

Waving his leave to the councillors, Garric walked to the carriage rather than ordering the guards to let Liane through their lines. The Blood Eagles took their orders very literally—and given that one King of the Isles had been murdered by his own mother, perhaps that careful literalness was as it should be.

Garric squeezed Liane's hand, then swung up onto the rear-facing seat paired back-to-back with the one on which she and Tenoctris sat. "To the palace?" he asked, turning so that he sat sideways on the bench. He leaned forward to put his head between those of the two women.

"If you're done here," Liane said as she clucked the mules around in a tight circle. She touched the ear of the inside beast with her whip, as lightly as the brush of a butterfly's wing.

The guards assigned to Liane and Tenoctris fell in before and behind. The rank which guarded Garric himself ran for its horses and would clop along at a gallop until it caught the carriage. Garric thought of suggesting to Liane that she take it easy, but driving fast was one of the few things that really relaxed her.

"I wanted to see how the new crews were shaping up," Garric said, shouting over the roar of the iron tires on the pavement. His seat behind the axle jounced significantly more than the front one did. Tenoctris had started to offer him hers, but the old woman needed the relative comfort much more than Garric did. "And I wanted my councillors to see them also. Traditionally the fleet has been crewed by fishermen and bargees, so the concept of using laborers is new to Ornifal nobles."

"They aren't sailors?" Tenoctris asked curiously. The practical questions of kingship were of no real concern to her, but she had an inquiring mind that found interest in any puzzle or seeming paradox.

"Not when they're hired," Garric agreed. "But they're used to work—and to hardship. And there's worse things we could do than show the poorest folk, day laborers from Valles and the countryside, that they too can serve the kingdom if they like."

He stretched, one arm and then the other so that he could keep a hand firmly on the seat's railing. Liane brought the mules along with pops of her whip. The tip never quite touched the beasts, but it left them in no doubt as to what would happen if they slacked. At each *snap!* the mules' ears twitched.

"Tenoctris has reached a temporary impasse with her researches," Liane said, giving the wizard the brief nod that was all that could be spared from the driving.

"Ah," Tenoctris said, taking up her cue. She turned toward Garric while continuing to cling to the seat with both hands. "I haven't been able to penetrate the barriers separating me from the other plane in which the bridge is anchored, Garric. That would take more power than I have, or better tools; and the tools at least are available. This evening I hope to visit a wizard named Alman who has a viewing crystal. I normally couldn't, but I hope the bridge will ease my task sufficiently."

"And I'm going with her, to carry her equipment," Liane said, pointedly *not* looking at Garric. "You and I can review the petitions first, of course."

Garric laughed. They'd reached the outskirts of Valles proper; even with the Blood Eagles for outriders, Liane was having to slow down. He for one was thankful.

"Of course I'll go with you," he said affectionately in answer to the implied question.

"But you're busy," Tenoctris said. "There shouldn't be danger in this. I trust you beside me as I could few others, but I know you have more important duties."

"I have to be king," Garric said, "and it may be that I'll have to be a general. But if I can't be Garric or-Reise part of the time, I'll get as addled as last year's egg."

He put a hand on the shoulder of either woman. They

all three laughed together; and Carus, who'd never had even Garric's tolerance for the grinding *business* of kingship, guffawed in Garric's mind.

Ilna looked over the stern railing at the weeds and colorful fish as the vessel rocked at anchor in the clear water. On both ships the passengers stretched, gathered personal belongings they wanted to take ashore with them, and snarled at servants for clumsiness or stupidity, or simply because the voyage was uncomfortable and folk of rank liked to snarl at their inferiors.

"Is something wrong, Ilna?" Merota asked with a note of worry. The girl had been cheerful most of the day, excited by the glimpses of unfamiliar birds and fish.

"Wrong with the world?" Ilna said, barking a laugh. "Yes, but it isn't a new problem. Nothing to do with you, Merota."

Ilna grinned with amusement, an expression very different from her laugh of a moment before. The problem didn't affect her either. Nobody was going to take his bad temper out on Ilna os-Kenset.

Lord Neyral had been lounging amidships in the shade of the embroidered awning with Tadai and his top aides. When Vonculo called that they'd made the day's landfall, it took the nominal captain more than a minute to get up and walk back to the stern.

"Surely we can go farther today, Vonculo?" Neyral said as he joined his sailing master. "There's half the afternoon left, and the weather's fine."

"I think it's best that we overnight here, milord," Vonculo said. "There's firewood and firm ground to stake your tents on. And I'm not so confident about good weather as you are, though Your Lordship is doubtless my superior in reading the sky."

His tone was dismissive rather than directly insulting. It was, Ilna recalled with a flash of anger, much like the tone

Neyral himself had used when Ilna warned the commanders about the threat of mutiny.

"Is it really going to storm, Ilna?" Merota whispered. The warship's stern was very narrow, and much of the space was taken by the helmsman who stood holding the bar that worked the tillers of both steering oars together. The officers were close enough that Ilna could have touched them, but they were too focused on one another and their mutual anger to take note of what Merota or anyone else was saying.

Ilna glanced at the sky, clear except for high haze and cirrus clouds. Any countryman, let alone an experienced sailor like Vonculo, knew that there wouldn't be a storm this day or the next. "No, of course not," she said to the girl.

Mastyn watched the officers with an expression of sneering contempt from the trireme's bow. He held the line of the kedge anchor he'd cast over the side to hold the vessel while Neyral made a final decision about the landfall. The *Ravager* waited a bowshot away. Four oars bow and stern stroked slowly to keep the ship from drifting on the light current.

"Sister take it, man!" Neyral said. "How long are we to be bobbing hither and yon like this? I'd understood there was a good chance, a very good chance, that we'd be ashore in Erdin in three days' sail. It seems it'll take a *week* at the rate you've been going!"

"Perhaps the fine gentlemen in Valles told you the voyage would take a few days, my *lord*," Vonculo said, looking down the bridge of his nose at his captain. "The same ones who calculated the headway we'd make using only one bank of oars on ships loaded like priests coming home from a temple banquet! A sailor with practical experience could have told them that the currents set wrong for sailing west at this time of year, of course."

Ilna's eyes narrowed. Vonculo was lying. She knew nothing about currents and winds, but she could hear the way words shaped and wove. Neyral knew as little of seamanship as she did, and unlike Ilna anger shut his mind off completely. Not that the captain was ever going to be praised as one of the great thinkers of this age.

Lord Neyral flushed. "Well, you know what I th-think?" he cried in a high voice. "I th-think you're a, you're a—you're no good, Vonculo. I think that's why it's taking us so long on these Sister-cursed ships that roll all over the sea!"

Vonculo folded his arms across his chest. "Well, milord, you can replace me as you choose," he said distantly. "Perhaps you'd be better acting as your own sailing master. I can only offer you my best opinion, and if you prefer not to take it—well, that is Your Lordship's option."

Merota kept her eyes on the frigate birds circling overhead, but her little hand squeezed Ilna's hard. Ilna found a certain beauty in the birds' red throat sacs and their wings—long, narrow, and as crooked as sickle blades—but she knew that the girl was really watching distant things because she was so afraid of what was happening close by.

Lord Tadai had risen from his couch and was making his way sternward with Roubos and the other five Blood Eagles aboard. Despite their care, the weight of so many men moving made the vessel's narrow hull roll violently. Tadai's complexion was greenish, and two of his bodyguards seemed in little better condition.

"What's the problem?" Tadai asked. "Are we landing or aren't we?"

"I think we should go on, Tadai," Neyral said, his brow ridged with frustration. "We'll never get to Erdin if we don't use the daylight we have!"

Vonculo continued to stand with his arms folded. "Whatever the captain wishes," he said. "If the captain will direct me, I will carry out his orders precisely—even if that means tearing the bottoms out of the ships and drowning every man of us!"

Tadai looked in bilious amazement from one man to the other. "For pity's sake, Neyral," he said. "What's wrong with this place? It looks better than the one we camped on last night. And I for one wouldn't mind having something under my feet that didn't move!"

The captain clenched his fist, though who or what he'd thought of striking wasn't clear. He was obviously furious with Tadai for taking the sailing master's part; but Vonculo, the ship itself, and the whole pattern of reality were equally frustrating to him.

Ilna looked over the island with the experience of someone who'd traveled more than she cared to and who had a good eye for details. The islet rose a dozen feet above the sea though the tide was scarcely past full. It had no large trees, but beach plums and holly covered everything down to the surf. When the sea withdrew between sweeps of curling foam, Ilna saw rocks rather than sand or even coarse shingle like that on the shore of Barca's Hamlet.

Still, if they could get ashore it looked like a solid place to overnight. There was no sign of permanent habitation, which probably meant there was no drinkable water save what pooled after rainstorms.

"Yes, all right," Neyral said abruptly. "Yes, this is probably best. Bring the ship up on the beach. And—"

He glanced toward the second trireme. It was drifting closer to theirs on wind pressure, though the slow oar-strokes kept it headed into the current.

"—signal Captain Perra to land also."

"Rather than beach the ships, milord . . ." the sailing master said quickly. Vonculo had trembled with relief when Neyral gave in; his tone now was feverishly cheerful instead of sneering. "We'll hold them against the shore on oars until the passengers have landed, then back off a cable's length and anchor. The beach is too rocky to bring the ships up it. Besides, so steep a slope would break their spines."

"What?" Neyral said in surprise. Lord Tadai stopped and turned; he'd started forward when it looked as though the matter was decided. "Come now, Vonculo, if it's not safe to land here, then surely we *must* find a better place."

Ilna smiled faintly as she saw how matters were tending. Being marooned on this islet was a survivable way out of the impasse caused by a mutinous crew and commanders whose response to difficulty was to wish it wasn't happening. They were in a well-traveled region. She'd seen several vessels close enough to hail on each day of the voyage, so it shouldn't be long before she and the rest of the passengers were rescued.

Ilna had only duty before her in Erdin; Merota had less than that to draw her. They could afford to spend a few days drinking brackish water and eating clams.

"It's quite safe, milord," Vonculo said. His voice had the quivering brightness of gnats circling in a shaft of sunlight. "We'll leave half the crew aboard as an anchor watch. None of the other islands within the distance we could sail before dark are high enough for our passengers."

"The men can sleep on board?" Neyral said in mild surprise. "Well, if you say so, Vonculo."

Neyral turned away from the sailing master, muttering as he did so, "I'll be thankful to see Erdin and have a proper roof over my head, that I can tell you!"

Vonculo cupped his hands to bellow directions to the *Ravager*. Mastyn was already ordering the *Terror*'s crew into action.

Chalcus, the scarred sailor who'd watched with Ilna as the bosun preached mutiny, sat at the stroke oar on the starboard side. When he saw Ilna looking in his direction, he tapped the side of his nose with his index finger and grinned broadly.

Ilna glared back. *That one is far too full of his own cleverness!*

"Ilna?" Merota said in a small voice. "Is everything going to be all right?"

Ilna put her hand on the girl's shoulder. "Yes," she said, speaking quietly but not whispering; if the mutineers heard her, they could think what they would. "Your uncle's plans are about to change, and I suppose we'll be spending a few days on this island; but it's probably better this way."

Ilna checked the silken noose she wore around her waist, then the hank of short cords she carried in her left sleeve, and almost as an afterthought the sharp, bone-cased paring knife stuck through her sash. "We'll be fine," she said to the girl.

Ten of the bow oarsmen began a slow stroke. The flautist seated cross-legged beside Vonculo set the rhythm, blowing a stopped note for the pull and lifting his finger for a higher tone when the oars were to come out of the water. The trireme crunched slowly into the beach.

Mistress Kaline lay in the trireme's bow like a bundle of black rags. Merota's tutor didn't have enough status to claim a place under the awning amidships, and she'd been unwilling—or afraid—to come near Ilna since their first meeting.

Lord Tadai and many of his suite were bad sailors. Mistress Kaline was no sailor at all. She hadn't been able to eat since the ships left Valles, but she still lifted herself to the railing to retch every time a swell made the vessel pitch.

Ilna smiled harshly. At least the woman had learned to huddle by the lee rail after her first experience.

Under Mastyn's snarling direction, the ship's dozen deck crewmen hopped from the prow into the low surf. The bosun swung them the line of the light anchor he'd used to hold the vessel while Lord Neyral made up his mind to land here. The sailors ran well up the slope with it before hooking the flukes in the crevice of a weathered outcrop.

Oarsmen got up from their benches and unpinned a length of the extra decking that covered what had been the inner rows of benches on the port side. It had been fashioned to fit into mortises in the starboard bow, forming a gangplank for dignitaries who couldn't be expected to swarm down the sides of a warship.

Mistress Kaline had to move for the men to do their jobs. When she was slow getting to her feet, two sailors grabbed her like a roll of old sail and slung her onto the feet of the folk standing near the vessel's centerline.

Sailors on shore staked the gangplank's foot into the rocky soil. Foam washed the boards, but by now occasional waves had combed the vessel's deck often enough to soak the footgear of Lord Tadai and all his aides. A warship might be the surest method of traveling from one island to another, but no one would call it a comfortable one.

The first down the gangplank were servants, Mistress Kaline among them. The vessel shuddered side to side, but rowers kept it upright by thrusting the blades of their oars into the land.

Tadai's party moved forward behind a pair of Blood Eagles. The guards were armed with shields, helmets and body armor, and their spears were poised to thrust or throw. They were ready for any enemy who lurked among the twisted stems of the vegetation.

Ilna smiled; or sneered, it probably depended on the state of mind of whoever might be watching. "Let's go," she said to Merota, slinging her own modest bindle of effects. "The sooner this is over with, the sooner we can get on with our real business."

Empty and bleak though that prospect seemed for both of them. Well, Ilna hadn't designed the pattern into which the world had chosen to weave her.

Shepherding the girl carefully ahead of her, Ilna walked to the trireme's bow. A sailor more intent on his work than his surroundings blocked them. Merota shied away; Ilna cleared the human obstruction with a crisp "Watch yourself!"

She didn't voice the rest of the sentence—"Or it'll be the worse for you!"—but her tone commanded obedience.

She smiled. Perhaps she was wrong to believe the implied threat had anything to do with it: all these sailors might be decent fellows who leaped with embarrassment when reminded of their manners.

"Did you say something, Ilna?" Merota asked nervously.

"I was thinking," Ilna said truthfully, "that perhaps pigs would fly. But not, I think, in my lifetime."

They'd reached the gangplank. The trireme was lively,

now. With so many of the passengers and crew ashore, the vessel was fully afloat except for the long bronze-sheathed ram driven hard into the slope. If the ship was being drawn on shore for the night, it would have had its curving stern-post to the land.

Chalcus, braced against his oarloom, grinned as Ilna and the girl passed him. "May your stay be a fortunate one, mistress," he said, forcing a lilt into his voice despite the obvious strain of fighting gravity to hold the warship steady.

The bosun glared at them both. Mastyn moved with stiff-limbed tension like a cat preparing for a fight. Ilna glanced coldly at him as she followed Merota onto the gangplank. She didn't bother to acknowledge Chalcus in any way.

Merota wore a sensible tunic and cape instead of the ridiculous outfit in which she'd been draped at the start of the voyage. Mistress Kaline was too sick to badger her charge into foolishness, and Tadai had other things on his mind. Ilna wished the child had sturdier footgear than the velvet slippers she was wearing, but there wasn't time to worry about that now.

Merota gasped when she stepped onto the rocky ground. She tried to walk on the balls of her feet, hopping stiff-legged like a stilt-walker. Ilna caught the girl by the shoulders and half-carried her up the beach to where the soil hadn't been washed away by every tide.

Ilna herself was barefoot, but she'd gone barefoot eight months of the year in Barca's Hamlet. Her calluses might have softened some on the soft turf of the palace grounds in Valles, but they were still thick enough to help Merota over the worst of these rocks.

"Be careful or you'll sprain your ankle," Ilna said tartly. "That's *all* we need."

"Lady Merota!" Mistress Kaline called in peevish anxiety. "Where are you—there you are, my lady! Come here at once."

Sharina had once told Ilna of a monster of legend—"legend" meant it wasn't really true, though Ilna had never understood why folk would tell stories that weren't true and even write them in books—who took his strength from the ground. Mistress Kaline seemed to be of the same race: the tutor had recovered as soon as she stepped onto more-or-less dry land. She was her old unpleasant self again.

Merota looked at Ilna questioningly. "Yes, go on," Ilna said, patting the girl on the shoulder.

Merota trotted off, calling, "Mistress Kaline? Do you have my box? The one with my parents' things?"

Ilna sighed and surveyed the island. Most of the vegetation was no taller than her shoulder, but the land rose from where she was standing near the shore. She started toward higher ground, not that she expected to find anything of great interest. It seemed a good idea to explore territory that she'd be spending days or possibly longer in.

"Mistress?" called an unfamiliar voice from behind Ilna. She ignored it until it continued at a higher note, "Mistress Ilna os-Kenset?"

Ilna turned. The speaker was some minor functionary of Tadai's suite who traveled on the other vessel. She hadn't bothered to learn his name. "Yes?" she said, with no pretense of wanting to waste time in the fellow's company.

"Mistress," he said, "I'm Understeward Mizo or-Doson, in charge of Lord Tadai's commissary for the voyage. You've been issued food and drink as though you were a member of Lord Tadai's suite, but in fact you're a private citizen. You shouldn't—"

His eyes met Ilna's; the flow of self-important nonsense stopped. An additional gurgle or two dribbled from Mizo's throat.

Ilna was of two minds about how to deal with this business. She'd considered three, really, but the third was no proper use for her powers. She reached for a silver piece to fling to the ground, sufficient pay and more for the simple fare she'd taken from the servant's store. She caught herself, though, not because she didn't have the money to spend but because she wasn't going to be imposed on by a worm like Mizo.

"Very well," Ilna said in syllables chipped from a glacier. "You will render me an account for the food and water—not drink, mind you, because I haven't touched your wine and I wouldn't use what passes for ale on this vessel to wash my floor with. I will pay the amount to you in the presence of Lord Tadai. Do you under—"

A trumpet blew harshly from the *Terror*. Sailors who'd come ashore stopped whatever they were doing and scrambled back aboard the triremes.

Lord Tadai glanced over his shoulder and returned to a discussion of the night's dinner with his cook, but Lord Neyral shouted angrily at the men who were nominally under his command. He'd been personally directing the party that would clear brush to erect his tent and that of the ambassador.

Ilna smiled faintly. "As I was saying—" she resumed. Merota screamed.

Ilna turned with a terrible lack of expression. The girl should be perfectly safe with Mistress Kaline, but—

The sailors had thrown down the gangplanks—cast them loose from the railing instead of pulling the stakes up from the rocky shore. Merota, the red silk lining of her cape flaring, struggled in the arms of a man in the *Terror*'s bow. She clutched a casket made of blackwood and mother-of-pearl.

The girl had asked about "my parents' things" as she joined her tutor. Ilna suddenly realized that Merota would have very little by which to remember her parents and the childhood which had perished in flame with them. Mistress Kaline had been in no condition to bring the casket of mementos or anything else as she'd staggered from the ship.

So Merota had gone back to get them.

Ilna started toward the vessel. Lieutenant Roubos and the handful of Blood Eagles closest to him rushed into the water, bellowing with their shields held high. Other soldiers formed a loose knot around Lord Tadai.

Most of the crewmen had moved toward the trireme's

stern. Some rowed, while the rest used their weight to lower the stern and lift the bow. A dozen sailors under Mastyn had taken cutlasses and pikes from the arms chest. They waited in the bow to confront the oncoming Blood Eagles.

"Come back here!" Lord Neyral shouted. "What are you doing? Vonculo! What are you doing?"

Exactly what I told you they were going to do, you titled fool, Ilna thought as she waded into the sea. She snatched up the hem of her tunic and tucked it under the sash so that it wouldn't drag in the salt water. She was already up to her mid-thighs; she couldn't swim, and she didn't know how quickly the beach dropped off.

The trireme backed very slowly, but it had cleared its ram and the rest of the oarsmen were seating themselves at their benches. The Blood Eagles splashed out after the vessel, though Ilna couldn't imagine what they thought they were going to achieve. A sailor thrust with his pike. Roubos blocked the point with his shield. The sailor leaned his weight onto the shaft, pushing Roubos over in the water. Sailors cheered and catcalled at the soldiers floundering below them.

The flautist blew time. Oarblades poised, then threshed forward in unison. Ilna judged the rhythm. She caught the nearest blade with both arms and pulled herself up the shaft.

The oarsman blatted in surprise at the unexpected burden. Ilna squirmed to avoid being scissored as the next oar sternward clacked into the one she was climbing. She clamped her knees on the shaft and twitched her noose free with one hand. The fibers were damp, but they'd run freely nonetheless.

The rower looked over the railing to see what was binding his oar. Ilna tossed the noose over his neck.

The sailor squawked once as the cord pulled tight. Ilna climbed the rest of the way aboard, using her victim's weight to anchor her. His limbs flailed and his tongue protruded stiffly from his lips.

The *Terror* floated freely, sliding seaward in a curve now because Ilna's appearance had disrupted the stroke of the rowers in the starboard bow. They sat too far inboard to see what was happening close by the hull. They shouted when they saw Ilna coming over the side as if she were some monster of myth. She'd approached from the side of the ship unnoticed while Mastyn and his henchmen concentrated on the soldiers rushing straight at the prow.

Ilna's face was a mask of cold anger. *They'll find me worse than any lying myth could be!*

She dropped the noose. The strangling sailor's fellows pulled him away, loosening the cord that hadn't quite killed him. He lay in his friends' arms, wheezing and gasping obliviously as they stared at the sea-dripping woman who'd throttled him.

Ilna slipped cords out of her sleeve; her fingers knotted several lengths together. The pattern hidden by her palms was as complex as a dragonfly's darting flight above a pond in summer.

Vonculo was in the stern, shouting as he tried to see what was happening farther forward. Some men were still at their oars, but others had risen to their feet and blocked the sailing master's view.

Shouts behind them turned the armed sailors under Mastyn in the bow; they'd been gibing as the Blood Eagles sloshed back to dry ground. Roubos leaned on the arm of a subordinate, coughing and spluttering. His weak leg and the weight of his armor had kept him under water for a dangerously long time when the pikeman tipped him over.

"Let go of the child!" Ilna said to the man holding Merota.

"Easy, mistress," the fellow said. It was Chalcus! He took his left arm from about Merota's waist and sent the girl down the deck toward Ilna with a pat. "I was only keeping her safe till you arrived."

Chalcus was grinning. His right hand held a single-edged sword whose tip bent downward in an inward curve that would put more weight behind a stroke. It wasn't one of the cheap weapons from the ship's store: the blade had gold chasing near the hilt and was as sharp as vain regret.

"I'm safe now!" Merota said, burying her face against Ilna's side. "They won't hurt me!"

"Throw them in the sea!" Mastyn said. "Prick the bitch with your pikes if you don't want to touch her!"

In the confusion the oarsmen had stopped rowing, but the trireme continued to wallow outward on a combination of momentum and the mild current. The bow was a hundred feet from the shore, and the water under the keel was too deep for Ilna to see the bottom when she glanced down.

The *Ravager* had backed off the island at the same time and was under proper control. Its helmsman—the sailing master was on shore with the abandoned passengers— shouted "What's going on there?" across the water to Vonculo.

None of the armed sailors moved toward Ilna. Mastyn tried to push one forward; the fellow shrugged away from the pressure.

"May sea demons drown every one of you pack of cowards!" Mastyn cried. He strode toward Ilna with his cutlass raised. Chalcus cocked an eyebrow in query to Ilna, then stepped out of the bosun's way.

Ilna spun her pattern of cords toward Mastyn. He screamed and slashed wildly at something no one else could see. Chalcus dropped flat on the deck; the cutlass smacked wetly into the shoulder of a pikeman beside him.

Mastyn snatched his cutlass free among screams and a welter of blood, then chopped downward. Chips of pine decking and three of the bosun's own toes flew up at the *thunk!* of the blade.

A sailor grabbed Mastyn from behind. The madman twisted free and cut downward again, lopping off his left foot above the ankle.

The man who'd tried to help ducked out of the way. Mastyn toppled forward and went over the side. He was still screaming at an invisible horror when the sea covered his face

"Now the rest of you . . ." Chalcus said, stepping between Ilna and the remainder of his armed fellows. "Step back and give our guest some room. Mastyn like to have topped me when he nutted, and I don't need one of you lot finishing the job."

The sailor Mastyn had wounded when he went berserk lay on the deck with two of his fellows trying to stanch the blood. Ilna doubted they could do much for the victim. The cutlass had cut to the bone, a remarkable blow with a blade that was none too sharp. The bosun had used a madman's strength in his last moments, of that there was no doubt.

A sailor near the jib pole bitts raised his pike tentatively. Chalcus pointed his own weapon at the fellow's face and said, "Did you hear me, Andro?"

The pikeman lowered his point. Disease had left deep pits on his face above the line of his beard and mustache. "Getting soft, Chalcus?" he snarled.

"Maybe, Andro," Chalcus said in a tone that lilted as pleasantly as it did in his chanteys. Despite the kink in the blade's tip, a thrust with Chalcus' shoulders behind it would carry the sharp point through the front and back both of Andro's chest. "But not so soft that I won't feed you bits of your own liver if you cross me on this."

Ilna smiled despite herself. Now, *that* was a promise she'd be willing to wager her small hope of redemption on.

Vonculo and two sailors with capstan bars struggled through the press amidships to halt a dozen feet from Ilna. The sailing master held a bow with an arrow nocked. "What's going on here?" he said. His voice shimmered with rage and fear. "What's happened to Mastyn?"

"He started swinging his cutlass at whoever was close," Chalcus said mildly, turning to face the sailing master. He lowered his sword so that the point was near the deck. "He went over the side, but he's killed Ipis or I'm a nun."

Chalcus' sword flicked in the direction of the victim.

His fellows seemed to have stanched the blood, but the wounded man's face was sallow and his whole body was beginning to shiver despite the hot sun.

Ilna grimaced. She broke the knots into which she'd fixed another set of cords and retied them in a wholly different pattern.

"Sister take him!" Vonculo said in bitter desperation. "I have the course but he's the only one who knew anything more."

His eyes focused on Ilna and Merota again. "What are you doing here?" he demanded.

"The girl came aboard," Ilna said. "I came after her."

"She's a wizard," muttered someone behind his hand; maybe the pikeman, Andro.

"I've heard that," Vonculo said without expression. He stared at Ilna coldly, then went on, "You can go over the side now, mistress, or you can come with us to where we're going. Which will it be?"

Ilna detached Merota's arms gently and knelt beside the wounded sailor. The men holding him flinched back. She spread her new pattern of knots before the victim's blank eyes. His body relaxed and color started to return to his skin.

Ilna stood. "Get the cut bandaged properly," she snapped to the men who'd acted as nurses. "I can bring him out of shock, but that won't help long if all his blood drains out."

She turned and looked at the sailing master. Reaching out, she linked her hand with Merota's again. The island and the folk marooned upon it were a good bowshot away by now.

"Lady Merota and I will accompany you," Ilna said without expression. There were too many of them to fight, even with her weapons, and what would she do if she did manage to send them all over the side? Drift till she and the girl starved, she supposed.

"Glad to have you aboard, mistress," Chalcus said from behind her. "Some of us are, at any rate."

Chapter Eleven

The bridge was still transparent—Garric could see occasional lanterns on the far shore of the Beltis, gleaming through the fabric of light—but it had become solid. It seemed more real than the silent buildings on the riverside, in fact.

"The streets are so *dead*," Liane said, looking around at the nearby tenements. "Where has everybody gone?"

When Garric first visited, the Bridge District had been bustlingly full of people—ordinary residents going on with their lives as well as the crowd viewing the apparition hanging above the river. The activity had reminded him of the way termites pour out of their nests in late spring, spreading to new habitations. Cheap wine, vegetables cooking, fish offal, human wastes, and a thousand lesser odors blended to give the atmosphere a bubbling, vibrant life.

Now the smells were stale. Smoke from charcoal fires no longer hung in the air. The shops on the ground floors of the buildings had their shutters locked down, and the stairs to the apartments on the upper levels were silent instead of echoing with the cries of children and the adults responsible for them.

A creature of red light ran down the street, tossing its head in anger. It looked like a bull, but it was eight feet tall at the shoulder and its nostrils snorted flame. For an instant its hooves hammered and sparked on the cobblestones; then the sound ceased and the creature's image began to fade. It started across the bridge before vanishing from the eyes of Garric and his companions. He thought he heard another flurry of hoof strikes; then nothing.

"The residents left because they're afraid," Tenoctris said as Liane helped her out of the sedan chair. The others in the party were on foot; the guards because Garric was, and Liane for the same reason though he'd have been as happy to have her carried at his side in another chair. "They're right to be afraid."

The escort of Blood Eagles shouldered their shields again when the bull disappeared, though they couldn't be said to have relaxed. Besimon, the commander of the escort, grimaced at Garric, but he didn't try to urge his prince to leave this dangerous location.

Garric would rather walk than be carried—and he'd rather have crawled than ride a horse, though sometimes horses were the only practical means of transportation. King Carus had been an experienced rider; his reflexes would keep Garric on even a mettlesome animal. But Garric's muscles would be the ones aching the next morning, and nothing could make him *like* being at the mercy of a beast that weighed six or eight times as much as he did.

"It reminds me of Klestis when I'm dreaming," Garric said. "The buildings still stand, but everybody's gone from them."

"Like a city that's been captured after a siege," Carus said, watching through Garric's eyes but analyzing their surroundings with the mind of an experienced man of war. *"Though there'd be more smoke then. And there'd be the smell of death; that you wouldn't miss."*

A detachment of the City Watch approached, jogging down a side street; they must've been warned that the prince was visiting the district. There were four in the squad instead of the six that would have been its full strength.

Besimon went to meet the City Watchmen. The squad's officer wore a silvered helmet and carried a sword; the three ordinary Watchmen had brass helmets and hardwood staves with a knob on one end. Their metal equipment shimmered with the cold blue glare of the bridge.

"Danger from the bull?" Liane asked.

"Danger from things like the thing that took the semblance of a bull," Tenoctris said. "There's always a risk when planes of the cosmos leak into one another; and there are some planes whose inhabitants pose a very great risk to any humans with whom they come in contact."

Garric turned from watching Besimon and the Watchmen. "And to Sharina?" he asked.

Liane took the satchel with Tenoctris' paraphernalia from the tray under the chair. The old wizard shrugged. "I'm sure by now that Sharina was abducted deliberately, not simply taken by one of the entities entering through this weak point in the cosmos. There's risk to her, of course; but—"

She smiled. Tenoctris looked decades younger when she did that.

"—probably less danger than there is to the rest of us, standing here. I need the bridge's weight on the fabric of the cosmos to pass us to where we'll find Alman; but the sooner we're away, the safer we'll be."

"Ah," said Garric as another thought struck him. "Do you need me to help set up?"

"I need only someone to hold the lantern," Tenoctris said. "Liane can do that."

"Right," Garric said, nodding. "I'll join you soon."

He walked over to Besimon and the Watchmen. Instead of letting Garric step through them, thirty of the Blood Eagles strode forward to preserve their cordon about him. The other twelve moved toward the bridge with the two women, the parties for whose safety they were responsible.

The two bearers stood beside the sedan chair. They looked nervously after the soldiers, though Garric wondered how much protection the troops' weapons really gave against threats like the bull-thing that had passed a moment before.

"Undercommander Copelo here has been telling me that the buildings for three blocks around are deserted during the nighttime, Your Highness," Besimon said as he turned to face Garric. He used a professional tone, but it was obvious from the way the Blood Eagle stood—slightly shielding the Watchman with his body—that he sympathized with the fellow. "He and his men patrol the edges of the area, but not as a general rule along the river itself."

"Residents come back during daylight, some of them," Copelo said. His jaws worked, chewing moisture out of his dry cheeks. "Maybe half of them. But there's not the folks from the big houses visiting to gawk, and at night there's not even the thieves you'd expect with places empty the way they are. So we don't . . ."

His voice trailed off. He rubbed the pommel of his sword, staring at the cobblestones, and went on, "Ah, there's a lot of sickness in the squad already, and we don't . . ."

"I understand completely," Garric said. These men were braver than their fellows who claimed to be sick; and maybe those men weren't cowards either. If Garric let himself think about it, he'd be nervous too; the bridge had an eery *wrongness* as he stood beside it now, though when he crossed it in his dreams it was no more than an incident of his journey. "Take your men back to their normal patrol route."

Garric smiled; engagingly, he hoped. His own lips were dry. "Normal until my friends and I manage to remove this bridge, that is, I mean," he added.

The squad leader gave Garric a look of enormous relief and turned. "Let's—"

He paused and spun around again. "That is, yes, Your Highness!" He saluted by crossing right arm over his chest.

Garric waved Copelo away, smiling in amusement this time. "Besimon," he went on, "I want you to take your men—and those with Ladies Tenoctris and Liane—back a bowshot from here also. You won't be any use to us, and—"

"Your Highness, we're here to guard you," the Blood Eagle interrupted. "You can't—"

"We're not going to *be* here," Garric said. "This is a dangerous location, but Tenoctris is taking us through it to another place. When we come back, you can return to your duty."

"Oh," Besimon said. He glanced at the women. Tenoctris had sketched a figure on the cobblestones with a stick of lead and was now adding words of power around the perimeter. "We should come with you to—"

"Not unless you're a wizard yourself," Garric said, trampling the protest before Besimon got it out. "Tenoctris can only take the three of us."

"Oh," Besimon repeated. "Well, I—"

He caught himself. Drawing up in a brace, he saluted so firmly that his blackened-bronze cuirass bonged at the impact. "Yes, Your Highness."

Turning, Besimon shouted, "Form column of fours! His Highness has stationed us at the fountain we passed just up the street. On the double!"

The Blood Eagles trotted toward the nearby intersection with as much noise as a dozen brewer's drays: their hobnails crashed on the stone pavement, their aprons of studded leather strips rattled, and they drummed their spears against their shield bosses every time their right heels came down. The troops were obeying orders, but nobody could imagine that they were skulking away in fear.

Tenoctris was ready; she and Liane watched Garric as he stepped quickly back to them. The wizard had drawn a seven-pointed star in lime-wash on a slab that had been part of the abutments of the Old Kingdom bridge. The bridge that spanned universes, not the river, was close enough that Garric could have put his foot on its approaches. Would it support him as it did in his dreams?

"It'll be solid enough to walk on soon," Tenoctris said, demonstrating again a striking awareness of what those around her were thinking. "And I think we'll need to do that, or someone will. But for now I'm just using its presence to help us to Alman through—"

Carus' instincts, not Garric's eyes, warned Garric to turn before even Liane, who was looking toward Garric, reacted. He wasn't wearing body armor or a helmet, but he drew his long sword in a *sring!* of the patterned-steel blade against the scabbard's iron lip.

The man running toward them from the shadow of a tenement was a bulky blur. The wizard-light distorted the objects around it. Garric didn't see a weapon, but—

"Wait!" the figure cried in a squeal of rising fright. It flung its arms up in the air. "Garric, it's me!"

Garric slid his sword back in its sheath. He was trembling between laughter and fury. His mind understood that there was no danger, but his body would be keyed up to fight or flee for the Lady knew *how* long!

"Katchin," Garric said, "if one of Besimon's men had looked back and seen you, you'd have had a javelin between your shoulder blades. And that's just what you deserved."

The Blood Eagles faced around in front of the cracked stone basin, all that remained of the fountain which had graced the plaza under the Old Kingdom. The bronze statue—*"A nymph on a sea horse,"* Carus remembered inconsequentially, and Garric had a vision of these same streets when his ancestor paraded through Valles a thousand years before—had been stolen or melted into coins centuries past. If Besimon noticed in the deceptive lighting that Garric's party was now four, not three, he nonetheless kept himself and his troops where Garric had ordered them to be.

"Now Garric, Garric," Katchin the Miller said in a tone of oily fullness. "It's your own fault that I had to meet you this way. Your fault for not keeping your servants in check, that is, but I well know how hard it is to get decent help these days."

Garric had known the miller all his life. He recognized the manner as the one Katchin displayed to wealthy drovers who came to Barca's Hamlet during the Sheep Fair. Its bantering attempt to claim equality was very different from the way Katchin abjectly fawned on real nobles, and more different still from the boastfully superior fashion in which he treated—or tried to treat—all his neighbors in the borough.

Liane looked furious. If Garric hadn't been so clearly in charge, she'd have shouted for Besimon to come rid them of this distraction. As it was, her habit of polite deference trapped her.

Tenoctris looked on with her usual expression of mild interest toward matters that didn't affect her directly. She held the brush with which she'd drawn the figure for her incantation. Apparently she intended to use it as her wand as well.

"You didn't hear what I said, Katchin," Garric said quietly. "Those men there would have *killed* you if they'd seen you running toward me. They practice with their weapons for three hours a day."

"But Gar—" Katchin began.

Garric reached out and took the older man's chin between his right thumb and forefinger. He didn't squeeze hard, but he lifted Katchin's jaw slightly and clipped the words off behind the teeth.

"Katchin, you knew you had no business here," Garric said. "You're too foolish to realize that you were risking your life, even now that I've told you in the clearest words I can imagine. You know that you gave up all pride to beg for a job, though."

He released Katchin, who stepped back gasping and wide-eyed. For a moment Garric thought that he'd understood, but a moment later Katchin's face re-formed itself into familiar lines.

"Well, I knew you'd want to have me in a position of trust," Katchin said, his voice returning to fullness and roundness with each syllable. "Tried friends from your home are too rare to waste. And the truth is, of course, I'm the only person in the borough with the experience to serve in this larger arena. I'm Count Lascarg's bailiff, you know."

"Katchin, you're right that I know you well," Garric said. He smiled in amusement that the miller could say all those things not only with a straight face but with obvious belief. Everybody in the borough knew that Katchin the Miller was a windbag, a liar, and a cheat; albeit a wealthy windbag, liar, and cheat.

Everybody knew that but Katchin himself, apparently.

"Ah!" Katchin said. "Now I don't want to complain about Reise, Garric—"

Garric raised a hand. Katchin continued, "I know he raised you, but—"

Garric reached out again. Katchin clapped both hands over his mouth and fell silent. His eyes bulged at Garric in horror.

"I'm sure that with the way the royal service has expanded . . ." Garric said. He tried to keep his voice steady, but a little of the passion came through. He'd always hated bullies, even after he'd grown to where they couldn't bully *him*. "I'm sure we've employed other men as bad as you are, Katchin: petty tyrants who grind down their subordinates and the citizens who have to deal with them, but who fawn on anybody who seems to have power. I'm sure we've employed such men."

He leaned forward. Katchin was of average height for Haft; Garric was taller than most people from Ornifal, where men averaged a handspan taller than those of Haft. He towered over the miller.

"But they were hired because I didn't know them," Garric said, letting his voice rise. He wasn't shouting; not yet at least. "I do know you. Go home, Katchin. Go home now!"

"But I've come all this way at my own expense!" the miller wailed through the fence of his fingers. He sounded on the verge of crying.

"And I'm telling you to go back!" Garric said. "Go treat your neighbors like neighbors, not as sheep to be sheared by loans at crippling interest—the way you robbed your own brother! Not like dirt to be trampled on for the sake of your pretensions. If you can prove to me that you're a man worthy of promotion, then maybe at some day in the

future I'll come back to Barca's Hamlet and take you into
my service. And even if I don't, Katchin, then you'll still
have had the good fortune to have become a worthy man!"

"But . . ." Katchin said. He *was* crying.

"Get away from here," Liane said in a vibrant contralto.
Her tone gave Garric the mental image of a cultured lady
removing a dead rat from her best parlor. "You don't belong, and besides it's dangerous. Go away or I'll call the
soldiers to remove you."

Katchin turned and blundered off. He walked like a
drunkard.

Garric put his fingertips on his brows and kneaded his
cheeks hard with his palms. He felt queasy. "Tenoctris,"
he said with his eyes still closed, "can you start now?
Maybe I'll feel better if I can get away from this place."

"Yes, of course," the old wizard said.

Tenoctris put her left hand on Garric's wrist to steady
herself, then settled to the pavement by crossing her legs
beneath her. Liane held the small cushion which she'd
taken from the satchel. Waiting till she was sure where the
old woman would light, she slid it beneath her thin but-
tocks.

Tenoctris sighed and let go of Garric. "You might keep
a hand on my shoulder, though," she said apologetically to
him. "In case I get dizzy and fall over."

"Sure," said Garric. He rested his fingertips on Tenoctris' collarbone.

Sometimes Garric wondered if the work of reuniting the
Isles might be easier if Tenoctris were younger and health-
ier, but . . . Tenoctris' mind, not her body, was the important factor.

If Tenoctris' flesh had been stronger, perhaps her pre-
ternatural awareness of how cosmic forces interplayed
would have been less acute. Others could help the wizard
with physical strength, as Garric was doing now. No one
but Tenoctris—no one Garric or King Carus before him
had met—could thread through the maze of power and
chaos to reach the world's survival on the other side.

"Are we to call out the spell with you?" Liane asked softly. She stood across the seven-pointed star from Garric; her hands were tented before her breast.

"No, I'll speak this myself," Tenoctris said. She gave a wry smile and added, "Since we're so close to the bridge, I think one iteration will be enough. I hope so, at least."

Garric looked along the span of light dwindling into the distance. It looked real, as though formed of sunlit blue stone. The shimmer of its surface was no more than a normal roadway might show at noon in summer.

"Pan," murmured Tenoctris. Her wand dipped and rose. *"Paipan, epaipan . . ."*

The waning moon was low over the west bank of the Beltis. Its silver crescent glowed red, then blue and back again to red, alternating with each syllable from the wizard's mouth. Garric swallowed.

"Kore bazagra oreochore . . ." Tenoctris said. Garric felt her heart beating faster and her body tremble. A vortex of blue wizard-light spun from the center of the star, expanding to envelop the three of them. Its touch was like the edge of an ice sword, slicing through Garric's flesh and soul together.

"Iphibe," Tenoctris said. She breathed explosively between words now. *"Amphibe, erode, antheme . . ."*

The vortex froze, encircling Garric and his friends like a cone of blazng sapphire. The world outside, the bridge and the buildings of Valles in Garric's own day, began to spin widdershins. The motion was slow at first. It built to the speed of a pirouetting dancer, then that of a top.

"Kolasseis!" Tenoctris cried. *"Poine! Rheneia!"*

The world swelled around them. The tenements rose into vast monoliths, taller than the cliffs of dream, and the soldiers standing at the next intersection with their shields advanced were giants painted in quick flickering sheets of red and blue wizard-light.

Garric fell out of the waking world. His right hand gripped Tenoctris by the shoulder, his left linked with Liane's hand. Her fingers were the only warmth in a cold as penetrating as that of the sunless depths of the sea.

Beyond the blazing wall around them Garric saw vortices of light spin sunwise into the night. Cobblestones writhed and lifted beneath them. Besimon must have shouted an order, because the troops cocked their spears ready to throw.

The universe sucked in on itself. The wall of wizardlight vanished, though the memory of its glare danced orange and purple at the back of Garric's eyeballs.

The world changed. Garric's feet had never left the ground, but instead of cobblestones there was sand beneath his boots. He staggered with an impact that was not of his weight shifting. Liane cried out and sank to her knees.

Garric caught Tenoctris in both arms to keep her from sprawling. Her face was pale and her pulse fluttered like a bird's.

They were in a desert creeping over the ruins of a once-great city. The skeletons of mighty buildings stood around them, some of them half-buried by pale dunes.

The air seemed thin and the stars were holes in the black sky. Coarse shrubs wriggled in the cold breeze.

Tenoctris raised her head. Garric kept an arm around her, for support and because this was no place to be without the touch of another human being. Liane's fingers linked with his again.

"I'd say that getting here was harder than I'd expected," Tenoctris said, managing a smile, "but in truth I wasn't sure that I was strong enough to bring us here at all. Now we need to find Alman."

"Someone lives here?" Liane said. The only movement about them was that caused by the wind.

"Alman didn't want to be disturbed," Tenoctris said softly. "He came to a place where no one else would choose to come."

"But we did," said Garric.

The wizard's smile transfigured her face the way sunrise brightens the gray sea. "I wouldn't say that we *chose* to come here," she said. "We didn't have a choice—if we want to preserve civilization."

Using Garric and Liane as braces, Tenoctris rose to her feet. She still held the brush. She pointed it toward the largest of the buildings on the horizon. "We'll try that, I think," she said. "If Alman isn't there, I'll have to speak another incantation."

"Will you be able to do that?" Garric asked. Tenoctris was panting just to stand in the thin air.

"If I have to," the old wizard said. She tried to smile. "If I have to."

She didn't object when Garric put his arm around her. They set off across the vast ruin, letting Tenoctris' small steps govern their pace.

The wind made a sound like steel rubbing steel, and the stars never blinked.

"Oh, sure," Krias shrilled from the ring. "Wander in here like one of your sheep, kill my master the first thing you do, and then you expect *me* to help you! That's just like your type."

Cashel wondered what his type was. It probably didn't matter. It was the sort of thing people said when they were mad and it wasn't enough to blame a man for what he'd done: you told him he was a type of fellow who did things, and that made it worse.

Apparently ring demons did that just like people did.

"Well, I haven't been long enough in this place to know what to expect," Cashel said calmly. "Where I come from, folks would give directions to a stranger who asked them politely, that's true."

Of course there was Aron or-Raddid with the rocky farm north of Barca's Hamlet. Sour Aron and this ring ought to get along pretty well together. They'd make a pair in harness, at any rate.

"Most folks would, anyhow," Cashel added to be completely accurate.

The ring was heavy gold, but its surface was covered with chains of tiny beads fixed on in some fashion that didn't mar their perfect roundness. Cashel had never seen anything made that way before. It wasn't much to his taste, but he could appreciate the craftsmanship of whoever the goldsmith was.

He cleared his throat. "And I'm sorry about your master," he added. "I came here to see him, but things didn't work out the way either of us would've wanted."

"I told him a hundred times if I told him once," Krias said. His tone was still waspish but not quite as he'd used a moment before. " 'Landure, calm down or one day you'll meet somebody just as stupid as you are and stronger besides!' But would he listen? No, no, he kept on the same way until you showed up, sheep-boy. And now who's to keep all the slime from the Underworld from oozing across the cosmos, hey?"

Cashel looked down at the figure quivering in the heart of the stone. He didn't speak for a moment. Krias knew without being told that Cashel was a shepherd. Did the ring maybe know the route that would take Cashel . . . ?

He was starting to feel more hopeful than he had been since the moment he realized he'd bashed out the brains of the fellow he was supposed to ask for help, but it wasn't time yet to ask about Sharina. He cleared his throat again and said, "About Master Landure. I was wondering where to bury him, here or at his house. Or, well, where? Can you tell me?"

"Bury him?" Krias snapped. "Bury his meat, you mean, and a silly waste of time that would be. Not that your time is of much value, is it?"

Cashel started to put the ring down. Put it back on Landure's finger, he supposed, and carry the body to the mansion as he'd started to do. There was a nice spot in front of the door where the morning sun would fall on the grave, and—

"Landure has any number of *bodies*, sheep-boy," Krias said. "It's his life that's important, and that he keeps under his tongue. Bodies, indeed! Some of us get along perfectly well without any body at all."

Cashel paused. "Ah," he said. He laid his staff crossways on his knees while still holding the ring. With his free hand he opened Landure's jaws by squeezing at the back of the hinge. The dead wizard had good teeth, white and strong.

Cashel lifted the tongue and took out the wafer beneath it. Blood had dried on the teeth but didn't stick to this thing.

The wafer was a little smaller than the circle Cashel could span between his thumb and index finger. It was as thin as the touch-piece some folk carried for luck, but its edges had a rounded feel instead of being sharper than a knife the way something so thin ought to be.

It was crystalline and clear, but it had color. The hue changed when Cashel moved the wafer and even when he didn't.

"How is this Landure's life?" he asked.

"How is dirt dirt?" Krias said. "How are sheep stupid? It just is. Put it under the tongue of another of Landure's bodies and there he is again—just as full of himself as he was before you knocked his fool head in."

"Oh," said Cashel. He continued to squat as he considered what Krias had said, and what the ring demon had told him beyond the words he'd used. Cashel often wished people—and rings—would just say what they meant instead of playing games with words and not-words. Life would be simpler.

Though come to think, that was pretty much the way his sister Ilna acted—say whatever it was she thought and say it in words that nobody could mistake. You could argue that Ilna *did* have a simpler time than most people, but you could also look at her and see why other folks chose to do things in a different way.

"Well?" Krias demanded. "Are you just going to sit there like a bump on a log? You're good at it, though, I'll admit. Maybe you can be reincarnated as a lichen!"

Cashel looked down at his bare, tanned arm. "I'm the

wrong color for a lichen," he said. "But that's not what I wanted to talk about. Where does—"

"Are you really that stupid?" the ring shrilled. "You couldn't be, not and remember to breathe!"

"That's not what I want to talk about either," Cashel said calmly. He'd learned a long time ago that if he let other people wander all over the field instead of answering his questions, he'd *never* get answers. "Where does Landure keep his extra bodies?"

He held the crystal in his callused palm, letting light tremble across its face. Sometimes he thought he saw something moving in its depths . . . but it really didn't have depth, being so thin.

"He doesn't keep anything now, does he?" Krias said with a sniff. "Except I suppose he'll soon be keeping worms for a while. If you mean where are the bodies, they're in Landure's other mansion—the one at the bottom of the Underworld, three levels down."

"Ah," Cashel repeated. "And I just put this—"

He tossed the disk in his palm. He wasn't sure that Krias saw things, saw them with eyes, anyway; but it was the way Cashel would've called attention to the crystal if he'd been talking to another person.

"—under his tongue, like it was on the body here when I took it out?"

The birds had started to sing again, and Cashel thought he heard a squirrel chatter. He didn't have strong feelings about birdsong and a squirrel's own mother wouldn't be able to find anything good to say about *its* voice, but they were normal sounds for a woodland. Cashel liked that better than the grim silence he'd waked up to.

"Are you deaf, sheep-boy?" Krias said. "I said the palace is in the *Underworld*. Through those bronze doors there and past all the frights and monsters that were locked away from the waking world—till you came and killed the guardian!"

"I heard you," Cashel said calmly. "Is it far to this other mansion?"

He thought of adding that he was trying to bring Landure back to life—back to body?—now that it turned out he could, but Krias already knew that. The ring was just being difficult, and there wasn't any point in Cashel letting it upset him.

Cashel could imagine burying the ring with this Landure and getting on about the job of reviving the wizard in a new body, though. If Krias didn't squeak some useful information pretty quick—

"Far?" the ring said. "It's farther than you're likely to get in a lifetime. Only a great wizard like Landure the Guardian could expect to survive any length of time in the Underworld!"

Cashel snorted, but thought of Sharina kept him from stomping the ring into the ground right now and being done with its noise. The best way to Sharina was through Landure's help, and the best way to Landure—alive and able to help—was through Krias.

Besides, Cashel sort of owed Landure for, well, killing the wizard when he was just trying to lock up a monster. Listening to Krias yammer like a squirrel was a better thing to do than choking the ring under a foot of dirt and maybe make a second mistake as bad as killing Landure in the first place.

Rather than say anything for a moment, Cashel set the ring on the dead man's palm. He scraped up a wad of moss, wrapped it around the crystal disk, put it all in his belt wallet.

The squirrel chattered. Cashel looked up over his shoulder and went *"Tsk-tsk-tsk!"* with his tongue against the roof of his mouth. The squirrel froze on its branch, then resumed scolding at twice the rate.

Grinning, his normal good humor restored, Cashel picked up the ring again and stood. "The other thing I need to know," he said, "is is there food down in the Underworld or should I bring some from the house up here? And I'd appreciate if you'd tell me how many days distant the place I'm going is likely to be.

"If I get there alive, I mean," he added to keep the ring from bursting like a long-dead woodchuck, but he couldn't help but let his grin grow broader.

"Do you think you can just bash your way through the Underworld with that quarterstaff?" Krias demanded. Cashel was starting to get used to the demon's voice; but by Duzi, the little God of shepherds, Krias made the squirrel sound like Garric calming the sheep with his pipes.

Cashel balanced the staff in his right palm. "Well," he said, trying not to sound too boastful, "I bashed it through Landure the Guardian, that great wizard, didn't I? But I do need to eat."

"There's food in the Underworld," Krias said. That was about the first time he'd just answered a question, wasn't it? Though Cashel'd had to ask twice. "There's food if you're strong enough to take it."

"Right," said Cashel. He bent and slipped the ring back on Landure's middle finger. The corpse had been dead long enough that the flesh was as supple as soft wax.

After thinking about it, Cashel had decided that this clearing was a better place for the grave than up by Landure's house would be. It was here, trying to defend the world, that he'd been killed.

"I'll be back with a shovel," Cashel called over his shoulder as he started up the path. "I know you don't think the body matters, but the animals didn't feel that way; and I don't either."

"Sheep-boy!" Krias called. Cashel walked on through the galax.

"Master Cashel or-Kenset!" Krias said. "Listen to me!"

Cashel turned, his hand resting on the rough bark of the nearby dogwood. "Master Krias?" he said.

"You should take me with you," Krias said. Loud as the demon's piping voice seemed close by, it faded quick as the whine of a mosquito once you got a few paces away.

Cashel rubbed his chin with his knuckles. He wasn't happy to be alone, that was the truth. Cashel hadn't spent as much time around other people as the innkeeper's children did, that was true, but sheep had personality as sure as humans did. There wasn't a lot to choose between people and sheep for being contrary, either.

That didn't mean being alone wouldn't be better than having Krias for company, though.

"Well, after all, he's going to want me when he's alive again, isn't he?" the ring said; and by Duzi! it was sounding a little desperate through the usual peevishness. "It stands to reason!"

"I guess you're right," Cashel said. He walked back to the corpse and removed the ring. It fit perfectly on his left little finger.

After staying silent half the way back to the house, Krias said, "You know, at the rate you're going, you may die of old age before you even *enter* the Underworld."

Cashel smiled. He walked at his own pace instead of trotting along like a dog in a hurry, so he'd heard that before plenty of times. It didn't bother him now either.

"Any notion where Landure keeps his shovels?" he asked.

"By the black heart of the cosmos!" the ring spluttered. "You lower the intellectual standard of any flock you're herding!"

Cashel chuckled. It *was* good to have company.

Ilna and Merota sat side by side against the bow railing. They held hands: left in left, right in right, their arms plaited before them. Without the contact Merota trembled like a rag in a breeze, though she didn't complain or ask for consideration.

The flautist piped the stroke with his usual two notes, a slower pace than that at which the trireme had cruised earlier in the voyage. Even so an oarsman shouted, "Hoist the sail, Vonculo! Or at least rig the jib!"

"Aye!" cried another crewman, though he continued to haul back on the loom of his long oar. "We're as good as you are, Vonculo. If we're caught, we'll all hang on the same gibbet!"

Vonculo was in the stern, holding the music box he'd taken from Mastyn's small bundle of personal effects. He'd tilted the box and was turning it so that the light of the setting sun fell across the marks etched on its ivory base. His face was grimly set, and he made no response to the complaints.

"And if we run aground on these shoals we're threading through, Titin," said Chalcus from the stroke oar, "hang or starve is just what we *will* do. Shut your mouth and pray that Ambian at the masthead can conn us through!"

"Did the Lady wed you in the Shepherd's place, Chalcus?" Titin muttered from his oar. Ilna could hear the comment and doubtless Chalcus could as well; but Titin continued rowing without speaking further.

Titin didn't want a fight. Nobody who'd understood the way Chalcus held his sword *would* want to fight him.

Merota was watching the chanteyman's back as he rowed. Chalcus had scars from flogging, from weapons, from teeth, and there were a number of marks that Ilna couldn't identify. At rest he looked slim, but his muscles stood out like cables under the stress of rowing.

Ilna laughed. Merota looked up at her. "Ilna?" she asked.

Ilna shook her head curtly. "Not now," she said.

She didn't want to say aloud what had just occurred to her: the rest of the trireme's crew had mutinied and become pirates. Chalcus almost certainly had done both those things in the past; those things and worse.

And Chalcus appeared to be the closest thing Ilna and Merota had to a friend in this assemblage. Though why he should be a friend, or at least act like one . . . that part of the pattern hadn't formed yet.

"A point starboard!" the lookout called. There wasn't a basket at the masthead; his legs were wrapped around the stayrope he'd climbed, and he took most of his weight on his arms crossed over the mast truck.

The helmsman leaned against his whipstaff, using his

weight to twist the steering oars crosswise to the water flowing past the hull. Vonculo looked up from the box. His expression would have had to brighten to be called grim. The red silk cover was tucked under his belt. He tugged it free and began to wrap the box, then paused.

"Mistress Ilna!" he called over the squeal of oars in the rowlocks. "Come here, if you will. We need to talk."

"Go on, mistress," Chalcus said as his arms thrust down and he leaned forward, lifting his oarblade from the sea and swinging it back for another stroke. "The child will be well enough where she is."

He spoke in a normal tone with only the hint of a gasp as he started to draw back on the oar. That showed a degree of control which Ilna could well appreciate.

She grinned. She could appreciate the harsh pride that would make the chanteyman act in such a pointlessly boastful way, too.

"On your honor, Master Chalcus?" Ilna said as she rose, disengaging Merota's hands. The girl nodded and managed a smile.

Chalcus laughed, a gust of sound as he drew back on his oar. "On my sword, mistress!" he said. "That you can believe in."

Ilna sniffed and began working her way aft over the gear bundled down the center of the deck. *She* trusted the chanteyman's honor, and he probably knew it. Though why he'd chosen to make allies of her and Merota was a question she wasn't prepared to answer.

"A point to port!" the lookout called with new urgency in his voice. "*Two* points to port!"

The trireme heeled slightly as the helmsman leaned grunting into the whipstaff. Foam spurted not far off the starboard bow. *A fish?* Ilna thought, but it was the sea itself dancing on a reef. The water was shallow here, and the sun was getting low.

Vonculo watched her approach without speaking. He stood between a pair of burly sailors who each held a bare

272 / DAVID DRAKE

cutlass. Ilna wondered if they were supposed to guard the sailing master or threaten her.

She smiled dismissively. They'd be as little use for the one as for the other. Standing with her hands crossed into the opposite sleeves, she said, "If you're done staring at me, Vonculo, I'll go back to the bow where the company's better."

"We have a problem," Vonculo said. "We have the sailing directions—"

"A point starboard!" Ambian called. The helmsman shifted his grip and pulled the blackened oak whipstaff toward him. Scores of men had rubbed their skin and body oils into the smooth wood.

Vonculo winced, but he kept his tone level as he resumed. "The sailing directions are here," he said, holding out the music box. "Scratched on the bottom. Go on, take it."

Ilna shook her head; she kept her hands where they were. "I don't know anything about sailing," she said.

She didn't know how to read either, but she didn't say that. Ilna wasn't ashamed of her ignorance—or much of anything else—but she didn't choose to volunteer information to such as Vonculo.

Vonculo scowled, but he was worried rather than angry. He forced a smile through his concern and said, "Come, mistress, we need to be friends. Will you have some wine?"

He gestured to one of his bodyguards. "Tayguch, break out a bottle of the—"

"No," Ilna interrupted; and then, because the offer had been made politely, she added a curt, "No thank you. The water does well enough for me."

In truth the water had been poor when it was poured into tarred storage jars in Valles, and days sloshing in the trireme's hold had done nothing to improve the flavor. Ilna still preferred the water to wine, and she wouldn't have accepted a favor from Vonculo if it meant she could drink tankards of Reise's best ale.

"You see, the problem is . . ." Vonculo resumed. He paused to lick his dry lips. "The problem is that the fellow you killed, Mastyn, was the only one of us who'd actually met the rulers of the place where we're going. He said . . ."

Vonculo looked at the men nearby: the guards, the helmsman, the flautist sitting at the sailing master's feet as he blew time. Even the first few ranks of oarsmen could hear anything Vonculo said unless he chose to whisper it in Ilna's ear, and that wished-for secrecy would be more of a risk to his position—and life—than anything he might say aloud. The crewman who'd gibed that they were all equal now had said no more than the truth.

"Mastyn said he was a wizard, you see," Vonculo went on in a studiedly even tone. "That's how could he get this box—"

He held the music box as if weighing it in his hand. It was a complex piece of workmanship even on the outside, the gold in spirals and the ivory panels carved in floral patterns. Rather too busy for Ilna's taste, but it would do for some, she supposed.

"—to sing the way it did, you see," Vonculo continued. "And Mastyn said that the rulers of the island where we're going are wizards also. So you see, while in many ways I'm not sorry that the fellow went over the side in pieces—"

Vonculo's smile was perhaps meant to be ingratiating. To Ilna, "terrified" would have been a more accurate description.

"—it does leave us with a lack."

"I don't see that it leaves me with anything at all," Ilna said, meeting Vonculo's cringing gaze with her own steadfast one. The sun was below the horizon. The sky was still bright, but it no longer lighted the surface well. Ilna supposed the lookout could see froth against the dark water, but shoals that didn't break the surface would be another matter.

Vonculo inserted the gold key in a slot in the base of the music box and turned it several times against the clicking of a mechanism. When he withdrew the key and lifted the rock crystal lid, pins inside played scales instead of the haunting tune Ilna had heard when Mastyn held the device.

The box ran down. Everyone near the trireme's stern stared at the two of them, but none of the crewmen tried to interfere.

Vonculo held the box toward Ilna again. "Can you make it work, mistress?" he said, trying to keep the desperation out of his voice.

"I don't care to try," Ilna said. The box seemed harmless and was certainly an interesting piece of workmanship, but she preferred not to get involved in things that she didn't understand. "Anyway, I don't see how that would help you; or Merota and me, either."

Vonculo closed the box and wrapped the silk around it with a sailor's quick, sure movements. "They say that you're a wizard yourself, mistress," he said to his hands.

Ilna sniffed. "I've met wizards," she said, "and none of them were in the least like me. And only one of the wizards I've met is someone that I'd be willing to sit down to a meal with."

"A point starboard," the lookout cried. "*Two* points! By the Lady, two points starboard!"

"Don't you understand?" Vonculo said. His hands were trembling. He suddenly turned and thrust the music box at one of his bodyguards. The sailor clasped the silken bundle against his belly with his left hand—the one that didn't hold a cutlass.

"Listen!" Vonculo shouted at Ilna. "We're going to an island ruled by wizards. There's gold and jewels in the street, I've seen them when the box plays, but they're wizards . . . and we should have a wizard on our side too. You see that, don't you?"

Ilna sniffed and said nothing. She saw that Vonculo was afraid of the course he'd chosen but even more afraid of going back on it now.

Did the sailing master believe in the gold and jewels? Perhaps. But he certainly believed that if the triremes put in at any port in the Isles capable of supplying their considerable crews, they'd all be hanged; and the provisions aboard would last only a few days at most with so many mouths devouring them.

"What do you think your own chances will be, woman?" Vonculo said, his voice rising. "We've been summoned, but you'll arrive on the island as an interloper! Help me, and I'll protect you and the girl."

Ilna laughed. "You're afraid that you won't be able to protect yourself, Master Vonculo," she said. "And as for us—Merota has me to watch over her, and when *I* need help it'll be from something more impressive than the likes of you."

Vonculo glared at her in frustration. The guards looked from him to Ilna uneasily. The man with the music box set it on the deck and rose, edging away from the object.

Ilna grimaced. She'd been angry because the sailing master had tried to manipulate her, claiming he and she were allies by virtue of the fact that he'd kidnapped her. Anger was something she had to fight or it would rule her; and besides, she and Merota did have some common interests with the mutineers, however that fact had arisen.

"What I will do is this . . ." she said. "I will treat you as I'd treat anyone else: politely so long as you behave politely to me, and honestly under any circumstances. We're neighbors, so to speak, and neighbors help one another."

Vonculo made an expression which Ilna supposed was meant for a smile. "We had no wish to inconvenience you, mistress," he said. "Or Lady Merota, of course. But since we're together, it only makes sense that we work for our mutual good."

Ilna nodded, more a dismissal than agreement. She would have turned had not Vonculo suddenly added, "Can you tell the future, mistress?"

"That's a fool's question," Ilna snapped. "You're the one that weaves the pattern of your life. Why do you ask me about it?"

"Wait!" Vonculo said as she would have stepped away.

"Tell me how our venture will succeed. *Tell me!*"

"All right," Ilna said pleasantly. "I'll need some hairs from your beard and threads from a garment. The frayed end of your sash should do very well. And some of the ship's cordage."

Ilna drew the paring knife from her sash and used it to cut off frayed strands of the twine that whipped the mainspar's lifting tackle. She was trembling with rage. She'd let her anger speak, knowing that she shouldn't; but shouts reached Ilna's soul and called up responses that in other circumstances she'd have been better able to control.

When Ilna turned, Vonculo was sawing at his beard with a knife that wasn't sharp enough for the job. "Hold still," she said with a grim smile. She stepped close to snip away half a dozen strands.

Vonculo's beard was reddish and luxuriant, with a scattering of gray. He flinched as Ilna drew her blade past his throat, but he didn't try to jerk away from her.

"Land a point to port!" the lookout cried. "It's big enough to beach on!"

The sailing master hopped to the backstay and climbed it like a frog, hunching on the pull of his arms, then thrusting himself higher on the strength of his legs. Sailors peered from the railing, and some of the rowers slacked their oars despite the curses of the section bosses seated on every fifth bench.

Ilna looked forward as her fingers wove the disparate bits she'd gathered. Merota's hand were folded. She watched Ilna in silent concern. Chalcus, drawing back his oar with the ease of strength and practice, threw Ilna a familiar grin. None of the oarsmen under his immediate direction had stopped rowing.

Vonculo and the lookout muttered at the mast truck. After a moment the sailing master called, "All right, we'll put in here for the night!"

"There'll be no water!" a sailor called from the deck. "That's a sand spit that'll be under water by high tide."

"We'll be away before high tide!" Vonculo said as he

shimmied down the stay backward. "By daylight we'll find a place with water. It's spend the night here or spend the night on a shoal, can't you see?"

The lookout and a sailor forward called directions to the helmsman. "Half stroke!" Vonculo said to the flautist as he returned to his place by Ilna.

To her he added, "Sister take Leser for a fool! Does he think we can sail through the East Shoals in darkness?"

"If they weren't fools, most of them," Ilna said without emphasis, "would they have followed you in this hare-brained nonsense?"

Vonculo scowled. "Maybe you're too fine a lady to care about gold," he said. "Men like us who've gone hungry are willing to take risks for wealth like we've been offered."

Ilna smiled with a mouth like a fishhook. "Here," she said, giving the sailing master the design she'd quickly plaited for him. "Hold it where there's enough light to see."

She didn't say that two children left orphaned at age seven in a rural hamlet knew about hunger. Her life was no business of Vonculo's, and he wouldn't understand anyway. Vonculo's sort thought that wealth was the magic balm that made all troubles go away. Even getting rich wouldn't make him see the truth: he'd just decide that *more* wealth was the answer, because what he'd gotten thus far didn't cure his ills.

"Give me the lamp, Tayguch," Vonculo said. The lantern hanging from the curved sternpost was a complex affair of wood with horn lenses. It drew air through twisting passages so that spray wouldn't douse the flame. The nearer sailor unhooked it and held it close to Ilna's weaving.

"I don't see—" Vonculo said; then he screamed. He flung the scrap of cloth and hair over the side, raising his other hand to shield his eyes.

Tayguch leaped back, the lantern swinging violently. He stepped on the flautist, who jumped to his feet, losing the rhythm of his call. Oars clattered together and a sailor cried angrily.

"That's a lie!" Vonculo shouted. For a moment Ilna thought he might reach for his belt knife. Instead he glared at her and rubbed his palms fiercely on the railing as if to clean them of whatever might have clung from the little pattern they had held.

"Get away from me!" he said. "Get forward or go over the side, it's all one to me!"

The other trireme was coming alongside. A sailor stood in the bow with a brass speaking trumpet; sunset turned its bell into a fiery half-moon. "Hold up!" he called.

"Hold the oars!" Vonculo ordered. The flautist blew three long trills, but the rowers had already raised their oars. Ilna scrambled between the lines as quickly as dignity permitted, reaching her original location beside Merota.

"He asked you to tell his fortune, did he?" Chalcus said, grinning over his shoulder at the women. "What did you show him, mistress?"

Ilna shrugged. The girl's hands felt warm and sweaty in hers. "I have no idea," she said. "The pattern was his life, not mine."

Sailors shouted plans and objections to one another across the water separating the ships. At this rate the moon would be near zenith before they came to a decision.

"Ilna?" Merota asked. "Could you see your future if you wanted to?"

"In my experience, child," Ilna said, "the things that come are quite bad enough when they arrive. I don't see any reason to worry about them ahead of time as well."

Chalcus laughed. "Aye, child," he said. "But I think you'll find the future is worse for those who stand in her way."

"And your enemies, Chacus?" Merota asked unexpectedly. "What happens to them?"

The chanteyman looked at her. "Often enough they'd have been wiser to make me a friend, that's so," he said.

After a moment he laughed. He was still chuckling when the flute ordered them onto the looming islet for the night.

Sharina didn't have her brother's gusto for the classics, but she'd followed Reise's course of instruction as an intelligent student and a dutiful daughter. As she picked her way through the time-ravaged stonework, she tried to place it in the context of what she had read.

She couldn't. There were hints in Rigal's epic *The Wanderings of Dann* and shadowings in Almsdor's equally ancient *The Birth of the Gods*. The sources contradicted each other—and in the case of Almsdor, contradicted himself. This palace, this ancient *city*, was older than myth itself.

But it was real.

Occasionally blocks had tumbled into her path, displaying squared features and intricate carvings to the moonlight, but they weren't a serious obstacle. The trees growing in what had been a plaza were the real barrier, and in some places Sharina found them almost impenetrable.

The buildings to either side of the boulevard were so overgrown that by daylight she wouldn't have been certain they were there except that hills weren't so regularly linear. The moon's white light slipped between the trunks to brilliantly illuminate the stones beneath. Sometimes the black rectangle of a doorway gaped; sometimes a face, stylized but recognizably reptilian, glared out at her.

Nothing remained of this place in Sharina's day. Nothing at all.

Historians—Herfa, Palatch the Hermit, and even some of the lyrics of Celondre—told how Lorcan the First founded the Kingdom of the Isles with the help of a great wizard from a prehuman reptilian race. All that was nearly a thousand years in the past even when Herfa began writing.

What sort of sources could Herfa and the others have

used? The annals of great families, perhaps—written to glorify members of their own house. Temple records, cursory at best. Besides, for the most part the temple lists were transferred to stone from painted boards only when the originals had been copied many times by bored, careless scribes. Minstrels' tales, told to entertain rather than inform and embellished in whatever fashion the singer thought would earn him the highest pay.

And imagination. Sharina knew that the historians of the Old Kingdom had been human. Like other humans they generally preferred to invent explanations rather than admit they were ignorant.

None of what Sharina knew about King Lorcan was as trustworthy as the gossip about Lady Sharina that teamsters told in the taverns of Valles. The stories about Lorcan's inhuman companion had even less grounding than that.

But King Lorcan *had* existed: the Kingdom of the Isles proved he was real. It was easier to believe that a great wizard had aided Lorcan than it was to imagine that a minor noble on the island of Haft had arisen from chaos to unite the Isles *without* the help of wizardry. And while the Dragon might not be "real" in the sense that Cashel was real to the touch, Sharina had certainly met someone in these ruins tonight.

She grinned. Perhaps the Dragon could dictate to her a true history of Lorcan and the founding of the Kingdom of the Isles. If she published such a work, however, the scholars of Valles and Erdin would dismiss her text as a naive attempt to euhemerize myth. Well, she wasn't cut out to be a historian.

Something hopped in front of her. *A mouse,* she thought, but its second hop took it into a patch of moonlight and she saw it was a gray-mottled toad.

The air was full of insects—many of them mosquitoes with a taste for Sharina—and she'd seen lizards scurrying over the stones. There were no bats, and the birds she'd seen and heard in the surrounding woods didn't call within the compound.

Sharina had wondered why the settlers who'd pursued her had been unwilling to step through the gateway. To her the ruin seemed little different from the woods near Barca's Hamlet, but the feeling of discomfort that barred the villagers worked on other warm-blooded creatures as well.

The Dragon had welcomed Sharina. Almost certainly the creature that brought her to this place had been the Dragon's minion; but she'd given her oath to serve the Dragon, and even on reflection she didn't see that she'd had any better choice.

She wondered "when" in the greater fabric of time the present was. The Dragon had said she was on Cordin—what would be Cordin. She'd seen the shark's-head standard outside the raw settlement. Rigal spoke of the shark's head being the symbol of Cordin's first ruling dynasty.

But Rigal was alluding to events many millennia in his past, and he'd been dead for thousands of years when Sharina was born. *A myth of a myth . . .*

She smiled. She might as well smile.

Sharina had started to climb over the rock in front of her before she realized this was the throne that the Dragon had sent her to find. It was of the same material as most of the city around it: light-colored granite, very fine-grained and hard.

The throne's back and arms were low and perfectly smooth instead of being chased with complex designs. The wide seat had been mortised into the block that formed the rest of the structure.

Sharina eyed it, then cut a length of rattan for a prybar with two blows of the Pewle knife. She worked the end of the rattan into the back joint, then levered the seat forward enough to give her fingers a grip. Rootlets had found purchase between other, equally tightly fitted stones, but the throne was as bare as the day the masons finished with it.

If masons and not wizards had formed it.

The seat slid forward like a drawer, moving easily despite its weight. Sharina left it in the grooves when she'd pulled it open far enough to remove the objects in the alcove beneath.

The material folded on top looked like cloth, but she felt the dry rustle beneath her fingers as she picked it up: it was a snakeskin. It had girdled a body as thick as Sharina's thigh, but it was only six feet long. No snake she knew of had those dimensions.

She held the skin to the moonlight. It was subtly mottled, but it had stretched when the snake cast it and the markings were faint anyway. Sharina couldn't tell anything from the pattern. She wasn't even certain there *was* a pattern.

Sharina wore her knife on a belt that had been cut for a stocky man. The belt's tongue was long enough to double Sharina's waist, but she hadn't been willing to trim the heavy leather to fit her more closely. Now she loosed the buckle. Twisting the skin lightly as though it were silk, she wrapped it twice around her waist and cinched the belt over it.

Her neighbors in Barca's Hamlet would have thought anyone dressed in a snakeskin had gone mad, but Sharina had seen fine ladies in Erdin and Valles wearing far more exotic garments. She grinned. Perhaps she'd return to the capital to start a new fashion.

Sharina reached into the hollow seat and brought out the other object: a plaque, slightly trapezoidal, and stamped from thin gold. There were holes at the four corners; Sharina guessed it was meant to be worn as a pectoral on a priest's breast.

Embossed on the metal was the head of a humanoid reptile: the Dragon or a member of the Dragon's race. Its jaws were open slightly, baring the pointed teeth in what could be either a smile or a snarl.

Around the plaque's border was a line of nonrepeating symbols, sharply incised wedges. At first glance Sharina took them for decoration, but closer appraisal suggested they might be writing. They were beyond her ability or that of any other human to translate, though, and she no longer had time for whimsy: the moon was nearing zenith.

Sharina pulled open the neck of her tunic and slid the plaque inside to nestle against her belly where the sash caught it. Gold is heavy, and even a thin sheet like this was a noticeable weight. In sheer metal value, the plaque was worth more than her father's inn.

She wormed through the stand of gnarled beech trees between her and the archway. Their roots had managed to find lodging between blocks of the pavement, but the meager nutrients available stunted them.

Sharina paused to catch her breath when she'd gotten past the beeches. Almost as an afterthought she looked around and realized that she'd reached her destination: a pillar rose from either side, leaning inward to meet above her in a corbeled arch.

The arch was of black stone unlike anything else in the city. Like the throne, its surfaces were unadorned. Vegetation brushed and shrouded it, but the roots and tendrils hadn't worked their way into the stone fabric.

Sharina placed herself between the pillars. Their shadow, black like the stone itself, pooled around her but a blur of light wavered in the center. She twisted to look straight overhead.

There was a small hole in the very top of the arch. Light channeled through the opening showed that its raised stone lip was crosshatched, or perhaps covered by the same wedge-shaped markings as the pectoral beneath Sharina's tunic.

Small though the opening was, the moon was in perfect alignment with it. The edge of the white disk blazed coldly through a tunnel of stone. In a moment it would—

The light tugged at her eyes. Once a mummer had brought his camera obscura to the Sheep Fair and amazed spectators by projecting an image of the world upside down onto the curtain behind him. Wizardry, he claimed, and the folk who watched—visiting merchants as well as locals—were willing for the most part to believe him.

Reise alone said that it was only a trick of the light streaming through the pinhole at one end of the box—

marvelous, but no more wizard's work than a rainbow is. Sharina had taken her father's word for it—Reise was no more likely to lie than he was to dance naked in the street—but she'd thought even then that perhaps there was more magic in a rainbow than her father thought.

This arch was another camera obscura, only that. But the opening was toward the empty sky, and the images that it threw onto Sharina were—

She felt her body dissolving like salt in creek water. She was part of time, flowing through eternity: every rock, every tree, every living thing was Sharina os-Reise, and she was all of them. The cosmos shone as a brilliant tapestry about her. Momentarily she wondered if this was how Ilna always viewed the world—

But it couldn't be, because this was perfect beauty. The world in which Ilna lived was a bleak expanse of misery and desperation. Sharina knew her friend too well to doubt that; and now, seeing *this* cosmos, she pitied Ilna as well. Everyone chose her own life. . . .

Existence slowed. Time had no duration in Sharina's eternal present, but she could feel boundaries closing about her.

She was standing. For a moment she thought she'd gone blind, but that was because she was seeing with the eyes of her body alone instead of *being* all the cosmos.

It was late in the afternoon, and the air was warmer than that of the ruin Sharina had left. Beyond the mouth of the alley in which she stood were buildings, two stories high and three, in which people wearing kilts and light wrappers went about their ordinary business.

A man walking past the alley mouth saw Sharina and frowned, lengthening his pace. He didn't seem surprised, just mildly disapproving.

Sharina was shaking. She couldn't remember any clear image from the transition that brought her here, but lack of that oneness with eternity gnawed her soul like a cancer. She had been . . . she'd been everything! And now . . .

Sharina squatted and lowered her head, forcing herself

to breathe deeply. After a moment her body's shuddering stopped and she could straighten up, feeling embarrassed at her reaction. Though perhaps—

When a man is rescued from drowning, he gasps and splutters on the shore. Sharina knew she'd been drowning also, submerged and dissolving in the flow of eternity.

More pedestrians crossed the alley mouth, some of them glancing in her direction. Their chatter and the street cries were no different than what she'd heard often when walking through Valles. Though the speakers used a dialect broader than Sharina was used to, she could generally understand the words.

She looked at herself and decided to hang the big knife over one shoulder so that her cape would conceal it; the folk in the street didn't go armed. The pectoral was a heavy presence within her tunic. Taking another deep breath, Sharina prepared to go out.

It was only then that she noticed the side of the building to her left. It had been plastered but not recently, and some of the coating had flaked off. The wall beneath was built from the inscribed blocks of the city where Sharina had met the Dragon.

Katchin the Miller stumbled on cobblestones as he left Garric and the two women. The bridge's wavering light distorted the joins between stones, and Katchin was half-blind with tears of frustration besides.

What had happened? How *could* little Garric or-Reise, a boy who'd been exposed to Katchin's worth every day of his life, send him away?

Katchin heard the old woman mumbling behind him. Light flared, throwing Katchin's long shadow across the pavement. Suddenly frightened, he glanced over his shoulder. An upward-flaring cone of light surrounded the trio who'd just dismissed him; its blue glare filtered their bodies into figures of smoke. The air buzzed, like a cicada but louder. The note rose steadily.

Katchin started to run. He'd bought new shoes in Valles to be sure he'd be in style. The uppers were red leather; the toes curled like crooked fingers and were finished by little tassels of gold cord.

The soles were as smooth as the uppers, though, and these cobblestones had been polished like glass by ages of use. Katchin slipped and fell, crying out with pain and anger at the world's injustice toward him.

The light surrounding Garric and the others brightened further, but it no longer cast shadows. The cone started to spin. Cobblestones at the edge of the vortex rippled and began lifting from their bed. The sound keened too high to be heard with ears, but Katchin felt his teeth quiver.

He got onto all fours, wheezing and gasping. To be treated like some common peasant—and then this!

There was no one in sight. Katchin was close to the buildings, so the soldiers down the cross street couldn't see him nor he them. The windows facing the street were shuttered and the rooms behind them empty.

A vortex of whirling light spun off the greater cone which enclosed Garric. It wandered across the pavement, illuminating nothing but showing within itself glimpses of other worlds, other times.

Three more cones spat away from the mother cone, each turning its own drunken path into the night. One wobbled toward Katchin.

He got to his feet and ran, this time placing his feet with the care of a townsman trying to cross a plowed field. He was wearing his best clothing: his short cape had gold trim, and his saffron tunics were layered so that the appliquéd border of the inner one showed beneath that of the outer. The sash of crimson silk around Katchin's waist had cost him the price of a dozen sheep. It was water-damaged now because he'd had his wife Feyda wash the garment rather than asking his niece Ilna to clean it.

Ilna wouldn't have refused. No, she'd have sneered at Katchin, done the work perfectly as she did everything having to do with fabric, and sneered again as she dropped

Katchin's payment back in the dirt at his feet. He loved money, but the insult of having Ilna fling it back at him would have been worse than the cost; though it meant half-ruining the sash as a consequence.

Katchin was the most important man in Barca's Hamlet! He was the bailiff of Count Lascarg! How could everyone treat him with contempt?

Sometimes Katchin almost managed to convince himself that on his trips to Carcosa he dined with the count instead of being dismissed from the palace by an underclerk when he offered his report. But nobody else in the borough believed Katchin, even though he was the richest of them by far. He deserved respect!

He felt a buzzing, bone deep and as piercing as a rabbit's scream. He looked over his shoulder. A vortex skated toward him. He screamed. The vortex pirouetted as though it were his partner in a reel dance.

Katchin sprang away from it—

slipped—

and fell into flat, gray light with no color and no shadows. A woman stood facing him. She wore a robe of bleached linen, and her skin was painted with white lead.

"Where am I?" Katchin said. His voice didn't echo. The street, the bridge of wizard-light—the vortex itself that he thought had enveloped him—all were gone. There was nothing but a woman as colorless as old bone. "Who are— Did you bring me here?"

The shrill buzzing had stopped. It was as though the gray ambience were a wall isolating Katchin from the world he had left.

The woman raised her right hand and dangled a human neck vertebra from her index finger. It hung on a cord of the particular red-blond color of hair growing on the heads of dead men.

The woman twitched the bangle with her other hand. It rotated sunwise, then widdershins, before Katchin's staring eyes.

"We have things to discuss, Katchin the Miller," the

woman said. Her voice was toneless. "You will come with me."

"I will come with you," Katchin's lips said. His voice was a dead echo of her own. "We have things to discuss."

The woman walked into the grayness, her steps as slow as a pallbearer's. She held the neck bone at her side, spinning one direction and then the other. Katchin followed, his eyes on the bangle.

"I will come with you," his lips repeated.

Chapter Twelve

The courtyard in which Garric stood with Tenoctris and Liane was big enough to swallow the Field of Monuments in Carcosa. Sand had swept in from the west, covering whatever walls or buildings had stood on that side.

"Is this a city or all one building?" Liane asked. "It looks as though it's all connected."

"It's both, really," Tenoctris said. "A vast building to contain all of mankind. The builders called it Alae, which meant Wings in their language, and it was man's last city."

Though Tenoctris had claimed she could walk by herself, Garric made sure his left arm was taking most of her weight. He breathed deeply but his lungs didn't seem to fill properly. He certainly wasn't going to let her strain herself physically if he could help it.

"The last?" Liane said. It was hard to hear her voice. The air didn't carry sound well, but Liane was speaking softly besides. The thought must have disturbed her. Garric was too focused on his own problems to worry about those of a city long dead.

"The last of mankind on this world," Tenoctris said quietly. "There has to be an end some time, you know. What we must do is see to it that it's a natural end, not because chaos triumphed and wiped life away before its time."

She squeezed Garric's biceps affectionately and reached out to pat Liane's arm with the other hand. "That's what we have to try to do, I mean."

"Evil won't win while I'm standing," Garric said, echoing the thought of the king in his mind. He laughed and added, "While any of us are."

Though hidden, the western structures stabilized the dune and prevented it from devouring the remainder of the plaza with a single sinuous bound. Tendrils of glistening sand had squirmed to the first of the five terraces rising from the central hollow, but the small-leafed bushes rooting in cracks in the pavement were visibly different from the vegetation that grew on the dune itself.

They mounted three steps to the first terrace. Garric had seen fields where the ground was shored up to hold rainwater and to flatten the surface to make cultivating easier. This—changing the contours of the land on an enormous scale merely to create a vista for those beholding it—was new to him.

From Carus' memory cascaded images of the great cities of the Old Kingdom. Carcosa, Valles, and a dozen metropolitan centers had structures built on an impressive scale, but no single unified artifact like this one.

At about every twenty yards around the edge, as though looking down into the pit, were statues of crouching beasts. They'd been heavily worn by blowing sand.

"Are these lions?" Garric asked. There were humps on the backs of the stone creatures.

The moon was well up. Though it seemed larger than the orb which shone on the world to which he'd been born, its light was reddish and not as clear as he expected.

"They're sphinxes, Garric," Liane said. "Winged sphinxes. They couldn't fly with little wings like that, though."

She looked at Tenoctris. "Could they?" she added. Garric wasn't sure from Liane's tone whether the question was serious.

"The statues are just a decoration," Tenoctris said, eyeing them as they climbed past to the next terrace. "Though the men who carved them could fly. At least they could have flown if they'd wanted to. They'd given it up long before the last of them had died."

Garric missed a step in amazement. "How could anybody give up flying?" he asked.

Often while minding sheep he'd put down whatever book he'd brought and watched instead the gulls gliding above the sea. Land birds didn't impress him. The little ones darted from place to place with no thought but safety or another bite to eat. Vultures wheeled all day above a sunlit field, but their circles were even more obviously empty than the punctuated fluttering of their lesser brethren.

But the whole world belonged to the gulls. Their gray wings coursed from island to island, and they made their home for the night wherever they chose.

"The people who built Alae had other concerns," Tenoctris said. She looked back at the rank of downward-looking sphinxes. "Perhaps they'd have been better off to remember flight," she added. "Though I shouldn't judge other people."

The third terrace was surrounded by a railing. Blowing sand had sculpted its spiral banisters thinner yet; some had been worn to stubs reaching toward one another like pairs of stalactites and stalagmites.

An ornamental gateway, square and massive, framed the steps. Its flat surfaces were carved in low relief. The wind must always come from the northwest, because the figures on the sheltered angles were still sharp. There were willowy humans, nude but sexless, carrying out rituals that involved pouring fluid from basin to basin and over one another. Their faces were almond-shaped and without expression.

Liane carried the collapsible desk that held her writing

equipment and whatever documents she felt she'd need for her present endeavors. Though the case was no heavier than a traveler's wallet, she paused to switch the strap from her right shoulder to her left. Garric was tiring fast in the thin air, too.

"Alman is the last of his race, then?" Liane asked.

"Alman bor-Hallimann was a wizard in the time of King Lorcan," Tenoctris said, smiling faintly. "He was horrified by the upheaval that attended the founding of the kingdom and wanted to go somewhere where he'd have peace for his studies. He came to Alae after other men were gone from the city."

She looked around at the windswept magnificence. "He has a scrying glass made from the lens of the Behemoth's single eye," she added. "I want to borrow it to view the other side of the bridge."

"Will Alman help us?" Liane asked. "If he came here for peace . . . ?"

"He'll help us because he's human and mankind needs help," Garric said. "Or if Alman no longer cares about humanity—"

He touched his sword hilt, reassuring himself that it was where he knew it was.

"—then I don't care very much about Alman's willingness."

The slabs paving the fourth terrace were a material different from the ruddy stone of which the remainder of the city was made. *Water*! Garric's eyes told him, but a dusting of sand had blown onto even this relatively high surface. Aloud he said, "Is it glass?"

The surface was smooth, dangerously smooth. Garric placed his feet carefully, stepping straight down, because he knew that otherwise he'd fall and take Tenoctris with him. Sand grains scrunched beneath his boots.

"It's too hard for glass, Garric," Liane said. "The blowing sand hasn't etched it at all."

She swallowed; the thin air seemed to dry throats abnormally fast. "It could be sapphire, though," she added quietly.

Garric frowned, trying to see the pavement as a creation rather than an obstacle as dangerous to cross as a narrow ledge. The surface was flat: it reflected the surrounding buildings without distortion, and on it the stars glittered as motionless points in the same relation to one another as they had in the cold heavens.

Garric wasn't sure whether the pavement had color. Perhaps it was blue or blue-black, but he might be seeing the sky echoed deep in a crystal of white purity.

They reached the highest terrace. Garric sighed with relief as he set his boot on the border of pale sandstone. It was hard and originally highly polished to judge from corners which blowing grit hadn't scored, but it was safe to walk on so long as it was dry. "How did they get across that without breaking their necks?" he complained.

"Mostly they didn't leave the building," Tenoctris explained. "Toward the end, everyone stayed in his room, being fed by the beings they'd created. And finally, of course, the last of them died."

"How can anyone choose to live here?" Liane asked. "Alman could have gone other places for privacy. Alae isn't just dead—it was never alive."

"The men who built it didn't think as we do," Tenoctris said. "For which I'm very thankful. And as for Alman, I can't say; but he has the power to leave at any time, so this is where he wants to be."

"Still, it's beautiful," Garric said. "I don't think I'd be comfortable here myself, but it's very peaceful."

"Which you are not, lad," King Carus said. *"There were wise, peaceful folk in my day too—priests, some of them; philosophers; even ordinary people who'd decided that they couldn't live with themselves if they took away the life even of someone bent on their destruction."*

The ancient king saw more through Garric's eyes than Garric himself did: a niche that would conceal an assassin, a parapet from which bowmen could step to rain arrows

on those in the courtyard below; a sand-sawn cornice that
even a child could lever down on an enemy approaching
the wall. With a harshness that Carus rarely showed, he
added, *"Perhaps the Lady delights in their presence; but
by what they were afraid or unwilling to do, the kingdom
and the lives of their neighbors all went smash."*

Garric looked at Liane, then Tenoctris. Aloud he said,
"The world has room enough for peaceful folk. I think
they're as likely to be advancing the cause of good as ever
I am when I put my hand to my sword."

The women looked at him—Tenoctris knowingly, Liane
with a quizzical lift of the eyebrows. In Garric's mind, his
ancestor laughed approval.

They entered the building through a portal that was perfectly square and high enough for a giant. The doorleaves
were of silvery metal that the sand had worn more than
the stone in which they were set. One valve hung on its
hinges; the other was a tangle of scraps half-in, half-out of
the hallway beyond. The metal surfaces were chased,
though the patterns might have been those of the skirling
wind using sand for burins.

From a distance the building seemed monolithic, un-
marred and unchangeable. Closer by, Garric could tell that
sand had burnished off the fine detail of the lower carvings,
and that many woody-stemmed, spiky plants had found
cracks in the stonework in which to grow. The walls would
trap dew in the mornings and channel the droplets down
to niches at the margins, providing a constant source of
water in this barren waste.

A first glimpse of the vaulted hallway showed that
time's tendrils of destruction had worked on the interior as
well. Even so, Garric touched his sword and Liane gasped
to see gigantic faces smiling at them from the walls.

A black beetle the size of Garric's little fingernail scurried out of sight in the joint between the blocks forming
the right and left side of the nearest face's lips. It was the
first form of animal life that Garric had seen in this place.

"Who are they?" Liane asked. Moonlight filtering from

openings high above gave the ten faces—five on either wall—a sinister cast, but their expressions were probably intended to be serene under proper lighting. Their lips were fleshy, their noses broad, and their cheeks heavy in contrast to the epicene grace of the figures on the terrace archway.

Tenoctris looked at the carvings with only the general interest she showed for all that came her way. Each wore a complex headdress of porticos and dancers. Despite the dim light, Garric could tell that the sculptors had distorted the figures to compensate for the foreshortening of seeing them from the floor.

"I suspect they're meant for mankind as a whole," Tenoctris said. "But I can't be sure."

She smiled at her companions. "The only one who knew anything of Alae were Alman himself and the student from his own time who helped him as he studied the city," she explained. "The student—we don't have his name, he's just the Acolyte from Shengy—left an account which others copied in part for their almagests."

Tenoctris coughed in slight embarrassment at what was for her boastfulness. "I'm not a powerful wizard," she said, "but there are more ways to learn things than by wizardry. I connected several accounts that didn't mention Alman by name with one that did, but which didn't say anything about him viewing Alae. I realized that it was here that he must have taken refuge from the Wars of Unification, carrying his paraphernalia of art. I was very proud of myself."

She looked at the towering faces about them, her own expression oddly similar to the stone smiles despite the contrast with her fine-drawn, birdlike features. "But I never thought," Tenoctris said, "that I'd be able to see Alae with my own eyes. I don't have the power to view this place, let alone visit it in the flesh. The bridge draws the cosmos to a single flat sheet in which all time is one time. That made it possible for us to be here."

Liane nodded. "And makes it necessary for us to remove the bridge," she said, "before Alae and Valles and all time mix. I don't know exactly what the result would be, but I suspect—"

She grinned and squeezed Garric's hand, reassurance for both of them.

"—a repeat of the way the Old Kingdom ended would be preferable."

"Well, that's why we're here," Garric said carefully.

Tenoctris laughed. "Yes, indeed," she said. She paused to cough and clear her dry throat. "I'm so used to thinking of myself as a scholar that sometimes I forget the times require me to be a person of action.

"Now, how to find Alman?" she went on. Her eyes darted toward each of the three hallways leading from the anteroom. "The incantation I spoke should have brought us by the principle of congruity to the point where Alman entered this plane: the same action in the same medium will cause the same response. That doesn't tell us where he may have walked after he arrived here, however."

The sand on the floor was unmarked except for whorls drawn by the moving air itself. Garric looked back. The three of them had left clear prints. The wind would erase them eventually, but the air was too thin to shovel sand grains quickly.

"Will he be growing crops?" Garric asked. "Or does he get his food through wizardry?"

"I can't say for a wizard as powerful as Alman," Tenoctris said with a wry smile. "But the amount of effort to create or transmute matter by art on the scale that a human needs it to live would take most of the waking hours of most wizards."

She looked behind her, out the open doorway toward the barren plaza. "It might be equally difficult to grow things here, though. I'm not an expert on farming. Or much else that doesn't involve a book."

Garric laughed. "I can't tell you much about raising crops in this desert myself," he said, "but if Alman chose to come here we can assume he had a plan to keep himself fed. Let's walk straight through—"

He stretched out his arm.

"—and see if we come to another courtyard on the other side. I don't see how he could be farming in the building itself."

"The roof of the right wing may have fallen in," Liane suggested. "It looked as though it had from where we stood when we arrived."

Garric stamped his foot. "The floor's still stone," he said mildly, "even if plants could get light."

He remembered how confused he'd been the first time he entered a city; how confusing he *still* found cities. City-dwellers snarled or sneered at people who asked them questions they thought were obvious. Liane simply explained without ever suggesting that Garric was stupid because he was ignorant. That attitude was one of Liane's many virtues that Garric was trying to copy.

They walked down the hallway, their footsteps echoing. Tenoctris' toes dragged audibly; Garric paused to shift his grip, spreading his hand on the old woman's hipbone to lift her without making it harder for her to breathe.

"Tenoctris?" Liane asked. "Why didn't Alman's acolyte come here with him?"

"What?" said the wizard. "I'm not sure, Liane; none of the preserved fragments of his account say anything about that, though . . ."

She looked toward the younger woman. Garric, glancing over Tenoctris' head, was surprised to see how solemn Liane's expression was.

"I expect, since Alman's purpose was to leave his world completely," Tenoctris resumed carefully, "that he never intended his acolyte to accompany him."

"That seemed likely to me too," Liane said. "I wonder how the acolyte felt about being abandoned."

It wasn't really a question, so Garric didn't say anything in reply. If Tenoctris hadn't been between them, though, he would have hugged Liane.

Doorways—some with their metal panels closed, others standing ajar—were spaced every twenty feet on either

side of the passageway. Occasional rents in the outer walls
let in light. The rooms were as empty as the hall, though
sometimes the vividly carved wall reliefs startled Garric
into thinking people were watching him.

For the most part the only illumination was the ghostly
haze from above. Garric's eyes adapted to it, but he felt as
though he were walking through a cave by the light of
glowing fungus.

"Tenoctris?" he said. "There weren't any windows in the
rooms originally. How did the people see? By wizardry?"

"They didn't call it that," Tenoctris said. "They had arts
they thought were as natural as you do lighting a candle.
Of course, the spell that brought us here was perfectly natural also. I suppose anything's unnatural if you can't do it
yourself."

She laughed. "And I certainly couldn't light these halls
the way the builders did," she added.

When they'd come a quarter mile from the anteroom,
Garric saw a rotunda opening ahead. They walked on. The
hall and the rooms lying off it had twenty-foot ceilings,
making the rooms perfect cubes. The rotunda was over a
hundred feet in diameter and as high as it was wide. Another giant doorway gaped on the other side. Some light
spilled through it, but more came from the hatch in the
ceiling to which a flight of metal steps climbed in a tight
helix.

"He's been coming in and out of that door," Garric said,
nodding toward the smudged sand. "I'm going to look
closer."

Without being asked, Liane took Tenoctris' weight. Garric strode quickly across the circular space with both hands
free. He didn't expect danger to come at them through the
doorway—the beetle was still the only animal he'd seen
in this world—but he didn't need Carus' vivid memories
of ambush and surprise to remind him that he didn't *know*
anything about this place except that he'd never seen anything similar in the past.

The wind moaned, echoing in the high cylinder. Nothing

else moved. Around the walls was a relief of men using the body of an enormous serpent as a capstan bar to turn millstones centered on the doorway. Two-legged creatures with gills and scales were gobbling the parts of men who'd fallen into the mill.

Stuffed into the carvings of the lower register were bulbs the size of a man's head and seedpods like those of the locust tree. What Garric had taken for rubbish was actually a collection of gathered food.

Garric turned. The women had followed him at a pace set by the old wizard's frailty. "I think we've found Alman," he said. "If his larder's here, he can't be far away."

All three looked at the silvery spiral rising to the ceiling. It was as delicate as spiderweb, and they'd seen repeated proof that the metal weathered here more quickly than the stone around it. The steps bore fresh scratches from feet grinding sand grains into the treads.

"Then I think we should go see him," Tenoctris said, starting for the stairs on Liane's arm.

"Let me lead," Garric said quietly. He slid his sword a finger's breadth up in its sheath and let it drop back.

The wind moaned.

Not that there was any danger . . .

Cashel stretched, first raising his arms and standing on tiptoe, then bending backward with his staff planted behind him as the third leg of a tripod to keep him from falling over. He felt unusually—

Well, he wasn't sure what to call it. Not unusually *strong*, because strength was something Cashel took for granted the same way he did sunrise. You wouldn't talk about an unusually rising sun, would you?

"Clean" was more like the right word. He'd slept like the dead after Colva fled from him, but there was more to it than a good night's rest. He felt like all the dross had been burned out of him the way a fever would do. He guessed that was Colva's doing.

Cashel grinned. Maybe he ought to thank her, but he guessed that like a fever she was at least as likely to kill as cure.

"What are you smirking about?" Krias demanded. "Have you realized you'd better turn and run the other way?"

Cashel looked down at the ring. Usually the figure was a blur inside the stone, but just now the little demon glittered like a purple spark on the surface.

"No," Cashel said, "I was just about to start down. Should I close the door behind me?"

"The door won't keep the monsters out," Krias said. "Only the Guardian could do that, and you've killed him!"

"So I did," Cashel agreed mildly. He checked his wallet once more, then laced the flap tightly over the bread and cheese he'd brought from Valles—and the little wafer of Landure's life. The disk seemed sturdy enough, but he'd wrapped it in moss nonetheless and tied the bundle with a stem of rye grass.

"I guess I'll close it anyway," he said as he stepped through the bronze portal. He didn't understand why people—and generally little people, though never before anyone as little as Krias was—tried to get him angry. Mostly it was after they'd had more ale than was good for them.

"Do you drink, Krias?" Cashel asked. "Drink ale and cider, I mean?"

"What?" Krias shrilled. "Of course not, you ninny! I'm a demon, don't you remember?"

Just naturally cantankerous, Cashel decided. Well, a lot of people were. He sighed and looked the portal over.

The door had no latch or bar, just a vertical staple on either side for a handgrip. The lower half of the grip was polished by use. Landure hadn't spent his time outside with his sword drawn. He must have ruled his Underworld the way Cashel tended sheep, always present to keep an eye on them and to take care of things when they got into some foolishness or other.

Cashel stepped into the cavern. For as far as he could see there was just rock with no marking except for a patch of damp just at the edge of the light. That was going to be a problem, now that he thought about it: the light. Still, Landure had gotten along—and Colva too, it seemed like—so Cashel would. Maybe Krias would guide him.

Cashel put his left hand on the inner staple and pulled the door closed. The door swung easily once he got it moving to start with. He wondered what the builders used for hinges to carry so much weight without binding.

Come to think, he wondered who the builders *were*.

The bronze door closed with a soft thump. The fit between jamb and valve was so close that they trapped air in between for a cushion.

It wasn't a cave anymore. Light as red as rusted iron shone all around him. Everything had changed.

Cashel stood on an outcrop overlooking a pine-covered valley. He could see for, well, as far as he'd ever seen. It was like looking out to sea from the pastures south of Barca's Hamlet, but he was a lot higher up here.

He glanced over his shoulder. Now the door was set into the face of a bluff that pretty much mirrored what he'd seen from the outside. Stunted pines and rhododendrons grew from the rock face, though they didn't look quite right. The limbs were a little too sinuous, and he'd never seen a pine with bark as smooth as the one bobbing just above his head. Well, you had to expect differences when you traveled.

"I suppose you're wondering where the light comes from, aren't you?" Krias said.

Cashel thought about it. "No," he said, "but I'm glad it's here. I was wondering if it'd be dark."

He coughed, clearing his throat. The air still had a touch of sulfur to it; it nipped at the back of his nose when he breathed. He guessed he'd get used to it. The trees looked healthy enough, even if they were a bit funny.

"Do I just head down there and follow the river?" Cashel asked, pointing his staff toward what looked like a reasonable track into the valley. He didn't see a river, but that was what you got at the bottom of valleys.

Cashel could get around on the rocks, but he wasn't an enthusiastic climber. It wasn't a matter of strength or a head for heights; it was simply weight. He crumbled niches and knobs that supported smaller fellows just fine.

"You don't care, do you?" Krias said. The demon sounded really amazed instead of just being peevish. "Here you go into what you think is a cave and you don't care where the light comes from! It doesn't come *from* anywhere! It's a part of the Underworld, like the rocks and everything else except the monsters. It's part of their cage!"

"Oh," said Cashel. It didn't sound like he was going to get an answer to his question, so he started down the slope. He'd thought carrying the quarterstaff might be a problem, but when he butted it in the roots of trees below him, it braced his body as he climbed down.

"You're going to drive me mad!" Krias said.

Cashel didn't say he was sorry—which would've been a lie—but he tried not to smile too broadly either. That happened a lot, people going into shrieking rages because Cashel wouldn't get mad at them. Krias didn't realize that he was playing an old tune that Cashel had learned long since to counterpoint.

Things chattered in the trees, but they didn't sound much like the woodland creatures Cashel knew from home. They didn't sound like anything he wanted to get to know, either. One sort clicked like rattling bones, and the rest hooted like owls that knew something nasty about you.

Cashel gripped a little dogwood, gave it a firm tug to make sure its roots would stay anchored, and let himself down another long step. Just below was a proper ledge, so big it had grass growing. After that the slope eased enough that he'd be able to walk normally.

He thought about Landure the Guardian, who hadn't been dressed for rock climbing during the brief time he and Cashel knew one another. Of course, he might have changed into a short tunic and taken off those silly boots before he entered the cave, but the long sword was at best going to get in the way.

"What did Landure do, Master Krias?" Cashel asked as he stepped onto the ledge and caught his breath for a moment. "Climbing down into the valley, I mean? Did he have a different route?"

He wriggled his toes. The roots of the plants who'd first colonized the rock trapped grit and windblown dust, creating a more welcoming terrain for later comers. You couldn't call the result sod, but it felt pretty good nonetheless.

"Landure didn't walk like a sheep-boy!" Krias said. "He was a great wizard. He floated through the air with his arms crossed."

"Ah," said Cashel, nodding. He should've guessed it'd be something like that.

He stepped off the end of the ledge carefully, thrusting his staff in front of him. It might not be steep enough now that he'd break his neck, but he could still make himself no end of a fool if he slipped. Rolling downslope like a round of cheese wouldn't be the way to meet any of the locals either. Colva had been bad enough, and Cashel didn't doubt there could be worse where she came from.

"You could fly too, you know," Krias piped unexpectedly. "Sail majestically over the treetops."

"What?" said Cashel. "This is fine. I'm not a wizard."

He walked on, keeping his staff pointed well out in front of him, but he didn't worry anymore that he was going to fall. He was just being careful, as usual.

"I'm a demon with powers beyond your imagining!" Krias said. "*I* can make you fly!"

Cashel grinned. He might not have much imagination, but he'd seen things since he left home that he didn't think a puny little fellow like Krias was going to better. Aloud he said, "Oh, I don't mind walking. I just wondered about Landure."

Krias gabbled to himself. He sounded like a cote full of doves going to sleep, only madder.

If he'd asked, Cashel would've explained that he wanted to have his feet planted if it came to trouble, and from what Krias himself had said it was going to do that sooner or later. Cashel didn't volunteer that because Krias was the sort who'd jeer at whatever reason Cashel gave him; and anyway, Cashel didn't generally volunteer what he was thinking.

He'd gotten down into the forest proper. It was mostly pine like it had seemed from above, but there were red maples and dogwoods where the taller trees let light through. There were outcrops of bare rock, too, as well as places where moss had found a lodging but nothing larger was able to. The moss wriggled under Cashel's toes in a fashion that struck him as more active than a small plant ought to be.

He heard music. It was a fluting sound, very pure and sweet. Usually high notes like those didn't travel far in a forest, but Cashel was pretty sure that this wasn't a usual forest.

"What's that noise, Krias?" Cashel asked. He'd been about to rest the staff over his shoulder as he walked, but the sound made him change his mind. He kept the sturdy length of hickory in both hands, slanted crossways.

"I know and you're going to learn, sheep-boy!" the ring cried gleefully. "Oh! you will! You're going to wish you'd never come down to the Underworld!"

Cashel thought about that. The horn—or was it just a throat, a singer loud enough to sound like a horn?—continued to call. The golden notes seemed to come from several different directions, but that might have been tricks of echoes.

Cashel could imagine he wouldn't like what he found in the Underworld, that was true. But that he'd regret coming? No, that wouldn't happen. This was the direction that took him closer to Sharina. He couldn't imagine going any way but that one.

"Well, aren't you going to ask me what it is?" Krias

said, pouting because Cashel hadn't begged or yelled or whatever for the information.

"That's all right," Cashel said. "I guess I'll learn before long."

Sure, he'd have liked to know what was calling—that's why he'd asked in the first place. But you didn't get anywhere by playing silly games with folks who wanted to be difficult. Trying to wheedle the ring into telling would be as big a waste of time as chasing a chicken around the house when you wanted dinner. Much better to drop a pinch of oats between your spread feet while you sat on the back step.

And wring the bird's fool neck when she came to peck up the food.

Cashel grinned. He wondered if you could stew a demon. Krias would probably taste worse than a fish crow.

This was an open forest, not much different from the woodland owned in common by the householders of Barca's Hamlet. There dead limbs were gathered—and dead trees felled—for fuel, while hogs rooting for mast kept the undergrowth clear. Maybe the same thing was going on here, but Cashel would've smelled woodsmoke if he'd been anywhere close to Barca's Hamlet.

He didn't smell the sulfur either, but his throat was dry and getting drier so he knew it hadn't gone away. That was the thing about a really bad stink: it didn't take long before you didn't notice it anymore. Ermand or-Pile didn't mind how his tanyard smelled, but any other villager who came close gagged at the stench of urine, alum, and rotting fat.

Cashel caught movement out of the corners of his eyes. Things were flitting between the trees, though it seemed more like they were flitting *within* the trees some of the time. Were they women? But then, Colva had looked like a woman when he first met her.

The horns had stopped calling. Now Cashel heard plucked strings and somebody singing to the tune. He couldn't make out the words.

Cashel gave his quarterstaff a practice spin, in front of

him and then over his head. The ferrules swept in a grace-ful figure eight, smooth as butter. Cashel crossed his wrists, swapped hands, and repeated the set of movements to bring the staff back just as it was when he started.

He was glad there wasn't much undergrowth. A quar-terstaff takes up a lot of room even at rest, and when seven feet of iron-capped hickory is moving at the speed Cashel's thick wrists could bring it to—Duzi knew, you wouldn't be able to see for ivy leaves and splinters of saplings!

"So, you're going to fight them with your stick, sheep-boy?" Krias said.

"I'm not going to fight anybody if I can help it," Cashel said, slowing his breathing back down to where it ought to be. It wasn't so much the exercise of whirling the quar-terstaff that made Cashel's heart race as the chance he was coming to the fight he'd told Krias—truthfully—that he wasn't looking for.

Cashel never had gone looking for a fight. But he'd never turned his back on one that came to him, either.

Ahead of him was the gurgle of water moving over rocks at a good clip. That was the sort of sound that fooled you. It didn't seem loud, but it smothered all the other noises that usually warned you about things you couldn't—

A man stepped out of the forest in front of Cashel. Stepped out of a giant beech tree? But maybe he'd just been in the shade beside it. He carried a bow made of gold instead of ashwood or yew, and the arrows in his quiver had silver shafts. He was tall but not as tall as Cashel, and his build was as slim and supple as a young girl's.

"Greetings, stranger," he said. "We People don't get many visitors."

His eyes kept drifting toward the iron ferrules of Cashel's staff and the glint of Krias on his little finger. The fellow had the same expression as old Kifer did, sitting in a corner of Reise's taproom staring at his neighbors drink-ing jacks of ale that Kifer couldn't afford since he'd drunk away his land and lived by casual labor.

Cashel spread his legs. He turned his head slightly, side

to side; nothing furtive, just openly checking to see if he had more company.

He did. There were at least four handsful of them, males and equally willowy females, standing in a wide circle among the trees. Only the first would have been within reach of Cashel's quarterstaff.

"Good day, sir," Cashel said. "I'm Cashel or-Kenset, and I'm just passing through this region. I don't intend to trouble you."

The strangers were bare-chested, wearing kilts cut to hang lower on their right leg than the left. Most of them held golden bows like the fellow who'd greeted Cashel. Three had slender horns coiled over one shoulder and about their chests; these had swords thrust beneath their girdles. The blades writhed like snakes.

Only one of the group was unarmed, a lanky boy with a shock of red hair instead of the golden curls of the others. He carried a double-strung lyre, and he glared in disgust at Cashel.

"I am Wella, Cashel," said the man who'd greeted him first. He stared at the ring with hungry eyes. "We People are honored by your presence. You must stay with us tonight so that we can feast you as you deserve."

One of the females stepped toward Cashel, her slim-fingered hand reaching out as if to touch something perfect and fragile. He saw the movement and turned quickly. She sprang back immediately, smiling.

"I . . ." Cashel said. He didn't want to spend any longer with the People than it took his legs to carry him away; but there were a lot of them, and they had bows. He thought of asking Krias what to do, but he couldn't trust the demon to say anything helpful. Besides, the People were already a bit too interested in the ring.

"Come, Cashel," Wella said, stretching out the hand that didn't hold his bow. "Come to the home of the People."

Cashel moved slightly; the quarterstaff bobbed its iron cap a hair's breadth closer to Wella. He jerked back, his topaz eyes blazing.

"Elfin, lead our guest," Wella said.

The youth with the lyre stepped forward and put his hand on Cashel's arm. "Come, heavy person," Elfin said. His voice was as pure as the sound of ice cracking in a hard winter. "Come and we People will treat you as we should."

"Well, I guess I need to eat somewhere," Cashel said. The youth's touch was reassuringly warm. Cashel had expected something smooth and metallic, somehow.

The People turned and started off through the forest. Cashel was in the midst of the party; Elfin's fingers never left his biceps.

"I know and you're going to learn," chimed the ring's tiny voice.

"How old are you, my pretty little miss?" sang Chalcus at one of the mutineers' pair of driftwood fires. *"How old are you, sweet marrow?"*

Ilna thought of Garric's piping; and turned her thoughts back, because there was no sense and less joy in the direction they were going. Four sailors danced on the sand, their hands on their hips and their legs kicking high. The only accompaniment came from another man with miniature cymbals made from hollowed nutshells on his thumbs and forefingers. He clacked them together, giving the beat with his right hand and a complex rustling counterpoint with the other.

"If I don't die of a broken heart," Chalcus sang, now in a falsetto, *"I'm sixteen come tomorrow."*

Ilna looked down at the child sleeping beside her. Merota had a bit of her cloak's hem in her mouth and was chewing it as she dreamed. Ilna thought of tugging the cloth free, but there wasn't any real harm in what the girl was doing.

Ilna sighed also. She had to remind herself to pass over the many things that might be wrong but didn't do any harm. And some of them weren't wrong, even though Ilna os-Kenset thought they were. Her head accepted that, but her heart would never believe it as long as she lived.

There was nothing wrong with the music, for example. Ilna wasn't in a mood to listen to it, though, and unlike Merota she wasn't so wrung out by the day's events that she could sleep despite it.

The provisions intended for Lord Tadai and his suite had still been aboard when Mastyn sprang his mutiny. Tonight the sailors had eaten food they'd never known existed— eaten some and wasted more, actually. To sailors from the south coast of Ornifal, eggs preserved in a sauce of rotted sheep's entrails were simply rotten eggs, while the tastes of the royal court ran to far more exotic dishes than that.

Ilna smiled faintly. Prince Garric's taste in food wasn't that different from the sailors', actually, though the one was heavier on mutton with porridge and the other on porridge with fish. The courtiers were appalled.

Tadai's wines had found universal acceptance, though. The vintages came from all over the Isles, some of them spiced and many fermented from fruits other than grapes, but that made no matter. The sailors' attitude seemed to be that when you'd drunk enough, it didn't matter if the stuff smelled like worms had died in the vat. The party would be going on till dawn. Vonculo and the other leaders would have their work cut out to get the ships relaunched by midday.

Ilna stood, glanced again to be sure Merota was still quiet, and walked toward the fire at the other end of the long crescent. Behind her a dozen sailors joined Chalcus to chorus, *"Ti di diddly di, ti diddle do!"*

It didn't disturb Ilna to hear other people having fun. Her lips quirked in an almost-smile. It shouldn't disturb her, at least.

Vonculo and four other sailors sat around the fire at the other end of the islet. They'd knocked the top off the long-necked jug that stood upright in the sand beside them, but the atmosphere here was in dismal contrast to that of the larger grouping.

Ilna had no intention of joining Vonculo. The common sailors were fools and presently drunk besides, but they'd still be better company than the men who planned this nonsense.

For now, all Ilna intended was to put distance between herself and noisy happiness until she mastered her anger enough to go back and sleep beside Merota. She didn't expect to be happy. Some people were, some people weren't. It didn't seem to matter what happened around them—it was how they were made inside.

Cashel was happy. Not all the time, but more of the time than any other person Ilna had met. She supposed that she and her brother had a normal amount of happiness between them; but you weren't going to mistake a garment with black and white stripes for a gray one.

Just now Ilna was furious at the world; and that in turn made her angry with herself for such a *foolish* reaction. Clouds didn't care who they rained on, and the world didn't care that Ilna os-Kenset saw life as a tangle of yarn greater than any human being could be expected to sort out.

The world didn't expect Ilna to sort things out. That was a duty she put on herself, more *fool* her.

Ilna seated herself against a hummock of sand cemented roughly by lime in the crushed shells that made up much of the whole. She looked up at the stars, wondering if the people who inhabited the heavenly spheres on which the stars turned were happier than she was.

She smiled again. The people like Cashel were, she supposed. No doubt there was balance in the heavens as well as here.

Vonculo and his fellows carried on a morose conversation without noticing Ilna. She hadn't made any attempt to conceal herself, but she'd been quiet and the dark blue cloak hid her better in the night than true black would have done.

Ilna was too far away to overhear the men's conversation, not that she'd have wanted to. They'd be making a series of despondent observations about the mess they'd put themselves in. At any rate, Ilna would have been doing that if she'd been fool enough to have joined them.

The *Ravager*'s helmsman stirred up the fire with a salt-crusted pine bough, then tossed his poker on the rekindled flames as fresh fuel. Vonculo inserted the key in the music box and wound it.

Ilna's eyes had been drawn by the flare of sparks, but when she saw Vonculo with the device she continued to watch. She wasn't spying—she was in plain sight, after all, if any of the seamen bothered to look around—but neither was she particularly pleased with herself.

Vonculo released the key. It turned, glittering, and the box began a tuneless chime as if someone were tapping the blade of a good sword. The sound was empty rhythm—

But sparks rising from the fire whirled into images of flesh. Didn't Vonculo and the others see what was happening? Their eyes remained fixed on the music box, ignoring the fiery dance in their midst.

Ilna watched the patterns the sparks drew. Six wizards and a mummy stood in a circle chanting. She could hear the words—meaningless to her, meaningless to anyone but the powers they commanded—in the whorls of light.

Above Ilna the stars wheeled; before her the sparks spun. Together in the tinkle of the music box they made a purposeful unity, like cogs turning Katchin's millstones and grinding grain to flour. She wasn't on an islet of the Inner Sea, though part of her mind remembered that place; and remembered Valles and Barca's Hamlet and all her past.

Inside the circle of wizards knelt a seventh: his right hand raised with a dagger, his left holding a bound child on the floor in front of him. A man taller than anyone of Ilna's acquaintance was tied to a pillar beside the coven of wizards. He screamed, and his muscles were knotted like kinks in an anchor chain.

The wizards chanted, then paused. Their leader in the center shouted the final verse of the incantation and stabbed downward.

Wood cracked in the fire like sudden lightning. Sparks exploded upward, dissolving the scene. Ilna shivered in the warm night as the final note rang from the mechanism of the box.

Vonculo removed the key and wrapped the box again in its silk brocade. He and the others drank and talked and cursed the luck they had made for themselves.

After a time, Ilna got to her feet and walked toward the other fire, where Merota slept and Chalcus sang of a black-haired girl with lips as sweet as honey.

Sharina took a deep breath, squared her shoulders, and stepped out of the alley. A trio of women with market baskets on their heads bore down on her, chattering among themselves. She squeezed against the wall. The women swept by, giving her only a cursory glance. The trussed capon in the middle basket craned its neck to glare at Sharina as long as they were in sight of one another.

She grimaced. She didn't know what the bird had against her: it wouldn't be going into *her* oven.

Sharina wanted to sell the gold pectoral, but she wanted to know more about where she was first. She started walking, east so that the lowering sun would be on the faces and in the eyes of people coming toward her. She listened to talk and street cries, not for the information they contained but rather to be sure that she could understand and be understood here before she tried to do business.

She was getting awfully hungry. She passed a woman carrying a tray of wheat loaves under a piece of worsted cloth. Sharina's stomach cramped with longing at the smell of fresh bread.

The streets meandered. This city had been laid out by sheep walking to market or by men who had as little regard for straight lines as sheep did. The thoroughfare down which Sharina started split into two branches, each so narrow that the women talking to one another across the second-floor balconies could have touched hands if they'd wanted to. She went left.

The shops on the ground floor here sold pottery. It was utilitarian stuff, not even as good as the salt-glazed earthenware manufactured at Dashen's Place, on the road across Haft from Barca's Hamlet to Carcosa. The shapes were clumsy, and the crudely brushed slip decoration added color but no beauty to the beige field.

Sometimes shoppers glanced at Sharina. She was taller than other pedestrians, men as well as women, and her long blond tresses were an exception among swarthy, dark-haired folk.

The same had been true in Barca's Hamlet, of course. The people back home had had eighteen years to get used to Sharina's appearance, though. Still, nobody here screamed when they saw Sharina and she didn't think she'd have any trouble being understood.

She waited till she got to an intersection where three streets met and a fourth split off a few steps down the widest. A doctor had set up at a corner booth. His paraphernalia were displayed on the open counter before him: stoneware medicine jars and a rank of surgical tools. The blades were iron but had gilt and silver chasing on the bronze handles to lure custom by their flash.

At the back of the doctor's booth hung a creature like nothing Sharina had ever seen before. It had the shape and claws of a scorpion, but its many legs were flat paddles and the body was six feet long. She supposed it was for show rather than some part of the doctor's real medicaments. She certainly *hoped* it was for show, not that she intended to patronize the fellow professionally.

The doctor had just finished weighing the chunk of copper he'd gotten as his fee for putting ointment on the sores of a man with yaws. He wiped his spatula with a wad of straw which he tossed into the street as Sharina approached.

"What can I do for the lovely lady?" the doctor asked.

His eyes narrowed slightly. "If it's a matter of a personal nature, we—"

"I need only information," Sharina said, hoping to avoid a discussion which would embarrass her. "Can you direct me to the street of goldsmiths?"

"Ah," said the doctor, setting back on his stool. "Where was the lovely lady born, if I may ask?"

Sharina would have liked to walk off, but that might be more dangerous than answering. She didn't know where she was or *when* she was, though at least the people of this day had iron tools.

"I'm from Ornifal," Sharina said curtly. Her blood father had been an Ornifal noble, and her looks favored his side of the family. She turned away and called over her shoulder, "I hope you get all the custom your courtesy deserves."

"My apologies, mistress," the doctor said. "If you'll follow Fagot Lane—"

Sharina looked back; the doctor was pointing up one of the intersecting streets.

"—to the plaza, you'll find the goldsmiths down the street on your left."

"Thank you," Sharina said. She smiled, but the expression felt stiff. She hadn't realized how nervous she was until she collided with something as innocent as a busybody's curiosity. And of course she was hungry.

She started down the street. "I wish you luck in your dealings, lovely lady from Ornifal," the doctor called to her back.

A well with a low curb and a stone trough for watering animals sat in the center of the plaza. Entertainers had set up where each of the streets entered the circular open space.

One man sang and played a monochord while a child of six or younger sang a descant beside him. Either the words were unintelligible or the pair were using their voices as instruments to make sound rather than convey meaning.

Across the plaza a man juggled knives, occasionally snatching one from the air with his teeth.

Sharina turned to the left. Here a bird the size of a human being danced. Beside him was a strip of blanket on which spectators had dropped a few finger-length iron wedges.

Sharina looked around to find the owner of the performing animal. A balding fellow wearing a leather apron over his tunic was the only person who didn't glance and walk on, or simply walk on. He reached into his belt purse, fingered the money within, and then strode away quickly without dropping anything on the blanket.

The bird was its own master.

Despite the complaints of her stomach, Sharina stayed to watch. The creature moved with the same smooth grace as a gull flying along a shoreline. It had arms, not wings, though the short limbs bent the way a bird's did rather than those of a man or a dog. It was covered with fine down like a baby chick—though this was a gray, not yellowish—and it wore a harness of coarse fibers knotted in the fashion of macramé.

The bird's head was slightly smaller than that of a human so tall: this wasn't a man wearing a clever costume. Besides, no human could possibly execute the creature's dance. Repeatedly it leaped high, aiming one blunt-clawed foot heavenward while the other pointed to the ground.

Unwillingly, Sharina walked past the dancer and down Fagot Lane. The bird paid her no attention. It continued its dance, rotating its body slowly and punctuating each sequence of mini-steps with another vertical kick.

In a line on the left side of the narrow street were five goldsmiths, each in his separate booth. They faced the blank back wall of a stone building, a temple judging from the corner of a pediment that Sharina had glimpsed over the roofs of buildings fronting the plaza.

The booths were open-fronted, but a husky guard with a bare sword or a broad-bladed axe stood at the street side of each. The smiths sat on their strongboxes behind a table, across from an ivory stool for the client. At the right front of each booth was a tiny shrine.

A chest-high curtain drawn across the front of one booth gave privacy for what was probably a pawn rather than a purchase. A personal maid waited in the street beside the guard, alternately wringing her hands and trying to look nonchalant.

Sharina looked over the smiths who were free for the moment. Three of them met her glance with stone-faced professionalism. The last raised an eyebrow in query. His guard was neatly dressed though not as ornately as those of his neighbors, and his shrine was a simple ivory plaque of the Shepherd in contrast to gilt and jeweled images of the Lady of Fortune.

Sharina generally prayed to the Lady, but it was more than thought of Cashel that sent her into the booth of the man with the Shepherd on his wall. His guard nodded politely to her, but his eyes hardened as they lighted on the vague outline of the Pewle knife under her cape. Instead of drawing the curtain behind Sharina, he stepped into the booth with her.

The goldsmith rose from his seat, looking quizzically at his guard. Sharina said, "Your man is concerned that I'm carrying a knife. If this concerns you as well, sir, I'll go elsewhere with my affairs."

The goldsmith smiled slightly. "Thank you, Tilar," he said to the guard, "but I think the lady and I can be left to ourselves. It's understandable that someone with valuables would take steps to protect herself."

To Sharina he went on, "I am Milco of Rasoc, milady." He extended a hand toward the stool.

The guard stepped away and slid the curtain across. Plenty of light still came through the wooden grate in the ceiling.

Sharina sat, carefully picking her words as she did so. The folk here didn't use the patronymic form of address that was general in the Isles of her own time.

"My name is Sharina," she said. Milco was thin, old,

and very precise, with eyes that didn't miss anything. "I have an heirloom that I need to turn into money."

The goldsmith's mouth smiled; his eyes did not. "Since you're a stranger, milady"—either the accent or Sharina's appearance alone would have told him that—"I'll mention to you, without offense, I hope, that if you've innocently come into possession of a stolen object, I don't even want to see it. None of the dealers here would. I'll further mention that the chances of myself or my colleagues not knowing what's been stolen in Valhocca or the surrounding region isn't worth the risk a thief would run by displaying such an object to us."

Sharina smiled. *Very smart.* "I appreciate your candor," she said. "The object involved was given me by its owner for me to sell. Before we get deeper into details, though, may I ask about your attitude toward religion?"

She'd heard of Valhocca in epics of the Silver Age, the epoch following the thousand-year reign of the Yellow King; the city didn't figure in the geographical writings of Old Kingdom authors. Valhocca was the capital of the Sea Lords of Cordin.

Everything told about the Sea Lords was mythical. This city was real enough, though, and there was nothing impossible about an ancient kingdom uniting the southern isles millennia before King Lorcan welded together the whole archipelago.

If Valhocca was real, then Sharina had to wonder how real were the stories of the city's destruction. Supposedly the last and greatest Sea Lord, Mantys, put to death a wizard and threw his body into the sea. The wizard had returned with an army of sea demons which floated through the streets like airborne jellyfish. They'd stung to death everyone they met and tore down buildings with their tentacles.

That was all fancy, of course. The philosopher Brancome claimed to have found the story in ancient Serian records, but many thought he'd invented it to make a point in his essay on divine retribution.

Well, Sharina didn't expect to be in Valhocca long. With luck she'd never have to learn how much truth there was in Brancome's tale.

Milco nodded toward the ivory tableau of the Shepherd with two goats. "I worship the Shepherd," he said. "Most of us in Rasoc do, though worship of the Lady is more general in the city proper."

"I myself worship the Lady first," Sharina said, "but my concern is how you feel about artifacts of other faiths of former times."

The settlers who'd chased her into the Dragon's ruined palace had been reacting to a supernatural event. Sharina didn't want to learn that their descendants, the folk of Valhocca, felt the same way about the Dragon. If that was the case, she'd have to batter the pectoral shapeless with rocks before she tried to sell it.

"Ah," said Milco, nodding with understanding. "If perhaps you've been digging in ancient tombs, well . . . there are differing attitudes on the subject, but my own is that when men return an object to the earth, then the one who rediscovers it is no more to be censured than the one who dug the ore in the first place. But you're right to discuss the possibilities beforehand."

Sharina threw back her cape. She pulled loose the neck of her tunic with one hand and fished out the pectoral with the other. She placed it, warm from her body, on the empty table between them.

Milco's eyes widened very slightly when he saw the size of the Pewle knife. "I did Tilar an injustice," he said mildly. "I couldn't imagine why he was concerned that a lady carried a dagger for protection. Not that I regret admitting you, milady."

"It was a friend's," Sharina said curtly. It still hurt to remember Nonnus. She set the thin gold stamping in the center of the table. "I carry it in remembrance of him."

And to use, if the need arose. As she had used it in the past.

Milco nodded absently, but he'd transferred his whole

attention to the pectoral. "May I?" he asked. Sharina flicked her fingers toward him and he picked up the plaque.

"Quite a perfect example," Milco said judiciously, holding the piece by the edges and rotating it under the light. "Gold doesn't tarnish, of course, but I would still have expected discoloration from debris deposited *on* the piece."

Sharina shrugged, then smiled to soften her refusal to give any more information than the pectoral itself provided.

Milco took a steelyard from the shelf of implements behind him and hung it from a ceiling hook on a long copper chain. Next he took gold weights cast in the image of demons from the strongbox and set three of them against the plaque. To bring the two pans into perfect balance he adjusted the beam by one notch.

Sharina waited quietly while Milco carried out the operation. The goldsmith worked without haste but quickly nonetheless; he never wasted a motion. When he'd finished, he took a small knife from his sleeve and with it notched a tallystick of willow.

"I hope you'll not feel insulted if I test the piece for alloys, milady?" he said. He raised an eyebrow. "Sometimes the luster can be deceptive."

"Go ahead," Sharina said. "I have no idea how pure the gold is myself."

Milco took what Sharina had thought was a mixing bowl for wine from the shelf where the steelyard was kept. It was of much higher quality than the pottery Sharina had passed on her way to his booth. It was already about half-full of clear water.

The vessel's interior glaze was decorated with a harpy drawn in remarkable detail. The tips of her spread wings touched the rim so that the trailing edges of the feathers formed a series of minute notches up the sides.

Milco slid the pectoral into the water with great care. Sharina stood so that she could look into the vessel with him, though she didn't have the faintest notion of what she should be looking for.

Milco shook his head in pleased amazement. He pointed to where the water rose against the harpy's wings—precisely on the tip of one feather, while halfway between a pair on the other wing.

"Absolutely pure," he said. "I guessed as much from the greasy feel. I harden my weights with copper. Metal as soft as yours can't be touched without being diminished."

He set the vessel to one side of the table and sat down, gesturing Sharina onto the stool. "This leaves the question of how you choose to proceed," Milco said. "As you clearly surmised, there are elements in our society which would be offended by the object you've brought me. Offended enough to do violence against the owner."

With a minute grin, Milco added, "At least to attempt violence. I wouldn't choose to be the person who attacked you, milady. But that's only one side of the matter. There are others who might very well pay a considerable sum to gain an object of this sort, regardless of the material of which it was made."

"Collectors?" Sharina asked. She didn't think Milco meant collectors.

"Of a sort," Milco replied. "As you noted, the item has religious significance. I could make discreet inquiries if you like; some of them would be within the palace itself. The amount you could realize on the sale would be potentially much greater than the object's bullion value."

Sharina shrugged in turn. "No thank you," she said. "I'll sell it to you as a weight of metal."

Milco nodded. He unhooked the first steelyard and replaced it with another whose counterweight arm was much longer than that for the pan holding the objects being weighed.

The goldsmith would probably advance her something for food, but Sharina didn't have time to wait for him to make cautious inquiries to those with secret interest in demon worship. At least she didn't think she had time. Conceivably she'd have to stay in Valhocca for months or years before the Dragon sent her on the next stage of her journey—or until her friends rescued her. She thought of Cashel, striding toward her through whatever happened to be in his way.

As she waited, Sharina smiled to imagine Valhoccans secretly worshipping the Dragon. He wasn't a God or even a demon—though she wouldn't be surprised to learn that the Dragon had demonic powers. Sharina doubted prayer would be a very good way to get him to help, though.

"Because you're a stranger," Milco said as he set the three gold demons in the pan of his counterweight, "I'll mention that we exchange twenty weights of silver for one gold, and twelve copper for one weight of silver. Iron is ten to one against copper."

"What sort of coins do you use here?" Sharina said. She'd seen the little iron wedges tossed to the street entertainers and once she'd noticed a lump of copper being offered in exchange in a shop she'd passed, but she hadn't seen real money.

"Coins?" Milco said, repeating a word that obviously had no meaning for him.

Sharina realized her mistake. Well, the goldsmith already knew that she'd come from far away—though he probably thought the distance was in space rather than time and space both.

"In my country," Sharina said, "the ruler stamps his face on metal of a given weight and purity so that it doesn't have to be weighed for every transaction."

Milco smiled thinly. "You're a very trusting people," he said as he began counting small ingots of silver into the pan of the steelyard. "If I were offered silver by one of my colleagues here, I would be certain that their weight was correct—but I'd reweigh the piece nonetheless. And if Lord Mutums were to offer the ingot, I'd first nick it to be sure that it wasn't lead under a silver wash."

Sharina laughed. "The custom of the country," she said. "Though you should recall that the ruler's face tells a merchant what the metal *is*; what value the merchant puts on that is another matter. Historians say that the coinage of some rulers has passed at the value of lead."

Milco displayed the steelyard; the counterweight hung slightly lower than the pan of silver. The goldsmith took down a third, much smaller, balance and set it on the table. He put the tiny silver image of a pig in the counterweight and set copper strips in the pan to be weighed.

Sharina frowned. The silver weighed at least four pounds and was of considerable bulk besides. The sturdy leather wallet that had come with the Pewle knife's harness would hold that amount, but it was going to be an unpleasant burden to walk around with.

Not as unpleasant as going hungry, though. She grinned, wondering what the price of a meal in Valhocca was.

Milco took the silver from the hanging steelyard, added three strips of copper, and laid four iron wedges on top. The silver and copper had been stamped, sometimes scores of times, with the hallmark of each goldsmith through whose hands it had passed and—each time—a series of circles and dots to indicate the weight.

Milco reached into his strongbox again and came out with two more silver ingots, a large one and a piece of about a fifth the size of the first. He added them to the end of the pile.

"I'm giving you a premium over the bullion value," the goldsmith said. His mouth and eyes both smiled—minutely. "If I can sell the artifact in its present form, my profit will still be considerable."

Instead of taking the metal at once, Sharina said, "You don't have to do that. We made a bargain."

"So we did," Milco agreed. "Perhaps the Gods will favor me in the future because I didn't take advantage of a stranger, do you think?"

He laughed. With something more than humor in his voice, though, he added, "And there's also the fact that I believe you when you say that the owner of the object—"

The pectoral had vanished into his strongbox as soon as he removed it from the steelyard.

"—gave it to you to sell. I worship the Shepherd, as I said. But I wouldn't willingly offend the personage whose object that was."

"I see," said Sharina. She began placing the silver in the leather wallet. The copper and iron would fit in the brocade purse she kept in her left sleeve.

She remembered the Dragon's tone when he spoke of those who were using his body for purposes of their own wizardry. She gave Milco a tight smile and said, "Yes, I think that shows good judgment on your part."

Chapter Thirteen

*I*nto the nursery crept we in secret," sang Elfin. His fingers plucked the paired strings of his lyre with spare precision. Instead of playing the full melody, the lyre touched the musical high spots while the youth's silver voice carried the burden of the tune. *"There as she slept did we fall on the nurse."*

The People laughed like the tinkle of brooks, chatting among themselves as they led Cashel through the great trees. Occasionally one would look back over a shoulder at their guest; then they'd all laugh louder.

"Silver the wires we used, sewing her lips shut," Elfin sang. *"Golden the nails that we drove through her wrists."*

He had a lovely voice, as high and pure as the singers Cashel had heard perform the first time Garric gave a banquet in the palace. When Garric learned how it was that grown men could sing that way, he'd sent them away with a pension . . . not that anything was going to grow back just because Prince Garric didn't want to hear geldings sing anymore.

Cashel glanced sideways surreptitiously at Elfin. The

fabric of the youth's tunic was flowing but you couldn't see through it. Elfin seemed pretty normal, though, except for his voice.

"Out of their sockets plucked we her eyes twain," Elfin sang. *"Sacred and gilded we wear them as jewels."*

"Do you like our music, Master Cashel?" Wella asked. When the king of the People smiled, the tip of his tongue licked out quick as a fly's wing.

"Elfin's great," Cashel said. "My friend Garric plays the pipes, but this is even better."

A further thought struck him and he frowned. "I don't know how the sheep would take to it, though," he added. "Garric can pipe them to sleep in the middle of a thunderstorm, or he used to anyway."

Wella blinked, but it wasn't the regular lids that moved: a clear membrane wiped over each eye side to side. Cashel had never seen that before, except on snakes.

"Into her nose did we winkle our pincers," Elfin sang. *"Pincers of gold for to seize on her brain."*

The People had led Cashel over the river on a bridge woven from osiers. The wood was still growing; narrow green leaves half-concealed the latticework. The trees on this side of the water were all big, broad about as well as tall, but the white oak directly ahead was the biggest tree Cashel had ever seen in his life. It was like walking into a clearing, though the branches formed a roof overhead.

Cashel frowned slightly. The oak was a wolf tree, hogging ground that could have supported a dozen ordinary trees. In the borough it would have been cut down generations ago and a dozen acorns planted in its stead.

Well, this wasn't the common wood attached to Barca's Hamlet. The People had nothing *but* forest here, so Cashel guessed they didn't have to think about how best to use their woods.

"Welcome to the King of the Forest, Master Cashel," Wella said over his shoulder. "This is the home of the People. We will provide you with fitting entertainment, dear guest."

Elfin had stopped singing; he held his lyre under his arm. He met Cashel's eyes with a nervous, angry glare. Cashel couldn't imagine what the boy had against him. Elfin acted like a dog whose master beat it when he was drunk.

"Ah, I'm glad to be here," Cashel said because his hosts expected him to say something. They twittered like flock of swallows as they led him toward a split in the side of the oak tree.

Cashel couldn't complain that they were unfriendly, any except maybe Elfin, but they'd get on his nerves if he had to stay around them any length of time. He'd rather be back in the court at Valles. Though in truth there was a lot of similarity between the People and the way courtiers acted.

Cashel raised his left fist to his cheek like he was rubbing his jaw and muttered, "Krias, is this on the way where we want to go?"

Elfin stared at Cashel with an expression of . . . well, something other than hatred. Longing? Envy, certainly.

"It's on the way to where you're going, fool that you are," the demon said. "As to it being on the way to Landure's mansion—it would be, sheep-boy, if you got beyond it."

Krias' spiky little voice was as different as could be from Elfin's singing. The funny thing was that Cashel found himself *liking* to hear the demon. It was like a bite of salt meat after too many mouthfuls of honey.

The People knew about Krias, that was certain. One by one they slipped through the opening in the great trunk. Each before he did so glanced back at the ring. They had narrow, double-pointed eyes, except for Elfin.

It bothered Cashel—sort of an itch in his mind—that the ring demon had quit squeaking his usual litany of insults and complaints when Cashel went off with the People. Cashel didn't like to be insulted, but neither did it bother him a lot. It never had; which was a good thing, since he'd had plenty of it from growing up poor and being, well, not as bright as most folks.

The truth was, he'd gotten used to Krias grumbling. There was a lot going on around Cashel that was new and worrisome; he'd just as soon that the demon, at least, had stayed the same. Well, he still had his iron-shod quarter-staff. . . .

"Enter, honored guest," Wella said, gesturing toward the split in the tree bark. "Enter the home of the People, dear Cashel."

"It's not big enough for . . ." Cashel said; and paused, because it *was* big enough now. It'd be a tight fit for him, even sideways; but the opening had been glove tight on the People who'd preceded Cashel, and none of them were half his girth or as tall either.

"Enter, that the People may entertain you," Wella said. Cashel thrust his staff out in front of him and, behind it, entered the hollow of the King of the Forest.

Whatever there was beyond the crack in the bark, it wasn't the insides of a tree. The oak was huge, sure, but this room was bigger yet and its walls seemed to have been dripped from colored wax. Stepping sideways to clear the entrance, Cashel patted the surface with his left hand. It was warm but stone-hard.

The room's greenish illumination came from inside the walls. It wasn't bright to look at, but Cashel could see bones through the flesh of his fingers when he touched the wall. The ring was a sharp black emptiness.

Under the peak of the light-vaulted hall stood a table shaped like a horseshoe with high-backed chairs around the outside. The only seat on the interior of the horseshoe was a stool facing the throne of gold and ivory in the center of the other side.

Wella slipped in behind Cashel, the last of the People to enter the chamber. A look of triumph transfigured the king's face. "Elfin," he said, "lead our guest to the seat of honor."

Elfin took Cashel by the left hand. "Come," he said. "Come."

The youth's voice sounded like distant wind chimes. As

he led Cashel to the stool across from King Wella's throne, his fingers crept down Cashel's palm toward—but not quite to—the ring. Elfin looked sidelong at Cashel the way a rabbit views a snake.

The People seated themselves on the outside of the arc, moving like thistledown on a light breeze. Their garments rippled the way a creek falls over rocks, each now with its own color instead of taking that of the light from the walls. Gold, beige, blue—all sorts of colors. All of them shifted, except Wella's robe stayed a fierce fiery red with the gleam of metal.

A high sound filled the hall, though it was almost too faint to hear. Cashel couldn't tell where it was coming from, or whether he was really hearing music rather than the thin calls of insects.

It was like sitting at the edge of a wood during late spring, when the meadow and trees were in flower and glittering bees buzzed between the blossoms. Elfin alone was plain; his garment was green, and the light threw the same sickly hue over the youth's face.

Cashel sat. The stool held his weight, though he heard it creak. It wasn't bleached oak like he'd thought. Somebody had carved it out of bones. The carpenter had fitted small pieces together with only the different textures of rib and shoulder blade and marrowbone to show the joins.

It was a nice piece of work, but Cashel didn't much like it. Sheep bones, he figured. They just about had to be sheep bones.

The People had hung their weapons on pegs about the walls when they entered. There were shields there already, curved things like crescent moons, that seemed to be made of metal, and golden spears too.

Elfin moved back against the wall. There wasn't a seat on the other side for him. Cashel wasn't sure how many of the People were present. Two double handfuls, he thought, but the number of chairs and people seemed different every time he looked across at them.

One of the People stepped from the wall itself, carrying

a tray of steaming meat. Cashel didn't know whether this servant was someone he'd seen before or if there were more of the People than he was seeing. Their robes changed color, though never exactly *when* he was looking at one of his hosts.

The servant set the tray before Wella and stepped back— into the wall again or to sit around the table with his fellows, Cashel couldn't be sure. The king rose to his feet. He took a strip of braised flesh, held it high, and nipped off the lower portion with his teeth. When Wella swallowed, Cashel realized that the throats of the People didn't swell for their voice boxes.

Wella reached across the table, holding out the rest of the piece of meat. "Eat with us, dear Cashel," he said.

Cashel had his quarterstaff upright between his legs, but it got in the way like that. He set it crossways on his knees, taking care that he didn't bang against the table that curved around him from either side.

He took the meat. It was still hot but only slightly greasy. Another of the People—a woman this time—came out of the wall, holding an ivory cup with gold and silver mountings.

"Thank you," Cashel said. He didn't trust his teeth to cut the strip as cleanly as the king's had, so he dropped the whole piece into his mouth. He chewed carefully to keep from burning himself.

Wella raised the cup and drank. He smiled at Cashel. The cup wasn't ivory. There was a human skull under all that gold and silver filigree.

"Have you figured out what the meat is, sheep-boy?" Krias said.

Cashel spat out the meat, then spit again to clear his mouth of as much juice as he hadn't already swallowed. He rose to his feet, bringing up the quarterstaff, but the People were already standing.

Their mouths opened so wide their faces seemed to split. They had teeth like glittering needles, three rows of them interlocking when the jaws closed. Walla's tongue licked out like a whiplash and wrapped about Cashel's right wrist. It was sticky and as strong as braided silk.

Cashel jerked back, pulling the king across the table toward him. The cup and tray clattered to the floor, each in its own crazy arc. Another tongue snaked about Cashel's neck. A third caught his left thigh—a handful, a double handful, the tongues of all the People, surrounding Cashel and pulling him in all directions at once.

Cashel shouted. A tongue wrapped around his head, covering his eyes. He dropped the quarterstaff and gripped the tongue that was blinding him despite the tug of others trying to drag his arms down.

Cashel pulled with all his strength against the cool, gummy appendage. He freed his eyes, but even his strength wasn't enough to rip the tongue in two. The People hissed through their open mouths, and in the sound Cashel heard laughter.

"Now a lot of people who were lucky enough to own a ring of power," Krias said in a voice like a mosquito's wings, "would want to use it. Obviously you prefer to be eaten instead, *master*."

"Do something, then!" Cashel said. The tongue wrapping his throat began to tighten. Out of the corner of his eye he saw his staff spin away, licked by another creature. A ferrule struck the wall with a flash of blue fire. It left a patch of blackness on the green, like mold on a rose leaf.

"You have to use my name!" the demon cried. "You can't command me without using my name!"

"Do something, Krias!" Cashel said, twisting his torso to take some of the strain off his neck. It didn't help. At least three of the People were choking him while others strained to pull his arms and legs out like those of a squashed roach. "Do something, or by Duzi I'll grind you to powder!"

Cashel's skin tingled. He tried to get a hand around the triple noose of flesh that was choking him, wondering if the burning sensation meant the People's touch was poisoning him as well. Right now that seemed pretty unnecessary, though Cashel wasn't about to give up.

His skin *burned*. The tongues that gripped him were shriveling like slugs caught on a hot stone. The People screamed with the high horror of axles rubbing their hubs. Wella's eyes bulged at Cashel like a frog on the tines of a gig. The king's skin blackened and his back arched as all his muscles contracted in death.

The spasm of heat passed. Cashel felt dizzy. He was sitting on the floor; he must have fallen while he struggled with the People. He started to get up, then settled again and plucked the tongues from him the way he'd have cleaned himself of cobwebs after walking through a spider-festooned woodland at evening.

The People's flesh was black and shrunken; sometimes the strands broke when Cashel unrolled them. Their touch left sticky smears on his skin; he'd want to wash as soon as he found water.

Elfin stood by the wall as he'd done since leading Cashel to his seat. The youth's fingers rested on the strings of his lyre, but he didn't pluck them or sing. Cashel couldn't read the expression on his face.

"Thank you, Krias," Cashel said. Croaked, really; he must have shouted his throat raw in the fight.

"Not bad, if I do say myself," the demon chirped. "And not before time, either. It's no concern to me whose dinner pot you fill, but I'd regret having to serve King Wella for the rest of eternity."

Cashel's skin prickled worse than a bad sunburn. He looked at his forearm and saw what he'd thought was true: the fine hairs on it were gone like he'd reached too close to a fire. He patted his forehead and found he'd singed his eyebrows, too.

The People lay scattered across the floor of the chamber, shriveled and dead. Cashel could tell which was the king by the red robe. The blackened flesh was sloughing away from bones that looked less human than the People had seemed in life.

Cashel found his quarterstaff against the far wall. He

picked it up and let the touch of smooth hickory against his palms settle him. He felt . . .

The People hadn't deserved any better than they got; but what they got wasn't something Cashel would have wished on anybody. Well, it was over, and he wasn't about to complain about a result that left him able to continue on after Sharina.

The light within the chamber was fading. The walls still had color, but it was the sullen shimmer of a coal about to go black.

"I don't mean to intrude on your philosophical reverie, master," said Krias, "but the King of the Forest is dying. Far be it from me to dissuade you if you've chosen to end your miserable existence in this fashion, but if you *don't* want a tree to collapse on you . . . ?"

"Oh," Cashel said. "Thanks."

He crossed the quarterstaff before him and twisted his torso right, then left, working the kinks out of his shoulder muscles. It hadn't been much of a fight on Cashel's part; more like trying to swim in a block of ice that gripped him everywhere and wouldn't move. He'd put everything he had into it, though, he'd tell the world!

The oak groaned like a storm was twisting it. It wouldn't stand long; and Cashel guessed it'd stood longer already than it should've.

He strode toward the opening and found it larger than he remembered; punk wood was flaking away from the edges the way it did when the wind ripped a limb from an old elm and showed the hollow heart.

Elfin stood motionless. It was so dark now that he could have been a stain on the dank wood.

"Are you coming?" Cashel said.

Elfin said nothing, but Cashel heard the lyre whisper.

"Do as you please!" Cashel said, and stepped out into the forest. He felt weak and angry, and the red light outside had an evil shimmer that brought no balm to his soul.

*   *   *

Garric stepped onto the roof of Alae. Even the wind blowing fiercely in his face didn't fill his lungs with air. He felt as though he were being whipped with cobwebs too fine to see.

Near the edge of the building, facing west over the barren desert, was a sapphire throne that had been made for giants. A man of normal size sat in it now.

The roof was empty of all except the wind, the throne, and the person on it. Garric helped Tenoctris up the last step. His tunic fluttered and his sword shivered against its scabbard.

"He's there, I think," Garric murmured with a nod toward the throne. "Somebody is."

Tenoctris smiled, but she didn't waste breath speaking. Between her two younger friends, she walked with short steps to the side of the throne.

Close up it seemed even bigger than it had from the head of the stairs. It was in scale with its surroundings: the flat plain of the roof; the horizon beyond the city's half-submerged limits, empty in all directions; and a sky of brilliant, unwinking stars.

"Lord Alman," Tenoctris said in a surprisingly firm voice. From here only the head of the seated man was visible over the throne's crystal arm. "We've come from a time past your own to ask your help in forestalling chaos."

For a moment nothing happened. Then, as slow as a winter dawn, the man turned on the stone seat to look down at them. He placed his hand on the chair arm.

"Am I dreaming, I wonder?" he said. His voice cracked with disuse and dry air.

Garric reached up to squeeze Alman's hand. The wizard's bones and sinews were prominent beneath a thin coating of flesh. "We're real, sir," he said.

"So it seems," Alman said. "Or else I've lost my mind entirely, of course. In either case I suppose I'd better join you. A moment, please."

Alman turned, then slowly backed down the three high steps from the seat. Garric didn't think the throne had ever been meant for use; though on the other hand, an empty chair made an odd monument.

"I didn't think anyone could find me here," Alman said, looking at his visitors with a mixture of interest and puzzlement. He was younger than Garric had first thought: no older than Reise, certainly. Alman's hair had thinned back from his forehead, but the half that remained was black. His skin was dry and wind-cracked, but his face wasn't a mass of wrinkles like that of Tenoctris.

"Your power meant people were aware of you despite your reclusiveness," Tenoctris said. "Even so I wouldn't have been able to locate you, let alone visit you in your seclusion, except for the crisis that my age faces."

She made a slight gesture to wipe away a partial misstatement. "The age which I now call mine," she said, correcting herself.

Alman shrugged. "I suppose we may as well go down," he said. "Now that you've awakened me, I find I'm thirsty. And I suppose I should eat something as well."

Alman moved and spoke with the frailty of the very old. Tenoctris *was* old, but that was only a weakness of her body: her intellect and personality were as sprightly as a three-year-old's. Alman had one foot in another world. Everything about him projected an aura of gray dullness.

Head bowed, he walked to the head of the staircase. Garric strode ahead to lead as he'd done on the way up. No threat would follow them from the empty roof. There probably wouldn't be any danger below either, but Garric knew without King Carus' approving nod that this was no place to take unnecessary chances.

"There is *no place to take unnecessary chances, lad,"* the king whispered in Garric's mind. *"Of course, there's no place for a leader who won't take necessary chances, either."*

Garric thought of offering Alman his arm, but on consideration he decided that might be taken as an insult. The wizard had climbed the stairs unaided, after all, and he almost certainly made the journey up and down on a regular basis.

"We've come to borrow the Lens of Rushila, Lord Alman," Tenoctris said. "I say 'borrow,' but it may be that I'll be unable to return the Lens to you if I'm successful in ridding our age of the gateway that threatens us."

Tenoctris was last down the stairs, her hand on Liane's shoulder. The treads were narrow, and the lack of a railing made even Garric frown. It'd be a bad place to fall.

"The Lens of Rushila?" Alman said after a pause so long that Garric had given up on an answer. "Yes, I have that. I think I do, anyway. I don't really remember what I brought with me to Alae."

"A wizard has opened a gateway to our age," Tenoctris said, though Alman hadn't asked for an explanation. "I'm not strong enough to reach him through an ordinary scrying ritual. With the Lens I can view the wizard and get a better idea of what his purpose might be."

"The Lens of Rushila," Alman repeated with an expression of wonder. "I was so very proud when I split the rock and raised it to the light for the first time since . . ."

He shook his head. "Since time began as men know time, perhaps," he said. "Since our world was formed."

Garric reached the ground and sighed with relief. The staircase trembled like a sparrow's heart through the soles of his boots, vibrating to the rhythm of the wind. The spiral seemed as solid as the day it was built, but . . . well, it was good to stand on stone again.

"The Lens came from the eye of a creature older than the stars," Alman said. He walked toward the part of the relief where Garric had found the trove of foraged food. "Rushila conjectured its existence but he never found the Lens. I alone could do that!"

For a moment Garric saw a different Alman—a wizard of unexcelled power, arrogant in his strength. His words woke echoes from the rotunda's high ceiling. Then the memory passed and Alman, weak from privations and older than his years, hunched in on himself in a series of racking coughs.

Garric put an arm around him for support and said, "Sir, do you have water here? I'll get you a drink."

Alman raised a hand in denial. "No," he said when he regained control of his throat. "No, I was only laughing at myself."

He shuffled to the collection of food, holding Garric's arm for the first few steps. He took a knife with a gold-chased blade from the sheath tucked into his sash. Removing a bulb the size of his head from the store, he stabbed through the top in a circular coring motion. Alman lifted the plug between the thumb and forefinger of the hand that held the dagger, then tilted the bulb to suck deeply from the opening.

"Is that your only source of water?" Liane asked.

"It's mine!" Alman said, hugging the bulb to his chest with one arm and waggling the dagger wildly with the other. His eyes and expression cleared. "Oh," he said. "I . . . I've been remiss; you're my guests, after all. Would you like . . . ?"

He offered the bulb hesitantly. A trickle of pulp leaked from the opening. It was the consistency of thin gruel and smelled strongly of turpentine. The odor and the thought of drinking it made Garric's stomach turn, though he hoped he managed to keep his reaction off his face.

"No thank you," Liane said calmly. "We'll be going back soon."

She glanced toward Tenoctris. "Yes, that's right," the old wizard said. "As soon as we have the Lens, we'll leave you in peace, Lord Alman. Unless . . . Would you like to come back with us?"

"It's only that the water roots are getting harder to find," Alman said apologetically. "I have to go farther and farther to find them. And I don't want to leave Alae, because of the throne."

He looked up the spiral length of the staircase to the roof opening. "In my room in Sandine I had a glass," he said, "in which I summoned the wizards of former times. I drew Rushila to me. He came and answered my questions, for he was dead and I had the power of living over the dead. I called up others, gained their knowledge, and added to it my own researches. I had the wisdom of all ages at my fingertips!"

Again Garric heard the power that underlay the speech. The vast building, or at least Garric's perception of it, shimmered to the rhythm of Alman's words.

"Then I realized," Alman said, shrinking into a man again and a frail man besides, "that despite my power someday I would die. Another wizard would arise and I would be a shadow in *his* glass, dancing to his tune for eternities to come. So I smashed my glass and came here to Alae. When I die there will be no one left to command me. I sit on the throne of God and watch the sun set, waiting for the day it will no longer rise."

"May we borrow the Lens now, Lord Alman?" Tenoctris said quietly. "We should be going, and you have your own affairs to attend."

"Yes, yes," said Alman. He drank again from the bulb, this time sucking with desperate insistence to gain the last of the moisture from the thick rind. He capped the hole carefully with the plug and set the bulb back into a niche of the mural.

"Sometimes more drains down if I let it sit for a little while," he explained.

Garric was afraid to speak. Anything he said might have sounded like an insult, and they needed Alman's help. In his mind, the stone-faced Carus said, *"If anybody treated a prisoner of mine this way, I'd have the skin off his back as quick as I could uncoil a whip. But this man's done it to himself."*

Alman paused, then noticed his three visitors again. "Oh!" he said in mild surprise. "You're still here. Yes, I was going to give you the Lens of Rushila. It's in the place where I sleep. Out of the wind, you see."

He shuffled toward the vast double doors and slipped

between them into the starlit night. Tenoctris nodded; Garric followed at Alman's heels while Liane and the older woman came after. Outside was a semicircular plaza bordered by a low coping. Drifting sand had covered what once was the vista beyond.

For all the wind's echoing whistle in the rotunda, its force was noticeably greater outside. Here at ground level the thin air used sand grains for teeth, nibbling at the skin of Garric's calves above his boot tops.

"Sometimes I fall asleep on the throne," Alman said. "It's so cold there, though. Once I had to crawl down the stairs because I was too stiff to stand."

They were shuffling toward the mouth of a storm drain set into the coping. Garric looked out at the horizon, amazed at the thought of violent rain buffeting this dry wasteland. That—more than the ruined state of the buildings—drove home to him how extremely old Alae must be.

"Here it is," Alman said, kneeling at the entrance. The stone was recessed for a metal grate, but that had perished long since. Alman crawled through, his bare feet vanishing like those of a vole hopping into a crack in the rocks.

Garric squatted at the entrance. He could fit, even with his sword slung, but he wasn't sure he wanted to crawl down a dark hole without some better notion of what waited for him there. "Do you have light, sir?" he called.

"Light?" Alman repeated. "Oh. Oh, I'm sure I can find it . . ."

Tenoctris sat before the figure she'd scratched in the sand with one of the bamboo splints from the satchel Liane carried. *"Thai picale,"* she murmured, tapping the miniature wand on the syllables as she pronounced them. *"Huprista . . ."*

"I'm sure it must be here somewhere," Alman said a muffled voice. Garric heard objects clack. He winced, though the Lens of Rushila must be fairly sturdy to have been blasted out of rock to begin with. "It couldn't have gone anywhere, after all."

The plaza was paved in swirling patterns of white and gray stone, or perhaps white and colors which Garric couldn't determine in the faint starlight. Sand had risen to this level in something more than a dusting but not yet a complete layer.

In the sand near the drain were marks that could have been the prints of shod feet—not his own.

Or the marks could be insect paths. Whatever had caused them, they were sharp and recent.

"Konaioi!" said Tenoctris. Blue light bloomed in the center of her hexagon, a fist-sized ball as faint as foxfire. It rolled like thistledown across the pavement and down the mouth of the drain. Without pausing to ask, Garric followed the light.

He was in a masonry chamber so low that he had to squat for his head to clear the ceiling. A pipe joined on either hand. Sand choked the one on the left; the other was blocked by human debris—containers made of wood, glass, and stone, some broken, lying every which way. Alman was rummaging in the collection, discarding the unwanted pieces onto the pile of fabric on the chamber's floor.

"See?" he said without turning around. His voice reverberated from the pipe, blurring without gaining strength. "This is my athame. The Lens should be with it."

He tossed the spell knife behind him. It had been forged from strips of iron and silver woven into patterns as ornate as any creation of Ilna's. The metals gleamed with their different lusters in the bluish wizard-light.

Garric lifted the pieces of cloth, a velvet robe and the tatters of a tunic of transparently fine silk, and sorted through it while the wizard dug. Another little beetle tumbled out and scuttled to a shadowed corner. The cloth was empty except for the things Alman had just tossed onto it.

"I don't understand," Alman said. He reached as deeply into the pipe as his arm would stretch. "Where could it have gone? Did I not bring the Lens with me after all?"

"Let me try," said Garric. He moved the wizard aside—

not harshly, but Alman's thin frame seemed to have no weight at all. The wizard-light drifted to the mouth of the pipe, then slipped inside. Garric could see the seams between blocks in a regular pattern that went on for—

He jerked himself back and blinked, then rubbed his eyes. There was something hypnotizing about the pattern within the masonry: the builders had done more than join stone to stone. Garric was sure there was nothing bigger than a grain of sand within the pipe.

The drain inlet was pale and the only light remaining within the chamber. "Let's get out now, Lord Alman," Garric said. "I don't think we're going to find the Lens."

Garric pulled himself up, feeling weak. His head was beginning to ache, and his eyes itched from grit and dryness. "Tenoctris," he said. "It isn't here. I think someone's been here before us."

Garric frowned as he thought of how fresh the maybe-footprints looked. He couldn't be sure, but . . .

"I think somebody may have taken the Lens while we were looking for Lord Alman," he said. "Is that possible?"

Tenoctris nodded. "Yes," she said. "It is. Someone watching me could follow, if they were powerful enough. I don't know precisely what it means, but—"

She flashed her smile at Garric and Liane.

"—I'm confident that it doesn't mean anything that would please me."

Alman climbed out of the drain. He moved with the aged care of a tortoise.

"Lord Alman?" Tenoctris said. "Thank you for attempting to help us. We won't trouble you again."

"I can't think where it could have gone," Alman said, shaking his head in puzzlement. "I'm sure I would have brought it here to Alae with me. I was so proud of owning the Lens of Rushila."

A shooting star flashed across the heaven, looking much closer than the ones Garric had seen at night on Haft. It was briefly as vivid as a comet.

Alman had watched the streak of fire also. "The Lens

of Rushila was part of the eye of a creature older than our world," he said musingly. "Older than our portion of the cosmos. And yet it died. All things die."

"In order to return, I need to draw my spell where we entered this plane," Tenoctris said quietly. She took a grip on Liane's arm.

"Sir?" said Garric. "Lord Alman?"

Alman had started back toward the palace. At Garric's call, he turned. He looked surprised to see other people.

"Sir, won't you please come back with us?" Garric said. He gestured toward the horizon of sand. "This is no place for a human. It's no place for anything that's alive."

"Leave?" Alman said. He smiled faintly. "You're trying to be kind, I see, but you're quite wrong. Here I can sit on the throne and watch the sun set. I'll continue to do that until the night that the sun no longer rises, for the world or for me. It's all the same, you see. And there's nothing else anywhere—nothing but darkness or the promise of darkness."

Alman resumed walking toward the palace. Garric watched him for a moment, then lifted Tenoctris in his arms.

"I'll carry you," he said. He was strong enough for this, for the brief distance involved. "It'll be quicker that way. And I want very much to get out of this place. I don't like what it does to human beings."

A pair of men with yellow stripes on their sleeves were watching the bird perform when Sharina returned to the plaza. One of them tossed down an iron wedge to clink against the two already on the cloth. Talking of dinner, the men walked on.

The bird stopped dancing and squatted, startling Sharina subconsciously because its knees bent backward. It began folding the cloth by the corners.

"Wait," Sharina said, stepping close to the dancer with her thumb and index finger in her purse. "I watched you earlier but I didn't have money then. Here."

She brought out a short copper strip, its edges smoothed by the touch of those among whom it'd been passed and repassed. She offered the metal, uncertain whether to hand it to the dancer or to wait for him to reopen the cloth to avoid direct contact. Sharina had seen enough of the world to know that customs differed from place to place. She'd also seen that people kept to customary ways with a determination that they rarely granted their laws.

The bird stood, holding the cloth as a neat bundle in both hands. It was taller than Sharina by a hand's breadth, but most of that difference was a feather crest. A circle of down petaled outward from either round eye, making the orbs seem larger than they actually were.

"No thank you, mistress," the bird said. "I have earned sufficient money today."

She hadn't been sure it *could* speak. In fact its voice could pass as that of a Valhoccan, at least to Sharina's foreign ears. Its words were half a tone higher than the goldsmith's, still well within normal human range.

"Yes, but I want you to have this," Sharina said, raising the copper a trifle to call attention to it. "I watched you earlier and I was unable to pay you. Now I'm paying my debt."

She knew that the strip was at least twice the value of the three bits of iron the dancer had collected. There was a small wicker basket on the ground, apparently the bird's only possession beyond its harness and the square of cloth for donations. Perhaps it had transferred earlier takings there, but Sharina doubted it. The basket's lid was knotted on with pale hemp cords which would have been discolored if they were tied and untied every day.

"I am Dalar, the youngest son and bodyguard of Rokonar," the bird said. "I guarded my sister as she sailed to become Testig's bride. I could not save her from the storm that engulfed the ship. It blew me to this far land on the wreckage, when I might better have died."

Dalar raised his face to the twilight and hooted like the

scream of a black sea eagle, once, twice, and again. People in the plaza looked around, startled, and a barrow woman shouted curses as she picked up quinces she'd spilled to the ground.

"Because I choose to live," the bird said in his normal voice, staring eye to eye at Sharina again, "I humiliate myself by performing the Battledance of Rokonar. But I have not lost all honor, so I take only what I *need* to live, mistress."

He raised the fabric covering the iron wedges. "This covers my needs."

"Wait," Sharina said as Dalar turned away from her. His head rotated so that the bird's great eyes stared at her over his thin shoulders. "I'm a stranger in Valhocca. I come from even farther away than you do."

Dalar turned his body so that he and Sharina faced one another normally again. The tiny adjustments his feet made were themselves a dance.

"I don't know anything about the city, and I don't know how long I'll have to stay," Sharina continued, licking her lips. "My name is Sharina os-Reise."

She hadn't jumped away in horror when Dalar appeared to wring his own neck, but she hadn't missed doing that by very much either. She suspected the bird used his inhuman suppleness to create a barrier between himself and the curious.

"You wish me to direct you to a guide, Sharina os-Reise?" Dalar said. He spoke with a studied lack of inflection.

"I wish to employ you as a bodyguard," Sharina said. She forced herself to stare straight at Dalar because that appeared to be his choice of interaction. The bird's eyes were amber around wide black pupils. "I didn't have money earlier; now I do, and I need protection in this strange city."

She'd meant no more in approaching the bird than she'd said at the time: to offer a unique performer a mite from her bounty. The plan had rooted and blossomed at she spoke with him. Sharina didn't know what Dalar would be like in a fight—though she for one wouldn't choose to be kicked by those clawed toes—but she was certain that a warrior whose honor forbade him to take more than bare life from strangers wasn't going to cut her throat for a wallet of silver.

The sun was setting. Oil lamps gleamed from a few east-facing windows, though those across the plaza were still making do with sky glow.

"I am Dalar son of Rokonar," the bird said. He spoke quietly, though the words had in them a hint of the proud scream of moments before. "The wind blew me north for thirty days. I drank the rain that soaked my feathers, and I ate fish that surfaced beside my raft of decking. There is no one in Valhocca who came from farther away than I did, mistress."

"And yet I have," Sharina said. "We're both strangers. I may need your strength, Master Dalar, but I need your honor more. Will you serve me?"

"I will take from you a warrior's scot of meals and lodging, Sharina os-Reise," the bird said. "And each Year Day you will provide me with new silver bindings for my toes. It's traditional in the house of Rokonar to offer the chief bodyguard one of the females from your harem as a mark of special respect after a victory, but I think—"

Dalar opened his short beak amazingly wide and clucked like an angry hen. It was a moment before Sharina realized that the bird was laughing.

"I think, as I say," Dalar resumed, "that we can pass over that for the time being."

Sharina let out her breath, surprised at how relieved she felt. She did need a guard, that was true enough; Milco had been an honorable man, but she had no doubt that Valhoccans included a normal human percentage of thieves and worse. A lone woman leaving a goldsmith's with a full wallet was likely to arouse interest of the wrong sort.

But there was more to it than material need. Sharina was just as much a stranger as she'd told Dalar she was. The presence of someone who belonged with her was more important to Sharina than the bird's ability to kick a footpad into the middle of tomorrow.

"Well," said Sharina, "I'll begin my duties with the food and lodging—and I hope to find a sufficiency of the same for myself. Especially the food. Is there an inn of any quality in Valhocca?"

A further thought struck her. Before Dalar could reply, she added, "An inn that won't object to strangers from far away, that is."

The bird clucked with laughter again. "I sleep in the stables of the Golden Tunny for an iron stiver a night," he said. "They are clean, as stables go. They have rooms that would be suitable for a lady of the quality expressed by the weight of your purse, mistress; and they will not quibble at a warrior of Rokonar sleeping on his employer's doorsill."

Sharina nodded. "Let's go, then," she said. "Ah— Dalar?"

"Mistress?" the bird said. He'd started to unknot the crossties binding the lid of his wicker basket. Including the "thumb," Dalar had four fingers. Like his arms, they were shorter than would be normal for a man of his height.

"I'll be leaving Valhocca, I don't know when," Sharina said. "And I don't know where I'll be going, except that it'll be another long way. I've been told that there'll be risk, which I can readily believe."

She grinned, then wondered if Dalar recognized human facial expressions. He probably did.

"Anyway," she went on, "if it were possible for you to accompany me, would you be willing to do so?"

Dalar laughed again. "A warrior of Rokonar is willing to stick his arm in a furnace if his master desires it, mistress," he said.

"Yes, well, I hope it won't come to that," Sharina said, though her words made her wonder just what the Dragon *did* have in mind when he warned her. "Let's get me some supper, shall we?"

"One moment, mistress," Dalar said. He loosed the final knot and removed the lid of his basket. He took out the contents and dropped the wicker at his feet.

"When I was a street entertainer," he said, pouring the contents from one hand to the other, "I had no right to touch these. Now I am a warrior again."

He opened his stubby hands to Sharina. There was an eight-faced weight made like two pyramids joined base to base in either palm. A length of fine chain joined them. Everything was made of the same dark metal. Sharina couldn't tell the length of the chain, because it flowed like a liquid.

Dalar spun out the weight in his right hand on a yard or so of chain. It blurred in the air, visible only because the lamps of passersby woke glints from its luster. There was a *whack* and the basket leaped off the pavement sawn into two ragged pieces of wicker.

Dalar reached out; the spinning weight vanished into his closed palm. The links of the chain whined minusculely against one another.

"What's it made of?" Sharina said, forcing herself to say *something*. She shouldn't have been surprised. She'd seen Dalar dance, after all. "I don't recognize the metal."

"A kind of bronze," the bird said. He clucked softly. "A very hard kind of bronze. As hard as steel, mistress, but it will not rust."

He held the two weights and chain in one hand; the combination took up as little space as a pair of hen's eggs. Sharina smiled and said, "I'll let you lead us to the Golden Tunny, Dalar. Since you know the way."

The bird nodded. Very deliberately he opened his bundle of cloth with his free hand, flicking the bits of iron into the night. He dropped the cloth on the ground and strode down the street, his crest erect. Sharina walked at his heels; Dalar appeared to have better night vision than she did, besides knowing where he was going.

Well, Sharina knew where she was going also: she was following Dalar. She chuckled.

Barrowfolk were trundling their rigs off the streets, and most of the shopkeepers lowered shutters across the front of their establishments. Cookshops and taverns were just gearing up for the night's activities, and down a cross street Sharina saw women in gaudy outfits seating themselves in windows.

A narrow alley led between two shops, both closed for the night. Dalar paused at the opening and said, "Mistress? If you'd rather, we can go around, but this leads directly to the inn."

"The shortcut is fine," Sharina said. She touched the hilt of the Pewle knife, which still hung under her arm for concealment's sake. The gesture was reflex, not because she was worried about the route.

A baby was crying in the second-floor apartment to their right. There were no real windows, just bamboo-grated ventilators near the roofline. Somebody was boiling cabbage in the building to the left. She could see Dalar's gangling form ahead of her, silhouetted against the faint light from the street beyond.

The dry reptilian odor warned her. She stopped. "Dalar!" she called. "Wait!"

The Dragon sat in an alcove to her left, which a moment before had been a blank wall from which most of the stucco had flaked. "Greetings, Sharina, my servant," he said. "You're ready to continue with your journey?"

Dalar had turned back. "Mistress?" he said. "Is something wrong?"

"Your companion isn't aware of me," the Dragon said. "Reassure him if you will, so that I can get on with the instructions."

"Dalar, I'm having a vision," Sharina said quickly. She supposed that was more true than not, though just now she was willing to shade the truth in order to simplify the situation. "I need to concentrate for a moment."

"Very good," said the Dragon with a nod. His voice was within her mind as she'd heard him before. "Just before you reach the head of this alley, you'll see a block of white stone used in the foundation course of the building to your left. It was once the seat of my throne."

He gave a clicking laugh. "That was a very long time ago. It will slide out of the wall despite the efforts of the folk of this day to mortar it into place. You must remove the stone and crawl through the opening."

"Sir?" said Sharina. She'd been extremely hungry a moment before, but now her stomach was too knotted to think of food. "I have a companion. He'll be coming with me—if that's all right?"

The Dragon laughed again. "So long as my servants carry out their duties faithfully," his cold soundless voice said, "I don't care how they live their own lives. Farewell for now, Sharina."

The pattern of light—volume holding a creature—dissipated like the constellations at sunrise. Sharina faced the blank wall again. Dalar stood beside her, his body turned toward the end of the alley but his eyes watching his employer.

"We aren't going to the Golden Tunny after all, Dalar," Sharina said. She was trembling. Too much had happened too suddenly, and she *needed* food even though she doubted that she'd be able to get anything to stay down right now. "We're looking for a block of white stone in this foundation."

She tapped the wall behind her with her foot.

"And then we're going somewhere else, you and I," Sharina added. "May the Lady shelter us with Her favor!"

"Shoals ahead!" the lookout at the *Ravager*'s mast truck called across the water. His voice had the same high rawness as those of the gulls wheeling above the triremes.

"Shoals!" snorted Chalcus from the rail beside Ilna, two paces back from the prow. "Those aren't shoals, they're the shells of the Great Ones."

His expression hardened and he added, "Though I never saw so many on the surface together, that I'll admit. And

I never saw an island in these waters before, I'll say that too."

Vonculo and his four lieutenants stood in the far bow. The *Terror* was proceeding on the pull of twenty oars, even those few at half-stroke. A common sailor had taken the tiller, freeing the helmsman to join the other leaders.

Ilna sneered. If "leader" was a word that described any of this gang of buffoons.

"You've been here before, Master Chalcus?" Merota asked, leaning back from the rail so that she could see the sailor past Ilna's slim self.

"So I have, mistress," Chalcus said. "Though that was long since. A lifetime ago, you might say. Isn't that right, Ilna-girl?"

He grinned at her.

"I don't know anything about your life or lives," Ilna said coldly. "I know that I'd prefer you never call me 'girl' again."

She didn't add a threat. She wasn't sure what she'd do if Chalcus repeated his "Ilna-girl," but she did know that if she spoke a threat now she'd have to carry it out later—whether she wanted to or not.

"Ah," said Chalcus with a nod. "Then I'd best be careful not to do that, hadn't I? But calling you 'Ilna,' there's no harm in that?"

"It's my name," Ilna said. "Of course there's no harm in using it."

Chalcus was . . . interesting. He'd understood exactly what she'd meant: why she hadn't threatened to send him over the side screaming, for example. And also that Ilna might do exactly that thing without warning, if the occasion arose and she felt angry enough.

That would be a terrible overreaction, of course, but Ilna had done worse things than that in her life. And so, she was quite certain, had Chalcus. An interesting man.

The triremes were heading into the sunset. The sides of the island ahead were covered with vegetation, but there was a muddy freshness on the land breeze.

The sea shimmered with sunlight on the opalescent shells of the Great Ones clogging the water. Garric called the creatures ammonites when he meant the sea animal with tentacles and a coiled shell instead of the bogeys, the ancient Gods and now black evil. Looking at these, Ilna thought that Chalcus had been right: these were the Great Ones.

The triremes advanced, no faster than babies crawling. Men shouted to one another across the water between the vessels.

"They're trying to make each other feel better about this," Chalcus said with a chuckle.

"Yes, and themselves as well, I shouldn't wonder," Ilna agreed.

She didn't find the creatures frightening. A poor girl trying to keep herself and a brother growing to the size of any two other men learns to cook whatever's available and cheap. Sometimes that meant ammonites. Shelled and sliced into rings they weren't bad, once Ilna learned that if you did more than sauté them lightly you'd find them as hard to chew as ox gristle.

Tentacles waved suddenly; the Great Ones vanished beneath the sea, leaving the water astir with foam. The swells tonight were sullen as though the waves themselves misliked their present surroundings.

Ilna didn't mind the Great Ones; but if the island ahead was Vonculo's destination, Chalcus' doubts that the mutineers would find a sailors' paradise were well-taken. From this angle the hills dropped to the water in darkly wooded slopes; high bluffs overhung the sea not far to the south. There was nothing obviously threatening, but the landscape nonetheless made Ilna think of the temporary corrals built in the fall when Stallert the Butcher culled the borough's flocks.

Vonculo turned. "Get to your benches!" he ordered with a wave of his arm. The gesture was meant to be brusk but looked nearly desperate. "We'll bring her up within bowshot, then reverse onto the beach!"

"He'll do wonders," Chalcus murmured to Ilna with a grin. He patted Merota on the shoulder as he sauntered to the lead oarbench. Adjusting the sheath of his curved sword so that the hilt wouldn't foul his wrists as he leaned into his oarloom, he bellowed, "Bow section, out oars!"

For half an eyeblink, Ilna had thought Chalcus was going to pat *her*. She'd have—

She blinked in confusion, then chuckled. Ilna didn't know what she'd have done. Well, it hadn't happened.

"Ilna?" the child asked. "Is something funny?"

"I'm laughing at myself, Merota," Ilna said. "Perhaps that's funny, yes."

Chalcus *was* a leader. Certainly he could have led a more impressive gang than these bumbling mutineers. Mastyn had been the only one of them with real drive, and Chalcus could have handled the fellow as easily as Ilna herself had.

"Is that where we're spending the night?" Merota asked. She kept her voice calm, but Ilna could hear the tension underlying the words. Even Vonculo and his fellows could see this island was no place to land, but they let hope and desperation pull them forward regardless.

"This night at least," Ilna said quietly. "I don't see any sign of streets covered with gold and jewels, but perhaps that's because the light's bad."

The *Ravager* was surging forward. The *Terror* had been slower getting under way than her consort, but the rowers were driving them on strongly now.

Chalcus grinned at Ilna over his oar. The island's shadow fell across the ship, but she could see the wink of the chanteyman's teeth.

The *Ravager*'s lookout screamed and pitched forward from his perch. Oars flailed wildly as the rowers rolled off their benches.

"Hold on to me, child!" Ilna said. She squatted and wrapped her arms around Merota, then gripped the railing on the other side of the girl.

"Reverse stroke!" Chalcus shouted, jumping up to brace

himself between his bench and the loom of his oar.

The *Terror* slid to a sucking halt. Crewmen, bits of gear, and baggage that hadn't been secured properly after the mutineers rummaged through it bounced toward the trireme's bow.

The lookout saw the trouble coming and slid to safety down the backstay, but the mast itself whipped forward under the sudden stress. It didn't snap, but Ilna heard wood crackle dangerously over the shouts of startled sailors. They'd have to splint the mast before putting the strain of a sail on it.

Ilna smiled without humor. It might be premature to consider how the ships were going to be repaired.

She rose, still sheltering Merota. The trireme remained upright, though the *Ravager* several lengths ahead was slowly tilting onto her left side. The water around both vessels swirled in dark patterns.

Chalcus made his way back to them. The *Terror*'s helmsman had pitched over the bow railing at the impact. Vonculo and another sailor had jumped down onto the trireme's ram to help the fellow back aboard. Half a dozen men were shouting orders, none of them to any purpose that Ilna could see.

"And again," said the chanteyman, "It might be that a school of the Great Ones was swimming over a mud bottom not a pace below the surface. Another thing I've never seen before, but I should've told Vonculo to put out a leadsman before we shifted closer."

He looked toward the shore. The island was in full darkness. Lamps gleamed on the other vessel. The *Ravager* carried a skiff, and a party was sliding her across the deck tilted like a ramp.

"What should we do, Ilna?" Merota asked quietly. She was watching Chalcus.

Ilna shrugged. "Wait or swim, I suppose," she said. "And speaking for myself, I can't swim. Can the ship get free of this, Master Chalcus?"

"After the tide turns," the chanteyman said, "which

should be in about six hours. When the moon's *there*."

He pointed his left arm toward a spot midway between zenith and the western horizon. Two fingers of his right hand rested lightly on his sword's eared pommel in what Ilna didn't think was a conscious gesture.

"That's if we haven't sprung the hull strakes," he added with a sour grimace. "Which I doubt we have on mud, but I've seen eggshells built sturdier than a warship's hull. Pine's light and easy to work, I'll grant you, but give me an ironwood Lataeene two-banker if I'm going to come aboard another ship under way."

"The Lataeene Islands are the Pirate Islands, aren't they, Master Chalcus?" Merota asked. Innocently, Ilna supposed, because the child really *was* innocent.

"I've heard them called that, mistress," Chalcus said, his voice as flowing and normal as ever. "But you mustn't believe everything you hear."

He looked over Merota's head to Ilna. "Though some might be true, that's so," he added with the same false unconcern.

"Someday I may tell you about what I did when I first lived in Erdin," Ilna said evenly, her eyes on the skiff drawing closer to the land. A sailor stood in the bow with a lantern, though it couldn't have shone any distance ahead. The scouts going ashore were frightened and using the light to reassure themselves.

In fact Ilna didn't intend ever to tell Chalcus in detail about the amulets she'd woven for any woman who had the money. Love charms that really worked, visual spells that drew men despite any bonds of love or duty or honor that worked to hold them back.

Ilna had no idea of how many murders and suicides, how much misery in a thousand other ways, she'd caused with the ribbons she wove. The cost hadn't mattered to her at the time Evil ruled her, and it didn't really matter now. All that mattered was Ilna's knowledge that though she spent her whole lifetime trying to repay the damage she'd caused, she'd never be able to do enough.

So Chalcus had been a pirate? There were people who had a right to judge him for that, but Ilna os-Kenset wasn't among them.

The skiff must have reached the shore, though except for the lantern there was no way of distinguishing the sailors from the island. The sky looked bright, but it cast no light on the surface beneath. The *Ravager* was closer to land than it was to the *Terror*; the leading vessel had been following a channel of sorts through the underwater mudbank.

"The tide has another hour to fall," Chalcus said, watching the land. Ilna wondered if the sailor could see more in the darkness than she could. "I think we bellied deep enough into the mud that we won't topple over the way that lot did."

He nodded toward the *Ravager*, now lying on her side with her port rail in the water. Men were crawling over the trireme with lamps and tools, cursing one another and shouting demands to their fellows on the *Terror*. Vonculo shouted back, but for the most part the *Terror*'s crew seemed ready to wait for news from their consort's scouting party.

"And while it's cramped quarters if we spend the night aboard," Chalcus added with a broader specimen of his usual grin, "I think I'd just as soon be here as there tonight. Not so?"

"Yes, I agree," Ilna said. She squeezed Merota's shoulder.

"I have some bread and cheese," Ilna went on. "Since we won't have a cooking fire—"

The lantern ashore spun in a high arc, starting to drop just before it went out. *Why don't they shout something?* Ilna thought, but the scream was only a few heartbeats behind the sparks of spinning light. She'd forgotten the distance to the shore.

The scream cut off suddenly. For a moment there was silence, marked only by the whisper of waves and the sobbing of a sailor nearby.

Something on shore started laughing. The sound was too loud and terrible to come from a human throat. It continued in echoing peals, fading slowly, until it ended as though the creature had gone behind a hill. Ilna thought she still heard hints of the manic hilarity, ever fainter.

"Ilna os-Kenset!" Vonculo shouted. "Wizard! Come here!"

Chapter Fourteen

Anhira panton phrougi," Tenoctris said; then, jabbing her little wand down into the center of the figure, *"Atithe!"*

A whirlwind spun upward, swifter and carrying more material than the thin air of this desert could have lifted. The vortex scavenged down to the pavement beneath the drifted sand, then dug deeper yet as it expanded.

Azure sparks spun among the sand grains. Garric leaned backward, putting a hand on each of the women as the walls of the vortex swept over them. The hole at their feet plunged down to—

Garric, Liane, and Tenoctris crouched at the mouth of a tunnel, not a pit toward the center of the world. The walls had a fiery blue translucence, sometimes sagging inward as though something heavy constricted the tube.

Tenoctris slumped forward; Garric caught her. "We have to go on," she whispered, her eyes closed with exhaustion. "Help me if you can."

If I can! Garric thought. He scooped the old woman up in his arms, resting her head on his right shoulder. Liane gave him a nod and a tight smile. She'd already shouldered the satchel holding the paraphernalia of Tenoctris' art. Side by side, they started down the glowing tunnel.

The air was dry and without character, but at least it was thick enough to breathe. Garric felt as though he'd surfaced after too long underwater. He didn't understand how Alman could choose to live the way he did.

He glanced back over his shoulder, but the tunnel stretched infinitely far in that direction also. Liane saw the gesture and said, "It wouldn't have been right to drag Lord Alman back against his will." Then, "Would it?

"I didn't think so," Garric said. He shook his head. "He's safe where he is, I suppose."

"He could be safer still," said Carus, *"if he hanged himself. I can forgive a lot in a man, but not cowardice. That one's afraid to live!"*

Garric thought of the times he'd been frightened. The most recent occasion had been while he waited at the Valles riverfront, while Tenoctris spoke her spell and the bridge glowered behind them as a symbol of uncanny power.

Garric could follow the line of memories back to when he was three if not younger. He'd trembled as he waited in the common room for his father to learn he hadn't done the reading lesson he'd been set. . . .

All the memories had the same thing in common: Garric hadn't been able to act, or it was too late to act. So long as there was something for him to do, he was fine.

Garric let out a peal of honest laughter as King Carus laughed in his mind. Liane glanced at him. Tenoctris, barely conscious on Garric's shoulder, murmured something unintelligible.

"I was just thinking," Garric said to his friends. "It's good that I'm, well, Prince Garric now. That means I won't run out of things to do any time soon."

Liane blinked. She reached past Tenoctris to grip Garric's hand and said, "I don't know if you're joking or serious, Garric. I—You confuse me. But I'm glad I'm with you."

She sounded half-desperate; not afraid, but confused almost past bearing. Garric squeezed her hand and said,

"Mostly serious, I guess. I'm fine if I don't have to sit still and wait for something to happen."

He cleared his throat. "I'm glad we're together too," he added.

The tunnel's walls were becoming either thinner or clearer as the three continued. At first Garric thought the speckles and lines he saw were flaws in the blue translucence itself, but the spots had motion of their own. By the time Garric and his friends were another hundred paces down the corridor, he could see images moving alongside them.

Liane eyed the tunnel walls, her face serious but calm. She glanced toward Garric.

"Yeah," he said, "I see them too."

He bent his head slightly to look at Tenoctris, but the old wizard had fallen back into the sleep of exhaustion. The visit to Alman had made physical demands on all of them, and Tenoctris had the effort of the incantations besides.

"I think there's something ahead of us," Garric said, resisting the impulse to start running. All he could see was a change in the featureless azure light. The tunnel didn't constrain them tightly—Garric couldn't have jumped high enough to reach the curved ceiling—but its smooth emptiness was as confining as the desert outside Alae's ruins.

The walls were now a thin shimmer; Garric felt his feet sinking deeply into the floor as he strode forward. If he'd been walking on the log bridge, he'd have thought the wood was rotten and likely to give way at any instant. He glanced at Liane, but she didn't seem to notice anything. She didn't weigh half what Garric and Tenoctris did together, of course.

Garric grinned wryly. Besides, noblewomen didn't have much experience of walking on rotten logs.

"Umm?" said Liane, smiling in response to Garric's smile.

"I was thinking that some folk's education is sadly lacking," Garric said cheerfully. He didn't intend to lie to Liane, but he didn't see much good in spreading gloom either.

A barrier of scintillant gold closed the tunnel ahead of them. Garric's stomach drew in, wondering whether it would open or recede or— ˉ

Or maybe neither of those things.

The tunnel walls had become as clear as the isinglass curtains of a wealthy traveler's carriage. Marching beside them were men in armor, cavalry and footmen alike. The troops shambled forward silently, holding their ranks but moving with a lack of interaction that surprised Garric and amazed the king watching through his eyes. The figures were as shadowy as those of an army seen at twilight, but they were human beyond doubt.

"They're walking on the bridge," Liane said quietly. "The bridge we see in Valles."

She was right. Garric had been more interested in the soldiers, but the structure on which the army marched had the same filigree railings, the same twisted, multi-spired finials as the bridge that glowed at night over the River Beltis.

The same bridge by which the dreaming Garric had crossed to Klestis.

"I can see their standard," Liane said in an urgent undertone. "It's a crab, I think. I don't know any principality that uses a crab for its symbol, though."

"Tenoctris?" Garric said. He didn't want to disturb the old wizard, but he didn't know what would happen if he touched the barrier.

Tenoctris murmured in his arms. Her eyes opened and quickly focused on the figures marching alongside, paying no attention to the wall of light. Garric took another step, the last before they'd reach the barrier.

"Should I keep going?" he said urgently.

The tunnel dissolved like chaff in a bonfire. Garric stumbled forward on hard pavement, catching himself on one knee without dropping Tenoctris. Liane gasped beside him, and the detachment of Blood Eagles crashed down the street toward them at double time.

Garric and his friends were on the Valles riverfront again. False dawn had brightened the east, though the sun would still be a finger's breadth below the horizon.

The bridge of wizardlight was fading. On it, becoming gray and transparent with the structure, the army continued to march. It was going toward Klestis.

"I can tell you about the Crab, lad," King Carus said grimly. *"It's the standard of the Dukes of Yole. But the army of Yole drowned when I did, a thousand years ago."*

Sharina squatted beside the slab. There wasn't any question which block the Dragon had meant: this three-foot length of hard white granite looked nothing like the crude limestone ashlars that made up the rest of the foundation layer. Identification aside, though, she couldn't imagine how she and Dalar were going to remove it.

Dalar stood between her and the street, facing forward and back over his shoulder blades in quick succession. He looked like an extreme example of a spectator watching both sides of a game of netball. Sharina was afraid that the bird's movements were going to attract more attention than they'd help, but she was too unsure of what *she* was doing to tell him to stop jerking his head around.

"Well, he said . . ." she murmured, trying to grip the stone with her fingertips. To her amazement, it *did* have a greasy willingness to move; but whatever had happened to normal friction, the stone still weighed twice what she and Dalar did together.

Sharina drew the Pewle knife and thrust it into the gap between the altar stone and the block to its left. She didn't like to use her only physical reminder of Nonnus as a prybar—but she needed a prybar, and this was what she had. Nonnus himself had trained her to remember that objects were only objects, and that human beings alone were worthy of real concern. Sharina's memory of her friend and the lessons he'd taught her were important; his knife was just a tool.

She worked the blade gently sideways. Bits of mortar cascaded from the joints as though she were moving a block of ice, not stone. Sharina set a pebble in the crack to brace the stone, then slid the knife into the opposite joint. The steel was thick and of the best quality. It wouldn't snap under Sharina's careful use, though there'd be scratches to polish out as soon as she had a chance.

The stone pivoted out a full two fingers' breadth. Sharina wiped grit from the blade unconsciously before sheathing it. "Help me, Dalar," she said as she set the fingers of both hands against the left side of the stone.

Dalar knelt on the other side of the block. Sharina pressed hard, sliding the stone forward at an angle. As it straightened, Dalar pressed and pulled also.

The block scraped half its depth out into the alley before Sharina had to shift her grip. They could use their palms now. She'd wondered how strong the bird's thin arms really were. The answer appeared to be "Quite strong enough."

"Hey, what're you doing there?" someone shouted from the alley mouth. His shadow blocked half the dim light from the street.

"We're fixing the foundation so the wall doesn't fall in!" Sharina shouted back. She made eye contact with Dalar and murmured, "Now."

They heaved, scrambling backward as the block slid completely clear of the wall. Sharina's hands were on the verge of cramping from the strain. The edges of the granite were sharp. They didn't cut flesh, but they clamped off circulation in fingers pressed hard against them.

"Fixing the foundation?" the voice said. "Hey, that don't make any sense. Leimon, come here and look at this."

If Sharina had to, she'd fling a handful of silver ingots into the street. *That* should prove an adequate distraction to let her and Dalar escape.

Though "escape" probably wasn't the right word.

"Once more," she said, and gripped the back edge of the altar stone for a straight pull outward. They tugged together. The stone's weight resisted while Sharina's biceps bunched and the bird made a faint wheezing noise through his closed beak.

When the block moved, it was with a frictionless rush that made the pair of them jump up quickly to avoid being crushed. *Foolish!* Sharina thought. *As silly as cutting vegetables against the palm of my hand, and a good deal more dangerous!*

"Hey, you guys got no business here," the speaker said, coming a step farther into the alley. Two friends had joined him. The fellow didn't sound angry—or drunk, which was much the same thing. He was simply a busybody.

"Go!" Sharina muttered, gesturing Dalar to the opening. The wall above was holding together for the time being, but she wouldn't bet it would stay that way forever.

Dalar slid through the rectangular hole, leading with his clawed feet. "Hey, what's he doing?" whined one of the strangers.

"See here, my man," Sharina said, trying to sound as snooty as she could in a foreign dialect, while squatting in the filth of an alley. "You go check with the building's owner and he'll tell you that he's hired us to do this. And he'll probably put a flea in your ear for nosing into his affairs!"

She took off the belt with wallet and sheath. The rig was under her cape, so even though she'd slung it over her shoulder she had to unclasp the buckle first. It was carved from the dense bone of a sea mammal.

"I don't believe a word you say!" the first man said. He glanced back at his companions before he decided what to do next.

Sharina drew the Pewle knife, then slung the wallet and harness through the opening. "By the Lady!" a man cried. All three of them backed hastily, stumbling on one another's feet. "Hey, what *is* this?"

Sharina thrust her feet through the opening, then pushed

herself backward with her left hand. The knife wobbled, not a threat unless one of the men decided he ought to stop her. They'd run back to the street, though, shouting for help.

Rain dampened Sharina's feet. She tensed her belly muscles against the lip of the wall and dropped to the ground no more than a foot beneath her. "Oh!" she gasped, glad of Dalar's hand bracing her.

They stood in the ruins of a city. It was early afternoon. The warm drizzle must have been falling all day, because puddles filled every hollow and indentation.

Dalar handed Sharina her belt. She sheathed the knife and took stock of herself. She'd scratched her thighs— nothing serious—and hiked her tunic up to her navel. Her cape had caught on something as she went over the edge. The wing of the cloisonne butterfly pin had bitten at her throat, but when she rubbed herself she found the skin hadn't been broken.

"I see what you meant about coming from far away," Dalar said. He clucked with laughter. "Is it possible, do you think, that you could go to Rokonar?"

Sharina noticed that as the bird spoke, his short fingers manipulated the chained weights in his right palm. He surveyed the landscape in quick jerks of his head.

"I don't think so," she said. She fitted the belt again over the snakeskin sash, concentrating on the task so that she didn't have to look at Dalar. Not that she'd have been able to read pain in the bird's expression. "I go where the person I serve sends me. All I know is that I'll continue to move until I'm where he wants me to be."

She met Dalar's eyes. He nodded; she didn't know whether that was a gesture of his own race or something he'd learned to do in human society. "A warrior of the Rokonar doesn't question where his lord takes him," he said. "It was a matter of personal curiosity that might better have remained unspoken."

Sharina took her first real look at the landscape. Behind her was a wall, limestone except for the granite slab she and Dalar had removed in Valhocca. The hard stone was noticeably worn, and half had split off on a ragged diagonal.

"I saw you crawling over it," Dalar said, nodding to the slab. "Your feet appeared, then the rest of you. Out of the air."

The granite was on top of the remaining portion of the wall, but the building of which it had been part must have been enormous before it collapsed. *Probably a temple; at any rate, the stone drums of fallen pillars line what should be the front of the structure.*

Dalar waited silently. He occasionally spun a weight between two fingers on an inch of chain, perhaps implying that he'd like his mistress to direct him. Sharina would like somebody to direct her, too.

"I have no idea where we are," she said. "Or where we should go next. The Dragon—the person who, whom I serve—appears as you saw."

She smiled. "Well, you saw me," she corrected. "I had no warning the first times he came to me with directions, and I doubt it'll be different in the future."

The ruins could have been of Valhocca, but the destruction was so complete that it could have been any city in the Isles—centuries after a cataclysm. "The legend of my time," Sharina said evenly, "was that a wizard destroyed Valhocca and cursed it so that it was never rebuilt. That was in the mythical past of *my* age, however. No one could really have known."

Dalar clucked. "Indeed, you're from very far away, mistress," he said.

His downy feathers slicked as the rain wet them; the warrior looked like a larger version of a chicken that Sharina had scalded and plucked for dinner. To keep from giggling—and because they had to do something—Sharina said, "Let's see if we can find some cover. And do you suppose there's anything to eat in this forest?"

It was past berry season and Sharina didn't see any nut trees on a quick survey of their surrounding. The vegetation was mostly broad-leafed and succulent, quite different from the woods she'd been chased through on her way to meet the Dragon.

Something hooted raucously from the forest south of them. Sharina couldn't guess how far away it might be. She started to say, "Probably a bird," but she closed her mouth again without speaking.

That would have sounded like she was hoping away danger. She simply didn't know what had been calling. And while anything *could* have made the sound, it hadn't really sounded like a bird.

She grinned at Dalar and drew the Pewle knife. "We'll go this way," she said, nodding northward along the line of a boulevard separating rows of ruins.

"It might be edible," the bird said. His head flicked in tiny movements as quick and uncertain as light wobbling from faceted glass.

"So might we," Sharina said.

They started off, moving parallel on either side of the street's centerline. The trees were just as large here as elsewhere in the ruins—many were too thick for Sharina and Dalar to have spanned if they linked arms—but the footing was easier than if they'd had to clamber over piles of rubble which once had been buildings.

The drizzle made it harder to concentrate on anything that was more than an arm's length ahead. Sharina repeatedly reminded herself that she *had* to be aware of her wider surroundings, but she kept finding her eyes focused on the ground just ahead of her feet.

She giggled. The bird glanced at her and said, "Mistress?"

"It isn't fair we have to be uncomfortable *and* in danger both," Sharina said.

"I've been contemplating a severe complaint to the Gods about just that situation," Dalar agreed with a straight face. "All that's holding me back is deciding precisely which God is primarily responsible for the conditions. My race has ten thousand separate deities, you see, so it's difficult to correctly apportion blame."

Sharina giggled again. Not that the bird had much option about the straight face, since instead of mobile lips he had a beak as rigid as cow horn. It pleased Sharina to see that her companion not only had a sense of humor, it was a sense of humor that agreed with her own.

They heard the call again and both paused. "It sounded farther away than before," Sharina said. She spoke instead of swallowing her words because this time she could make a truthful statement instead of expressing a frightened wish.

"Yes," said Dalar, "and well to our right. Whatever it is."

A ghoul with yellow tusks and skin the color of lichened rock stepped out of the ruined building beside Sharina. It walked on two legs like a human, but it was eight feet tall despite its slumped carriage. Its broad hips were cocked back to balance the weight of its canted forequarters.

Sharina shifted slightly, settling both feet for a good grip on the soil. Dalar stepped around her right side so that they were both facing the creature.

The ghoul lifted its head and hooted to its fellows who'd been calling in the distance. Close up the sound was deafening, like a bull roaring through a crude iron trumpet.

The ghoul's arms were long enough to touch the ground, but at present it held a headless rabbit in one clawed hand and picked bits of flesh from its teeth with the other. Six teats flapped against the creature's belly; it was a female.

The ghoul grinned and dropped the remains of the rabbit. Sharina raised the Pewle knife, gripping the hilt with both hands. Her only chance was to chop into the creature's rush with all her strength. Running would be useless.

She heard a whistling sound from the side, but she didn't dare take her eyes off the ghoul. If her timing was perfect, they might surv—

The ghoul leaped. The mushy *choonk* of impact sounded like an axe hitting a melon.

The creature's hairless skull twisted sideways and deformed. One of Dalar's bronze weights froze momentarily in the misty air, having transferred all the momentum of its spin to the misshapen head.

Dalar snatched the weight back into his palm and set the other one spinning on six feet of chain. After two quick twists of the bird's wrist, the bronze was a shimmer in the air rather than a discrete object. He tilted the weapon slightly so that it was safely above Sharina's head on that side of its circuit.

The ghoul hit the ground at Sharina's side, hopped backward with its arms flailing—she jumped away but wasn't quick enough to avoid a claw-slash on her left calf—and finally flopped on its back and continued to thrash. Each of its four limbs jerked in a different rhythm.

Its jaws opened, displaying interlocking canines as long as Sharina's little finger. The tongue and lining of the ghoul's mouth were white, streaked with blue veins. It said, "*Kuk kuk kuk*," and stopped. The long body arched in a convulsion that made it wheeze. The limbs drummed briefly; then the ghoul went flaccid.

Sharina let out her breath. Her hands were trembling so badly that after two failures to sheathe the Pewle knife, she continued to hold the weapon as she examined the scratch on her leg. It normally wouldn't have been serious, but given the condition of the ghoul's claws she'd better clean it immediately.

She looked up at her companion. She said, "That was good work, Dalar."

"I am pleased to have been of service to my mistress," the bird said. A tone of crowing delight colored the neutral simplicity of the words. He added, "The creature was new to me."

"And me," said Sharina. "I want to rub this cut clean with a dock leaf and then see if we can find some spider-webs to pack it with. Nonnus—"

A ghoul called in the middle distance. Another responded from farther away. Before that cry ended, at least a dozen more of the creatures were giving tongue. All of them seemed to be south of where Sharina and Dalar stood, but some sounded very close.

"Or again, the cut can wait," Sharina said. Together they began jogging northward out of the ruins.

Elfin sang somewhere nearby, though not so close that Cashel could make out the words. That was just as well, he guessed.

He thumbed the last of the pine nuts into his left palm, then dropped the stripped cone on the ground beside him. He rose to his feet, chewing the little nuts. Cashel didn't know if he'd be able to get used to them as a steady diet— they had an aftertaste of turpentine, though he didn't notice it when each mouthful was going down—but for keeping him fed here in the Underworld they were fine.

"The woods here seem really quiet," he said to the ring. "Except for Elfin, I mean. Is it always like this?"

"The other inhabitants on this level are afraid of you," Krias said. "They're still here, never fear. They'll come out when you're gone."

"Ah," said Cashel, nodding. "But you mean they're afraid of *you*."

"It's all the same, sheep-boy," the ring said.

"No," said Cashel, "it's not."

He smiled at the ring to show he wasn't angry or anything. He wasn't going to leave stand a false statement that touched him, though.

Cashel stretched and gave a quick spin of his staff. He looked over his shoulder in the direction of the singing and called, "Hey Elfin! Come here if you like. I won't hurt you."

The music stopped, then resumed. It wasn't coming closer.

"He didn't, you know, attack me the way the rest of his people did," Cashel explained to the ring. Not that he had to answer to Krias for the company he kept. "And he sure can play and sing, can't he?"

"The rest of *his* people?" Krias said. The little demon cackled with laughter. "*You're* Elfin's people, sheep-boy. The People stole him from his cradle as an infant. Didn't you listen to *what* he was singing?"

"Well," Cashel said. "Songs don't really mean anything, Krias. Granny Brisa used to sing about her love across the sea or the gray-eyed lad who loved her, all sorts of things like that. Nobody'd loved *her* since her husband died back before I was born."

The ring demon gave a sigh that wasn't as theatrical as his usual. "Well, that's not what the People sing about," he said. "They made that song when they killed the nurse and stole Elfin—not that his name was Elfin, of course. And they've got a thousand more songs like it, every one of them true."

"Duzi!" Cashel said in amazement. "Why, that's terrible!"

Krias cackled. "They weren't singing when we last saw them, were they?" he added gleefully.

Cashel made a trumpet of his hands, leaning the staff in the crook of his right elbow, and bellowed, "Elfin! Come to me! I'll take you back home as soon as I'm done with my business here!"

The boy didn't even pause in his singing. It was awful to think that those words were real.

"Well, maybe he'll catch up with us later," Cashel said. "And anyway, we'll be coming back this way, won't we?"

"I'm a magic ring," Krias snapped, "not a fortune-telling ring. I don't have the slightest idea what you'll be doing, sheep-boy, except that it'll be stupid."

"Well, we may as well move on," Cashel said. He couldn't help smiling at the ring's fussiness.

"You know?" he added. "Back in the borough boys poke straws into an anthill and watch the ants run around in circles. I guess it doesn't hurt anybody, and sometimes it's pretty funny to watch."

Krias spluttered like a kettle on the boil. Cashel continued to grin as he walked on.

Cashel had been seeing a rocky hill ahead every time the trees overhead were thin. He stepped through a copse of beeches—almost beeches, anyway; the leaves were the right saw-edged shape but they were way too big for adult trees—and saw it rising right there, a stone's throw away.

He'd seen it before, or near enough. "This is the same place where I met Landure," he said. "Did we just go around in a circle, Master Krias?"

"Look at the portal, sheep-boy," the ring said. "Does *that* look like where we came through before? No! Because this is the gateway to the second level."

"Yeah, I see it now," Cashel said, walking around the spur of rock that pretty well hid the opening from the angle they'd approached. The door was wood, not bronze, true enough.

He didn't bother telling Krias he hadn't seen the door at first. The demon already knew that, and excuses weren't worth much even when they were better than "I didn't see what was in plain sight."

It was a big, heavy door, all oak and fastened with tre-nails instead of iron. The workmen had been more interested in weight than craftsmanship. The staves weren't dovetailed, so despite how thick they were Cashel could see light through the cracks.

The light was a sickly green. Well, it'd be a change from the red he'd been walking under since he came through the bronze door. Neither one was a color Cashel much cared for.

"So I go through this?" Cashel said to the ring.

"How do I know what you do?" Krias snarled. "You're free to wander like a fuzzy animal with just *about* enough sense to wake up in the morning. You don't have to ride on some boob's finger like I do!"

"Master Krias," Cashel said, "you're not going to get me mad, so you may as well stop trying. Besides, I guess you want Landure alive again the same as I do. Now, is this door on the way to find Landure's new body?"

"Yeah, this door and another one like it, if you get that

far," the demon said. "That's *if*, remember."

He sounded peeved—well, he always did, except when he'd been talking about things Cashel wished hadn't happened, even to the People—but he was a little more subdued than usual too. It couldn't be a lot of fun being cooped up in a little ring the way Krias was.

"Thanks," Cashel said as he gripped the handle, a horizontal pole long enough for three men to hold at the same time. When Cashel pulled, the panel creaked and groaned instead of opening.

Cashel was beginning to think that it was barred on the other side when he thought to lift as well as pull. That worked and he backed up, holding the panel off the ground. It was too heavy and saggy for its hinge pegs. For all its size, it wasn't made any better than a stable door.

The terrain through the open doorway was pretty much like what Cashel had seen when he opened the bronze door earlier. The vegetation, though, was like nothing he'd ever come across.

Just inside grew something more like a young willow than anything else familiar, but it didn't look much like a willow. Its limbs were snaky like a weeping willow's, but they didn't have any leaves at all that Cashel could see. It hadn't lost them for winter, either: the breeze coming up from below was warm and wet, like a summer noon in the marshes.

Cashel hefted his quarterstaff and sighed. "Do the People live down here too, Master Krias?" he asked.

"Them?" said the ring demon. "No, not them, but there's worse things, sheep-boy. Much worse!"

"Well, let's hope we stay clear of them," Cashel said mildly. He stepped through the doorway.

"You're not going to close it?" Krias said. "What's the matter—are you so worn out already that you don't think you can move the door again?"

"No, I'm all right," said Cashel, stroking the smooth hickory. He wished Garric could be here with him, but the quarterstaff itself was a friend from home. "I just thought

I'd leave it in case Elfin wants to come with us anyway. I don't think he could open the door if I was to close it."

Krias sneered. "Somehow I doubt that you're quite up to Elfin's cultural standards," he said.

"Still, he might be getting lonely," Cashel said. He walked into the vast green-lit cavern. As with the place he was leaving, there wasn't anything overhead that looked like a cave's roof. He might have been standing under an open sky.

The trees on the slopes below quivered gently, like a barley field in an autumn breeze. It didn't look like the trees were all blowing in the same direction, though. Each one shook to a little different rhythm.

"That's funny," Cashel said. He was about to ask the ring about what he saw. As his mouth opened he heard in his mind the string of insults that'd be all he got from that quarter. Instead, Cashel stepped over to examine the little not-willow. The sapling's trunk was about three fingers' breadth across and as supple as a bamboo fishing pole. The bark was smooth.

"You'll be sor-ree!" Kiras piped.

The tree's long, whippy limbs wrapped around Cashel. It was like being caught in a net.

"Call on me!" Krias said. "Call on me, sheep-boy!"

Cashel let go of his quarterstaff; it wasn't going to help him now. The tree limbs squirmed over him like so many snakes.

He tried to pull back, not seriously but to test what would happen. Limbs interwove themselves between Cashel and safety, forming a barrier of living wickerwork. He grinned, because that was what he'd expected. The tree didn't meet many wrestlers, he guessed.

"Are you a lunatic?" Krias shrilled. "Use my name!"

Cashel hunched down and stepped toward the tree. He gripped it low around the trunk, the same way he'd have gone for the ankles of an opponent who'd fallen for his initial feint.

No man living had ever broken free once Cashel had got

his grip on him. He slowly straightened his flexed knees, letting his leg muscles do the work. As he did so, he leaned back slightly, putting tension on the trunk.

For some moments the branches pulled at Cashel—hard, hard enough to leave welts where they wrapped his arms and torso. The tree didn't know *anything* about a fight. Everything it did was just helping its opponent!

Cashel's teeth were bared and his gasping breaths blew spit from his lower lip, but he could feel the roots start to give. The tree must have known what was about to happen. Its branches stopped tugging and instead lashed at Cashel like a drover with a stubborn mule.

Cashel tucked his face into his left armpit to save his eyes, and for the rest—well, whip-cuts weren't going to change anything. Not when he could see the taproot pulling up from the soil, fat and yellow and covered with little broken tendrils twisting like earthworms cut with a shovel.

The tree made a sound. It wasn't a scream, really; it was more like the rattle of a pot at a roiling boil. The limbs stopped whipping Cashel and the trunk went as limp in his hands as the tongue of a dead sheep.

Cashel let go of the tree and straightened slowly, breathing in gasps. His head was swimming and he knew he had to be careful not to fall straight down the side of the bluff. "Oh!" he said.

"And what do you think you proved by that?" Krias said, sounding more puzzled than petulant.

"I didn't prove anything," Cashel said. "The tree started a fight and I finished one."

He stretched his arms out carefully and looked himself over. He hadn't pulled any muscles, but he stung all over and he was bleeding in a few places from the tree slashing at him. He hoped there'd be water in the valley below so he could wash off.

Cashel didn't know what he was going to do for clothing, though. The tree had torn off the right sleeve of his tunic, and he'd split the back all the way down to his belt when he flexed to pull out the root. He wished Ilna was here to mend it.

Truth to tell, he wished any of his friends were here. Well, he'd be back with them soon enough. First Sharina, then they'd rejoin the others.

"*I* could have taken care of the problem a lot easier, you know," Krias said.

Cashel picked up his staff and twirled it, being careful to keep it clear of the bluff behind him. "I won't always have you around," Cashel said. "Anyway, I'd rather scotch my own snakes."

He chuckled. "Or trees."

Cashel leaned over the slope, picking a route. It shouldn't be any worse than the first climb was. He braced his staff a long step down.

"Sheep-boy?" said the ring.

"Umm?" said Cashel.

"You could eat the root of that tree you killed," Krias said. "It's supposed to be tasty, even. If you're the sort of lower life-form that needs solid food."

"Ah," said Cashel. He straightened and drew his belt knife. "Thank you, Master Krias. Those pine nuts were starting to get old."

Cashel whittled just below the line of the bark. Somewhere back of him, still on the other side of the open door, he heard Elfin singing.

Vonculo gripped the hilt of his broad-bladed sword in both hands, though the weapon was still sheathed. He was holding it for a lucky charm. His bearded face looked like a beast's in the lamplight.

"Keep the child out of trouble," Ilna said curtly to Chalcus. She stepped toward the sailing master.

"We can—" Chalcus said, nodding toward Vonculo and the others.

"Take her into a crowd of frightened fools?" Ilna snapped. "I think not!"

Half the crew had pressed toward the bow and their leaders, desperate for information. They squeezed aside for Ilna just as they'd have made way for a viper crawling down the deck.

There *wasn't* any information, a point that should've been obvious to anybody with the brains of a pigeon, but this lot seemed to be hoping for a miracle. A miracle seemed the most likely source of salvation to Ilna as well, given that the ships had been caught this way.

"Well, Mistress Merota," she heard the chanteyman saying, "I'll teach you the woman's part of 'The Gambling Suitor' and we'll sing together."

"All right, mistress," Vonculo said. "You're a wizard, and if that we heard on shore isn't wizard's work, then it's demons'. We need you to make us safe!"

He and the men around him were frightened enough to do anything. Ilna kept her empty hands in plain sight, knowing that if she touched her cords she'd be clubbed— or stabbed—by one of the sailors behind her. There wasn't enough light, anyway, for her to bind all those present.

"I'm not that kind of wizard," Ilna said. "I can weave patterns that have an effect. My art isn't of any good to you."

"By the Shepherd's *tool*, mistress!" the sailing master swore. "If you're no help to us, then you've been a waste of the rations you've eaten. You and the girl both!"

Ilna sniffed. "I can't weave you safety, Master Vonculo," she said. "I'll go ashore and use my senses to find out what's going on, though. The same as any of you could do—"

She turned and raked her eyes across the men behind her. They flinched as she'd expected they would.

In the silence, Ilna heard Merota sing, " 'Sir, I see you've come again—' " Chalcus met Ilna's eyes over the girl's head. The chanteyman grinned like a hook-bladed knife.

Ilna turned to Vonculo again. "—If there were men among you!"

"You mean . . . ?" Vonculo said. He blinked. The answer had gone in a direction he hadn't been expecting, so his stunned mind had to pause before it could interpret the words.

"I mean that I'll wade ashore and see what really did happen to the men from the other ship," Ilna said contemptuously. "Personally, I don't see anything supernatural about a man screaming. You're ready to do the same yourself the next time a fish jumps."

"Sure, that's all right," the helmsman said. "We'll have the girl here, so—"

"No, Tias," said Chalcus in a voice clear enough to carry to the island, "Merota will be accompanying Mistress Ilna and myself as we go view the land."

"I'm not taking Merota into that!" Ilna said, turning as quick as a squirrel.

"There's no risk we'll find there, mistress," Chalcus said, his left hand on the child's shoulder, "that's so great as leaving her by herself with folk I wouldn't trust to pour piss out of a boot. Not sparing yourself from the description, Master Vonculo."

Chalcus was angry; this Ilna could see despite the chanteyman's grin and pleasant voice. But there was still more to what he was doing than that. There was a streak in the fellow which, if pushed far enough, might lead him to do absolutely anything regardless of consequences. The present situation, the result of the mutineers' stupidity, brutality, and fear, had brought Chalcus to that point.

Ilna didn't recall ever having seen a more dangerous man—except possibly when she glanced into water clear enough to give a reflection.

"But . . ." said a sailor hidden in the crowd. "How do we know they'll come back?"

"Now that's a fine question, Skogara," Chalcus said with a friendly smile. "Do you want to come along and keep watch on our wizard?"

There was a muffled curse from the sailor but no other response. Chalcus grinned even more broadly and continued, "I thought not; but never fear, we'll be back. What I saw of the island by daylight didn't encourage *me* to pick it as a place to retire, that I can tell you."

Ilna's mind slid like a shuttle through choices. Chalcus was right about Merota being better off with the two of them than alone, and Ilna wasn't fool enough to think that she could force the chanteyman to stay aboard with the child. Indeed, they might all three be safer ashore than in the midst of fifty frightened fools.

"We'll need a float of some sort for Merota and what we carry with us," she said loudly. "I'm not trusting the child to this mud."

"We'll use Lord Tadai's mattress," Chalcus said with a cheery lilt. "It's feathers in a waxed linen cover. And *think* how the poor man must be suffering without it, Vonculo."

"By the Lady's tits!" Vonculo said. "You're a madman, Chalcus. Mad!"

Ilna agreed completely; but the chanteyman wasn't stupid, not at all. And unless she missed her bet, Chalcus had survived in circumstances when many others had not.

He turned and slashed twice across the baggage in the belly of the ship, severing the cargo net. The feather bed, on top of other gear as a cover and compressed by the tight-drawn net, sprang up as though volunteering.

Chalcus had slid the sword from its sheath as part of the same motion as the double cut. It was quite as pretty a movement as those of mountebanks juggling for coppers at the fair.

He sheathed the weapon. "If you'll get over the side, Ilna dear," Chalcus said as the other sailors watched nervously, "I'll hand this down to you and send the child after it. If you've got anything more to carry, I'll take care of that too."

Ilna tossed her slight bindle to the chanteyman, then stepped onto an oar and walked herself into the water. "I'm not your dear," she called over her shoulder without particular emphasis.

"And how would you know, mistress?" Chalcus said.

Laughing, he handed her the mattress to lower into the water—it floated like the ducks whose feathers filled it—and then stuck his left arm out like a beam by which Merota lowered herself onto the float. Ilna nodded with approval: if Chalcus had held onto the child, his grip would likely have bruised her.

The seawater was cold and was sticky with salt. It came waist high to Ilna or a little deeper; nothing dangerous, but wading in it was a thoroughly unpleasant business.

Ilna grinned tightly. Like so much else about this journey.

She didn't mind the squelch underfoot, but her bare toes stirred gases out of the ooze. The stench of ancient death was choking, far worse than the margins of Pattern Creek in the borough after the tide slunk back.

"Oh," Merota gasped as she bobbed on the float. "Oh, what smells so awful, Ilna? Oh, I can't breathe!"

Chalcus slipped over the side with as little stir as a goose bobbing. "We'll get to shore, child," he said, "and we'll hope that the air's better there . . . though I don't promise that, nor anything else good about this island."

"Your sword will get wet," Ilna said as she started shoreward, tugging the float along with her left hand. The girl's weight made the mattress sag in the middle, letting a stream of water dribble over her knees. Merota winced but didn't complain.

"Aye," said Chalcus, "and the steel's so good that it'll rust if it hears the splash of a woman's tear . . . but it's a seaman's blade, Ilna, and I've a swatch of raw fleece in my wallet to wipe the salt off it as soon as we reach land. If I don't have other use for the blade, that is."

He laughed. To Ilna's surprise, Merota giggled along with him. Chalcus' good humor made even Ilna want to smile, though she restrained herself.

Though the sea wasn't dangerously deep, it remained at the same awkward depth for step after step. The mud slid around Ilna's toes and didn't give a good grip when she tried to push forward. Water sucked at her garments.

Ilna chuckled. Well, the mud and water weren't going to prevent her from carrying on with her plan, such as it was; and discomfort was merely a part of life. The greater part of life, she'd found, though others might have another opinion.

"Mistress?" said Chalcus, responding to her chuckle. He and Ilna towed the float like a yoke of—what? Not oxen, surely. Carriage horses, perhaps; not a nobleman's team, but certainly a healthy, well-kept pair. And by no means ill matched.

"I was wondering," Ilna said aloud, "how Lady Liane bos-Benliman views life."

"A friend of yours, Ilna?" Chalcus said; pressing, but with a tone of mild disinterest that would permit her to ignore the question without creating a problem. Ilna wondered what if anything the chanteyman knew of her, beyond what he'd seen and what he'd seen in her eyes.

"Liane has always acted as a friend to me," Ilna said carefully. A tag of Celondre's poem ran through her mind as she spoke: *Follow a proper goal, for it's doom to wish for what the Gods have placed beyond your grasp.* "And I hope I've been a friend to her this past while as well."

They'd gotten inshore of the other trireme, a glitter of lamplight and curses well off to their right, and the muddy bottom had finally begun to shelve. There was nothing to see on land, though a thin line of foam and debris marked the shore now that they'd gotten this close.

Chalcus pulled the float in exactly Ilna's rhythm; setting his pace to hers, she was sure, since he was stronger and likely more familiar with the sort of task chance had set them. Ilna noticed that she hadn't been thinking about the stench, the slime, and the cold.

Working with another person was surprisingly easy, if the person had the same habit of fitting tasks into the most efficient pattern. That wasn't very many people, of course.

"If I can ask question for question," she said aloud, "why were you aboard the *Terror*, Master Chalcus?"

He chuckled. "A question I've asked myself often," he said. "The short of it, mistress, is that I'd left my former employment and thought I'd put some distance between myself and the region as well. The Royal Fleet, such as it was, was hiring . . . and bless me if my first voyage out of the Pool of the Beltis isn't right back to the southern waters I'd left!"

Chalcus gave a loud, caroling laugh that echoed from the shore ahead. Ilna imagined the nervousness on the triremes as the mutineers heard the sound and mistook its source.

"That sort of luck makes a fellow wonder if he's been sacrificing to the wrong Gods, doesn't it, mistress?" Chalcus said. "That, or sacrificing the wrong things!"

"Chalcus?" said Merota. "Do you mean you don't want to meet your former master?"

"My associates, you mean, child," the chanteyman said with a careful mildness. "And I won't be meeting any of them this side of the grave; though on the other there'll be some looking for me, I have no doubt."

In a different tone he went on, "I think it's time for you to walk the last cable length on your own legs, child, though hold Ilna's hand if you please."

He dropped his corner of the mattress. The water was only ankle deep, but Ilna's feet sank that depth again into the muck.

Chalcus drew his curved sword; the steel gave a vibrant sigh. "And myself," he said, "I'll go on a little ahead to make sure there's no hole here at the shoreline that you might fall into, hey?"

"Yes, go ahead," Ilna said. "Hold on to my tunic, Merota. I need both hands for a moment."

Splashing inshore had dampened the noose she carried in her right sleeve. She ran it between thumb and forefinger, squeezing it dry or dry enough. The white silk would flow like poured milk if she had to cast it.

Chalcus grinned approval, then started walking directly

ahead of them. His feet lifted in and out of the soup with scarcely a splash.

"Not too far, Chalcus," Merota called.

"Not far at all, child," Chalcus replied cheerfully, but he didn't turn his head to look at her. The area behind him was for Ilna to deal with.

The water became shallower, the soil underneath firmer and finally dry. Chalcus' tunic, a blur in the starlight ahead of them, halted.

"We're coming up behind you, Master Chalcus," Ilna warned.

"Why did you say that, Ilna?" Merota asked.

"Because Ilna knows I'm nervous as a cat," the chanteyman said with a grin, "and we'd all be very sorry if I whacked your head off because I mistook a noise, wouldn't we, child?"

He chucked Merota under the chin, though all the time his eyes were scanning the vegetation which grew to the line of the spring tides. There weren't any tall trees, but shrubs and saplings in profusion interlocked branches.

"Well, the rest of us'd be sorry," Chalcus added.

"Shall we strike inland?" Ilna asked. She didn't see an obvious route through the vegetation, but she felt exposed on this muddy beach.

"Now that we're together again," Chalcus said, "I thought we'd walk down to where the others landed. All right?"

"Yes, of course," Ilna snapped. "Merota, stay between me and Master Chalcus, if you please."

Chalcus paused. "The thing is, Merota," he said, "Ilna and I don't know what's going on any better than you do. That comes out different ways, but nothing either of us does or says means we're mad at you. Do you understand?"

"Yes, Chalcus," Merota said. She looked from him to Ilna and went on, "I'm not afraid when I'm with the two of you."

"Oh, so young and such a liar!" the chanteyman said with a peal of laughter. "But I will say that in the past it's been the wiser choice to be standing with us than to be on the other side."

He cocked an eyebrow at Ilna. "Not so, mistress?"

She snorted. "More true than not, I suppose," she admitted. "That doesn't predict the future, you know."

"Ah, we've had that discussion already," said Chalcus as he strode forward, checking the sea to his right as well as the foliage at the edge of the tideline to their left as they followed the shore.

Ilna watched also. She didn't spend much time in the raw countryside, but anything that violated the normal pattern would be as obvious to her as a bonfire.

She smiled. Although . . . what was normal in this place might be dragons with mouths large enough to swallow the triremes. Still, dragons that big should be obvious enough even though they did fit in.

The smell was the first warning. "Merota," Ilna said, "something's been killed here and the chances are it was a man. Maybe several men. Don't scream when you see it."

"Keep the girl back!" Chalcus said.

"We can save her life if we keep our minds on our work!" Ilna said sharply. "But we can't hide the kind of place this is, and if we try to do that, we'll make mistakes we can't afford!"

"It's all right, Chalcus," Merota said. "I saw my parents. After the fire."

They walked the three steps to where Chalcus stood. "That's far enough," he said. "Or you'll trip on his guts."

The corpse hung upside down from the crotch of a sapling, its fingers touching the ground. One of the sailors, Ilna supposed, though she wouldn't have been able to identify the victim even in better light. Besides his having been stripped and gutted like a trout, something had bitten his face off.

The skiff was smashed to bits on the mud, with pieces lying thirty feet from the main pile of wreckage. Ilna hadn't heard the boat's violent destruction. Perhaps the laughter had masked the crackling wood.

The mixed odors of blood, feces, and fear made the beach stink like a slaughter yard. Back home the blood would've been sopped into a bowl of oatmeal for sausage and puddings. Of course, back home the cadaver would have been a sheep or a pig.

Though the lungs and intestines had simply been dragged out across the sand, the heart and liver were missing. "Ah!" said Ilna.

Both her companions were looking at her. Ilna made a moue of displeasure—she shouldn't have made her surprise public—and said with scrupulous honesty, "I was just thinking that the killer's tastes didn't run to puddings and sausage."

Chalcus laughed and squeezed Merota's shoulder with his left hand. "You'll be all right with us, child," he said. "I swear you will!"

Merota looked at the chanteyman. "Was he a bad man, Chalcus?" she asked.

"Three-finger Sinou?" he said, looking at the victim. "He's a lazy bugger who couldn't keep stroke if his life depended on it . . . which it didn't, not when he was rowing for me, but I glad when they moved him to the *Ravager* and made him Plestin's problem. Maybe Plestin's discipline is tighter than mine, do you think?"

He laughed. Ilna wasn't sure whether he really thought his joke was funny or if he was just trying to jolly the child along. Both, she suspected; and she found she was smiling also.

"There's a gap in the woods here," Chalcus said, gesturing with his sword. "The others likely went off through it, since we'd see their tracks in the mud if they'd gone up the beach. My thought is that we wait here till we get some light and then head inland."

"Instead of going back to the ship?" Ilna said.

"Every decision Vonculo's made has put us deeper in

the muck, Ilna-darling," the chanteyman said. "I think we're better on our own."

"I suppose you're right," Ilna said. "Particularly since the locals appear to have had dinner already."

She found a hollow at the roots of a fig whose stems would make a springy rest for her back. She wouldn't sleep, but she might as well be as comfortable as possible under the circumstances.

"Come here, Merota," Ilna said. "Put your head in my lap and get some sleep. It's been a long day."

"Indeed it has," Chalcus agreed cheerfully. He positioned himself at the head of the track through the vegetation; moonlight danced as he wiped the blade with his wad of fleece, again and again as he waited.

As Merota settled herself, Ilna heard the chanteyman sing in a low, lilting voice, " *'So I will marry who I please, as you can do as well.'* "

Chapter Fifteen

Garric leaned his elbows on the table of the conference room and put his head in his hands. He knew there were people around him—he could hear Liane murmuring to Chancellor Royhas and three senior aides. The city burgesses of Herax, in the east of Ornifal, had challenged the imposition of royal law in their community, citing their charter from Duke Valbolg the Strong as proof of their judicial independence.

Valbolg had died 705 years ago. According to Royhas the government's position was that even if the charter was legitimate, the assumption of kingship by the ducal line had voided all contrary acts of the dynasty previous thereto. The matter would be in the courts for at least five years, however, if not twenty, and it imperiled the whole process of rationalizing the judiciary until it was resolved.

"Oh, Shepherd help me," Garric moaned. His lips moved, but nobody outside his own head could have heard the words. "I know it's important but I just can't keep my eyes open."

"I'd have mounted my bodyguard and ridden all night to Herax," King Carus said. *"Pull the burgesses out of their beds, march them to the main square, and hold them in a ring of swords while I informed the citizenry what the law was going to be henceforth."*

"I'm not going to do that," said Garric, though he grinned.

"I shouldn't have either," Carus said with a bellowing laugh. The king wore service garb, but though the cloth was sturdy wool, the short tunic was bright yellow and the breeches tucked into high boots were dyed orange. He stood like a flame in Garric's mind, cheerful and vibrant. *"I did it twice, and both cities closed their gates to me the next time a halfway credible usurper appeared on the scene. You're too smart to let your anger make worse trouble down the road for you, lad."*

"At any rate, I'm well advised," Garric said, grinning tiredly at the thought of his ancestor.

He rose to his feet. The others looked around in surprise. *They're probably expecting me to fall on my face,* Garric thought. *They might be right, too.*

"Gentlemen!" Garric said. They jumped, even Royhas, who'd gotten to know Garric pretty well over the past months. Garric hadn't meant to shout, but he'd been concentrating so hard on getting intelligible words out that he'd managed to bellow.

Liane, who knew Garric better than *anybody* else, wasn't startled, but worry underlay her smile of greeting. She recognized the signs of Garric being asleep on his feet.

It wasn't this business with Herax, though even by itself that was enough to bore anybody to tears. The day, starting in the watch before dawn, had been a series of similar problems. Cordage for the fleet, promotions within the military, floods in Tall Springs County that had washed out the barley crop—the locals said; the treasury beadle for the district was sure that the harvest had been complete and the grain secreted.

Those things and at least a dozen more; every one of them important, every one of them intractable—what was Garric supposed to do? search every cave and cow byre in Tall Springs County looking for baskets of barley?—and in concert they were mind-numbing beyond the imagination of Garric or-Reise.

Prince Garric had been here before, and the life he saw ahead of him was an unending procession of similar days.

"What I suggest is this, gentlemen," Garric said more quietly. His vision blurred, then refocused. He tried a smile, though he wasn't sure it worked. "Ask the burgesses to stipulate that the royal justices will remain in place pending the outcome of the matter in the high court. The government will post bond in the amount of, oh, one year's tax revenue from Herax and the surrounding district. The amount is negotiable."

"They'll never agree to that, Your Majesty!" said one of the chancellor's aides before Royhas could shush him. "We've already made a similar, a *very* similar offer."

"In the same communication as the request for a stipulation," Garric continued, "you will politely request a list of accommodations for up to eight thousand soldiers. You'll explain that the government is considering a plan to quarter the army outside the capital, and that Herax will be the first site so chosen if the plan comes into effect."

"*Are* we planning that, Your Majesty?" another aide blurted in surprise. "Herax has only four hundred and twelve assessed houses, and—"

Royhas pointed his index finger. The aide swallowed the rest of his observations.

"On my oath by Duzi!" Garric said. "We *will* consider it if the burgesses don't accept a reasonable compromise!"

"Which I rather think they will," Royhas said. "I'll see to drafting the documents, Your Majesty."

Then to his aides, crisply, he added, "Come! We needn't trouble Prince Garric any more today!"

Garric sat down again. Sat or slumped; he was lucky he'd managed to brace himself with his elbows on the table. Bright sunlight slanted through the window jalousies, but Garric saw only a faceted blur. He heard Liane speak—to him? to Royhas?—and then close the door.

"Aye, you have good advisors, lad," King Carus said. *"But we have a good prince as well."*

Garric laughed with his ancestor; and, laughing, fell with no transition into his dream of movement. He and Carus beside him walked through the wall of the conference room, following a course in which time as well as the streets of Valles unreeled before them.

Night and daylight interchanged randomly from one step to the next. Occasionally Garric recognized someone on the street, but more often even the fashions people wore were unfamiliar. Once he glimpsed a procession bearing the great chryselephantine statue of the Lady, the work of the sculptor Gudgin of Charis, which had burned with the temple of the Lady of Valles generations before Carus himself was born.

Carus grinned at his descendant. As before the ancient king showed the strain of joining Garric on a journey meant for Garric alone; but as before, Carus came along. They were going toward the river and the wizard-bridge; that alone was beyond question.

With their first steps onto the structure, the images of Valles past and present faded away. The bridge was solid and splendid, with spiked finials rising from the supports. Long pennons fluttered in breezes that didn't stir Garric's clothing or that of his companion.

Others were crossing, mostly pedestrians but some on horseback. There was even a high-sided carriage with outriders before and behind. Garric could see the other travelers, but instead of jostling they interpenetrated. Everyone was crossing a different bridge, a structure whose existence was immaterial but real nonetheless, across multiple planes of the cosmos.

Garric clasped hands with Carus. There was no worse feeling than to be alone in a strange and hostile world. Whatever else happened, Garric was spared that.

This time the controlling power whisked them through the time-eaten shell of Klestis, then the stone fabric of Ansalem's palace, without the charade of climbing the external staircase. They stood in Ansalem's chamber. Soft illumination poured through the alabaster and more vivid light gleamed on the electrum grating of the window to the east.

"Oh?" said Ansalem, rising from the couch of patterned marble. He peered at Carus. "Why, I think I know you, don't I, sir? Of course, you're the king!"

"We met during my lifetime," Carus said, standing straight and clasping his hands at the small of his back. Garric suspected Carus was preventing himself from grasping the hilt of his sword. He hated wizards in general, and he had no reason to love Ansalem. "And we've met since, in this place."

"You brought us here before, Lord Ansalem," Garric said. He found it hard to concentrate with the amphisbaena shifting in and out of the travertine couch. It was like light flickering from a mirror onto the corner of his eye while he was trying to think. "What is it you want us to do, sir?"

Ansalem walked to the outside window, shaking his head. "I really don't recall summoning you, young man," he said. "I don't remember you at all, to be honest."

He looked over his shoulder at Carus, his face changing slightly. "I remember you, though. You wanted me to become a man of blood. Like yourself."

Carus shrugged. The tension in his muscular frame would have been obvious even to a stranger, let alone Garric.

"I wanted things of you that you didn't want to provide," Carus said. "And I've let blood, sometimes when I shouldn't have. I made a lot of mistakes in life; but fewer, I hope, as I am now."

"What did you want, Lord Ansalem?" Garric asked. "Did you bring us here to help you with *your* plans?"

"Oh, I don't think so," Ansalem said with a half-concealed smile. "You're not a wizard, are you? And I didn't need any help anyway. Come see."

He gestured to the grating and moved aside to make room for the others. Garric looked at his ancestor. Carus forced a wry smile and squeezed Garric's shoulder; they stepped together to look out over Klestis.

King Carus had seen wizardry as the cause rather than the symptom of the stresses tearing apart the Kingdom of the Isles. He knew now that he'd been wrong, but he couldn't help his feelings; and it took as much willpower for Carus to be polite to Ansalem as it would for Garric to let a spider run across his face.

The view through the electrum filigree wasn't the ruined Klestis on this side of the bridge, nor yet the living city that Carus had seen when he visited Ansalem in the flesh. Garric looked down on citizens gathering fruit and nuts from trees in the parks among the gleaming buildings. Gardens with a profusion of vegetables as well as flowers graced rooftops and boulevard medians. Even the balcony railings were green with lush plantings.

Cattle, plump and sleek, wandered among the people in the streets, browsing at will on the vegetation. The bounty was sufficient for them and the human residents of Klestis as well.

Occasionally Garric saw a man or woman with a cow on a milking tether, a little stake and halter meant not to hold the beast but merely to show it where to stand while its udders were stripped. Ewes provided most of the dairy products for Barca's Hamlet, but Garric knew the quantity that a good milch cow gave. The folk below drew bucket after bucket from their herd, many times what was possible.

"That isn't real," he said. "The milk, the fruit on the trees—that's not real."

"It could have been real," said the plump wizard with a brief frown. "It would have been real, except . . ."

Ansalem looked back at his stone couch. "I thought it was a mistake, but it really can't be," he said. "I went to sleep after I took Klestis out of time, and my acolytes knotted the amphisbaena to hold me in my chamber forever. Why would they have done that?"

"Because they wanted your power to use for their own ends," Carus said harshly. "Because they wanted to rule the Isles, I shouldn't wonder. And because you thought you were too good to concern yourself with any world but the one you wanted to create, they were able to do it."

"Purlio did that?" Ansalem said. His face screwed up into a look of wondering horror. "But I suppose he must have, him and the others."

"My friend, the wizard Tenoctris," Garric said, "says that you'd gathered objects of power that didn't affect you; but others weren't as strong as you are. She met you once, but she left Klestis for fear of what the forces here would do to her."

"I don't remember your friend," Ansalem said, shaking his head sadly. "I don't remember very much, I'm afraid. I did pick up baubles here and there. I liked to have them, and it did no harm. Besides, some of them could have been very dangerous in other hands. I have one of the Great Ones from a time before ours, changed to marcasite but still alive in its own way. I couldn't leave that where someone else might get it, could I?"

"Somebody else did get it," Carus said. His face was granite hard, and his lips chipped out the syllables. "Your Purlio, it seems."

"I made a mistake, didn't I?" Ansalem said softly. He looked into the king's cold eyes. "Should I have done what you wanted me to, sir?"

For a moment Carus didn't move or speak. Then he laughed, a gust of honest humor, and took the wizard's hands in both of his. "No, you shouldn't have done that, Lord Ansalem," he said, "because I didn't know what I was doing any better than you did. Together we could have made things different—for a time, at least. But it wouldn't have been better. I know that now."

Carus shook his head and stepped back from Ansalem; he was no longer tense. "I just wish," the king said, "we'd both had somebody to tell us what to do. I meant well, I swear it."

"Sir?" Garric said to Ansalem. "Can we get you out of this . . . trap? Cage? Maybe that's why you brought us."

"The encystment has to be broken from outside," said the wizard sadly, "and the amphisbaena itself is the only key. It's here with me, you see."

Garric forced himself to look at the serpentine form shimmering in time and space. Sometimes both heads were visible; often the stone couch and the air above it were bare, untenanted except for a pulsating imminence as real as the amphisbaena's physical form.

"Sir, can we take the talisman to our friend?" Garric asked. "Maybe she can open the encystment—or she can find someone more powerful if she can't do it herself."

"I appreciate the thought, young man," Ansalem said in the sort of tone an adult uses to a child who's asked why the sky is blue, "but you see, you're not real. Nothing here is real except me."

The chamber dissolved, or Garric dissolved through it. He was crossing the bridge again with Carus at his side. Klestis was a ruin behind them, trapped in an eternal twilight without hope or future.

"I feel sorry for him now," the king said. He shouted, but Garric as much read the words on his companion's lips as heard them. "I wish he could have another chance, the way I do through you, lad."

An army was marching across the bridge in the opposite direction. Garric saw the troops clearly this time: the corpses of men on the corpses of horses. Crab pincers and the teeth of fish had nibbled away here a nose, there the skin from a finger, but the cold abyss had held at bay the normal processes of decay.

Over the army floated a gonfalon bearing a black crab on the white fabric. Beneath it walked a man all in white. Despite the face paint, Garric recognized the figure as one of the acolytes who'd met King Carus when he visited Ansalem in the last days of the Old Kingdom.

The wizard turned his head slightly as he and Garric passed on their different planes. There was no more feeling in the wizard's eye than in the eyes of a spider.

". . . another chance," Carus whispered as Garric shuddered back to the waking reality of his conference room.

As she ran, Sharina held the Pewle knife before her with her right hand on the hilt and her left fingertips gripping the back of the blade near the point. She was too tired to hold the weapon safely in one hand, and she didn't trust herself to be able to unsheathe it quickly when danger threatened.

When, not if; the cries of the ghouls sounded in a broad semicircle whose ends had already drawn ahead of Sharina and Dalar. Before long the horns of the crescent would curve inward, forming a noose around their prey.

"I can't . . ." she gasped to Dalar, "go on . . . much farther . . ."

"Nor I," said the bird. He didn't wheeze or gasp—maybe his throat wasn't constructed so that he could—but his words had a clipped thinness now. "We will find a tree for our backs and make a stand."

He clucked and added with bitter humor, "For propery's sake I should compose my death lay first, but I do not know that our enemies have a sense of honor."

Live oaks and some relative of the hemlock or juniper were the most common trees. Some of them were huge: Sharina had seen Cordin being colonized when the bird first dropped her, but the wilderness had returned in full funereal glory in the millennia which had passed.

Moss hung in gray tangles from tree limbs. All the foliage dripped, though the drizzle had paused for the moment.

The ghouls were calling more frequently as they closed in. Sharina judged there were at least a score of them. It occurred to her that neither she nor Dalar had eaten for a long time. Not that a good meal a few hours ago would've made any real difference in the way the present situation ended.

"There!" she said. She pointed the knife at arm's length toward the half-overgrown building. The gesture unbalanced her so that she almost fell forward. "There, we can get in where the yew's growing on the roof!"

The building was rectangular. Its steeply peaked roof was, like the walls, built of ashlars reused from earlier buildings. The crude result looked like a step pyramid on a dais, but it had proved sturdy enough to withstand the forces that devoured the walls and towers of the more sophisticated structures of the ancient city.

The area around the building had been cleared repeatedly in past ages. Cedar stumps, none of them more than six inches in diameter, dotted the ground within twenty paces of the walls; pits in the soil remained where the roots of trees less resistant to weathering had grown in past ages.

No one had cut the vegetation for the past generation or more, though, and the forest was growing back quickly in the damp heat. A sticky yew berry had lodged among the roof corbels and sprouted to drive stones apart. The crack was narrow, but Sharina was slender and Dalar looked skeletal with his down slicked to his skin by the rain. They'd manage.

They had to manage.

The walls were only eight courses high, shoulder height for Sharina. At another time she could have jumped to the top, catching the wall midway with her right foot and bouncing the rest of the way up on her running momentum.

Another time. She laid her knife on the first mossy step of the roof and crawled up gasping, thrusting her bare toes into the gaps between courses. Even then she might not have made it in time without a boost from Dalar's stubby fingers.

The walls were blank on all sides: the builders hadn't provided a door or other opening.

"Dalar," Sharina said, turning to give her companion a hand up; he was as exhausted as she was. "This is a tomb."

The bird gave a series of low-voiced clucks. "That is fitting, I fear."

He didn't sound as though he were afraid. Neither was Sharina, which surprised her. One advantage to being so completely worn out was that she had no energy left for strong emotions, fear or hope either one.

"Go through!" Dalar ordered. His weights were circling in opposite directions, each out on six feet of chain while the remaining length quivered in a short loop between his hands. The weapon whistled softly, like a hound straining to slip its leash.

Sharina would have sent Dalar ahead of her: the bird was even slimmer, and if the first person into the opening got stuck it would cut them both off from safety. This wasn't a time to argue precedence, though.

She snatched up the Pewle knife and wormed through the crack in the masonry. As she did so, a ghoul broke through the edge of the forest. It was a male and considerably larger than the creature Dalar had killed. It screamed like ripping metal when it saw its prey.

The gap between the blocks narrowed at the inner end. Sharina had her head through to the other side when her shoulders caught. She stretched her right arm out as far as it would go and twisted to the left.

Her tunic tore. The yew's hairy root scraped the side of her ribs, but that was no price to pay for safety. Sharina gave another twist and tumbled free into the darkness. Outside the ghoul's cry ended with the sharp *whack!* of bronze on bone.

Sharina had been mentally prepared for the floor to be less than her own height below the opening. It was at least twice that. She was lucky to have curled her feet beneath her, but her legs still flew sideways on the slimy stone. She landed on her spine, hard enough to jar the world into a flare of buzzing light.

She'd kept hold of the knife, though. Nonnus would've been proud of her.

Sharina's feet dangled in open air. She blinked to get her vision back: there was a pit in the center of the small enclosure. She could have skidded. . . .

Dalar's body blocked the light through the opening; he was coming in feet first. "There's a hole in the floor!" Sharina shouted. She tried to act as a human guardrail without getting in the way of whatever gyrations her companion needed to wrench through the strait entrance.

Dalar fell inside. Sharina bunted him forward with her shoulder, away from the hole. She couldn't tell how deep it was, but she hadn't seen bottom in the glimpse she'd gotten.

The light faded again; a long, clawed arm reached into the enclosure and groped in the air. Dalar poised, looking upward with a weight in either hand.

"No!" said Sharina. "Boost me."

The bird dropped his weights and squatted, lacing his hands together. "Now," Sharina said, stepping into the stirrup.

Dalar straightened and lifted Sharina to the height of his shoulders in a smooth motion. The Pewle knife arced forward in an overhead chop into the ghoul's elbow.

Gristle and porous bones crunched. The ghoul's claws spasmed; the forearm dangled for an instant, then fell to the tomb floor. The edge of the masonry had torn the remaining tags of flesh away when the creature jerked back.

Sharina landed with flexed knees; Dalar steadied her. Outside the moaning cry of the wounded ghoul merged with the eager yelps of its fellows as they reached the clearing.

Sharina squatted on the tomb floor; she wasn't sure her legs would hold her any longer. Her shaking hands made light quiver across the knifeblade. Almost absently she wiped the weapon with the hem of her tunic.

She found herself smiling. The battered garment wasn't good for much but wiping rags after what it'd been through.

The ghouls crooned outside the tomb. None of them reached through the hole, but Sharina heard grunts of effort as some of the pack tried to move stones.

"There is an odor here," Dalar said. "We are in the den of something."

Sharina looked up. Her first thought was a leap of relief—*We've been saved!* Her face hardened. Aloud she said, "Yes, we're in a snake's den. I thought for a moment that my master was coming to . . . take us to the next stage."

"A snake?" Dalar said. The weights twitched out an inch or two before his palms swallowed them again. They weren't a good weapon for a tight enclosure like this, though Sharina didn't doubt that her bodyguard would make the best of whatever situation he was in. "I see. A large one, it would appear."

The interior walls of the tomb—was it really a tomb? There was no bier or coffin, merely what looked like a natural pit in the limestone—were plastered and frescoed. A great root had penetrated a lower corner and rotted when the tree it fed was cut down. Seepage and small animals had enlarged the cavity until a block fell from the wall.

The snake that laired here had polished the stones on the top and bottom of the entrance as it passed in and out. A scale stuck to the edge of a block. It was bigger than Sharina could have circled with her thumb and forefinger together.

"We can crawl out the tunnel," Dalar said quietly. "Possibly it is wide enough."

There wasn't a great deal of light, but Sharina's eyes had adapted. She could see that she'd be a tighter fit for the snake's tunnel than she'd been for the hole in the roof.

They couldn't be sure how long it was, but it might well extend to the edge of the original clearing.

"Yes," Sharina said. The enclosure darkened as a ghoul stepped between the hole and the light. She and Dalar looked up with the quick, cold deliberation of cats noticing motion on the pantry floor.

The ghoul moved away. Several of the creatures grunted together; a roof stone grated, then stopped. The grunts rose to snarls of frustrated anger.

"Yes," Sharina repeated. "I suppose we'll have to do that. But right now I think I need to rest for a while."

"I as well," Dalar said. "We should have . . . an hour or so? That is what I estimate. We will be better for relaxing during that time."

Outside wood clunked on stone. The ghouls were using branches to lever the roof apart. Sharina wasn't sure she and Dalar would have a full hour before there was an opening big enough to let the ghouls enter, but there'd be some time.

"Yes, we'll relax," she said. Her weary laughter echoed in the small enclosure.

"Well, Mistress Ilna," Chalcus said in a voice as smooth as sap flowing, "the sky's not so bright that we'd change from the night watch to the first morning watch—but we can tell it from the land, as you see. If you and the child are up to moving . . . ?"

"Yes, of course we are," Ilna said, shaking Merota gently awake. She wouldn't have the chanteyman thinking that Merota was a dangerous burden just because she was young and female. Ilna had been on her own and caring for her brother before she was Merota's age!

Not that there was any similarity between Ilna and this well-born child . . . and not that Chalcus was going to abandon either one of them if the going got tough. Tougher.

"Umm?" said Merota. "Oh!" She sat bolt upright, looking around wildly for danger.

"We're going for a walk now, mistress," Chalcus said soothingly. "There's nothing whatever wrong, but there's light enough to see and we'd best use it, not so?"

Ilna peered toward the sea. The lamps on the triremes had gone out by midnight. Though the sky *was* brightening, the light wasn't good enough to differentiate the vessels from the water. From what the chanteyman said, the ships should've floated off the mud bar by now, but she supposed she'd have heard if they'd gotten under way during the night.

"Yes, Chalcus," Merota said as she stood. "Chalcus? I'm thirsty."

"We'll see about that too," the chanteyman said. "As much brush as there is, we should find a spring soon enough. But there's other things we may find too, mistress, so keep those sharp young eyes of yours open, hey?"

"Yes, Chalcus!" the girl said, beaming. They started up the trail in single file, with Merota sandwiched closely between the two adults.

He has a way with women, killer and pirate though he is. Or perhaps that's why *he has a way with women. . . .*

The track rose sharply. The larger trees were elms, sweet gums and live oaks, but they were young and the tallest were less than thirty feet high. They weren't full enough to shade out the evening olive and blackberries, which therefore wove a thick, prickly mass to either side.

Chalcus proceeded cautiously, snapping olive stems and bending blackberry canes with his foot when he thought they'd be a barrier to the females behind him. His callused soles ignored the thorns.

He held the sword vertical before him, the hilt at waist height. He never used the blade on the vegetation, and his eyes combed the thickets ahead and to either side.

As they neared the crest of the hill, Ilna turned to look back at the ships. The vegetation was too dense for her to see anything but the trail immediately behind her. She didn't suppose it mattered.

Chalcus reached the top of the ridge that paralleled the seacoast. He didn't crawl the last of the way; rather, he slipped into a crouch that was less for concealment than to add spring to whichever direction he jumped.

"Well, may mermaids come out and play with my toes," he said, relaxing slightly. "Ilna, dear thing, come here and tell me what you think of what we're seeing."

Ilna frowned, but she didn't let her irritation reach her tongue. Chalcus probably couldn't help his silliness; and if he could, well, they still had more important things to worry about. Bringing Merota along by a gentle push between the shoulder blades, she moved up to where the chanteyman stood.

Ilna expected to see more tangled wilderness. Instead she was looking down on a neatly planted orchard. Though the fruit trees were unmistakable, she didn't recognize the globular fruit itself. They weren't apples, and they were too brightly colored for the peaches which were the borough's only other orchard crop.

"Oranges!" squealed Merota. "Oh, Chalcus, can we pick some? I'm *so* thirsty!"

"I don't think anybody'd object to thirsty castaways helping themselves from such bounty," the chanteyman said. He raised an eyebrow to Ilna. "What do you think, dear one?"

Ilna had seen oranges before, at banquets in Erdin and Valles. Apparently they grew on trees like apples. She'd thought they were vegetables.

"I suppose that's all right," she said aloud. *Even children and sailors know more than I do!* "If the owner comes, we can pay him then."

Chalcus started down the reverse slope at a saunter that seemed careless if you ignored the way he scanned their surroundings like a nervous vole. His sword was still in his hand, though now that they'd gotten out of the heavy brush he slanted the point down to his left in a slightly less threatening manner.

"The island looks completely wild from the sea," Ilna said deliberately. "But these trees must have been planted some time ago. The ridge conceals them."

"It's more interesting than you'd know, mistress," Chalcus said, "seeing as you've not sailed these waters as I have. I can take a star sight as well as Vonculo can, so I know we're between Seres and Kanbesa. But you see, dear ones, the last time I was here we were afloat, and there was nothing but open water for hours in either direction."

They'd reached the orchard. Chalcus plucked an orange with his left hand. He tossed it over his shoulder to Merota without seeming to look back at her.

He turned to Ilna smiling, his fingers rubbing the rough bark of the branch. "Not three months ago this was salt sea, mistress. An island may rise from the sea . . . but it doesn't grow trees like this in a few months only. Not without wizards' work."

"Well, we knew there were wizards involved," Ilna replied coldly. Her lips twitched into a grin of sorts. "Even Vonculo knew there were wizards, though that and the direction of sunrise were about all I'd trust him on."

Chalcus laughed like brass chimes. He picked two more oranges, then tossed the larger of the pair to Ilna. He flicked his with his thumbnail and began to peel the fruit one-handed. Ilna watched him, then peeled hers with the paring knife from her sash. Merota 'had simply bitten a piece from the rind to squeeze and suck the contents directly into her mouth.

"Why do you suppose the folk doing this . . ." Chalcus paused to spit out seeds and a scrap of the inner membrane. ". . . want our ships? Or their crews, perhaps, though they're a poor enough lot if I do say so, who was one of them."

"Maybe nobody lives here," Merota said through sticky lips. "We haven't seen anybody."

"Someone tends these trees," Ilna said. She wasn't an

orchardist, but she knew that an apple or peach tree left to its own devices quickly becomes insect-ridden. The sweet sap that filled the fruit seemed to draw pests the way fresh meat drew flies.

"The trees looked no more than forty rows deep when we sighted them from the ridge," Chalcus said, tossing the orange rind through the branches of the tree to his side. *Through*, not into, Ilna noticed, though the chanteyman had been looking in the other direction at the time. "There's fields to the other side. I'd say we look there, then report to Vonculo on what we've seen?"

"Yes," said Ilna. "Much good it'll do him."

They started forward. The trees were aligned not only in rows but across rows; each step disconcertingly opened new aisles half-left and half-right while closing the aisles glimpsed a step before.

Chalcus chuckled. "The only thing that'd do Vonculo good would be a coil of strong rope," he said. "But then, many have said the same of me."

Insects—bees and swift clear-winged moths—buzzed about them. The patterns of their flight were subtly wrong, though even Ilna couldn't describe what was *off*. If she'd been an insect, her path would have differed minutely from the paths of *these* insects. The reason eluded her; and she didn't mention it to her companions.

"Gently, now," Chalcus said. They'd reached the last row of trees but one. The chanteyman paused beside a gnarled trunk, his left hand resting lightly on the bark, as he looked beyond.

A paved road, disarrayed by time or other stresses into a jumble of canted stone blocks, separated the orchard from a barley field on the gentle slope opposite. A crew had begun harvesting the grain, starting at the top of the field. They were too distant for Ilna to make out individual details, but the harvesters' movements were as wrong as those of the bees around her.

"Should we go talk to them, Ilna?" Merota asked in a

small voice. She'd tented her hands primly before her, but they trembled slightly.

"Hush, child," Ilna said. After she spoke it occurred to her to hope she'd been gentle about it, but that wasn't as important as other things.

They were harvesting the grain with cradles, scythes with a wicker tray to hold the stalks as the blade severed them. A woman followed each man. She removed the stalks from the cradle, then bound them with a twist of rye straw and set the bundle in the little cart she pulled behind her.

Every motion was normal, familiar in general thrust to any peasant in a county where grain was grown. The sum of the motions was wrong, because the crew was *only* harvesting.

They weren't a team, chattering to one another about the quality of the crop, the heat, the fever that had gotten into Sincarf's hogs and whether it was going to spread through the borough. Twenty individuals sheared their way down the field, with no more interaction than so many stones bouncing in a rockslide.

"Their clothes are ragged," Merota said very softly.

"Their skin's ragged, child," Chalcus said. "They're dead men, they are, though they're moving well enough."

"The insects are dead also," Ilna said. "They fly and crawl, but they're dead. I think we should return to the ships and do whatever's required to convince Vonculo to leave at once."

"Aye," said the chanteyman. "I for one haven't seen any gold lying in the streets."

He nodded to Ilna. "Perhaps you'll lead and I'll take my leisure at the back, mistress?" he said.

"Yes, all right," Ilna said. She set off at a swinging pace through the orchard, down an aisle alongside the one they'd taken in the other direction.

It was hard to tell from which direction they were threatened. Chalcus apparently thought the rear was the place of danger. Ilna suspected it could be anywhere, in the ground or the air they breathed, but since they had to walk in some order it didn't matter.

It was almost a relief to reach the brush that screened the orchard. Ilna twisted sideways to slide through the narrow jaws of the path.

"A moment, dears," said Chalcus. "There's something on the road now. We can wait a moment more."

A procession was making its way up the broken roadway from the south. A battalion of corpses dressed as footmen preceded a pair of open-topped carriages, each drawn by eight skeletal horses. Despite their large wheels, the vehicles rocked and sometimes yawed so far to one side or the other that they threatened to tip over.

Pairs of women danced in the beds of the carriages. They'd been women, at least, before death claimed them. The slime of ages stained their clothing, but even at this distance Ilna could see that they were dressed as only princesses could afford. Their jewels and gold winked and glittered in the rising sun.

One of the dancers wore bracelets set with rubies and diamonds from right wrist to right elbow. At one time her left forearm might have been similarly bedizened, but that limb was only bones and the sinews connecting them. The crabs had been at her.

At the end of the parade of death was a sexless figure who neither walked nor rode: its arms were crossed before its chest, and its slippered feet floated above the road's surface. Its hooded robe was black wool, and soot mixed with grease covered the exposed skin.

The figure was as motionless as a statue carved from coal, and as evil to look on as a boil oozing pus.

"We'll go now," said Ilna clearly. It wasn't a question. Her companions fell in behind her without comment, though at least Chalcus probably wondered where the edge in her voice had come from.

Ilna's fingers played with the silk noose, forming it into quick, complex knots and loosing them almost before they appeared. Aloud, because not to speak would have meant she feared to admit the truth, Ilna said, "Looking at that fellow—the wizard, I suppose he is. I was reminded of seeing myself in the mirror when I lived in Erdin not so very long ago."

"But I don't think, milady," said Chalcus easily, "that you'll ever see that reflection in the future. And I very much doubt the one back there will see any face *but* the one he wears at present. Not so?"

"We'll hope it's so," Ilna said. She snorted. "Yes, of course; I'll make it so. On my soul, I will!"

She stepped out of the brush onto the mud beach. The tide had begun to fall, though it was still much higher than when Ilna and her companions first landed.

"The ships are gone," she said in a clear voice that was only a hair louder than it needed to be for Chalcus to hear her.

"Are we in the—" the chanteyman said, stepping to Ilna's side. In embarrassment he added almost as part of the same sentence, "Yes, of course we are; and I shouldn't even have needed my late friend Sinou as a signpost to remind me that Ilna os-Kenset wouldn't lead me wrong."

He strode toward the water, then paused and called over his shoulder, "Stay close, little one; and you too, mistress, if you please."

"Come," said Ilna, but Merota was already scurrying after Chalcus. He looked down the beach to southward.

"There they are," Chalcus said. "Just rounding the headland."

Ilna shaded her eyes with her right hand. The ships were moving with minute, jerky motions. One was still fully visible, while only the curved sternpost of the other showed around the edge of the high cliffs south of the landfall.

"I don't see anyone on deck," Ilna said, wondering if only her ignorance made the vessel's appearance seem so wrong. "And the oars aren't moving."

"Look at the color around the hulls, dear one," said Chalcus. "That's not the sun on waves, you know."

"Ah," said Ilna. "No, it's the shells of the Great Ones. And they're towing the ships."

Cashel wiped sweat from his forehead with his sleeve. The green light didn't come from any sun, so he couldn't say the sun was hot today; but *he* was hot, he'd tell the world!

A poppy grew, goodness knew how, from a crack in the stony soil. Cashel guessed the petals'd be bright red under normal light, but here they were mostly brown. It was still a treat to see them.

He'd first thought he saw a half dozen dark-skinned men in a circle up ahead, waiting for him. Closer up he could tell they were trees, though the spindly limbs didn't look as big as the gnarled trunks should support. There was a knob right above where the branches sprayed out, too.

"Those trees really do look like people," he said to Krias, just being friendly. Cashel talked to the sheep he was tending also. He wasn't sure they understood him, but the sheep seemed to like being noticed; and he wasn't sure they *didn't* understand, either.

"Well, they ought to," said the ring demon, "since that's what they are. What they were till they didn't hold their tongues when they should've, that is. *That* was a mistake they won't be able to make again!"

Cashel sighed to hear the gusto in the demon's voice. Those fellows—were they women as well as men? Cashel decided he didn't want to know—might have deserved what they got, but it wasn't something you ought to be pleased about. Well, he guessed the world had as much right to have a Krias as it did a Cashel.

There was a flat gleam in the middle of the trees. Cashel didn't want to get his hopes up, but if that was water it'd be welcome indeed. He'd been eating the shaved root of the tree that attacked him. It had an oily richness, but plain water would go down a treat.

Rather than ask about the maybe-water, Cashel said,

"Did those fellows get on the wrong side of a wizard, then, Master Krias?"

"That might have happened," the demon replied with a tart smugness that made Cashel think of Sharina's mother, Lora; not a woman he or anybody else he knew had ever cared for. "Or it might have been a God, because in the Underworld more things visit than any sheep-boy could imagine. Or it just possibly was a demon who wasn't *always* trapped in a sapphire on a fool's finger, you know."

"Ah," said Cashel. Well, he didn't want to get into the rights and wrongs of a business that'd probably happened longer ago than even Garric had read about. Especially not with Krias doing the telling.

He cleared his throat. "That looks like a pool of water," he said.

"Oh, there's water there, all right," Krias said. "You won't like the taste, but it won't kill you. Getting it out of the middle of the tar it lies on, *that* may kill you."

Cashel stopped a few paces out from the trees. The water shimmered—green with the sky's reflection and pretty awful to look at—in the middle of a greater expanse of tar. That had crusted in a coating of dust, but Cashel knew that chances were it was soft underneath and Duzi knew how deep.

He thought for a moment, then said, "Master Krias? Are the trees going to attack if I go near them?"

"Worried, sheep-boy?"

"No," Cashel said truthfully. "But I like to know what's going on before I get into it."

Krias sniffed. "Them? No, they won't attack anybody. Least of all somebody wearing me."

"I'm glad to hear that," Cashel said, walking to the edge of the tar. The pool of rainwater was still a long double pace, left heel to left heel, beyond where he stood.

Cashel thought he'd heard one of the trees sigh as he passed through them, but that could've been imagination. They weren't a familiar kind, but their spines and horny bark were a lot like what he'd seen in dry country else-where.

The light was fading; it'd be pitch dark soon. There wasn't a moon down here any more than there was a sun, nor was there anything that'd pass for moonlight.

"It's going to get cold tonight, I shouldn't wonder," Cashel said as he unreeved the strap that bound his water bottle to his belt. Even empty it was a sturdy piece of stoneware, sealed with a pale cream glaze. He uncorked it.

"So build a fire!" Krias said. "And if you've forgotten how since last night, I'll light it for you. Just break off some branches."

Cashel wound the strap around one end of the quarter-staff. He looked at the nearest trees. They were ugly things for a fact.

"I don't guess I'll do that," he said. "I've been cold often enough before."

Cashel backed a little from the edge of the tar and lay flat. He moved with cautious deliberation, as he always did unless he saw a need for haste. Cashel saw the need for haste so rarely that many folk assumed he *couldn't* move fast. Those who presumed on such a belief often had broken bones or worse to pay them for their mistake.

He slid his staff forward and held the mouth of the water bottle under the surface of the shallow pool. He didn't need Krias to tell him it'd taste awful, but it had been a hot day and there was no reason to expect a change tomorrow.

"You could burn chunks of dried tar, I suppose," Krias muttered. "You'd want to sleep upwind, but I guess you'd do that anyhow. Of course if you're too sensitive to use the dead twigs lying around for kindling, you'll never get the asphalt to light without my help."

Cashel lifted the staff and filled bottle, then got to his feet with his usual slow grace. He looked down at the sapphire. "Thank you, Master Krias," he said. "I wouldn't have thought of that."

"Of course you wouldn't, sheep-boy!" the demon shrilled. "Of course you wouldn't!"

The water was just as foul as Cashel'd expected. He hoped he'd be able to wash the bottle clean when he next found a clear spring. He grinned.

"What do you have to laugh about?" Krias demanded.

"I'm getting ahead of myself," Cashel said. "I should've been hoping I'd *find* a clear spring, not wondering whether I could wash my bottle in it."

He took another swig and added, "But this will do."

He wondered what Sharina was drinking now. He'd be able to ask her soon enough, he supposed.

Still grinning, Cashel used the side of his foot to scuff clear an arc of ground not far from the pool. The hard soil was covered with stones, mostly flat and about the size of a duck egg sliced the long way. They were all right to walk on—they didn't have sharp edges—but he'd prefer not to sleep on them since he had the choice.

Duzi, the soil *was* hard. Cashel drew his knife and used the broad point for a mattock to break up a patch big enough to cradle his hip bone.

"I can do that," Krias said. "*I* can make you a feather bed to sleep on, sheep-boy."

"This is fine," Cashel said, scooping the dirt away with his palm and the back of the knife blade. He didn't like anything soft under him when he slept. He'd heard feather beds were warm, but so were the wool blankets his sister wove.

Krias muttered. Cashel couldn't make out the words, but he could guess them. Pretty much the same sort of words the demon used most times and most places, which you'd think would get old after a while. It didn't seem to, though; not with demons nor that sort of people either one.

Cashel made a little fireset from fallen wood on the inside of the arc he'd cleared. The twigs wept a sap that hardened clear, and some of them had dead leaves still attached.

The pool's surface cracked when it hardened. Cashel levered fist-sized chunks loose, then put them close to the wood. He was as careful as he could be not to get the sticky blackness underneath onto the blade of his knife. The trees' coarse bark would clean the iron a treat, but he didn't think he'd do that either. There'd be other trees farther on, he figured. Trees that were just trees.

Cashel used one of the desert stones to tick sparks from the back of his knife into a bed of punk. He carried a small flint in his wallet, but the local rocks were plenty hard enough and a better size to use. The punk lit the twigs into a quick, hot flame which in turn got the tar going.

The tar burned deep red with a lot of oily smoke. The air had cooled off fast when it got dark. Cashel was glad of the warmth, but the whiff he'd gotten when he lit the fire made him hope the mild breeze didn't change direction while he was sleeping.

"Good night, Master Krias," he said. He settled himself with the crook of his right arm for a pillow and his left hand grasping his quarterstaff at the balance.

"*Good* night indeed!" Krias said. "Or any other kind of night. I hope you don't think that *I* care whether it's dark or light outside?"

Cashel wondered what the demon did care about. Something, that was for sure. Krias wouldn't be so prickly if there wasn't something bothering him. Asking wouldn't bring anything more than an insult, though; and it wasn't Cashel's habit to go prying into other people's affairs.

The ring's mutterings were a lot like cicadas chirping when you got used to them. Smiling and thinking of Sharina, Cashel drifted off into sleep.

He wasn't sure what waked him or how long he'd slept. The fire was burning much the way it had been when it first fully caught; the chunks of tar grew smaller, but they didn't form ash that smothered the open flame the way wood did.

Cashel wasn't alone anymore. The trees from around the pond now stood close together across the fire from him.

"Ah," Cashel said, rising onto his elbow. He didn't jump to his feet nor lift the quarterstaff. Krias had said they wouldn't attack him; and they hadn't, after all, when they walked past him sleeping.

Clearing his throat, Cashel said, "It's a cold night, sure enough. Would you like me to put some more wood on the fire? Fuel, I mean."

The trees didn't move or make a sound. He'd have thought they'd grown right where they were if he didn't know better.

"Do you expect them to answer you, sheep-boy?" Krias said.

"Well, I wasn't sure," said Cashel. To the trees he went on, "Good night to you, sirs. And ladies, if, you know; if you are."

Somewhere in the distance he thought he heard Elfin singing. It could have been the wind, though. It was a pretty sound, whatever it was.

Cashel turned himself end for end, putting his left side down this time. It was a cold night for fair!

When the sky brightened at what would have been dawn in the upper world, the fire had burned out and the trees were back where he'd first seen them. It might have been a dream.

Cashel refilled his water bottle. Before he walked on in the direction Krias indicated, he tapped his forelock in salute to the grove.

Chapter Sixteen

"P lease," said Merota as the ships disappeared around the point of land. She looked from Ilna to Chalcus with pleading eyes; very young, very controlled, and very frightened. "What should we do?"

The chanteyman laughed. "I'd be inclined to say that

you've as much judgment on the matter as I do, child, but I won't lay that burden on your young shoulders."

He glanced at Ilna and raised an eyebrow. "Mistress?"

"Can we sail a ship off this island by ourselves?" she asked crisply. "Can you sail us off by yourself, that is? I know nothing of the business."

"Build a boat and sail it off, that'd be," Chalcus said, frowning toward the horizon as he considered the question. "Yes, if I had long enough and I knew that our lives depended on just that thing; but I think the better choice is that we leave on the *Terror* with enough others aboard to crew her. Even if the others are Vonculo and the widdifus who believed his tales of treasure."

"Then let's follow," Ilna said. "Back up on the ridge, I think; the waves are washing that headland, and the cliff looks too steep for me to climb."

They had very little information; that meant weaving it into a plan was simpler. Standing on mud to stare at an empty sea was as complete a waste of time as Ilna could imagine, and the chances were that she and her companions had only a little time.

"Well said," said Chalcus. "But I'll lead, I think."

The chanteyman walked as fast as he could, though his legs were more at home on shipboard than on land. Merota had to scramble to keep up, but she didn't complain. Indeed, the child would probably have been treading on Chalcus' heels out of nervousness if he'd not been pressing.

Ilna followed without difficulty. She was used to walking quickly; and if she didn't have the stride of her long-legged friend Sharina, she could certainly match that of a sailor!

Merota was red-faced when they reached the ridgeline again, but that was more excitement than exhaustion. The child was glad simply to be moving when she was frightened. She hadn't learned that blind action was as likely to take you into hidden danger as out of it.

Ilna did know that; but she felt better for stretching her

legs as well. She grinned. Another proof that she was human, she supposed. It was a pity that usually when she thought that, she also thought she was being foolish.

With Chalcus continuing in the lead they followed the ridge to the left, southward. The harvesters were still at work in the barley, but the wizard and his procession of corpses were by now out of sight.

Ilna heard the clicks and buzzing of insects rubbing their wing cases together. Birds hopped silently among the brushwood. The ground south of the orchard and field became a bog. In it frogs dived with a plop at the approach of humans—but they didn't croak, shrill, or peep.

Most of the birds flitting through the reeds had lost their feathers, and a few were little more than frameworks of fine, hollow bone. Merota watched a crow scud past low, watching the humans with an empty eye socket. The child lowered her eyes to the ground, but she didn't cry or even gasp.

Chalcus whistled a dance tune as he walked, his gaze shifting as quickly as a butterfly's wings. There wasn't a path for them to follow, but he found a route of sorts a short way down from the edge. Here the ground was dry enough that their feet didn't sink in but too wet for woody plants to grow into an impenetrable tangle. The risen sun boiled a miasma from stagnant water. A light breeze blew inland, but within bowshot of the ridge the reeds and horsetails became wan forms among whorls of gray.

"Now I would judge," said Chalcus, "that the headland is there—"

He stretched out his left arm. They'd had to bear inland because of the footing or lack of it. Ilna saw nothing where the chanteyman pointed but solid brush, at least as tall and solid as what they'd climbed through from the shore. If Chalcus thought they'd come the correct distance down this blinkered path, though, she was confident he was right.

"Now, getting to where we can see again . . ." he said. "Still, I think . . ."

Even as the chanteyman spoke, he stepped into the unappealing wall of vegetation. Blackberry canes which grew amid the general mass of weeds and shrubs crackled beneath the soles of his horny feet.

"Follow him closely, child," Ilna said. "Don't worry if your clothing catches. I can mend tears."

Which assumed a number of things, not least that she and Merota would live long enough for mending clothes to be a worthwhile occupation; but Ilna *did* assume that. She smiled wryly. Perhaps she was more of an optimist than most of those who knew her would have guessed.

"Ah, who would not be cheerful with heroes like you and me protecting them?" called Chalcus without turning his head. "Not so?"

Is the man reading my mind?

"We'll hope that's so," Ilna said aloud.

Merota's hem hung on a blackberry. Before Ilna could reach down and loose it, the girl jerked the cloth free.

Ilna smiled in silent approval. The child took direction as few adults seemed able to do, and the embroidered fabric hadn't ripped after all. Ilna liked to see evidence of good craftsmanship . . . which, like the ability to take direction, wasn't something she met with every day.

"There we are," said Chalcus, sounding pleased though not triumphant. "Nothing but lichen and a pine wedged in the rock ahead."

Ilna wondered what the chanteyman would think was worth him feeling triumphant about. It might be that she'd learn before long.

The headland was a wedge of dense gray sandstone which remained like a doorpost when tides wore away the walls of softer rock to either side. Ilna thankfully followed Merota out of the brush and onto bare stone. Though vertical—even undercut—on the seaward edge, as Ilna had seen from their original landfall, this side of the slab lay at a shallow slope that she could walk up with ease.

Chalcus already lay at the top with his legs spread, leaning far out into the air. "Come look at this," he called.

Merota paused at the bottom of the slope. "Ilna," she

whispered. "I don't like heights. I really don't. . . ."

"Yes, all right," Ilna said. She understood the difference between the fear that everyone felt about one thing or another, and the blind, clutching terror that she saw in the child's eyes. "Wait for us here."

Ilna crawled up the slope on all fours. She could have walked to the chanteyman's side, but since she was going to lie down on the rock anyway she saw no point in doing so. It wasn't as though she had anything to prove to Chalcus; or to anyone in the world if it came to that.

By looking straight down—not an experience Ilna liked, though it didn't freeze her heart the way it might have Merota's—she could see the stern of a trireme being worked around the rock. The water must be deep, because the vessel was very close inshore.

"Nobody on the deck," Chalcus observed. "And the water full of those devils."

The sea was in direct sunlight. The ammonites shimmered and rippled around the vessels like maggots in a rotting corpse.

The trireme slowly disappeared beneath the overhang, edging forward much as it had when Ilna watched it being launched by pulleys from the shiphouse in Valles. She wondered why the vessel didn't reappear around the other face of the headland. The warships were so long that she should see the prow of the second, and the first should be completely in sight.

"Now where do you suppose the ships are going, my dear?" Chalcus said, rising to his feet with a nonchalance that Ilna could never have equaled when perched so high above a sheer drop. "Wizards' work, do you think?"

"I know as little of wizards' work as you do," Ilna said—tartly and perhaps not quite truthfully, if she let herself think about it. "My first guess would be that there's a hole in the cliff, and they're being drawn inside it."

The chanteyman slapped his left palm with the fingers of his right hand, callus cracking on callus with a sound like sudden lightning. "Yes!" he said. "Now, how shall we get a look at this tunnel, as it may be?"

He leaned out again; the second ship had disappeared as completely as the first. To Ilna's shock and surprise, Chalcus sheathed his sword and swung himself over the lip of the rock.

"I can't come with you!" Ilna said. It wasn't that she was afraid—though she certainly had a healthy fear of plunging a distance sure to be fatal—but that she simply didn't have the physical ability to hold herself by her toes and fingertips on a face so sheer. Garric and Cashel gathered eggs when the seabirds nested on the spires of rock off the coast of Haft, but even they would have found this hard sandstone daunting.

Well, Chalcus probably couldn't weave anything more complex than a rope splice. And she wasn't competing with him!

"One's enough for the task," Chalcus said. He pitched his voice normally, but Ilna could hear the strain in it. This wasn't a time to bother him. "You just keep an eye on Mistress Merota till I'm back, hey?"

Ilna looked over her shoulder. She hadn't been thinking about the—

The girl was gone.

"Merota!" Ilna said. *The child couldn't have been carried off without sound! Unless the wind over the rock was louder than—*

"I'm all right!" Merota called from the bushes just below the bare rock. "Please, I just want some privacy!"

Oh. Well, I can scarcely blame the poor child. All these days on the ship with fifty men watching everything—

"Ah!" Chalcus cried. "I've found something indeed!"

Merota screamed. The brush crackled as though an ox were charging through it. Ilna, flicking her supple noose open in her hands, sprang toward the sound. Bushes and the crowns of saplings quivered as something raced through the thicket, headed away from her.

Merota's scream stopped as if her throat had been—

As though someone had clapped a hand over the child's mouth. Laughter, the horrible cackling laughter that they'd heard when the *Ravager*'s skiff landed, filled the sunlit air.

Ilna shouted over her shoulder "I'm going after the girl!" as she plunged into the brush. She didn't know if Chalcus heard her or not, but he couldn't possibly get up the cliff soon enough to help.

Ilna didn't suppose she could do anything useful either, but she had to try. *This is my fault. . . .*

If she'd thought about it, Ilna would have expected the thick vegetation to delay her. In fact she slipped between trunks that seemed too close to pass her and around brambles that she barely noticed as she went by. There wasn't time to think or worry; the same instincts that guided her weaving chose Ilna's path now.

The maniac laughter still drew away from her. Ilna heard splashes, then a final trill of hideous joy.

She reached the edge of the bog where woody shrubs gave way to reeds and mud. A door thumped, or perhaps it was a bubble of mephitic vapors bursting on the surface.

Ilna paused. The bog was astir with ripples and counter-ripples reflected from the stems of the soft-bodied plants. The water showed no tracks, and there was no obvious path across it.

But there *was* a path, to the thing that had taken Merota and to Ilna os-Kenset as well. She walked into the bog. Her feet sank ankle deep on the first step, to mid-shin on the second—

And the third step was onto the top of a stone pillar hidden just beneath the surface of water dark with mud and the black effluvium of rotting vegetation. Ilna strode on, her smile more terrible than a snarl on most faces.

The rope flowed between her fingers; she caressed the noose the way an old spinster pets her cat. Ilna didn't know what she was going to meet at the end of her trail, but she knew that it, whatever it was, would meet her.

Walking as though she were in her own kitchen, Ilna wove a winding course among the tussocks. Each support

was a long stride from the one nearest and no bigger than
was sufficient to hold the ball of a person's foot. She never
slipped. The black water gurgled as if in sullen anger to
be balked of its prey.

The mist wrapped her. Occasionally Ilna could see as
much as twenty feet in one direction or the other, but more
often her hands would have faded from sight if she'd
stretched them out.

Ilna grinned with at least a morsel of humor. She'd been
in worse places than this. She wasn't sure that was a recommendation, but it was something.

A shape loomed ahead of her. At first Ilna thought she
was seeing another phantasm of mist, but this held its form
despite the surrounding whorls and caracoles of gray. It
was an island, and there was a hut near the edge of it.

She stepped onto firm, dry soil. There was grass, though
the blades had the yellowish pallor of vegetation covered
almost long enough to kill it completely. What she'd taken
for a building was a boulder the size of a building. There
was a bronze door let into its face.

Ilna looked around, not that she'd be able to see much
unless it came charging through the fog. She doubted the
island was of any great extent, through she couldn't be sure
under the present conditions. Bubbles and perhaps frogs
plopped; nothing moved but the mist. There was no sign
of Merota or whatever it was that had taken the child.

Ilna gripped the door's bar handle; the bronze was dry
and felt distinctly warm. Perhaps she should be pleased not
to be touching metal that dripped with the swamp's cold
sweat, but it hadn't been what she expected. Ilna doubted
that the unexpected was ever a good thing in this place.

The door swung toward her easily. Ilna hadn't thought
it would open. The panel's face was bare of anything but
the handle, but she'd still thought there'd be a lock—
concealed from any but a wizard, perhaps.

A staircase cut in living rock curved downward. Ilna
grimaced. She didn't like stone, but neither had she come
this far in order to turn around again. She started down.

Ilna was less than a full circuit below the ground when she heard a soft thump and the feeling of air being compressed. The wan light she'd had to that point cut off. The door had closed, perhaps pushed by the faint breeze. Perhaps. She paused for long moments, but there was nothing to hear save her heartbeats echoing through her bloodstream.

She went on, moving without haste. It wasn't likely that whatever waited below was something she'd want to hurry to meet.

Light shone into the staircase below. Ilna didn't walk faster, but she frowned slightly. The glow had the balance of sunlight outdoors, not the yellowish quivering of a lamp forty feet below ground.

With another turn of the stairs she came to the slit carved into the rock. If she'd been in a tower she'd have said it was a window looking out onto a bustling city. Folk shopped in kiosks and lounged in the open square below her. The three-story buildings were made of brick with red tile roofs. The women leaning out of windows to talk with their neighbors were close enough that Ilna could have shouted to them—if her apparent vantage point and the women themselves had been real.

A troop of armored cavalry rode through the square beneath a banner figured with a crab. People made way for the soldiers sullenly but without exceptional concern.

Ilna continued downward. Whatever the "window" showed, it wasn't this island at this time. All the people she'd seen were alive.

There were more windows—onto fields worked by teams of horses and living humans; onto the sea, across which a squadron of warships rowed swiftly; onto a palace courtyard in which a burly man in black armor and a crown harangued a crowd of courtiers and citizens alike.

Ilna gave them only passing glances. She was interested in reality alone, and they weren't part of her present reality.

She wasn't sure how far down she went. She hadn't been

counting the steps, and anyway she couldn't have counted
so far without a tally.

The door at the bottom of the stairs was wooden and
stood ajar. There was no light in the room beyond, but
enough of a subdued haze filtered from the slits into time
and space above for Ilna's adapted eyes to view the portal
clearly.

She pushed it open with her left hand and stepped inside.
When her foot crossed the threshold, the walls themselves
lighted to display a circular treasure room.

Ilna felt her diaphragm suck in. When she was a child
she'd had to scramble to earn enough for her and Cashel
to live on, but "enough" was all that had concerned her.
After she'd established herself as the finest weaver on the
east coast of Haft—and beyond—she'd made a point of
being paid what her work was worth, because she would
no more let herself be robbed than she would rob another.

Ilna had never cared about other people's money,
though; and because she was without avarice, the concept
of wealth beyond avarice was meaningless to her. Even so,
she had to gasp at the sheer volume of coins and jewels
and bracelets, the gleaming platters and vases of silver
where they weren't solid gold. The white light, though not
harsh, was shadowless because it flooded from all directions at once.

She gave a throaty chuckle. The stories with which Mastyn and Vonculo had lured the others to mutiny had been
true after all; though the chance of any of this wealth reaching the hands of the sailors was as slight as that of Ilna
letting treasure turn her from her duty.

Bags and pots of coins and other small items sat in piles.
Some had split and spilled their contents again. Among the
riches were objects whose value was less obvious: a small
wooden coffin; a device of globes and spindles, made of
brass; a clear disk the size of a plate but convex on both
sides; and a score of others, all jumbled together with the
gold.

Ilna noticed a rolled tapestry under a stack of plate. She

grasped it, intending to pull it out to examine. When her fingers touched the slick weave, she felt a heart-freezing image of waves on all sides towering above houses as people screamed in their final terror.

Ilna drew her hand back with a grim smile. Her fingers tingled. Fabric had always spoken to her, and it did so with a particular clarity since she returned from Hell. More often than not what her talent told her was unpleasant. Rarely as unpleasant as this, however, feeling thousands die together as an island sank in a foaming sea.

When Ilna entered the chamber, the door had closed behind her of its own accord. The inside walls were unmarked and as smooth as polished flint, but she could find the door easily enough. There were other doors as well, hidden in the walls.

One of them opened. A figure all in white stepped in and the portal closed behind him. *Him,* though he was as sexless as a spindle; and as evil as a spider lurking in a tunnel of white silk.

"Welcome to Yole, mistress," he said. "I wasn't expecting to find a visitor, but I'm not sorry to see you. I am Ewis of Zampt."

He made a half-bow; his eyes never left her face. Ewis' pupils were the only parts of his person that weren't white.

"I'm Ilna os-Kenset," Ilna said. "I've come looking for the child who's in my care. Have you taken her?"

"Me?" said Ewis with a giggle. "Goodness, no, neither I nor any of my colleagues. I suspect the Tall Thing has your little friend. He's eaten recently, so there's no immediate danger."

Ewis took a faceted ivory bead from his sleeve and tossed it in his palm. "Besides," he added, "it rather likes little children. Not adults, though; and especially not wizards."

"Fine," Ilna said, though nothing about the situation was really fine. "Where will I find the Tall Thing? Is it a wild beast?"

"Oh, goodness, goodness!" Ewis laughed. "What shall I

say? It's wild enough, and it's beyond question bestial—
but a wild beast? I think not."

He sobered and focused eyes as black as a spider's on
Ilna. "And I'm afraid I can't tell you where it is, either.
We have to avoid it, you see, my colleagues and I. It's
rather angry at us, I'm afraid."

"If you're avoiding the Tall Thing . . ." Ilna said. She
viewed so much of life and the world with loathing that it
was natural now to keep her tone emotionless as she spoke
to this *creature*. ". . . then you have to know where it is.
Tell me."

"Why, you might be right at that," said Ewis. "Yes, perhaps I should do that. Perhaps I should. But first, won't
you look at the treasures my colleagues and I have gathered?"

He rummaged with his left hand in a tumble of silver
salvers and brought out an earthenware bowl. "You could
call anyone in the world to you with this," he said. "He
would come. Alive or dead, he would come."

"I want the child Merota," Ilna said. Her fingers were
still, but the soft supple noose they held restrained an anger
that would otherwise, otherwise . . . "That's all I want from
you, wizard."

"Not amused by the Bowl of Longing?" Ewis said, tit-
tering. "Goodness, goodness."

He set down the bowl and stepped over to the crystal
disk Ilna had noticed already. "Perhaps this new acquisition
will pique your interest, mistress. It's the Lens of Rushila,
and it can show you anything in the cosmos. No wizard
can protect himself from the eye of whoever wields this
wonder. Is it not fine?"

In Erdin and Valles, Ilna had seen windows of plate as
smooth as human skill could roll it. Even so the glass distorted shapes. This crystal, though doubly convex, was as
clear as air when Ilna looked through it straight on.

"If you're so powerful, wizard," she said, "then why do
you fear the Tall Thing? Tell me where he has Merota!"

Ewis giggled, but Ilna noticed that his hand trembled as

he set the Lens down. He continued to bounce the ivory bead in his other palm.

"Ah, the Tall Thing," he said. "That's a bit of a problem, I said. We needed him—"

He looked at Ilna again, his gaze as disconcerting as before. "Him, you see," Ewis continued, his voice thin and insectile. "At the time he was still a man. His name was Castigan. My colleagues and I bound him and used his rage as part of the incantation that sealed our mentor Ansalem out of eternity. The anger was just as important as the blood, you see."

Ilna remembered the images of sparks quivering over Vonculo's campfire as the music box played silently. "You killed a child," she said. "You killed *his* child. As he watched."

"Well, we had to, you know," Ewis giggled. "If Ansalem had awakened, well, he wouldn't have been very happy, would he? But the trouble is, having bound the Tall Thing once we can't bind him again. He's no longer a man, you see. He's only rage . . . and hunger."

"Ewis," Ilna said. "Wizard. I'm going to leave here now. Tell me where to find Merota."

Ewis looked at her. His left hand still trembled. "You want to leave here, mistress?" he said. "Do you think you can find a door?"

"Yes," said Ilna. She let the noose out into a white circle spinning before her. The door by which she'd entered was behind where Ewis now stood, but she was beginning to see the pattern and it didn't take her in that direction after all. . . .

"Do you really think so?" said the wizard in faint surprise. "Perhaps you can at that, perhaps you can. Then there's only one thing to do, isn't there?"

The ivory bead left his palm. Ewis didn't throw it, only freed it as though slipping the leash of an eager hound.

Ilna cast her noose. The silk fell short because light glancing from the bead's facets wove her into a soft cocoon; a gentle constraint now but one she could feel start to tighten.

Ewis grinned brightly at Ilna and said, "Now I have to kill you."

Valence III, King of the Isles, was playing chess with a footman when Garric and Liane joined him on the loggia overlooking an ornamental pond. Black swans paddled in graceful circles. Their flight feathers were clipped, but the birds were too well fed to fly anyway.

"Why, Prince Garric!" the king said. "It's always a pleasure to see you. And your lovely friend too!"

"He's put on weight since you took over the kingdom," Carus muttered, eyeing the king critically through Garric's eyes. *"He'd walked away from the responsibility long before you took it on, but he was a decent enough man to be ashamed of himself."*

"I wanted to tell you about some recent occurrences, Your Majesty," Garric said, bowing to the king. Beside him, Liane curtsied gracefully.

"Nothing that I have to do, is there?" Valence said warily. He hunched away from Garric, threatening to overset the ivory stool on which he sat. The footman had hopped to his feet as soon as Garric entered; now he moved to the other side of the king to catch him if necessary.

"Not at all, Your Majesty," Garric said. "I just wanted your advice on a few matters."

He hoped he sounded reassuring instead of just disgusted. Garric was tired—he was always tired since he'd become ruler—and sometimes that made him snappish.

The notion of meeting with Valence at least once every ten days was Liane's. To most citizens of Ornifal the king was merely a symbol, no more a part of their daily lives than a visit from the Lady, Queen of Heaven. To that majority, Valence III was King of the Isles now as surely as he had been at his accession twenty years before.

That meant it was to everybody's advantage that Valence remain happy with the situation. For now, what he wanted to do was play chess, chat with old friends, and display himself in gorgeous robes at public functions. Occasionally Valence's adopted son and heir apparent, Prince Garric, stood at the king's right hand, but for the most part the king's presence was all that was required. Regular meetings with Garric lessened the danger that Valence would awaken some morning and decide he'd been kept in the dark—and that his honor demanded that he seize real power again.

"Good luck to him in that!" Carus said, speaking with the disdain that Garric didn't dare allow to stain *his* voice. *"He couldn't hold power when it was handed to him at birth!"*

Which was true, Garric knew, but it wasn't the point—as his ancestor knew as well. Valence couldn't rule the Isles, no matter how angry he got—but he could make it very difficult for Garric and his government to rule. It was always easier to prevent things from working than it was to make them work.

"Ah," said Valence, nodding agreement. He still had a wary look, but he eased forward so that the stool's four legs were all on the tile floor again. "Well, I'm very glad to see you, then."

"The reorganization of Ornifal continues to go well, Your Majesty," Garric said. "We've reasserted your authority in all the districts by now. Though there are complaints, we haven't met with anything that could be called rebellion."

He squatted at the king's feet. According to protocol, visitors should stand before the seated king; but that would have meant Garric towering over Valence. Garric—and Liane and Royhas—thought that implied threat would have risked worse than a technical breach of etiquette. Valence was still very fragile mentally.

"As I told you when we last met," Garric continued, "we're moving toward discussions with the rulers of Sandrakkan and Blaise as well. There's been a slight delay in

422 / DAVID DRAKE

the embassy to Erdin—Lord Tadai's crew mutinied and
stranded him on a islet. He's been rescued, though, and
he'll resume his journey shortly. With better results, we
hope."

"Tadai lost?" Valence said, frowning in concentration.
"No, that's not what you told me. You told me your *sister*
had been lost, Lady Sharina. I remember you saying that
very clearly!"

Garric cleared his throat and swallowed, giving himself
time. Liane saw the veins pulsing and interjected, "That's
correct, Your Majesty, Lady Sharina was carried off. Lord
Tadai's mishap was more recent, but it's been cleared up
already."

"I do hope nothing serious has happened to Sharina,"
the king said. He looked aside and noticed the game board,
blinking as if seeing it for the first time. It was very hard
to tell how much of any conversation would stick in his
mind. "She's quite beautiful. A true princess, don't you
think?"

"Indeed she is, Your Majesty," Garric said, forcing himself to smile. "Her fiancé, Master Cashel, has gone after
her. I have every confidence in Cashel's abilities—and in
Sharina's abilities as well, of course. She'll be all right."

Taking nothing away from Cashel or Sharina either one,
Garric wished he were really as confident about her safety
as he tried to sound. Their best hope was that the creature
which abducted Sharina did so for a purpose—beyond that
of filling its belly, that is.

"You've mentioned this Cashel before," Valence said.
He was frowning again, this time in brooding anger instead
of mere concentration. "He's not of noble birth, is he?"

"Master Cashel's birth is shrouded in mystery, Your
Majesty," Liane said quickly. "The wizard, Lady Tenoctris,
suggests that the Lady may have sent him to support you
in this crisis."

Garric turned to Liane in surprise, then blanked his face
and hoped Valence hadn't read anything into his expression. Liane's words were just to distract the king from a

line of thought that Garric would have found irritating even if Cashel hadn't been his friend.

"Really?" said Valence. "Oh, I hadn't realized that. I thought Master Cashel was just . . . well, he's so *rural*, you know."

Tenoctris didn't believe in the Gods, whether in the forms they took in temples or as philosophical abstractions called Fate, Chance, or whatever. She certainly wouldn't have described Cashel as a gift of the Gods . . . at least not in those words. Neither Garric nor the Kingdom of the Isles would have survived these past months without Cashel's support, though.

"Only a few people are able to penetrate Cashel's disguise, Your Majesty," Liane said. The warmth of her tone was even more soothing than the words themselves, and in combination they were drawing Valence back from the peevishness into which he'd begun to retreat. "Lady Tenoctris is one of those; and Lady Sharina herself, of course."

"Ah, yes, I see," the king said, nodding sagely. Valence looked the perfect monarch when he was calm, but it took very little to upset him. When Valence was upset, no one would mistake him for anything but a puling coward. "Yes, of course, Sharina would know."

There was a mumble of low conversation in the room which opened onto the loggia. Liane looked over her shoulder, then turned back and made a tiny gesture with her hand to Garric.

"I hope I haven't disturbed your afternoon, Your Majesty," Garric said, rising to his feet and backing a pace. "But I did want to inform you of the generally positive way things are going."

"You have to go," said Valence. Was that sadness in his tone? "I understand."

Garric bowed deeply. Instead of formally dismissing him—or going back to his chess game without any acknowledgment—Valence said, "I really did stand at the Stone Wall, you know. It seems now as though it all happened to somebody else. I remember the Sandrakkan cavalry charge and thinking I was going to die. Do you suppose I did die then, Garric?"

Garric looked at him; really *looked* at Valence for a change. Considered him as a man rather than a bundle of whims and petulance which Prince Garric had to manipulate for the good of the kingdom.

"No, Your Majesty," Garric said. "You didn't die then. You're still the hub that holds the wheel together while Tenoctris and Royhas and all the rest of us try to fit the spokes into you. We need you. The kingdom needs you."

"Do you really think so?" said Valence, brightening like a woman complimented on the way her hair was arranged. "Well, perhaps. Keep me informed, Prince Garric."

Garric bowed again as he backed away. He didn't turn until he was through the door and a servant had closed it between him and the monarch.

He was in a semicircular reception room with benches and low tables around the curved wall. Instead of tapestries, the wall was frescoed with a red ground and, framed by painted pillars, individual cells each holding a mythical animal.

Tenoctris stood with her hands folded. From the angle at which Garric saw her, the wizard seemed to have a golden hippogriff tangled in her gray hair. She smiled in greeting, but there was tension beneath the expression.

"Which we knew already, lad," Carus noted. *"Or she'd not have called you out of a conference with the 'king' in there."*

With Tenoctris in the chamber were her guards, the guards accompanying Garric and Liane, and the four guards responsible for Valence's safety besides. Along with the servants, they made for a larger gathering than had been seen here in the last five years of Valence's reign—when power slipped from the king's fingers and he became increasingly reclusive. People avoid someone they see sliding downward, as though they think failure is contagious.

Now there was no lack of wealthy citizens who wanted

to meet the king. Valence hosted formal dinners on a regular basis—that was part of the duties of his present position—but for leisure he played chess with a footman. Perhaps he'd learned something during his five years as a pariah.

"I've been examining the bridge," Tenoctris said quietly as Garric and Liane joined her against the red wall. "Through my art." The Blood Eagles formed an impassive semicircle between the trio and the rest of the world; even here, in the palace. Good guards don't take anything for granted.

"Can you?" Garric said. "That is, we weren't able to find . . . ?"

Tenoctris smiled wanly. "I could learn more, and more easily," she said, "if I had the Lens of Rushila; but even I can accomplish surprising things when there's so terribly much power concentrated by the bridge itself."

Her face hardened. "Unfortunately, it takes a toll. I've slept the past six hours through. I interrupted you because I was afraid to let the information wait still longer. I think we're in danger of invasion from Yole."

"The island of Yole sank a thousand years ago, Tenoctris," Liane said. "Everyone on the island died but you yourself."

"Yes, I haven't forgotten that," Tenoctris said, smiling to take away the sting of what for her was a slashing reproof. "Someone has made Yole rise from the sea. I suspect it's one of Ansalem's acolytes or more likely all of them together, but that isn't important."

She sighed and suddenly looked very frail. "The ones who raised Yole," she continued, "are necromancers. They're raising the dead of Yole as well. We saw them ourselves when we returned from Alae."

"That was real?" Garric said. "Real in our time, I mean, Tenoctris?"

"Yes," she said. "I think so. And using the bridge from Klestis to here—which sooner or later, I think they'll be able to do—they'll be able to march straight into Valles. But that isn't the worst of it."

Garric felt Liane's hand in his. Her touch strengthened and relaxed him more than he would have believed possible. Acting on impulse, he reached out with his free hand and cupped Tenoctris' interlaced fingers.

"We can beat Yole," Garric said. In his mind, King Carus nodded with a grim eagerness that no one could misunderstand.

Tenoctris smiled brightly and held the smile as she said, "I don't doubt that you can. We can. But if the bridge stands, and if the necromancers are as powerful as all evidence suggests, then they won't be limited to Yole. Have you ever considered how much the dead of past ages outnumber those living at present?"

"Ah," said Garric, nodding as he understood. He thought of Valence making the same gesture a few minutes before and managed a half smile. Never forget that you're only human, just like the other fellow. . . .

"Then we'd best do something about the bridge immediately, hadn't we?" he said. "I'll take the army to Klestis. If the bridge is solid enough for material bodies to cross it, then we can free Ansalem by breaking down the walls around him."

"I don't think so," Tenoctris said. "But I hope I'm wrong, because I can't think of a better way. And judging from your dream, neither can Ansalem."

Sharina had been staring for some minutes at the images frescoed onto the tomb walls before her mind encompassed what her eyes were seeing. "Dalar," she said, "this is a story. They're not just pictures."

Stone scraped above her. The ghouls had moved a block enough to chip a bit of rock from its edge. The pebble clicked on the floor, then bounced into the pit in the center of the enclosure. It finally hit the bottom with a glutinous splash.

Sharina looked at the walls again. She'd glanced upward instinctively, screening her eyes with her fingers against falling debris. She'd thought, she'd feared . . .

"They have not made much headway," the bird said quietly. "When the fragment fell, I thought perhaps they were breaking in."

"Me too," said Sharina. She still wasn't in shape to squeeze into—and hopefully through—the snake's tunnel, though she supposed she'd rather do that than battle a pack of ghouls.

She took a deep breath and pointed with the Pewle knife. The tomb was painted in columns reading downward from the top, each with four registers. The snake's scales had rubbed away all the bottom row except for portions in the corners; seeping water had flaked off great chunks of plaster and stained much of what remained. Despite the damage, Sharina could follow the story reasonably well.

"The Rokonar do not use pictures the way your people do," Dalar said. He cocked his head as if to bring the frescoes into better focus, then clucked despair. "Our art is of colors shading into one another to induce an emotion. All I see on these walls are daubs cruder than the youngest chick of my people could present."

Above them, several ghouls whooped together on a note of rising triumph. A stone block groaned, then clunked twice as it rolled from the tomb. Sharina and Dalar tensed.

The roof seemed as solid as it ever had been. There was a crunch. A ghoul shrieked with pain and continued shrieking until its voice faded into a whimper.

"Somebody got in the way of more stone than he could carry," Sharina said with a faint smile. "They're not very bright—"

Blocks at the corner of the roof finally sagged inward, doubling the amount of wan daylight entering the enclosure.

"But they're strong," she concluded. "And I suppose they're bright enough."

"We have time still," said Dalar. "Read me the pictures, mistress."

He clucked his laughter. "I have decided to hold my death lay for another time, you see," he added. "I do not believe this audience would appreciate the intricacies of the meter."

Smiling, Sharina pointed again. "That figure is a wizard," she said. "He comes to the city—which must be Valhocca—walking on the waves in a circle of red light."

"The spiky things are waves?" Dalar said. "Amazing. I was thirty days *in* the waves and I never saw anything that looked the least like that."

"It's a convention," Sharina said, feeling a little defensive. She burst out laughing. "My friend Liane would be a better one to discuss it with you. I'm sure she was taught Art Appreciation at Mistress Gudea's Academy for Girls. My father was only concerned with literature."

"I will look forward to meeting your friend," the bird said solemnly. Blocks scraped, then slammed back together and loosed a shower of dirt and pebbles. It didn't bother Sharina now.

"The wizard does a variety of things in Valhocca," she continued, dipping her blade to indicate each panel in turn. "Some of them are pretty unpleasant. The others are mostly worse."

The frescoes were executed in bright primary colors on a white ground. They had no subtlety whatever, but scenes of children being boiled alive in a cauldron didn't call for subtlety.

"A mob," Sharina said, moving to the wall to the right of the first one, "chased the wizard through the streets and captured him. I don't know how he was discovered; that must have been on one of the parts we can't see. He was tried before a tribunal—no, the man in the center must be the Sea Lord of Cordin. The women to either side are allegorical figures for the islands of Shengy and Tisamur which Valhocca ruled at the time."

"Those are women?" asked the bird. "And if they *are* women, how can they be islands as well?"

"In the mind of the painter, they were both," Sharina said. That wasn't an explanation, but it was the truth. "And to the people seeing it, too, even if they couldn't read."

"But who would have been meant to see it, mistress?" Dalar asked. "There was no way in."

A slab gave a high-pitched squeal as ghouls slid it across several of its fellows. The sound cut off abruptly with a *clack* of stone against stone. A further sliver of light crept in from above.

"I think it was meant to warn people who broke in," Sharina said as she examined the next range of frescoes. "Looking for treasure, perhaps."

The ghouls had much simpler desires, and the paintings would mean as little to them as they did to Dalar.

"The wizard was beheaded on a pier in the harbor so that as many people as possible could watch," Sharina said. "His body was quartered, put in a weighted chest, and then dumped in the sea. One—this is a moon, but I don't know if it means one night or one month—one something later, the wizard walked back up from the harbor. His body parts had rejoined, but . . . not the way they should have been together."

She moved to the next column. The light didn't fall as clearly on this wall as on the first, but it was more than clear enough. "He killed the people he met and absorbed them, merged with them. Soldiers attacked him, attacked the *creature* it was by now. Their weapons tore its body, but the body flowed back together and kept growing as the thing absorbed the soldiers also."

The next wall was very badly water-damaged. Sharina paused, trying to make out the meaning of the remnant.

A ghoul reached through an opening directly above her. Its clawed fist clenched, nowhere close to its would-be victim. Dalar's arm shot out, curving a weight up in an arc that just cleared the back wall. It smashed the ghoul's wrist with a quick crunch. The creature's scream echoed painfully in the tomb as it jerked its flopping hand away.

"The thing grew much bigger," Sharina said. "A hundred feet tall, unless this is just a convention for great size. It looked like a jellyfish with tentacles around its upper mantle to grasp with. Everyone fled the city. The thing didn't follow them far; it stayed and pulled down the buildings."

More blocks shifted above them. Quite a lot of sky was visible, but the tomb's interior was getting darker because the sun was so low on the horizon. "Perhaps we should leave now, mistress," Dalar said.

"We'll leave soon!" said Sharina, lost in the description of an ancient tragedy. In a calmer voice she continued, "The thing stayed in the ruins. There wasn't anyone for it to eat, to absorb, anymore. It shrank, but it didn't die. Finally a band of men caught it in nets and dropped it into a well—no, a natural hole in the limestone. And they built this building, this tomb, over it so that it could never eat enough to grow and escape again."

The ghouls gave a howl. A block bounced away on the outside. Two more sagged into the tomb, then jammed one another by the corners. The whole corbeled roof was in danger of collapse.

"Mistress!" Dalar cried. "We must go!"

Sharina ran the fingers of her left hand through her hair, combing out debris from the room. "I'll lead," she said to Dalar. She wormed into the snake's tunnel with her arms outstretched before her. The knife was in her right hand.

The stones scraped Sharina's shoulders on her way past them, but the compacted earth beyond was smooth and damp enough to feel slick. She kicked out, getting her hips through the opening, and used her elbows to squirm forward.

Sharina couldn't breathe. She thought she was panicking at the tight space and twisted, pushing up from the edge of the tomb wall with her toes.

She *couldn't* breathe. Neither will nor intelligence could override a terror squeezing her brain at the level of the first creatures to develop spinal cords.

"Dalar!" Sharina said as she braced to elbow herself backward. Her voice was a muffled grunt. "The tunnel's blocked! This isn't a way out af—"

Something touched Sharina's hands. She jerked her head, thumping on the dirt ceiling hard enough to stun the scream that would have followed. *A snake crawled on me!*

But it wasn't a snake. It was the snake's tongue. The tomb's present inhabitant was coming home.

Sharina got her legs into the open air and kicked violently to help wring her body out of the opening. The darkening sky showed through a dozen places in the tomb roof; the whole structure was moments from collapse. Dalar had hopped to the other side when Sharina thrashed back into the enclosure.

"There's a snake," she gasped. "It's coming through!"

Sharina looked at the roof, trying to estimate whether the whole thing would fall in before the ghouls made a hole big enough for them to enter. Their huge figures capered. Perhaps if Dalar looped his chain around a stone roof beam, he and she could pull themselves up before the ghouls reacted. A slim hope, but the best one on offer.

"Dalar—" she said.

The bird stood transfixed with terror, a stuffed caricature of the active, graceful, person Sharina had known. He was staring at the tunnel opening.

The snake's tongue flicked the air of the tomb; then the wedge-shaped head, as large as Sharina's chest, slid inside. Rosettes mottled the snake's skin, though Sharina couldn't tell what the colors were in this dim light.

The snake focused on Dalar. Six feet of neck and body followed in an S-curve that kept the head at the same point in the air. The snake was gathering to strike.

Sharina brought the Pewle knife down with the strength of both arms, severing the snake's spine and most of the musculature that supported the head. The lower jaw dropped open. The snake writhed into the tomb in a series of convulsions, threatening to fill the enclosure like a flood of water.

A touch slammed Sharina against a wall. She sat down hard in a cloud of plaster dust from the frescoes. Coils of the serpent's body rolled over her. The reptile was huge, over a hundred feet long in reality and seemingly endless as Sharina watched it thrash liquidly from the wall.

For a moment Sharina thought she would be crushed, suffocated by the snake she'd killed. She couldn't see Dalar; he'd probably been trapped in the corner opposite hers. She'd have laughed at the irony of the snake's revenge if she could have gotten her breath.

The mass of scaly flesh suddenly began to diminish. The snake's dangling head had flopped into the central pit; now the rest of the body followed. Gravity was doing what no human strength could have accomplished, dragging the serpent off Sharina.

The snake's tail—a surprisingly sharp termination for a body which was the same diameter for most of its massive length—waved for an instant, then vanished. Sharina still held the Pewle knife, but she was too weak to lift it. She couldn't get to her feet, and she wasn't even sure that she could crawl. The tunnel was clear, but it was too late. . . .

Two blocks tumbled away from the roof; three more fell inward, one of them missing Sharina's sprawled leg by less than a finger's breadth. A ghoul howled and dropped through the opening.

Dalar had gotten one foot under him. He cocked his weights back for a quick, slashing blow—useless at this short distance.

A creature glowing with red wizard-light rose from the central pit. It sizzled like the ground near where lightning has just struck. Its translucent mantle pulsed out and back as if it were a jellyfish swimming.

The ghoul lashed the creature with the hand that had been reaching for Dalar. Its claws tore three deep wounds in the glowing flesh. Tentacles—or cilia—swept from beneath the mantle, enfolding the ghoul and drawing it inward.

The ghoul convulsed at the first touch, its muscles knotting. The beginning of a scream choked in its throat.

Another ghoul jumped down. Cilia caught it in the air. Again the ghoul twisted into a tetanic arc as the strong muscles of its back tried to pull its head and feet together. The first ghoul was melting into the flesh of the monster from the pit.

The creature rose further. Its mantle—the purplish lump on top couldn't really be described as a head—touched the sagging remnants of the roof.

The central column on which it balanced swelled, flinging tons of rock aside the way toadstools lift paving stones after the autumn rains. Cilia swept out, snatching several more ghouls as the pack howled in surprise.

Sharina stood frozen; kitty-corner from her, Dalar knelt like a statue. Only his eyes moved; there was no fear in them now.

The creature braced its mantle on the tomb's walls and sucked the central tube up, climbing the rest of the way out of the pit. Its sluglike foot slid up the side of the wall, then down the tumble of stones that had been the tomb's roof.

Two of the ghouls had dissolved almost completely into the creature's shimmering flesh, and the others were melting like snow on an oven. Wobbling among the treetops like a cloud of distant fire, the creature disappeared into the forest.

Sharina let out her breath. She was trembling, but her strength was coming back.

"We can get away now," said Dalar. He was standing, but his voice wasn't as strong as it usually was. "I think we should."

The moon wasn't up and the sun had set an hour before. All the plaster had been rubbed from the wall across from Sharina. Instead of bare stone, she saw a faint bluish tremor.

"Wait . . ." she said to Dalar; at least her lips formed the words. She wasn't sure she'd managed to be audible.

The Dragon sat behind his table, watching Sharina with

unblinking eyes. She thought of the snake and began to tremble again.

"You are well, Sharina?" he said. "You are able to go on at this time?"

"I'm alive," Sharina said. A natural smile found its way to her lips. "I don't think we'll be alive for long if we wait till the creature we shared this place with returns."

"Ah, yes, Ohmqat," the Dragon said. His jaws gaped in a lipless, reptilian equivalent of a smile. "It was not human, though it took on a human semblance when first it came to Valhocca. It will go to the ruins and stay there. In a few days the coastline will sink and take Ohmqat back to the seabottom where it belongs."

Sharina stood carefully. "I'd still like to get out of here as soon as possible," she said. "Although . . . Dalar, do you want to leave immediately?"

The bird's eyes moved back and forth from Sharina to what he obviously saw only as a patch of wall. He shrugged his thin shoulders. "I will go when and where my master requires," he said. "But if I had an opinion—"

He clucked merrily.

"—I would leave this place as soon as possible. Or sooner."

The Dragon's laughter trilled in Sharina's mind. "The way out," he said, "is at the bottom of the cenote; the pit, that is, where Ohmqat was confined. His captors placed a stone on him to hold him in place. That was vain, but the depth of the cenote was enough. You will tilt up the stone and go through the hole you find beneath it."

"How deep is the pit?" Sharina asked. She felt surprisingly good, though she supposed she might just be getting light-headed from the stress of the past however-long.

"Thirty feet and a half foot," the Dragon said. His form and the alcove in which he sat were fading. With a last whisper he added, "The moon will give you light if you wait a few minutes."

"It'll take longer than that to get ready," Sharina said, as much to herself as to the vanished phantasm.

To her companion she said, "Dalar, we need thirty feet of vine to reach down into the pit. That's the way we'll be going out. And I guess enough more to tie around one of these blocks to anchor us. I don't trust myself to climb to the bottom without a line to help."

"Nor do I, Sharina," the bird said. "Though if it were jump straight down or stay, I would jump."

He laughed again. "My distaste for a place where my life was unexpectedly saved is most unfair," he said. "No doubt it will cost me a long journey of penance in the afterlife."

The moon, waxing beyond its first quarter, had risen above the treetops. Dalar found a thumb-thick strand of trumpet vine attached to a cedar at the edge of the former clearing. Sharina cut it off at the base but it was barely within her strength and that of Dalar combined to rip the vine loose above.

"The Dragon says that the thing from the tomb here won't come back," she muttered as they strode back to the building, now in ruins. "I'll still be glad to be away."

"I too," Dalar agreed. "The creature seemed as unlikely to appreciate my death lay as the ghouls were."

Sharina tied the vine around a block that greatly outweighed the two of them together. The makeshift rope was too stiff for trustworthy knots, but the two half-hitches wouldn't unravel easily.

"I will lead," said Dalar as she turned from her task. He was already stepping into the pit, holding the vine with one hand and the weights dangling on short lengths of chain in the other.

Sharina waited as the vine swayed, chafing on the limestone but not to a dangerous extent. Only when Dalar called "I've reached the bottom!" in a booming, ghostly voice did she start down hand over hand. The vine would probably have held both their weights together, but she didn't want to take a needless risk when the necessary ones were so terrible.

Midway down the hole narrowed to a throat half the size

of the opening at the top. Sharina brushed the coarse stone uncomfortably. There was almost no light in the shaft. *Dalar would have said something if there wasn't room for both of us at the bottom.*

Sharina slipped free, turning as the vine straightened under her weight. Water rich in acids from decaying vegetation had eaten a hollow deep in the stone, like an abscess at the base of a tooth. Her outstretched legs touched nothing till Dalar caught her ankle and guided her the last few feet down. His fingers were noticeably warmer than a man's.

There was still no light. Bones, *old* bones, scrunched beneath her bare feet.

"They are human," Dalar said quietly. "The skull is on the other side of the chamber. There is no sign of the serpent."

He clucked. "Not that I was looking forward to meeting it again," he added.

"Nor what the snake's body fed," Sharina said. "But it saved us by coming when it did. Ohmqat saved us."

No light at all . . . but there could be no doubt about the stone slab in the center of the chamber. Sharina's fingers explored it. The block had been smoothed on five of its six faces, but the last was jaggedly diagonal. It had been broken off a larger slab—

"The seat of the throne!" Sharina said. "Dalar, this is the other half of the stone that we pulled out of the wall in Valhocca. Not that it matters."

"If I were sure what mattered in this business," the bird said, "I would be much wiser than I am today."

"I think if we pull it toward ourselves . . ." Sharina said. She gripped the long edge of the block with both hands but waited for Dalar to position himself before she shifted her weight against it.

They tugged together. Nothing happened till Sharina was almost ready to call a gasping halt; then the block slid and continued sliding until it was completely clear of the spot where it had lain for a millennium.

Sharina felt the uncovered space. Instead of rock, there was a hole of uncertain depth. The granite cap had acted to concentrate water seeping through the walls of the pit, and acid erosion had resumed under its shelter.

"I'll lead," Sharina said, gathering herself on the edge of the opening. It was barely big enough for her to squeeze into, and she was taking it on faith that this really *was* a portal. If it was merely a deep crevice in the limestone, she was going to die in a very unpleasant way.

"Dalar?" she said before she stepped in feet first. "Do you wish you'd been wise enough to turn me down when I came to you in Valhocca?"

"No, Sharina," the bird said. "That is the only thing in my existence since the storm that I do *not* regret."

Grinning, Sharina let herself through the opening.

"I hope Elfin is all right," Cashel said as he ambled through the forest. "I guess we don't hear him just because the leaves are so thick; but, you know, I wish he'd come with us."

The trees here didn't have bark, just slick green skins. The leaves were any number of different kinds, but they were all big—none smaller than Cashel's hand with the fingers spread, and some the size of towels. There were blossoms, too: dangling blue and yellow things the size of a grain measure, and towering cones of white fluffiness.

Everything dripped. Cashel wasn't sure if it was raining somewhere above the forest or if water was just wringing out of the air. Duzi! There were drops falling off the end of his nose and the ferrules of his staff!

"You're worried about Elfin?" Krias crowed. "Don't worry about the changeling, sheep-boy, worry about yourself! You have no idea of how dangerous the Underworld is!"

Cashel thought about that for a moment. "I wouldn't want to be somebody who worried about himself, Master

Krias," he said. "There's plenty of folk who do, but they
aren't folks I like to be around; and I'm around myself,
well, all the time."

Krias sniffed. "If ever Elfin does come near enough," he
said, "Knock his head in with that stick of yours. Or tell
me to deal with him. He's not human after living down
here all his life—and I *don't* mean living with the People
made him as stupid as a sheep, either!"

"I don't much care for the place myself," Cashel admitted. "But there're parts of the world I came from that I
wouldn't choose to go back to either."

He chuckled. "I don't remember ever being this wet before that I wasn't trying to swim, though."

"The Sun rules in your waking world," the ring demon
said. "Oh, not everywhere, and not all the time . . . and not
anywhere *completely*. But the Sun rules there, and here
Malkar rules to the same degree."

Two birds launched themselves from oddly green
branches and beat away through the soggy air. They must
dislike this weather as much as Cashel did. One was an
owl, the other an eagle or a really big hawk. They carried
strips of dark flesh in their beaks.

Cashel thought a while about what Krias had said. "So
Master Landure is fighting Malkar here in the Underworld?" he asked at last.

Over the squish of his feet settling into leaf mold—the
soil beneath was slick, dense clay—Cashel thought he
heard Elfin's lute at last. A good thing it had silver
strings. Gut would stretch like the truth in Uncle Katchin's
mouth.

"Thanks to you, sheep-boy," the ring snapped, "what
Landure *does* is fertilize a patch of forest. And he never
fought Malkar, since he had better sense. What he did was
to keep monsters of the Underworld *in* the Underworld
instead of them invading the waking world."

"Could he have, well, made things better down here?"
Cashel said. "If he'd tried to?"

"Don't you listen?" Krias shrilled. "There's a balance,

the Sun and Malkar, Light and Dark. You can't have one without the other, you just try to keep them as much apart as you can!"

Sort of like Ilna and her patterns, Cashel decided. If she'd mixed all her threads together, the cloth would be a muddy gray. She didn't do that, of course.

"Master Krias?" Cashel said. "Who weaves the patterns of good and evil?"

He didn't talk about the Sun and Malkar, or even dark and light. That was all right for a scholar like Tenoctris who had to see things from every direction, but Cashel wasn't a scholar. He was a shepherd, and if something was bad for his flock—or his friends, or his world—he called it by its right name: evil.

"Pattern?" said Krias. "There's no pattern, sheep-boy, it's all random chance!"

"But you just said that there had to be balance, Master Krias," Cashel said in a reasonable tone. "Balance doesn't just happen. If it did, farming would be a lot simpler than it is. Who keeps the world's balance? The balance of all the worlds, I suppose?"

"You're talking nonsense!" the ring demon said. "What, do you expect me to build an altar to the Lady here in my spacious apartments?"

"No, but I guess it wouldn't hurt for me to offer the Shepherd a little of my next meal," Cashel said. "Before, I always crumbled a bit of bread and cheese to Duzi when I ate my lunch. I don't know if a little God like Duzi would, you know, hear me down here."

"Nobody can hear you!" Krias said. "It's just you and me, sheepboy."

"I guess I'll set up a stone and make an offering anyway," Cashel said. He didn't want to argue with the demon. Krias knew a lot of things, sure, but he thought he knew things that nobody could know for certain. Cashel figured to keep going along the way he always had, no matter what other people—or demons—said. That had worked for him in the past.

For most of today the forest had been as flat as the best plowland in the borough, but just ahead was a hill that looked rugged though not especially high. Cashel hadn't been following a trail, exactly, but what he'd judged to be the natural course was apparently the right one. Anyway, Krias hadn't objected.

This, though . . .

"Master Krias?" Cashel asked. "Should I go over this hill or work my way around it?"

"How do I know what you should do?" the ring said. "Go back to your home and herd sheep, I suppose."

After the pause Cashel had learned to wait for, Krias went on, "Tian here is wider than it's tall. And if you go around, you'll find yourself in places that you may not want to be. Not that I pretend to know what goes on in a minuscule brain like yours."

"Thank you, Master Krias," Cashel said as he started up the hill. Instead of clay, the ground was all blocks and outcrops of stone with a thin layer of dirt. He raised his feet high for each step. Though he sometimes braced his quarterstaff behind him, the going was never so steep that he had to use his hands to climb.

It was getting darker. The rain—wet air? whatever you ought to call it—was slowing down, but there didn't seem much chance of dry wood for a fire.

The vegetation was a little different from what Cashel'd been walking through earlier. The trees had normal bark, for one thing. There were vines, too, with fist-sized translucent fruit hanging in bunches. They looked a lot like grapes except for the size.

Cashel said, "Can I eat these, Master Krias? Without it hurting me, I mean."

"That depends on what you mean by hurting you, sheepboy," Krias said. "Fruit from Tian may expand your mind, which isn't an experience you could have had very often before. It hasn't hurt other people in the past."

Cashel reached what he judged was the top of the hill, though he couldn't be sure with the forest as thick as it was. A hollow at the base of the roots of a big oak looked as dry a place as he was going to find to sleep.

First things first: he tilted up a block and used his knife pommel to scratch the outline of a face onto the moss. It was a simple thing, but so was the stone dedicated to Duzi back in the pasture. Duzi wasn't a fancy God for fancy worshippers.

"Please help me find Sharina, Duzi," Cashel said. "She probably doesn't need our help . . . but please help me if you can."

He sighed and twisted one of the big fruit loose, then squatted and cut two slivers with his knife. He set one before the crude image. The flesh of the fruit looked a little like creek water after a storm, more clear than not but with dark bits swirled into it.

"Guess I'll give it a try if others have," Cashel said, biting into the slice. It was both tart and sweet, like a segment of orange, and it was deliciously cool. He'd figured to slurp rainwater from the hollow of a stone, but the fruit ought to take care of his thirst better than water.

Cashel ate the whole fruit, and then plucked another one. He couldn't complain about his meals here in the Underworld—he'd never gone hungry, at any rate—but this was the first time that he'd eaten something because it tasted good rather than just to fill his belly.

Smiling and feeling pretty comfortable despite the occasional drop from the oak that splashed him, Cashel curled up and went to sleep. And began to dream . . .

Chapter Seventeen

Cashel or-Kenset, his quarterstaff slanted back over his right shoulder, sauntered between fields of swaying wheat toward the city that floated in the air. The road's clay surface sloped into gutters on either side. It was well made, but it didn't seem to get much traffic.

The bright sun glinted from the city's conical golden roofs and the helmets of soldiers on the battlements. Rainbow-colored pennons fluttered from the spires.

There was something puzzling about it all.

Cashel blinked, then chortled at himself. There was a city, all shimmer and beauty, hanging high in the air with no support but a slender, serpentine ramp from the ground to the main gate. Of course it was puzzling!

But even so he glanced at his left little finger, somehow expecting to see a sapphire ring there. He'd never worn a ring; why should he think he had one now?

A horn called from a gate tower. A second horn from deeper within the city echoed it. Cashel continued at his usual pace. More people appeared on the battlements, some of them leaning over for a better look as Cashel drew near. The women's silken head scarves trailed in the wind like pastel bunting.

Two double handfuls of armed men quick-marched through the gateway and rattled down the ramp. Their helmets and the shoulders of their armor flared fantastically, and they'd painted monstrous faces on their jointed breastplates. Most wore scabbarded swords which they gripped with both hands as they ran; one man, by far the largest of the troop, carried a glaive.

Cashel kept walking, though he slowed his already leisurely stride a tad so that he'd reach the bottom of the ramp when the warriors did instead of just ahead of them. They seemed more nervous than you'd expect, but maybe they didn't get many strangers.

Cashel frowned. He couldn't remember whether he'd met anybody on his way here.

He frowned more deeply. He couldn't even remember why he was here at all. He'd been going somewhere to meet Sharina; but she wasn't in this place, surely. Was she?

The warriors slid to a halt in front of Cashel. The ramp was wide enough for all these men to stand abreast. It seemed spindly only because Cashel was looking at it against the hanging majesty of the city.

The ramp wasn't made of metal the way he'd thought, either. It was some kind of glittery crystal that scattered light or passed it, depending on the angle, and the whole bottom of the city was the same material. It was so smooth that when Cashel looked up, he saw a reflection of wheat fields and the hills far beyond to the west. The road stopped here.

"Halt, monster!" called the leader of the troop. Gold tassels streamed from both his shoulders; the others only had one. "If you try to enter Tian, we will slay you!"

Cashel straightened up and planted his staff vertical at his side. "My name is Cashel or-Kenset," he said. "I wasn't raised to push in where I'm not wanted. If you don't want me in your Tian or whatever, I'll just keep on my way."

He cleared his throat. Trying to keep the growl out of his voice but not succeeding very well, he added, "But I'm no monster. And this isn't how we treat people where I come from."

"He's not the giant of the prophecy," one of the men said to the leader.

"He's pretty big," another man said. "We can't take a chance."

The warriors facing Cashel weren't children—the leader's face in particular had the lines of considerable age around the eyes—but they weren't any bigger than boys.

Even the biggest, the one with the glaive, would've passed for ordinary in the borough—unlike Cashel himself, or Garric, who was even taller.

"Oh, come on, Penya!" another man said. "How's he going to tear down the walls of Tian, tell me? Besides, according to the prophecy, the giant's supposed to appear tomorrow, not today."

"The prophecy might be wrong, Sia," said the leader. "We can't—"

"The prophecy might be complete superstitious claptrap that sensible people ignore!" Sia snapped back. "Look, King Liew, if you believe in the existence of Gods none of us have ever seen—"

"That's blasphemy!" cried the man with the glaive. The broad blade was etched in a pattern of clouds with silver inlays.

"I don't have an opinion on the Gods myself, Mah," Sia continued, "but I *am* of the opinion that killing farmers passing through the countryside is no way to get on the good side of any Gods that do exist."

"I'm a shepherd," Cashel said in a voice that came from the back of his throat. "And if you're talking about killing, I might have something to say about that myself."

He shifted his stance slightly and brought the staff up crossways before him. Cashel was used to people talking about him like he was a side of mutton, unable to think or speak for himself. He was used to it—but he'd never gotten to like the experience.

"Sia's right, you know," another warrior said. "He's not a giant, it's not the day of the prophecy, and anyhow, why are we threatening the first visitor Tian has had in a generation? We should be feasting him!"

King Liew sighed and lifted his helmet with his left hand. His hair was white and as fine as a baby's. "We can't dismiss the prophecy," he said in a troubled voice, "but you're right, Peng; this Cashel is a guest, and we should treat him as one."

He extended his hand to Cashel, clasping him forearm

to forearm. For Cashel it was like greeting a half-grown child. "I am King Liew," he said, "and the men with me are the knights of Tian. We're having a banquet today on the eve of the prophecy, Master Cashel. I hope you'll join us."

Cashel cleared his throat again. His mouth had gotten dry when it sounded like . . . well, what it had sounded like. Now his muscles were trembling with the energy they'd stored for the fight that didn't happen.

"I'd be pleased to eat with you, sir," he said. "And especially I'd be thankful for a drink of water right now."

"Water!" said Sia merrily as he and the others swept off their helmets. "Only the best of wine for our visiting shepherd!"

Sia had sharp features and clever eyes. It struck Cashel that the fellow hadn't so much been helping Cashel in the earlier discussion as showing the others how much superior his mind was to theirs. Tian wasn't the only place Cashel had met fellows like that.

The warriors started back up the ramp with Cashel walking in their midst beside King Tiew. When he'd glimpsed the ramp from the side, he'd seen it was as thin as a knife-blade. It had no more spring beneath his weight than stone would have given, though.

"I don't think we should be taking him inside," muttered the man with the glaive, walking right ahead of Cashel. "The prophecy's a thousand years old. Maybe this was what a giant looked like a thousand years ago."

"Oh, brave Mah!" mocked Sia from the back of the group. "Determined to protect Tian from shepherds."

Cashel swallowed. He didn't like Sia much more than he did Mah; but then, he was a stranger here, and everybody was wary about strangers except in a big city where they were all strangers. Everybody was wary about *everybody* in a big city.

"I've never seen a place hang in the air like this one does," Cashel said to the king as a way to avoid the byplay between Mah and Sia. "How do you make it do that?"

"Tian is a gift of the Gods," Liew said seriously. "It's the only true paradise, formed by Sky and Earth for their most favored children. The first Priest of the City, Lan Tee, raised an altar to Earth and Sky; and Tian sprang from the smoke of that altar fire."

"*And* Lan Tee said that after a thousand years, a giant would destroy Tian," said Penya, turning to sweep Cashel with a deliberately aloof glance. "But we're bringing this Cashel inside anyway."

"What we ought to do," called a warrior from the back of the group, "is tear down the causeway. Let the giant do whatever he wants down below. We don't need grain when the orchards within the city give such bounty!"

"It's our duty as knights of Tian . . ." King Tiew said. More forcefully he continued, "Our duty and *honor*, Lau, to defend the causeway with our swords and our lives. If we fail, then those we died protecting can sever the causeway and find safety in that fashion."

Cashel thought about it. Common sense said Liew should break down the ramp right now, but that'd mean the people in Tian would have to stay there all their lives. Of course, if Sharina hadn't decided to leave home with King Valence's ambassadors, Cashel himself would have spent all his life in Barca's Hamlet. The hanging city wasn't a whole lot smaller than the borough.

The ramp snaked back and forth in graceful curves, but Cashel and the knights were finally nearing the gate. The long walk had worked the shivering out of Cashel's muscles, pretty much. The gate towers and walls to either side of them were stone, not the gleaming crystal of the ramp. Each block had an indented border around delicately carved flower patterns.

From the walls above, men cheered and women waved scarfs. Their eyes were almond-shaped, and their hair ranged from the rich brown of sourwood honey to glossy black.

One of the most beautiful of the women tossed a wreath of roses and ivy down to Cashel. He snatched it out of the air without thinking. As he did so he caught a glimpse of Mah's face, contorted into a silent snarl.

The king and his knights entered the city to even wilder cheers. The gate at once began to close—the panels swinging shut from either side and a spiked grating sliding straight down from the arch behind them. The machinery was so quiet that Cashel didn't hear it groan or squeal over the human noise. And all this was a thousand years old?

Among the slender, languorous folk in pastel silk were shorter, much stockier people. The darker clothing and darker complexions of the second race set them apart even more than their stature did. They glanced down or aside when Cashel looked at them instead of meeting his eyes boldly like those in silk.

The band of knights continued straight along a boulevard between buildings whose upper stories jutted out slightly from the ground floor. All were built of the same dense, rust-colored sandstone; in fact, it looked as though there was only one building of many interlocked rooms, and that the outer walls of Tian were part of the same great structure. It was a huge beehive.

"Sir?" Cashel asked. "There's people in silk—"

He was Ilna's brother; he could identify fabrics at a distance as few women and fewer men could.

"—and there's people in linen and dark colors. What's the difference between . . . ?"

"People in linen?" Liew said. "Oh, I see what you mean. No, those are the servants. They take care of the work that we citizens of course can't do—the food and the cleaning, those sorts of things."

"Ah," said Cashel, nodding to show he understood. He understood all right. Well, it was no different most other places he'd been.

The citizens were coming down from the walls and balconies to fall in behind King Liew and his knights. Servants stepped aside for their betters, smiling and bowing to the willowy folk who paid them as little attention as they did the cobblestones.

Cashel half-smiled. The nobles didn't treat him that way—not that it was really a bad way—because he was a stranger in a place that saw very few strangers; and maybe because Cashel was as big as any two of them together.

The procession was headed toward a pillared entrance of the building at the end of the boulevard. The porch was gorgeously ornate, not in big ways but in the detailed floral carvings that covered every hand's breadth of the hard stone.

A woman who moved like a lavender breeze came up beside Cashel and took his arm. She plucked from Cashel's hand the wreath he held and set it on top of his head, leaning against him to reach so high. "Silly," she said in a liquid voice. "I didn't toss it to you to carry in your hand. My name's Lia."

Cashel cleared his throat. "Ah," he said. "I don't . . . I never wore flowers before. I, ah, I'm Cashel or-Kenset."

"I grew them myself, you know," Lia said. "You'll sit by me at the banquet, won't you, Cashel dear?"

Mah turned around and stared cold-eyed at them. Lia giggled and stuck out her tongue. Mah flushed dark red, then stumbled on the first of seven steps up to the porch. He dropped his glaive with a clang, causing the knights ahead of him to shout, "Hey!" and "Watch it, Mah, or you'll kill somebody!"

That's what Mah wanted to do, of course, and for a moment as the knight fumbled the glaive back into his hands Cashel thought he was going to try. Instead Mah pushed ahead of his companions and entered through the triple-arched doorway.

"I, ah . . ." Cashel said, wishing he was someplace else. He felt sorry for Mah—though not nearly as sorry as he'd be if Mah hadn't taken against Cashel from the first.

Thinking about that and grinning again, Cashel stepped into the building's domed anteroom alongside King Liew. Servants ran up to them, several to each warrior, and began stripping off their equipment. The knights stood like horses being curried. The armor was made of metal tubes strung on light chains. When the men moved, they sounded like wind chimes on a blustery day.

A pair of servants came toward Cashel on either side. Lia stepped away, which Cashel thought was a mercy, but when one of the little men tried to take his quarterstaff he bellowed "No!" in surprise.

Everything stopped for a moment. That was what usually happened when Cashel shouted, especially if he was indoors.

"Did we give offense, Cashel?" the king said. "If so, my deepest apologies on behalf of Tian. We took the staff as a mere tool, but if it's a religious object that you must keep with you even when you eat . . . ?"

Cashel was blushing. "It's not religious," he muttered. "But if it's all the same, I'd like to keep it, you know, close by. It's, well, it reminds me of home."

"Oh, that's darling!" Lia said. "You're so sensitive, dear Cashel."

Which would've been embarrassing enough by itself. When Lia stood on tiptoes to kiss Cashel's cheek, he wanted to sink right through the floor.

A consort of horns and pipes called from pillared lofts to either side of the anteroom. The inner doors opened and King Liew entered the banquet hall beyond. Cashel, with Lia clinging and directing him all at the same time, followed the king.

Side columns carried the arched ceiling so everybody in the hall could see the high table at the end. King Liew seated himself at the center of it, beside a gravely beautiful woman of his own age. Lia led Cashel to the seat on the king's right hand.

Cashel hesitated, but Liew nodded welcome and even touched the high-backed chair—though a bowing servant pulled it out for Cashel. He couldn't keep holding the quarterstaff, much as he'd like to, so he leaned it against the wall back of him before he sat down.

Lia sat beside Cashel. He'd expected that, but he sighed anyway. He really wished Sharina was here. Or Garric, or *anybody* who knew how to deal with this sort of business.

The knights entered according to some order more complicated than who got his armor off first. A woman joined each knight at the entrance. The pairs were seated at the high table, alternately to the left or right of Liew and his queen.

Cashel grinned.

"Cashel, dear?" Lia said, putting a finger on the lobe of Cashel's ear. "You're smiling because something pleases you?"

"I was thinking," Cashel said honestly, "that it's a lot like watching a flock come in to be milked in the evening. In order, and all the others get upset if some ewe pushes ahead."

"Very amusing!" Lia said with a trill of false laughter. "A flock, you say?"

It occurred to Cashel that she'd never heard the term before. Did she even know what a ewe was? He hadn't seen a scrap of wool—or leather either, come to think—in the clothing here.

A servant set before them porcelain goblets so thin that candlelight shone through the rims. Cashel seized his, glad both of a drink and the chance to avoid explaining to his companion what a sheep was. The wine was the clear red of pomegranate juice, but it sparkled on his lips and tongue.

All the hall's many seats were filling with lithe men and willowy, beautiful women. The servants were everywhere but almost unnoticeable: they were deft, quiet, and seemed to blend into the walnut-paneled walls when at rest. Porcelain dishes, some white but others in a rainbow of pale hues, appeared and were whisked silently away when emptied or refused.

Cashel was used to eating with his knife and his hands, but Reise offered horn spoons to the guests in his inn and Cashel had learned to use forks for banquets in Valles. The folk of Tian ate instead with skewers. All the food was bite-sized. Servers capped short tubes with their thumbs to pick up varied sauces and uncapped them to apply the contents according to the diners' taste.

Cashel looked at Lia to see how to proceed. That was a mistake; she promptly began to feed him, like he was a baby just being weaned. Cashel colored—again—but there didn't seem anything to do about it that wouldn't make for a worse embarrassment.

"Did you come to Tian because of the prophecy, Cashel?" Lia asked as she searched a platter for the next tidbit to feed him.

Cashel quickly speared something and stuffed it into his mouth to forestall her. Around the morsel—it was a chopped paste of mushroom and spinach, he thought, fried in a wrapper of paper-thin dough—he said, "That a giant is going to destroy Tian? No, I'd never even heard of the city."

He frowned as he tried to cast his mind back and found nothing but fog about the past. "I don't remember where I'm going, even, except that I'm to meet Sharina . . . Somewhere."

"Well, I'm glad that you came," Lia said. She tittered. "Maybe you came to see me."

In a more sober tone—though there'd been nothing casual about the way she'd watched Cashel sidelong at her last quip—Lia continued, "Anyway, I think the prophecy is just silly—ancient superstition, that's all. But I wish dear Liew would tear down the causeway."

"You'll have time for that if I and my knights fail, Lia," Liew said, leaning forward to see the woman past Cashel. "I expect that our courage and skill will protect the city, though it may be at the cost of our lives."

"Oh, I *wish* you wouldn't talk that way!" said the queen, whose name Cashel hadn't heard. "It gives me shivers to think of watching you fight a monster tomorrow."

"As you know, my dear . . ." said the man on the other side of her. He looked an older version of Sia, but his voice had the oily fullness of a much heavier man. "I and my immediate predecessors as Priest of the City believe that

Lan Tee's so-called prophecy was an allegorical injunction to preserve the sacred rites on which our polity depends. 'A thousand years' is a figurative phrase which in context means 'a very long time' or, better, 'forever.' "

"Shan, you know I find your commonsense so comforting," the queen said. "But I can't help worrying nonetheless about my Liew. We women don't have the strength of you men."

Cashel choked. Imagine somebody saying that to Ilna! For that matter, he'd met weasels with less predatory determination than Lia was showing; and if Cashel wasn't mistaking the note in the queen's voice, *she* didn't have much to learn about getting her way either.

"When the giant comes," said Mah—shouting to be sure that Cashel could hear him; he'd been seated far on the king's other side—"he'll find we're ready for him. Mere size means nothing compared to the courage and true nobility of a Knight of Tian!"

Cashel jabbed what looked like a small white carnation. It was a carved turnip, dusted with spices that Cashel decided he liked once he got over his surprise. He chewed stolidly, ignoring Mah's bragging and the gibes Sia cast at the other knight.

"Are you happy now, Cashel?" Lia asked, her lips as close to Cashel's ear as they could be without her tugging him toward her.

"Sure," said Cashel, and washed the bite down with a draft that emptied his goblet. Emptied it again, he realized; the servants kept filling it up almost before Cashel set it back on the table.

He didn't usually like wine, but this was refreshing without the aftertaste of vintages he'd drunk before. The food here was great, even though it came in bits no bigger than a nibble, but the wine, well, it almost convinced him that Tian *was* paradise.

"I'm so glad," Lia breathed, leaning against him again. In a different voice she added, "Cashel, do *you* believe in the prophecy?"

Frowning as he thought about the question, Cashel took another drink. "Well, I couldn't say," he said. "I just heard about it today, you know. I didn't even know about Tian."

"But what do you think?" Lia said. She was suddenly a person, not just an appetite. "You've been out in the world, not like us. What do you *think*, Cashel or-Kenset?"

Cashel turned to look at her, the refilled goblet in his hand. Lia was as lovely as a spray of orchids, but all he felt seeing her was loneliness.

"Lia," he said, "I don't know about giants, and I don't think about things that I can't change. All I know is this."

He drank, still meeting her eyes. "Tomorrow we'll all know the truth," he said. "And nothing you or I or a priest says tonight is going to change the truth one whit."

Lia suddenly shivered. Her hand drew away from his arm as if of its own volition.

Cashel didn't remember much more of the evening. Tian's wine, however fresh and clean-tasting, was a great deal stronger than the bitter beer of home. Cashel had a flash of awareness, sometime later in the night, of many small hands carrying him along a corridor; and later still, of a bed canopy above him as he lay on a mattress softer than he liked.

But mostly Cashel slept, the sleep of the dead.

As the wizard's net of power squeezed down on her, Ilna heard Merota calling from somewhere beyond the walls of the treasure room. A peal of manic laughter crashed over and through the girl's attenuated voice. *That* clutched Ilna's heart tighter than Ewis' bindings of red fire did her body.

For the moment Ilna could still move. Instead of trying to reach the giggling wizard—useless; his spinning ivory bead would have choked out Ilna's life before she managed the second step—she twisted toward the creamy, almost-featureless wall behind her. She extended her index finger in a motion that seemed to her as slow as watching ice melt.

Ewis must have understood. He stopped giggling and shouted, "No, you—"

Ilna touched what looked like a swirling gray blemish somewhere beneath the surface of the stone. A door swung silently inward.

"—mustn't do—" Ewis shrieked.

A skeletally gaunt creature leaped into the chamber, flinging Ilna aside. Once it had been a man over seven feet tall; a sunburst medallion hung around its neck.

It stank. It was covered in filth that no wild beast would have permitted unless it had been too desperately ill to clean itself.

Ewis made a hand gesture; the twirling bead changed its pattern. Ilna shrugged free, and a cocoon of rosy wizard-light enfolded the Tall Thing. It laughed like all the demons of Hell and leaped across the room, trailing the would-be bonds like a wild boar slashing through gossamer. It gripped Ewis with hands like a crab's pincers and began to chew the wizard's face off.

"Ilna!" Merota cried. Ilna got to her feet, coiling again the noose that she'd dropped as the net of light wrapped her. The girl ran through the doorway that had released the Tall Thing.

"No, child!" Ilna cried, sweeping Merota back down the corridor from which she'd come. Other portals opened around the circumference of the treasure room. A band of men with swords and spears ran in, their equipment clanging.

Ilna turned to shut the door. A dozen guards were hacking at the Tall Thing, but it continued its gurgling laughter. Bone splinters and brains dribbled from its mouth.

The door slammed. Ilna could still hear the laughter. She hugged Merota fiercely. Holding the girl's right hand in her left, she started off down a lightless corridor. The walls had been blank stone for as far as Ilna could see before the door closed.

"Ilna, I was afraid," Merota said.

"I should hope you had enough sense to be afraid!" Ilna said. She swallowed. "I was afraid too."

Not afraid for herself: afraid that she would fail Merota. But Ilna didn't—couldn't—say that aloud. The girl mustn't think there was ever a chance that Ilna wouldn't rescue her.

"Someone's coming," Merota said, her voice rising. Ilna froze, holding the girl firmly. She herself didn't hear anything but the echoes of their footsteps, shuffling down the corridor ahead of them. That and her own pulse . . .

"Ah, and would that be you, Ilna dear?" Chalcus called from the darkness. "And the child with you, I'm glad to hear. I regret coming back to you by such a twisty road, but I was looking for a way that I thought might be more suitable for the two of you than the spider's path I crawled down."

"Oh, Chalcus!" Merota cried. "I'm so glad you're here."

"As am I," said Ilna. "Though I hope you've a better notion of where 'here' is than I do—and a better route out of it than going back the way I came. I'm as glad to have left Ewis and his visitor, truth to tell."

"We'll go the way I came, then," Chalcus said. There was no light at all in the corridor. The chanteyman was a presence in her mind nonetheless, down to his mocking grin and the gleam in his eyes. "If you'll give me a sash to hold or the like . . . ?"

"That won't be necessary," Ilna said. She didn't like the thought of being led like a milch ewe, and it seemed to her that Chalcus might need both hands quickly. "We'll follow well enough."

They started down the corridor. Chalcus used his scabbard like a cane, tapping it along the wall to his left. Occasionally the iron chape struck a spark.

"How did you find us, Chalcus?" Merota asked. "I was afraid I wouldn't see you again. I didn't think I'd see either one of you."

"Well, child," Chalcus said, "I found an opening in the

cliff and followed it back to a gallery above the biggest harbor I've ever seen in my life—and all cut in the rock, would you believe? The entrance they dragged our ships through, that closes with doors an army couldn't force in a lifetime . . . but there's vents above it, and one of those was my entrance."

Merota said, almost whispering, "Everything was dark and smelly, and then the door opened and he let me go and I saw Ilna. And then you came, Chalcus. The Lady was with me."

"I took another passage out of the gallery," the chanteyman said. "A vent on the land side I thought, and a chance to circle back and find you. As I did, thanks be to the Lady of Sailors. And perhaps to the Shepherd of the Little Ones, hey?"

He was talking to Ilna: Merota was too obviously lost in wonder at her own survival to understand what he was saying. Ilna suspected the child was steadier, though, for hearing human voices after the time she'd spent as the captive of a laughing maniac.

"Huh!" Ilna said aloud. "If the Great Gods step in and help people in this place, then that's a change from what happened when I was at home in Barca's Hamlet. You came to us in a treasure room that had many doors. I don't wonder that the passage you took led to one of those many."

There was faint light ahead of them; so faint that only the sight of Chalcus in dim silhouette convinced Ilna that her mind wasn't tricking her with an illusion. She didn't fear the darkness, much less hate it; but they'd learned already in this place, this *Yole*, that hostile creatures could appear at any moment. Being able to see didn't guarantee a warning, but at least it might be some help.

"Now here," Chalcus said, lowering the outstretched scabbard and sliding it again through the folds of his sash, "is the harbor. I wouldn't choose to leap about and wave my hands, but in all its hugeness there wasn't a soul save myself when I came through the first time."

The trio stepped out of the tunnel onto a gallery eight feet wide, cut from the side of the enormous cavern it encircled. Light entered through slits in the rock ceiling. Though modest by ordinary standards, it seemed as bright as summer midday to eyes that had come from total darkness.

The gallery had no railing. Merota squeezed against the back wall. Ilna, determined not to let the girl's fear infect her—terror spreads faster than croup does—walked to the edge and looked down.

Far down. The dozen ships in their masonry cradles appeared as small as they had when Ilna watched the triremes from the top of the cliff.

"How did we get so high?" she said in puzzlement. "I had to go down to reach the treasure room."

"Did you, mistress?" Chalcus said with a raised eyebrow. "Water wouldn't have flowed in the tunnels I've been following, neither the vent nor the passage to where I met you fine ladies. The floors were that flat."

The cavern was alive with echoes, most of them no more than the slap of water against the quays. Sounds could go on forever in this place, rebounding from smooth stone until the sun froze.

"I see," said Ilna. "Let's get to the ships and see if there's sign of what's happened to the crews."

The corkscrew staircase she'd followed in search of Merota had worked on her mind in some fashion. She should have guessed. Those "windows" showing scenes from the past weren't part of the normal world.

"There's steps cut down just ahead here," Chalcus said, "and on the other side as well, you can see."

He turned to Merota and went on, "Now take my left hand, Your Ladyship. We'll keep each other from slipping on the stairs, will we not? And you can turn your face to the wall as we go if you choose."

His eyes met Ilna's over the child's head. Ilna nodded and took the lead. She held the noose in her hands in a loose coil; not that there was any reason to be concerned. She laughed harshly.

"Mistress?" the chanteyman said.

"I think that we're as safe here as we are anywhere on Yole," Ilna said. "And therefore we should expect to be attacked."

Chalcus laughed; and a moment later, Merota laughed as well. *If the poor child goes to court balls in Erdin laughing at the sort of things Chalcus and I think are funny,* Ilna thought, *they'll look at her like she has two heads.*

And that was funny as well, so Ilna laughed again.

The stairs were cut into the rock instead of being built out from it, narrowing the gallery by half for the length of the descent to the waterside. The treads were narrower and steeper than was comfortable, more like a loft ladder than a proper staircase.

"Did you notice the line of barnacles on the cliff face, mistress?" Chalcus said from a safe distance behind. Ilna didn't turn around; all her attention was on each next step down.

"Barnacles?" she said. "No, but what of it? You said yourself that this island was under water as recently as last month."

"Ah, but under a thousand fathoms of water, dear one," the chanteyman explained. "Barnacles fix themselves at the tide line, not so deep that they'd starve, the poor things. It seems to me that this island didn't rise so high when last it was above the surface, do you see? This harbor was under water."

"Then who built it?" Ilna said. "It isn't new."

Wizards might be able to excavate rock by their art, doing years of work in a day and a night. Ilna could see the tool marks on the stone here, however, and a coating of dried slime flaked off the walls whenever she touched them. This place had been made by hands.

But she wasn't sure they'd been human hands.

"Aye, that's the question, isn't it?" Chalcus said. "We'll

puzzle over it for years, I'm sure, after we've gotten away from this place. Not so?"

"I'll let you know after we've gotten away," Ilna snapped. The chanteyman's attitude irritated her in more ways than she could number, but it was good he'd come with them. He calmed Merota, after all.

She reached the bottom of the staircase and waited for her companions. The water had an ancient smell, nothing like that of other harbors Ilna had known—nor even that of mudflats drying at low tide.

"I hadn't noticed this from above," Chalcus said in a tone of mild wonderment. He gestured toward the nearest stone slip. "The water's just a fathom down, do you see?"

"I see," Ilna said, "but what of it?"

"The tide's out by now," Chalcus explained, "or nearly so. The doors at the cliff face—they're lock gates, they are. Otherwise the basin here would be dry as an oarsman's throat."

He gestured with the curved sword. "Let's view the ships," he said. "It strikes me that one of those merchanters might have a dinghy on deck, and at this point I'd think of that as the better choice than spending any longer in this place."

"The island's named Yole," Ilna said. "That's what Ewis called it."

After a moment she added, "And I agree with you."

The cavern had both slips for sailing ships and ramps for drawing oared warships out of the water between voyages. The numbers of each available were far beyond Ilna's limited ability to count.

At present the ramps held only the two triremes that Mastyn's directions had brought to Yole, and in the slips were a double handful of the merchant ships whose hulls could hold cargo instead of expensive oarsmen.

The ships were grouped together near the entrance. After Ilna and her companions had walked some minutes toward them around the curving quay, she had a new appreciation of the size of the enclosed harbor.

"I feel little here," Merota said.

"Aye, we're small folk in a big world, child," the chanteyman said easily. "It's like the seashore, don't you think—all that sound, the surf or here the walls' echoing; and it doesn't mean a thing."

He reached over and rubbed Merota's scalp; salt air and sand hadn't been kind to what once had been a primly lustrous coif. "We're small, but we're together," Chalcus said. "And we've faced the sea already, haven't we, milady?"

"Yes, Chalcus," Merota said. "Sometimes I forget, is all."

Ilna's mouth was tight, her eyes questing for . . . she didn't know what. She felt exposed here, as indeed the three of them were on a featureless waterfront, but she wasn't searching so much for threats as for patterns.

She grinned. The threats would come without her looking for them.

Tunnels entered at half a dozen places around the cavern's circumference. Most were at the level of the waterfront, but a few opened partway up the wall and were reached by flights of steps. On the far side of the basin was another stairway to the gallery.

"No lack of ways to get out of here, is there?" Chalcus said brightly. *Or enter,* he must be thinking, as Ilna was; but the chanteyman spoke to ease Merota's mind.

"But we want to take a ship, don't we?" Merota said.

Ilna smiled tightly as the girl proved she wasn't a fool. Aloud Ilna said, "Yes, but we may have to wait till the tide is right, and we've learned how to open the doors to the sea. Until then, we want to be able to run like mice in the pantry."

The chanteyman grinned at the women.

Water seeped between layers of rock, forming gleaming sheets on the walls. Though the cavern had been carved from one large block rather than built, even the hardest stone can have flaws.

There were vertical cracks as well. A blanket of dry

warmth puffed from one as the trio passed. Ilna paused
with a hand signal to Chalcus. The right side of the crack
was a hand's breadth higher than the left, as the faintly
striped layers of stone showed clearly. A narrow triangle
wide enough for a human to squeeze through had opened
at the bottom.

"Something interesting?" the chanteyman asked, trying
to disguise his tension with the lilt in his voice.

"Something that wasn't made by whoever made the harbor," Ilna said. "Since the wizards using the harbor aren't
any friends to us—yes, I think it's interesting. But let's go
on."

When Ilna stepped away from the split in the rock, she
was back in the cavern's natural dank atmosphere. She
shivered, then scowled at her body's uncontrollable reaction.

They'd reached the ships. Most were nondescript vessels
of moderate size. Their spars and sails had been tumbled
down so carelessly that when they were viewed from the
gallery there might have been a dinghy concealed on their
decks. From here, close alongside, it was obvious that
Chalcus' hope was vain.

"Now, let me see about this one," the chanteyman said
in a nonchalant tone. "A pleasure yacht, I shouldn't wonder, for a rich man who isn't in such a hurry he wants the
discomfort of oars."

The ships were berthed alongside one another, two to a
slip, but in most cases at least six feet separated the side
rail of one and that of the ship moored to the opposite
quay. Instead of walking around the stone promenade to
reach the small vessel two slips over, Chalcus jumped from
one to the next.

He wasn't showing off—Ilna was sure the chanteyman
didn't think there was anything remarkable in what he was
doing. He continued to hold the sword. Obviously he was
more concerned about what might be hiding aboard one of
the ships than he was of having his hands free in case he
fell.

"Chalcus, is there any sign of the men?" Ilna called. She noticed that she was resting her left hand on Merota's shoulder. The girl seemed happy enough with the contact, but Ilna suspected that it was her own desire to touch another human being that had caused her hand to move without her conscious intention.

"Not so much as a drop of blood," Chalcus said as he eyed the yacht critically. He disappeared briefly down the vessel's forward scuttle, then hopped back on deck.

"There's food aboard," he announced as he started back toward his companions. "The wine jars were opened with a hammer—there's bits of the necks and handles where they were stored—and dumped over the side empty, I'd guess. As with *Ravager* and *Terror*, no doubt."

He jumped to the stone before them. "What's left in the bottom of the water casks is so slimy that we'd have to eat it rather than drink it, but needs must it might last us till we landed somewhere with a spring. And I *think* I might be able to sail her myself, once we got her out of this cave."

Chalcus raised an eyebrow in question.

"Please," Merota said, staring at her clasped hands. "I'd like it if we left now. If we can."

Ilna stood silent for a moment as she considered their choices: bad and worse, though which was which . . .

"Yes," she said. "If we don't need the help of the crewmen, then I for one will be glad of their absence. I think the mechanism for the doors should be—"

Near the entrance, she'd intended to say to finish her comment. Merota interrupted with, "Someone's coming!" The girl pointed toward the nearest tunnel opening, a little farther away than Ilna could have thrown a pebble.

How can she possibly hear in this bedlam? Ilna thought, but she shook her noose out with a quick motion as she turned. Chalcus shifted his stance minutely. He held the sword a little higher, slanted across his breast. He was grinning.

A sailor stepped out of the tunnel carrying a cutlass. Ilna

recognized the man, though she didn't know his name. More sailors were shuffling out behind him.

"Daltro!" the chanteyman called in barely suppressed glee. "Piezo, Cant—you're a sight for sore—"

The sailors appeared to ignore him. There were scores of them, all of them armed. Ilna didn't recognize some of the faces, though the light wasn't very—

"Chalcus, their throats have been cut!" Ilna shouted.

A wizard in white robes and skin paint strode from the tunnel behind the walking dead. He pointed toward the trio. "Get them!" he cried in a voice as shrill as a gull shrieking over the rumbling surf. "Kill them!"

"This way!" Ilna said. She reached for Merota but Chalcus had already flung the child over his shoulder like a sack of wool. "Into the crack! The corpses don't get tired!"

She'd seen that when they watched the harvesters, back a seeming lifetime ago. This pursuit wouldn't stop, and the minds of the dead couldn't be bound by Ilna's craft. The split in the rock was too narrow for more than one pursuer to come at them at a time. The passage led to a place where the air was warm and dry.

Not necessarily by a route that humans could take, of course; but a bad chance was better than no chance.

"Take her!" Chalcus said, dropping Merota at the entrance, but there was no need to worry about the child— she scrambled through like a squirrel. Ilna crawled after on all fours. The chanteyman's feet brushed hers, but he was backing to face outward.

Chalcus grunted. Steel sang on steel, then crunched into something that damped the vibrations.

"That'll slow them!" he said in a muffled voice. "You'll be pleased to know that being dead doesn't prevent our shipments from being killed again, dear ladies."

"Yes," said Ilna as she followed Merota into a crevice so narrow it rubbed both her shoulders. "I *am* glad of that."

Ahead of her, the darkness seemed to breathe.

*   *   *

Sharina wriggled in empty air, then dropped with an echoing splash into a masonry chamber. The water on the floor only came up to her ankles, but it got deeper in a series of steps toward far end. The blunt claws of Dalar's feet thrust from the square inlet above her head; she quickly sloshed clear. It was no surprise that the block forming one edge of the opening was the familiar piece of pale granite.

The bird landed with considerably more grace than Sharina had. Dalar's head rotated once, back and forth like a weathercock on a gusty day. His body remained poised; the weights were already humming in his hands. Sharina backed against a damp wall, more to stay clear of Dalar than as protection from an enemy. She could hear people nearby, and enough light crept in through the doorway behind them to indicate it was daytime.

Dalar relaxed noticeably. "We're in a cistern," he said. He clucked with good humor. "I am pleased that we came through at this end rather than the other—"

He gestured toward the wall opposite the doorway.

"—since I cannot swim."

"A cistern this big?" Sharina said in amazement. The millhouse which Ilna and Cashel split with their uncle's family had a cistern, built during the Old Kingdom. The slate roof channeled water through pipes into the cistern, a plastered brick pit at the inner corner of the building.

Ilna said rain was better for cleaning delicate fabrics than well water—and she should know—but this room was big enough to hold the millhouse and the inn combined. It didn't serve just a house or even a village.

Sharina took a deep breath. "If they've rebuilt Valhocca," she said, "then there shouldn't be ghouls waiting for us above. And—"

She tapped a reassuring clink from the wallet holding her silver.

"—we might find something to eat. I'd *really* like to find something to eat."

Dalar clucked merrily as he splashed with Sharina to the inward-opening door.

Which was locked. From the outside.

"Can we break it down?" Dalar said. The panel was heavily braced wood with no inside handle or lock. The builders would want to keep out everyone except the occasional cleaning crews. Quite occasional, from the level of mud and leaves Sharina could see on the stonework.

"We don't need to," she said, raising her knife in both hands. She chopped, severing the upper hinge strap with a clang and a spray of sparks. The door was already beginning to sag when she squatted and cut the lower strap.

"Indeed, I serve a hero," Dalar said. He clucked, then added, "I was jesting; but I need not have been."

They pulled the door toward them, wriggling it free of the bar and hasp. Sharina sheathed the knife beneath her cloak and started through. Dalar shifted his hips to block her and stepped out in the lead, his weights concealed in his palms.

Sharina followed, grinning faintly. Part of her chided herself for not pausing to sharpen the fresh nick out of her blade, but the demands of her ravenous stomach had first claim.

It was midafternoon, and they were in a bustling city with a much more modern aspect than the Valhocca in which she'd met Dalar. The narrow-fronted buildings were three and four stories high, brick on the lower levels and lath faced with terra-cotta tilework higher up to save on weight. Some were set back slightly from the street with openwork walls enclosing small forecourts.

"Ah," said Dalar in a pleased tone as he surveyed the building from which they'd emerged. "Not a cistern, but a settling tank for an aqueduct. I never thought that while I was an exile I would see a water system to equal those of Rokonar."

A pair of prosperous-looking men with attendants at their heels strode down the pavement, so deep in conversation that they almost walked into Dalar. They stopped and gaped at the bird. One man flung wide his blue cape in theatrical gesture and shouted to passers-by, "Look! A

portent! The Gods announce the arrival of Mykon the Protector!"

Sharina stepped in front of Dalar. "My friend is from a
far country!" she said. She had no difficulty understanding
the local accent, and she hoped the reverse was true.
"We're strangers, but we have nothing to do with the
Gods!"

At least not that we know of, she added in her mind.

A woman passing in a sedan chair stopped. She whispered in the ear of a footman, who pushed past the fellow
still declaiming with flourishes of his cape. "Is he real?"
the footman said to Sharina.

Dalar batted away the man's attempt to tug at his beak.
Since the bronze weight was in the bird's palm, the footman understandably yelped.

"Of course he's real!" Sharina said. "He's a gentleman
of Rokonar here for a visit!"

"Why is that?" demanded the man who'd first noticed
them. "Are you in Port Hocc to meet Prince Mykon?"

Sharina had read about Mykon the Protector, Prince of
Cordin, but that didn't mean she'd really believed he was
a historical figure. That somebody named Mykon had
united the island of Cordin in the age before Lorcan
founded the Kingdom of the Isles—that she was willing to
accept. The rest of the story claimed that Mykon was
younger brother to Brut the Storm God and that he sometimes ate in Brut's cloud palace. It seemed to Sharina that
if part of the tale was fancy, then the rest likely was also.

*Apparently not. And who knows? Maybe Mykon does
visit Brut's palace.*

"Come on, Garamon," said the companion of the fellow
making the fuss. "Don't be a fool. This is some mounte-
bank who's come to Hocc with the Boats. Mykon won't
thank you for crowing that some feathered juggler is proof
of the Protector's divinity."

"The Gods will smite you one day for your blasphemy,
Malat," Garamon said in a pointedly sincere tone. He
wrapped his cape around him, then said more quietly to

Sharina, "Is that true? Are you from the Boats?"

"Yes," Sharina said decisively. "Where can we find a meal and an inn for the night?"

"Why do you ask me?" the local said with a surprised frown. "Down at the harbor with your fellows, I suppose."

Garamon and his companion hurried on with their flunkies. The rest of the crowd was breaking up also, though the heads of people walking by often swiveled to stare at Dalar—and at Sharina herself as well. They might have seen more tall blondes than they had intelligent birds, but they appreciated the blondes nonetheless.

"Unless the waterfront changed directions," she murmured to Dalar, "we need to go south."

She set off in the lead; traffic was too heavy for them to walk abreast. A fountain and pool quivered at the other end of the masonry tank, fed by a siphon inside. Women filled buckets of painted terra-cotta, chattering to one another and sometimes calling to friends on overlooking balconies.

In Sharina's ear Dalar said, "What are the Boats, Sharina?"

She grinned wryly over her shoulder. "I don't have the faintest notion," she said, "but I think it's a better choice than being portents sent by the Gods."

The street they were following wasn't paved except for the gutter down the center, but the broad waterfront boulevard was completely bricked and had stone curbs. Troops wearing silvered equipment and carrying batons rather than spears kept open a travel lane along the landward curb, but the harborside was packed with people. Some were city residents in patterned garments, but the majority were rural folk wearing homespun and bearing the mud of a long journey well up the calves of their legs.

The harbor itself was clogged with sailing barges: broad, bluff-bowed vessels with low freeboards and a profusion of goods and manufactures on their flat decks. Even a quick glance showed Sharina poultry, textiles, and fruit in baskets—and several dram shops as well. A smith's ham-

mer clanged from a barge moored with a safe span of water
between its hull and those of its fellows.

"It may be," said Dalar in a tone too cautious to be
described as hopeful, "that in this gathering there is another
person of the Rokonar."

Sharina looked at her companion. "Dalar?" she said.
"Remember we're here thousands of years after you were
shipwrecked."

"Yes," said the bird with the same lack of emotion as
before. "And in any event, Sharina, I have given you the
bond of my honor. But if I could, I would speak to another
of my fellows before I die."

He clucked laughter, though it sounded false to Sharina.
"I will begin the process of deciding which of my ten thousand deities should receive my prayers."

The vessels themselves were for the most part an extension of the land, moored side to side so that no gangplanks
were necessary for those wanting to walk from one to another. Sharina nodded toward a barge in the third tier back
from the shoreline. "That looks like a cookshop," she said.
Together she and Dalar squeezed through the crowd.

She'd seen hawkers working the land with barrows and
trays, but as well as eating she wanted to learn something
about the Boats. Nothing in the extensive reading Reise set
his children had mentioned them.

Though come to think, when you eliminated Gods and
demigods, battles and palace intrigue—and love affairs—
you'd eliminated most of Reise's library of classics. Sharina tried to imagine Rigal describing his wandering hero
Dann in search of chicken stew; she began giggling.

"Sharina?" Dalar asked in concern.

"I'm all right," she said as she got control of herself.
"I'm a little hysterical, is all."

But it was *funny*.

They hopped from the brick quay to the first barge, already crowded with locals bargaining for cloth of many
different patterns. Sharina didn't have Ilna's understanding
of fabric, but she knew enough to doubt that any one place

had generated all these styles. A heavyset man accompanied by two servants—or slaves—was trying to sell rolls of baize *to* the barge owner. Women in Port Hocc used similar cloth as an overlay to their dresses. The Boats clearly spread the specialties of many localities over the whole region.

The folk of the barges were of identifiably slight build and pale complexion; instead of tanning, their faces weathered red. They chaffered fluently with their customers, but Sharina noticed that they spoke among themselves in an argot that had only slight resemblance to any language she was familiar with.

The second barge was loaded with potatoes in loose-woven baskets that shifted like wineskins when the proprietor poured six into the pan of his hanging balance. He nodded with a neutral expression as Sharina and Dalar crossed his deck, but his many children stopped their various tasks to stare openly at the bird. If the attention disturbed Dalar, he didn't show it. In fact, he stiffened his crest even higher and turned his hop to the third barge into a prancing dance step.

The staff of the floating cookshop was a middle-aged woman at the grill, with a trim-looking youth of twenty or so chopping fish and vegetables, then rolling them in thin rounds of flatbread. A boy of ten served the broiled pastries in a square of seaweed and took the customers' money.

The food smelled delicious to Sharina; she was so hungry that the raw seaweed made her mouth water. When the elderly farm couple ahead of her moved aside, prodding in wonder at their single sausage roll—there were worse new experiences to come to the city for—Sharina said, "Three of those, and my friend will have . . . ?"

She glanced at Dalar. "Three," the bird said. "To begin with."

"So, you're not from around here, mistress," said the youth. He smiled engagingly to Sharina, but his left hand kept feeding fish under the big knife which his right hand rapped up and down on the cutting board. "Nor anywhere on our circuit, I'd judge."

The boy handed Sharina two pastries; the woman was flipping two more over the charcoal. She eyed Sharina and Dalar sidelong, but she let the youth carry the burden of the questioning.

"I'm from Haft, and my friend is from farther away than that," Sharina said as she reached into her wallet. She'd lost the copper and iron change from her sleeve miles and thousands of years ago, but she still had the silver. "I've no coins, I'm afraid. Is that . . . ?"

"Ah, we in the Boats can give you better value for bullion than you'll get on land, mistress," the youth said. "Now, Haft—where would that be?"

The woman, still silent, wrapped the next two rolls and left the grill empty while she eyed the small ingot Sharina offered. The youth wiped his knife on his apron and handed it to her; she put the ingot on the cutting board and set the knife on its corner. With a quick forward stroke and enough pressure to turn her knuckles white, she clipped off a small portion of the silver.

"Pure?" said the youth.

"Soft enough to be," the woman grunted. She returned the ingot to Sharina, then set the clipping in one plate of a knife balance and matched it with grains of corn before dropping it into a wash-leather purse hung inside the bodice of her tunic.

"Haft is an island north of here," Sharina said. The woman handed her three worn bronze coins from a sack hanging beside the grill. The only markings were a single letter stamped on the obverse.

"Ah, we in the Boats sail the southern coasts," the youth said. "East on the currents, west with our sails. My name's Bantrus, and I own *Columbine* here with my mother Brasca."

He pointed a thumb to the boy. "Pilf is a nephew, but we're all related more or less, all of us in the Boats. If you're strangers from the north, you might not know that."

Nor had she. "I'm Sharina, and my friend is Dalar," she said around a mouthful of pastry. Grilling warmed the stuffing, but it couldn't be said to be cooked. At another time Sharina might have objected to raw fish, but right now she'd have swallowed a mullet while it was still flapping.

"You've come to Port Hocc to watch Mykon's procession?" Bantrus asked. He'd returned to work, but his smile was an obvious attempt to keep the conversation going even though Pilf was wrapping the last pair of pastries. "We've seen it ourselves now the sixth time, but it's a fine performance."

"Mykon's following us down the length of the coast," Pilf said as he handed Sharina and Dalar the last of their food. "My brother Jem says Mykon knows he can't gather a crowd for his nonsense, so he rides along the shore beside us."

"Don't talk politics with strangers, Pilf!" Brasca said. "And don't talk *land* politics with anybody. Jem hasn't the sense of a sea urchin, but I do—and I'll send you back to the *Tailwind* with the hide off your butt if you forget what I've just said."

"Yes'm," Pilf muttered. Without being told, he lit a twist of woven grass from the grill and shinnied ten feet up the barge's mast to light the lantern hanging there. It was protected by dried fish skin on a wicker frame.

Trumpets blew from well up the waterfront. The sky was purple, and stars winked brightly above the eastern horizon.

"Say, they're starting the procession!" Bantrus said. "Mom, how about I take our guests here up the mast for a better view? You know there won't be any business while the entertainment's going on."

"Seems to me that they could climb by themselves," Brasca said, eyeing Sharina without warmth. She shrugged. "You're an adult now and not beholden to your mother— you made that clear over the business with—"

"Mom!" the youth said. "I told you what—"

"I think we'd best be going now," Sharina said loudly.

Her voice rang more clearly than it might have done before she'd become Lady Sharina of Haft. She hadn't wanted or liked to be a noble, but she'd learned to do it as well as she'd served food to drunken strangers during the Sheep Fair.

Sharina turned. Dalar bolted the last of his pastries as he stepped between her and Bantrus. There wasn't any threat from that direction, but it was the bodyguard's re-action to any sort of raised emotion.

"Wait, there's no point in this," Bantrus said in a con-trolled voice. He sounded like a man again instead of the furious boy who'd answered his mother a moment before. "Sharina, ah, Dalar?"

The bird nodded agreement. It didn't strike either of them as surprising that the youth had remembered her name better than that of her companion.

"Come up to the spar with me and we'll have a good view of the procession," Bantrus said. He made a slight bow toward his mother. She stared stolidly off the stern of the barge, refusing to acknowledge him.

"Thank you," Sharina said. "We will."

A knotted rope dangled from the mast truck in place of a ladder. Sharina deliberately ignored it, climbing instead with her hands and bare feet. She'd climbed trees at home, and she wasn't going to have Bantrus thinking of her as a delicate city girl ripe for his protection.

Twinges in her pectoral muscles reminded her she hadn't climbed trees in a while, though. Odds were she was going to feel the strain tomorrow morning.

She seated herself on the furled sail, far enough out along the spar to place Dalar between her and Bantrus. Bantrus couldn't take a hint—or perhaps he mistakenly thought he *was* taking a hint when he turned at the mast truck to sit beside Sharina. Sharina started to say some-thing. Dalar leaped onto the spar from six feet down the mast; his claws gave him a grip that no human acrobat could have equaled. From his perch he bowed to Bantrus.

The youth started to look angry, then barked a laugh and

settled on the other side of the mast from his guests. He pointed up the waterfront to where the trumpets were calling again. "There," he said mildly. "They'll start soon."

The shoreline was crowded, but Sharina noticed by the light of hanging lanterns that those watching from the spars of other barges were landsmen rather than folk who lived on the fleet. She remembered what Bantrus had said about Mykon following the Boats. Torches gleamed where the trumpets were calling, and more were lit as Sharina watched. She could see horses; one lifted its head in the harness and whinnied. A spectator screamed in apparent delight.

"Mykon tells people he's the brother to Brut the Storm God," Bantrus said in a voice pitched low enough that his mother on deck couldn't overhear him. "I guess people believe him—the farmers from the backcountry, anyhow. It wouldn't make sense go to this trouble if they didn't."

"It has not been my experience that humans invariably do things because they make sense," Dalar said, his eyes on the preparations. "Nor was it my experience of my own people when I lived with them."

Bantrus paused to process the words he'd just heard. He didn't strike Sharina as stupid, but she suspected he was used to getting more content from the tone of a comment than from the words themselves. Dalar never let emotions color his speech, and Sharina doubted that the warrior ever said anything that he didn't mean precisely as he said it.

"Well, anyhow," Bantrus said, "it makes a good show, especially for the first time."

He cleared his throat. In a conspiratorial tone he went on, "This Prince Mykon, he hasn't done the Boats any harm, not yet, but he's not . . . friendly, you see? He's set on bringing everything under him personally, all Cordin and I shouldn't wonder if he plans to go farther before he flutters back to the clouds on a lightning bolt—or however he figures to go."

"You have all the sea," Sharina said. "Can't you keep

away from Mykon? Keep away from Cordin, if you have to."

"That we cannot," Bantrus explained. "The Boats put in to land every night, mistress. Look at us—"

His gesture indicated the whole harborful of flat-bottomed, bluff-ended vessels. "We can run up on any shore and do, when there's no community to overnight us. But sail from Pare to Yole—not in *our* ships. The business of the Boats is trade, not seafaring."

"Yole?" Sharina said. She hadn't meant to speak.

"It's an island to the east, mistress," Bantrus explained equably, thinking she'd repeated the name because it was unfamiliar. "They do a fine trade in grains and citrus fruit. Also casks of what they call orange wine."

"Ah," said Sharina. She'd forgotten that in this age—and for the next thousand years—Yole was simply one of the Isles. The wizard's error that sank the island into the depths and made "Yole" a byword for evil was yet to come.

"The Boats serve the people of the land, mistress," Bantrus said. Sharina heard pride in his voice, but also a note of concern. "The rivers to the Outer Sea run down steep valleys on all the islands of our route. It's easy for inland folk to raft down, trade with us, and trek back to their farms. They may only be a few miles from the people in the next valley, but that's miles of hills with no roads and few passes."

Something had begun happening high up the waterfront, but Sharina continued to lean forward to hold Bantrus' eyes. He was telling her things she hadn't known; and quite apart from the scholarly curiosity with which Reise had infected his children, she might have to know what was going on in order to stay alive.

"The people of the land need us," Bantrus continued. He paused to swallow. "But the Boats can't exist without the land either. In my great-grandfather's day, every little patch of coast had its own chief and its own law . . . some better and some worse, but they all knew they needed the Boats. Now . . ."

He shrugged. "Mykon is putting all Cordin under him," he said. "He doesn't like anything that doesn't kneel to him—worship him, he's saying, now that he claims to be a God. We in the Boats don't bow to anyone on land; and even if we were willing, we couldn't serve Mykon *and* the Priestess of Guelf on Shengy, and Ragga of Tisamur. And who knows how many others, before I'm my mother's age?"

"The princes of whole islands may not need the Boats the way village chiefs did," Sharina said, trying to be both logical and reassuring. "But they're better off with you serving them than they would be by making it impossible for you to operate."

"There are people among my race," said Dalar, "who would rather have less for themselves than to know that they'd let something go free when they might have squeezed it in their hand. In this too, I have seen much similar between humans and my people."

Bantrus grimaced and gestured toward the shore. "I don't want you to miss the show," he said. "And unless you're Gods yourself, there's nothing you can do to help us."

The trumpets, now at least a score of them, blew a long note and fell silent. A man using a megaphone bellowed, "Hail Mykon, Protector of Cordin and brother of the Storm God!"

"That's thunder," Sharina said. She could see a man standing erect in a chariot that rolled slowly down the boulevard. Torchlight winked from his silvered armor and that of the soldiers walking beside the vehicle. The sound, though . . . the night sky was clear!

A squad of servants in simple tunics and headbands ran from behind the chariot and down the street in front of it. They were carrying—

Sharina started to laugh. "They're carrying sheets of bronze," she said. "They're laying it on the street ahead of the chariot so the wheels make it rumble against the bricks. That's all there is to Mykon's divinity!"

"Hail Mykon, Protector and God!" the man with the megaphone called, though only familiarity made the words intelligible over the thundering bronze. Soldiers cheered as they marched ahead of and alongside the chariot, keeping the way clear for Mykon and the bronze sheets.

Ordinary spectators took up the cries. Sharina thought of the man who'd accosted her and Dalar when they emerged from the settling tank. Aloud she said, "Some of them do believe it, or anyway they're willing to go along with Mykon for their own reasons. And not just country folk."

"Yeah," said Bantrus. "And even those landsmen who don't believe or don't care—not one of them in ten would object if Mykon said he was taking over the Boats."

The youth leaned closer and lowered his voice still more. "If we're to survive, we have to fight for ourselves," he whispered. "At least be *willing* to fight. My mother won't ever admit that, but me and some of my friends have been making plans."

Sharina nodded solemnly, hoping she wouldn't be asked to comment on the notion. If the Boats were inadequate as long-distance sailing vessels, they made an even less likely pirate fleet. The princes of the islands could survive without the Boats, but the Boats were completely at the mercy of the princes' goodwill—or at least forbearance.

She could understand why no mention of the Boats survived to her day. They were a footnote at the margin where myth became history; they'd disappeared in Bantrus' generation, just as he feared.

The waterfront procession continued at the speed of a slow walk, rumbling and flashing. It had a sinister appearance in Sharina's mind now.

Bantrus was looking nearer by. A man came toward the *Columbine* across a long line of barges starting at the eastern end of the harbor.

"That's Jem," Bantrus said. "Something must've happened."

He looked at his guests. "I'm going to talk to him," he said. "You can stay here and watch—"

"No, I think we've seen enough," Sharina said. Dalar gave a tiny nod of agreement and followed Bantrus down the mast ahead of her.

They reached the deck just as Jem, a husky youth with a scar running from his right eyebrow almost to the peak of his shaven scalp, arrived. Brasca glared from him to her son and said, "You needn't think you can stay here and talk your foolishness. You think I don't know what you're planning? I do!"

"They're here!" Jem said, staring at Dalar. To Bantrus he added, "He's real?"

"I am real," Dalar said, and for emphasis he kicked his right leg high in the air. The central toe of the other foot gouged splinters from the deck. No one watching could imagine that Dalar was a man wearing a bird suit.

"What did you mean by, 'They're here'?" Sharina said with a cold feeling.

"You're the ones that Mykon's looking for!" Jem said. "Somebody told him there was a huge bird and a beautiful princess with the Boats. Mykon says his brother Brut the Storm God sent them to him. He's got his men working down the harbor looking for you."

To Bantrus he added, "I didn't think it was true, but I figured Mykon had *some* reason he was searching the Boats, so I came to warn you. I never thought . . ."

He stared at Dalar. "Is it true?" he asked the bird. "Have the Gods sent you to Mykon?"

"You've got to leave here!" Brasca shrilled to Sharina. She'd picked up the butcher knife, her eyes wide with terror. "Now! Leave!"

Dalar poised. Sharina stepped in front of him. "Yes, we have to leave," she said. She didn't know what Mykon had in mind for Dalar, but she could guess what her own role in the prince's court would be. "And no, we don't want anything to do with Mykon. Is there a place we can go?"

"She can't stay here!" Brasca said. Her arms trembled and her eyes no longer focused. She was a strong, competent woman, but fear for a bleak future had virtually paralyzed her.

"Jem?" said Bantrus. "If we sail to Klestis tonight, we'll have time to get things ready. We have to act sometime."

"Right," said the other youth after a moment's hesitation. To Sharina he added, "Come on, we'll get aboard the *Tailwind* and out of here. You'll be a symbol, all right, but you'll be *our* symbol!"

He turned and jumped from the *Columbine*'s bow to the stern of the next barge in this rank, retracing the route by which he'd arrived. Sharina followed him without hesitation. She didn't know what she was getting into, but she had a good idea of what she was escaping.

Behind her, Bantrus was gathering a few possessions into a blanket. His mother had dropped the knife onto the deck. She was sobbing.

Lord Waldron bowed to acknowledge Garric's question and said, "Eight battalions are ready to march on four hours' warning . . ." His lips made a sour moue before he added, ". . . Your Majesty. That includes the phalanx. As a practical matter I can have the leading companies moving in a few minutes and the rest can join as they fall in."

The proud old nobleman glared across the table at Lord Attaper. "Does the commander of the Blood Eagles have anything to add from his years of experience?"

For all the sneering way Waldron put the question, it was an intelligent attempt to keep the emotional temperature in the room low. Waldron knew that Garric would ask for Attaper's opinion as a check—which Waldron would view as an insult. By asking himself, everybody avoided embarrassment.

"I'd take the phalanx into battle without hesitation," Attaper said. "Lord Zettin and his drillmasters from the Blood

Eagles have done a splendid job . . . under the general direction of the commander of the Royal Army."

He made a slight bow to Waldron.

"Then tonight—" Garric began.

The door behind him opened. He turned. The others at the table looked angry—Waldron angry enough that he reached for his sword—but Garric felt hollow fear. An interruption *now* meant something very bad had happened.

His father stepped into the room, leading a man with a roughly bandaged head and blood down the front of his gray tunic. From the injured man's white hem and high-laced boots, he was one of the men who carried the sedan chairs and palanquins of high palace officials.

Lord Pitre opened his mouth; Reise peremptorily gestured him silent. "Tell them what you told me!" he ordered the chairman in an iron voice.

"A fat rube come to Lady Tenoctris while Hiller and me was on duty in case she needed her chair," the fellow said. He paused, wincing and squeezing the bandage; it oozed red.

Liane dropped her tablets and stepped to the wounded man, snatching up a bowl of wine and water from the serving table. "Katchin the Miller," Reise explained to his son and the others. "It's my fault. The ushers at the gate knew I'd admitted Katchin once, so they believed him when he said he had business in the private domains."

Garric waved curtly. This was no time for recriminations; and no one, not even Reise, could consider all the possibilities of who might wheedle entry to the palace.

"I heard him," the chairman said. He continued speaking though he closed his eyes as Liane dampened her sash and dabbed it at the ragged cut on his scalp. "He said you'd sent him to bring her to a place in White Street, a stables that's built on the foundations of an old temple. Right away and no bodyguards."

"No bodyguards?" Attaper said. His words clanged.

"*He* said, the rube did," the chairman explained, "but the guards said they were with her till their commander said so, and they didn't care if the Lady herself come down and told them different."

Attaper nodded crisply. Garric wouldn't have wanted to call the Blood Eagle's expression a smile, but it was as close to a smile as a block of granite could show.

"We went off with the rube," the chairman said. "He had his own chair, a hired one, waiting outside the gates. Lady Tenoctris had her bag of gear along. She was doing something as we run along, but I don't know what."

The man took the bowl from Liane's hand and slurped enough to fill a drinking cup. Liane winced, but the chairman didn't care that his own blood stained the contents, if he even noticed.

"We get to the place and it's a stables, like the rube says," he went on. He still sounded hoarse but the edge of near hysteria in his tone had dulled. "It's closed up now and empty, but the rube goes to the trapdoor and unlocks it with a key. He takes Lady Tenoctris down and the guards go with her. Hiller and me, we're waiting with the chair but we can hear it all inside."

We know his partner's name, Garric thought, *but not his. And under normal circumstances I'd never have been aware of him as an individual.*

"Lady Tenoctris says something about the stone and what it must be," the chairman said. "And a guard says something about a statue, and somebody shouts something. And then there's a flash of red light, only . . ."

He raised his eyes from the floor he'd been looking at and with a grimace of confusion said, "By the Lady, sirs, it came *through* the stones, not just out the doorway. I swear that's what I seen."

"Go on," said Garric motionlessly. King Carus in his mind stood like a tensed spring, but he and Garric both knew that they had to have information before they acted. Attaper and Waldron had sent aides scrambling out of the room; troops would be ready to go at once, if that was the proper response.

"Me and Hiller both run to the stairs," the chairman said.

"He's right ahead of me as we go down. It's just a basement, but there's no *wall* on the fourth side—it's an ice field instead and there's two of the godawfulest things you ever saw standing there. They're like spiders or worse, only they stand on two legs and they're as big as oxen. They come at us, and the guards go at them."

The chairman gave a look of longing to the carafe of pure wine on the mixing table. Garric reached over and handed it to him, ignoring Reise's frown. *"Protocol be hanged,"* King Carus muttered. *"The poor devil needs a drink if ever a man did."*

"Hiller came back and I froze," the man went on. Liane had finished bathing the fellow's cut. She sliced off the hem of her outer tunic with the dagger she kept in one sleeve for protection. "Hiller and me tangled and rolled down the stairs. There was a man in white come in with the monsters. Lady Tenoctris is saying something but this guy spins something in front of her. She goes stiff and the guy leads her away."

"What are the guards doing while this is going on?" Attaper said. His question was perfectly enunciated, but the words quivered like racehorses poised at the starting gate.

The chairman looked at him. "Dying, milord," he said. "I told you, these things was the size of an ox and got claws on all six legs. One knocked *me* down, that's how I got this—"

He pointed to his forehead, careful not to interfere with Liane binding on the fresh bandage.

"—and I was just trying to get away. At that, I was luckier than Hiller."

"By the Lady!" Lord Waldron said. "You ran? You should have—"

"He should have come here to inform us of the situation, milord," Liane said, looking over her shoulder as her fingers fastened the bandage with a gold fibula from somewhere within her garments. "As he has done."

Garric pointed to the chairman. "Can you ride a horse?" he asked.

"What?" the man said. "Me, a horse? No, milord."

Much as Garric had expected. "Then we'll all go afoot and you'll guide us," he said. Perhaps they should put the fellow in a palanquin himself? "Can you make it back on your own feet?"

"Sure, I could run unless they cut my head clean off," the man said, contemptuously boastful. "Which is what they did to Hiller, the bastards."

He raised his eyes again and added, "Let's go. *I'll* take you there."

Garric looked at Attaper and said, "All the on-duty Blood Eagles. The off-duty shift stands ready here at the palace for further orders."

"Done," said Attaper as another aide sprinted out the door. "I've already ordered the whole battalion to stand to."

"Lord Waldron," Garric continued, "alert the Royal Army but hold the troops in barracks until further orders."

"Yes, Your Majesty," Waldron said. Garric didn't know if it was the crisis or the steely certainty Carus put in Garric's voice *during* a crisis, but he noticed that there was nothing grudging in the honorific this time. "They're being called to arms now."

"Then let's go," Garric said, taking his sword belt from the servant who held it while he was in conference.

Chapter Eighteen

The Blood Eagles in half-armor—shields, breastplates, and helmets—rammed a path down White Street through any pedestrians who hadn't been warned clear by the mounted trumpeters at the rear of the column. They used their spearbutts, not the points, but it was still a brutal process that Garric hated to watch.

He couldn't delay now if they were to rescue Tenoctris. If that meant knocking a few citizens off the pavement, so be it. Without Tenoctris to guide them, the Isles would slip into chaos as surely as the sun rose.

Streets on the outskirts of the city like this one had begun as drove roads, laid out by sheep who didn't care about distance but could sense a rise in the ground that wasn't enough to make a ball roll. The chairman—his name was Maylo—pointed as Garric's company pounded around another turn and cried, "There it is!"

A squad of the city watch stood at the side entrance of a stables. None of the the watchmen looked comfortable, and one had taken off his brass helmet to vomit in the street. Civilian spectators watched from a slight distance. Hawkers with water skins and trays of food had already begun to work the crowd.

The squad leader looked relieved when he saw troops arriving. "There's been killings!" he called—to Attaper; Garric was merely a civilian, while Attaper's gold-inlaid cuirass had drawn his attention. "There's a thing down there dead and men. May the Shepherd guard me, I don't know how many men there are!"

The hundred-plus troops clashed to a halt. At least one man behind Garric skidded and fell with a crash of equipment. The soldiers' hobnailed boots weren't meant for brick pavers with the slime of garbage inevitable on a city street, and it had been a long run for troops dressed for battle.

The chairman wasn't even breathing hard. Garric was; he'd been spending too much time sitting. He trained with his sword daily, but that didn't make him as fit for running as he'd have hoped.

Garric prayed to the Shepherd daily also, something he couldn't imagine doing when he was a peasant. Becoming Prince Garic hadn't exactly made him more religious, but it certainly made him aware that he was going to need a lot of help to succeed.

He drew his sword, feeling the ghost of King Carus thrill to the *string* of the blade's chine against scabbard's iron cap. The watchman started back, surprised to see a civilian with a bare sword in this company.

"Attaper," Garric ordered, his words echoing those of Carus in his mind, "ten men down with us, the rest ready to follow."

Attaper shouted a curt command as he and Garric took a squad to the rough stairs down from the slanted trapdoor. Attaper would have led if he'd been quick enough, but Garric was younger and didn't have the burden of armor.

The basement was an abattoir. The four Blood Eagles had been dismembered. A heavy blow had crushed one man's breastplate against the back of his cuirass, and the dead chairman's head had splashed its brains against a support pillar.

Katchin the Miller sat in a corner of the room, trying to stuff coils of his intestines through the rip in his belly. His eyes followed Garric down the stairs, but he didn't speak.

One of the killers lay dead as well; Garric heard Attaper grunt approval. Plates of slick, dirty-white chitin, hard enough to turn a blade that struck glancingly, covered the monster's body and six limbs. Hair sprouted from the joints.

Where swords had penetrated, the gashes leaked yellowish ichor. A sword was stuck through one of the compound eyes. The monster had been trying to pull the blade free when it died. The point was too firmly embedded to move, but the pincered "hands" had twisted the good steel like a strand of taffy.

Maylo had said the creatures were as big as oxen. They were at least that large. The jaw plates opened sideways and meshed like rows of broken glass.

"What happened, Katchin?" Garric asked quietly. He squatted beside the dying man, cocking up the scabbard of his long sword so that it didn't catch on the floor.

"It wasn't supposed to be this way," Katchin said. "I was supposed to bring the old woman here and put the statuette they gave me into the niche in the wall."

He spoke in a normal voice; shock had apparently kept him from feeling pain. Did he know he was as surely a dead man as any of the dismembered corpses around him?

Garric looked at the wall where Katchin's gaze had wandered. He saw the niche, carved at the junction of two of the blocks, but there was no statue in it.

"Who told you to do that, Katchin?" Garric asked. Attaper was trying the monster's chitinous armor with his dagger point, first at a joint and then on the smooth carapace. Most of the other Blood Eagles watched with their commander, but one man held his spear leveled at Katchin's breast and another was gathering the parts of dead men into separate piles.

Katchin frowned. His fingers moved as if by their own volition; slimy coils leaked out of his body cavity again and again.

"I don't know," he said. "I don't remember. Though there was a man in white . . . a wizard, perhaps? A wizard told me."

He seemed oddly detached. Katchin had never cared about much except himself and his own dignity. Now he didn't care about anything, and that was far worse. Garric was talking to a corpse; nothing more.

"Your Majesty?" a soldier said. He poked his spearpoint toward an object lying in the corner of the wall, almost covered by one of the monster's pincered legs. "Is this something? The statue?"

Garric shifted his stance to look. He still saw only the sheen of ivory.

"Pick it—" he said. He realized that the soldier was afraid to touch the object. Garric started to get up rather than order the man to do something that frightened him the way physical danger would not.

Liane had slipped down the stairs while Garric was talking to Katchin. She'd followed the soldiers in a sedan chair. Garric hadn't intended her to enter this charnel house, but he wasn't surprised—or entirely displeased— that she was here anyway, looking as calm as a statue of the Lady.

Liane stepped past the soldier's armored bulk and picked up the statuette. It was an intricate cone holding more cones, carved each within the next larger. The layers rustled softly as Liane handed the object to Garric.

Elongated female nudes formed the sides of the cone. Though distorted, their shapes had a cool beauty that made Garric think of waves on a bright winter day.

"Does the statue have to face in a particular direction, Katchin?" Garric asked. The surface of the outermost cone had turned a creamy yellow from handling, but the layers within—each increasingly delicate—were the cold white of sun on a snowfield.

Katchin smiled faintly; he didn't speak. His fingers no longer moved, though he was still breathing.

"Right," said Garric, rising to his feet with the carving in his left hand. The patterned steel of his swordblade shimmered like a crawling snake.

"Liane, stay behind the first squad," Garric said, because he wasn't going to waste breath telling her she couldn't come. He grinned at Attaper. "Let's see what happens."

He set the carving in the niche and backed a step. The ivory vanished and the ancient stones flared into a wall of crimson light beyond which shapes loomed. The stables trembled as if an earthquake had struck; dirt sifted down from the ceiling joists.

"Garric and the Isles!" Attaper shouted as he and Garric led the squad into the unknown.

Garric's skin tingled as he entered the portal. For a blind instant he thought the blast of cold wind racking him was wizardry as well.

He stumbled on coarse gravel and his eyesight cleared. Garric and the men following through a shimmer of rosy light—much paler on this side of the portal than in the

Valles basement—had entered a cold wasteland. Moss and trees no taller than his little finger grew among the stones. A wall of ice, horizon to horizon, gleamed in the near distance, lighted by a sun that barely rose over the rocky waste to the south.

"There's Tenoctris!" Liane called, pointing to the western sky. A bridge—*the* bridge of light—arched from the windswept plain. At its far end Garric saw the glittering buildings of Klestis.

A man in white glided rather than walked midway along the span; in front of him shambled four servants who were human but not necessarily alive, carrying the frozen figure of Tenoctris on a litter. Behind the wizard, step for step, the bridge was disintegrating into sparkles of light. He and his party were beyond even bowshot from the ground. It was impossible to reach Tenoctris from where Garric was now.

And there were things closer to hand which needed his attention.

"Help me!" cried the nude woman staggering toward them from the direction of the ice sheet. She was clearly exhausted. Her body was scratched and bruised, and there was a more serious cut on her right thigh. "Sirs, your protection for the Lady's sake!"

A second squad of Blood Eagles plunged through the curtain of light. More would be following, which was good—because a pair of the insectoid monsters were following the woman closely. They generally ran along on the four rear legs, but sometimes one or the other would rise onto its hindmost pair alone and scream like slates rubbing.

"Ranks by squads!" Attaper ordered. "Close order! First rank receives the enemy with spearpoints, second rank will launch javelins on command before engaging with swords!"

He turned to Garric. "You and the Lady Liane—" Attaper said. The running woman stumbled, barely managing to keep her feet. She was twenty yards from the double line of soldiers, and the monsters were not much farther than that behind.

Garric sheathed his sword and sprinted toward the woman.

"Charge!" Attaper shouted.

"Garric and the Isles!" Liane cried. If either of them was thinking, *Garric is an idiot!*, they kept the opinion to themselves for the time being.

Carus was shouting encouragement in his mind, but the decision to go after the woman was Garric's alone. Garric caught her around the waist and flung her over his right shoulder as part of the same motion by which he turned to run back to relative safety. He could smell old corpses on the fetid breath of the monsters pursuing; he would've been able to guess their usual diet even without the half-picked human rib cage that dangled from the foreclaws of the one on the right.

From the way they were chasing the woman, they were also willing to eat living prey if such were offered.

The gravel was too coarse to give safe footing, but the beach beneath Barca's Hamlet was shingle and Garric had often walked there. Besides, keyed up as he was now, Garric thought he could dance along a sword edge if that was what had to be done.

"May the Lady bless you, sir!" the woman gasped. Her flesh felt as warm as if she'd just come from a heated room instead of running across tundra. She was remarkably supple, and she didn't seem as heavy as Garric had guessed.

The Blood Eagles strode forward, their studded aprons jingling and their hobnails sparking on stones. The front rank held its shields high so that each man peered around the right edge of the round of laminated wood. Their spears were in an underhand grip so that they could thrust upward or brace the butts on the ground behind them. The rear rank—and more soldiers were spilling forward through the portal—had its spears cocked back to throw on command.

Garric skidded around the advancing Blood Eagles. He caught himself on his left hand. The woman over his other arm got her feet down; Liane embraced her, keeping her from falling.

"Loose!" Attaper said. His voice was as loud and harsh as a bronze trumpet.

"Garric!" bellowed the rank of soldiers behind him. Their arms lashed forward, sending their heavy javelins at the pair of oncoming monsters.

There'd been no time to plan, so six men cast their spears at the creature on the left and only four at the other. Every missile struck its target, though one glanced away after cracking a belly plate.

The monster on the right fell sideways. Three of its legs thrashed; the three on the other side froze in the position they'd held when the javelin punched through a compound eye.

The remaining monster continued with a clicking, multijointed gait. Ichor dripped down the shafts of the five spears projecting from its thorax and abdomen. The front rank of Blood Eagles strode into the wounded monster like a hammer coming down. Spears thrust; veterans shouted with murderous rage.

A shield split into layers and splinters; the strong glue between laminations held, but the birch itself sheared from the force of the monster's blow. The creature flung two men aside with simultaneous twitches of its forelegs. It continued on.

The second rank met the monster with swords while their fellows—those still able to move—prodded at the flanks of the armored body. Two more spears dangled from the creature, and there were many more gashes and dents in the chitin. Its right middle leg dangled from where the joint was torn, but as the creature advanced it used the limb as a flail, crushing the hip of another soldier.

Garric drew his sword.

". . . Necromancers captured me," the woman he'd saved was saying, her voice dancing through a gap in the clash of battle. She might have information, but that wasn't important now.

Nothing was going to be important unless Garric survived the next few moments.

The monster continued to advance, leaving a wrack of bodies in its wake. The Blood Eagles were as brave and skilled as any warriors in the Isles, but they were trained to fight men—and there were too *many* of them to handle this as the hand-to-hand combat it'd become.

"Lord Attaper!" Carus called in Garric's voice. "Call your men back. I've done this before!"

And so they had, Carus and Garric both: fought monsters, using skill and quickness where strength was insufficient and armor a burden rather than a benefit.

"Call them back, or on my *honor* you'll all be emptying cesspits!"

All the survivors, anyway, which wouldn't be many of them.

Attaper had lost his helmet and sword; a gouge across the front of his cuirass trailed curls of bright bronze. He'd been crawling toward the body of one of his men whose sword was still in its sheath.

The Blood Eagles' commander looked at Garric—looked at his *prince*. He shouted, "Section, withdraw!"

Garric stepped forward, laughing with a surge of emotions he couldn't have imagined a few months before when he was a peasant. Fighting this creature alone wasn't braggadocio: the Blood Eagles' flailing swords and javelins would be a greater risk to him than they were to the monster.

Nor was it braggadocio for Garric to fight when he could have scampered back through the portal, leaving the struggle to the soldiers. It was their job, sure; but it was as surely the job of Prince Garric to lead them. At least part of the time, leadership has to come from the front.

Maybe a little of it's braggadocio.

Laughing at a joke only warriors or madmen would understand, Garric stepped into the monster with his blade singing in a flat arc. The sword tip sheared through a joint of the forelimb reaching for him. The pincers spun away, clacking open and shut in the cold air.

Garric jumped back.

The creature rose on its hind legs and screamed, towering over Garric. A slash had destroyed one of its eyes. The yellow ichor that filled the creature's veins painted the underside of its abdomen and much of its smooth carapace as well.

Garric lunged, thrusting through the monster's back-folding knee. The remaining front pincer scissored shut close enough to snip a lock of Garric's hair. He rolled free, ignoring the stones and frozen ground. He'd bruise, sure, but that would be tomorrow. . . .

The monster screamed again and fell sideways like a tree toppling. It hit as hard as a great oak, jolting stones in the air; Garric heard a crunch that could only be the creature's own legs flattening under the impact of the massive body.

The jaws opened and clashed shut; the creature was trying to skid itself forward with the strength of its remaining limbs. Garric stood, trembling and exhausted.

"Your Majesty?" Attaper said. He held a sword again. From this side Garric could see the commander had a scalp wound as well as the tear in his breastplate. "Shall we finish him?"

Garric looked at the horizon. Six more of the great creatures had left their caves in the ice and were coming toward the humans.

"No," he said as he backed away, "we'll leave that to its friends. We'll go back, but we'll take our dead with us."

"Always, Your Majesty!" Attaper said, shocked at what he took as a slight on the Blood Eagles' honor. He glanced toward the oncoming monsters and added in a milder tone, "But yes, especially here."

The last of the detachment stood on the tundra, waiting for orders. The portal behind them wavered, shrinking and swelling like a flag in the wind.

"Sir?" an officer said, looking at Attaper but shouting to

be heard by Garric as well. "The stables aren't going to last much longer, the way the ground's shaking."

Attaper glanced at Garric, caught his nod, and shouted, "Right! Move it! Squads from the front first, carrying the dead and wounded!"

Liane embraced Garric. He hugged her awkwardly with his left hand; ichor gummed the blade of his sword, so he hadn't been able to sheathe it. Until this moment, he hadn't remembered he *should* sheathe it.

"Your Majesty," said Attaper. His face was hard as the distant icewall.

"Right, I've been fool enough today," Garric said. Holding Liane, he walked clumsily toward the portal.

The woman he'd saved stood nearby with Liane's lace wrapper over her shoulders. The garment did nothing either to conceal her body or to block the cutting wind, but it at least provided a sop to her dignity. When she saw Garric coming toward her, her face brightened in a smile.

Pairs of Blood Eagles, each carrying a third man—and sometimes the bearers themselves used spears as crutches— were lurching through the portal. The soldiers' set faces showed how much they hated and feared wizardry, but they'd followed Garric because their oath demanded it.

"Good men," whispered Carus. *"Whatever they may be in their personal lives, good men to serve a king."*

And may the Shepherd make me a good king for them to serve, Garric thought.

Two Blood Eagles carrying a decapitated fellow stopped when they saw Garric approach. One of them even managed to bow, despite the fact that he limped and his face looked gray.

Rather than argue with the men, Garric said "Come!" to the women in an unintentionally harsh voice. He plunged through the square of light. On the other side, the basement was pitching like a ship. The air was warm but full of dust shaken from the walls and floor.

"Into the street!" he shouted. "Before it all comes down!"

When Katchin placed the carving in the wall niche, tremors had shaken it out. Garric had wedged the piece tightly between the blocks of ancient stone. It would stay till the violence of the forces it unlocked brought down the wall with it.

Garric bent to grab the corpse of one of Tenoctris' guards. He was still holding his sword.

"I'll take it!" said a female voice close to his ear. Delicate hands closed over Garric's. He let go of the weapon and waddled to the stairs carrying all that was left of a man who'd been faithful unto death.

Garric came up from the vibrating dust cloud into a street full of soldiers. Waldron was there with at least a battalion of the Royal Army.

"Your Majesty?" the old noble said in disbelief. He snapped an order to a pair of common soldiers; they took the corpse from their prince's arms.

"We couldn't get her," Garric said, suddenly aware of failure. "We're going to have to go another way. Is the army ready for action?"

"Yes," said Waldron with a haughty assurance that disdained to boast.

"Then they're going to have it, as soon as night falls and we can cross the bridge to Klestis," Garric said, articulating the plan he'd made as he stepped into daylight. There wasn't time to dither, just act. He couldn't follow the wizards who'd taken Tenoctris, but he could go to where he'd seen them headed.

And with the help of Duzi and whatever God instilled discipline, perhaps the army would follow him. Though he'd go alone if he had to.

Lord Waldron nodded and gave orders to the aides waiting at his back. Blood Eagles were pouring into the street, coming up the stairs faster now because all the wounded men were out. The building shook even more violently. Thank Duzi, its roof like many of those on the outskirts of Valles was thatch rather than tile.

Attaper burst into the street, covered with grit and wobbling with the pain of his injuries. "I'm the last," he muttered; and in Garric's mind, King Carus nodded grimly and echoed, *"Of course."*

"Clear the street!" Garric said. Even as he spoke, the lengthy roar of the stables falling in on itself drowned his words.

He held Liane and stumbled forward as best he could with his eyes shut. The trumpeter at Waldron's side was blowing retreat, though how he could fill his lungs in the dust mushrooming from the wreckage was more than Garric could imagine.

The tremors had ceased at the beginning of the collapse. The carving had finally been flung from its niche or more likely had been crushed to powder when the blocks shifted. It didn't matter: the plain to which it was the key wasn't a place that Garric wanted ever to see again.

Half a block from the ruin, clear at last of the spreading dust cloud, Garric stepped with Liane into the entrance of a mews to take stock. Civilians living in the apartments around the courtyard had come out to see what all the commotion was about. Blood Eagles entered with Garric and pushed them back.

Liane was with him. So was the woman he'd rescued, now wearing a military cape that fell to midthigh on her short frame. She reached forward, holding Garric's sword to him hilt first; the cape gapped open.

"Here, Lord Garric," she said in a voice like honey flowing. With her other hand she dropped Liane's gauzy wrapper, now wadded and stained with fluids from the monster's body. "I've wiped the steel for you."

Garric took the sword. He put his left arm around Liane possessively.

The stranger smiled and added, "My name is Colva."

The trumpet calls awakened Cashel before dawn. For a moment he couldn't remember where he was. He'd been dreaming that he slept on a vine-covered hill beneath a sky of rock. With him was spiky little man who had a tongue on him worse than Ilna's. . . .

Cashel got up from the low couch. He was wearing some kind of loose silk garment that covered him neck to ankles. His tunics and boots hung on a rack by the wall. They'd been cleaned, which they'd probably needed; the sturdy wool was still slightly damp. He ought to be grateful, but the kindness reminded him of how helpless he must have been.

Cashel wriggled out of the nightdress and flung it toward the couch. It made him feel like he'd walked into a huge cobweb at night in the forest.

There was a bowl and a ewer of water on the night stand. Cashel drank deeply, straight from the ewer, before it occurred to him that he'd probably been meant to wash with it instead. His hands and face didn't need water near as bad as his dry throat did. He remembered drinking the local wine, but he wasn't sure just how much he'd drunk. More than was good for him this morning, that he was sure of.

Trumpets continued to skirl and tremble in the morning air. The eastern sky out the window was already too bright to show stars; there were no clouds to color the sunrise.

The quarterstaff leaned discreetly against the clothes rack. Cashel took it and ran his fingers over the smooth hickory, thinking it'd dispel the formless disquiet that had settled over him as soon as he awakened. The familiar touch didn't help. That disturbed Cashel worse than the original feeling had.

He rattled aside the door curtain of jasper, quartz, and carnelian beads and strode into the hallway. It was empty but he heard voices coming from the right so he turned that way. As soon as he met somebody, he was going to ask them how he could get out of Tian. Getting out was the thing Cashel most wanted to do right now.

The end of the corridor kinked to the right and joined the hall where Cashel had come into the palace the evening before. Servants crowded it, chattering among themselves. They fell silent when they saw Cashel.

"Excuse me," he said, but the crowd parted ahead of him as soon as he appeared. "I'm just looking for the way down."

Cashel spoke for politeness' sake, because now he knew where he was and was already striding toward the gateway at the opposite end of the avenue. Servants lowered their eyes or looked away, pretending not to be aware of him. There was nothing hostile in their behavior. They were just silently rejecting what was alien.

Cashel didn't resent the way they acted, but it made him even more uncomfortable than he already was. Well, he'd wanted to get away from Tian, so he couldn't blame the city's residents for wanting to be shut of him as well.

He walked along the empty avenue, flanked by the whispers of servants gathering in every doorway that he passed. Cashel didn't see any of Tian's silk-clad nobles until a swirl of bright motion made him look up. The great folk packed the battlements, talking in lilting voices as they watched the eastern horizon from coigns of vantage.

Cashel walked to the open gates. A group of nobles clustered around the great windlass that worked them through gears made of the same shimmering metal as supported all Tian. One man even touched a capstan bar like he was thinking of turning it.

"Well, I think somebody should summon them!" a corpulent fellow with flaring white moustaches said. "What kind of servants are they if they don't serve?"

"I'm sure the king will take care of it when he's . . ." another man said, looking out the gate in puzzled concern. "After he's come back, you know."

Cashel strode past, his staff slanted across his chest, feeling the nobles' eyes on him. He tried to look relaxed, but he felt like a child in a roomful of frightened adults.

He stepped through the gateway and out of Tian. As he passed beneath the stone arches, he looked up at the faces craning over the battlements. He couldn't tell their features apart in this predawn dimness, but he thought one of the pale ovals was that of Lia.

King Liew and his knights stood at the bottom of the sweeping ramp, their weapons in their hands as they faced sunrise. Cashel, letting the slope lengthen his strides, followed the curves down to them.

A few knights looked back. None spoke, and their eyes glanced away from Cashel's big figure like sunlight splashing from a crystal.

Cashel turned his head once more. Sunlight reddened the upper towers of Tian, though the ground beneath was still in shadow.

"King Liew!" Cashel said. "If there's an enemy coming, I'll stand with you to meet him."

He spoke more loudly than he'd have chosen to. The king and his knights were ignoring him, and to get their attention Cashel had either to force his way past or shout. As edgy as he felt, a part of him would just as soon have pushed . . . but he couldn't blame the knights for being, well, nervous too.

Mah turned, his broad-bladed glaive trembling in his angry grip. "Get out of here!" he snarled. "You've had your guest rights—now go back where you belong!"

Sia also turned. His expression was shuttered; hostile not only toward Cashel but to all the world outside himself. His lips drew back in a grimace more threatening than Mah's open anger.

"We are gentlemen of Tian!" said King Liew sharply to his knights. "A gentleman should always behave as if the next moment might be his last. That's especially true this morning."

Sia muttered a curse and looked away. Mah continued to stare at Cashel, looking ever so much like a terrier desperate to attack a bear.

"But as for you, Master Cashel," the king resumed, "you have no place here today. This is the duty and the honor of the Knights of Tian. Either go your way or rejoin the others in the city to await our return."

Liew looked at the sky; a bright arc was creeping over the distant hills. "It shouldn't be long, now," he said, but his tone suggested he was speaking mostly to himself.

"Thanks for the meal and bed," Cashel said curtly. "I'll be going now."

The knights made no more reaction than so many trees lining the path. As Cashel passed through them he heard a knight exclaim, "What's that? What's happening in the city, Your Majesty?"

Cashel looked over his shoulder. Through the gates came people crowding together like a flock being driven through narrow city streets. Early dawn lighted their bundles and drab clothing.

Nobles called in anger and amazement from the battlements. The servants of Tian were leaving. From their numbers, filling the ramp in a brown-gray-dun mass, *all* the servants were leaving.

"They can't do that!" Sia shouted. "We can't let them do that! They're running away!"

"There's smoke from the high tower," Mah said wonderingly. "Shan is lighting the beacon of sacrifice. He's never done that except on the winter solstice."

King Liew looked at the city and the servants' silent approach, then turned again to face the dawn. "Let them go," he said in the shrill, fearless tones of a hawk hovering in the morning sky. "It's beneath our honor as knights to concern ourselves with such things!"

Cashel started down the road that led back to a place he couldn't remember clearly. Sharina wasn't in Tian; and by the goodness of the Lady, might she *never* be here. By the time he was a few furlongs away, his spirits had started to lift.

The morning dimmed. Though the sky overhead was clear, clouds were beginning to pile up on the eastern horizon to block the sun.

Cashel eyed them and frowned. There was no shelter closer than an hour's hike. As black and boiling as the clouds rising over the hills appeared, they were going to bring a storm like few he'd experienced. He slipped the thong of his countryman's hat down over his chin, knowing that if there was hail—as there well might be—the broad leather brim could be the difference between discomfort and outright injury.

Spectators in Tian screamed. Cashel looked at the horizon again. It wasn't a storm rising over the hills; it was a striding figure of cloud.

The storm giant was black and swirling gray. Red lightning flashed in his head like angry eyes, and in his right hand was a club greater than the tallest tree that ever grew.

The nobles wailed from the battlements, but their joined voices were less than a lamb's bleat against the howl of oncoming destruction. The giant strode forward. His head towered high above the floating city, and his cloud arms raised the club.

Cashel watched the figure approach. He started to poise his quaterstaff, then stood it firmly on the ground beside him. There was nothing a man could do except watch or flee. Cashel or-Kenset wouldn't flee, but neither would he make a fool of himself.

The servants were a dull mass in the near distance, staying together like ants crowded onto a floating leaf when their hill flooded. The cloud giant ignored them as he ignored the knights of Tian praying or slashing at the air like madmen beneath him.

The club came down with gathering speed and struck the center of the floating city. Stone shattered. Tian rocked like a sheep, suddenly aware and trying to back away from the slaughterer's hammer.

The cloud giant struck again, this time a two-handed blow from the side and slightly below. The ramp flew away like a ribbon in a sea breeze, twisting and vanishing into no more than a scatter of droplets when it hit the ground. The shimmering underplate on which the city floated, dented down by the first impact, now collapsed around the club head.

The club of storm withdrew. The plate was disintegrating, thinning and vanishing like mist in the late morning. Stone blocks, no longer supported, dribbled out of the sky.

They took a surprising length of time to fall before drumming on the ground, leaping and bouncing and shattering on one another. The city was a burial mound for her knights.

The nobles of Tian were among the rain of objects. Their bright silks fluttered all the long way down.

Cashel turned his head and resumed walking away from what had been a city. He was still walking when green light awakened him on the hillside where he'd eaten the huge grapes in another lifetime.

"Well, did you learn something, sheep-boy?" Krias asked.

Instead of answering, Cashel ran his index finger down the hickory shaft of his staff, then touched the sapphire as well. The purple stone felt warm and reassuring.

"Hey!" cried the ring demon. "What's that about? I just asked a civil question!"

"Just glad to see you're still with me," Cashel said. "This isn't much of a place to be alone, is it?"

"I was alone for so long," Krias said, and for once his voice didn't seem really harsh. "Then Landure came and chipped me out of the rock; but he wouldn't free me from the sapphire, sheep-boy, no matter how I begged him. But I had Landure, then, so that was all right. Even though Landure was a fool, he was all I had."

Cashel rubbed his thumb against the stone he'd pillowed his head on. One side was heavily carved with vines and flowers like those of the dining hall. All the walls of Tian were decorated, though; this block might have come from anywhere in the city.

"Master Krias?" Cashel said. "Was the dream I just had real?"

" 'Real' isn't a useful word here," the ring demon said. "Not for sheep-boys, and especially not for me."

Cashel rose to his feet. He was hungry enough to eat again, but he thought he'd wait until he could find something growing at a distance from here. He started across the overgrown mound, headed in the same direction as before.

"Master Krias?" he said. "Could you raise a palace into the air and make it float there?"

"Nobody can do that now, sheep-boy," the ring said. "Not here, not without Malkar's aid, I mean. And I won't invoke Malkar, not for you or for anybody!"

Cashel cleared his throat. "I wouldn't ask you to," he said apologetically. "I was just wondering. Ah . . . I'm not sure it's good for people to live like that anyway."

"All decent people can do now in the Underworld," Krias continued, talking perhaps to himself but loud enough that Cashel could hear the words by straining, "is to keep it shut off from the waking world. And Landure the Guardian is dead."

Ilna twisted out of the narrow crack and settled her tunics. They'd become disarrayed by brushing through the walls of rock. Merota waited with her hands folded and her eyes wide, saying nothing.

The walls of the cavern were banded; several of the narrow layers exuded light. It was faint as foxfire but sufficient as a contrast to the total darkness of the crevice.

Ilna rubbed a lighted streak, thinking she'd feel powdery lichen. There was nothing but the grittiness of stone.

Chalcus slipped through, turning as soon as he entered the greater cavity. He chuckled and slid his sword back into its scabbard. "I don't think we'll have a problem with them, good ladies," he said.

"Chalcus?" the girl said. Her quiet voice almost drowned in its own whispering echoes. "Did you kill them?"

"Kill them again, child?" the chanteyman said cheerfully. "That I did not, when I saw that Tirling was the leader of them coming after us. He's broad as an ox, is Tirling, and nigh as stupid even when his throat hadn't been cut. They were a determined lot, our crewmen. I figured that if Tirling was bound to wedge himself into a crack that Mistress Ilna and myself found tight passage, who was I to hinder him?"

"Let's go," Ilna said, nodding toward the farther end of the cavern. She didn't know where it went, but a breeze came from somewhere. The other end wasn't going to be worse than the place they'd just escaped.

"Aye, mistress," Chalcus said, stepping into the lead without comment. "You know, there were times I'd have cut Tirling's throat myself, so stupid and lazy did I find him. It would be a wonderful gift to the king's fleet if all the rowers showed the dedication to their task that Tirling did when he crammed himself into a place he couldn't possibly fit."

"There were times," Ilna said, "that I thought the world would be a better place if I could put people in place the way I do threads. I've learned, though, master pirate, that I liked that world worse than I did the one I was born in."

They went on, going slightly downward more often than they went up so far as Ilna could tell—but she knew from past experience that she couldn't tell much at all, here on Yole. The walls of the cavern were hard stone. The surfaces were generally smooth, but knobs swelled from the floor in some places like giant toadstools.

"Now, how would you say this cave was made, ladies?" Chalcus asked, walking a pace or two ahead. The cavern was generally broad enough for the three of them to go abreast, but its twists and turns meant frequent blind corners. Chalcus wanted room for his sword strokes if the need arose.

"I wouldn't," Ilna said. "I've never seen anything like this. It's sandstone."

"Nor, I," said the chanteyman. "Well, we shan't quibble at the gifts the Lady gives us, shall we?"

Ilna snorted at the thought of the Great Gods creating this place as a bolthole for Chalcus and his companions to escape. Still, something had wormed a passage through hard rock that water wouldn't dissolve. Natural forces of some sort, she supposed; but neither water nor wind, and the walls were too smooth for this to be some sort of fracture from the earth moving.

Aloud she said, "I suppose that's as good an explanation as any."

"Aye, we'll all three of us build her an altar when we've won free, shall we?" Chalcus said with a laugh. But he walked at the front like a hunting lynx, and Ilna's hands bunched and loosed the soft, strong cord of her noose as she paced along behind Merota.

The cavern went *on*. Ilna realized that she'd assumed it was leading somewhere; and so it must be, but not nearly as soon as she'd thought. The rock continued to supply light—sometimes more, sometimes less. One of the glowing layers formed the floor of a stretch a bowshot long. Ilna saw the silhouette of her feet with each step forward.

Occasionally water oozed from between the bands of rock. The first time they passed it by. The second time Merota said softly that she was thirsty. They stopped and held Ilna's scarf to the wall until the wool had sucked up water for them to chew out of the fabric.

It wasn't much—the source was slow and the cave's dry air absorbed the liquid almost as quickly as the scarf could. It was what they had, though, so it would be sufficient.

Merota didn't complain. As for Chalcus—

"Around Cape Ice in frost and snow," the chanteyman sang, soft and sweet as Garric's pipes. *"Around that cape we all must go. . . ."*

They walked on steadily. When Chalcus finished a song, he started another. *"Oh stretch your backs and haul away, and make your port and take your pay. . . ."*

"Shall I sing with you, Chalcus?" Merota said after a pause. "We could sing 'The Gambling Suitor' like you taught me."

"Ah, child, not this time, if you please," the chanteyman said. His voice was hoarse beneath the lilt when he spoke, though when he sang it rang as clear as a warbler's trill. "Leave me be to show off on my own, if you will, for I'm a vain man."

And so he is, Ilna thought. *But he's a man first, and that's not a small thing in this world.*

They came to a patch of wall where the bands of rock swirled and jumbled like burl in a piece of walnut. The light from within was brighter, throwing the dark striations into sharp relief. Ilna frowned.

"I don't know about you ladies," Chalcus said at last, "but I'm about done in. Shall we make our beds here for the night and go on in the morning?"

He knows perfectly well how we are, because he just glanced back and saw Merota wobbling with fatigue. Aloud Ilna said, "Yes, but let's keep on till we find another water seep."

Ilna didn't like the patch of twisted light on the wall. Water was a good reason—a reason she could point to—to go on, so she didn't mention the way the shadow patterns made her feel.

"Aye," said Chalcus, nodding as he sauntered forward again. "I smell water just up ahead."

Merota didn't move. She was staring at the pattern on the wall with a hunger that didn't belong on a face so young and innocent.

"Merota," Ilna said sharply. "Go on."

The child still remained where she was. *"Now!"*

Ilna stepped between Merota and the patch of rock. Only then did she finally come back to waking reality with a shudder.

"Oh, Ilna!" she said, staring up at the older woman's stern face. "I was . . ."

She frowned. "I don't remember where I was."

"No place you should have been," Ilna said, shepherding the girl along with a hand on her shoulder. "We'll all be better for water and some sleep."

"And water we have!" the chanteyman called at another bend in the passageway. "Would I could say it's a gusher like the spring on my uncle's farm on Shengy, but it's wet and will do us, I trust."

Thirsty as they were, it was still almost more effort than

benefit to trap moisture in the cloth and suck it away. They didn't have many other demands on their time, of course.

Chalcus stripped Merota's sandals off and examined the child's soles with a practiced eye, prodding gently with his thumbs. "They'll do, I suppose," he said, giving Merota a friendly pat on the instep as he turned her loose. "I was afraid you'd have bruised yourself on this hard stone, but you walk like a feather, and it's saved you."

He cocked his head toward Ilna. "And you, mistress?" he asked. The soft light gave the chanteyman's smile an incongruous fairy quality.

Ilna shrugged. "My feet are all right," she said. Then—and she didn't know why, it was unlike her to say anything at all about herself—she went on, "I understand cloth, Master Chalcus, better than anyone else you'll ever know. But rock like this—"

She waved her fingertips toward the cavern's wall.

"—if it has feelings, it hates me; and such feelings as I have toward it, that is hatred too."

The chanteyman frowned. "Then this journey we're making must be very difficult for you," he said. "Sorry I am to hear that, lass. I didn't know."

Ilna sniffed. "I expect life to be difficult," she said without particular emphasis. "And in that, at least, it's rarely disappointed me."

Chalcus chuckled. He rubbed Merota's tousled hair and said, "The sooner we sleep, the sooner we'll rise to get to back to the open air. Goodnight, ladies."

Ilna wrapped herself in her cloak, lying beside Merota; Chalcus settled on the child's other side. As tired and hungry as they were, they couldn't keep watch; but a predator that tried to harm Merota would have to get past one or the other of the adults. Whatever tried that would find it an expensive meal.

Ilna hadn't been sure she could sleep. She could, and it was dreamless.

* * *

It wasn't sound or even the absence of Merota's warmth that awakened Ilna, but rather change at a level below even her sleeping consciousness. A pattern had shifted.

And Merota was gone.

"Chalcus," she said, but the chanteyman was already rising. His swordblade was a tongue of curved light.

With no more sound than a weft thread sliding through the warp, Ilna paced back in the direction they'd come. Merota stood in front of the wall of twisted light.

"Merota!" Ilna called with a rush of relief. She'd been sure that the girl was irretrievably lost, snatched away by— something, nothing; by the fabric of the cave itself.

Instead of answering or even looking at her companions, Merota stepped into the wall and disappeared. The pattern of light and shadow swirled momentarily, then froze in the form it had first taken.

Shouting like a madman, Chalcus leaped forward and hammered the stone with the heel of his left hand. His sword was raised to slash at the least sign of threat or give in the wall which had swallowed the child.

It was solid rock, as Ilna had known.

"Get back!" she said, facing the lighted wall. Her hands looped the noose around her waist in a running knot, then twitched separate lengths of cord from her left sleeve. "You're in the way. I have to see the pattern!"

"See" wasn't the right word for the way Ilna viewed, *lived*, patterns. She was vaguely aware that the chanteyman had stepped clear, but even that didn't matter any more. A portion would be enough for Ilna to understand the whole. There was no longer rock before her, merely a passage of light swirling in a way that was as obvious as the stars wheeling on a clear night once she—

Ilna stepped into what had been stone, entering a chamber out of time and space.

"Hello, Merota," she said mildly. "I've come to take you home."

"Ilna?" the girl said from the nest of inward-pointing spines. "Ilna, I can't move!"

WHAT IS THIS THAT CAME UNSUMMONED? demanded a voice in Ilna's head. It was as cold as the heart of a dead star.

She was in a hollow nodule. The walls were varicolored crystals like the interior of a geode, but these glowed and quivered with life. Scores of them had extended into spikes as thin and sharp as yucca leaves, enclosing Merota with their points.

"I'm responsible for the child," Ilna said. She could hear the crystals rustle all around her; the light at the heart of each pulsed to an individual rhythm. "I've come to bring her back where she belongs."

THIS CANNOT HAVE COME THROUGH THE WEB, the voice said. It was the melding of hundreds, perhaps thousands, of inhuman minds speaking as one. THE WEB IS CLOSED, AND WE ARE INVIOLABLE.

Ilna laughed. "Then I'm not here," she said. "Release the girl and we'll go away. Then you'll never have to know if I'm an illusion."

If rock feels anything for me, it's hatred. And I hate rock, beyond any question.

"Oh, Ilna," Merota said. "I'm so sorry . . ."

Rock quivered. Words that were not sound danced and whispered just beneath Ilna's understanding. It was like listening to a dying fire; hisses and sighs, and sometimes a muted pop.

WE WILL RELEASE THE CHILD, the voice said. COME AND TAKE HER AWAY.

Colored spines began to withdraw, returning to squat forms against the nodule's walls. Three remained at their full length, centered on Merota's chest. The light at their cores was blood red.

Ilna tossed up the pattern she'd been knotting while the crystals whispered and lied to her. The cords spun in the air, lighted by the rock itself.

The nodule screamed. Crystals twisted, shattered, slumped like butter melting. One of the swords of red light imprisoning Merota wrenched in on itself to stab through its own base, shivering into a thousand fragments from which the light died slowly.

Merota pitched toward Ilna, bawling with terror. Ilna had been holding her ears in pointless reaction to pain that wasn't sound. She threw her arms around the child, glad to have something to hold that was life of the kind she understood.

The nodule was growing dim. The light that remained was the muddy color of a badly dyed garment.

"Help me Ilna help me!" Merota bawled.

The rock—the world—spasmed. Ilna and the child flew forward, sliding on slick stone. Chalcus caught them left-handed and held them to his chest.

"Ladies?" he said. "You're all right?"

Ilna's eyes readapted. She gave Merota a pat and set her free, then shrugged out of the chanteyman's grip.

"You can put up your sword now, Master Chalcus," she said. "I appreciate the thought, though."

The panel that took Merota was dull as sand. Cracks webbed its surface like those in shattered ice. Bits and then more bits crumbled away from the wall. The whole section was slumping into gravel.

"Yes, we're all right," Ilna said, finally answering the chanteyman's question. "I'm ready to go on, though. I very much doubt either Merota or I will be able to sleep for some time to come."

The girl hugged Ilna tightly. Her throat worked, but she couldn't get words out and instead nodded her agreement.

Six barges traveled together in the bright sunshine, their square sails plump from the following breeze. There was little to choose among individual elements of the Boats, but Sharina thought the *Tailwind*, owned by Jem and three of his brothers, was a little larger than the *Columbine*; a little newer; and a great deal dirtier.

"When we land in Klestis," said Bantrus, standing with her and Dalar in the bow, "we'll go straight to Palace

Square and declare the Boats' independence from Prince Mykon. The people will join us, and the movement will spread along the whole south coast of Cordin!"

The youth's forceful delivery was disconcerting, though Sharina realized that Bantrus was trying to convince himself by sounding certain. Dalar, less used to the way humans tricked themselves into disastrous errors or perhaps just less sensitive than Sharina, said, "Why will the people join you, Master Bantrus?"

Jem had been talking with his brothers near the helm of the barge. Now he and a pair of slightly older siblings came forward along the gunwales, skirting the stacks of earthenware vessels netted down on the center of the deck.

"What?" Bantrus said, frowning with unconscious anger at having his fantasy probed. "Well, you'll be with us, of course, messengers from the Gods. And Klestis needs the Boats, all the islands do. All they need is a spark to, well, show people the path to their own salvation."

Jem and his brothers joined them. One of the barges, not so heavily laden as the others because its cargo was wickerwork, had drawn a bowshot ahead of the rest. Two others were lashed together some distance behind, and the remaining pair were closing with the *Tailwind*.

While the barges were a motley assortment as to cargo—the pair approaching were a dram shop and a brothel, if Sharina read the signs correctly—none of the folk on their decks was older than his mid-twenties. Apart from two flashily dressed women on the brothel, all of them were males as well.

"Tiglath's coming alongside," one of Jems's brothers said, nodding to the tavern vessel. Bunting fluttered from a net drawn between the mast truck and poles fore and aft. A canvas awning on a pole framework sheltered the deck. Three men were trimming the sail. A fourth, black-bearded and squatly powerful, manned the steering oar.

"Better get the fenders out," Bantrus muttered. "I think he *tries* to stave in other boats so that they'll give him landside space in harbor out of proper order."

Deliberately to avoid talking further about the Boats' future, Sharina said, "Here, I'll help with that. These are the fenders?"

The doughnuts of woven coir on the railings could scarcely be anything else, but it was proper to ask. She'd gripped one and was loosing the clove hitch that held it to a stanchion before Jem could say, "Oh, you needn't do that. . . ."

"No need of those, little lady," called the black-bearded man in coincidental parallel. "You'll never meet a man as smooth as me—when I want to be!"

Sharina looked up, judging the other barge's line. That wasn't hard: the closing speed would have seemed sluggish to a ewe. She hung three fenders along the gunwale at the points the vessels were most likely to come in contact, hoping she kept her expression neutral when she looked at the black-bearded man.

He barked a harsh laugh, then said, "Make ready, *Tailwind*, I'm coming aboard."

"Aye, Tiglath," the eldest of Jem's brothers said sourly. "So you are."

The tavern barge coasted against the *Tailwind* with no more thump than Sharina's heel coming down when she was walking. If so skillful a helmsman regularly crunched into other vessels, it was indeed deliberate bullying.

"Diccon, take the helm!" Tiglath ordered. Without waiting for a crewman to replace him at the tiller, he hopped to the *Tailwind* carrying a line. Another of his fellows tossed a line from the bow to Jem, who bound it off to a stanchion without comment.

The brothel vessel bumped up on the tavern's port side. There were three men aboard her, all of them husky and sharing facial features with one of the women. They kept a flat-eyed silence as they lashed their barge to Tiglath's.

"We'll make better time separate, Tiglath," Bantrus said as the black-bearded man sauntered forward.

"We're not in such a hurry, I think," Tiglath said. "Klestis isn't going anywhere, and the prince isn't going to chase us down, is he? I thought I'd get a better look at the visitors the Gods have sent us."

He reached out, giving every indication of planning to chuck Sharina under the chin. She jerked away, angered but not surprised. She'd met Tiglath's sort before, among the guards and badgers at the Sheep Fair. The wealthy drovers and traders were generally more sophisticated, if not necessarily different at heart.

"I'm Sharina os-Reise," she said in a ringing voice. "I'm a traveler, not the messenger of any God."

Dalar stepped between her and Tiglath. His weights hung from short lengths of chain, but he wasn't spinning them.

"And this is my friend Dalar," Sharina continued smoothly. "Also a traveler."

"I am honored that Sharina calls me her friend," said the bird. "But I am her champion as well, Master Tiglath. Her bodyguard."

Tiglath put his hands on his hips, leaned backward, and laughed even louder than before. "My, such a pretty lady deserves something better for her body than it be guarded by a walking feather duster!" he said. "But I'm impressed. I had a crow that talked, but he wasn't near as good as you."

Sharina gripped a backstay overhead for support, then flipped herself lithely to the other side of the deck. Her feet didn't touch the chest-high rank of cargo. Dalar dipped his head twice in Tiglath's direction—the gesture looked like a human's nod, but Sharina suspected there was more to it than that. He somersaulted over the cargo without the help of his hands.

Tiglath glanced at them. His expression was blended of surprise and anger.

"Look, Tiglath," said Bantrus. "If you've got something to say, say it and cast off. We've got enough facing us without you making trouble."

"Now, that's just what I wanted to talk to you about, boy," the black-bearded man said. He swaggered forward, forcing Bantrus to retreat if he wanted to avoid contact. Jem was trying to back his friend, but Jem's three brothers were in a tight group in the *Tailwind*'s stern. "Who is it died and made you Commodore of the Boats, hey? I think it's time we decide just who's in charge of this show now that we're on our own."

"My money's on you, Tiglath!" a brothel crewman said. He slammed a knotted cudgel into the palm of his other hand. "My money and this!"

"Are you crazy, Tiglath?" Bantrus said. "Save your fighting for Prince Mykon!"

Tiglath extended his left index finger and jabbed Bantrus in the center of the chest. "Now there you go, little fella," Tiglath said. "Calling people crazy just because they don't believe you're God. Now, *I* said that I'm the leader. If you think something else, then you can fight me. Is that clear enough?"

"I am not one of the Gods either, Master Tiglath," Dalar said. He hopped to the ridge of cargo, landing with delicate precision on a five-bushel storage jar which was in turn packed with finer ware. "Nor do I wish to lead your heroic band. But I will fight you, if you feel the need to fight."

Tiglath glared at the bird with a molten expression. Dalar began to spin his weights, moving his stubby arms alternately and letting out another hand's breadth of chain with each shimmering circuit.

"This isn't any business of yours!" Bantrus cried in startled irritation.

Sharina looked from Dalar to Tiglath. *Oh, yes, I know the type,* she thought. Aloud, facing Bantrus, she said, "Yes, it is—because Dalar is my bodyguard. I have a notion of where Master Tiglath believes my place in the new order would be."

"You've got that right, little lady!" Tiglath brayed. Sharina's comment had probably decided him to go ahead openly with what she was sure would be his certain intention whether he admitted it or not.

"Boss, those spinners . . ." warned one of Tiglath's crewmen.

Tiglath spread his arms wide, his empty palms turned up. "Sure, I'll fight you, bird," he said. He jerked his thumb toward his own vessel. "Bare hands, and on the *Horn of Plenty*. The awning'll keep the sun out of our eyes."

The awning would prevent Dalar from making his splendid vertical leaps. Sharina's face didn't change, but her eyes flicked across the tavern boat, absorbing its features. She'd expected the fight to take place on land. . . .

"Otherwise," Tiglath added with the smile of a man about to start carving dinner, "you can fight us all. Right, boys?"

The crewmen—Tiglath's and the men from the brothel—cheered or snarled, depending on their individual temperament. All of them held clubs or tools that could be used as clubs. The Pewle knife concealed beneath Sharina's cape dragged at her, demanding to be drawn.

No. Not yet.

"Yes, I accept your terms," Dalar said equably. He snatched the spinning weights into his palms, brought his hands together, and tossed the weapon in a coil to Sharina without seeming to look in her direction.

She caught it left-handed; the chain clinked faintly as she closed her fingers around the bundle. The ruddy bronze was heavier than she'd subconsciously expected.

"Wix, Twenus!" Jem called desperately to his brothers. "Talla! We can't let this happen!"

"Jem, you've done enough last night and today," the eldest said. "Done too much, I'm beginning to think, you and Mistress Brasca's boy. Now shut up and come here with us!"

Dalar pointed to the men backing Tiglath. "Only ourselves on the *Horn of Plenty*. That is correct?"

"Yeah, get back aboard the *Sweet Goddess*," Tiglath said with a careless gesture. He gave Jem's brothers a hard look. "And you lot stay this side of my gunwale, too, you hear? Although if clever-pants here—"

He prodded at Bantrus again. The youth jumped back in time to avoid the probing finger.

"—wants to join in, I wouldn't mind taking care of him at the same time. Of course, then we'll have to decide which of 'em we want to stew for dinner, won't we, boys?"

Sharina sidled toward the bow of the *Tailwind*. Bantrus was alone amidships; Jem had gone to the stern with his brothers, as they'd demanded. Bantrus saw Sharina move. He might have joined her but her cold glare fixed him in place, even more miserable than before.

The laughing crewmen backed onto the brothel. Diccon paused to hook a wineskin out of the low deckhouse near the stern.

Tiglath jumped to the center of the *Horn of Plenty* and flexed his muscles again. He was a large man by the standards of the Boats and would rate as a strong man anywhere. "Coming, bird?" he shouted. Dalar was half his weight, or less.

Dalar hopped to the *Horn of Plenty*'s gunwale and wobbled there like a mockingbird on a twig. He thrust his short arms behind him like balance poles. Tiglath roared and swung right-handed at the bird's lower abdomen while his left arm guarded his face against a beak thrust.

Dalar kicked Tiglath's fist, twisting the bully sunwise and flinging his arm up into the awning. Blood spotted the canvas.

Dalar stepped down lightly from the ankle-high railing. He raised his beak and caroled a fluting cry like nothing Sharina had heard from him before. There was blood on his claws.

Tiglath backed and circled, crouching slightly now. He touched his right hand with his left, probing gently for broken bones. He was an experienced fighter and no coward; this wasn't the first time he'd been hurt in a brawl. His fingers dripped on the decking, but the number of small blood vessels in the hands meant a wound there was going to look bad no matter what.

"Now I *will* eat your liver!" Tiglath said, spreading his

fingers to grasp. He lunged with his arms stretched forward
to protect his face.

Dalar kicked flat-footed from the deck. His legs were
longer than Tiglath's arms. The main claw whacked Tiglath's forehead so hard that the bully turned a backward
somersault. His beard flared into a black ruff as blood
sprayed from the gash at his hairline.

Dalar hooted musically again. His arms were folded
across his chest; he'd been so sure of his timing that he
hadn't bothered spreading them to fend off Tiglath's
clutching hands.

The bird pranced, taking tiny steps, then kicking high.
His physical display was even more insulting than his calls.
The men aboard the *Tailwind* were cheering while those
on the brothel had fallen silent. Diccon kneaded the wineskin like a throat, unaware of the liquid spurting onto his
tunic.

Tiglath got his arms under him and raised his face from
the deck. Blood from his scalp blinded one eye and
gummed his beard.

"Do you yield, Champion of the *Horn of Plenty*?" Dalar
shrilled. "Do you yield to my master Sharina os-Reise?"

"By the Sister I do n—" Tiglath said in a voice clotted
with rage. He lurched into a kneeling position.

Dalar kicked him in the face. Bones crunched. Tiglath's
torso hit the mast and bounced forward again, leaving the
bully doubled over as though taking a seated bow.

Diccon let out an inarticulate cry and sprang onto the
Horn of Plenty, grappling with Dalar from behind. The bird
bent at the waist with acrobatic suddenness, flipping Diccon over his back. The thug hit the deck face-first.

"Dalar!" Sharina shouted as her hands came out from
beneath her cloak swinging the Pewle knife. The bird
leaped to the *Tailwind* with the grace of a curvetting swallow.

The men from the brothel and the two remaining members of Tiglath's crew jumped aboard the *Horn of Plenty*.

Their man had lost the duel; they intended to win the brawl that followed.

Sharina's heavy blade sheared the post and both stays supporting the bow end of the awning. Falling ropes, canvas, and the brails that stiffened the fabric netted Tiglath's followers like so many fish in a weir.

Dalar, hooting and crowing like a whole chorus of cockerels, hopped back aboard the tavern barge. Every time a man tried to rise, the bird sprang onto the hump in the canvas. For some seconds his clawed feet danced swiftly; then the activity beneath the awning subsided to squirming and muted groans.

The women on the *Sweet Goddess* watched in amazement. The one with a family resemblance to the men running the barge began to cackle with high-pitched hilarity.

"Master Dalar!" Bantrus cried. "Master Dalar, stop that! You've won, don't you see?"

Dalar stepped back aboard the *Tailwind* and uncrossed his arms for the first time since the fight—could you call it a fight?—began. Sharina laid the bundle of weights and chain back in her champion's palm.

Dalar bowed to the four brothers around the barge's tiller, then faced Bantrus. "It may be that men understand war differently from my people, young human," he said. "Or it may be that I understand war and you do not."

The bird looked disdainfully toward the shambles aboard the *Horn of Plenty*. A man who'd crawled to the far railing poked his head out from under the canvas. He was anonymous, his features masked by his own blood. He saw Dalar looking and hid himself again.

"If you think that a fight with such bandits is over before they are plucked and hanged by their toes," the bird continued, "so be it. This place is yours; it is not for me to decide."

"He isn't serious, is he?" said one of Jem's brothers. "I don't like to hear things like that even as a joke."

Dalar's head rotated to stare at the man who'd spoken.

The speaker flinched back. Dalar nodded, then faced Bantrus again. The youth looked queasy.

"So be it," the bird repeated. "But my master Sharina and I will not go to battle with you again, because you choose to fight the same battles twice when you need not."

"Let's get the lines loose," Sharina said quietly. The big knife trembled, shimmering with sunlight reflected from the polished blade. She sheathed the weapon carefully, using both hands.

"Yes," Bantrus whispered. He bent and cast off the line before him while Jem did the same for the other. "I think that's a good idea. We'll put you ashore in Klestis."

The barges began to drift apart. Injured men aboard the *Horn of Plenty* were crawling into the light with dazed expressions.

"Young humans?" Dalar said in a tone like that of a trumpet. "I will not tell you your business. But it is my belief that Prince Mykon and your Master Tiglath understand war in the same way as I do; and if you do not, you would be wise not to go to war with either of them."

As a coda, the bird kicked high with his right foot, then his left. The toes of both were bright with blood.

Chapter Nineteen

Please," said Colva, placing her hands in Garric's as she stood with him and Liane beside the River Beltis, "I'm still shivering."

Colva now wore a pair of tunics cut for women—they fell to just above and below midcalf, instead of being knee-length as a man would wear—and a cloak, bought for her from a peddler who'd been lucky not to have his barrow overturned when Waldron's troops charged toward the stables and their prince. The garments were used, but they were of excellent quality and thick. Despite proper clothing and the warm evening, Colva's hands were icy.

Garric shook his hands free. "Tell us who we're facing," he said brusquely. From the corner of his eye he saw Liane relax minutely.

The royal astrologer stood beside the waterclock he and his assistants had erected on the bank, calibrating it with a portable sundial while there was still light enough to throw the gnomon's shadow crisply across the inscribed lines. He saw Garric glance in his direction and called in a self-important voice, "Twelve minutes to full sunset, Your Majesty."

Waldron and his officers were marshaling the available troops on the riverbank both up- and downstream. The bridge was already a shimmer of azure highlights above the water, but it wouldn't become sufficiently solid for ordinary humans to cross until the sun went down. Twelve minutes . . .

Garric had four battalions of the pike-armed phalanx, two battalions of skirmishers with bundles of light javelins, and two more of heavy infantry with swords, short spears, and full armor. He didn't have the faintest notion of whether they'd be enough for the army they'd face when they crossed the bridge.

"You never know, lad," King Carus said with resignation. *"You can plan and hope and pray, but you never know till it's over."*

"They are necromancers, seven of them," Colva said. "They've raised Yole from the sea, but they do their works of real power in Klestis. They captured me after my husband Landure the Guardian entered the Underworld with a stranger named Cashel. I think they intended me for a blood sacrifice."

"Cashel's all right?" Garric blurted. He'd had no idea that Colva would have met his friend.

"Nothing in the Underworld can harm Landure the Guardian," Colva said with an odd smile. "They know that by now. They may try to escape past Landure to the waking world, your world, but few manage even that."

Garric grimaced. Apparently Landure had left his wife unprotected to go off with Cashel. That wouldn't have happened except that Garric had allowed his sister to be snatched away from his presence.

Liane touched the back of Garric's hand, just for the contact. He wished that Tenoctris were here so that she could tell him what was waiting on the other side of the bridge; but in his heart of hearts, he knew he'd rather have Liane's presence than Tenoctris' knowledge. He grinned wryly at the realization.

"The necromancers have an army of the dead," Colva continued. "Eventually they will have an army of all the dead of all times. Perhaps that's why they wanted your friend: to sacrifice a wizard for even greater power than they'd gain from a child, say, or from me."

"Eight minutes, Your Majesty!" the astrologer called. The bridge already had form, though it tended to blur into cloudy evanescence.

Garric wondered what would happen to a man who was standing on the structure of wizard-light when it vanished. He'd fall, certainly; but Garric suspected the victim would drown in something worse than the muddy waters of the Beltis.

"You're so brave to attack them, Prince Garric," Colva said. Her black eyes met Garric's with a molten intensity. "When I saw you fight the ice beetle, I knew there'd never been a hero like you."

"Don't say that!" Garric said, more harshly than the comment justified. The woman's flattering nonsense was understandable in someone whose life had been saved, after all.

The trouble was that although Garric knew the words were nonsense, it warmed him to hear Colva say them. He didn't need Carus glaring in his mind, nor the sudden hardness around Liane's eyes, to warn him how dangerous it would be to like flattery.

Lord Waldron strode over to Garric. Half a dozen aides followed like a swirl of dry leaves. Attaper saw Waldron coming and approached from where he'd been waiting ten feet away with the 170 Blood Eagles fit for duty.

"The army is ready for your command, Your Majesty," Waldron said with hard-lipped precision.

"Four minutes, Your Majesty!" called the astrologer as another of the water clock's bowls filled and overturned.

Garric looked past his officers to the ranks of soldiers. The uplifted pikes stood like groves of twenty-foot saplings planted as far as eye could see, up and down the water-front. The men's faces were bleak and frightened.

Garric grimaced, bitterly aware of his own fears. *Afraid of failing Tenoctris and the kingdom. Afraid of what'll happen to Liane and everybody who depends on me* if *I fail.*

"I don't know how many will refuse to advance," said an aide, a blond young man with fine features and enough wealth that his armor was gilded. He shook his head. "They're afraid of wizardry."

"By the Lady, they took an oath!" Waldron said. "A soldier who isn't afraid is a fool, but they'll follow orders regardless—or they'll stay here decorating gibbets! I swear it on my honor!"

"They'll obey," Colva said with her odd, *expectant*, smile. "They'll follow Prince Garric. Everyone in the army's heard how he fought the ice beetle alone."

Attaper nodded. "She's right, Waldron," he said. "If Garric leads, they'll follow."

"We put plowmen and shopclerks in our phalanx, lad," Carus said. Memories of a score of battles seen through the king's eyes, against men and things not men, cascaded through Garric's mind. *"They'll follow you to Hell, because you said they were as worthy to defend the kingdom as nobles like Waldron. And the other battalions of landholders and the noblemen's retainers—they'll follow too, because they're afraid of being shown up as cowards by plowmen and shopclerks."*

Garric laughed, looser than he'd been since he'd stumbled back from the ice world and realized what he'd have to do to rescue Tenoctris. "Then it's easy enough, isn't it?" he said. "Because I'm surely going to lead."

"One minute, Your Majesty!"

Though the bridge of stone and timber had washed away centuries before, the abutments still remained. Garric grinned at his closest companions and jumped atop a waist-high buttress. Everyone in the army could see him even if they couldn't hear his voice. Blue wizard-light, grown firm and steady as the color died out of the sky, lit his features from the left and silhouetted him to the troops on his right.

"Men of the Isles!" Garric shouted. He drew his sword and waved it like a banner. "Fellow soldiers! Our kingdom, our families, and our honor lie across this bridge of light. Follow me!"

"Sunset!" cried the astrologer. Garric saw the man's lips move, but his voice was inaudible against the approval bellowing from the throats of eight thousand soldiers.

Garric jumped onto the structure of light. It was as solid as granite. Platoons of Blood Eagles double-timed past him to either side, shouting, "Garric and the Isles!"

Liane was at his side; Garric grinned at her. He hadn't even bothered to tell her not to come. They both knew there was danger on the other side of the bridge, but there was no safety anywhere in the Isles if this attempt failed.

He glanced over his shoulder. The regular army was behind him with a battalion of the phalanx in the lead. The front rank saw Garric's glance and cheered.

Colva was coming also, a step behind Garric and Liane. She smiled. Garric turned from her expression, blinking. He couldn't read the emotions on the woman's face.

The towers of Klestis gleamed in the distance. Garric raised his sword again and swept it forward.

Klestis and what waited there was enough to worry about for now.

* * *

Cashel recognized the cliff. He guessed he ought to, since he'd seen it in Valles and then at the entrance to each of the Underworld's two previous levels. This time a boulder had been rolled across the mouth of the cave in place of a proper gate.

"Is this the last one, Master Krias?" he asked, leaning on his staff as he eyed the situation. The stone would take a bit of effort, but nothing he couldn't handle.

"I told you it was!" the ring said. "Do you want me to tell you there's three more layers now? Or is the problem that you can't count to three?"

Cashel smiled. He could hear Elfin singing somewhere in the forest, close enough that you could just about make out the words. The youth seemed to be moving nearer each night since Cashel killed the King of the Forest.

"I can count to three," Cashel said. He leaned his quarterstaff against the bluff and let his hands explore the boulder. Touch would find them a better grip than his eyes would.

"I can move that," Krias said. He sounded hopeful.

"That's all right, Master Krias," Cashel said. He settled his left buttock against the face of the bluff to brace him, then leaned into the boulder.

It didn't come at once, but he hadn't expected it to: a stone so large would've dented a nest for itself into the ground. Cashel felt his face flush and the ligaments stand out on his neck.

"I don't know why you even bothered to bring me—" said Krias; and as the demon spoke, the boulder started to roll. Once Cashel had broken the soil's grip, it was no more effort than rolling an egg. He walked it two short paces to the side, gasping for breath.

He rubbed the ring affectionately. "I brought you for the company, Master Krias," he said, "and for what you know. But I also remember it was you that saved me from Elfin's folk."

Cashel brushed his palms together, then got off the last of the grit on the breast of his tunic. He picked up his staff, twirled it once, and stepped into a world of cold, purple light.

"They weren't his folk," the ring said in a pleased mutter. "They just kept him for a pet, though he didn't have sense enough to see it. Still doesn't, *I'll* bet."

Cashel started down a slope that had become as familiar as the bluff itself. There weren't any trees this time. There was no vegetation at all; things that Cashel thought at first were plants always turned out to be lumps of rock. Even what looked like vines snaking across the landscape were really veins of crystal.

There wasn't a watercourse at the base of the cliffs on this level of the Underworld. An undulating plain, broken only by outcrops, stretched for as far as Cashel could see into the purple distance. He wasn't hungry, but . . .

"Is there anything to drink down here, Master Krias?" he asked. "Ah, that's safe to drink, I mean. For me."

"There's water," the demon said. "The water of life itself, sheep-boy; water that will cure your ills and make you immortal if you bathe in it every day. But first you have to reach the fountain, and I doubt you'll be able to do that."

"I'd settle for plain water," Cashel said as he started off with his staff over his right shoulder. "But I'll take what I get, I guess."

To tell the truth, Cashel would a lot rather have plain water. If Krias said this "water of life" wouldn't hurt him, then it wouldn't; but though the fruit from Tian hadn't hurt him either, he could've done without the dreams he'd had that night.

The good thing about the empty landscape was that Cashel didn't have to pick his way through undergrowth and around trees like in the woods of the upper levels. He felt cold, though; cold enough that he sort of expected to see his breath when he opened his mouth and puffed out. He didn't, though.

"Does anybody live here, Master Krias?" Cashel asked as he surveyed the bleakness again. He hadn't seen any animals either, though that might be just as well.

"Colva lived here, sheep-boy," Krias said. "Before you let her loose, I mean."

"Ah," said Cashel, nodding. He hadn't exactly let Colva loose, but it was his fault she stayed loose. He wasn't going to quibble about words when the truth at the bottom of them was that he'd made a bad mistake.

There was somebody ahead of him. A couple of shaggy-looking fellows at a campfire.

They stood up slowly, laughing from deep in their chests. Cashel could feel the ground quiver. The strangers weren't right over the slight rise he was climbing. They were farther away than he could fling a stone.

Which meant they were as tall as trees. The clubs they carried *were* trees.

One of the giants took a bite out of the human leg in his left hand; it looked no bigger than a pigeon drumstick. Juices dribbled down his bushy beard.

"Well, brother," the other giant said, "more dinner's coming before we've even finished what we had."

Cashel continued walking onward. His first thought was to bring his quarterstaff down across his body, but he didn't like to act hostile till he was sure there was need. He'd have plenty of time for that if things went on the way they looked they were going to.

Also he wasn't sure how much good the staff was going to be.

"Master Krias?" he asked. "What do you think I ought to do now?"

Even as Cashel spoke, he braced himself for Krias to give him a smart answer instead of a real answer. To his surprise, the ring demon said, "Since they're illusions, sheep-boy, what you ought to do is ignore them. Do you think you can do that?"

As if repenting the fact he'd spoken clearly, Krias added, "Using 'think' loosely, of course!"

Cashel chuckled. "Ignore them?" he said. "Sure. That's a *lot* easier than what I had in mind."

"We'll play bowls with his skull, brother," said the giant who'd spoken before. "After I've sucked his brains out, I mean."

The other giant stripped the calf muscle off the leg he was holding and tossed the limb away. Tendons still articulated the bones. "Say!" he said. "You got the brains of the last one!"

Their voices were like nearby thunder. Though . . . if the giants weren't real, then Cashel guessed their voices weren't real either. But maybe that didn't follow in this place.

"How far is it to the water, Master Krias?" he asked. He was walking right between the two giants. They stunk awful. It was as bad as the summer Old Todler hung himself and nobody thought to look in his hut for three days. "A lifetime if you flinch, sheep-boy!"

Todler hadn't been much for baths even when he was alive, either.

"Oh," Cashel said aloud. "It isn't that bad."

One of the giants slammed the head of his club straight down in front of Cashel. It'd been a pine bole, though use had worn away half the scaly bark.

Cashel walked through it. He didn't feel anything at all, though for a moment he couldn't see. Then he was past and the giants had vanished, leaving him and Krias alone in the rocky wasteland.

"Will there be more of them, Master Krias?" he said.

The jewel in the ring sparkled brighter for a moment. The light down here brought the sapphire's color out better than the sun had back above ground.

"There might," said Krias. "I doubt it, though. You've passed the test, after all."

"Ah," said Cashel, nodding. "That was a test?"

"They're all tests, sheep-boy!" the demon said. "Do you think just anybody can visit Landure's castle?"

"I didn't think about it one way or the other," Cashel said truthfully. He thought he saw something on the far horizon. It might be a tree, which would be a nice change; but he didn't want to get his hopes up.

"Weren't you afraid?" Krias said unexpectedly.

Cashel shrugged. "You said they weren't real," he replied. "I guess I'd have been afraid if I thought they were real."

Cashel wasn't sure that was true, but he didn't want to sound like he was bragging. He'd been scared often enough, but it had always been for what might happen to somebody else—usually one of his sheep. He guessed he figured that he could handle most anything he ran into. And so far, at least, that'd been true.

"If you'd flinched, they *would* have been real," Krias said. "I didn't know what would happen if I'd told you that before we were past them."

Cashel laughed. "Well, I wasn't going to flinch, Master Krias," he said. "Whether they were going to eat me or not."

He thought about the situation for a moment and added in a sober tone, "Look, I'm not the brightest fellow around, and I don't even mean compared to Garric or Tenoctris. But I don't run away, Master Krias. I've never done that."

"No," said the ring demon in a voice Cashel didn't remember him using before, "I haven't seen any evidence that you would."

Krias made a metallic sound that seemed to be the way he cleared his throat. He said, "The Fountain of Life is right there ahead of us. You'll be able to eat and drink."

That really was a tree, then, growing on a little island in a pond. The branches were heavy with fruit, but it was fruit of all different sorts. Cashel had thought it was another illusion like the giants, though least it was something he liked to look at.

"How long will it take us to get to Landure's palace?" Cashel asked. As best as he could see, the landscape on the other side of this little oasis was pretty much the same as what he'd crossed to get here. "I mean, if everything goes all right."

"It's gone all right thus far, hasn't it, sheep-boy?" Krias snapped. "At least it has since you decided that killing Landure the Guardian wasn't such a great idea after all."

Cashel didn't say anything. The little demon had as many moods as a ewe in the springtime.

Last week a lady in the palace had gushed to him about how placid sheep were. Cashel could only shake his head about how little some people knew.

"You should get there by midday tomorrow," Krias said as Cashel approached the oasis. "That's if you get up with the light and walk the way you've done in the past. If you hurry, you could get there even sooner."

Ankle-high vegetation covered the margins of the pond. Soft leaves caressed Cashel's feet; he squatted to look more closely. No two of the little plants were the same, and many looked like miniature versions of shrubs and trees.

He stood, wriggling his toes. It felt good. "Is there some reason we need to hurry special, Master Krias?" he asked.

"Not that *I* know of, sheep-boy," Krias said in a sneering voice. "But I thought you wanted to find your beloved Sharina?"

"I do," Cashel said, walking forward. "Thing is, I get along better by going steady than I do by rushing. And I break a whole lot less."

He prodded his staff into the pond to judge the depth. The bottom was firm. If it sloped at the rate it started out, the water wouldn't more than come up to his waist at the middle.

Cashel stepped in, keeping his staff slanted out in front of him. There was no point in taking chances of a sudden drop-off, after all. The water wasn't hot or cold either one, but it made him tingle.

The bottom rose just the same as it'd gone down, gentle and not even quite as deep as he'd figured. The island was covered with the same sort of vegetation as the pond's outer margin had been: real plants, but as soft and delicate as moss.

When Cashel lifted his foot, the foliage popped right up

as well. He'd thought that he must be crushing the soft leaves flat, but you couldn't even tell where he'd been walking.

"The other possibility that you might want to consider . . ." Krias said. There was a lot of intensity in the demon's voice, but no anger for a wonder. "Is that you might want to stay here."

Cashel laughed. "Oh, I wouldn't want to do that," he said.

"You don't think so?" Krias said. "Look at your staff, sheep-boy!"

Cashel blinked. "Wow!" he said.

There was nothing in the world Cashel knew better than he did his quarterstaff. He'd felled a huge hickory tree for a farmer, taking one arrow-straight branch as his pay. He'd trimmed the branch down using first an axe, then a curved block with sand held in grease to smooth the wood better than a blade could; and finally he'd finished the job with wads of raw wool rich in lanolin, passing over and over the close-grained wood until the surface was as smooth as a stream-turned pebble.

The end that Cashel had dipped in the pond was sprouting leaves around the iron ferrule. Another unfolded as he watched, the bright green of new growth and bigger than you'd get on a mature tree.

"Is it going to keep on doing that?" Cashel asked. The staff wouldn't be much use if it did. How could he spin it if instead of bare wood he was swishing a leafy branch through the air?

"It'll shrink back to what it was unless you dip it in the Fountain of Life every day," the ring said. "But you could, you know. You could stay here forever, living on the fruit and bathing yourself in the water every day."

Mention of fruit reminded Cashel of how hungry he was. The tree's branches were so laden that they hung down to the ground like the fronds of a weeping willow. The foliage was more like a cherry's pointy ovals than the slender leaves were of a willow, though.

He plucked something that looked like an apple, though it was hard to tell with everything being colored by the indigo light. There were all sorts of hanging fruit, some of it as big as melons, and no two alike that he could tell.

"This is all right to eat, then, Master Krias?" Cashel asked. He remembered what the ring demon had said, but when there were way more different kinds than he could count without a tally stick, well, he didn't want Krias crowing that the one Cashel had just swallowed would make him turn black and bust.

Although . . . Krias hadn't ever tried to trick Cashel into anything that was really going to hurt him. The demon had a tongue on him, that he did; but so did Ilna, and Ilna wouldn't have let anybody, not even Uncle Katchin, drown from his own stupidity.

"All *right*?" Krias said. "It's not 'all right,' sheep-boy, it's food fit for the Gods! It's better than the best thing you've ever eaten—and better than anything you'll ever eat again if you're fool enough to leave here."

Cashel bit down. It was like—well, it was nothing he could describe as a flavor. It was more like morning on a sun-swept meadow, the air clean and everything more perfect than it could ever be in life.

"I see," Cashel said. He didn't remember swallowing, but his mouth was empty except for the tingle. He took another bite. The fruit didn't have a core like an apple, and there weren't seeds in the flesh either.

He ate the fruit down to the stem by which he'd plucked it. Every bite was just as wonderful as the first. It didn't have an aftertaste, but it left him with a general memory of wonderfulness.

"You could eat the fruit every day," the demon said. "You'd live forever, just from that. One of these fruits would bring life back to a dead man!"

Cashel shook his head. The demon seemed to be serious about him staying in this place. He supposed he could get used to the funny light, but it was such a silly notion.

"What would I do here, Master Krias?" Cashel said.

"There aren't any sheep to watch, are there? And even if there was, I need to find Sharina. Not that I think that she isn't fine wherever she is, but . . ."

He stopped talking. He'd already said more than he liked to. Cashel had never been one to talk about the way he felt, and he didn't guess the vinegar-tongued demon would be the one he'd choose to unburden himself to anyhow.

"You could live forever, sheep-boy," Krias said. His voice buzzed, but it didn't have quite the usual edge.

"But *why*?" Cashel said in honest wonder. He took another fruit, this time one that looked more like an eggplant than anything he'd seen on a tree before. "I mean, living forever's all right for you, but I'm just a shepherd."

"Do you think it's all right for me, Cashel or-Kenset?" the ring demon said. "But I see what you mean: this island isn't greatly different from the jewel that holds me. We'll spend the night here and then revive Landure."

Cashel bit into the second fruit. The flavor differed from the first—this tasted like a summer evening just after the stars appeared in the west, with a soft breeze and the sheep murmuring in the fold—but it was equally wonderful.

"But take one of the fruits in your wallet, sheep-boy," Krias said in a voice like a bee crossing a meadow. "It'll keep for a time. Time matters to you, after all. And life too, you'll find."

Ilna's feet had felt the pulse of water racing through a channel for some while. Closer on she heard the stream as well, but the roar that met her and her companions when they stepped into the domed chamber was a surprise even so.

The air was as wet as that of a meadow after an evening storm, and condensate gave the walls a glassy sheen. A chasm split the chamber; on this side the rock floor was no more than a few spans wide, scarcely a ledge compared to the canyon beyond. She couldn't see across. Clouds of chill mist filtered and muted the light coming from the abyss.

A cable as thick as a man's torso crossed the chasm— or at any rate vanished into the mist, sagging slightly. This end was attached to the rock face by some means that Ilna couldn't see from where she stood.

A man, tall and very thin despite the hooded cape that covered all but his face, waited at the head of the cable.

"Good day, my friend," said Chalcus as he stepped out, bowing deeply. He flourished his left arm forward and his right behind him, managing to make the gesture courtly despite the sword still bare in his right hand.

The chanteyman walked on, keeping the blade down at his side to suggest it was simply too much effort to sheathe it. "My name is Chalcus and I'm a stranger here. May I ask your name?"

"I am Harn," said the tall man—very tall, now that Chalcus had come close enough to provide scale. "Do you wish to use my bridge?"

Harn's voice seemed thin, but it penetrated the roar of the torrent even better than the chanteyman's practiced tenor did. Penetrated—and rasped on Ilna's mind like the scrape of slate on slate.

"I don't like him," Merota said quietly.

Ilna had one arm around the girl's shoulders and the noose ready in her other hand. "Nor do I, child," she said. "But then, I don't like very many people, so perhaps you should ignore my opinion."

"We'd indeed like to use your bridge, Master Harn," said Chalcus as he stepped very slightly closer to the bridgeman. "We'd be much beholden to you."

"You will not be beholden," Harn said. "You will pay me and cross; or you will not cross."

Ilna stepped forward. She tried to ease Merota behind her, but the girl stayed at her side.

"Where does your bridge go?" Ilna demanded. She was starting to feel a pattern, as though the passage they'd followed was one strand and that just ahead was a joining beyond even her skill to fully comprehend.

"My bridge takes you to wherever you wish to go," Harn said. With his arms crossed beneath his cape he looked more like a draped post than he did a man. "There is no other way to go than by my bridge or back by the way you came; but you must pay me."

The floor on which they stood was a niche, though a considerable one. Within a bowshot to either side the chamber's walls closed over the chasm. There was no path skirting the abyss for Ilna and her companions to follow, and no imaginable way to cross the torrent thundering in the depths even if the two females could have climbed down the cliff.

"Why, we're all three honest folk, Master Harn," Chalcus said cheerfully, "even those of us who might have been something else in the past. What would your price be for us to use your fine bridge?"

"There are three of you," said Harn. "One will be mine as the toll for passing the other two to their desire."

Ilna smiled faintly. It was always good to know where matters stood. She felt Merota stiffen beside her, but the girl didn't whimper.

"That's a high price indeed," said the chanteyman, "but I'll offer you even a greater one, Master Harn. My friends and I will cross your bridge, and for payment I'll leave your head—"

His curved blade sang as it flickered a finger's breadth short of Harn's shadowed face.

"—on those narrow shoulders of yours."

Harn leaped—not toward Chalcus, certain death on the sword's point as the chanteyman drew his dagger with his left hand—but sideways. He scuttled to the chamber's curving wall and turned to watch them. With the light from the abyss no longer silhouetting Harn, his face was triangular and less than human.

"Go!" Chalcus said to Ilna, a snarled command that the circumstances justified. He stood between Harn and the women: swordblade slanting down and dagger point up.

The cable appeared to be glued or even melted onto the cliff face. "Hold the back of my sash, Merota," Ilna said as she stepped onto it. "And *don't* look down."

The cable beneath Ilna's bare feet was silk: numberless gossamer strands had been braided into a hawser that would support the weight of a city. Though firm as the rock and even stronger, it thrummed with suppressed energy.

Ilna strode on, unconcerned for herself. She was used to crossing streams on fallen trees or stepping-stones polished by generations of use.

She glanced over her shoulder. Merota met her eyes with a calm, trusting stare.

Ilna smiled approval. "We're well clear, Master Chalcus!" she called to the chanteyman poised at the head of the cable, his back to the chasm.

Harn flung his cape to the ground. He—*it*—had eight slender, multijointed legs. It scrambled up the sheer rock like a spider on a stone wall.

Ilna continued walking at the same measured pace. She heard Harn's chittering despite the boom of the torrent below. Harn reached the arched ceiling and continued across it, clinging to the smooth rock.

Chalcus was on the rope, staying far enough back that he wouldn't crowd Merota. His face was turned upward, and Ilna thought she heard a snatch of something he was singing.

The light came from so far below that it was a milky blur even when Ilna looked down into the abyss. Cold spray soaked her garments. She laughed.

Cocking her head back to meet Merota's eyes, she said, "Our luck's changed, child. We'll drink well when we get to the other side."

The girl managed a smile, but drops of more than condensate were running down her cheeks. Ilna felt a sudden rush of affection.

Courage doesn't mean you're not afraid. Courage means you go on anyway.

"And yet you will pay me, humans," Harn called from the rock high above. Its body was long and slender like that of a dragonfly, and its hindmost pair of limbs were working a billowy *something* from the tip of its abdomen. "You will pay, as all pay who cross!"

The silken cable had began to slant upward by the same slight degree it had sagged when they started across. Ilna saw hard angles before her. The start of the bridge had long vanished in the mist, but they were nearing the far terminus at last.

"Ilna!" Chalcus cried. "It's a net!"

Ilna looked up. Harn's bundle quivered down like a flung stone, then snapped open at a twitch of the line still attached to the creature's abdomen. *Not a net but a web, fluttering toward Merota.*

Ilna twisted, leaning so that her body covered the child. Chalcus was running toward them, but she knew as the silk settled onto her that the sword's keen edge would be useless against this gummy fabric.

"Don't try to cut it!" she shouted. She expected Chalcus to ignore her and tangle his blade hopelessly in silk both sticky and too light to cut except under tension.

He didn't, for a wonder. Chalcus *listened* to her, and that was almost enough to make Ilna believe in the Gods in these last moments of her life!

Merota hadn't moved. She was singing a child's prayer for bedtime, her hands still gripping Ilna's sash. Harn clicked and giggled above, but the creature hadn't yet put strain on its net because that might permit a blade as sharp as the chanteyman's to shear it through.

As Chalcus poised with his sword raised and his face stark with fury, Ilna gave a flick of her wrist to wrap her own noose about the cable. She caught the loop end in her other hand. She could still move within close limits.

"Let go of me, Merota!" Ilna said, wondering if the girl would obey the order. *If she doesn't, she'll die. Death is the way of the world.* "Now, close your eyes and run for the far side!"

Ilna hurled herself off the cable, carrying Harn's web with her.

She heard the creature shriek like a cicada, but it loosed the loop of silk it held in its hind legs. The reserve of line was long enough that Ilna's doubled noose rather than the net took the weight of her falling body.

"Ilna! Ilna! Ilna!" Merota cried as she scampered across the last twenty feet of the bridge like a squirrel on a twig. Safe! Chalcus would see to the future. . . .

Only if Ilna let go of the noose could Chalcus cut Harn's line. Her plunge into the abyss would keep her out of the creature's belly—or worse.

"Hold on or may the gulls eat your eyeballs!" Chalcus said. As Merota reached the far ledge, he knelt and drove his dagger into the bridge cable at a slant. What was he—

Ilna laughed with the delight of a craftsman learning a trick from an equal craftsman. The dagger would be Chalcus' handgrip if the cable broke.

He brought the sword down behind him in a slashing blow. The cable was strong beyond the imagining of anyone but Ilna and Harn itself, but it was soft nonetheless. The steel edge cut a hand's breadth deep. The strands' own tension pulled them apart when severed, making a broad V across the surface to direct the chanteyman's second draw-cut.

Which was perfectly placed and as powerful as the first. *Of course!*

Harn was screaming, but Ilna had no time for the creature. She twisted her hands to loop her noose around her wrists. If her fingers lost their grip, the cord would still support her for the few moments she'd need to recover. Normally Ilna didn't doubt her strength, but the test facing her in a moment—

The sword flashed down. Ilna had expected six or more cuts, but she hadn't reckoned with the chanteyman's strength.

Silk sheared; the few remaining strands stretched and began to snap. A wisp of silk is lighter than the breeze, but these wisps had been spun into a hawser so thick and long that both Uncle Katchin's millstones together had nothing like its weight.

Chalcus sheathed his blade with a cry of triumph, then wrapped his legs and right arm around the cable. The chanteyman's left hand held the dagger hilt in a grip that death couldn't break.

The last threads gave way. The bridge's greater length sprang backward toward the side from which Ilna and her companions had come. The short end, four or five times a man's height, swung toward the cliff.

Harn had spun enough slack to keep Ilna's leap into space from freeing her, but this sudden additional drop was beyond his capacity. She felt the net grab around her head and torso, clinging by the strength of the adhesive and trying to lift her away from the cable.

Ilna held and the bridge fragment continued to swing down. She expected Harn to release its end of the net. The creature couldn't do that because the silk was a part of its body beyond easy separation.

Harn jerked away from the ceiling to hurtle down in a long arc toward the stone wall.

Ilna tried to keep her feet in front of her to take the shock, but the silk cable was twisting as it shrank under the release of tension. She hit the stone sideways, a stunning blow but not quite enough to jerk her fingers loose. Her looped cord and Chalcus' support—the chanteyman behind her must have landed like a bird—were insurance that she didn't need.

Harn, the end player in a monstrous game of Crack the Whip, snapped into the cliff face and shattered like a crab dropped from a height. Its muscles spasmed, then relaxed; now at last the creature's abdominal sphincter released the silk that held it.

Harn dropped into the mists. Its jerking form was visible

longer than Ilna would have believed possible; but even so, it finally vanished.

"Can you climb, Ilna?" Chalcus said. "Shall I carry you?"

"I can climb," Ilna said. Because she'd spoken, she wrapped her legs around the thick cable and started to creep upward. The net still lay over her like a bath in honey, disgusting if she let herself think about it but actually useful because it helped her cling to the hawser.

She was going to make it to the top; but after she did, she was going to lie down for a very long time.

"Ah, you were magnificent, love!" Chalcus cried from behind her. "I'd never have thought to pull the skinny wretch loose had you not shown me the way."

"I think you're lying," Ilna said, because she was Ilna. But for the same reason she added, "But I'm grateful to you, and anyway, it's a kindly lie."

She touched the edge of the cliff and felt Merota's tiny hands grip her wrist. Chalcus began to sing merrily, *"This night my soul has caught new fire! I felt the Shepherd drawing nigher. . . ."*

"Half stroke!" called Jem from the *Tailwind*'s tiller. His brothers and Bantrus were doubled on the pair of sweeps that the barge used to move in light winds and tight spaces. The stars were hard sparks in the dome of the sky, though the moon hadn't come up as yet.

"Back water!"

The oarsmen rose, pushing instead of pulling on the oarlooms, until the barge grounded easily on the muddy waterfront. It was a warm night. Lamps gleamed from the unshuttered windows of buildings around the harbor, and somewhere in the distance a musician was bowing his fiddle.

Dalar and Sharina stepped ashore. They'd stayed quietly in the vessel's bluff bow since the fight with Tiglath that morning. They were out of the crew's way there; and more important, Bantrus and his friends could pretend their passengers didn't exist. Portions of food were set out for them, but even then there'd been only a few words exchanged.

Dalar stretched by doing splits, right foot forward and then reversing with a kick that seemed scarcely to lift his body off the ground. He stood and bowed to the *Tailwind*'s crew, dark shapes in the starlight.

"Peace is a wonderful thing," the bird said quietly to Sharina. "But a folk so peaceful that even the rebels grow ill to see a bully put down—they would have no business among my people. Nor among yours for long, I fear, Sharina."

Sharina nodded. She was about to walk away when Bantrus left his fellows and came forward.

"Master Bantrus," Sharina called in a voice the others could hear as well. "Thank you and your friends for the hospitality you've shown us. I regret any difficulties that we've caused you."

"That's all right," Bantrus muttered, sounding as though he were deciding the manner of his own execution. He looked at the city and added, "We don't usually travel after dark."

The comment wasn't inconsequential: the other four barges in the small squadron had landed at a creek mouth to shelter some hours before. The *Tailwind*'s crew had held a brief conclave—excluding Bantrus as well as the strangers—and gone on. Quite obviously they wanted to be shut of their passengers more than they minded the risk of traveling in the dark.

"If some money would repay the trouble—" Sharina began.

"No!" cried one of Jem's brothers. "We don't need your money. We have no part of you, nor you of us!"

"Thank you again," Sharina said. She turned and strode off as quickly as she safely could. Dalar walked behind her for the first few steps, then moved to her side when reflex decided Bantrus and his fellows were no longer a threat.

Sharina smiled at the thought of Bantrus *ever* being a threat, but it was a sad smile. Dalar was right: the folk of the Boats deserved better of life than they were likely to receive.

Klestis had a fine natural harbor, but it lacked the quays and paved frontage of Port Hocc. Fishing boats were drawn up on the shore. In a few of them men sat under hanging lamps and mended nets; their quiet conversations paused when they saw a blond woman and a bird the size of a man, but no one called to the strangers. The community beyond was more than a village, but it fell far short of the glittering metropolis which the legends of Sharina's day said Ansalem would rule in a thousand years.

"I did not like ships before I was wrecked on one and blown to this land," Dalar said as they neared the first buildings. "Thus far, greater experience has not make me like them more; but perhaps some God is determined to make me more accepting despite myself."

"I'd like to find a place to sleep," Sharina said. She supposed she should be hungry, but the atmosphere aboard the *Tailwind* had soured her stomach.

The houses were single story with roofs of reed thatching. Klestis didn't have real streets, just passages between buildings which weren't necessarily parallel. Dalar stepped in front of Sharina as they entered an alley that narrowed toward the far end.

"Will your master be able to contact you in this new place?" the bird asked as they picked their way along. He clucked cheerfully. "Not that I would prefer that we'd stayed in Port Hocc, Sharina."

"I don't know," Sharina said. She felt a surge of bleak despair. What if she had to remain here for the rest of her life? Away from Cashel, away from all her friends; away from the time and place she *belonged*.

Sharina didn't doubt that she could survive. The silver in her wallet amounted to a considerable fortune, and she trusted that her wit and willingness to work hard would parlay the capital into support for the rest of her life. She could run an inn, perhaps. But . . .

Aloud she said, "I could live if we had to stay here. But I'm not sure I'd really want to."

"I know what it is to be taken forever from one's home," Dalar said. "But we would go on, as I went on before you hired me."

Sharina smelled the reptilian odor before she saw the square of light in what had been a blank wall when Dalar passed it. "Wait!" she said to her companion.

The Dragon gave her a toothy smile from behind his counter. "Greetings, Sharina os-Reise," he said. "You needn't fear that we'll lose touch. One place is much like another to me."

The lizard-man trilled his laughter. "That was true even when I was alive," he said. "A very long time ago."

"Still, I'm glad to see a familiar face," Sharina said. She smiled faintly and added, "Greetings, master. What do we do next?"

"Your travels on my behalf are almost complete," the Dragon said. "In what passes for the central square in Klestis of this day, you'll find a well with a curb to keep out surface water. The curb is built of ballast from ships which arrived here light and left with full cargoes. One of the blocks should by now be familiar to you. Remove it and crawl through the opening."

Sharina nodded. She glanced to where Dalar waited as silent as the stars. His weights were in his hands.

"Lord Dragon?" Sharina said. "When—*if* I succeed in carrying out my duties to you, can you send my bodyguard Dalar back to his home?"

"When you carry out the last of your duties," the Dragon said, "I will no longer exist."

He gave his inhuman smile. "Which is as it should be, since I've been dead for so many thousands of years. Did you think to add that as a condition for your service?"

"Of course not!" Sharina said. "I pledged my honor."

"And I pledged mine," said the Dragon, "that you and

your friends would gain because you served me. All your friends."

"Ah," said Sharina. The Dragon meant as much by his promises as she—she and her friends—did by theirs. "I'll proceed with the present task, then."

The Dragon didn't speak; his long jaws smiled as his image faded from view. Dalar's head rotated to stare at Sharina.

"There's a well in the plaza," Sharina said. "The stone is part of the wall around it. We take it out and go through, as usual."

The bird strode forward, pausing for Sharina to come to his side when they were past the narrows. Lights from some of the houses set off the ragged open space beyond. It could be used for community meetings, but Sharina suspected that for the most part it pastured flocks driven into Klestis to be sold.

"Dalar, did you hear our discussion?" Sharina said.

The bird cocked his head toward her momentarily. "I heard your words, Sharina," he said. "I do not see or hear your master."

"The Dragon considers it his duty to aid my friends in payment for my service," Sharina explained. "And you're my friend."

"First, of course," Dalar said in sober whimsy, "we must survive. Though I suppose we could be said to have solved our problems ourselves if we do *not* survive."

"I don't consider our deaths to be the result of choice," Sharina said with equal gravity. "But of course, I'm merely a servant and cannot be expected to understand greater truths."

They laughed together in their different fashions. *When I pray to the Lady tonight,* Sharina thought, *one of the things I'll mention is how grateful I am for a companion with a sense of humor.*

The moon had risen above the roofs, giving Sharina a real view of the plaza. The waist-high well curb and stone bases where temporary wooden stands could be erected were the only signs of public construction. A few people sat on benches in front of their homes, watching the strangers silently. Sharina didn't see an inn or even a tavern.

She bent to examine the curb. Klestis must have no quarries of its own if the citizens mortared together pieces of rough stone ballast for their constructions. That made the wonderful city Ansalem ruled—according to legend and the journey Garric had made in dream—even more amazing.

A pale granite slab stood out from its darker neighbors in the moonlight: the other half of the block built into the cistern of Port Hocc. It was part of the curb's base course. "Here—" Sharina said.

"Who comes toward my master?" Dalar demanded in a ringing voice. His weights began to spin, building to a hum that now had lethal significance in Sharina's mind.

"Sharina?" a man called. *Bantrus, following us after all.* "It's me, Bantrus. Look, I couldn't let you go away like that. Come back with us and—"

Dalar caught his weights, slapping them loudly into his palms. *He must have calluses like a blacksmith.*

"Master Bantrus, we have to go," Sharina said. "Your friend was right: we have nothing to do with one another, your folk and mine. Go back to your friends."

"But—" Bantrus said. He tried to come closer.

Dalar hopped in front of Bantrus, then moved the youth back simply by taking small steps toward him. Sharina frowned, then realized that Dalar was providing vivid proof of what she'd meant by her words. Bantrus was heavier than the lightly built bird, but he obviously didn't consider holding his ground.

"Go to your friends," Dalar said in tones as gentle as his beak could make them. "Make your peace with Prince Mykon, young human; all of you, make peace. For helping us escape, I offer you the only advice that may save your lives. But *go*."

Dalar spun on his clawed heels, hanging his weights from a loop of harness to free his hands. "Let us move the block and leave this place, Sharina," he said.

They knelt. Sharina wriggled the slab with her fingers. As before in Valhocca, they had only its weight to contend with: the stone moved slickly.

"But . . . ?" Bantrus said.

"Toward you first," Sharina said, pushing the block outward with her fingertips. She gained a finger's breadth.

"Toward you," Dalar repeated, pushing in turn as Sharina braced her side. Rather than pause when the block started to move, they kept it moving outward by shifting one hand at a time.

"We have gained a skill, master," Dalar said. "We will be able to support ourselves in later life."

Flickers like stars or distant firelight showed through the gap where the block had been. Bantrus stared in amazement at the play of ghostly colors where he'd expected only shadow. "Are you Gods?" he said. "Was it really true that . . . ?"

Dalar cocked his head, fixing the youth with eyes as hard as an eagle's to silence him. "I will follow you, I think, master," he said.

"Yes, all right," said Sharina. She slid feet-first through the opening. For the first time she felt they were moving toward closure instead of merely escaping an unpleasant present.

The present was pretty unpleasant. In a way, the doom facing the Boats disturbed Sharina more than physical danger from ghouls in the ruins of ancient Valhocca had. The Boats were too gentle to exist in a world that was becoming civilized.

The moonlit square spun like water going down a spout. Dalar and Bantrus, motionless in their present, danced to the rhythm of the cosmos; then they vanished. Sharina was climbing through the side of the well curb into the center of a transformed Klestis.

A new canopy covered the well, built as protection for an ancient monument. The plaza was paved with smooth slabs interrupted by planters and fountains to provide shade and comfort.

The structure before Sharina was a palace. *All* the surrounding buildings were magnificent, tall and clad in shining metal. Their surfaces now gleamed beneath a dome of red wizard-light where the sky should be.

Thousands of people stood in the plaza, though there was room for many more. Their eyes were fixed on the palace. None of those nearby seemed to notice Sharina's arrival, nor Dalar moments later squirming backward from the well.

The bird looked up at the sky, a haze shot with occasional angry flashes. The air itself hummed. The red light muddied the spectators' vivid garments into hues that were more in keeping with the present atmosphere.

"Sir?" Sharina asked the man closest to her. He was middle-aged; beside him stood a younger woman and a line of six children down to an infant in the arms of her nurse.

He turned and stared at her. *He's terrified. They're all terrified.* "What?" he said. "Did you speak, mistress?"

Sharina knew enough about wizardry to expect they were right to be terrified.

"My friend and I are strangers here," Sharina said. She found she had to raise her voice to be heard clearly over the hum. "Can you tell us what—"

She grimaced, because she didn't want to speak directly about the sound or the light closing the sky of Klestis.

"—is happening here today?"

The citizen's eyes brushed over Dalar. He didn't have enough energy to look surprised at a man-sized bird. The whole sky flashed scarlet, then dimmed to its usual sullen hue.

The man winced, but he said, "This is the work of Ansalem the Wise, our leader. The kingdom is about to fall into chaos. Ansalem and his disciples are working to preserve us from that—"

The citizen's dry throat choked on the next word. He swallowed, closing his eyes as though he were squeezing back tears. His whole family stared past him toward the strangers, but none of them spoke.

"Ansalem is preserving us from that *end*," the man said. "That's all that's happening. Ansalem is our protector!"

"They're on the roof of the palace," the nurse said in a voice with a Sandrakkan burr. "Ansalem and the other wizards. That's where they're going to save us."

Despite the crowd in the square, nothing moved behind the windows of the palace. The door facing the plaza was open and unguarded.

"Has Ansalem told you this, sir?" said Dalar. The bird moved only his head, but his body was as tense as a sapling bent into a snare.

"We know it!" the man shouted. "Ansalem has always protected us! He's protecting us now!"

From the roof of the palace an unseen man screamed, "My son! Not my son!"

Sharina felt her guts knot. She looked at Dalar.

The man screamed inarticulately; only the fact the timbre was familiar indicated that the sound came from a human being. The sky flashed like sunlit blood.

The man and his wife were holding hands. The nurse sank to her knees, whimpering, "Ansalem will save us! Ansalem will save us all!"

Sharina drew the Pewle knife as she ran for the palace entrance. Dalar, his weights spinning close to his hands, sprang past her to lead.

Chapter Twenty

They've got heavy cavalry!" cried the commander of the first section of Blood Eagles to step from the bridge of light into Klestis. Instants later a trumpet signaled *Enemy in Sight*.

"And a lot of good cavalry is going to do them!" King Carus sneered. *"Trust a wizard to think horses on stone pavements are any more use than they'd be on ice."*

The Blood Eagles formed a skirmish line, screening the bridgehead. The first sections of the phalanx were swinging into position in a cacophony of horns, shouted orders, and the ring of boots on stone. Garric jogged to the right flank, sheathing his sword now that he was a commander again instead of a guide and cheerleader.

Lord Waldron and the army staff of aides, standard-bearers, signalers, couriers—and the personal guard detachment—came with Garric perforce. Normally they'd have been mounted for visibility, but Garric hadn't wanted to risk having horses panic in the face of wizardry. The men were nervous enough.

The right flank was as good a place as any for the command group. It was the point from which King Carus had usually directed his battles.

"Your Majesty, keep back!" Attaper snarled when he saw Garric beside him. As the phalanx deployed, the Blood Eagles shifted from an open array in front to tight masses of swordsmen on either flank. Attaper had gone with the right-hand platoons.

The sixteen-rank phalanx was a terrifying, almost irresistible force to its front, but it was next to impossible to swing the pikes quickly to meet attacks from the flanks or rear. Until the four battalions of heavy infantry made it across the bridge, the Blood Eagles—the best-trained soldiers in the Isles—would fill the need for flank guards just as they'd acted as skirmishers because the light troops were also still somewhere in the rear.

"I'm not here as a fighter, Attaper," Garric said. "But I need to view the situation to command . . . and I *am* in command, milord!"

The snap in Garric's voice came from his ancient ancestor—but Garric meant the words, and they were the right thing to say. Attaper, Waldron, and the other royal officers were used to acting for themselves because King

Valence had been no more than a figurehead even when he was younger. Prince Garric of Haft, with the help of King Carus, would *rule* the Isles.

Or die trying, of course.

Klestis was the same glittering ruin that Garric had seen in his dreams. Beneath a sun muted by a dome of wizard-light was a landscape of rank grass, tilted pavement blocks, and buildings from which the metal sheathing had begun to slip. Garric's eyes picked out the alabaster filigree around the audience chamber on the palace roof.

To reach the palace, he'd have to get through the mass of armored horsemen marshaling in the plaza. Besides the cavalry there were eight shaggy mammoths with armored breastplates; the platforms on their backs held soldiers with javelins and long pikes.

The mammoths' hair was falling away in patches. Fish or crabs had eaten half of one's trunk. The cavalrymen's armor was rusty, and where their visors were open Garric saw empty eyesockets and ravaged flesh. Yet they moved. . . .

Attaper and Waldron were expressionless. The trumpeter at Waldron's side began to tremble. Though he clutched his instrument to his chest, it still rattled on his bronze breastplate.

Garric put his arm around the trumpeter's shoulders; the soldier was younger even than Garric himself, and he didn't have the benefit of King Carus to steady him.

"They died once, lad," Garric said in a cheerful voice, loud enough for everyone in sight to hear despite the noise of troops rushing into position. "They'll die again—and by Duzi, they'll start doing it soon!"

Three wizards stood around a brazier placed on a decorative arch at the western side of the plaza. Two were in black, one in white. Their sex was uncertain at Garric's distance from them, and inconsequential besides. As their hands moved, smoke from the brazier twisted and the cavalry below them charged.

Waldron gave a crisp command; the trumpeter echoed

it. The phalanx shuddered forward, opening ranks as it did so. Though the pikemen had never been in battle before, they'd drilled thoroughly with oars and their weapons. Their execution of the present complicated maneuver made Garric cheer. Carus smiled with grim approval.

Several hundred javelin men slipped through the opened phalanx, jogging forward to meet the oncoming cavalry. If there'd been time to deploy properly, the skirmishers would already have been in position. . . .

"Welcome to war, lad," Carus said. *"The only thing that ought to surprise you is when everything goes the way you planned."*

Garric had imagined a cavalry charge would resemble a horse race, but the squadrons advancing behind the crab banner of Yole started at a walk and built speed slowly. The weight of an armored man was a burden even for a powerful horse. The necromancers could bring armies back from the dead, but they apparently couldn't change the nature of the men and beasts they revivified.

The heavy infantry battalions were the last to cross the bridge and take their position on the ends of the phalanx. The men rushing past Garric and the command group wheezed with the weight of their weapons and armor. Their officers gasped their orders; signalers paused and breathed quickly several times before they put their horns to their mouths.

"The last man in a march line always has to run," King Carus explained. *"The lead battalion'll have pitched its tents and eaten by the time the last one straggles in. I don't know why any more than I know why the sky's blue, but both things are the truth."*

The phalanx tightened files again as it crashed forward, now that the skirmishers had passed through. The command group was a knot on the phalanx's right edge, and a regular battalion with body armor, swords, and short spears closed the flank to the right of the officers and Blood Eagles.

Even Lord Waldron seemed to approve of the formation.

Valence III and his forefathers had stood in the center of the royal line, but Waldron could accept that the phalanx needed to display an unbroken array of pike points to the enemy.

Carus grinned with fierce anticipation. His hand was closed on the hilt of a sword that existed only in Garric's mind.

Garric wore a silvered breastplate and helmet, though he didn't carry a shield. His task wasn't to fight, but a commander can't predict how a battle will develop—

"Or even what he'll do in the middle of the fight," Carus murmured. *"Try to guess what they'll do and try to control yourself . . . but be ready just in case you have to cut your way through a shield wall!"*

The king didn't sound as though the prospect displeased him. Right now, as emotions raced through Garric's blood like a spring tide, Garric himself felt a thrill of delight to imagine leaping into the oncoming line.

The javelin men screening the Royal Army wore leather caps and carried wicker shields. One of them gave a shout and hurled the first of his three javelins toward the Yole cavalry. As if that were the signal, the whole skirmish line began casting their javelins as they continued to jog forward.

The missiles were short-shafted with slender iron heads. Thrown for the most part in high arcs, they slanted down on the mass of cavalry like windblown rain. Though the spikes might find their way through the joints of a rider's armor, their targets today were the horses, which already stumbled over the broken pavement. Javelins plunged deep into the necks and withers of the cavalry mounts. Horses fell, throwing their riders and tripping those in the next rank.

The wounded animals didn't kick high in pain and wheel violently, though, transforming injuries into chaos. Those that hadn't been hit continued forward at a trot building into a canter. They didn't smell blood, nor did they panic because of the screams of their fellows.

One gelding ran with a loop of intestine wrapped around a hind leg; every stride pulled more gut through the rent in its own belly. It managed twenty strides before it finally collapsed.

"Recall them!" Garric shouted as he understood what was about to happen. "Get 'em back or they'll be overrun!"

Waldron opened his mouth to pass the order to his trumpeter. The skirmishers had realized the danger themselves and scampered toward the safety of the armored line.

For many of them it was already too late. The Yole cavalry swept on like a torrent through a canyon. Though many had fallen, the remaining riders and mounts alike were fearless in the face of death and pain. Lances caught fleeing skirmishers and flung the bodies aside with quick twists to clear the point.

Death and revival hadn't robbed the horsemen of their skill. Only rarely did a misdirected lancehead spark on the pavement, breaking the shaft or lifting the rider out of his saddle.

The surviving skirmishers dived beneath the shields of the phalanx and heavy infantry like voles reaching safety in the rocks. Attaper shouted an order. Eight ranks of Blood Eagles pushed their way in front of the command group, shield rim to shield rim.

Garric saw the Yole horsemen loom above the infantry the way the surf curls when it reaches the shore. The lines crashed together: metal on metal, metal on stone; metal on crunching bone. The sound and the stench were like nothing that belonged in the world of men.

"Horses wouldn't charge home!" Carus shouted. *"But these stopped being horses when they died. May the Sister eat the hearts of all wizards!"*

The mounts and armored men weighed tons; they hit the royal army at a full canter. Men shouted, pikeshafts snapped like crackling lightning. The front rank of the phalanx recoiled into the shields and breastplates of the rank behind them, and that rank sagged back as well.

But the phalanx was sixteen ranks deep. All the horses

accomplished by their speed and fearlessness was to ram themselves and their riders hard enough to pierce even plate armor on a hedge of pikepoints.

The Yole charge splashed like a mudball on stone. The rearmost horsemen were as mindlessly brave as the front; they rode into the pileup, raising their lances to clear the windrow of twice-dead men and beasts. Some even managed to climb their mounts over the carnage. They met pikes and died again in turn. Even broken pikestaves pointed long ashwood splinters toward the face of the enemy.

Cheering, cursing—pressed on by their officers and their own fierce determination—the men of the phalanx resumed their advance. Their hobnails bit into rotting flesh or skidded on slimy paving stones, but when a man stumbled the comrades close behind and to either side braced him till he found his feet again. Horsemen continued to ride into the wrack of their fallen fellows, and the phalanx continued to spike down those not already felled by their own side.

"No more generalship than a wheat field has," said Carus. *"And we are the scythe!"*

The wizards had formed their troops in the plaza, but the Royal Army had deployed on a wider front on the outskirts of the city. Because the leaders *were* wizards, and not soldiers, even bad soldiers, they'd sent their army of the dead straight ahead so that the pikes of the phalanx in the center caught almost the entire charge.

"Almost" was a score of armored horsemen riding into Garric's guards. Four of the shaggy mammoths followed close behind.

The pikemen slung light oval shields from neckstraps so that they had both hands for their weapons. The Blood Eagles instead wore heavy shields on their left forearms. They raised them now to guard their faces against the oncoming lances while their own shorter spears thrust for the chests and throats of the horses.

Some of the horsemen broke through the front rank, though their mounts were already dying again. Soldiers

who'd lost their spears drew swords and stooped to hock
and gut the horses, then to hack through the riders falling
from their backs. Soldiers from the rear ranks thrust back
the riders they could reach with their spears, and the regular infantry on the flank started forward to encircle the
enemy.

Garric saw a Yole champion trying to swing his long
sword despite the spear protruding from the gorget around
his throat. He went over backward with a clang that could
be heard over the general din.

The mammoths, so dead that they sloughed patches of
skin as they moved, walked into the royal line. Their
strides were slow, but each one covered more ground than
a man lying full-length.

The commander of the flank battalion bellowed an order.
His troops hurled their spears, puncturing the shaggy monsters scores of times. The rain of heavy missiles killed the
drivers seated on each animal's neck and swept away all
but two of the sixteen soldiers in the fighting platforms on
their backs.

The mammoths, walking dead before they received their
first wound from the Royal Army, continued to pace forward. Their concentrated mass carried them into the ranks
dented by the cavalry charge, then on into the raised
shields of the men behind.

"Cut the tendons!" Garric shouted. No man on Ornifal
today had fought mammoths, but King Carus had met them
as he crushed the rebellions flaring all across his kingdom.
"Hamstring them!"

Garric eased backward, along with Waldron and his
staff. Lord Attaper was at the front of the line, but that
was his place as commander of the guards. Garric had
drawn his sword, but he wasn't here to—

"Colva!" Liane cried in a clear voice. "Come back!"

Garric tried to glance over his shoulder, but to see past
the cheekpiece of his helmet he had to lean back and twist
at the waist. Colva slipped by, moving toward the melee.

Garric grabbed the woman with his left hand. She turned

and looked at him with a transfigured expression, then shrugged free. She seemed to have no more skeleton than a stream of water.

The dying mammoth strode through the shouting, stabbing soldiers who were no more hindrance to a creature of its size than a thicket of blackberries. A sweep of its curving tusks flung ranks of tight-packed troops sideways. Its trunk was curled high against its forehead.

Colva stood with her face lifted and her hands spread at her sides. There was now nothing between her and the mammoth.

Garric stepped forward, shouldering the woman aside. He didn't think about what he was doing: it was the sort of thing you don't do if you think about it.

The tusks spread to either side of him. He swung his sword in a vertical stroke. The tip of his blade severed the mammoth's trunk and sliced deep into the spongy frontal bone. Noxious black fluid sprayed from the great blood vessels that fed the trunk.

The mammoth paced onward, shoving Garric back. His heel turned on the arm of a fallen soldier. He stopped trying to free the sword and grabbed the tusks with both arms.

The mammoth lowered its head to crush him. One of its eyesockets was empty; the other stared at the man between the tusks with no more emotion than a stone. The stub of the trunk twitched; had the appendage been whole, the beast would have shoved Garric to the ground and knelt on him. Now it could only splash him with its last dribble of reliquefied blood.

The eye glazed. The mammoth sagged forward, dead again and finally at peace. Garric shoved himself clear of the toppling ruin. He thought he'd lost his sword—it wouldn't be hard to replace it on this field of carnage—but the beast rolled over on its left side with the hilt sticking out. Garric sawed the blade up and down like a pump handle, then drew it free.

The battle was over. The Yole squadrons had been

slaughtered to a man. Except they hadn't been men anymore. . . .

Liane held Colva from behind, twisting her arms. Liane's face was as blank as a cobblestone—and despite that
control, utterly furious.

"I'm so sorry," Colva said in a liquid voice, as though
she were in the throes of passion. "The powers drew me.
Such powers are loose here!"

Garric was drenched in the fluids of a beast dead a thousand years and surrounded by corpses, *his* men some of
them as well as the dead of the ancient past. He looked
into Colva's expressive eyes and felt queasy.

A Blood Eagle officer glanced from the two women to
Garric and mimed a question. "Hold her!" Garric said.
"Not Liane, the other one. Just . . ."

Garric turned away. "Just hold her, keep her out of the
way," he added as he almost fell; from reaction to the
battle, he supposed. And from what he thought he'd seen
in Colva's eyes.

Liane touched Garric's shoulder. That steadied him even
more than the hand he dabbed down to the ground.

The three necromancers were climbing down a ladder
leaned against the arch. They moved as if they themselves
were the walking dead. Great wizardry was as draining as
great age.

Garric pointed his sword. "Get them!" he shouted. "*Kill*
them!"

Because as long as they lived, they were dangerous.

The empty despair Garric had seen in the mammoth's
single eye had eliminated any possibility he'd grant mercy
to the wizards responsible. No doubt they were responsible
for worse; but *that* Garric had seen.

He started forward. At first he had to climb over
mounded corpses, but the dead weren't the barrier on the
flanks that they presented to the center of the Royal Army.

Beyond the line of slaughter, broken pavement made the
footing dangerous. Garric ran anyway, bouncing from one

tilted block to the next with no more hesitation than a squirrel leaping between trees.

The trio of necromancers had knocked over their brazier when they fled; a faint haze spread from the top of the arch. A new column of smoke, thick and formed by alternate streams of black and white, twisted skyward from the palace roof.

Garric knew he'd be a wobbling wreck when he tumbled down from his present emotional heights—but that would be later. For now he had to get to the palace.

Officers were sorting out the phalanx. Its ranks had been badly disordered by victory—though not nearly as badly as they'd have been by defeat. Those troops couldn't pursue the necromancers anyway unless they flung down their long pikes.

The Blood Eagles and regular infantry were almost as heavily burdened. Those who heard Garric's order clumped off in pursuit of the wizards, but they weren't likely to catch the trio before it reached the palace.

The skirmishers, those who'd survived the mindless courage of the Yole charge, sprinted forward through the ranks of their heavy-armed fellows. If Garric sprang like a squirrel, the skirmishers were a nest of hornets flying past him for their revenge.

The three leading skirmishers reached the wizards while Garric was still twenty yards behind. They'd used up their javelins, but they still had the short hatchets that smallholders in the east of Ornifal used for farm tasks.

The necromancer in white turned and extended his hands toward the soldiers. The nearest man sank his hatchet to the helve in the wizard's face. The pair wearing black managed another step each before quick strokes severed their spines.

"Your Majesty, wait!" Attaper gasped. "By the Lady, Your Majesty!"

Garric glanced sideways. The Blood Eagles' commander had thrown down his shield and helmet; now he was struggling with the side laces of his gilded breastplate. A score of his men were following closely, one of them even carrying a spear.

"May the Sister take you, Your Majesty!" Attaper cried. He flung his elaborate breastplate away with a clang and at last drew level with the far-younger prince.

"Not the palace door," King Carus warned. During the moments Garric faced the mammoth, Carus had been as much in control of Garric's actions as the youth himself was, but now the ancient king had slipped back to his usual presence in the back of Garric's mind. *"Up the outside stairs to the roof!"*

The dead necromancers lay like cast-off clothing. The white-painted hand protruding from one's sleeve was as thin as an articulated skeleton. The power these wizards controlled had worn them away like steel on a grindstone; soon there would've been nothing left. Garric's attack had speeded their doom only slightly.

But that slight difference might be enough to save the world the wizards would have brought down with them.

"Take the stair tower!" Garric said, pointing with the sword still bare in his hand. He'd even wiped the blade, though he didn't remember doing it. Some reflex of Carus', he supposed. "The door from the inside'll be barred!"

The alabaster screen was an effective barrier against citizens who tried to push closer to their ruler. It wouldn't stop soldiers in a hurry.

Garric wasn't the first to the spiral staircase. The javelin men were ready for further work now that they'd run down the necromancers. More than a score of them raced ahead of Garric's pointing blade. Some had even picked up missiles from the volleys thrown into the beginnings of the Yole charge.

The reanimated corpses began to decay as soon as life left them again. Carus, glancing over the battlefield through Garric's eyes, wore a puzzled frown. His memory was full of similar scenes, but always the birds had settled by now: vultures and eagles, crows; and especially, since no part of the Isles was far from the sea, the gulls with their great, hooked beaks.

Klestis was a city of the dead. Only coarse plants and a few insects survived in what the necromancers had made of Ansalem's paradise.

Garric ran up the stairs, taking three of the low steps with each stride. He couldn't do this forever, but he wouldn't have to. They didn't have forever, Garric or the Isles either one.

As Garric climbed, he glanced out over Klestis through the serpentine stone pillars. It was just as he'd seen when Ansalem called him here in dreams, except that now the Royal Army was advancing in ordered battalions over the bodies strewn across the plaza. Lord Waldron was doing his job as army commander.

Prince Garric of Haft was doing his job also, one that he alone of those present knew enough to perform.

Liane watched from the plaza, waving her white silk scarf. That was a change from Garric's dreams also, one worth any number of soldiers to him now.

The bridge from Valles touched the curtain of light by which Ansalem had separated Klestis from the rest of the universe. That was familiar—

But instead of a single bridge, an infinite number of spans overlay one another all around the barrier's circuit. The surviving necromancers were opening other passages to Klestis, and from Klestis to the Isles.

With Attaper somehow still on his heels and more of the Blood Eagles behind, Garric ran onto the roof garden. The javelin men hadn't bothered to lift a planter for a battering ram. They were hacking at the soft alabaster with their hatchets, eating a hole in the pierced stone big enough for men.

A brazier carved from dolomite in the shape of a dragon's maw stood in the center of Ansalem's chamber. Smoke spewed from its mouth and filtered through the screen, then re-formed into a single strand above.

Tenoctris lay in frozen silence on the bier where Ansalem

rested in the dreamworld. At her head stood a necromancer dressed in white. Beneath the paint Garric recognized a thin, terrified face from the band of acolytes Carus had met in Ansalem's palace. She held a dagger above Tenoctris' throat, ready to slash when the order came.

The figure at the foot of the bier was Purlio. His left side was black, his right was white.

In Purlio's hands was the fossilized ammonite. Evil pulsed from the gleaming marcasite shell. The chamber wavered from its place in the cosmos as Purlio mounted an incantation.

"Stop them!" Garric shouted. He kicked his right heel into the screen. Weakened stone flew inward, leaving a hole as big as a man's head.

Blood Eagles shouted, following Garric's lead to hammer the alabaster with their hobnails. Several of the light troops continued chopping at the screen, though by now their hatchets were more danger than benefit.

The wizard in white dropped her dagger and stumbled away. Purlio shouted a word of power in a terrible voice. He lifted the marcasite fossil against his face.

There was a flash of red as deep as sunset on a dying world. The shell—the Great One—merged with Purlio's flesh to rest on his shoulders in place of his skull. Hazy tentacles wobbled from the opening just as fleshy ones had done in life.

Soldiers threw down their weapons and scrambled away. Attaper shouted, "Forward! Forward!" and banged his sword hilt on the alabaster, but even he was blind with horror at what he'd seen.

The fleeing wizard turned and looked at her former leader. She started to scream. The Great One's arms wrapped her head and drew her against the parrotlike beak. Bone crunched repeatedly before the screaming stopped.

Garric jumped against the screen, this time hitting with both feet. A section the size of a palace door toppled inward, shattering into a thousand creamy fragments.

Purlio turned, staring at Garric through the ammonite's eyes. Its pupils were curved slits. The dead wizard lay on her back; her face had been chewed away. The Great One's tentacles were now blood-red muscle.

Garric swung his sword in a slanting arc. Purlio became a sparkle of scarlet light. It swirled and vanished as the bright steel snicked through it.

The air was empty.

Tenoctris stirred on the stone couch like a sparrow awakening. Garric slumped to his knees. He let the sword slip from his nerveless fingers and clutched the bier for support.

"By the Lady!" cried a soldier outside on the roof. "There's armies coming across all those bridges! By the Lady! There's a million soldiers coming at us and they're all dead!"

"Behold the Palace of Landure, sheep-boy," said the ring demon. In a half-wondering tone he added, "We've arrived. I really didn't think we would."

"It wasn't so bad," Cashel said truthfully. "With you to help me, I mean."

The structure was set into—cut into—the face of a bluff like the one which had opened every stage of Cashel's journey through the Underworld. In front was a porch with four stone pillars carved to look like palm trees. The bases were one color, the uplifted fronds forming the capital another, and the shafts were painted in contrasting stripes—though Cashel couldn't guess what any of the colors would've been under a real sun.

The blue light here was cold. It made the building look like a tomb.

Instead of a wooden or metal panel, a curtain of silver beads fell across the doorway. They shimmered as the slight breeze stirred them. Cashel couldn't read the pattern of their motions, but he knew there was one.

"I guess I'll go on in," Cashel said. "Unless there's

something else I ought to do, Master Krias?"

"Nothing at all, sheep-boy," the ring said. "All you have to do is go inside and place the wafer where I tell you; then you're done. You're free."

"Right," said Cashel, striding toward the porch. There was more in the demon's voice than the words themselves, but Cashel couldn't figure out what. Life would be a lot simpler if people just said what they meant; but generally they didn't, and he'd learned a long time ago that it didn't help if he asked them slap out what they really wanted.

Sheep would likely be just as bad if they could talk. Thankfully, they couldn't.

As he pushed the curtain aside with his outstretched left hand, Cashel heard a chord from the distance behind him mingle with the silver beads' tinkling. Elfin was out there somewhere still. Cashel grimaced, though Elfin's problems weren't Cashel's doing; or at least not much.

White light from no visible source flooded the long, shallow room beyond the curtain. Cashel touched his quarterstaff to the floor to see which way the shadow fell. There wasn't a shadow, from the hickory or from his own body either.

The ceiling was high by peasant standards, but not exceptional for the palaces Cashel had seen since he left home; he could've touched it with his staff if he'd wanted to. He couldn't tell how far it stretched to right and left, though. If not forever, then certainly beyond the range of Cashel's own keen eyesight. The inner wall was painted with a mural of Landure in an endless series of occupations.

"Turn right," Krias said sourly. "It isn't far."

"Wow," said Cashel as he walked slowly down the passageway. When he looked closer, he saw there wasn't a lot of variety in what Landure was doing, though the settings changed. The wizard's sword struck down a winged creature that would've been a bat if it hadn't been bigger than a plow ox; the wizard held out his clenched fist so his sapphire ring could incinerate men the size of voles who swarmed out of rocky soil; the wizard stood on a beach, driving shark-headed creatures back into the sea; the wizard—

"Didn't Landure do anything but fight, Master Krias?" Cashel asked.

"Once he died, sheep-boy," the demon said. "As I recall, you were present when it happened."

They'd come to a scene of Landure seated on a throne of light. The artist had made Landure's grim expression look regal rather than merely peevish. Before him, bowing so deeply they rubbed their foreheads on the ground, were the front rows of an assembly stretching widely to right and left.

The assembly was of monsters: half-men and non-men, slender folk Cashel recognized as the People who'd have devoured him, creatures with insect antennae and faceted insect eyes, giants and dwarfs and all manner of differing unpleasantness. Those disappearing into the distance on either side were still shown precisely. Cashel was sure that he could have told their expressions apart if he had a magnifying crystal to examine the painting with.

Landure's image glared outward, making Cashel a member of the obsequious crowd. Cashel's right hand squeezed his staff a little tighter.

Cashel was generally pretty easygoing—he was too big and strong to be anything else if he was going to live around decent people. Even as a painting, though, Landure sure knew how to get his back up.

"Well, what're you waiting for, sheep-boy?" Krias demanded shrilly. "You said you wanted to be free, didn't you? Put the life under Landure's tongue in the picture and your job's done!"

"Ah," said Cashel. People were always and forever getting mad because Cashel hadn't known to do things they hadn't bothered to tell him in a way he understood. That was mostly because they were impatient, he supposed; or because they were just folks who liked to get mad.

He reached into his wallet, rummaging past the plum-sized fruit he'd brought from the tree, and brought out the crystal wafer. It gleamed like a rainbow in the hall's shadowless illumination.

Cashel looked at his ring; Krias was barely a spark in the heart of the purple sapphire. He raised the wafer to the mouth of the painted Landure and found it slipped easily into—

What was no longer a wall, but rather the man himself stepping forward imperiously to snarl, "Who are you and what are you doing here?"

Cashel stepped back. The painted throne was empty. "I'm Cashel or-Kenset—" he said.

"He's the fellow returning the life you lost, master," Krias said. "Or hadn't you noticed?"

"Silence!" the wizard said. "I see I could die of old age if I waited for a peasant to tell me what I need to know."

Symbols and words were set into the mosaic floor already. Landure undid his shoulder cape's gold clasp—it was fashioned to look like a leech humping toward his throat—and knelt. *"Sukk kala bowe,"* he muttered, using the pin as a wand. *"Badawa balaha war-ry."*

Cashel stood silently with the staff vertical at his side. His skin prickled; it always did around wizardry. For choice he'd have planted the staff square in front of him, but he guessed that'd look hostile.

He *felt* hostile, that was no lie. Landure the Guardian wasn't wearing any better the second time than he had the first, but there wasn't any help for that.

"Risauda!" the wizard cried as he struck his pin at the center of the mosaic pentacle before him. Lights whirled in the air. Sometimes Cashel thought he saw figures, but it was all spinning too fast for him to focus.

Landure stood up. For a moment he seemed a little shaky from the incantation, but he was too mad for that to delay him long. "So, peasant, you killed me!"

"Yes sir, I did," Cashel said. He didn't raise his voice, he didn't try to explain what the wizard must already know; and especially, he didn't flinch away from Landure's angry gaze.

Landure didn't flinch either, but his tone was a bit more reasonable when he continued, "I see you brought my ring back. Where's my sword?"

Cashel twisted the ring one way, then the other, and drew it over his knuckle. The gold circuit was as tight on his little finger as you could have and be comfortable.

"Here's Krias," he said, handing the ring to the wizard. "He's been a big help to me. As for your sword, I left it where it lay. I don't have anything to do with swords."

"Except occasionally to kill fools who try to use them on him," piped the ring demon. "Fools whose faithful servant has tried to warn them."

Landure gave the ring a fierce look as he slipped it onto the middle finger of his left hand. With it in place his gaze returned to Cashel.

"I suppose you know what you've done?" the wizard said. He pinned his cape back in place. "Besides letting Colva loose, I mean? There's a flood of demon-souls entering the waking world to animate the armies a necromancer is raising!"

"I didn't know that," Cashel said calmly. He was taller than Landure, stronger than three Landures put together—

And if it came to that, he'd killed Landure once. The wizard was mad and sure, he had reason to be; but he wasn't going to back Cashel down, no matter what he said or tried.

"The souls would be entering the waking world anyway," Krias said. "The necromancers are using the Dragon's body as a talisman."

"I could have stopped—" Landure said.

"You could have stood against the Dragon, master?" shrilled the ring demon. "You, who couldn't keep a *peasant* from knocking your fool head in? My, you've come back to life as Landure the Court Jester, I see!"

The wizard's face went red. For a momen Cashel thought he was going to shout a curse—a real curse, not the sort of thing you said when a skittish ox trod on your foot during yoking.

Instead, Landure took a deep breath and settled back. "I could have driven some of them back," he said softly, "but there's no point in talking about that now. There's much to be done, and I'll need my sword to do it."

"Tell him why you came to him, sheep-boy!" Krias said. "Or do you just want to waste your trip?"

"What?" said Landure. A touch of the usual choler was back in his voice.

"I'm looking for my friend Sharina," Cashel said, feeling his face get warm. "Tenoctris said that you might be able to help me. She said finding Sharina is maybe important. I mean, not just for me."

Landure frowned. "Tenoctris of Guelf?" he said. "I've heard of her, but I don't see what . . ."

He shrugged. "Anyway," he said, "I don't have time. You can come with me to the surface and I'll send you home from there."

"He doesn't want to go to the surface," Krias said unexpectedly. "He wants to go to the Chasm and cross it to where the girl is."

"He can't cross the Chasm!" Landure said. He held his hand out as he spoke to the ring.

"He can with help, as you—"

"Demon, shall I lock you in a cliff of basalt that will stand till time stops?" the wizard shouted. *"This fool of a peasant killed me and loosed monsters on his own world!"*

"You died not because this *man* didn't listen," said the ring demon, "but because you didn't explain. And you live now, master, because this *man* made a journey that not one in a thousand would even have attempted!"

"Look," Cashel said with dry lips. "If you'll point me to this Chasm, Master Krias, I'll take care of the rest myself. I don't need help from folks who're too busy to give it."

Landure bunched his ring hand into a fist. "I don't need

lectures on duty from servants!" he said. "Or from a peasant either!"

"You need them from somebody," Krias said. "And as
for servants—I've stopped serving you, Landure the
Guardian. Now that I've seen how a man behaves, I'm
going to do the same from now on. Even if you boil me
in amber, the way you threatened before!"

Landure blinked. He cocked his head like he was hearing
voices that Cashel couldn't. The anger went out of him and
he slid the ring from his finger.

"Here," he said, handing it to Cashel. "I owe you this
for returning me to life. The demon Krias will guide and
protect you, wherever your way may lead."

Cashel worked the ring onto his finger again. It felt
good. Landure glared at the sapphire and added, "Krias
knows he'll suffer the consequences if he fails you."

"I'm not afraid of your consequences!" Krias said.
Cashel didn't believe Krias, exactly; but he *did* take him
for a fellow who'd do what he'd said even though it flat
terrified him. "As for helping Master Cashel, why, that'll
be a pleasure. You can't imagine what a change it is, Landure, to be the companion of a real man."

Krias snickered. "Of course, he's a really *stupid* man as
well," he added, "but that's all right."

Cashel laughed. He said to the fuming wizard, "I was
afraid something'd happened to the Krias I knew, but now
I see it's still him."

He rapped his staff on the floor to close the previous
discussion. "Master Krias?" he said formally. "Where do
we go now?"

Landure himself pointed down the hall in the direction
they'd been traveling. "You'll find it fifty yards that way,"
the wizard said. He correctly read the doubt in Cashel's
expression and added, "Let's say the height of a tall tree,
if that helps you more."

"I'll tell you when we get there, sheep-boy," the demon
said. "Just start walking."

Cashel bowed to Landure and walked away. The wizard

was frowning. Not with anger this time, but apparently out of puzzlement.

Cashel grinned. He supposed he and Krias made a pretty funny pair at that. The grin faded as he wondered how Sharina would take to the little fellow. Still, most everybody got along with Sharina.

The scenes painted on the wall were more of the same: Landure laying down the law, which mostly meant Landure driving all manner of monsters where he wanted them, and slaughtering them if they didn't move fast enough to please him.

Cashel frowned, but he knew there were folk you pretty well *had* to treat that way. The People, if it came to that. Being polite to them hadn't got Cashel anything more than the chance to be the main dish at dinner. . . .

"I guess I see how your Landure gets, ah, short-tempered," Cashel said to the ring.

"Huh!" Krias snapped. "Landure got short-tempered by being born. If you listen to him tell it, he's a martyr sacrificing himself to guard the waking world—but the truth is, he made this job for himself so he'd have a chance to behave the way he was going to behave anyhow."

In a different voice the demon said, "Stop here! You're going to go right past it. Are you blind?"

Cashel stopped before a panel showing a landscape. Landure wasn't in the picture, nor was anybody else Cashel could see, but given the enormous scale there might be whole regiments of people hidden among the trees.

Ragged cliffs faced a misty chasm. In the middle ground, flat-topped peaks lifted above the swirls. There was maybe even a far wall of cliffs, but that wasn't anything Cashel could've sworn to.

A rainbow crossed the gorge. When Cashel turned his head a little to one side or the other, the band of light seemed to shift too.

"Well, walk into it!" Krias said. "Just step forward! Or is that too complicated for you?"

"No, Master Krias," Cashel said. Smiling faintly—he

didn't know that he'd ever warm to the demon, exactly, but at least you didn't have to worry about the little fellow saying things behind your back that he wouldn't say to your face—Cashel stepped forward.

There wasn't a wall. It was pretty much like Cashel had walked from meadow into the woods fringing it, though these trees were huge. They were firs and hemlocks, and they didn't start to have branches before you were higher up the trunk than the tops of most trees Cashel had seen.

He gave his staff a trial spin. In front of him, then over his head; and for a climax he used the hickory as a spinning brace and whirled his body around in a circle beneath it.

"Very cute, sheep-boy," said the ring demon sourly. "Do you think you're going to leap the Chasm, then?"

"No, Master Krias," Cashel said as he walked through the aisles of trees. "But I don't want to be stiff if I have to climb down the cliff, either. How deep is your Chasm, then?"

Krias sniffed. "Deeper than you'd live to reach the bottom of," he said, "even if you jumped off the edge. Which I *don't* recommend, sheep-boy; and anyhow, there's a bridge."

Cashel walked on quietly for a moment. He could see the cliffs past the last of the trees. A wedge of stone jutted out into the clouds like a ship's prow. There wasn't anything that looked like a bridge to him, that was for sure.

"How do I find the bridge, Master Krias?" Cashel asked. He walked onto the spit of rock and looked over the waste of boiling cloud. The air sparkled with life and moisture, the way it did in the pause between the halves of a fierce storm.

"You just call it to you, sheep-boy," the ring said. "But before you do that, you should know that there's a guard, and even you can't fight him."

Cashel cocked an eyebrow, though he didn't say anything.

Krias tittered nervously. "Oh, I don't doubt that you'd try," he said, "but you can't win unless you first cease to be human. Are you willing to do that, Cashel or-Kenset?"

Cashel frowned. "Being human" wasn't one of those things he thought about; it was just what he was. But if he stopped being what he was, he might as well be dead.

"No, Master Krias," Cashel said. "I guess I'll fight him the way I am now. If that's not enough, well, it wasn't enough."

He gave his quarterstaff a series of slow twirls to make sure that everything still worked. Cashel knew he could lose a fight—but he hadn't yet, not since he was a boy too young to talk in sentences.

"I can fight him," Krias said. The demon's voice was all sparks and prickles; *much* more was going on in Krias' mind that he meant to put into words. "I can fight him, but you'd have to free me."

"Free you?" Cashel said in surprise. "Why, I'll do that anyway. I didn't know that I could, Master Krias."

"You didn't know?" Krias said. His voice started shrill and ended like the whine of mosquitoes' wings. "I've spent more ages trapped in this sapphire than there are sand grains on a beach, and you didn't know I wanted to be free?"

"I didn't know that *I* could free you," Cashel said calmly. "Tell me what to do and I'll take care of it now."

Lots of people thought they had to squirm and twist to get what they wanted. There must be some good reason to act that way or there wouldn't be so many people doing it, but Cashel sure couldn't see what it was.

The times he needed something Cashel asked straight out; and asking him straight was likewise the best way to get him to do something. If only because he generally didn't understand what people were asking when they tried to do it some other way.

"I'll fight the guard for you," Krias said in the same spiky nervousness as before. "But after that you have no hold on me. I won't take any orders!"

Cashel smiled. "Master Krias," he said, "I don't recall giving you any orders before now, except when you told

me I had to say the words. As for fighting my battles—
I've never asked anybody to do that, and I'm *sure* not
asking now. Tell me how to free you. You can go off on
your own business while I deal with mine."

Krias was silent longer than Cashel had expected. "All
right, sheep-boy," the demon said at last. "That's what
we'll do. Set me on a stone. Call, 'Bridge, bear me to my
Sharina.' Just that. And then smash the jewel with the butt
of your staff—or a lump of stone, if you'd rather."

"Oh, I think my staff will do," Cashel said. He worked
the ring off his finger. "It's done. . . ."

Cashel's voice trailed off as he set the ring on the
ground, then had to adjust it when the wind tipped it off
the knob. There was a lot of wind up here. It didn't seem
to affect the mist bubbling in the Chasm like a pot on a
rolling boil, but Cashel's sleeves and the skirt of his tunic
fluttered like a baby bird demanding food.

"It's done harder things than that for me," Cashel concluded quietly. He faced the Chasm. "Bridge, carry me to
Sharina!" he called.

He looked down, determining exactly where the ring
was. The sapphire winked at him. Holding the quarterstaff
heel-to-thumb like a pestle, Cashel brought the iron cap
down squarely on the stone. It shattered with a crash.

Cashel lifted the staff and crossed it before him. The
gold setting had smeared; the sapphire was purple dust that
began to swirl in the wind.

"Master Krias?" Cashel said. Nothing answered, though
his voice began to echo, "Sharina . . . Sharina . . . Sharina . . ."

Cashel turned, frowning. The mist was congealing into
the shimmers of light. It looked like—it looked like a rainbow forming, only this was right in front of him.

It was a rainbow. It was also a bridge. It spanned the
Chasm, from the crag where Cashel stood to a point too
distant for his eyes to reach.

"Thank you for your guidance, Master Krias," Cashel
said. He'd thought something would happen when he

smashed the ring. Had he maybe misunderstood and flattened the demon along with the gold of the setting? "I guess, well, I'll be getting on my way."

Sharina . . . Sharina . . . Sharina . . . whispered the cloudy distance.

The mist was piling up in the middle of the Chasm. If Cashel had seen the same thing high in the summer sky, he'd have said that a storm cloud was rising. This time the cloud had shoulders and a lump of a head in which glittered flashes of red lightning.

He *had* seen this before. At Tian.

The colors of the bridge changed in a continuing cascade but they always shimmered and were as real as sunlight on the deep sea. Cashel had been reaching out the tip of his staff to check how solid the bridge really was; now he pulled it back.

He wasn't going to be standing over an abyss when he fought the storm giant; not that it'd matter much. He wondered if he looked as pitiful as King Liew and his knights had done the morning Tian died.

Sharina would be all right without him. Sure she would.

Cashel started his staff spinning, getting into the rhythm. A blue spark spat from one ferrule, then the other. Wizardlight, not that Cashel claimed to be a wizard.

The giant continued to swell out of the mist like a man climbing from the sea on a shelving beach. It raised its club, a mass of writhing thunderheads. The weapon looked as solid as if carved from basalt. Judging from what it'd done to Tian, that was no illusion.

Even if Cashel was a greater wizard than any he'd met—and he'd met some—he doubted it'd be enough. The storm giant was just too big to be stopped by any spell that wouldn't as surely sink the ground the wizard stood on. Just too big . . .

Poor Lia. Poor Tian.

The ground beside Cashel crackled. The hair on his arms stood on end and his neck was prickly. He looked down. Purple lightning sizzled where he'd smashed the ring, growing with the sudden speed of a spark catching in this-tledown.

Cashel stepped back, blinking as burned air stung his eyes and nostrils. The snarling lightning continued to swell into a figure.

Into the figure of Krias.

The demon was as tall as a house, then as tall as a tree. He stepped from one crag to another, bunching his flashing limbs—

And leaped toward the storm giant as the latter swung its club.

The figures crashed together, lighting both sky and the depths of the Chasm from which the giant had risen. A cloud arm flung Krias into the cliff, blasting a section of rock into pebbles. Krias sprang up like a ball and lunged for his opponent's throat. He caught the shoulder instead and bit into thunder. Rain slashed from the wound, clearing the mist beneath it for farther than an eye could see.

"Go on, sheep-boy!" crackled a voice of purple fire. "Go off on your own business while I deal with mine!"

Cashel shouldered his staff and started across the bridge. The surface was cold and had no spring, like sod frozen before the snow falls to soften it. He lengthened his stride. He wasn't running, but he'd seen enough fights to have a bad feeling about how this one was going to come out. Sharina was on the other side of the bridge. Now that Cashel had decided he was going to live after all, that was important to him.

Krias' crackling violet presence was huge, but the cloud giant had swelled to the size of an island. This was like watching a rat battle a bulldog.

The ring demon spun free and hunched in mid air. The giant's club rose. Krias leaped, under the weapon but try-ing again for the giant's throat. Teeth of sizzling lightning savaged another flood of rain from the wrist the giant man-aged to put in the way.

Krias wasn't a rat. Krias was a weasel, and just possi-bly . . .

Cashel started to jog. He was past the middle of the span. He still couldn't see to the other side, but his feet were descending the chill, rigid slope. When he looked straight down into the Chasm, he saw twinkles of light as numerous as the stars on a winter's night.

They *were* stars. Cashel recognized constellations: the Lady's Train, Hell Mouth with its two guardian stars, the Flock—

He jerked his eyes away as vertigo swept over him in a sudden rush. If the stars were below . . .

The bridge, the shifting solid light, was coming to an end ahead of Cashel. He couldn't see anything beyond it, just an absence the way a tree rises into the sky and stops.

If the stars were below him, would he fall forever?

Thunder crashed and lightning turned the sky violet. Cashel looked around, though he kept trotting forward.

A wrack of clouds was beginning to dissipate over the Chasm. In the midst of them, capering like the demon he was, Krias shouted, "Free! I'm free! I'm free forevermore!"

Cashel stepped into a wall of chill darkness. He wasn't sure whether he really heard the final shout, "Cashel, I'm free!"

But he hoped it was true.

"Now, if Harn's bridge took us where you wished to go, Mistress Ilna," said Chalcus as he led them through the ice cave with his sword bare, "then your tastes and mine differ."

"As I'm sure they do!" Ilna said tartly. The cave was a wormhole, not a straight course from the ledge where the stub of Harn's cable still hung, but blue light through the ceiling and walls illuminated the passage sufficiently. "I wouldn't think they were as different as this, however. Perhaps Harn was joking with us. His final joke."

"I see soldiers in the ice," Merota said in a tiny voice. "Do you think they're real, Ilna?"

Ilna grimaced. The light was a little better than it needed

to be: it showed not only the trio's path but also the figures frozen into the walls of the glacier. Their spiked helmets had veils of of bronze links. Lower-ranking troops wore tabards of scarlet with gold embroidery over mail cuirasses, but their leaders were splendid in jewel-accented breast-plates of silver and gold.

"I suppose they are," Ilna said truthfully. "But they can't hurt us, so I don't see that it matters."

The second half of Ilna's statement was too assured. She'd have phrased it more circumspectly if she were *quite* as truthful as she knew she ought to be. She pursed her lips.

"Just so, child," the chanteyman said cheerfully. He picked up a scrap of metal from the cave's floor and waved it behind him for the others to see. It was half the blade of a dagger, engraved with a hunting scene barely visible beneath the verdigris. "Their blades are bronze."

Chalcus cast the metal aside with a laugh and continued, "How many ages has it been since men fought with bronze, do you think? Whoever put our cold friends beneath this ice has kept them there for long enough that we needn't fear for the little while we'll be traipsing past them."

What Ilna noticed—and from the way Chalcus carried his sword, he had too—was that the dagger blade appeared to have been *chewed* off. She and her companions were in no danger from those dead, but whatever dug through the heart of the glacier to eat the dead was perhaps another matter.

"We're coming clear of the tunnel, I think," the chanteyman said. "I won't miss it."

His laughter caroled cheerfully despite the whistle of a fierce wind past the mouth of the tunnel. "Though I shouldn't say that, do you think, lest I tempt the Lady to prove me wrong?"

"If I believed in the Lady," Ilna said more sharply than she'd intended, "then the Lady *I* believed in would have better uses for her time than playing grim jokes."

"Don't you believe in the Lady, Mistress Ilna?" Merota said in surprise.

"I don't know what I believe in anymore," Ilna said curtly. "I used to think the world was a simpler place than I've found it recently. It's not a *better* place, child, but it's not simple."

They stepped, side by side, onto a windswept plain. Their tunnel was one of many in the face of a glacier stretching across the horizon; rivulets from each snaked across the stony ground, braiding into streams. Lichens and stunted vegetation softened the outlines of rocks toward the sun in the far south.

"I wouldn't mind sharing this place with others," said Chalcus softly as he eyed six figures standing a bowshot away. "But I don't think I'm willing to share it with those fellows, eh, mistress?"

"No," Ilna said, slinging her noose and taking the hank of cords from her sleeve. This wasn't going to be easy, if it was even possible. "I doubt they'd accept our presence either; but regardless, we can't let whatever they're doing continue."

A wizard whose garments were half black, half white, stood on one side of a brazier; across from him was the mummified corpse of something man-sized but not human. The mummy's age-browned linen wrappings fluttered in the wind. They—both—were chanting. Ilna felt the words she couldn't hear, the way she'd felt the pulse of the torrent before she entered Harn's cavern.

Another wizard was present, all in black, but he had no part in the incantation. He'd been watching a rod of light which stood upright in the center of a circle. The light bent toward Ilna, then vanished.

The wizard looked up and shouted an order. The words were only a puff of sound by the time they reached Ilna.

"The other man doesn't have a head," Merota said, her voice a skin of calm over boiling hysteria. "He has a thing where his head ought to be. One of the Great Ones."

"Indeed that's so, child," the chanteyman said, "but I

dare say it'll come off just the way real heads do."

His sword made a graceful figure in the air. "Though that may have to wait a time for more pressing business."

The other three figures were huge insectlike monsters. At the wizard's summons, they rose on their jointed legs and started toward the interlopers. Their jaws opened sideways and clashed edges of ragged chitin together when they closed again.

"I'll deal with the wizard," Ilna said. *I'll try to deal with the wizard.* "I'm afraid the rest are for you, Master Chalcus."

"I'll help," Merota said.

Ilna and the chanteyman glanced down at her. Neither spoke.

"I will!" the child said angrily. "They'll chase me and you can kill them!"

"Indeed," said Chalcus, "if they're no brighter than they look and with Mistress Ilna occupying the fellow who'd be directing them. . . . I think you're very likely right, milady."

Ilna squatted to make her body a better shield against the wind that wanted to disrupt her pattern. Her companions walked forward, moving to their right at an angle to the direct line between Ilna and the brazier where a wizard and a mummy still concentrated on matters not of the present world.

Neither Ilna nor Chalcus bothered to say that Merota would be in danger. The child knew that; and anyway, there was no safety in this chill wasteland.

In particular, there's no safety for our enemies. On my honor!

Ilna's fingers wove with the silent certainty of stars wheeling in the black heavens. The black-clad wizard intoned his spell in a singsong which reached Ilna only as a faint rhythm. As he sang, he held his left arm out toward Chalcus with three fingers extended.

The monsters shambled forward like a leash of hounds, spreading apart slightly as they advanced. One of them

would be in position to cut the chanteyman off if he
dodged in either direction.

Ilna smiled faintly and tugged her pattern tight. The wizard gasped. His arm twisted down, the fingers cramping into an arthritic knot. He turned and, instead of watching the swordsman, met Ilna's eyes across the scree of rocks.

Chalcus must have said something to the girl. The chanteyman froze; Merota sprinted toward the left. Released from the wizard's control, the three monsters turned as one to follow her.

The wizard looked toward his leader, but the headless thing at the brazier was intent on its own incantation. The wizard knelt. He drew an athame of chased silver from his sash and started to scrape a circle in the rocky soil.

Ilna tightened another knot. The wizard's hand jerked inward. The athame's edge was too dull to pierce the wizard's robe, but the point jabbed hard enough into his belly to double him up in pain.

Ilna was breathing hoarsely, but her fingers continued to loop cords into complex patterns. She was still smiling.

Chalcus danced forward, flicking his sword in a figure eight as he passed behind the first insect. He cut from the inside and severed the lowest joint of the creature's hindmost legs. Though the insect limbs didn't have hamstrings, they nonetheless had equivalent connections.

The monster twisted backward on its remaining pairs of legs and gave a shrill cry. Chalcus was already crippling the second creature with a similar pair of cuts. The motion was as graceful as the curve of a gull's wing, but the blade's kinked edge slung drops of ichor through the air like an amber necklace as the stroke finished.

The black-clad wizard staggered toward Ilna, his lips twisting as he spoke words of power. Ilna felt the air around her thicken as though lightning was about to strike nearby. She opened a gap in her pattern, then locked it with another knot. The wizard stumbled and fell hard, knocking the breath from his lungs.

Ilna was sweating like a scytheman in high summer. The

wind made her shiver, but still beads formed on her forehead and trickled down her spine beneath her tunics. All her muscles were trembling; all except those of her fingers, knotting a pattern as subtle as the interplay of high cirrus clouds.

The third creature was turning to meet Chalcus. Instead of dodging backward, the chanteyman leaped toward it and struck at the knee joints of the middle and hindmost leg on the side nearest him. The monster would've toppled over if it hadn't planted the left foreleg to support it. Chalcus laughed and struck again, severing the foreleg also. Only then did he jump clear as the creature rolled sideways like a maggot fallen from a carcass.

The wizard rose to his knees. Ilna twisted a cord and pulled it tight. She'd clamped her jaws together, but still her teeth chattered.

The wizard almost got to his feet before he fell on his face. Ilna had to put the flat of her hand to the ground to keep from toppling also. She closed her eyes and let her strength build, breathing deeply.

Chalcus gasped through his open mouth. He knelt on one knee, waving his sword to keep the attention of the two insects which were still mobile. Perhaps he thought that because the monsters were crippled, six yards was a sufficient margin.

It was, but barely. The creatures charged like rams battling to rule a flock, spurning large stones behind them. The chanteyman started to rise, realized the creatures were coming much too fast to flee, and hurled himself between them.

The monsters spun, both of them turning inward. Their mandibles tangled momentarily instead of either one clashing shut on Chalcus' chest. The chanteyman rolled under the massive abdomen of the insect on his right.

It turned again—the creatures' hind feet were dangling but the lack seemed to cost them nothing in terms of speed and agility—but this time Chalcus was ready. He slashed forehand and backhand in another figure eight, chopping both knee joints on the creature's left side. Like Chalcus' previous victim, it crashed down on its thorax and drove a furrow in the stony ground.

The chanteyman crouched, using the monster as a shield. The creature's two unbroken right legs tried to shove the body around to where its mandibles could reach its tormentor.

The wizard was coming toward Ilna again: crawling, now, but crawling steadily. He continued to speak his words of power. His right cheek bled from where he'd fallen on the rocks.

Ilna raised her pattern of knots. Her vision went gray and fuzzy. She thought her fingers were twisting the cords, but she couldn't be sure. . . .

Merota trotted across the waste, moving clumsily because she was carrying a large stone against her chest. The wizard must have heard her coming, because he turned his head toward her and raised a hand.

Ilna's awareness was crystal sharp again. She jerked her cords *hard* as if throttling a viper.

The wizard screamed; his arm jerked back to his side. Merota swung the rock, releasing it an instant before it thumped into the wizard's skull. The wizard went flat, his limbs splaying like a crushed spider. The child struggled to pick up the rock and repeat the blow.

The insect that still had four good legs hunched itself and started to crawl over its crippled fellow. Chalcus cocked his head upward to watch with a bemused smile. The creature he sheltered behind roared and squirmed, furious with what was happening.

The crawling insect thrust its head past the abdomen of its fellow. The chanteyman rose to his feet and stabbed upward, as smoothly as though the brief rest had refreshed him completely. The blade's slight inward bend didn't prevent it from plunging straight as an awl through the thin chitin of the creature's neck.

Chalcus withdrew his sword in a rush of ichor. The monster lurched forward. That was a convulsion rather than an attack, but the result would have been equally fatal if the chanteyman hadn't stepped aside. He was laughing.

The insect crunched down and began flailing its abdomen onto the rocks. From any angle but straight below, its armored head and thorax concealed the delicate neck joint. Had Chalcus planned this result, or had he simply let the fight develop and taken the opportunities it offered?

Perhaps both were true. Ilna got to her feet. The chanteyman was a very good man in a fight.

And in Ilna's terms, a very good man.

Merota hadn't managed to lift the rock again. She must be nearly as wrung out as Ilna herself. Ilna put a hand on the child's shoulder and said, "Never mind him, Merota. He won't bother us anymore."

The top of the wizard's skull was concave. The blood pooling under his ears and nostrils made a bright contrast to his black garments.

Chalcus stood at a cautious distance from the tangle of insectoid monsters. Only one was dead, and it thrashed more violently than its two crippled fellows.

A sleeve fluttered in the mandibles of one of the insects. Chalcus judged his distance, then stepped close and flicked the cloth away on his swordpoint. He used it to wipe ichor from his blade. The rush of the two creatures together had come closer than Ilna realized from where she squatted.

Chalcus nodded toward the unhuman figures chanting at the brazier. He raised an eyebrow. Ilna nodded curtly.

"Come, child," she said as she started forward. Her fingers had picked out the previous series of knots; she'd need something quite different to bind the remaining pair. This task would be like binding the universe itself as it plunged through time. "I'd like you to stay close to me. For as long as you can."

The chanteyman was strolling toward the brazier from his own angle, still breathing through his open mouth but managing a snatch of song as he did so. Instead of smoke, shapes of light seethed in a ball above the coals.

The chanting paused. The ammonite shell turned on the

human shoulders. Slit-pupiled eyes older than life on dry land glared at the humans from behind a screen of tentacles.

Merota had picked up another stone, not so big this time. Chalcus laughed gaily and stepped forward, swinging his blade. Ilna drew her first knot tight—

The air flashed red and congealed into solid ruby.

The screams that had drawn Sharina and Dalar into the palace's empty splendor were muted within the walls, but the humming was even more noticeable.

Sharina had expected a crowd inside. In Valles she'd gotten used to ordinary citizens, most of them merely spectators, thronging the public areas; ushers backed by guards to shunt minor petitioners to officials who'd at least make a pretense of listening to them; senior palace staff who oversaw magnates and important dispatches, separating out the relatively few who needed to see Prince Garric; and everywhere, so common they were generally ignored, the servants who cleaned and cooked and ran errands for the courtiers and visitors and officials.

Klestis was one city, not the capital of a kingdom, but even so there should have been at least the shadow of Valles' establishment. Instead, Ansalem's palace was an echoing tomb.

"We need to find—" Sharina said as her eyes surveyed the high entrance hall.

"Here are stairs," said Dalar, brushing aside a curtain concealed behind a pair of trefoil-section pillars. He started forward.

"I'll lead!" said Sharina. The bird's head rotated to look at her over the middle of his spine; he didn't give way.

"I'll lead," Sharina repeated, "because we'll be in a stairwell where your weights are use—"

She caught herself and continued, "Less useful than my knife."

Dalar laughed and stepped aside. "If we were going

down," he said, "I would remind you that I can kick. But as we are not . . ."

Sharina skipped forward, taking the stairs two at a time. She had long legs and the pitch of the steps was flatter than what she was used to. The folk who used this staircase expected their physical labors to be made as easy as possible.

The hum—a presence rather than a sound—was even more penetrating in the stairwell than it had been in the entrance hall. The sky's nervous sanguine glow illuminated the stairs through slit windows, wider on the outside than the inside. Wax-soaked cressets stood in wall sconces, ready to be lighted when night fell. If . . .

"Dalar, do you think that night will ever fall again here?" Sharina asked as she turned on the first landing.

The bird made a sound that was neither laughter nor a moan. "I would instead ask if the sun will ever rise again, Sharina," he said. "And I fear the answer is that the sun will not rise."

They turned the second landing and continued upward. Sharina heard the screams more clearly as she climbed.

She glanced through a narrow window. The citizens of Klestis stared upward like carp gulping air on a hot day. Some had begun to cry with terror and despair.

Sharina had survived things she hadn't expected to. That she still lived was a gift. If the Lady wanted to reclaim that gift, then Sharina hadn't been raised to whimper.

As if sharing the thought that went through Sharina's mind, Dalar said, "For thirty days I floated on a raft, eating the fish I could catch and drinking the rain that fell on me. Every day I met Death yet again. What have I to fear in this place, when Death and I are old dinner companions?"

Dalar was a friend and a stalwart warrior. Nonetheless, Sharina wished that Cashel was at her side, because he brought a kind of solidity to everything around him. Cashel could settle even this hell of hums and screaming.

She'd reached the head of the stairs and another curtained doorway. Dalar gestured.

Sharina nodded. Instead of sliding the tapestry aside, she gripped the cloth with her left hand and ripped it from the carrier railing. Dalar sprang through with his weights spinning, ready to strike right or left if an enemy waited in ambush.

No one did. Dalar caught his weights. Sharina followed him into a shallow anteroom. The screams came from the electrum-grated view slit of the door opposite. Dalar glanced through the opening, then stepped aside for Sharina to look.

Seven wizards wearing black or white or black-and-white stood in a circle around the butchered body of a young boy. The eighth figure, placed opposite the wizards' particolored leader and hissing the words of power with the others, was a reptilian mummy in cerements of browning linen. Sharina had finally met the Dragon in the flesh.

Against a sidewall a tall, lean man with muscles like splits of hickory watched the wizards and screamed. Serpents of red wizard-light writhed tightly about his limbs. On the stone couch beside him slept a plump man with a cherubic face and only a fringe of white hair remaining on his head.

"That's Ansalem," Sharina said. "My brother dreamed of him. We've—"

But there wasn't time for talk. Sharina stepped back, raising the Pewle knife overhead with both hands, and chopped down at where she judged the bar locking the door from the other side would be.

Her stroke split away a long splinter of wood veneer and sprang back from metal. Sharina's hands were numb and her blade still trembled. The core beneath the wood had the sheen of polished silver, but no metal Sharina knew could've taken that blow and remained completely unmarked.

"Back!" Dalar said. He spun the weight in his right hand at the gap in the veneer. It was a short stroke since the anteroom didn't give much scope for the chains, but Sharina had seen what Dalar could do with his weapon. Steel would have dented, stone would have chipped.

The weight bounced away with a *crack!* and wobbled limply, all its energy drained. The door didn't even ring from a blow that would've crushed a man's skull.

In the sanctum beyond, a ripple of golden light played across Ansalem. A serpent with a head on either end began shifting in and out of phase with the sleeping wizard. Ansalem's body had become as rigid as a statue.

"The wall, then!" Sharina said, but it was of dense sandstone blocks, set too tight for her knifepoint to enter. She looked for anything that might serve as a pick or a battering ram, but the room was as bare as a horse's stall.

They *had* to interrupt the spell. She knew from Garric's dream that if they didn't, they'd remain in Klestis: out of time and space, without hope or succor, until they and all the city's population died. Someone would defeat the wizards, of that Sharina was sure; but the victory would come long after she and Dalar were dust.

The bird stepped to the stairwell, searching for a tool. As he did so, the outer wall dissolved into rainbow light.

Sharina shouted and raised her knife. Dalar sprang to her side, setting his weights spinning. Something came toward them from the bright haze, gigantic and inexorable.

Cashel stepped from the light, his quarterstaff raised across his body. His face was alert but friendly; when he saw Sharina, he smiled broadly.

"Cashel!" Sharina shouted. "Dalar, a friend!"

Behind Cashel, the rainbow dissipated like quartz sand falling through sunlight. The cosmos sucked in on itself and closed, becoming a stone wall with a window looking down onto terrified citizens.

"Who . . . ?" said Dalar. He wasn't threatening the big stranger who'd appeared out of nowhere, but his weights continued to whirl.

"Cashel, we need to get into that room!" Sharina said, gesturing toward the door whose veneer she'd scarred. "There's wizards inside, and they've murdered a boy."

"Ah!" said Cashel. His face didn't change in an identifiable fashion, but there was no longer any softness to his expression. He shifted his grip on the quarterstaff. "Stand clear," he ordered without raising his voice.

"The door is steel or harder than steel!" Dalar said. "You can't—"

Cashel brought the end of his staff forward like a battering ram. The ferrule hit the center of the door. Instead of the crash of metal against metal, there was a flash of blue light that penetrated flesh and stone alike. The universe rang. Time froze.

Sound and movement resumed. Cashel staggered back from the blow. The door tore from its hinges and sailed across the room beyond.

The wizards were gone, all but the one lying on the floor as a faceless corpse. The dead child and his pinioned father were gone as well. Ages had racked the room, but a body lay on the bier and a band of armed men were crashing through the shattered screen that formed the far wall.

The figure on the bier tried to sit up.

"Tenoctris!" Sharina cried. Then, "Garric! It's me!"

"By the Lady!" someone was screaming. "There's a million soldiers coming at us and they're all dead!"

Garric stumbled to his knees. He dropped his sword and reached out to touch Tenoctris. Her fingers seemed as delicate as ivory wands when he clasped them in his own tanned, powerful hand.

Cashel stepped into the room, wobbly but walking on his own legs. Sharina threw her arms around him. She should have sheathed the Pewle knife first, but it was only the flat of the blade that rapped Cashel's shoulders.

From the way he lifted her and whirled her in the air, he wouldn't have cared if she'd slashed him with the edge. Attaper dodged back with a curse to avoid Sharina's feet, and Dalar twisted his head aside.

Garric fumbled for his sword. The air was choking with powdered alabaster, the fumes of the overturned brazier, and fluids leaking from the dead wizard.

*What had happened to the dead man? He was evil be-
yond doubt, but had Gar- ric . . . ?*

"Liane's in the plaza," Garric muttered. "I've got to get
down to her and the army."

"No!" said Tenoctris. She looked barely able to sit
straight without help, but her voice rang with authority.
"Where did Purlio go? The chief wizard?"

Cashel set Sharina down but continued to hold her. Dalar
stood with his back to the pair. His head twitched in quick
half-circuits that covered the room now filling with soldiers. The bird had caught his weights, and his face had
even less expression than it normally did.

"He vanished," Garric said, rising carefully to his feet.
His face was drawn and gray, even taking its covering of
grit into account. "He was standing there—"

He pointed to the foot of Tenoctris' bier.

"—and he vanished in a flash of red. But if armies are
attacking us, I've—"

"No," Tenoctris repeated. "Purlio has all the dead of all
time to send against us. We have to stop *him*; then his
armies won't matter. Now please, don't disturb me. I hope
I can open the gate he just used. This is a place of great
power, so I may possibly . . ."

She slid off the bier. Cashel guessed what she was doing
before anyone else did. He caught Tenoctris and lowered
her to the floor, where she sat cross-legged.

*You never had to wonder who would help you if Cashel
was around. . . .*

Tenoctris drew a hexagon in the dust with her index
finger, then made quick notations in the Old Script outside
each of the six faces. Sharina smiled wryly and handed the
old woman a splinter. It had been part of the veneer from
the door.

Tenoctris smiled back minusculely. *"Darzah howa
walab,"* she said, using the wood to tap the words of power
as she spoke them: *"Warzaho beha getayat. . . ."*

Trumpets called in the plaza below. Sharina heard shouts
and the clash of equipment as troops formed ranks in the

face of a new threat. *All the dead of all time. . . .*

"*Re sou lampse,*" said Tenoctris. "*Lak othi kalak. . . .*"

Sharina walked into the anteroom from which she'd come in a former age, wanting to put distance between her and the partly eaten corpse. Cashel fell into position behind her.

Dalar, demonstrating both alertness and athletic grace, leaped past to precede both the humans. Cashel grinned slightly. Sharina noticed for the first time that one ferrule of his staff had been blasted completely away from the hickory. The wood was merely scorched.

She glanced through the outside window. From this height Klestis was still a splendid metropolis, an expanse of shining buildings and luxuriant gardens. You had to look for the details which proved the beauty false: places where the cladding had slipped from many façades, and the way vegetation grew in uncontrolled masses of a single species that had destroyed those which had shared each planted bed.

Armies marched on Klestis all around the enclosing red membrane. Sharina couldn't count the banners, let alone the individual soldiers following them. Dead cavalrymen rode dead horses. Heavy infantry tramped along in mail and plate armor, but bone glinted beneath the visors of their helmets. Slingers and javelin men who were little more than armed skeletons capered on bridges that stretched as far as the eye could see.

"After they retake Klestis," Sharina said, "they'll go on into Valles and all the Isles."

Cashel shrugged. "They'll try," he said. "Garric will know what to do. And Tenoctris."

Dalar looked at him. Cashel smiled.

"*Nosaba!*" Tenoctris cried.

Sharina felt a shudder. The red light deepened, then cleared to become a pale winter sky. Everyone who'd been with Garric was still present, but there were other figures on the transfigured landscape as well.

The roof of Ansalem's palace was a glimmer in the air.

Instead of a tessellated floor, Sharina and her companions stood on a chill, rocky wasteland. The light of distant times glimmered over a brazier. In it miniature armies of the dead marched toward the end a wizard had determined for them. On the far side of the brazier was the Dragon's mummy, murmuring an enchantment.

Ilna stood close by like a grim-faced statue with cords in her hands; at her side was a young girl holding a rock. Near them a smiling man poised with his sword, curved like a scorpion's sting, in midstroke. Ruby light played around Ilna and her companions.

The sword stroke was aimed at a wizard whose robes were half black and half white; the marcasite fossil of an ammonite took the place of his head.

The Great One turned to stare at Sharina. The beast eyes within its mantle were yellow-green with slitted, S-curved pupils. The beak opened in a rasping cry. The human arms didn't move, but the tentacles quivered in a complex pattern. Sharina swung her knife—

Cashel thrust his staff—

Dalar's weights spun in accelerating circles—

Garric's sword cut in a long arc—

Spears, swords, and hatchets struck toward a figure that had once been human but was no more. Sharina felt a freezing lethargy of red light.

Ilna, relaxed from her restraint, drew a knot tight. The swordsman with her brought his weapon down and the girl half threw, half pushed her rock toward the necromancer.

The necromancer dissolved downward, inward with a scream both soundless and more intense than a living entity could grasp. The curved sword cut only air. Instants later other weapons clashed in the same empty space, Sharina's among them.

They were back in Ansalem's palace. Everyone was shouting. Tenoctris tried to gasp an explanation that the others were too excited to hear.

The necromancer was gone, but the mummy glared at Sharina across the brazier. She sheathed the Pewle knife and lifted the brazier by one tripod leg. She kicked the mummy onto the floor. The linen powdered at her touch, but the dry, scaly flesh beneath was firm. The mummy winked at her; that must have been a trick of the light.

Sharina dumped the blazing coals onto the Dragon's chest and belly. She jumped back quickly, but even so the fire bursting from a body impregnated with natron and cedar resins was so sudden that it singed the fine hairs off her right arm. Cashel snatched her away.

The flames billowed upward, mushrooming on the ceiling of Ansalem's chamber. "Out!" Garric ordered in a voice like a tree falling. "Out of here fast!"

Cashel put Sharina over his shoulder despite her cry and Dalar's cluck of protest. Two soldiers carried Tenoctris while Garric stood between the old wizard and the sudden conflagration. Instead of waiting for them to get through the existing hole, Cashel kicked the weakened screen. A piece flew outward.

Cashel paused as a further block of pierced alabaster the size of a tabletop wobbled, then decided to fall inward. He walked through without having to duck and deposited Sharina back on her feet.

The solid portion of the chamber's roof crumbled, eaten through by fire with a more than natural power. For a moment flames roared in windblown tendrils through the hole they'd burned; then the gout expanded into a figure thirty feet tall with a long, reptilian jaw.

"You have served me well, Sharina os-Reise!" said the Dragon. The figure of fire stretched out a three-fingered hand and swept the horizon. As the hand moved, the armies of the dead exploded like thistledown in a bonfire. Black smoke spewed from the cataclysm, then was sucked away. The bridges remained, delicate traceries of wizard-light, but the fire had scoured them bare of all life or once-life.

The Dragon continued turning until his gesture had covered and cleansed the horizon. Some of Garric's soldiers flinched as the flaming arm pointed past their heads, but

Sharina felt nothing save the prickling of nearness to great power.

The Dragon rocked with hissing laughter and leaped skyward. His flaming figure expanded, swelling until it splashed against the dome of light sealing Klestis out of time.

Fire spread across the wizard-light, merged—and vanished in a thunderclap. For long moments the echoes rolled across Klestis. They finally ceased, and there was no sound at all.

"We've won," said Garric. He sounded too exhausted to care.

"No," said Tenoctris. She strained, but only when Cashel caught her around the body was she able to rise. "No, Garric, I'm sorry, but we haven't won. Purlio has gone to a place no one living can follow, and the bridge . . ."

She pointed to the horizon. Sharina's eyes followed the gesture. She didn't know how Tenoctris could pick one bridge out of the apparent thousands which linked Klestis to other planes of existence, but neither did she doubt that beyond *that* span was Valles and Sharina's own time.

"The bridge remains, and so do all the certain dangers I described before," Tenoctris said. "The necromancers didn't create the bridge. So long as it remains, Purlio or something worse than Purlio will use it again; and again; and forever, until we fail and evil triumphs. Only Ansalem can remove the threat, and we can't reach Ansalem in the cyst Purlio formed around him."

"But Sharina and I *saw* Ansalem," Dalar said. "Only a moment ago."

Men who'd been involved in their own tasks and fears stared at the bird, some of them seeing him for the first time. A Blood Eagle raised his spear; Attaper rang a hard hand off the man's helmet to control him.

"You must have seen him at the moment the necromancers formed their cyst," Tenoctris said. "Only the amphisbaena, the double-headed serpent, can open it; and the amphisbaena is enclosed with Ansalem."

"Oh," said Sharina. She unwrapped the snakeskin which she'd been given in the ruins of the Dragon's palace. "I think this may be—"

Tenoctris' cry of delight cut off the rest of Sharina's words.

Chapter Twenty-one

Garric wanted to sleep, but he was too tired. He listened to Tenoctris while he focused his eyes on the sword he was sharpening with the small hand stone from his belt. When the emotions burned out of his blood and his mind re-formed from the shards of battle flickering through it in no particular order, then he might be able to sleep.

"When I'm myself again . . ." Tenoctris said. She managed a weak smile. Liane sat on one side of her with Sharina on the other. Cashel squatted behind the old wizard like a boulder.

"Such as that is, of course," Tenoctris continued, "I can at least try to unlock the place where Ansalem sleeps. I can't do anything about Purlio, though. He may not return to our time or any time for thousands of years, but we can't stop him from returning when he chooses to. When *it* chooses to, I should rather say."

Garric had sent Waldron and the bulk of the army back to Valles. Casualties had been light.

"Amazingly light," agreed Carus. *"Wizards are dangerous in their own way, but may we always be so lucky that the armies we fight have wizards for generals."*

The ghost in Garric's mind looked drained, though King Carus had no physical body to tire in the running, slashing chaos. Battle wears on more than muscles; and perhaps muscles least of all.

Garric and the remainder of his forces—the Blood Eagles and a company of javelin men, to honor the light troops for their initiative in dealing with the wizards—were camped in the overgrown medians of Klestis' boulevards. Garric didn't see the need for any troops at all, but Attaper wouldn't have obeyed an order to take his unit back across the bridge, and for a change Waldron would've agreed wholeheartedly with his rival.

Garric and his friends still had work to do in Klestis.

"You sent me to Landure," said Cashel in his usual slow rumble. "If you send me to where this Purlio is, I'll put him in a place he won't come back from."

Except for the perimeter guards, tents covered the soldiers in Klestis. The red dome over the city was harmless, but its light worked on men's nerves. Garric had thought of retreating to Valles until Tenoctris was strong enough for the incantation . . . but that would mean crossing the bridge twice, which would probably be worse for all concerned.

Garric's lips smiled. Himself included.

"Kill him, you mean," Tenoctris said with a touch of irritation. They were all exhausted, but the old wizard had been through more than the rest of them. "Purlio is *already* dead. Purlio died the moment he surrendered to the Great One, though I suppose he thought that was a last chance to save himself. But because he's dead, he's safe from those who live."

"With respect to your wisdom, mistress . . ." said Ilna's new friend. His name was Chalcus, and he was a sailor.

"A sailor?" King Carus snorted. *"Then I was a jockey because I sometimes rode a horse!"*

Chalcus squatted along one wall of the tent, with Ilna nearby and the child they'd appeared with sleeping between them. The girl—a niece of Lord Tadai, apparently—had absolutely refused to be separated from her companions, even though that meant staying in Klestis because Ilna had decided she was going "to see the business out."

Whatever *that* meant to Ilna's chill, knife-edged mind.

"But it's been my experience that men are much less trouble to me after they're dead than before," Chalcus went on. "If your wizard is dead, then so much the better."

"It's dead," Tenoctris said. Her voice sounded particularly reedy following Chalcus' honeyed tones. "Unfortunately it isn't a man. It's a thing that hasn't been alive as we understand it in more ages than you have years, Master Chalcus; but so long as it has a connection to our world, we'll never be safe from it."

Garric had soaked his whetstone in whale oil to float the particles of steel from its surface as he drew it along his sword edge, one side and then the other. He'd cut into the root of a tusk when he severed the mammoth's trunk; ivory had nicked the metal.

The rhythmic scritch of stone on steel settled Garric's mind as little else could have done. A simple, precise task, repeated over and over. It was calming, even soporific.

A three-wick lamp hung from the tent's ridgepole. The light barely illuminated the faces of those within, but it served to conceal the red glow leaking through the seams. The troops had built bonfires, feeding them with brush cut from plantings that had become thickets, but they'd quickly found that firelight alone wasn't sufficient protection from the scarlet miasma. Leather tent walls and a lamp made it possible—almost—to imagine you were back in the waking world.

Garric let his eyes close. He tried to put the whetstone away, but after fumbling twice—more?—he let it slip to the rank grass. He wiped grit and excess oil from the blade with a rag that had come from the tunic of a soldier now dead, then sheathed the sword with an instinct gained from King Carus. Even if the king had been beheaded, his hands could have placed his blade where it needed to be.

The nearby conversation dulled to a buzz. Liane spoke. Garric's lips smiled in reaction, but the words didn't reach his conscious mind through the interwoven layers of fatigue.

He was vaguely aware of his friends rising and filing

out of the tent. Liane was the last, and she carried the lamp with her.

Garric dreamed. He was in a deep forest. A storm rose, bending the trees and wrenching leaves, but the wind and rain were a protection. The fear that lay over Garric lessened during the violence. Lessened, though it never quite vanished.

The clouds cleared away. Stars in constellations that Garric didn't recognize glared down on him. There was a place that Garric knew he should be, but he couldn't remember where; and anyway, he couldn't move. He was a stone figure lying under an oak.

The moon rose. Garric thought the leafy branches would shield him, but light passed through as though the oak were transparent.

Tendrils from the moon's cold smile bathed Garric. His stone body began to crumble like gypsum in a furnace. Bits dissolved into powder and leaked into the ground. He watched and marveled as his form lost definition; became a mound, then merely a ripple, and finally merged with the grass as if he had never been.

The moon leaned down from the sky. It kissed the soil where once Garric had lain. Garric slipped through a barrier of light as chill as the dust between the stars. He felt nothing except the cold.

"Colva!" someone shouted in a world where Garric no longer had a place. He wanted to speak, but he didn't exist.

There was nothing but the cold.

Ilna ran the ivory comb through Merota's hair, taking only the width of a few teeth at each pass. The child's hair—and Ilna's—had gotten filthy during the days since the mutiny. Army soap was harsh, and Ilna hadn't waited for the brushwood fire to more than take the chill off the firkin of pond water, but the two of them were clean again. Grooming, the next project, was well in hand thanks to a comb borrowed from an officer.

"Will Uncle Tadai send me back to Erdin, now, Ilna?" Merota said in a small voice.

"I'm not a fortune-teller!" Ilna said before she thought about the question Merota was *really* asking; then she winced. The child hadn't complained at the fiery soap or the spurge bushes Ilna had used because she didn't have a proper loofa. The child hadn't complained about *anything* during all the time Ilna had known her.

"I'm not a fortune-teller," Ilna repeated mildly, "but I don't expect you to be sent to Erdin to be married off, no. Because I won't let that happen. Unless you want it to."

Merota twisted and hugged herself against Ilna's shoulder. "I don't want it to," she said. She was crying. "I don't. I never did."

Knucklebones rattled in the adjacent tent. The chanteyman's familiar voice cried, "The Lady! See how She forgives Her erring worshipper? Now, which of you fine soldiers will pay to prove that I can't make my point again?"

Cashel was sleeping the sleep of the just across the far end of the eight-man squad tent he shared with Ilna and the child. One of the soldiers pitching the tent had asked—innocently, Ilna now assumed—if the third blanket roll was for Chalcus. Ilna had come closer to throttling the fellow with her noose than he probably realized—but he did realize, babbling apologies as he backed away, that the suggestion hadn't been a welcome one.

She sniffed. She was Ilna os-Kenset, so she wouldn't lie to herself. The suggestion had been far too welcome; *that* was why she'd reacted as she did.

"Sit still and I'll plait your braids," Ilna said, taking a hank of the girl's long, fine hair and running it through her fingers. Touch would tell her how to interweave the strands and—

Ilna froze as she let herself understand what the pattern was telling her.

"Cashel, get up!" she said as she rose to her feet. Flinging back the tent flap she called, "Garric! Prince Garric!"

The pair of Blood Eagles posted at the entrance looked at her in surprise. "Come!" Ilna called, trotting in the direction of the large, silk-walled tent where she'd left Garric asleep.

Merota was at her heels. That was a good thing, because Cashel struck the forepole—he wasn't used to tents—and broke it in half as he followed his sister. The tent collapsed behind him.

"Garric!" Ilna called again. The dome of light provided as much illumination as the full moon, but it distorted as much as it displayed. A cherry tree threw a shadow like a troll's across the side of the royal tent. The limbs seemed to squirm though the air was still.

The squad of Blood Eagles guarding Garric were rigid as statues. A lantern hanging from the extended ridgepole lighted the circle around them through its horn lenses, but the men themselves were in shadow. Their officer wore a silvered cuirass instead of the black enamel equipment of his troops.

"We have to see Prince Garric *now*," Ilna said as she stepped up to him. She expected a refusal—and the pattern her fingers were knotting would be her response. The danger Ilna had seen, *felt* as Merota's hair wove into plaits, brooked no delay.

The Blood Eagles didn't blink. They *were* statues, locked into a frozen sleep as they stood.

"Get a light!" Ilna said. The lantern was too high for her. Chalcus leaped and came down with it in his left hand, holding it by its hot iron base. Chalcus pushed into the tent, bumping several of the guards aside with his shoulders. As the men toppled, they awakened with startled shouts.

Ilna followed her brother. Chalcus was beside her, holding the lantern now by its loop handle. He'd singed himself. The burned skin stank, but his rower's calluses were so thick that he probably hadn't felt the injury.

For an instant Ilna thought that Garric's body lay under

a tent of cobweb in the corner. The web shifted, turned. It had the face of a spider.

"Colva!" Cashel shouted. He stepped forward, holding his quarterstaff in both hands like a battering ram.

The tendrils of webbing solidified. The face swelled into that of an attractive woman instead of a creature of nightmare. Ilna didn't recognize her.

"Cashel, my hero—" the woman said.

"Colva!" Cashel repeated. He struck her face with his staff. The hickory drove through as though she were smoke.

"Iron!" cried Tenoctris from behind them. "You have to use—"

Ilna's noose settled over the woman's neck and slipped through the liquid flesh instead of drawing tight. Cashel spun his staff end for end to bring the remaining ferrule forward. The staff caught on the tent roof. Silk tore, but it clogged his motion.

Colva laughed. As Chalcus came toward her she stepped through the wall of the tent.

And staggered back inside. A small dagger with its hilt wrapped in gold wire protruded from her chest, just to the left of her breastbone. She screamed during the instant she had before the chanteyman beheaded her, but she was already dying.

The thing that called itself Colva began to shrink in on itself like a meringue congealing. The creature looked less and less human as successive layers of illusion failed.

The bottom of the tent wall humped. Liane squirmed through, her face pale. She still held the gilded sheath of her little dagger in her left hand.

"Is he . . . ?" she whispered to Ilna.

Tenoctris knelt beside Garric. As Sharina supported her, the old wizard touched her fingertips to Garric's throat. She closed her eyes, then opened them and faced the others again.

"We're too late," Tenoctris said. "I'm so sorry. Garric is dead."

There was complete silence. Then, for the first time in her life, Ilna cried openly.

Garric strode down a boulevard of the dead city, unaffected by the darkness or the miles of water over him. Yole had returned to the depths, but that didn't matter to Garric.

Because Garric was dead.

Fish that walked on their fins felt Garric's presence. They turned, launched themselves from the bottom, and swam off stiffly.

"I failed," Garric said. He'd gotten used to being with King Carus. In death he was completely alone, but he spoke anyway. "I died before I'd reunited the Isles. I failed."

On either side of the street were houses where wealthy citizens had lived in the days when Yole itself lived. Shutters hung open; the panes had fallen from most of the casements when wizardry engulfed Yole.

Tiles shaken from the roofs lay over the cobblestones. Garric saw them as red, though there was no color at this depth.

He smiled faintly. He was dead, but he still existed in this dead place; and he still had work to do.

The palace of the Dukes of Yole, fortified and a stark contrast to the comfortable luxury of the houses around it, stood before him. The gates were open when the island sank. The outer barbican had collapsed in the final earthquake, and the portcullis across the inner passage had decayed to a scale of salt-eaten iron on a frame of spongy wood.

It wouldn't have stopped Garric anyway. Nothing was going to stop him.

Three huge ammonites filled the palace courtyard. They adjusted the air trapped within their coiled shells to balance themselves just above the paving stones. As Garric approached, they waved their thickets of tentacles minusculely.

Garric laughed. "Do you think I fear you?" he asked. "I'm already dead!"

He bent to pick up a stone fallen from the façade. It was a gargoyle's nose, hooked and distorted. He would have shied it at the Great Ones, but his fingers slipped through the limestone.

The creatures lifted on lashing tentacles, moving as though parts of the same entity. When they'd risen above the courtyard walls, their siphons drove them backward and away. Their shells had the opalescent beauty of rainbows in the skies of Hell.

The last Garric saw of the Great Ones was their glaring, angry eyes.

He stepped into an anteroom which would have seemed dingy in the upper world. The thick walls and narrow windows required for defense meant a dark, narrow interior. The Duchy of Yole hadn't been rich enough to build on a scale that gave even this sort of architecture a stark majesty.

Light didn't matter to Garric any longer. He had one task remaining before he went down to the Sister's realm forevermore. Garric had failed the kingdom, but he would not fail to accomplish *this* thing.

He passed through a pointed archway; the curtain which once had closed it was a tangle of gold and silver wires, still clinging to a few of the linen warp threads. At the end of the high room beyond, a figure sat on the duke's throne.

"Greetings, brother," the figure called. Its lips didn't move, for it had no lips. "Greetings Garric, King of the World and of All Time."

Garric laughed. "Greetings, Purlio," he said. "I've come to kill you."

"No, brother, no," Purlio said. The ammonite which replaced his head waved its tentacles in a subtle pattern. "You can't kill me, because I'm already dead. But—"

"*I* can kill you, liar," Garric said.

He smiled as he might have done at a particularly fine

roast before he started to carve. He didn't have a sword in this existence, but that wouldn't matter.

"I'm not responsible for your death, Garric!" Purlio said. "But I can give you life again. Together nothing can stand against us!"

"You can't stand against me now, Purlio," Garric said as he continued to walk forward. He supposed movement was as much an illusion as the body he imagined himself wearing—but perhaps not. The drowned city seemed real, though the hand with which he'd tried to touch it was not.

The tentacles where Purlio's face should be grew agitated. "You wanted to be King of the Isles, *really* king. I can give you life *and* domination, brother. Garric, King of the World! Garric, Immortal!"

The throne stood in a bay framed on three sides by windows. It was intended to light the duke while his petitioners remained in shadow. Originally the casements had held colored glass, but only the twisted lead strips holding the pieces had survived the earthquake. Purlio looked as though he sat in a grape arbor after a killing frost.

"I'd have died before I became king on your terms, wizard," Garric said. He laughed. "I *did* die. Now the only thing keeping me in this world is the chance to see you out of it forever. Goodbye, Purlio!"

Garric leaped. The tentacles of Purlio's face wrapped Garric's right hand and drew his fingers toward the crushing beak.

Garric flung the wizard sideways. To his amazement, the throne crumbled under the impact of Purlio's body. Flakes of ivory inlay and gold leaf separated from the sodden framework. Purlio—or the monster that had taken control of Purlio—existed in the realm of the dead where Garric could reach him, but a part of the wizard still had a connection to the waking world.

Garric laughed and broke free. That connection was Purlio's doom.

The Great One's tentacles writhed. Ilna would understand the spell of binding they were trying to weave, but the pattern was a thing for flesh and the living. Garric stepped forward unfazed.

He'd been trying to fight a man, but the man Purlio had been no longer mattered. Garric grabbed the wizard by the waist. A human would've countered by seizing Garric by the throat or shoulders, but Purlio still didn't move his arms. The wizard bent, trying to bring the tentacles close enough to grip Garric's face.

Garric stepped into his opponent, shifting his weight. Running and wrestling were boys' chief sports in the borough, and Garric had excelled at both of them.

The Great One screamed in Garric's mind like a saw cutting glass. Garric's vision blurred with agony, but he threw Purlio headfirst into the sandstone pillar beside the throne.

The ammonite shattered. Fragments of marcasite, eggshell thin and the color of burnished gold, fluttered up in the turbulence. The flesh within the shell dissolved into a rosy pulp, the constituents from which the Great One had molded its physical being.

Purlio lay dead. His dried muscles were as fragile as his brittle bones. Flakes of the wizard's flesh drifted out of his robes, sloughed as a result of the mishandling they'd received from Garric.

Garric felt a force drawing him. The ruined city lost color; then its gray forms blurred into the grayness of eternity.

With the last spark of something that cared about success and failure, Garric shouted, "You'll never touch my world again, Purlio!"

And there was blackness.

Sharina felt the head pillowed in her lap stir; she prayed silently to the Lady that it wasn't a spasm in dead muscles. "He's coming around!" she said aloud.

"Master Krias wouldn't lie to me," Cashel said. "He said I'd need the fruit, after all, and he was right about that."

Cashel squatted with his quarterstaff upright beside him, pointedly a little apart from the group tending Garric. Sharina didn't think Cashel's concern that he'd smash things by accident was justified, but it was no less real for that.

Dalar was on the other side of the tent, directly across from Cashel. He remained perfectly still in this gathering of tense humans.

Liane held the plum Cashel had taken from his wallet. She squeezed a last drop into Garric's open mouth. He spluttered and his eyelids twitched, though they remained closed.

"Oh, Lady," Liane whispered. She'd remained dry-eyed, but now tears ran down her cheeks. "Thank You for Your mercy."

Tenoctris sank back against the support of Ilna's arm. "I wish I could believe in the Gods," she said, "so that I'd have someone to thank also. Perhaps you can pray for me, Liane."

She looked at Cashel. "I don't doubt the honesty of your demon friend, Cashel," she continued. "Not now, at least. But I don't understand why if the fruit was to work, it didn't work until now."

Garric mumbled like a man coming out of a deep sleep. He was speaking words, but they were too slurred for Sharina to understand them.

"Because it wasn't yet time to work that thread into the pattern," Ilna said, her eyes on Garric—and Liane. Ilna's smile meant as much as her smiles ever did: a great deal, but nothing that anyone else would be able to read. "Who do you suppose is at the loom, Tenoctris?"

"I would say rather," said Ilna's scarred friend Chalcus. "that Master Garric delayed to finish his work. Which may be the same thing, do you think?"

He smiled at Ilna in a way nobody had ever smiled at Ilna; but Sharina had seen Chalcus' sword move. Of all people, *that* man knew what Ilna was in her heart.

Garric coughed. His eyes opened in amazement. Sharina felt her brother start to lurch upright, but another fit of coughing interrupted him. He turned on his side instead so that he wouldn't choke.

At last Garric straightened. Liane threw her arms around his neck. She was trying to speak but the words were lost in her sobbing. Sharina got up, feeling a little embarrassed, and settled again at Cashel's side.

Liane pulled away, red-faced and smiling. She dabbed with a lace handkerchief from her sleeve, then nodded thanks as Ilna silently handed her the square of tight-woven linen *she* carried.

"But I'm dead," Garric said in wonderment.

"No," said Tenoctris, "but you were."

Garric held his hands out in front of him and flexed them, watching the play of muscles and tendons. He looked around the circle of his friends with a terrible smile.

"I see," he said. "But Purlio is dead, Tenoctris. And he's going to stay that way."

Chapter Twenty-two

On the floor of Ansalem's chamber lay shattered fragments of an ammonite fossil and a corpse wasted to skin over dry bones. The corpse was headless.

"Clear this rubbish!" Lord Attaper snapped to his detachment. His face froze. He looked at Garric and added, "Unless, Your Majesty . . . ?"

Garric shook his head. "Clear this rubbish," he said, deliberately echoing Attaper. "I'd say give it to the dogs to eat, but there aren't any dogs in Klestis."

"I *like* dogs," Liane said, eyeing the corpse with cold distaste.

Two soldiers grabbed the body. Purlio's right arm came off in the hand of the man holding it. He swore, but his partner didn't notice he was carrying the rest of the body by himself. The desiccated corpse weighed almost nothing.

Ilna spread her kerchief and brushed the bits of marcasite from the floor with it. She folded the fabric over the shell and handed it to a soldier. "Dispose of the cloth also," she said. "I don't want it back."

Garric exchanged glances with Tenoctris. He turned to his guard commander and said, "We're ready to proceed, Lord Attaper. If you'll hold your men on the roof garden, they'll be able to intervene if required."

"We can't possibly need soldiers," Tenoctris said to Garric in surprise.

"Humor me," Garric said with a smile. *While I humor Attaper. If I told him he was useless, he'd argue with me. If I tell him to hold himself in readiness but out of the way, he'll obey without question.*

King Carus chuckled, lounging in a garden of his youth where beech trees were espaliered against a brick wall. *"Half of kingship is considering what the other fellow is going to hear, rather than what you're going to say. You're better at it than I ever was, lad."*

The troop of guards filed out through the shattered screen. After the troops and Cashel had gotten done with it, you could drive a mammoth through what had started out as delicate filigree.

The atmosphere changed when the soldiers had left. It wasn't so much that the troops had crowded the chamber as the fact that they were more or less strangers to Garric and his friends.

Garric looked around the remaining group, smiling. There were still strangers present: the bird Dalar, whom Sharina said was a warrior and who certainly moved like one; the young Lady Merota, who met Garric's eyes with an aristocratic calm that extended quite a way—but not all the way—below the surface of her face; and Chalcus.

Chalcus grinned back at Garric. The sailor wore a broad leather belt dyed to match his equally new high-laced sandals. Those accessories and Chalcus' pair of embroidered tunics must have come from the personal effects of some of the wealthier Blood Eagles.

King Carus chuckled knowingly. *"Oh, yes, we can find a place for that one,"* he murmured to Garric. *"But an independent command—somewhere that he won't be meeting camp marshals or the City Watch either one."*

Tenoctris shook her head slightly. She took the packet Cashel carried for her and opened it.

The wizard had rolled Sharina's snakeskin in layers of fabric—a discarded tunic—to protect it. The skin was sepia with occasional golden highlights. The amphisbaena had been proportionately thicker than an ordinary snake; though less than six feet in length, it was well over a foot in diameter.

"I'm afraid to do this," Tenoctris said, trying to smile. "But it's not going to get easier if I wait."

"Is there danger?" Garric said. His hand twitched toward his sword hilt, though his conscious mind knew that a blade was unlikely to remedy any danger here.

The old woman shrugged. "Only of failure," she said. "My failure. In which case the continuing disruption will destroy the kingdom, I'm afraid."

Cashel frowned. "You won't fail, Tenoctris," he said. His tone would've seemed threatening to anyone who didn't know Cashel.

Ilna looked at Garric, then toward Tenoctris. "It isn't my pattern," she said, "but I doubt the craftsman at the loom would choose to weave disaster here."

"You're sure there's a pattern?" Tenocris said sharply.

Ilna held her palms up, then laced her fingers together. "As sure as I am of these hands," she said. "As sure as I am of anything in life."

"You're sure Good will defeat Evil?" Tenoctris demanded.

"I don't know about Good and Evil," Ilna said calmly. "I know about patterns; and craft."

Tenoctris gave a crisp nod. She walked to the empty bier and spread the snakeskin over the travertine surface.

The translucent scales blurred the stone's pattern of brown blotches in yellowish matrix. Lips pursed in concentration, Tenoctris adjusted the lie of the skin.

The mottled surfaces, skin and stone, merged into a single pattern.

"It's words," Liane whispered. "It forms words in the Old Script!"

Cashel beamed with calm satisfaction. He handed Tenoctris the sliver of bamboo he had ready.

"Tenoctris, can we help?" Sharina asked softly. "To speak the words, I mean?"

"One voice is enough, I think," Tenoctris said. "And ... while you, while several of you can read the Old Script as well as I can, I think this spell requires a wizard to speak it. Though I hope a wizard of my slight power will be sufficient."

Tenoctris took a deep breath. She had to stand to read the symbols on top of the bier. Garric stepped toward her but Ilna was already there, putting her arm around the old woman for support if the effort of the enchantment overcame her frail physique.

Since Tenoctris didn't need him, Garric turned his back. He knew his mind would try to pronounce the words of power if he let himself watch. Past experience had taught him that a spell formed for a wizard to speak would dry his throat and glue his tongue to the roof of his mouth.

"Horses for courses, lad," Carus said with a false laugh. *"The lady isn't much of a swordsman that I've noticed."*

Garric lacked a wizard's powers, but Carus had hated and even feared wizards during life. Carus' sword alone hadn't been enough to save the Isles; but it was true as well that no one, not even a wizard far more powerful than Tenoctris, could defeat the rising threat of chaos with only wizardry.

Garric flexed his sword hand and laughed. Horses for courses, indeed.

"Phouris chphouris on," Tenoctris said. *"Thala matro armatroa ..."*

Garric looked at the ruin of the alabaster screen. It saddened Garric to see such a work of art smashed, but there'd been no time to find another way to reach Purlio. Men had died that afternoon because only their sacrifice stood between the Isles and chaos. It would be perverse to mourn the mere product of a stonemason's craft and forget the lives.

Liane put her hand on Garric's shoulder. He took his right hand off his sword hilt and flexed it, working out the stiffness from his fierce grip. He put his arm around Liane and managed to chuckle.

"*Alaro alo aa,*" Tenoctris was saying. "*Marta max soumarta . . .*"

Dalar gave a croak of wonder. Garric turned instinctively. The bird was staring at the bier; so was Chalcus, his in-curved sword bare in his hand. So long as Ilna stood beside Tenoctris, Chalcus didn't have Garric's option of turning his back on the proceedings. Wizardry obviously frightened him, though.

A shimmer like that of a golden waterfall quivered above and through the stone bier. For an instant Garric saw a snake's head, its tongue darting to taste the air. That image vanished, but at the other end of the flowing light—

"*Zochraie satra!*" Tenoctris said, striking her slender wand in the center of the snakeskin. She stepped back and would have fallen if Ilna hadn't been there to catch her.

Ansalem the Wise lay on the bier, cushioned by a velvet pad. He turned his head toward his visitors and blinked in surprise.

"Who . . . ?" he said, trying to lift himself. Cashel put an arm behind the wizard and helped him straighten into a sitting position.

"Lord Ansalem?" Garric said. The kingdom's safety was *his* responsibility, not that of his friends. "We've awakened you so that you can remove the bridge that threatens our world."

"I remember you," Ansalem said. His expression had

been slightly vague; now it sharpened into focus. "From my dream. Where are my acolytes?"

"Dead," Garric said bluntly. "Before they could do more damage. Though they did enough."

Ansalem sighed. "Yes, I was afraid of that," he said. Placing his sandaled feet carefully on the floor beside the bier, he stood up. "I don't understand why they shut me away like that. I only wanted what was best for them and all my people."

"They weren't as strong as you," Tenoctris said. She seemed to have recovered herself, though Ilna was ready to catch her if necessary. "What to you were toys warped them in ways that . . . made them less than human."

"I know you too, don't I?" Ansalem said. His gaze was disconcertingly sharp. "But from before I took my city out of the coming collapse. You're a wizard of sorts yourself."

"Yes," said Tenoctris. "I visited Klestis, but I didn't belong here so I left before it was too late."

"You would have been welcome," Ansalem said in puzzlement. "You didn't have to leave just because you didn't have the strength Purlio and the others did."

"Your power was enough to doom all the citizens who trusted you, Lord Ansalem," Garric said. He didn't know if the words came from his own horror at what had happened or if King Carus spoke with Garric's lips. Either way, Garric was certain that the wizard had to know the truth in all its brutal clarity. "Without your art, the plants and animals here couldn't produce a tenth of what the people needed to live. They ate all there was, and then they must have eaten each other. And at last they died."

Ansalem's mouth dropped open. "But *I* didn't mean—" he said.

He stopped and swallowed. His cherubic face was suddenly gray. "I'm sorry, Carus," Ansalem said. "I was wrong. I was terribly wrong."

Garric clasped the wizard's arm, hand to elbow. "Everybody was wrong then," he said without trying to explain that he was Garric, not Garric's ancestor. "What's important is what happens now. Can you remove the bridge you formed to my world?"

Without comment, Ansalem walked to the window looking out over the city. He apparently expected people to get out of his way automatically—as they did, Sharina in one direction and Chalcus with Merota in the other.

Chalcus chose to sheathe his sword now; with a grin, but also with enough of a flourish to make the gesture a comment. In this gathering, Ansalem didn't have a monopoly on arrogance.

"I did that while I was dreaming?" Ansalem said, turning to face the others again.

"You formed one nexus," Tenoctris said. "I think your acolytes may have multiplied it in the fashion you see; but yes, it was your work."

"While I was dreaming!" the wizard repeated in a tone of delight. "Why, I don't think anyone else could possibly have done that. Not from a spell of encystment!"

"But can you *undo* it?" Tenoctris said. She spoke quietly and firmly, as though she were dealing with a child. "It's a great danger to other planes so long as it remains. A danger to all other planes."

"Yes, yes, it would be," Ansalem said, contrite again. "I'm so sorry, I never meant . . ."

His eyes suddenly focused on Dalar. "Why, my goodness," he said, losing the thread of his previous thought. "You're of the Rokonar, are you not? I didn't realize any of your folk had survived the catastrophe of the Third Age."

Garric saw Sharina wince. The bird merely nodded and said, "I am a warrior of the Rokonar, yes. I am far from my land and people, and I fear that I will never see my home again."

"Oh, sending you home isn't any trouble," Ansalem said. His surprise verged on irritation at the thought that he couldn't accomplish a task that seemed simple to him. "Is that what you want? I'll do that before I dissolve the nexuses."

The sudden sharp focus returned to the wizard's face. He looked at Tenoctris. "That is . . . will it be all right if I do that? I've made such terrible mistakes, I know."

Tenoctris glanced at Sharina. Sharina hugged Dalar and stepped away.

"The Dragon told me that my friends and I would gain by my service to him," she said. "I would gain greatly if you helped Dalar, who kept me alive on a long journey."

"I could have had no better master than you, Sharina," the bird said, bowing low and rising. "But yes, I would like to return home."

"We'd all be indebted to you for that, Lord Ansalem," Tenoctris said formally. "And for removing the weight of this nexus from our world."

"Yes, yes, of course," Ansalem said with a flash of peevishness. His face fell instantly. "Oh, I'm sorry," he went on. "I know it's all my fault. I'll take care of it as soon as you leave."

He frowned. "You do want to leave, don't you? Though if any of you would care to stay . . . ?"

"No," said Garric, breathing out a great sigh of relief. "We really want to return to our own world."

More than I could possibly have guessed, he thought, *before spending the better part of a day in this Paradise become Hell.*

"Lord Attaper," he called through the shattered screen. "Alert the troops for an immediate return to Valles!"

"It's dawn in Valles," Liane said as they approached the end of the bridge. "I've never been so glad to see *clean* light."

"Nor me," Garric said, feeling his heart lift at the sight. "Though I'm not going to cheer until I actually set foot on—"

Others were less inhibited. Chalcus, walking with Ilna and the child behind the leading section of javelin men, pointed his sword to the eastern horizon. "The sun!" he shouted.

Before the words were more than out of his mouth, a dozen throats echoed them. Instants later all the soldiers were shouting, the Blood Eagles no less than the skirmishers.

Attaper looked furious. Garric caught his eye, smiled, and cried, "The sun!" Attaper managed a lopsided grin.

Garric knew that Waldron would have drawn up the Royal Army along the streets facing the bridge, but the citizens packing roofs and balconies overlooking the troops were a surprise. When they heard the troops shouting, they too began to cheer hesitantly.

"They think we're cheering because we've won," Garric said, glancing from Liane on his left side to Sharina on his right. "They don't know we're just glad to have survived."

"We have won, Garric," said Cashel, beside Sharina and carrying Tenoctris in the crook of his right arm. Attaper had started to detail a pair of soldiers to build the wizard a litter from spearshafts and a cloak, but Cashel wouldn't hear of it. "Isn't that right, Tenoctris?"

"Yes, I think we did," she said, looking wan from her ordeal but satisfied nonetheless. Garric had to watch Tenoctris' lips to pick out the words over the cheering, though her smile would have been information enough. "We accomplished what we set out to do; or at any rate when Ansalem carries through, we will have."

Garric's hobnails clashed on the stone apron of the Old Kingdom bridge; the bridge of wood and masonry, not wizard-light. He drew his sword and waved it overhead. "The Isles!" he shouted. "To the kingdom and all her citizens!"

The cheers were as joyous as birdsong to ears returned from Klestis. Garric hugged Liane. If he didn't already have a bare blade in his hand, he'd have thrown her in the air like the climactic turn of the Harvest Dance.

Lord Waldron was at the head of the apron, in the midst of his staff and a dozen other noblemen. His face was as grim as a perched falcon's, showing neither fear nor hope. It was the face of the man who'd stood beside King Valence at the Stone Wall, certain the day was lost but untouched by the knowledge.

King Valence—the king's army—had ultimately won at the Stone Wall, just as Garric and his friends had succeeded in Klestis; but there were worse folk to have on your side than pessimists who'd die before they quit. Garric and the king inside his mind felt a sudden rush of affection for the old warrior.

Attaper hadn't let Garric be the last out of Klestis as he'd wanted to be. A final squad of Blood Eagles jogged off the bridge, bellowing and drumming their spears against their shield bosses. The crowd, even the ordered ranks of the army, gasped in a mixture of hope and terror.

Garric turned. The bridge sparkled like an outline of falling snow. Blue light that moments ago had been more solid than the limestone apron collapsed in on itself. Garric could see each bit rotating away in a direction that had nothing to do with ordinary distance.

The River Beltis, dark with silt and swollen from rainfall in the highlands, rolled toward the Inner Sea. The current roughened over the remains of the pier which once supported the Old Kingdom bridge.

Other than the ripples, the water and the air above it were empty. Garric slammed his sword home in its sheath.

"I suspect what's left of Klestis stands on the coast of Cordin again," Tenoctris said. "But I wonder what Ansalem himself will do. . . ."

After a dignified hesitation, Waldron and the other members of the council strode toward Garric. Lord Tadai remained where he'd been waiting, in discussion with Ilna. Garric was briefly surprised to see Chalcus several steps away, entertaining Merota by making a gold piece vanish and reappear from first the girl's ear, then her nose.

"Your friend doesn't need help to make her point," Carus noted with a grin. *"And when she's in the mood she is now, a wise man keeps his distance."*

Cashel set Tenoctris down but stood with his staff cross-ways to prevent well-wishers from trampling her and Sharina. Garric laughed and stepped with Liane behind the same protection. People shouted questions and congratulations—and Chancellor Royhas was saying something about the Earl of Sandrakkan.

That would wait. Sandrakkan was a threat, and there would be other threats worse than Sandrakkan before the kingdom was safe; but for today, they could all wait.

"The Kingdom of the Isles!" Garric shouted to the people, to *his* people. "May she stand forever in peace!"

"And may her rulers always be willing to stand against the enemies of that peace," King Carus shouted down the ages. *"As her ruler stands today!"*

http://www.herebedragons.co.uk/bfs/

The British Fantasy Society publishes fantasy and dark fantasy fiction, speculative articles, artwork, reviews, interviews, comment and much more. They also organise the annual FantasyCon convention to which publishers, editors, authors and fans flock to hear the announcement of the coveted British Fantasy Awards, voted on by the members.

Membership of the BFS is open to everyone. The annual UK subscription is £20.00 which covers the acclaimed bi-monthly Newsletter and additional BFS books and anthologies. To join, send moneys payable to the BFS together with your name and address to:

The BFS Secretary,
c/o 201 Reddish Road,
South Reddish,
Stockport
SK5 7HR

Overseas memberships, please write or email for current details.
The BFS reserves the right to raise membership fees.
Should the fee change, applicants for membership will be advised.

Email: syrinx.2112@btinternet.com